I0589651

Notes of a Self-Seeker

A Novel

Published in the United States of America by

Bar Nothing Books
P. O. Box 35
Adamant, Vermont 05640

802 229–0691

info@barnothingbooks.com

Created with Bookalope

SAN 256–615X

ISBN 978–0-9987709–5-6 (softback)
ISBN 978–0-9987709–6-3 (e-book)

FIRST EDITION

Library of Congress Control Number: 2021901888

Notes
Of A
Self-Seeker

A Novel

by Bill Porter

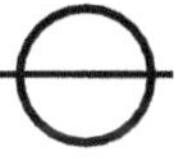

Bar Nothing Books
Adamant, Vermont

Table of Contents

Preface

Everyone who lived through 1968 in America knows what it feels like to stay put when a hurricane is bearing down on your house. A few people, a small band of timid or maybe super-brave souls, evacuated, disappearing into the anonymity of insane asylums or into drugs or into new citizenships in other countries. Those left behind, the vast majority, boarded up their own holdings as best they could and hunkered down; some prayed, some played, and some ran outside to rail at the winds and the gathering storm.

Over and over the tempest that was 1968 made surprise landfalls, leaving devastation that at times was too bleak to contemplate. Each disaster seemed utterly without precedent in its particular horror, and each made the next even more breathtaking in compounded magnitude.

As events overpowered the nation's collective imagination, virtually everyone became a news junkie. Bewildered and lost in a stormy wilderness, Walter Cronkite became our Moses, but even he lost his head and at one point blasphemed—on air—certain high authorities who had run amok.

It was a golden age for newsmen, at that time still a motley, unpredictable, barely respectable lot that constituted a group only under the loosest possible definition. These wretches, prospectors of history who didn't know that they already were themselves obsolete, stood in a roaring stream, grabbing giant news nuggets so fast that they totally forgot to search for the mother lode.

From thirty years' distance, here's an incomplete list of daily headlines in 1968:

- *A small enemy nation captured an American spy ship and held it captive while Washington sputtered in what appeared to be utter paralysis.*
- *Another undeveloped nation launched what came to be called the Tet Offensive, inflicting punishment at will on the forces of the nation with the greatest military and economic power the world had ever seen. Briefly, the Viet Cong occupied the U.S. embassy in Saigon.*
- *An obscure U.S. senator dethroned the most powerful leader in the world.*
- *Europe erupted in student riots that shook nearly every government.*

- *A prestigious national commission warned the U.S. had become two nations, black and white.*
- *Great cities burned.*
- *Martin Luther King, one of the century's true heroes, was murdered.*
- *Other cities burned.*
- *Robert Kennedy, one of thecentury'smost glittering icons, was murdered.*
- *Czechoslovakia revolted, nearly successfully, against the Soviet Union.*
- *The Democratic National Convention turned into a bloodbath of political repression, a "police riot" that trampled not the throwaway criminal class but the children of the great middle class.*
- *Richard Nixon was elected president.*

All of these events were highlights flashed against a background of unparalleled economic prosperity; a mysterious, sometimes mystic rebellion by the generation that expected to inherit the treasure being grabbed by the new middle class; and a confused and confusing distant war whose enormous destructive power was continuously recorded on video and replayed nightly as dinner table fare in millions of traumatized homes.

For those who practiced what by then was becoming the "profession" of peddling news, 1968 was a perpetual high, fueled by daily injections of sensations that boiled their emotions, chilled their brains, and sent their egos soaring. The old press was dead, the new media was crowned king; long live the media.

It was also the year, or at least the age, when newspapering lost its soul. After climbing to the top of the highest mountain, to the summit of power, prestige, and honor, the press made the one unforgivable mistake: it began to believe its own bullshit. Giddy with its own truth-seeking, the media came to believe it was too pure to be corrupted.

Bill Porter, 1998

Dedicated to Kendall Wild

No one, including my family members, influenced my life as directly as Kendall did. I spent twenty years working for Vermont newspapers and never was bored or uninterested in my work. Kendall was largely responsible for that interest. His deep commitment to newspapers passed directly to me. That influence was just as strong for others who worked under his guidance at the Rutland Herald.

Bill Porter, 2021

Notes of a Self-Seeker is a work of fiction. Names, characters, and nonhistorical events are products of the author's imagination.

Now Sam McGee was from Tennessee,
where the cotton blooms and blows.
Why he left his home in the South
to roam 'round the Pole,
God only knows.
He was always cold,
but the land of gold
seemed to hold him like a spell;
Though he'd often say in his homely way
that "he'd sooner live in hell."

The Cremation of Sam McGee
by Robert W. Service

CHAPTER ONE
Wednesday, January 3, 1968

His eyes popped open, staring, but it didn't make any difference. It was as dark looking out as it had been looking in. Icy cold lay on his right temple, a spot of pain but soothing at the same time. A draft cut across the side of his neck. His feet sweltered in a dry storm of heat that rose inside his right pant leg.

He slowly became aware of motion, forward but also swaying slightly side to side, then the distant, steady moan of an engine. His eye, an inch from the cold glass, peered hopelessly out the bus window into the blank night. His next awareness was from behind, a rustle at his elbow. He swiveled his head slowly until he could make out a small, dim form hunkered on the edge of the seat as far from his own sprawling hulk as it could get without falling into the aisle.

A child? He wondered whether he had been snoring, farting, or just spreading out into the other's space. He noticed the tail of his overcoat lying across the corner of his neighbor's seat and he pulled it back, wrapping it primly over his own lap.

Fuck it, he thought, rolling his head back to the window and closing his eyes. When they opened again, the engine rumble was louder but the bus was motionless. He breathed in diesel fumes that overwhelmed even the blended odor of stale tobacco smoke, dried-out sandwiches, and overripe fruit. Outside, people milled around on a snowy sidewalk, dark bundled-up shapes moving jerkily. He watched, an invisible spectator not connected even by curiosity, separated only by tinted glass but as far removed as deep space. They left in ones and twos, hurrying into the gloom outside the rim of light, disappearing into the dark.

The bus door whooshed shut. The motor revved, the gears engaged, and they were off, finished with their five-minute contribution to the history of this nameless town. He didn't turn to see if his seatmate was still there, but the space felt empty. He lowered his eyelids, shutting out the village even before they passed out of the two-block-long streetlighted area. Everything except the gentle swaying disappeared into background; the heat and cold mixed into warm, the engine rumble and tire-on-pavement zinging merged into murmur. Only the motion remained, timeless travel with no history, future, or even now—a trip that would leave him someplace else but one that he wasn't personally taking. His mind was as free of thought as his body was divorced from sensation, a being roving through time and space with no more friction than an idea.

It was a perfect state of consciousness—awareness stripped to a solitary feeling of absence but without regret or expectation. For miles his body and soul traveled independently of each other, a wonderful condition that disappeared the instant he thought it. His body was thrust forward, slammed rudely into the seat in front of him, and he heard the air brakes groan loudly. Fear rushed into his throat and anger sent blood gushing into his brain.

"Goddam hippie!" The shrieking voice guided Willis's racing senses to the front of the bus. The driver was raised half out of his seat, standing on the brake and struggling with the huge wheel. "Worthless fucking flatlander," he screamed and fired off a long, furious howl from the air horn. Willis hoisted himself up in the seat high enough to see the rear end of a VW van, the tassels on its back window curtain bouncing saucily in the glare of the headlights as the towering, groaning Greyhound bore down, now mere feet from its pygmy relative.

Willis watched until the distance between the vehicles began to lengthen, then he slumped back into his seat. Fear drained out of him, but it had stolen the numb oblivion and he silently cursed the bus driver. He noticed for the first time that he did indeed have a seatmate. She was maybe ten or twelve years old and she stared up at him as she gripped the aisle-side armrest with both of her small hands. Her hat had fallen off and rested on the crack between their seats. He picked it up, a dark wool beret, and held it out toward the girl. She looked at his face without moving for several seconds, then let go of the armrest to reach over and take the cap. Neither of them said a word.

The child's wide eyes fixed on him, round and shiny enough to reflect some distant pinpoint of light coming through the window. Was she terrified? He started to say something, but no words came out. Maybe she wasn't terrified but horrified. Maybe he'd been talking in his sleep. Or touched her, flailing out in a restless horror of his own. He looked away quickly, resting his forehead again on the icy window, and felt a throbbing pain jabbing just behind his right eye. A moment later he heard a small muffled sniff behind him, but by then the hangover had settled on him like a heavy weight and he dismissed the child's misery as insignificant compared to his own.

His mouth was dry and his throat thick. A pulse beat strongly in a neck that was weary from holding up his bloated head.

He closed his eyes, but sleep was somewhere far away, back behind the throb. Now, inescapably conscious of his small companion and all the other annoyances that surrounded him, he was acutely alert and sorely aware of his own body. His stomach was restless, empty but at the same time poised to heave out any intruder. His skin felt parched, except the soles of his feet. His scalp itched and his ears were hot.

Free of the Volkswagen, the bus gathered speed as it hurtled down the mountain. A wall of trees flashed by his window, and just above them he saw a quarter moon low in the clear eastern sky. He watched with increasing awe as it climbed, soon casting a dim light over the distant snow-covered hills. It was the moon, then, that he had seen glinting out of the girl's eyes. He turned to look and she was still staring up at him, the point of light still reflected out of her eye. He looked closely at her round face and suddenly realized that she was not scared or repulsed but merely curious, intently wondering about something that had to do with him.

"Where're you going?" he asked.

"Home."

She blinked but did not drop her gaze.

"Where're you coming from?"

"White River."

He remembered noticing an old woman with a child when he was waiting at the White River Junction bus station. Dredging that sort of extraneous detail out of memory was an occupational skill and he prided himself on being unusually good at it. He probed for more stored information, wondering if this was the same girl, but he couldn't recall the hat or any other useful observation from the bus station, a failure he attributed to the hangover. In the end, he just told himself it must be the same child.

"Are you okay?" He didn't mean to ask it, it just popped out.

"Yeah."

Still there was no change in expression and no shifting of her gaze. The beret sat perfectly straight on her head, the front band slicing a line neatly across the middle of her forehead.

"We nearly had an accident back there."

No response.

"Were you scared?"

"A little."

"Why do you keep staring at me?"

Her mouth pursed slightly as she thought it over silently, still looking directly into his face.

"I thought you were dying," she said in a small, toneless voice. "When you were sleeping, you gurgled like you might be dying."

"Gurgled?"

"Like a pig'll do sometimes when its throat's cut and it's choking on the blood."

They stared at each other. She evidently had no more to say. Now he wanted to say something; in fact, his mind spun around frantically looking for something to say. But in the end, he managed only a lame, "No, I'm not dead," and after one last look at her expressionless face, he turned back to the moon.

Twenty minutes later, when they rolled to a stop at the terminal, he was still staring out the window. He didn't move even when the overhead lights came on and he felt her stirring in the seat. When he finally turned toward the aisle, she was gone, hidden among a procession inching its way toward the front of the bus.

Willis waited until the last passenger in the line had passed his seat, then he looked at his watch and stood up. As he started down the steps of the bus, he caught a final glimpse of the beret, moving at the head of a small wedge of people slicing slowly through the crowd. Quarter to seven. Forty-five minutes to wait. Just about right.

After leaving his suitcase in a locker, Willis spent the next half an hour wandering around the town. The newspaper was in a big brick building on Main Street. He went into a small bar across the street. The sign on the door said The Oasis. Inside there was a long L-shaped bar, a shabby pool table and in the back six or seven booths. He and the bartender were the only ones in the bar. He slid onto a bar stool and stared through the dirty window at the newspaper building that sat on the corner. The front of the building sat on the level of the street. At the corner, the street dropped off quite sharply and the building followed so that the lower level could be accessed by delivery trucks. After bringing Willis a beer, the bartender looked at him for a long time, his eyes narrowing.

"Are you staying in town or just passing through?"

"Not sure," said Willis. "I'm thinking about seeing if there is a job for me."

When Willis finished his beer, he paid, crossed the street to the double glass doors, and stepped inside.

By the time he got to the door of the newsroom, he already was beginning to regret coming in, and he looked back quickly over his shoulder down the brightly lit hallway leading back to the big front doors. Suddenly he wanted to be back in the saloon and was about to turn around when the newsroom door opened and a gnomish, balding man stepped out, then stumbled quickly to the side, as far from Willis as he could get without letting the door slam. He bowed deeply, without irony, a pudgy hand sweeping Willis through the opened doorway.

He smelled the paste and the newsprint and he felt the ancient held-over excitement that waited like some inert gas to be reactivated. He breathed in deeply and it made him feel better.

He took in the huge room, filled helter-skelter with desks buried under mounds of papers, coffee cups, discarded jackets, photographs, and soda bottles. Why are they always slobs? Overflowing ashtrays perched atop the heaps on most of the desks. A few typewriters clacked in an erratic, patternless sound, like a band warming up, but he couldn't see the machines nestled down among the debris on sunken shelves. Probably they were ancient Underwoods and Royals, discards from the business office. They always gave them to the newsroom after the bean counters had depreciated them off the books.

About a dozen people were scattered around the room, most of them reading newspapers and all of them too preoccupied to notice Willis. It was seven thirty and no sense of urgency. That was a good sign — a late deadline. But why did they pretend not to know he had come in? A telephone rang and the blonde girl answered it, but no one else looked up.

Beyond the girl, at the far end of the room, a man was taking off his jacket in a small, glass-enclosed office. He was reading copy as it reeled out of a wire-service machine, and he tossed the jacket at the desk behind him without looking to see where it landed. Just back from dinner. Willis looked past the glass office where a double-sized open door led into the composing room, which seemed to be empty despite the haze of blue smoke hovering around the ceiling. Break time. A union shop.

The newsroom was noisy with voices, squeaking chairs, and desk drawers opening and closing. The Photofax machines whirred in a corner, and from time to time the pneumatic copy tubes rattled noisily as copy editors fired off little clear plastic missiles filled with rolled-up paper that moments later would slam into a wooden box somewhere in the composing room. Willis smiled. No copyboys here; this was a high-tech newsroom.

The room was loud the way a working bee colony is loud, a steady background hum that signaled idle comfort, and Willis, like a seasoned beekeeper, felt soothed rather than threatened by the drone. The faces were mostly youngish, mostly male. A couple of worried older faces, worn-out copy editors.

The door squeaked open behind him, sealing off that escape with a presence he felt but never saw, because instead of looking he started forward through the maze toward the glass office. They all glanced up at him without much interest, except the blonde girl. She was talking into the phone but she stared directly into his face as he walked by. Ballbuster.

Then he was at the open door of the office. Too late to turn around. A drop of cool sweat slid slowly past his ribs.

"Mr. Seymour? I'm Bud Willis. Uh, John Willis. I called you this afternoon from White River. I'm a reporter and I think we may be able to help each other." Willis paused. Christ, did he hear? "Assuming, that is, that you need a good reporter to work for you the way I need a good newspaper to work for."

So that's how they met—a supplicant seeking a benefactor, brought together by an improbable assortment of happenstances that neither of them ever untangled, two newsmen whose paths might have crossed without consequence, maybe even without notice, at any one of a thousand earlier junctions, or maybe never crossed at all. They talked for a while, sitting in the office like soap opera actors playing out their roles as the newsroom voyeurs watched suspiciously through the glass walls. They swapped insignificant but necessary pieces of information about themselves, and they talked perfunctorily of mutual acquaintances at other newspapers. Mostly the information flow came from Seymour's casual questions and Willis's careful answers.

"How'd you get to Vermont?"

"Luck. Good or bad, I don't know yet."

"Ever work for the *Birmingham News*?"

"Nope."

"That's good; it's a rag."

"But I did do a stint in Montgomery, at the *Advertiser*."

A raised eyebrow.

"Another rag but a pretty good gig for me."

"Family?"

"Not anymore—divorce"

And so on. They talked about politics and the war, about LBJ and history and the South and how Willis came to leave it for the North in frigid January. Mostly, though, they spoke of newspapering. It was, for each of them, the only real subject because all the others were folded into it. They talked about what newspapers could do if they would, and what they should do. They talked on and on, and after a while it was as though they were actually saying new things and conjuring new visions.

Finally, after nearly an hour, Seymour stood up abruptly and said, "Wait here. I'll be back in a few minutes."

Willis lit a cigarette and watched him walk into the newsroom and begin talking to a lanky, middle-aged guy whose desk was more or less in the center of the room. He nodded a couple of times and laughed at something Sy said. Twice he glanced over at Willis, but his face showed no interest whatsoever so Willis couldn't be sure whether they were talking about him. After a few minutes, the blonde girl walked up to Sy and they began talking while the graying editor went back to his work. She stood very close to him, her hands moving rapidly, eager and compelling participants in the conversation. Sy was still smiling but the easiness of the conversation with the tall guy was gone, replaced by something stiff that made him look pompous and shy at the same time.

Now Willis was the voyeur, the audience instead of the player, and he was amused by the pantomime. Sy backed up until his legs were pressed against a desk, bending slightly backward from the waist, grinning uncomfortably as she talked and gestured. She talked, smiled, brushed a fallen lock of hair out of her eyes with a quick, deft motion, and generally kept Willis's attention fixed on her. She had taken over the scene merely by stepping into Seymour's spotlight and pinning him down so he couldn't move to another spot. Finally, she smiled broadly, smoothed her hair back with both hands in a practiced move that for an instant left her in the posture of a hostage, then turned away and went back to her typewriter. Willis grinned. Ballbuster, all right.

Sy recovered and spoke something to her back that she acknowledged with a shrug without slowing or turning her head. He roved around the room, apparently without purpose, stopping a few times to speak briefly to someone, usually leaving the person laughing, but he never stopped long enough to get a reply. After a few minutes, he made his way back to his office and said to Willis, "Well, the city editor says he's willing to give you a try and I guess I am too, so when do you want to start?"

Willis was caught off guard. Until then, Seymour had not even let on whether he had a job open. They really had not talked directly about what kind of job he wanted or what kind of job Sy wanted him to do. Willis had assumed this would be a preliminary interview that might or might not lead to something. Christ, it'd only been two weeks since he quit newspapering for good. Permanently. He couldn't even remember why he'd called up Seymour in the first place, much less why he'd actually gotten on the bus and come over here. He suddenly realized that he had not even typed out a résumé.

"Great." It was his own voice and he felt a big grin forming on his face. "Great." His mind raced. Never let the other guy be cooler, more certain than you are. "I travel light. I could start tomorrow . . . uh, make it day after tomorrow."

"Good enough. Why don't you talk to the business manager about getting paid on your way out," Sy said as he crossed over to sit behind his desk. Willis realized suddenly that he was waiting for him to leave, so he stood up and stuck out his hand. Seymour looked startled by the gesture, then he gave him a bony, limp hand, just long enough to call it a handshake before he pulled it back.

Sy pulled a pocket watch out of the front pocket of his trousers. "I'll probably be done here about midnight. If you're around, stop in and we'll go out for a drink. Otherwise, I'll see you on Friday." He looked up at Willis for a long moment. "Unless you change your mind," he said. Willis started to laugh, then he realized that Sy was serious, so he just nodded his head and left the office.

Again, his passage through the newsroom was acknowledged only by the blonde girl. This time he smiled at her as he passed her desk. He didn't stop because she didn't smile back, and besides, his heart wasn't in it now. He moved slowly and alertly through the newsroom, peering intently at each person as if he were the store detective and they were potential shoplifters. No eyes tested his authority. But after closing the newsroom door, he hurried down the wide hall, through the tidy business office, out the front door, and straight across the street to The Oasis. Just as he reached the padded door, it swung outward and the newsroom gnome scuttled past, head down and arms pumping. They traded places wordlessly, and this time Willis was glad to be the one on the inside.

He didn't see the barman at first in the dimness, but by the time Willis had settled himself in the vinyl booth, he was standing beside the table. "That didn't take very long. You get the job?"

"Yeah," Willis said, "looks like it." He looked around the empty barroom. "You better hope so. It looks like you could use a steady customer. How many customers have been here since I left?"

"Don't worry about us," he said. "You eating or drinking or both?"

"First one, then maybe the other," Willis said. "I'll have another Bud."

When the bartender had brought the bottle and glass, Willis asked, "Who's the gnome?"

"Huh?"

"The little guy who left just as I came in."

"Oh, that's Merle."

"Merlin? Jesus, I knew this was Yankee country, but I figured it was Christian, at least. Merlin?"

"Not Merlin. Merle. M-E-R-L-E. Merle Scanlan."

"Well, it's the damnedest name I ever heard. Do they use it a lot around here?"

"Yeah. We use it a lot. You want a menu?"

Willis was taking a long drink and he just shook his head. The bartender spun around and was moving quickly but stiffly back to his post by the time Willis had swallowed and said, "Not yet. But bring me another beer in a minute."

Ten minutes later the surly bartender still had not surfaced from behind the closed door in back of the bar, and Willis, looser now, finally stood up and walked across the room. Just as he reached the bar, Mr. Hospitality came through the door, wiping his hands on a towel, pulled a beer out of the cooler, and took it over to Willis's table. He set it down, spilling a splash that he ignored, picked up the empty, and moved back behind the bar without saying anything or looking at Willis.

Touchy bastard.

Two couples came in and took a table on the far side of the barroom. It was another fifteen minutes before the bartender came back to Willis's table. He put a menu down in front of him and stood waiting with an order pad in his hand.

"Just bring me a cheeseburger and fries. And another beer."

When he brought the tray, he set it down in front of Willis, picked up the second empty bottle, and turned away without saying anything. Willis asked, "What's to do around here at night?"

"The movie's *Bonnie and Clyde*. Late show starts at nine." He started walking away, then turned around, tore out the check, set it down on the edge of the table, and left.

Willis shook his head. Christ, the moody bastard couldn't wait to shut off his best customer. One-horse town, one-horse movie theater, and horse's ass bartender. He looked around to see if the couples were paying attention, and he was glad to see they weren't. They were still the only others in the room.

He made it to the movie only a few minutes late but fell asleep about the time Clyde discovered that he was, after all, a fully equipped man. God, Willis thought as he closed his eyes, if Clyde had figured that out when he was about sixteen, like everybody else, just think how many lives would have been spared. The machine gun ambush waked him up just in time to see Faye Dunaway's wonderful body jumping and jerking as dozens of bullets tore her apart. "Should have known better," he mumbled out loud. First a stupid movie, then wake up with a headache. Bonnie Parker made Willis think of the girl in the newsroom, except he figured that one was a lot tougher.

He walked around the frozen, deserted town until he got too cold and ended up just after eleven back at the bus station, or rather, at a dangerous-looking bar next to the station. Two women and four men sat swearing, shouting, and laughing in a dark corner of the room, and three or four men were hunched over one end of the bar. He couldn't tell if they were actually watching the flickering television set over their heads but the bartender clearly was and none of them looked Willis's way. He sat on a stool at the other end of the bar and waited. After a few minutes, the bartender turned away from the TV and two of the others swung their heads toward Willis. Must be a commercial.

Willis got a beer and kept his head down and his eyes on the polished bar in front of him. About halfway through his beer, he suddenly knew that he was going to leave. He'd take the first bus out. He must have been crazy to come over here in the first place. Dead-end job in a dead-end town. Christ, he'd worked for nine different newspapers, none of them as small as this one. He was thirty-three years old and he'd covered some of the biggest stories of the last dozen years. Even if he wanted to get back into the business, which he didn't, what the hell was he doing here? He was ready to move up, maybe try one of the big Eastern papers. *Baltimore Sun*, maybe. Or the *Philadelphia Inquirer*. The *Providence Journal* was supposed to be a good paper too. But this job would be the end of the line. Who needed it?

Bullshit. Nine newspaper jobs all right—and three firings, five walkouts, and in this last case he didn't file any stories or even call in for more than two weeks, and when he finally did, they said they had just assumed he quit.

He looked sideways at his fellow drinkers. The two at the end of the bar, who had looked his way, were still watching him. No one in that crowd was talking. In the corner, one guy was pawing at one of the women. The front of her dress was half open and all six of them were roaring with laughter. The pawer seemed to be too drunk to coordinate his eyes with his paw. He reached out a groping hand and she jerked herself back just in time for him to miss her shirt front. His hand flopped on the table, then suddenly groped out again. Over and over, and every time they whooped.

A memory flooded into Willis's consciousness—a night years ago in Louisiana when he'd been working on a story about offshore oil drilling. It was late; after leaving a roadhouse, he'd been driving aimlessly around some narrow bayou roads when he came upon a giant bonfire in a clearing near a shrimp-processing plant. A bunch of shrimpers, still in their rolled-down rubber boots, were passing around a jug of whiskey and screaming insanely in their odd dialect at a drunken, undersized black bear chained to a stake near the fire. They were taking turns swinging a big, dripping fish under his nose, and with each pass he would rise up on his hind legs to snatch hopelessly for the receding treasure. Willis had been fascinated by the bizarre, awful scene and had gotten out of his car before he realized that could be a big mistake. The shrimpers appeared not to notice him, but he soon realized they had all but surrounded him, incorporating him into the circling group of jeering men so that he was close enough to see the bear's small, furious, but unfocused eyes. The fur on his right ankle was worn off by the rusty manacle and the hairy fringe on both sides was stained with dried blood. The bear's slowly rolling head would hesitate, his restless agitation interrupted by some sound or smell that sent his lips peeling back over yellow teeth in a silent snarl more piteous than fearsome. Willis was horrified, standing mere feet from the tormented bear, transfixed by pity or outrage or fear, until suddenly the cane pole on which the fish was tied was thrust into his hands. He felt his own head swinging wildly from side to side and everywhere he saw grinning, fire-lit faces. He shoved the pole forward, swinging the fish in a wide arc that never came near the bear but that on the backswing brought the fish slamming into Willis's own stomach. The crowd roared with a mocking cheer that quelled suspicion and freed Willis from the mob's invisible grasp so he could fling the pole to a leering neighbor and flee back to his car. Over the years he had thought about the bear from time to time, but he had never written about it or even told anyone the story.

He drained his glass, put a dollar on the bar, and left without looking back. He hurried into the bus station. A dopey-eyed, pimply-faced boy told him the next bus was due about one thirty on its way to New York from Montreal. His suitcase was still in the locker; he'd just wait here. The bus would put him in New York about nine. He sat down on one of the molded-plastic chairs hooked together into two lines facing the ticket counter. The kid behind the counter went back to his comic book, oblivious to Willis and the world.

Willis went to his locker to get his book, *The Death of a President*, and sat back down, but he only read for about five minutes. He couldn't concentrate. He didn't know if Manchester's version of the assassination would turn out to be good history, but it sure as hell wasn't particularly good writing, not even especially good as journalism. All the commotion about the Kennedys' complaints had hyped the damn book onto the bestseller lists and it still was, but it was headed for Willis's shit list. Hell, four years was too soon to be history and too old to be reporting.

He slammed the book shut, stuffed it back into the locker, and went out into the cold street. Maybe he ought to stop by and tell Seymour he didn't want the job. He had seemed like a pretty decent guy even if he was a little strange. There was plenty of time. Why not tell him? He didn't owe him anything. Just say he changed his mind and was going to New York instead.

Willis walked briskly, puffing steam with every breath. No one else was on the streets and he got to the newspaper building before he meant to, or at least he was there, standing in front of the big outside doors, before he knew it. He stopped briefly in the doorway then walked on. Hell, why bother. He didn't want to argue about it and what the hell difference would it make to Seymour anyway. He remembered how he had looked when he said, "Unless you change your mind." The bastard thought all along that he wasn't really going to take the job. Well, fuck him; let him gloat if he wanted.

Willis jammed his hands into his overcoat pockets and started back toward the bus station. Maybe he wouldn't even stop in New York. Maybe he'd just go on back to Atlanta or somewhere down South anyway. He could get half a dozen newspaper jobs down there if he ever did decide to get back into it. He was half a block away when he heard Seymour's shout.

"Willis! Willis, is that you?"

He stopped and turned around. Seymour was hurrying toward him. "God," he said while he was still ten yards away, "I just remembered that they've started locking up the front doors at midnight these days. How long were you standing out here?"

Willis didn't answer, he just shrugged. "God," Sy said, "I'm sorry. Christ, it's cold out here; come on back inside." He was in shirtsleeves and he turned back quickly, certain that Willis would follow him. And he did.

*
**

When they got to the newsroom, it was a made-over world. The place was a chaos of clacking machines, isolated shouts and curses, people hurrying in all directions carrying photographs, copy, and galley proofs. A few people, including the gnome, seemed to be out of the fray. They were sitting quietly at their desks, relaxed and unconcerned with the desperate rush of those all around them. Most of these idlers were reading newspapers, their feet resting on the debris that littered the desks in front of them. In the rear, beyond the glass office, the ceiling of the composing room was invisible behind thick, blue smoke. The hot smell of molten lead had escaped into the newsroom and the distant, soothing clatter of the Linotypes competed with the white-collar noises. Harried editors dashed back and forth between the two rooms, adjutants nervously flicking their pica rulers like swagger sticks. Long-bladed shears rose from their hip pockets, and most of them had cigarettes or cigars clamped in their mouths.

Sy turned around to speak to Willis but he didn't stop walking. "I've got a couple of things to do before I leave. Wander around if you want, or you can come in and wait in my office."

Willis unbuttoned his overcoat and leaned back against the door, smoking a cigarette and happily watching the paper come together.

He spotted the two reporters who were pushing the deadline—the stars of the production, for this night at least—writers whose stories were too good to hold even if they made the pressrun late. Others also were banging on their typewriters, but only these two were in the center ring. Christ, one of those boys looked too young to shave. Attendants hovered around, taking copy sheet by sheet as the writers rolled the widely spaced pages out of the machines. Both reporters were one-finger typists, jabbing at keys with single-minded aggression. The smooth-faced kid writhed and bounced slightly in his seat as he worked the keyboard, but the other one sat motionless, leaning far back with arms nearly fully extended, hands poised over the keyboard between strokes as his mind searched for the right signals to send the attacking index fingers.

After a while, Willis grew pleasantly bored and concentrated his gaze on Merle, staring until he caught the gnome sneaking a look at him over the top of his *New Republic*. He nodded, but Merle pretended not to see the greeting. Shy little bastard.

When Willis finally walked into the office, Sy was talking on the telephone and motioned him to sit down. "Okay, kiddo," Sy said to the phone. "You do good work. Thanks for hanging around. I had a hunch they might have something on Jackson's tax plan but if it's not in the early edition, we're probably safe. You checked the local section, right? Okay, thanks. You do good work. Right. Just tell her it's my fault."

Willis stood in front of the wire machine reading a long *Times* story about French agriculture. The last half dozen stories on the machine were advances for Sunday papers. He turned around when he heard the phone settle into its cradle. "Anything going on tonight?"

"Pretty routine," Sy said. "That conversation you just heard was our secret weapon. The opposition, the *Patriot Press*, has an earlier deadline. When we're worried about them breaking a story, one of our guys from the statehouse bureau goes over at twelve thirty to check their early pressrun."

"Pretty neat system," Willis said. "I take it they're not hurting you tonight?"

"Apparently not. Bob says they're running the usual drivel. We've got a reasonably good story on legislative committee assignments that'll get some attention in the morning at the statehouse, and both of those kids out there are working on good local stories."

Sy picked up some papers on his desk. "Sorry to keep you waiting. I'll be done in a couple of minutes."

Willis went back to the wire machine, two more advance *Times* features, and then Sy picked up his jacket and they left. Most of the reporters watched them as they walked through the newsroom and a couple spoke to Sy as they passed. In the hallway, a few steps away from the closed door, the clamor faded out and the newspaper smells were overwhelmed by the business office's furniture polish. A janitor rubbed silently and slowly at one of the bare desktops and did not notice their passing.

They spent most of an hour drinking slowly and talking about politics, Martin Luther King, Lyndon Johnson, and, of course, the war—or rather, Sy talked, pouring forth a stream of observations, thoughts, history, literary allusions, and anecdotes, talking easily, comfortably, without any objective except just conversation, and Willis listened, too weary to contribute more than a grunt or a chuckle but contented, interested, and entertained, soothed by the droning voice and stimulated by the words. They closed The Oasis and lit fresh cigars as they stepped back out to the deserted street.

"Hubris," Sy said, finishing up his assessment of how the president had gotten trapped into the Vietnam mess. "In the end, it's what brings them all down, and it's what will bring down this great, awesome country. It's the fatal flaw that Tocqueville couldn't see and it's the enemy that LBJ, for all his love of himself and life, doesn't recognize as a form of suicide."

It was just after two o'clock. Willis walked on the inside, peering sideways into the darkened storefronts but seeing mostly his own reflection. "I've got to get a place to stay," he said. "Where's a downtown hotel?"

"Christ," Sy said, "you don't have a place?" He walked a few steps. "The closest and probably the best bet is the Hotel Uptown, which isn't except in the sense of being at the end of upper Main Street. Come on, I'll walk you up there."

"Don't bother," Willis said. "Just point me in the right direction. I've got to get my suitcase out of the bus station."

Sy stopped and looked at him, then shrugged. "Okay. From the bus station, walk one block as though you were going back to the newspaper, then turn right and go up about three more blocks. It'll be on that same side of the street."

Willis thanked him and they set off in different directions. The no-name bar next to the bus station was closed and completely dark inside. As he retrieved his suitcase from the locker, the door to the bus station was flung open and a burly guy came in carrying a bundle of tied-up newspapers in each hand. He flopped them on the ticket counter and the dopey kid was just getting the string off when Willis dropped his dime on top of the pile. He scanned the top headlines and saw, without much interest, the story about the legislative committees, but he did like the clean, column-ruled layout of the paper. He realized with a jolt that he now worked for this newspaper, which he had never even seen before right now. He checked out the logo and folio line at the top of page one. The volume number on the left had so many Roman numerals he couldn't read it. Christ, it was an old paper. On the right, the date: January 4, 1968. In the middle, the state's motto: Freedom and Unity.

His mind sneered. Should say "or." You can't have both. But it stuck in his mind and he repeated it. Freedom and Unity. As he walked away, he was beginning to like the idea of a state that flaunted a bold but paradoxical slogan.

CHAPTER TWO
Friday, February 2, 1968

Sy lounged on the windowsill three stories above Main Street, drinking his coffee and idly considering the street's icy stillness as he scribbled his way through a journal entry. The sidewalks were empty and for nearly a block in both directions two cars and three delivery vans were moving, creeping along, spewing streams of gray exhaust into the cold, still air. *Thank God for winter*, he wrote. *It's the only force that cools the blood of commerce.* The new digital thermometer in front of the bank said minus five degrees and its little red lights suddenly blinked themselves into a new function to report the time as 11:27.

He dropped the journal on the sill and paced around the room. His place only had two rooms — or rather, he only used two. In fact, he rented the entire third floor because that was the only way the owner would let him have the two rooms he wanted and because that way he had only himself for a neighbor. Until he rented the space it had been unoccupied for a whole generation, ever since the feedstore had closed and the building was sold and became home to a series of failed retail stores that only used the ground and second floors.

He sniffed loudly, pulling in a long, deep breath. When it was a feedstore, the third floor was where they kept the hand tools and harnesses, and he could still detect a faint odor of leather but he might have imagined it because no one else ever noticed, or at least no one ever commented on the smell. He loved it, and now as he paced he held his breath and its real or imaginary smell until he felt mildly light-headed and dropped again to the windowsill to resume his musing.

One of his rooms looked out over Main Street and the other had a crow's nest vantage of Center Street. From the Main Street side where he now sat, he kept a watch over the town's retail center. From the other room, perched on its deep-set sills, he observed its nightlife on the rare nights when he didn't work until long after the street had shut down. The rooms were nearly identical, like messy twins with different haircuts. Separated by heavy wooden sliding doors, they were large with high ceilings, the same size and shape, and both dominated by books, magazines, and newspapers stacked, piled, and shelved in no identifiable scheme. The furniture in both rooms was heavy and characterless — in one, a perpetually unmade three-quarter bed, straight-backed chair, a large chest of drawers, and a footlocker, and in the other, a sofa, an armchair, a desk with a swivel chair, and in one corner a two-burner gas cookstove sandwiched between a tiny sink and a pint-sized refrigerator that was nearly buried under a pile of newspapers.

In the years he had lived here he had become more and more attached to the place. To other people, he called it his apartment, but he never really thought of it as an apartment. To him it was simply and completely "my place"—not a house exactly, and surely not "a home," but at the same time something more personal and private than merely temporary rented space. Without knowing when or how it happened, the place had become as important to his understanding of himself, to his private identity, as the newspaper or his secret journalized thoughts.

Maybe the place was too comfortable, too much of a soft refuge. Other men were tethered by the soft bond of family. Maybe this place, this snug corner, was just another self-set trap. It was a frequent thought and it had a place in more than one of his journal musings, but it was also an idle one, pushed aside easily by the sight of the publisher's car turning onto Main Street from Prospect, headed no doubt for home, where dinner would be waiting for him precisely at noon. Manny himself was punctual but not in the same league with Helen. More than just punctual, she was perfect, and everything within her realm was just as squared away. Midwest neat, in fact, since she was midwestern right down to her girdle. Thank Christ her domain stopped short of the newspaper. Be thankful, Sy thought, be thankful that the Helens were all taken, with none left over for him. And be thankful that whatever arrangement she and Manny had worked out kept her out of the newspaper. It was bad enough having Fletcher Junior, but he was manageable. Sy suspected Helen would be a more formidable enemy if he had to cross swords with her.

By now a few people were hurrying along the sidewalks, so bundled up you couldn't tell their gender except by their size and the colors of their bulky overcoats and hats. You could tell a lot more about them by which restaurant they chose. If they turned up Center Street, they probably were headed for the diner, and that was a loud mixed bunch where most of the conversations would be about sports, celebrities, or other people's romances. Center Street also was home to the new health-food restaurant, but you could easily spot the ones headed there. They wore Army Navy Store jackets instead of overcoats or, increasingly, serapes, and most of them had so much hair they either didn't need hats or couldn't find one big enough. Sy never could remember the name of the place, something to do with the zodiac; to him, it was just the Carrotjuice Club. He occasionally went there for lunch, more out of curiosity than for any other reason. He wondered about these people, mostly young and interesting looking, who were flooding into the state. They often seemed suspicious and unfriendly toward him, even though he instinctively liked them. He had rarely overheard any conversation in the Carrotjuice Club that didn't somehow relate to the war.

He turned to look in the other direction, up Main Street toward Mitch's Restaurant, the noontime hangout for the professional crowd. Several overcoats were jammed up at the entrance. Mitch's had an assortment of rooms separated from the main dining room where civic clubs and organizations held lunch meetings. Mitch was the brother of one of the town's most successful lawyers, who presided most noons over a tableful of early middle-aged practitioners of various kinds. Young Fletcher was a regular at Mitch's. Sy never ate there.

The Cafe, a block from Sy's place in the other direction on Main Street, was his favorite, or at least the place where he bought most of his meals, but, curiously, it was the local restaurant he would have the most trouble describing or explaining. The Cafe was just what it proclaimed itself to be—a place that sold decent meals of limited variety and moderate portions. They were served promptly, but not with a rush, at booths and tables that were generous if not interesting. It provided little atmosphere but large napkins, and the menu was what a reviewer might describe as plain Yankee, assuming any food reviewer would visit The Cafe, which none had ever done. Of all the downtown lunch spots, The Cafe was the one where on any given day you'd be most likely to see several single diners. The country must be full of these anonymous public kitchens because Sy had invariably found one wherever he had lighted for long enough to ferret it out.

Except for the twelve-stool lunch counter at the dime store, that was the extent of restaurant choices within sight of Sy's Main Street perch. If he had been sitting on the Center Street side of his place, he could have contemplated roughly the same number of public houses, some of which were reluctantly willing to dish out grill-cooked food upon request, though they all made it clear that drinking, not eating, was their chief interest, a value judgment shared by their patrons.

At this time of day, winter or summer, there was not much to see on Center Street since the customers had all gotten to their haunts earlier or would come much later.

Far up Main Street, a brightly colored knot of people hurried along the sidewalk, packed so closely together they looked like a single bouncing organism with no identifiable individuals. The hippie tangle turned up Center Street, still moving as one. Sy suddenly remembered the news from Vietnam and the wire services' frenzied, confused outpouring of last night.

He quickly finished up the day's entry by recording, as always, his own mood at the beginning of a new day, scrawling at the bottom of the page a code he had worked out many years ago that covered a surprisingly wide and subtle spectrum and that gave him more secret pleasure than he would ever admit, even to himself. He hurried toward the bathroom to shave. He wanted to be at the paper when Manny got back from lunch.

The newsroom was beginning to fill up by the time he got there, but it still had the relaxed, slow-motion feeling of a pregame warm-up. He was a little surprised to see Willis already at his desk, slouched down in his chair with the telephone cradled on his shoulder. The telex bell was ringing in his office and Sy hurried toward it without speaking to anyone in the newsroom. The morning's wire dispatches from the AP and the *Times* were filled with stories about what the news services were calling the Tet Offensive. He took off his jacket, skimmed the copy, and walked down the hall to the publisher's office, stepping faster and faster as he built his arguments for additional space in the paper.

Sy used to have the authority on his own to increase the size of the newspaper to accommodate space needs for breaking news. Then one day last fall, with no warning, Manny had suddenly told him that from that day on he would have to get permission to make the paper bigger than the advertising department had scheduled it to be. Sy had been stunned. He exploded in protest, but Manny calmly pulled out of his desk a sheet of paper tracking the size of the paper over nearly an entire year. On average, Sy had been overriding the advertising department 1.9 times a week, increasing the total number of pages printed by more than 400. The cost in extra newsprint alone, Manny read in a low monotone, was more than $10,000.

"That's a cost," he had said, raising his eyes to look levelly at Sy, "that comes right out of my pocket, not yours. So from now on, I've told the composing room not to increase the size of the paper unless I say so or the business manager says so."

Sy had tried to argue, but it was a feeble effort. Ten thousand dollars was two-thirds of his yearly salary. He had been blindsided. The business manager, the composing room foreman, and Fletcher Junior had mousetrapped him. They gave the report to Manny. Hell, he had only himself to blame since he had known they were getting more and more irritated every time he disrupted their plans and made them lay out the paper all over again. He should have headed it off. It was easy to beat those lightweights because Manny's instincts were all on the side of the newsroom, but he had to pay attention. Now he had to squander time and effort making a case for something that he ought to be able to do solely because it was the right thing. It was a waste. Manny didn't want to fret over the size of the paper any more than Sy did. They were both too old for nonsense.

Sy had worn away many hours thinking about Fletcher Monrose Sr.; in fact, he had spent more time than he would admit trying to analyze him. He believed he had peeled away most of the protective layers, but two of the publisher's most public features continued to startle Sy. First, there was his name; everyone called him Manny. How in hell did he ever get such a name and why in hell would he keep it? Even his wife called him Manny. It was unseemly.

The second disconcerting feature was that he was pink. His skin, wherever it was exposed, looked like the inside of a seashell, a soft, glowing pink that might have looked scalded had it not seemed at the same time to be so healthy and so comfortable to wear. His hair had been receding almost since puberty and for most of that time he had defied vanity by mowing it himself, using barber's clippers, into a stubble. Now, in his early seventies, it grew only in strips, a horizontal fringe connecting his ears with an intersecting narrow band that ran over the top of his round head but extended only halfway to his forehead. His hair had turned from blonde to gray during the decades of retreat, but the march of time had left his face practically unmarked—no wrinkles, no sags, and no puffs. Sy had talked with him almost daily for many years, but the serenity of his countenance still surprised him.

As usual the door was open, so he walked in and was already taking a seat before he took a good look at the publisher, who lifted his gaze but kept his fingers on the typewriter keyboard. He blinked and Sy thought he saw a shadow pass across his clear blue eyes. Neither of them spoke until Sy was settled in his wooden chair next to the desk.

Manny had just gotten back to the office after his two-hour lunch break. He looked freshly washed as usual, because he was. Every day after lunch with Helen he napped for twenty minutes and then swam for twenty minutes in the indoor pool attached to his house. Fifteen years earlier, in his mid-fifties, Manny had turned his two-car garage into a small swimming pool, a private refuge that, as far as Sy knew, no one else ever used. It was the only private indoor pool in town, possibly in the whole damn state, but Manny seemed to be neither proud nor embarrassed by it. Like everything else he considered to be his private possession, including his beloved editorial page, the rest of the world could take it or leave it.

The odd thing was that he didn't seem to feel the same way about the rest of the newspaper. He was the sole owner—or rather, he and Helen owned it—but except for the editorial page he made hardly any proprietary claims other than the owner's right to take all the profits, of course. He wanted the various managers to run their own small fiefdoms, and he invariably acted put-upon when he had to make a decision for one of the designated princes or settle a dispute between two of them.

Manny's attitude left Sy wonderfully free to run the news operation, but it also meant he could not count on the publisher to back the news decisions. More than once, in fact, Manny had written editorials that directly contradicted, sometimes even scolded, the slant taken in a particular news story.

"They've got it scheduled to be a thirty-six-page paper, but that's not big enough," Sy said abruptly. "Vietnam is falling apart and we need two more pages."

"You can't go up two pages," the publisher said. "You know you have to go up four at a time. And forty pages is too many for a Friday. The ad ratio would be too low."

Sy relaxed. It was a perfunctory argument. If he had meant it, he would have simply said no. "I checked. The ratio at thirty-six pages is top-heavy with ads," he said. "At forty, it would still be nearly half advertising."

Manny just stared, ever so slightly bug-eyed, his fingers still poised over the keyboard.

"Have you read the wire stories? This is a historic story. The Viet Cong have surrounded the U.S. embassy in Saigon. The brass keeps telling us we're winning, but the whole goddam country is falling." Sy paused and Manny, with a tired sigh, finally swiveled around away from his typewriter to face him.

Sy decided to throw in his ace, even though by now he was sure he didn't really need to use it. "You ought to know," he said with a seriousness in his voice reserved for delivering bad news to the publisher, "that we're running a shocking photo moved by the AP. It shows a high-ranking South Vietnamese police officer shooting a man to death in cold blood right on the street in Saigon."

He paused for effect. "It's a summary execution, a pistol shot to the head from about a foot away." He paused again but still no reaction from Manny. "It's pretty grisly. I just thought you ought to know because we'll sure as hell get howls of protest from the hawks."

Manny slumped back tiredly. "Do we really have to . . ." He closed his eyes and rubbed them with the tips of his index fingers, a characteristic gesture that usually made Sy feel sorry for him. "Can you at least get some local stories in the paper if we go up four pages? People are saying that all we have is war stories and statehouse news that nobody is interested in. Is there some local angle to this?"

Sy knew he had won, as he always did when he could position the conflict to be good newspapering versus journalistic philistinism. But he was puzzled by Manny's questions and the whining tone. "Goddam," he said, "what does that mean? Who says that's all we have in the paper—the boosters club?" A local angle to a Saigon murder? He almost asked it out loud but he didn't because it wasn't what Manny meant, of course, and it wouldn't be fair to tangle him up with word games.

Suddenly Sy understood that the whole conversation was a red herring, that something else was behind the odd comments by the old man. He looked carefully at the placid face but now he read nothing except a mild impatience, as though he wanted to get back to whatever he had been writing. Sy knew that he secretly and shyly wrote poetry but not during working hours. He glanced toward the typewriter, but it was turned so he couldn't see the words. Probably working on an editorial, although usually he liked to talk with Sy about his editorials.

Manny abruptly left his chair and stood peering out the window, his back to Sy. "How's your new man doing?" he said. "Willis. Still working out all right, is he?"

Had Willis had a run-in with Fletcher Junior? Damn. Why hadn't he mentioned it? Sy said stiffly, "Yes. He's doing just fine. Is someone complaining?"

"No. No, I haven't heard any complaints about him."

Sy's tone sharpened and he challenged the slump-shouldered back, "Well, then why did you ask about him? You've seen his stuff. It's good and getting better. He's barely been here a month yet."

Manny turned slowly away from the window and looked directly and calmly at Sy. Then his eyes flicked away and he said, "Oh, nothing. I just wondered if you still needed that reporter's slot as much as you had thought." His eyes returned to Sy's face, his gaze as open and pious as an acolyte's at the altar.

His frequent and worst fear flooded into Sy's mind. For a blinding instant he knew—just simply knew in his gut—that the publisher was thinking about selling the paper. That's what was troubling him, that's why he seemed distracted. Fletcher had talked him into selling out.

Sy had never talked to Manny about selling the paper, yet for years he had expected it to happen. He knew the big papers, the chains, had made offers. Hell, Manny himself used to show Sy the letters when the *Boston Globe* or the *New York Times* or, God forbid, the Thomson chain would make one of their periodic inquiries. Manny would just laugh and make a great show of dropping the letter into the wastebasket beside his desk. Sy would laugh too, but he always noticed that Manny didn't mention money. Several times Sy had slipped back into the office after the publisher had left, but before the night janitor made his rounds, to dig through the basket. Only once did he fail to find the letter, although none of the ones he did find ever actually mentioned a price. The one he couldn't find had been a multipage letter written on off-white paper that Manny had said was from a midwestern chain notorious for making money and producing awful newspapers. That night Sy had smoothed out every piece of paper in the basket but did not find the letter, although he remembered in painful detail how Manny had held it up like a prize, fanning out the pages before he dropped it with a flourish into the half-full can. Sy had examined the pile of trash twice and rifled through each stack of papers on the desk but he didn't find it, and the letter had never been mentioned again.

Manny moved back to his desk and looked directly at Sy, and the image of the smiling, pink-faced publisher holding up that mysterious letter flashed into Sy's mind. That's it. He's thinking about cutting the payroll to make the numbers come out better so they can sell it.

He said slowly and coldly, "I need the reporter, the slot, even more than I thought. Hell, I could use four more. You want to give me four more reporters?" Manny didn't even bother to reply. Sy went on. "Has Fletcher been complaining about Willis?"

Manny sat down again in his desk chair. "I told you nobody has complained. Forget it." He hurried on. "Okay, tell Rocky we're going to forty pages." He turned and reached toward the typewriter. "Oh, I'd like to see that picture when you get a chance. Will we play it big?"

Sy briefly considered reopening the talk about Willis, but he didn't because he suddenly was eager to get back to the newsroom. He wanted to read the war stories. And he wanted to take another look at the photo. He felt the mild squeamishness that often troubled him when he ran graphic, emotional news photos. He resolutely defended publication of personal-tragedy pictures — close-in shots of teenagers killed in cars, fire victims, grieving relatives, losing athletes. But in private moments of sheer honesty, he recognized the taint of voyeurism in such shots. This Saigon picture, he thought, will go to the top of the charts for brutal, violent news photography. The camera caught things nobody wanted to see — the ugly, angry look of the police executioner, the terrified look of the hands-bound prisoner, even the snapping motion of his head as the bullet smashed into it.

"Yeah," he said, "we'll run it big on Page One, and inside we'll use the whole sequence of shots."

Manny sighed mightily. "I suppose it'll give the peaceniks another reason for another protest. I just hope our people don't join in."

The comment stopped Sy before he reached the door. "What the hell does that mean? Who's going to join in what?"

Manny rolled his eyes. "Well, it just seems like the newsroom is mostly young liberals these days. I just meant — "

"Goddam it," Sy said, "I don't like the goddam war myself, but I'm not joining any protest. You've written editorials against it yourself. What are you getting at?"

Manny didn't answer and Sy again felt an urgent need to read the wire copy. He left hurriedly and started toward the composing room, but he changed his mind and went straight to the newsroom. He'd wait until Rocky had already gotten the paper all laid out before he made him redo it.

***

The Oasis was empty as usual so they took the large back booth, near the bathroom and angled so they could all see the entranceway. "Say, Merle," Willis said, "see if you can round up your friend the bartender."

"He's not my friend," Merle answered peevishly. "He's my cousin." He was halfway to the bar when Jake came through the door from the kitchen, drying his hands on a towel. "The bastard must spend most of his life washing dishes," Willis whispered, his voice edgy and his fingers tapping on the table.

"Nah," Ron whispered back, "he just stands back there peeping out of that little window in the door until the customers get up to get their own beer and then he pops out just before they get to the cooler."

Willis looked puzzled, not sure if it was a joke. Ron, still using a serious conspiratorial tone, said, "Yeah, you see, Jake secretly doesn't believe in drinking. Anywhere else in the country, he'd have some other line of work. But up here, not believing in something just means you don't do it yourself; if somebody else wants to drink, that's his business, and you might as well make a buck on it if he's going to do it anyway. But at the same time you don't want to make it too easy for him, so Jake hides out as long as he can until the poor customer can't wait any longer."

Merle spoke to the bartender then slipped back into the booth opposite Willis and Ron and they didn't talk again until Jake had brought the drinks, set them down silently, and gone away.

Willis said, "Nice friendly folks in your family, Merle."

"Yeah," Ron said, "masters of the social graces."

Merle, wiping beer foam off his mouth, sighed. "Worse than that," he said, "they're all Republicans. Goldwater Republicans. They think Nixon's soft on welfare cheats and draft dodgers."

Willis drained half his drink and slumped back heavily into the corner of the booth. Merle and Ron began to argue about whether America or the Viet Cong were really the aggressor. Willis was uninterested. At first he listened because he was mildly intrigued by the kid, Ron. Over the past month, the three of them had become after-work drinking buddies. Unless one or more of them were working on a late story, when the city desk knocked off about eleven each night they'd wander over to The Oasis for a few pops. They were the core of a small group of reporters who had no family attachments to take them home after work. Usually, they'd drink and argue until nearly the final deadline, then hurry back to the newsroom to hang around for the final balls-to-the-wall scramble, the nightly emergency that was absolutely predictable but at the same time just as exciting every time as though something truly unexpected had happened. The only thing better than being around when the paper was closing up was being the last reporter writing, the one racing against the deadline to bang out one or two more sentences in the story that, within a half hour, would be at the top of Page One as it rolled off the press, flashing by so fast that even the big headline was a blur and your byline couldn't even be seen, but that didn't matter because you knew it was there as the papers whizzed through the press and stacked up on the conveyor belt.

Willis knew this kid Ron was the real thing, one of the quiet, smart, tough reporters who got high on bylines. He was one of journalism's true disciples, vicarious participants, self-anointed vicars of the People. Willis once heard someone describe reporters as shy egomaniacs. He had seen Ron standing beside the press one night when the papers that were slapping down on the conveyor had his own byline at the top of the page. He'd watched his face twitch from anticipation, watched as he risked a confrontation with the feared pressroom foreman to snatch an early copy off the line, fouling up the stack count in defiance of the large Stay Back sign that ordered newsroom people to keep their hands off the papers. He'd seen Ron's eyes narrow as he read his story and then relax into a satisfied triumph when he found that the editors hadn't changed his lead. He loved it. He'd kill hell, he'd starve for a Page One byline.

Willis watched as Ron happily and calmly started to take apart Merle's informed but inarticulate thesis about America's true motives in Vietnam. He knew the kid was just toying with Merle because Ron despised the war as much as anyone. He had told Willis about pulling some mysterious strings with his Maryland draft board to keep himself out of it.

Willis grew bored and closed his eyes briefly, then reached forward to bring the glass of bourbon back with him into the corner.

He took another long drink, alone for an instant in the soft comfort of isolation, his mind screening out all outside distractions as the warm numbness seeped through him. He was warm the way you can be only if you've recently been cold, glowing inside and tingling on the surface. Had he ever been more comfortable, more fully at ease? It was an odd place to find such a sense of peace—a backwater town in a frozen land that was only now showing the first signs of entering the twentieth century. Even the South, with all its bluster about sacredness of place, had begun to shed its skin of parochialism, but this place was just as insular and didn't even seem to know it. In the South, the idea of proud poverty was a myth that applied, if at all, only to a tiny fraction of the population. Willis had seen a lot of angry, grasping, violent poverty in the Carolinas, rural Texas, Louisiana, Alabama, and Georgia, but he hadn't seen much of the self-respect that goes with real pride. What he had grown up with, observed, feared, and finally written about had been a bitter, brutal poverty. Up here, the trappings of life were threadbare for most people, with a statewide per-capita income that would make Big Jim Folsom feel right at home. The poverty was just as ferocious here as it was in Alabama but there was a difference; up here, Willis thought, it had not yet won. The struggle was constant and the enemy was unyielding, but they seemed to be still fighting.

A final swallow brought only ice cubes into his mouth, so Willis reluctantly abandoned the peace of his corner hideout so he could deal with the emptiness of his glass. He sat up straight and said in a loud voice, "I'll say one thing for your right-wing kinfolks, Merle, at least for the bartenders among them: they're not stingy." He raised his glass high above the table but Jake couldn't see it because he was standing with his back to them, watching the late news on a miniature television snuggled in among the rows of bottles at the back of the bar.

"That's Yankee conservatism," Ron said, looking over at the bartender then back to Willis. "He doubles up on your first drink so he can save steps for himself and save money for you. Of course, he doesn't make much money that way. But Vermonters expect to be poor all their lives anyway. They think it's natural justice; you can be poor and get to live in Vermont, or you can be rich and have to live somewhere else."

Willis snorted out a humorless laugh. "No, I'm serious," Ron said. "I think the people up here really believe in justice. I mean, they don't seem to have much interest in religion and they're generally not very sentimental. The most over-told joke in the state is the one about freezing the old folks in the winter and stacking them in the woodshed to save fuel. But they do sure as hell care about justice. All you've got to do to get a Vermonter to react is convince him that an injustice has been committed."

"Sure," Willis said. "Sure they believe in justice, just so long as they don't have to pay for it."

Ron shook his finger at Willis. "Hell, you ought to know better than that. Vermonters went south by the trainload to take the slaves away from your ancestors. Per capita, they sent more men to that war than any other state."

"Yeah," Merle added. "And in this war going on now, Vermont has sent the least per capita."

"That's right," Ron said. "The thing you've got to know about Vermonters is that justice is what they believe it is, not necessarily what somebody tells them it is. They just don't trust government very much."

Willis started to tell them some of the racist comments he had heard from these justice-minded Vermonters—mechanics and bartenders and all sorts of others who assumed that his southern accent made him a co-conspirator in their underground bigotry. He thought about telling them how the local police sergeant had volunteered out of the blue that he had learned in the army the only way to get a black soldier's attention was with a two-by-four. He started to say all that, then changed his mind. He was bored with the argument; racism was a fact, a condition built into being human, like greed or lust, and like them something to be curtailed by laws and punishments.

Ron and Merle were waiting for him to talk, but he abandoned the subject with a wave of his left hand, and with his right he shoved his empty glass across the table toward them.

Ron's glass was still full of beer, but Merle picked up his own empty beer bottle and Willis's glass and walked over to the bar. He stood watching the news until a commercial allowed Jake to turn around and take the order for refills. Merle started talking before he even got all the way back to the table. "That son-of-a-bitch Nixon says he's got a plan that's guaranteed to end the war but it's a secret and he won't tell anyone. Can you believe that?"

He slid into his seat and would have continued, but Willis called out to Jake, who was just leaving the bar with the drinks. "Your cousin here says Nixon's a liar, just trying to get elected. What do you think of that?"

Jake didn't answer until he had delivered the tray, then he said, "I think he's like the rest of the press; they know how to make trouble but they don't know shit about anything else. Don't even know enough to keep their mouths shut." He looked directly at Willis for a few seconds, then turned and walked stiffly back behind the bar and through the door into the kitchen.

Ron and Willis both laughed, but Merle was embarrassed. His head drooped and he stared for a long time at the table. Ron turned sideways toward Willis and asked, "Did you ever cover national politics?"

Ron gave the question a simple, offhand flavor, but the casualness was a lie. His lean, preppy face was taut and Willis felt the tension cast off by the body sitting next to him. The boy, barely old enough to drink on his own ID card, was intense about everything, and when it came to newspapering he was just short of electric. When his stories were rewritten, he fell ill. He regularly quizzed Willis about his earlier jobs, fascinated by details of past stories and other newspapers. He would have been a clown except that he was a damn good reporter and he could write like a natural. Poor Merle—as serious as Ron was ambitious, as humble as the boy was prideful. Poor Merle—a permanent backwater reporter because he looked like a clod, tripped on his own syntax, and displayed his moral judgment like a birthmark. He knew right from wrong instinctively and incorruptibly, but he was helpless when it came to choosing shirts, friends, causes, or adjectives. Willis began to laugh, remembering the night Sy had bellowed across the newsroom, "Goddam it, Merle, you'd miss the lead on the crucifixion story."

Ron was still looking at Willis, his face intent and his knees bouncing in place under the table. Merle doodled with his finger in a wet spot left on the table by his beer bottle. They all heard the outside door open, and when they looked, Connie, the blonde from the newsroom, was standing just inside, waiting for her eyes to adjust to the gloom. She spotted them and walked quickly toward the table, smiling broadly. Merle started to scoot over, then changed his mind and started to stand up, forgetting in his confusion that his legs were under the table. As he rose, he bumped hard into the edge of the table, spilling beer and knocking over the empty bottles. He sat back down quickly, and Connie, laughing, said, "Just slide over, Merle," which he did, but he went the wrong way and fell off the end of the booth at her feet.

Ron and Willis doubled over, both of them trying to speak but unable to get words past the roars of laughter coming out of their mouths. Connie started to step over Merle but he quickly scuttled out of the way in a clumsy crab-walk and she slid into the booth. She planted her purse on top of the napkin box, like someone staking a claim, and said to Willis, "That was a terrific advance you wrote on the New Hampshire primary. You must have pretty good sources over there."

He nodded, draining his glass. Connie leaned back in the booth, her arm resting on the back of the seat with her hand hanging limply over the edge. The cloth of her white dress stretched across her chest. Her eyes focused tightly on Willis's, but he looked down at her breasts anyway. It's always a mistake to take up that kind of dare and he tried hard not to, but he lost. Her chest at that moment was as irresistible and as tantalizing as a campfire. He looked and kept on looking and she didn't shift in her seat, not even enough to alter the creases in the cloth. But her composure came from will, not indifference, because when he finally got his eyes back to her face, spots of color showed under her cheeks, even in Oasis illumination. She was still staring straight into his face and he wondered if a person could blush and sneer at the same time.

Willis turned away and saw with some amusement that Ron was peering intently toward the other side of the bar, staring resolutely at the barely visible empty tables. Merle was still recovering from the fall, settling down with much shifting and shuffling, perched on the very edge of the seat with plenty of room for another adult between him and Connie. "Merle," Willis said, "since you're on the outside, how about getting another round of drinks." He dug a few bills out of his pocket and reached his arm across the table.

"Wait a minute, Merle, stay still," Connie said quickly. "I'll get my own beer." But after starting to slide across the seat, she realized that she couldn't get out of the booth because Merle was blocking her way, and her outburst confused him so that he couldn't decide whether to get up as Willis had said, or stay put as Connie told him to do. He bobbed up and down twice, like some strange oversized toy in a swimming pool, then finally sank back onto the seat and looked helplessly at Connie, then at Willis. They carefully did not look at each other. Finally, Ron jumped up. "Shit," he said, "I'll get the goddam drinks. What do you want, Connie? A Miller's, right?"

Willis edged back into his corner and watched Connie, who was looking intently at Ron with obvious friendliness. Whatever she wants, he might as well just go ahead and give it to her. The kid's smart, young, ferociously ambitious, and even seems to have been around a bit with girls. But all that won't do him any good this time. Not with her. By the time he knows what she wants, she'll already have it. What he'll get is a thank you — if he's lucky.

Maybe we never win, he thought. Can't win. Hell, maybe we never even know what the stakes are. But they know, all right. She knew what she wanted and how to get it. People always say women talk a lot. Well, that's subterfuge, a trick that we never catch on to. They talk a lot without ever telling the stuff that counts, like what they really expect from us, or rather, what they intend to get from us. Take Sheila. It had been five years since the divorce, she had been married to somebody else for the past three years, and she still was making him jump through hoops every time she saw him — senseless things, like making a fuss about him paying for the kid's camp for an extra week when he would have done it anyway if she had just asked outright. Not that Sheila was like this one. Connie was in a category all by herself, all straight talk with a chin-jutting forthrightness that defied normal skepticism, like a magician who not only shows you his empty hands but makes you roll up his shirtsleeves too so you know for yourself that either he really does do magic or else he's a hell of a lot too smart for you.

She was half turned in the booth, talking intently to Merle and gesturing, her hands moving up and down, inches away from the arm of his jacket. Willis tuned out the voices, focusing his consciousness on her and feeling the connection between them while the alcohol settled like smothering cotton around the parts of his brain that were not involved with Connie's presence. He was fully relaxed, yet at the same time he studied her turned-away face closely, sure that she was just as aware of him even though she appeared to have forgotten he was there.

And Merle really had forgotten Willis was there. He was so captivated by Connie's monologue that he had even forgotten to be nervous, just sitting there with a smile on his face, looking at her. Ron was gone for a long time, long enough for mild anxiety to bump gently against Willis's consciousness. He picked up his glass, but he knew before lifting it that he would get only a little melted ice water. He drained it off and set the glass down loudly on the table. Irritation toward Ron began to shove aside the pleasant absorption with Connie. He looked around and saw the kid starting over from the bar. He started to say something but changed his mind and just reached out for his new drink, pulling it back with him into the corner.

Merle looked up at Ron and said, "Connie thinks we need to change around the beats in the newsroom. Says reporters waste too much time covering local meetings and don't get to do any real writing." Ron, tracing his index finger around the rim of his beer bottle, said, "I don't know. I get some pretty good stories out of meetings sometimes."

"That's not the point, Ron. The point is that reporters end up working all day and half the nights." Connie leaned forward with her forearms on the edge of the table and both hands reaching toward Ron on the other side. She shook her head slightly, making the double-hoop earrings jingle. "Don't you see? When someone can write the way you can, it just doesn't make sense to have you warming a seat in some stupid meeting."

She looked at Willis. "You agree, don't you? Have you ever seen a newspaper that covered so many meetings?"

Willis was not listening. He wrestled down an impulse to reach over and touch her hands. They stared at each other until Ron reclaimed her attention by saying, "You're right. If we didn't have the damn meetings, we could cover stuff that needs to be reported, like Johnson's State of the State speech or like Aiken's Senate speech on Vietnam. That's the kind of stuff we ought to be writing."

"Jesus," Merle exploded. "Christ, I'd love to have covered Aiken's speech." He was talking to Connie, but she was watching Ron and didn't turn around to look at him, and the others ignored him too, but he didn't really even notice. "Willis, did you ever cover Washington?"

"What's that?" He heard his name but not the question. He had a mildly uneasy sense that this conversation had a hidden layer, some cryptic message that he wasn't getting. "What'd you say, Merle?"

"Washington. The capital. Did you ever cover national politics?"

Ron and Connie both turned to Willis and he slowly slid forward in the booth. Before answering, he shook out a cigarette and lighted it. "Not really," he said, blowing smoke out of the corner of his mouth. "I covered a bunch of congressional hearings and occasionally I'd go up there for a specific story, like the Civil Rights Act in '64."

"Damn," Merle said. "You covered that debate? Johnson's bill?"

"Sort of," Willis said. "I wrote a series on it for the *Charlotte Observer* and I spent a couple of weeks in DC."

The three of them watched him closely but silently as he took a long drag.

"Actually, that's a right good story. I'll tell y'all if you want." Willis, usually cautious about his accent, realized with a stab of worry that his guard had dropped. Maybe he was getting drunk? Naw, not yet. The drawl, the stretching of I to Ah, and the tip-off words often sneaked in when he talked on the phone to someone back home or even, like now, when he thought back about news stories — or Sheila.

He glanced quickly to see if the others had noticed. Connie had a small grin that could have been mocking, but the others didn't show anything except interest in his story. He hurried on. "I mean, the story about working on that story. The series set off a burst of activity by the Klan and I got a bunch of threats. They even evacuated the newsroom at one point."

"Christ," Merle said. "What happened?"

Connie interrupted, sliding across the seat and bumping into Merle. He jumped in his seat, like a comic-book character when a live coal is dropped into his lap. They all laughed. Connie turned back to Willis. "Sorry to miss y'all's war story but I've got to get back over there before they wrap up the paper. Remember to tell me the rest of it." He nodded, and she went on. "How about it? Will y'all help convince Sy that we can drop some of the damn meetings? He listens to you."

Now it was Willis who blushed. He said, "I didn't know he listened to anything except whatever it is inside himself that drives him to work eighteen hours a day. But, yeah, I'll agree with you about the meetings."

She smiled and looked directly into his eyes for a long moment, melting any lingering resistance, if there had been any. Then she stood up and left, leaving Willis restless and on edge, feeling a vague excitement — a strange hybrid sensation of mixed fear and joy. Once, in North Carolina, he had been driving fast on a twisting road, a little drunk, when he suddenly realized the car was out of control and he was no longer driving, just riding. He knew something important was going to happen but he didn't know what and he didn't mean for it to be that way but it was too late to stop, and besides, it was a terrific ride and he thought maybe at some point he would even be able to get the thing back under control. He remembered that exhilaration as he watched Connie walk out of the barroom. His head was clear and his senses were so alive the skin on his arms tingled, but everything was moving in slow motion.

*****

Merle and Ron were both looking at Willis, waiting for the rest of the story. "Damn," he said suddenly, "I feel like doing something. We need some action. Get one more round then let's wander back over to the paper and see what's going on." They finished the drinks long before he finished telling about Lyndon Johnson passing the civil rights bill, and he was still telling Texas stories about Johnson when they got back to the paper. The three of them walked in laughing, but the scene in the newsroom stopped them just inside the door.

Seymour and Connie stood squarely in front of each other, separated by three feet of charged space. Everyone else in the newsroom gaped at them openly, not even pretending to work. Seymour's face was red. His hand plowed in quick jerks through his messy hair. Connie seemed relaxed, a small smile on her face and her hand propped on her left hip in a curiously masculine, athletic stance, like an on-deck batter or a tennis player waiting for an opponent to recover his composure after a bad serve.

Both of them looked over as the three came in, but no one greeted them. Sy turned back to her and said angrily, "Look, Connie, here's what I think. I think I run this newsroom, and as long as I do we're going to cover local news the way I say we're going to cover it. And that means we're going to cover meetings. Period."

He was talking faster and louder with each sentence, working himself into a froth. Everyone in the newsroom had seen Seymour boil over into emotional anarchy, most often during confrontations with aggressive critics who dared challenge a reporter or the paper's coverage. Usually, the target of the anger withered and slunk away, sometimes murmuring about madmen. Now, though, Connie was standing her ground, watching Sy with a taunting smile that looked as though it might escalate into an open laugh.

Willis looked on in stunned anticipation. He heard a gasp as someone took in a large swallow of air, but then he realized he was holding his own breath so he didn't know if the noise came from himself or someone else. He looked around, but everyone in the room seemed to be holding his breath.

"That's what local news means and that's what it's always going to mean as long as I am editor of this goddam newspaper," he shouted.

"And if that means every goddam reporter has to go out every goddam night, then, by God, that's what they're going to do."

Connie waited with exaggerated patience until he stopped, either out of words or out of breath, then she moved a half step closer to Seymour and said, "And that means lots of overtime for everybody, right? Because reporters are people too, just like everybody else, and if we're going to work all night and all day, we're damn well going to get paid for it, just like anybody else would."

Her hands began to move as she warmed up. "We care about news just as much as you do, but we're not machines. We have lives outside this newsroom and we have a right to live them. And if we give up our nights, our time, to cover an assignment, then we have a right to be paid a premium for it." Her voice was low and calm and her words were carefully spoken, but by the end her right hand was chopping in front of her in tight little thrusts that sliced through a section of air running roughly from Seymour's chest to his belt line. "Other morning newspapers pay a premium for night work and there's no reason why this one shouldn't."

"Oh, and by the way," she said, looking around at her audience, "they already pay a premium for night work in the composing room here." She looked triumphant, Willis thought, maybe even a little smug, but when he looked over at Seymour, he was surprised to see his angry glower turned into an ironic smile.

"Well then, Connie," Sy said slowly, "why don't you get a job in the composing room? I expect Rocky would be glad to have you. Of course, every time you wanted to stop work for a little tirade, you'd have to punch out on the time clock."

For a moment, the room was frozen in place, as silent and as still as a theater set at the moment before the curtain goes up. Then, as if on cue, a dirty little man wearing a folded paper cap and stained green work trousers walked into the newsroom, shuffled passed the knot of people without looking up, and stopped in front of Seymour. He wiped his blackened hands on his t-shirt and said with a toothless grin, "Nine-Fingers wants to know when we'll get the last page tonight. Says to tell you if we get started late again, he's going to tell the old man."

Seymour snorted a short laugh and said to Connie, "Maybe instead of the composing room, you'd rather work in the pressroom. You could be a colleague of Eric here," he said, turning to the stunted, ageless messenger.

"As for you, Eric," he said, "fuck off. And go tell Nine-Fingers to fuck off too. He'll get the last page when we get the last news. And he'll run the press when we're ready to run the goddam press. As always."

The pressroom drone just stood there grinning, showing no self-consciousness and evidently oblivious to the charged atmosphere in the room. He pulled up the tail of his t-shirt to wipe the gray drops of sweat off his face, exposing a hairless belly and the filthy tops of his boxer shorts. He looked around at the fidgeting crowd and then across the room at the copy editor, Stebbins, who was the only person in the room doing any work. Eric tilted back his jug-eared head to leer up at Seymour and said, "Ayuh, I can see you're all going flat out. Well, don't let me hold you up." He turned around casually and strolled slowly out the door. If he knew any of the others that he passed on his way out, he didn't give any sign.

When the door had closed behind him, they all looked toward Seymour to see if the fight was over and he was going back to his office. He was not. He stood looking at Connie. "Do you know how Nine-Fingers got his name? No, of course you don't. Well, he got it one night when he was trying to coax another day's paper out of the obsolete, worn-out press that's been malfunctioning on a regular basis down in that black hole of a basement for the past seventy-five years. He was trying to unstick a roller without shutting the goddam thing off because he wasn't sure he could get it going again if he shut it down, and for him the most important thing in the world is getting a newspaper off that machine every day. He was sticking his hand in that monster and it by God mashed off his goddam finger. Mashed it off. And do you know what he did? What Nine-Fingers did in that very moment when he was getting christened with his new name? He jerked out the rest of his hand, tied a dirty rag around it, and ran off the whole pressrun before he went to the hospital.

"You want to know the funny part of that story? The funny part is that later, the press gang was speculating about whether he screamed when his finger got cut off. The press made so much noise that most of them didn't know anything had happened and no one heard him holler. So, later they asked him if he had screamed. 'I don't know,' he said, 'because I couldn't hear a goddam thing.' Then he said, 'But I'll bet the sonofabitch who got that paper yelled when my finger fell out into his cornflakes.'"

There was general laughter, and Willis thought, well he's got them again, Connie loses. But Seymour didn't stop. He called again to

Connie, "What makes you think you can manage these reporters' time better than they can manage it themselves?" She looked like someone who has been slapped, and Willis saw several reporters looking down at the floor. "They were getting along pretty well before they had a guardian angel." He paused but Connie didn't answer, and he was about to open up with another salvo when the shrill sound of the AP alarm bell rang out over the clatter of the wire. The frantic ringing stopped him and he whirled around toward the machine over in a corner behind the news editor's desk.

"Where the hell is Greenberg?" Seymour shouted. He glared at the empty chair behind the desk. "Goddam it, where the hell is Greenberg?"

Simmons called out from the outer ring of the crowd, "He's in the toilet."

"What?" Sy snapped his head toward the deep-voiced reporter. "How do you know?"

"Well," Simmons said, his voice rumbling slowly over the heads of the small crowd, "it's seventeen minutes past midnight, so where the hell else would Greenberg be?"

The reporters laughed. Everyone knew, but no one ever mentioned, that every night at 12:10 Greenberg left his desk, picked up the *Herald Tribune* from the table where all the newspapers were tossed each day, and went into the bathroom, where he stayed for twenty minutes, arriving back at his own desk at twelve thirty. Everyone knew this routine except Seymour, who still had an irritated, puzzled look on his face.

"That's right," Connie said cheerfully. "Greenberg's bowels are the only things that move on schedule around here."

The others roared, ignoring the renewed ringing of the AP urgent bell. Seymour's confusion turned to rage and he yelled, "Goddam it, somebody see what's on that wire. Where the hell is Greenberg?" Several of them jumped but he was already in full stride, dodging around desks, and he was the first to reach the AP machine. He grabbed the narrow, coarse paper and ripped it off along the edge of the plastic flap that covered the sputtering keys.

He scanned the widely spaced lines of type, then quickly checked through about a yard of copy before he turned around and said in a calm, low voice, "The Viet Cong are pounding our troops and the South Vietnamese all over the goddam country. Da Nang may be in trouble. A bunch of marines are surrounded."

No one replied, and Seymour turned to Ron. "Go tell Rocky we'll be having some late copy." He walked away toward his office, still holding the ripped-off AP copy. "Tell Greenberg to come see me when he gets back," he called over his shoulder to no one in particular.

*
**

All the others had bailed out early and Willis was pissed when he left The Oasis. His fury soared when the door slammed behind him so fast it actually hit his ass. He whirled around to kick it, but he was off-balance and nearly fell down. He was fairly drunk too, but he caught himself and spun to the side so goddam Jake couldn't see him. He knew he was on the other side of the goddam door, watching through the peephole.

Willis thought about checking to see if the nameless bar was still open, but he badly needed to use a bathroom so he walked slowly with careful balance across the street toward the office building, his shoulders squared and arms stiff at his sides. He reached the front door of the paper without a misstep, grabbed the door handle, and poured all his controlled fury into a mighty yank designed to show the door and anyone who might be watching who was in charge. But the locked door won and he found himself falling face first into the glass. He swore mightily, then recovered, found the key in his pocket, and slipped inside without daring to look around to see if anyone had seen.

The front office was dark and empty and he slipped quickly past the newsroom entry and into the bathroom. He found Greenberg's discarded *Herald Tribune* and when he came out ten minutes later and strolled into the newsroom, the paper was tucked under his arm. He tossed it onto Greenberg's desk and was about to make a wisecrack, but a quick look at the editor's face stopped him in his tracks. Willis heard a loud click, the unmistakable sound of a rifle bolt sliding home, and behind him a voice said, "Who the fuck are you?"

Willis's head snapped back, and as he started to turn around Greenberg said quietly, "Be careful. Go slow."

The man was sitting straight and tense in a wooden chair pushed against the wall behind the open door. He wore head-to-toe starched-stiff camouflage, complete with a small black corporal's insignia on the tip of his collar, black smudges under both eyes, and a rifle that Willis thought was an M14 cradled across his lap. He was young, no more than twenty, Willis figured, and when he raised his right hand to pull on his cigarette, it was trembling so hard he had to lurch forward and grab it with his lips.

He blew out a puff of smoke, dropped the hand back onto the trigger guard, and said, "I said, who the fuck are you?"

"Bud Willis. Who're you?"

The boy soldier just stared, eyes locked onto Willis's. "Are you the chief?"

"Chief what?" Willis said.

"The boss. This guy says he ain't," the soldier said, jerking the rifle toward Greenberg but not taking his eyes off Willis, "so are you the boss?"

"No," Willis said, just as the door, pushed from the hallway, slammed back against the sitting soldier.

"We've got a problem," Sy said as he hurried into the newsroom, "a big problem."

"We sure do," Greenberg said, gesturing at the young soldier, "bigger than you think."

Sy paid no attention to the pointing hand, moving quickly toward his office and saying over his shoulder, "They can't find a full-page furniture store ad and we've got to fill the goddam space."

"Sy," Greenberg called, "hold on. We've got another problem and it can't wait."

Sy wheeled around, scowling, but his mouth snapped shut when he saw the soldier, who had swiveled the rifle in his lap to point directly at Sy's stomach.

"Who the fuck are you?" Sy said.

The soldier simply blinked.

"That's his line," Willis said.

"Shut up, Willis. Now, what do you want, son?"

"You the boss? The one that runs this newspaper?"

"I run the newsroom. Why?"

The boy raised the cigarette again, his hand trembling more than ever. "Well," he said, "I don't like the stuff you put in the paper."

Sy moved a step closer to the soldier and reached out to drag over a chair from one of the desks. The boy tensed, his rifle barrel rising an inch or so. His left eyelid twitched several times.

"Relax," Sy said. "I'm tired, and if we're going to talk about what you don't like, I want to sit down." He settled into the chair, turned to Willis, and said, "You too, Willis. Sit down and relax."

"Now, son, my name is Sy. What's yours?"

"Roy."

"Okay, Roy, tell me what you don't like about the newspaper."

"All that stuff you write about the war and the soldiers. You make us sound like baby killers or something."

"Yeah," Sy said, "it's pretty lousy stuff they're writing about that war. Pretty lousy war, I think. What do you think?"

The boy just stared at him, his eye twitching again.

"I mean, no one believes you soldiers mean to kill babies—or anyone else, for that matter. We know you're just doing your job. And we know that at least some of you don't like it any better than we do. Right?

Sy picked an ashtray off a nearby desk and reached it out toward the soldier. The boy took it and ground out the cigarette, taking both hands off the rifle for the first time.

"Tell us, Roy, who'd you come in here to kill? You must be pretty upset."

"I came in here to kill you." His gaze faltered and his eyes swung away from Sy and toward Willis. "Or somebody. Somebody ought to pay."

"For what?"

"For saying we're losing the war. And that we ought not to be over there and all that."

"Well, you know, Roy, that's a really interesting idea. Because what you're talking about goes right to the heart of the reasons we Americans fight wars. At least, most of the time. We fight in part because we believe everyone has a right to his own opinion. That is, we think people can disagree without being punished—or shot. You've got to agree with that, don't you?"

"That's just words," the boy said. "Words don't mean a goddam thing."

Willis blurted out, "So why're you here? All we do is write words and if they don't mean anything, then—"

"Shut up," Sy said, jabbing a pointing finger at Willis. "Just shut up. Roy's here to talk to me, not you. So shut up."

He turned back to the soldier, who was still focusing his stare on Willis. "Say, Roy, I've got a big problem. And you can help me out. I've got this newspaper to put out, see, and we're already way behind schedule. And I need to find something to fill up a lot of space because some bozo out there in the composing room lost a big ad."

The soldier was watching Sy now, listening hard but clearly confused. "Anyway," Sy said, "I'd like to go on talking to you about this stuff but someone needs to finish making the newspaper. So how about letting Greenberg there—by the way, did you meet him, Matt Greenberg? He's sort of like a top sergeant in the newsroom. The one that gets things done. How about letting him go on and finish putting out the paper? Then you and I can go on talking."

The boy looked doubtful, shifting his eyes from Greenberg to Sy and back again, scowling slightly.

"Listen, Roy, I can promise you that he won't call the cops or anybody else. I just need to get this job finished before we can really talk. So, if you say so, I'm going to tell Matt to get up and finish his work. Willis can stay here or go help Matt, whichever way you want it to be."

The soldier still looked doubtful.

"Roy, I've got to tell you that if you don't trust me even that much, we can't get very far with this talk. I thought you wanted to get some things changed and you can't do that unless we can talk it out."

The soldier, brow furrowed under the stiff brim of the utility cap, looked as though he had a terrific headache and he sat for nearly a minute, saying nothing, his jaw muscles clinching and relaxing.

"Okay then," Sy said, turning to Greenberg, "Matt, you and Willis go ahead and get this damn paper out. We're way late and the delivery truck drivers will be going apeshit. Just find some photos—that's something Willis could do—and get the goddam page filled."

He glanced quickly at the soldier, then hurried on. "First, though, go tell Rocky what you're doing and tell him to stay out of the newsroom. Don't tell him or anybody else what's going on in here."

Roy still gave no sign of objection or agreement with these orders, and Sy hurried on. "And that goes for you too, Willis. Don't let anybody from the composing room into the newsroom. Got it?"

Greenberg and Willis both stood up, but not quickly, and both were watching hard to see what the soldier would do. Slowly they walked away, Greenberg toward the composing room and Willis into the little room where the AP Photofax machine was spitting out photos. He gathered up a handful of pictures from Vietnam, carried them out to his desk, and began sorting them.

Willis realized that he had become completely sober, and his head throbbed slightly. He sat with his face turned sideways from the doorway, carefully not looking at Sy and the soldier, but he could hear their voices plainly.

The boy was speaking, but his talk didn't make a lot of sense at first. He was telling some rambling, tangled-up story about how his old high school buddies now wouldn't have anything to do with him. Apparently, some girl had spit at him when he showed up for a school dance.

"I felt like hitting her," he said.

"You didn't do that, did you?" Sy said.

"No, but I felt like it."

"Did you used to have a crush on her?"

"That's none of your goddam business. And I didn't come here to talk about me, so just shut up."

Willis sneaked a sideways glance and when he saw that the rifle barrel had moved around again to point at Sy, he reached over slowly toward the telephone, but Sy shouted at him, "Don't make any phone calls, Willis. I don't care what you need, don't use the phone."

Sy's voice softened as he turned back to the soldier, "Well," he said, "I just want to tell you that I already knew you hadn't hurt her. Just like I know you didn't do anything like that in Vietnam."

He didn't wait for an answer. "You know how I already knew that? It's because I saw a war too. And I know what soldiers do and don't do and I also know how hard it is to come home from a war."

"What war?"

"The Second. World War II. I was in Europe."

"Did you get a honorable discharge?"

"Sure."

There was a long pause, and Willis took another quick glance at the young soldier. The rifle now was lying in his lap and both hands were off of it.

Sy said, "In those days, of course, it was a lot different from today. Lots of things were different. By the way, have you been discharged or do you have to go back to Vietnam?"

"I'm not going."

"So are you out of the army? I mean, are you home for good?"

The pause was so long that Willis again turned to look at them. The soldier's face was distorted into a tortured grin, the look of a frightened child being brave as he got a shot in the arm.

"I'm AWOL," he blurted. "I was supposed to go back last week but I'm not going to do it."

"Goddam," Sy said loudly, "now that's a real problem. I mean, that takes a lot of guts."

"Not for me," the soldier said. "I'm not going back because I'm scared. I'm a coward."

"Listen, Roy. I knew lots of guys, some real tough GIs who had seen a lot of action, who went missing. How long have you been AWOL?"

"Six days. A week tomorrow."

"Oh well," Sy said. "A week? That's not so big a deal. Hell, I bet we can fix that problem or at least make it be not so bad. A week? I knew guys who didn't show up for a month after a leave. One of my buddies—he was a sergeant—got drunk, went off to Italy, and didn't show up for six weeks. He got busted a couple of ranks, but that's all."

After a long silence, Sy went on, "Look, Roy, you haven't gotten in trouble on this leave, have you?"

"No. I spent a couple of days at home, then hitchhiked out here. I've been here three days but the army doesn't know it."

"Well, I think I can help you. Maybe we can figure out a plan—I mean, a new plan. You already had one when you came in here, didn't you?"

"Yeah. I was going to shoot you then shoot myself."

"Jesus," Sy said. "I guess in that case what I'm trying to do is help myself and you. Right?"

The soldier didn't answer and Willis saw that he had slumped down, the rifle in his lap and his arms hanging down over the arms of the wooden chair.

"Listen, Roy, have you got a place to stay? I mean, here in town?"

"I been staying with my sister. But her and her husband said I've got to leave because they don't really have enough room, with the baby and all."

"Okay, well, I think you better stay around for a while, while we try to figure out how to handle this problem. It's really not so bad, you know. We'll figure out something."

Sy stood up slowly, but the boy didn't move or speak, and he called to Willis, "We're leaving. Tell Matt to do whatever he needs to do to get the paper out. The two of you can handle it. But remember, Willis, don't say a word to anybody about any of this. Got it?"

Willis nodded and watched as Sy motioned to the soldier. "Come on, son, let's get out of here." Sy walked quickly to his office and snatched his jacket and scarf off the coatrack.

The boy stood up slowly, and when the overhead light caught his face Willis saw that the black camouflage smudges under his eyes were streaked with tears. He carried the rifle dangling from one hand, and he and Sy headed for the door. Sy said, "Don't you have a jacket?"

The soldier shook his head and Sy swerved over to the line of hooks adjacent to the door, grabbed an overcoat, and said over his shoulder, "Tell Greenberg I stole his coat. Fresh air will be good for him."

CHAPTER THREE
Tuesday, March 5, 1968

Andrew Johnson was on Sy's mind as he sauntered into the newspaper office, so he didn't even notice the cheerful greeting from the girl at the front counter. He had waked up thinking about how to cover the New Hampshire primary next week, and that led him to President Johnson, and that led to the first President Johnson. As an undergraduate, he had written a paper on Andrew Johnson in which he concluded that he had been a vastly misunderstood president.

As he walked toward the office, Sy's mind happily tortured the ironies that linked the two Johnsons so closely over the hundred-year gap. Two Southerners, they shared the burdens of war and civil rights conflicts; they both rode to power on political populism, a two-way tide that turned against them when they needed it the most; and above all they each suffered mightily from the intolerable scorn and derision of the northeastern elite, those self-righteous reformers and self-satisfied journalists who, Sy thought, would be insufferable except for one saving grace: they were right and both of the Johnsons were wrong.

The warmth of the building felt good. It might be spring in Washington but up here it was still cold in early March, even at midday, and Sy never wore an overcoat. Everyone believed it was because he was too apt to lose it, and he never bothered to disabuse them of that notion. And it was more or less true, but he also believed that he just couldn't afford to buy a good topcoat. He did wear a wool scarf, and as he unwound it from around his neck, his mind flipped from Johnson to Kennedy and then to Lincoln. Another parallel, of course—the Johnsons both plagued by the ghost of an assassinated legend. It was Sandburg's Lincoln that sprang into his mind, the Lincoln who spoke the admonition that gave Sy comfort in dark moments of self-doubt: "If both factions, or neither, abuse you, you will probably be about right."

He glanced around the newsroom and saw young Ron perched on the edge of Connie's desk talking to her but also watching the newsroom door. Sy wondered if journalism schools taught Lincoln's warning, and he was about to ask Ron when someone shouted to him from the other end of the room. "Hey, Sy, wearing a red scarf for a change, huh?" It was Hank, or Henry B. Walker, as he preferred for his byline, the other bright kid who came to the paper just about the same time as Ron, a little more saucy but a little less solid. Four or five people were hanging around the office and all of them except Alice laughed because one of the newsroom's standing jokes was Sy's propensity to wear uninteresting clothes, and a further refinement of that custom was to wear only red scarfs. He had several, and it seemed that every year someone gave him another one and they never wore out, so why buy any other color?

He spun around toward Hank and lashed the scarf out like a whip, saying in slow, theatrical tones, "Can you compose yourself the same as a bright bandana?" Everyone giggled although he was sure none of them knew the quote.

They laughed again as Sy flicked the scarf once more in Hank's direction before moving, with a slightly self-conscious hitch in his stride, toward his own office. Then he remembered why he had come in early. He stopped at his door and turned around. "All of you been to town meetings? What are they talking about out there?"

Ron shouted first. "Road graders, school budgets, and the deer herd. What else?"

Sy smiled and nodded his head. "Of course. What about politics? Big turnouts for the meetings?"

Lon Simmons, a newsroom fixture for two decades who normally covered only police and fire stories except for special occasions when everyone was thrown into a story, snorted loudly. "I've never seen so much politics, stupid politics, at town meeting. Every other speech was either directly political or at least had political overtones. One old guy made a blatant pitch for Davis, and a young woman jumped up to demand equal time for Oakes."

They were all looking at him, and Simmons, who usually was pretty much ignored and whose deep, rumbling voice often was mocked by the other reporters, cleared his throat like someone preparing to talk for a long time. But Hank cut him off. "It's really amazing, Sy. I went to three town meetings this morning, and at every one of them there were two distinct groups. You could just tell, just from looking and listening, how the town was divided. They fought over everything, even the purely local stuff; the same people stuck together on every issue."

Connie spoke for the first time. "Me too. I went to three meetings and it was the same way. You could tell just by the way they dressed and where they sat which side they were on. These people weren't even polite to each other. The old ladies serving lunch looked like they wanted to spit on the baked beans every time a longhair stuck out his plate."

Simmons cleared his throat again, but Connie hurried on. "It really seemed different even from last year, as though something important had changed. People seemed really angry."

Sy had become seriously intrigued by the talk. He wished he had gotten up early enough to go out to a town meeting. He had stopped to vote on his way to the paper, but in the city they didn't have a real town meeting. He couldn't remember exactly when he had covered his last town meeting, but it had been quite a while. Back long before anyone had ever heard of Vietnam.

"How about Aiken?" he asked. "Any sign that he'll have any trouble in the fall?"

"I saw a lot of Tufts bumper stickers," Hank said. "And there was a lot of talk at one meeting about gun control. Besides the Vietnam stuff, of course." He was eager for Sy to recognize his political perspicacity. Too eager.

Simmons snorted again. "Well, young Ace, if you think Aiken's in trouble, I've got a week's paycheck that says you're full of it." He looked around the room with a superior smile on his full lips. "The campaign hasn't even really started, but I saw George and Lola out shaking hands today and I know they've been in the state every other weekend since January. They'll toss Tufts aside like the right-wing nut he is." He turned a smug face toward Sy, who looked the other way.

Sy knew Simmons was right, but the pompous ass acted as if he had solved the riddle of the Sphinx when he was simply parroting fire station wisdom. Still, it was interesting that even the hard hats were not taking Tufts seriously despite Aiken's position on the war. Of course, by now Aiken could get away with just about anything. Even the know-nothings, the place-vain natives whose greatest lifetime achievement was to have been born in Vermont and who thought "liberal Republican" was an oxymoron, even they were secretly proud that their senator had become a national symbol. Buried deep inside nearly all of those jingoists was a gnawing, permanent fear that, because it was small and rural and insular, Vermont really was inferior and they, by extension, were doomed to suffer universal disdain in all serious matters. More, even, a fear that they indeed were inferior and could be independent and forthright and outspoken only as long as they remained inside the tight perimeter guarded by their own mountains. So even the ones who never had voted for him were proud of George Aiken, mainstay of the nightly news, confidante of the powerful Mike Mansfield, dinner companion of kings and presidents, and originator of the most famous political bon mot of the Vietnam war. The same Aiken who sounded and behaved like the men of the Robert Frost poems—hell, even looked like Frost himself—but who nevertheless commanded the attention even of those who criticized him. The same small, gnarled, ordinary hill farmer whose views were important enough to be criticized by the New Yorkers and Californians and Texans who ran the world.

They were proud because Aiken had succeeded by making the same choices they themselves would have made, or at least hoped and believed they would have made, not in politics or policies necessarily but in the real things, choosing self-respect over power whenever he couldn't have both and in the process achieving not only self-respect but universal respect that sometimes brought with it power's gaudy twin, the semblance of power. He and they knew, of course, the difference between power and faux power, but they all ignored or disregarded the distinction because the look-alike imposter often arrived in Vermont in the form of federal largess, which meant even the ones who refused to admit they were proud to have Aiken in Washington couldn't deny that having him there paid off in a thousand tangible ways, payoffs that in any guise other than democracy at work would have been called corrupt.

After five terms, Aiken had reached a state of political invincibility that could not be pierced even when he was at odds with the majority of Vermonters, as he surely was on the war and on gun control. So Simmons was right. Sy didn't like him, but he had to admit that he was right. Years of involved observation had given the old reporter's naturally dull mind an edge in such matters as politics over the smarter and better educated Hank, but none of them, including Hank, could quite accept time's unfair tipping of the scales because Simmons also was a decidedly less attractive specimen. Sy watched as Hank struggled with the challenge, looking for a way out of the trap without rewarding the smirking Simmons, who had a reporter's instinct for when a target was most vulnerable and now moved in on Hank. "How about it, Ace? Aiken versus Tufts—paycheck against paycheck?"

Sy decided to help the kid out. He lowered his head, looked at Simmons out of the tops of his eyes, and said flatly, "Sounds to me like we're paying you too much, Simmons. Better cut out the overtime." It was a joke. Everyone knew that Simmons used the police and fire beat to justify an inordinate amount of overtime, most of which was spent riding around in squad cars and hanging around the diner late at night with Callahan, the graveyard-shift sergeant who was waiting to retire and who was able to tolerate Simmons because he wore a hearing aid that he could turn off.

Simmons knew the overtime threat was a joke, but he considered the extra pay a deserved return for long service and he didn't like having it questioned, even in banter. But he was afraid of Sy's legendary temper, which everyone knew could rise full blown out of nowhere or even out of a playful exchange, like an argument over politics. He looked quickly at Sy but couldn't read the slight scowl with enough certainty, so he simply shrugged and turned away back to his desk. The others also were a little mystified by Sy's comment, or rather, by the way he delivered it, but they also were charmed by his rescue of Hank, except Connie, who started to say something then merely shook her head and walked off, muttering loudly about a power play. The others instantly grew very still, like a flock of feeding birds when the wind shifts suddenly. They waited tensely, but after turning his stern gaze in her direction momentarily, Sy smiled broadly at her back and headed off toward his office.

Inside, he looked quickly at a couple of telephone messages on his desk, then started to open some mail. Junk. Complaints. Two job applications that he barely read but that reminded him Willis wasn't at work yet. He looked out across the newsroom, but almost everybody had left. He looked just in time to see the door closing behind Merle, leaving the office empty except for Alice. Sy looked at the clock. He assumed they were all out on assignments, probably to do with town meeting, but the emptiness of the newsroom at two o'clock made Sy uneasy. Or rather, something was making him feel restless. He sat down at his desk and picked up the *Patriot Press*, but he'd already read most of it before he left home and even the witless Tory editorials didn't distract him. He stood up again and began reading the *Times* copy as it clacked out over the teletext machine. Even the *Times* bored him today, and besides, they didn't have anything useful on the New Hampshire primary. Most of the national reporters, including the *Times'*, were still quoting the *Time* magazine poll showing McCarthy out of the running, with only 11 percent of the vote. The stories made Sy nervous about Willis's analytical piece. He had rummaged around for a couple of days, meeting with students and some of the people he had hung out with before coming over to Vermont, and had concluded that McCarthy was going to put on a formidable showing. He had convinced Sy, and they had gotten some attention when they ran the story a week earlier. Now, though, Sy fretted that they would look foolish if Johnson swept the primary.

Irritation invaded him like some sort of instant flu. The vacant newsroom was an effrontery, his glass office a prison that made him dependent on the reporters, reporters who weren't even there, to know what was going on outside his tiny cage. He needed to know.

Sy took two steps over to his doorway and stood looking with repugnance at the back of Alice's gray head, slumped over her desk, with her multiple chins resting in the cup of her left hand supported by her stubby forearm. She was the widow of the publisher's boyhood friend, whose job, because she couldn't do anything else, was to answer the newsroom telephone from noon to nine. She sat near the door, her back to Sy's office. Maybe she slept between calls.

Alice plodded through her days toward Social Security with a profound self-absorption that puzzled Sy and infuriated everyone else. She never spoke except to complain. She never varied her routine, paying no attention to major fires, newsroom crises, or callers' hysterics. She plopped herself into her seat at five minutes before noon, took exactly twenty minutes for each of her two fifteen-minute work breaks, left for supper always at 6:30 and returned at 7:40, and turned off her telephone every night at ten minutes before 9:00, sometimes while it was ringing. Alice knew nothing and cared nothing about newspapers. If she had ever read one, nobody in this office had seen the remarkable event. She had been hired by the publisher and just appeared in the newsroom one afternoon soon after her husband died. She and the publisher had worked out terms of her employment between them and neither of them had ever told Sy what those terms were. She complained often about not having enough money, but after a while the sea of her general misery was so vast that the poor-mouthing did not register. Alice's unhappiness was so complete that for everyone else that's all there was to her. She had no friends in the newsroom, although in recent weeks several times Sy had noticed Connie sitting on the edge of Alice's desk, chatting away quietly.

Sy watched Alice for a few minutes but it was impossible to tell whether she was asleep. He strolled over to her desk. "I'll be back in an hour or so," he said.

"There's no one else here," she said. "I can't keep up with all these phones by myself."

"Don't worry about it, Alice. Just answer them one at a time and let the others ring. They'll wait for you."

"Well, it's Town Meeting Day, you know."

"I know that, Alice. I also know that they don't close the ballot boxes until six or seven and nobody's going to call in with election results until they close the polls. And if they do, I want to know about it."

He said it without any hint that it was a joke, and that's exactly how she took it. "Well, you can't get mad at me if they call with results and the polls aren't closed and I can't take the call because I'm talking to someone else," she said with impeccable logic. "Or in the bathroom."

Sy looked at her numbly. Finally, he looked around and said, "Where's everyone else?" as though he had just noticed the empty newsroom.

Alice looked away. "How would I know? No one ever tells me when they're leaving. Or coming back either, for that matter."

"How about Greenberg?" he asked. "Has he been in yet?"

"'Course not," she said, her face for the first time showing life, or rather, hatred—pure, undiluted, glint-eyed loathing. "He's always late. They're all like that."

"All who?" Sy asked. "Who's always late?" But when he looked closely and saw the tight-lipped, jowl-quivering fury, he just shook his head and hurried out of the newsroom, wrapping his scarf around his neck as he walked, because he really didn't want to hear her say who she was talking about. He had long observed with some degree of disgust that rank prejudice lay deep beneath the surface in some Vermonters, a subterranean pool of bitterness that occasionally oozed out in coded asides targeting black people, Jews, and homosexuals, the same fear-inspired wellspring that fed the more commonly heard jokes and sneers provoked by "flatlanders."

Sy was lugging a large cardboard box when he walked back into the newsroom an hour later. Five reporters were at their desks, including Connie, who looked up at him and smiled. Alice looked up as he passed her desk and said, "The new guy called." He paused, resting the corner of the box on the edge of her desk, but she didn't go on. Finally, he said, "What new guy, Alice?" He heard Connie laugh.

Alice's watery, magnified eyes peered at him through her pink-rimmed glasses. "That reporter you hired who nobody ever introduced me to. How'm I supposed to know his name?"

"For God's sake, Alice, that was two months ago." She stared ahead giving no sign that his implied logic had found a target. "Well," Sy said, "what did he say?"

"He said to tell you he'd be in about six. And that he had a good story."

"That's all?"

"That's all he said to me."

"Well, did he talk to anyone else?"

"How would I know?"

"Alice, goddam it, did Willis talk to anyone else in the newsroom?"

"No."

Sy tugged at his tie in irritation, then started toward his office, walking awkwardly, with the container in front of his stomach partially blocking his view.

"You needn't to swear," Alice said.

He balanced the box precariously on top of the piles of papers littering his own desk and took out his foot-long copy editor's scissors to open the lid. He tugged and pulled but couldn't dislodge the box's contents, so finally he simply cut away the front plate of cardboard, revealing to the amazed spectators in the newsroom a small television set.

For years Sy had batted away every suggestion of putting a TV in the newsroom, angered by the idea of admitting that the networks really did cover the news. More even, it felt like a capitulation to a hated enemy that somehow had sneaked past your guard and set up artillery aimed directly at your headquarters tent. He looked around, realized he had not prepared a place for the damn thing, and began clearing the top of an ancient oak filing cabinet standing at the back wall of his office. He lifted the television set into its place, then fished the rabbit ears out of the box and hooked them into the back of the set. When it was wired and plugged into the wall socket, he twisted the on-off switch and began dialing through the channels. Eventually, with several adjustments of the rabbit ears, he was able to pick up three stations with varying degrees of clarity. Only one offered anything that could be described as a clear picture, but it was the most important station, a CBS affiliate broadcasting from Burlington.

Sy backed up to view his new possession from his desk chair but realized he had piled most of the filing cabinet's load in the chair and he had to move it again, this time piling it on top of the other piles scattered around the office. Finally, he sat down, leaned back in the swivel chair, and began watching *As the World Turns*. That's when Fletcher H. Monrose Jr. walked into the office.

Sy looked up at the publisher's son but he didn't say anything. He just leaned further back and raised his feet to rest them cross-ankled on the desk, or rather, on the shortest stack of papers on the desk. He glanced at Fletcher standing silently in the doorway, then turned his eyes back to the television set. Fletcher seemed mesmerized by the television, staring with no sign of comprehension or emotion. Sy waited in silence, peering at the flickering black-and-white image through two long, wooden soap opera embraces before he finally looked again at Fletcher and said, "Did you want something?"

Fletcher broke his gaze away, picked up a stack of newspapers off of the chair beside Sy's desk, and sat down, his back turned to the television set. "I just wanted to tell you about a conversation I had yesterday at Rotary." He glanced over his shoulder at the television set, which Sy was watching again even though he still refused to mention it or in any other way help the conversation. Fletcher squared up his shoulders and plowed ahead. "Yeah, I was talking with Sandy Kittridge and he mentioned . . . that is, he sort of complained about our coverage of the tax legislation . . ."

Sy brought his eyes to Fletcher's face for the first time but he didn't say anything. "Yeah," Fletcher continued. "yeah, well, he seemed to think we had taken a position. That is, that our coverage was against the tax bill." He paused, then hurried on. "And I know that Dad hasn't taken a position. I mean, an editorial position. So I wanted to mention it to you. You know, just pass it along, sort of . . ."

Fletcher noticed that his necktie was hanging slightly to one side and he carefully stretched it down so the tip rested precisely on his belt buckle. He raised his head again, but Sy still was not looking at him. "I mean, I think a sales tax may be just what the state needs, don't you? We need the revenue, and we sure as hell don't want to increase the income tax." Still no response from Sy. "Sandy is a pretty good advertiser, you know. At least, his insurance agency is."

Sy slowly lifted his feet from the desk and leaned his chair forward, looking directly at Fletcher. "Fletcher," he said quietly, motioning toward the television set, "turn that goddam thing off, for Christ's sake." A puzzled look crossed Fletcher's face, but he stood up quickly and stepped over to turn the dial. The picture faded, and before he could get back into his seat, Sy asked, "How much did they fine you this time?"

"Huh?" Fletcher said. "Fine me?" He sat down again, carefully aligning the creases in his trousers.

"You know what I mean, Fletcher, don't play games. How much did they fine you at Rotary?"

"Thirty cents," he said. "A dime three different times. Three mistakes they said the paper . . . but that doesn't have anything to do with—"

"Look, Fletcher, we've talked about this before. Those guys just like to needle you. They're always going to have some complaint about the paper, and as long as you're in that stupid club, they're going to ride you. They're all shopkeepers, for God's sake. They think newspapers were invented to help the economy and to make them and their community look good to the rest of the world."

Fletcher was beginning to redden. "Look," Sy said in a more friendly tone, "I know you need to sell advertising to those guys, and I know it's no fun to listen to their gripes every week. But don't take it personally. If you think you need to stay in the club, then learn to roll with it. If they don't like something they read in the paper, tell them to call me. That's what your father does. Watch him. He never worries about the crap handed out by the Sandy Kittridges of the world."

Sy smiled but Fletcher didn't. "Maybe he'd be better off if he did worry about what they say," he said. "And maybe you would be too. This paper is part of the community and we ought to act like it."

It was an old argument and he knew his lines well enough to be comfortable. Sy knew that Fletcher had been going more and more often to newspaper meetings around the country, talking with other advertising directors, business managers, and publishers. He was developing strong views about how newspapers ought to be run and he was discovering that his father was not universally admired, or at least his style of managing his newspaper was not universally respected, even by some of the same publishers who did respect, or professed to respect, the paper that his father published.

Sy lifted his feet off his desk and dropped them with exaggerated weariness to the floor. He slumped down in his chair, cocked his head to the right, and said in a tired voice, "You ought to be ashamed, Fletcher. You of all people ought to know what your father has done for this community. You of all—"

"Wait a minute," Fletcher rose up halfway out of his chair. "Wait just a minute. I didn't mean to—"

"No, Fletcher, you wait just a goddam minute." Now Sy was sitting up straight, his hatchet face jutting forward and his index finger wagging at the end of an outstretched arm. "I'm going to tell you what your father has done for this community. And you're going to listen." He paused for breath but not long enough for Fletcher to recover his equilibrium. "So sit down and listen." Fletcher sat.

"Your father, as you ought to know, took a worn-out limp rag of a newspaper that was not worthy of the name and turned it into something that any newspaperman in the country would be proud to work for. He's spent forty years doing that. And you ought to be proud of it too. You don't have to be a newsman to understand what he has done. Community? He has given this community its most useful asset—a voice.

"And not just a voice either." Sy was approaching cruising speed. "It's an unafraid voice that speaks with a conscience. This paper, as much as any single institution, has made this community. And when I say community, I mean the whole goddam state. This newspaper has done more for this state than all the Rotary clubs and all the Kiwanis clubs and all the other goddam clubs combined. And your father has done more for the community than all the Sandy Kittridges combined, although God knows there are plenty of them."

Fletcher tried again to break in, but Sy stormed on. His voice was level and he leaned back comfortably in his chair so that from outside the glass walls the conversation appeared calm. It was only the words that raged. "And the business school refugees you talk to at newspaper conventions are no better. The advertising managers and general managers and hired-gun publishers are just Rotarians in better suits. When they brag about their return on investment, ask them how much they spend on news. When they're proud of cutting editorial budgets, tell them they ought to be embarrassed. And above all, for God's sake, tell them about your father. Tell them how your mother's father ran this newspaper into a debt-crippled hulk and then jumped off the roof. Tell them how your own father took it over in the middle of the Depression and not only made it profitable but made it into a real newspaper."

Sy knew Fletcher would be confused and therefore angered by the reference to his grandfather, so he was not surprised when the blood drained out of his face and he began to shake his head.

"And, Fletcher, one more thing before you go. Before you decide that your friends in the executive suites know more about how to run a newspaper than your father, before you get seduced by the Scrippses or the Gannetts, learn some history. Go and find out what happened when Louis the Sixteenth corrupted the newspaper publishers by making them fat and prosperous. Go learn something, for God's sake."

He was boring at another sore place, poking Fletcher's self-inflicted wound that was always either open or freshly scabbed over because being around the newspaper was a continual reminder for Fletcher of his own puny education. For him, college had been about serious drinking and partying and not-very-serious women and studies. In the dozen years since, reading had been a pursuit undertaken only when he couldn't get necessary information from some easier source. He just didn't talk about or even think about books and theories and history, all the things that seemed to be right on top of Sy's mind all the time, the things that Sy and his father spent hours talking about. Which one was Louie the Sixteenth? Sy saw him wince as self-doubt drove out anger. He considered jabbing him again with a Tocqueville quote about newspapers being essential to American unity but decided against it. A victim hemmed in too tightly by guilt and confusion can become dangerous, and Fletcher was beginning to have a bared-teeth look about him.

"Well, anyway," Sy said leaning back and smiling thinly at Fletcher, "thanks for taking the heat from Kittridge. But remember, you don't need to do that; you can just pass on the assholes to me anytime you want to."

Fletcher's confusion multiplied because now Sy not only was offering him a favor but had somehow conscripted him into a conspiracy that he didn't want to join, a plot against Kittridge, whom he considered to be an ally, not an enemy. And yet Sy had twisted the world around so that Fletcher's choice was not between Kittridge and Sy but between Kittridge and his own father, a choice between good and bad but with the poles turned upside down so he couldn't be sure which was which.

Sy was relentless. "Oh, and by the way," he said cheerfully, "you can quit worrying about the tax bill. Our statehouse people say it's not going anywhere this year; tax bills always get killed in election years, you know. And you can pass on that inside scoop to your Rotary friends if you want to. Maybe they'll take it easy on you next week."

Fletcher rose slowly to his feet, sighed, shrugged his shoulders, and actually opened his mouth to say, "Thanks," before he caught himself. Finally, he just turned away and left Sy's office, closing the door quietly behind him. Sy decided against telling him to turn the television set back on before he left. He sat quietly contemplating Fletcher for a minute, but replaying the victorious exchange didn't bring him much pleasure. In college, he often worked out on the speed bag, but no matter how long he punched or how perfect his timing, in the end his hands hurt and the Everlast bag just hung there, a permanent fixture absolutely unaffected by his assault. He'd felt pretty good, alert and focused, while he was taking Fletcher apart, but now his earlier mood of gloomy fretting returned and settled over him like a hooded robe. He sat hunched over his desk in such deep brooding that he didn't know anyone had come in until he heard Rocky's caustic voice from the doorway.

"Are we getting samwichees this year?"

He stood with his right hand resting high up on the jamb, a great swatch of gray hair sticking out of the armhole of his t-shirt. "'Cause I told 'em we were, and somebody goddam well better deliver 'em 'cause I ain't going to."

"What in the world are you talking about, Rocky?" Sy said in a tired, even voice. He made it a point never to be startled by the composing room foreman's manner or speech, which he knew were powerful tools that Rocky used with a craftsman's dexterity.

"I'm talking about them samwichees you said last year we'd have this year. Them samwichees they bring the goddam newsroom on Town Meeting Day night but never bring to the composing room."

Sy remembered, although in the intervening 364 days since he made the promise the subject had never been mentioned. "Well, Rocky," he said with a smile, "I sure hope so. For all of our sakes."

"Well, so don't I." Rocky glared once more at Sy, then left as abruptly as he had come, leaving the door to Sy's office open. He stalked through the newsroom without speaking to anyone or looking to either side, fully confident that anyone in his path would move. They did.

Sy noticed that most of the newsroom desks were full, so the town meetings must be over, but the high school kids who would be here to answer the phones hadn't come in yet. He figured roughly that, counting the kids and the composing room, he'd need sandwiches for at least fifty people. He realized with some alarm that it would cost him close to two hundred bucks, counting the cookies. Plus the beer for later. The numbers seemed to grow every year. Christ, when he started this town meeting feed, a couple dozen sandwiches was plenty. More than enough. He should have told Rocky that he'd have to pay for his own spread. But that would have meant letting him know that the company wasn't paying. Everyone, including Rocky, just assumed that the sandwiches were a gesture of thanks from the publisher for the long hours they worked on Town Meeting Day. Of course, it was really only the newsroom that worked extra hours. He'd have to be careful or the press room would start demanding sandwiches too. Maybe he ought to give the bill to the old man or maybe just try to pass it through the business office without saying what it was for. He picked up the telephone to call Pietro at the deli. Maybe he'd fix it next year. He was just worried because he had to take some cash out of his savings for the new television set; the money wasn't a big deal. Give it another year; it had only been a couple of years since the publisher had agreed to pay the high school kids that Sy brought in to take the town clerks' calls. He ordered a hundred sandwiches and fifty of Pietro's wife's homemade giant cookies.

Greenberg slouched into his office. His collar was open, his tie was not much more than half-staff, and his shirttail dangled out in back. His longish, gray-streaked hair was only finger combed, and the ash on the smoldering cigar was approaching dangerously close to his mouth. He slumped into the chair and turned his large, surprisingly warm eyes to Sy. He tossed the day's dummy on the desk. "They've really screwed us this time," he said with ancient bitterness. "The bastards have left us only one extra open page and a few partially open pages spread all over the goddam paper. How the hell can we make any sense out of the town meeting stuff with this kind of shit to work with?"

He paused to get Sy's reaction, then added, "And the whole thing is only about the size of a regular Wednesday. We've got to go up at least a couple of pages."

Sy thumbed quickly through the dummy pages. "Yeah," he said finally, "well, don't worry about it. I'll fix it."

They both looked at the wall clock. "You better hurry," Greenberg said. He sneered in contempt. "It's after four and you know the new edict: we can't go up unless the old man or Lyman okays it."

Sy dismissed him with a short wave of his hand. "Don't worry about it. I'll take care of it. I'll get you two facing pages with no ads and two others on either side of the double-truck that are more than half open. Okay?"

Greenberg stood up, made a halfhearted attempt to stuff his shirt into his trousers, and shrugged. "Sure. That'll be enough. If you can get it." Sy's head dropped into the top-of-the-eyeball stare and Greenberg turned and left, not exactly hurrying but clearly not interested in continuing the talk.

Sy watched him straggle through the newsroom until he reached his city editor's desk, where he slumped wearily onto his swivel chair. He hadn't even noticed the television set. Sy stood up and left the office, leaving his scarf hanging on the desk lamp although, after leaving the newsroom, he walked straight past the publisher's office without stopping and on out the front door into the cold.

The streetlights popped on as he walked through the overcast gloom of late afternoon. Sometimes mud season would be upon them by Town Meeting Day, but not this year. The heavy snows of January and February hadn't even begun to thaw outside of the city, but the sidewalks had a treacherous paving of dirty, slushy ice. He walked along briskly, missing his scarf, with his hands jammed far down in the pockets of his corduroy trousers. He walked for several blocks and was chilled enough by the time he pulled open the door of Vic's shop that the warmth inside felt like a blast furnace. The heat hit him first, then the wonderful smell of tobacco, coffee, and newsprint, all shut up together for so long that the aroma had become even stronger for being stale and inextricably blended.

Vic wasn't there, so no need to chat. The shop was empty except for the kid in back by the magazine rack, one more in an endless succession of high school boys who for years had given Vic his only off-duty hours by hanging around the shop during the slow hours of three to six, collecting customers' money but mostly expanding their own educations as they gulped knowledge from the city's most extensive collection of soft porn. They even earned minimum wage as a bonus payment for their academic diligence. Sy had already taken a fistful of cigars from the case before the kid noticed he was in the shop. He reluctantly put his *Penthouse* back on the shelf, crookedly, and shuffled toward the front. "Never mind," Sy said, waving him off, "I'll get the coffee myself." The kid must be new. Not an especially bad-looking one, as Vic's crew usually went, and even alert enough to be somewhat suspicious of Sy for taking the cigars. But too timid, or maybe just too eager to get back to *Penthouse*, to challenge a self-serving customer in his employer's interest.

Vic had the city's only espresso machine, a tribute to his own earlier life in San Francisco. He and Sy were the only locals who used it regularly. Next to the machine was a tiny round table and two soda fountain—style iron chairs. Sy made himself a coffee, ignoring the espresso cups that he and Vic had both discarded long ago in favor of regular white china mugs, and sat down at the table. He peeled the cellophane from a black cigar, slid off the band, and lighted up. Then he just sat, smoking and drinking his coffee, ignoring the kid and ignored by him so thoroughly that one or both of them could have been potted plants. He's got better things to occupy his mind, Sy thought, like Miss March and Peggy Sue, important things like what's going on down there between his legs, and maybe he's worried about SATs or, depending on his status, about the draft and Vietnam. Yeah, he's interested in—what? Maybe in whether he's going to graduate or whether he'll be rich or famous or, better yet, rich *and* famous. And the other one? The old codger sitting like the Buddha, with a pocketful of cigars he hasn't paid for yet—what's on his mind? Is he figuring out the final movement of a new symphony? Maybe devising a brilliant tax strategy that will bring him more millions or going over the potential complications from a life-saving surgery he just performed. Or maybe he's just sitting there passing time, enjoying the smells, the coffee, the cigar, and the isolation. Or maybe—unlikely, but maybe—he's sitting there brooding over his fiftieth birthday coming up next month.

Whatever they are thinking, the boy and the old man, whatever has them worried or entranced, they're doing it just right; they know, taught by instinct and further guided by custom, that what they should do is ignore each other, keep their distance, remain aloof, don't look, don't speak, don't notice. And they didn't. He, leaning against the rack, half turned away, the *Penthouse* held in both hands a foot from his face. Sy, sitting absolutely still, facing the door, eyes on the tiny table, moving first one hand to bring up the coffee cup, then the other with the cigar, each drug delivering its mysterious balm in turn.

It was fully dark and the cigar was nearly gone when he left the shop, paying the tab with a five dollar bill and pocketing his change without either man or boy breaking their now-sullen silence. The stored warmth of the shop lasted less than halfway back to the paper, so he hurried along, but still it was nearly five thirty when he walked back into the newsroom. The publisher, as punctual and predictable as a railroad conductor, had been gone since five and Lyman may have stayed around for a few minutes after the business office closed but he never lingered long. Sy figured he was afraid to be all alone with just the newsroom crowd in the front part of the building.

So it was too late to fight for more pages, a tussle he would have lost anyway since it obviously was no accident that the paper had been carefully dummied precisely to avoid giving up too much space for town meeting. The careful planning meant that Lyman and Fletcher had schemed the size of the paper together and that they would have gotten the publisher's assent, even if probably an absentminded okay, and in that case there would be no turning around because the old man couldn't let those two, his son and heir and his business manager and financial adviser, see him retreat in a confrontation with Sy. So all together, with the careful planning of the dummy and the earlier successful plot to take away his authority to increase the size of the paper, they seemed to have boxed him in, tied him down with lightweight trivialities that drained off strength he should be applying to some more-worthy work.

Sy walked through the newsroom without being noticed. Everyone appeared to be there, but most of them were gathered at the far end of the room around Willis's desk, and he heard loud laughter from the crowd as he reached his own office. Inside, he picked up the ad dummy book, took a packet of blank dummy sheets from the bottom drawer of his desk, and began redrawing the ad layouts. After fifteen or twenty minutes, he realized he could not squeeze out enough clear pages and still get all the ads in the paper. He sat back in his chair, made up his mind, and quickly threw away all the pages he had drawn and started all over. It took only a few minutes to make the changes he wanted, and he picked up both packs of dummy pages and headed for the composing room.

The night shift was in full bay, Linotypes hissing and screaming, lead slugs clattering, and Rocky bellowing threats at those who were not moving fast enough and profane warnings at those who were hustling but might at some time in their future careers consider slowing down. It was just a warm-up, a scrimmage that would get everyone loosened up for the real push later. They were still just setting ad type and putting finished block ads into the pages. They wouldn't really start working on the news columns, except for the editorial pages and the other early deadline copy, until midevening.

And tonight, with town meeting, the sweat wouldn't really pour until after midnight.

Rocky didn't have an office, preferring instead to direct the nightly production from a gray steel desk bolted to a six-inch-high wooden platform built squarely in the center of the room. The desktop was empty except for a brass pica rule, Rocky's scepter and gavel. He could slap the flat side of the rule against the bare desk loudly enough to be heard over the general chaos, and when he left the platform, he invariably snatched it up, incorporating it into his left hand like a long sixth digit. The desk was the only flat surface in the composing room that wasn't covered by a permanent layer of metallic grime. The final duty each night for Rocky's newest drudge was to clean the desk with alcohol and wipe it down with a thin coat of 3-in-1 oil, rubbed to a dull sheen that left no trace when Rocky yanked out his always-fresh white handkerchief and scrubbed it across the smooth surface. The desk was also the only flat surface in the huge, open composing room that was not occupied by lead type or chase forms or scraps of paper, dummy sheets, steel type-carrying trays, or some other paraphernalia accumulated over a hundred years of hot-metal printing. The desk had been used for a barely imaginable range of bizarre functions, including as a surgery table the time they had to strap down an apprentice to extract a bit of hot metal from his eye. But mostly the desk served as a symbol, an ever-present reminder that in this room, Rocky was not just the boss but the captain; more, even—a monarch who, for eight or ten hours each evening, exercised the absolute right to make this all-male kingdom do whatever he wanted it to do. There were no challengers to this absolute authority within his kingdom, and the internal security made him even more hostile to interlopers. Most outsiders, including even the publisher and the business manager, who ostensibly was his superior, dealt with Rocky only on their own turf, and since they worked days and he worked nights, such confrontations were rare.

Sy was one of the few who ventured into the composing room without in some way acknowledging Rocky's superior status. Most people behaved like a dog entering a larger dog's kennel. The composing room and the newsroom were inseparable, as symbiotic and as quarrelsome as a septuagenarian couple and, on the surface, mismatched from the beginning—dark versus light, sweet versus sour, cold versus hot, man versus woman. Standing in the doorway, page dummies in his hand, Sy surveyed Rocky's fiefdom with an unaccustomed queasiness that approached pity. He knew what these dirty, scurrying minions had not even dreamed: that they were on the brink of extinction, soon-to-be victims of technological evolution, that immutable force powered by an economic greed so powerful it made natural selection look namby-pamby. He knew that the publisher not only had decided to abandon the hot-metal printing process, but in fact had already ordered an offset press. By this time next year, the skills that some of these men had been perfecting for forty years would be as extraneous as their variform appendixes. Hun, the silent, Austria-born mechanic who had been coaxing type out of these decrepit Linotype machines since before the war, stood beside the desk, listening to Rocky and wiping his hands on a pink cloth. Tony, relaxed and chatting with Sal at the ad bench, was making up complex advertisements with an easy self-assurance that came from knowing he had not made a mistake in so long that even the foreman no longer bothered to check his work. Armand, who had been fully content with life and his own station in it since he first sat down in the sawed-off chair of a Linotype operator thirty years before, slammed away at the keyboard, squinting through the cigarette smoke that curled up from his mouth to mingle above his head with the darker, acrid smoke roiling out of the top of the machine. Next to him sat Mike, working fast but talking even faster, his own cigarette bobbing up and down as he spoke, unlit for ten years now but a permanent appendage to his face.

Sy quietly watched them all and the dozen others faithfully filling their own niches in this creaky subculture. In the back, as far from the purview of Rocky as they could get and still claim to be working, three young apprentices gossiped, the room's only occupants, whose hair was longer than the bristles on a shoe brush and the only ones who had personally felt the revolutionary winds of this stormy decade. They considered themselves lucky, these three—indeed, twice-blessed, for since tumbling out of high school last year, they each had found a path around the draft and then had landed these jobs at the newspaper. For generations, a printer's apprenticeship had been a lifetime ticket to ride for those who stayed reasonably sober and who could strike some sort of accommodation with Rocky or his vocational sires. These three had no reason to suppose their destinies would wobble from this venerable orbit. But Sy knew. He watched them grab-ass in the back corner by the bubbling lead pot and he knew this was the first generation of apprentices who would never graduate from toting pig iron to mastery of a trade they could transport to any city or, for that matter, any civilized country that was fueled by the printed word.

It was the civilized world, Sy thought, that had passed these boys by, displacing them by inventing sophisticated machines that relied on delicate finger agility and mathematic acuity rather than brawn, stamina, and affinity for mechanics. At some point, the world had come to value the skills of the typist, not the typographer, and had decided to pay top dollar for the broker and banker, not the tinkerer and maker, but no one thought to tell these guys. You lost, Rocky. The brokers and the typists are in the newsroom, not the composing room. Our war is over, yours and mine. My kids, the Hanks and Rons, won't even know your kids. And the irony, Rocky, oh the lovely irony—you have extincted yourself by making yourself so strong. A fortress, you thought, will keep them out. But that's not enough, Rocky. You have to go out and meet the bastards; you have to be willing to fight them wherever they are. If you don't, if you stay hunkered down in your fort, then you are committing suicide, the "self-overthrow" that Frost called "the splendidest sack since the forest Germans sacked Rome."

He moved purposefully through the composing room to Rocky's platform and dropped the dummy book on the desk. The foreman looked up in irritation, and Hun, still wiping his hands, nodded at Sy, then turned and walked off.

"What the hell is this?" Rocky growled. "I've already got the dummy."

"I've changed it," Sy said simply. "This is the new dummy."

Rocky looked at the wall clock. "Goddam it, it's almost six. You can't just remake the paper at six; most of them goddam ads are already in the goddam pages."

He looked at Sy, who stood silently with a slight smile on his face. "How many pages did you add?" Rocky said.

"None. Same number of pages. I've just changed some ads around."

Rocky began thumbing through the dummy pages.

"Oh," Sy said, "and I took out the comics."

"What do you mean? Where'd you put 'em?"

"Nowhere. I took them out. And the bridge column and the crossword and that stupid kids' puzzle. I cleared that whole page."

"Jesus H. Christ. You can't do that." Rocky stood up, grasping the pica rule. He slapped it down on the pile of dummy pages. "You can't just leave out the comics. That mat's all made. The company's already paid for all that stuff. You can't just leave it out."

"Rocky, that page is charged against me; the space is part of the newshole, right?" Sy's voice was still low and smooth but he didn't wait for an answer. "It shouldn't be that way, but as long as it is, as long as the amusement page is part of the newshole, then I can do whatever I damn well please with it. And what I please is to use that page for town meeting coverage."

He waited, but Rocky evidently had nothing to say. He just stood, a half-head taller than Sy, flicking the rule lightly like a finger drumming the desk.

"Besides," Sy said, "I am not amused by the amusement page."

Rocky squinted. "Huh?"

"Never mind, Rocky. Just set up another chase for this blank page. You'll also have to move some of the ads. Just on four or five pages. And you'll have to renumber some of the pages. I've grouped the town meeting pages together."

"Did you check all this out with Lyman?"

The blood rose on Sy's neck for the first time and his voice grew louder. "Listen, Rocky. You're right that I can't add pages on my own, but I damn well can still move ads around when I need to. I don't need to check this with Lyman or anybody else, including you. The new dummies are there on your desk. Just follow them."

He glared up at the foreman then turned around and walked slowly toward the door. Rocky watched him, his face distorted by bright red blotches and his hand flicking the rule faster and faster, but he didn't say anything until Sy had cleared the composing room.

A burst of laughter from the newsroom froze Sy at the door and he heard Willis say, "And that's when he spilled the beans." They laughed again, more of a snickering this time, and Sy held his breath; then he remembered Rocky was watching him from behind, so he pushed open the door into the newsroom. Willis looked up, over the heads of the crowd gathered around him, then went on with his story. "This old guy, Mr. Penn, the road commissioner, apparently had just had enough of the complaints. They'd been bitching all morning about the roads being dangerous, too much snow and ice, not enough sand and salt. They never mentioned Mr. Penn by name and never even directly blamed him or anyone else by name or title. It was as if the roads themselves were at fault."

Several people in his audience laughed softly. Sy was standing just outside the circle and Willis waved to him. "Listen to this, Sy, I'm telling them about the Hartland town meeting; you'll appreciate this."

He went back to his story. "Anyway, they just kept on complaining—worst winter in years, accidents every week, somebody going to get killed, that kind of stuff—for probably half an hour. And he just sat there in the front row, his jaw sticking out further every time one of them spoke but never saying a word. Finally, a woman stood up and it seemed to me she was trying to help him out. She said they ought to quit complaining because there was no way the road commissioner could have known this was going to be such a tough winter and it wasn't Mr. Penn's fault if the town ran out of sand and salt.

"Well, that was too much for him. He jumped up, red in the face, and said, 'Hold on, now. We got plenty of sand and salt both.'

"She looked hurt, then she got mad herself and said, 'Well, then, why in thunder don't you use them?'

"And he said, just as testy as she was, 'Can't. If we use 'em up, then we won't have enough and folks won't like it.'"

They all laughed, but Willis held up his hand and they grew quiet again. "That's not the end. After he said 'folks won't like it,' he snapped his jaw shut and looked around the meeting, as smug as William F. Buckley. In fact, he looked a little like Bill Buckley on steroids. Then he sat down and folded his arms. And the moderator popped up from somewhere—I had lost track of him—and banged the gavel on the podium and said, just as solemn as Moses, 'All right, and we thank Commissioner Penn. I guess we've settled that question to the satisfaction of everyone. Let's move on to Article 19.'

They all laughed again and Willis turned back to his own desk, but just as the little group began to break up, he stopped them by calling out, "That was the end of the controversy in Hartland, but being a good reporter, I went up afterward and asked the moderator for the name of the woman who had tried to defend Road Commissioner Penn. 'Oh,' he said, 'that's his wife.'"

Sy moved off toward his office, laughing with the rest of them, and motioned for Willis to follow him. Inside the glass cubicle, he leaned back in his chair and said, "What's your good story? I hope that wasn't it." The good humor fell out of Willis's face and he looked hurt. "I mean, Alice said you phoned in to say you would have a news story, not an anecdote. God knows we don't need any more cute Vermont fluff."

Willis leaned back and smiled. "Just for the record, I think that was a pretty good story, but it wasn't the one I told Alice about. No, I think I picked up a pretty good one. Not really a town meeting story, though."

Sy frowned. "Well, what is it? I was looking for a lead on the town meeting coverage."

"Well, you decide. Here it is: The governor is thinking seriously about splitting with LBJ on the war. He'd be the first Democratic governor to jump ship."

Sy picked up a pencil and began to tap lightly on the edge of his desk. "That is a pretty good story. Where'd you get it?"

Willis waited, the actor's pause for emphasis or maybe for suspense or maybe something more nefarious, then he said, "Cramer. I ran into him in Woodstock. He told me about it and said to call the governor tonight and he thinks he'll confirm it."

"Oh yeah, that's right," Sy said, "Cramer's from Woodstock, isn't he. Blue blood."

"More like Bluebeard, from what I hear."

Sy grinned. "How do you know Cramer? He could be a good source."

Willis paused again, holding back ever so slightly. Finally, he said, "I interviewed him for that story last week on the billboard law. And later we had a couple of drinks together."

"Oh yeah." Sy tapped his pencil. "Why do you think he told you about the governor shafting the president?"

"Well, I was thinking about that, and I think there are several reasons. Oh, I forgot to tell you about another story. This one I'll have to do some more work on later this week. Anyway, my three town meetings were all over by lunchtime so, since I was so close, I drove over to New Hampshire to poke around a little. Wallace is speaking at Dartmouth tomorrow night, and I just looked up a couple of the Democratic operatives I got to know over there before I left the *Constitution*. What I found out is that Johnson is incredibly weak, even more than I thought earlier. It's just a week before the primary election, and McCarthy is coming on like gangbusters. Even Wallace is taking away some LBJ votes, blue collars moving out of the Democratic primary. I think if I go back over there in the next couple of days, I can get a follow-up to the earlier piece.

"But that's another story. What I think is that our governor sees Johnson is vulnerable, and he's either timing this thing to give Johnson the maximum embarrassment or he wants to get this story out about his possible endorsement of McCarthy and use it to bargain with the president for something.

"Either way, whatever his reason, it's a good story for us. And I have it alone—at least, Cramer says no one else knows."

Sy was dubious. "Why would he give it to you? Why not the statehouse crew or maybe even the *Patriot Press* people; he owes them some favors."

Willis shrugged. "I didn't ask him. Who cares why?" Sy didn't answer, but he was not satisfied. "I don't know what's going on between the governor's office and our statehouse bureau," Willis said, "but I know Cramer seemed unhappy with them. And I know he's pissed at the *Patriot*; did you see that insane editorial they ran the other day on the billboard ban?

"And maybe Cramer just likes me and thinks I'm a good reporter. At the risk of being immodest, I do know that he and the governor both liked my billboard stories."

After a moment, Sy nodded, but he still wasn't easy about the story. He looked intently at Willis, who shifted slightly under his gaze but did not drop his eyes. Maybe it was Willis himself, not the story at all, that made him feel uneasy. The LBJ story seemed okay; in fact, it sounded completely in character for everyone involved. Was Willis trying to get one up on the statehouse guys? Sure he was. Hell, he ought to be. So what was wrong?

Willis sat quietly facing Sy but not looking directly at him, taking frequent, shallow pulls on his Winston. He blew the smoke sideways as his eyes roved slowly but steadily across the desk, up to Sy's face, then on to the piles of papers, photographs, and wire copy that formed a messy nest around the desk and wooden swivel chair. Willis had turned in consistently solid stories for the past three weeks and a few times he had moved beyond journeyman's work. His back-to-back stories had turned the campaign to take down the billboards from a pie-in-the-sky idea into a serious political issue. For the first time, the legislature, the reporters who covered it, and, most importantly, the lobbyists were taking it seriously. Every Volkswagen and Volvo in the state suddenly grew bumper stickers saying Ban All Signs Bigger Than This.

They had been good stories. Hell, Sy had worked on them nearly as hard as Willis; it had been his idea in the first place. So why was he uneasy about the LBJ story? Sy jammed his tongue up against the loose tooth in the back of his mouth, intensifying the slight pain that had been annoying him most of the day. He knew what was going on; he'd already lost two back teeth in the past year. The bone from which they grew was crumbling, like rotten ice in late winter. He pushed, then let off on the pressure, and the pain subsided immediately.

"Well, you better call the governor. If Cramer says he's ready to talk, he's almost certainly cleared it with him. You work on that and I'll get someone else to write the lead on the town meeting coverage. What about your meetings? Can you write anything on them?"

Willis stood up. "Yeah, I can wrap them up into one story and then break out the local elections and stuff at the tail end. All three towns I covered were voting on a regional school, and that'll be the lead." Sy nodded and Willis turned to go, then turned back. "You know, these town meetings really are amazing; I've never seen anything like them. I'll try to put some color in the story, but I need to spend some time on the political story too. Maybe I'll write another town meeting piece tomorrow."

He turned toward the door again and noticed the television set on top of the filing cabinet. "Hey, where'd that come from? You finally convinced the old man to let Satan in the newsroom?"

Sy nodded, but he didn't exactly answer the question. Instead, he stood up and stepped over to turn on the machine. "I want to see what they do with town meetings. They're supposed to be working with the AP to collect voting results and broadcast them."

A bluish light came on behind the blank screen and the machine began to hum. They both watched in motionless silence until an image finally appeared, the solemn, aging face of Bruce Hubbell, who read the local and state news every evening for Vermont's lone television station.

"Good evening," Hubbell said. "The turnout for town meeting today was said to be extremely heavy across the state."

"Who said?" Sy said in a loud, angry growl. "Who said it was heavy? And what the hell does heavy mean?"

". . . and we'll have more coverage throughout the night as results come in from town meetings, this annual Vermont tradition of grassroots democracy at work."

Willis started out the door. "That's enough clichés for me," he said. "If that droning old fool is our competition, I guess newspapering is safe."

Sy was back in his chair. "Ask Greenberg to come in here," he called after Willis. He watched as Hubbell read one story after another, looking up into the camera after each news brief as he noisily shuffled the top page to the bottom of the stack in front of him. Soon Sy realized that although he was listening intently to the sound of Hubbell's voice, the individual words were no more distinguished than raindrops in a storm. The sentences, even the entire stories, ran together into a stream that just disappeared into some crevice of unconsciousness.

"We'll be back after this," the broadcaster said, forcing a mirthless grin as his dull eyes locked onto the camera. Hubbell disappeared, replaced by the top half of a young woman who also served as the station's weather girl. She was posed beside an office copying machine, her long-nailed index finger outstretched to rest beside the on-off switch and her face turned directly into the camera. She's not very pretty, Sy thought. It was an ad for a local store that sold office supplies and was a stalwart sponsor for the Vermont newscast. Jennifer, the sometimes weather girl, was extolling the virtues of the copying machine as vigorously as she could manage without discarding the wide-angle smile. ". . . instantaneously and with incredible speed," she read from the teleprompter.

"If you could have only one of them, which would it be?" Greenberg said as he stepped through the door.

"Which what?" Sy answered.

"Which one would you choose: instantaneous or with incredible speed?" He slumped into the chair beside the desk. "God save me from these local ads." He waved toward the television set. "That's a nice addition, though. Is it just for the chief or can the Indians watch the news too?"

Sy didn't answer right away, instead looking steadily but without expression at Greenberg, who had half turned in his chair so he could see the screen. He was colorless, a gray, slumped sack of a human being who once had been, in Sy's judgment, a competent, maybe even inspired, all-around newspaper editor. He was a great copyreader, a level-headed, well-informed, sober man who was liked by the reporters who worked for him and who had the rare attribute called "institutional memory": he knew how today's events fit into yesterday's stories. He was smart and, most importantly of all, he considered himself a newsman, not a professional journalist, which meant that he would do whatever work needed to be done, first to get a story and then to get it in the paper and finally to get the paper on the street. He has one flaw, Sy thought, he doesn't care. Maybe he never did and maybe that's why he's here in my newsroom, but whether he ever did or not, right now what he cares most about is getting today's paper out and going home. Or maybe it's not that he doesn't care but that he doesn't believe in it anymore. That's right, the poor bastard doesn't believe in it. It's a job and he wants to finish so he can go home to do what he does believe in, so he can get up in the morning and see his wife and play chess with his kids and read history. It's his life, not his work that he has faith in, that he trusts. If we stopped giving him a paycheck or if he stopped needing one, he'd never come back into this newsroom and never even miss it or even wonder what was happening here.

Greenberg turned to Sy and lifted his eyebrows, which were conspicuous for being his only visible patches of hair that were still solidly black. "Sure," Sy said with a slight shrug that didn't entirely cover his irritation, "you can watch the news. I just didn't want the whole newsroom to shut down for an hour every night. But you can and even should watch, especially the local stuff."

Greenberg nodded. Sy picked up the packet of page dummy sheets and dropped it on the corner of the desk beside Greenberg. "Here you are—two blank and two nearly open pages, all together in the front section. And you can use as many of the others in that section as you need."

Greenberg picked up the packet and shuffled through the pages. "What'd you have to trade for these? Your manhood? Your firstborn child? Oops. That wouldn't be much of a sacrifice for you, would it."

"No trades," Sy said. "I just took out the comics and juggled around a few ads."

"Where'd you put the comics?"

"I didn't. I left them out."

"Azoy?" Greenberg's head snapped up and he looked as if he had nearly swallowed his cigar butt. Then he began to laugh. "By God, Sy, there's nothing wrong with your manhood. Your sanity may be in question, but you've got plenty of balls." He laughed again. "You know what's going to happen when they pick up the paper and can't find out what happened to *Mary Worth*? Much less *Nancy*. And when the fools are through with you, the *Peanuts* fans will start in. The phone'll go crazy tomorrow. And then Alice will flip out." He shook his head in merry wonderment, or maybe it was admiration, until he had another thought. "Christ, that's nothing compared to what Lyman and young Fletcher are going to do. They'll have your hide, Sy. At least, they'll try. You're toying with revenue now, you know. What's your excuse—just an oversight?"

Sy jumped up, slamming his chair back against the wall. "Goddam it, Greenberg, I don't need an excuse. They dummied the paper so tightly we couldn't get in the town meeting results even if we didn't run any other news. And then they left before I could get it changed. Well, by God, I'm not going to throw away all the extra money we spent on town meeting coverage. I'm not going to look like some rinky-dink shopper compared to the *Patriot Press*." He had moved around the desk, but then there was nowhere else to go, so he went back and sat down again. "And why are you so surprised? The comics and that other canned stuff don't have anything to do with news. You of all people ought to know that."

Greenberg had seen countless temper outbursts by Sy and he figured that about half of them at least were fake, just playacting, but he still hunched back in his chair, chewing hard on his cigar. "Listen, it's okay with me if you leave out the comics. I don't read 'em, at least, not usually. All I mean is that you better be ready for a storm tomorrow. That's all."

He stood up and started to back toward the door, but Sy said quietly, "Sit down, Matt. Sit down. We need to talk about the town meeting coverage." He opened his top desk drawer, took out two cigars, and tossed one over to Greenberg, who yanked the butt out of his mouth, looked it over closely, then stuck it back in and shoved the new one into his shirt pocket, at the same time nodding his thanks to Sy

"Willis has a pretty good state story. Politics. So he can't work on the lead for the town meeting coverage. Who else can do that?"

Greenberg took a copy pencil from behind his left ear and used the eraser to scratch slowly at a spot behind his right ear, then he said, "Well, I never thought of having Willis do that piece anyway. Hell, this is his first town meeting. I was going to have Connie write the lead story, just a general roundup, essentially a summary of the stories everybody else will be writing, plus whatever we get off the wire."

He paused to see if Sy would say anything, then went on. "What about the statehouse guys? Are they writing any town meeting stuff?"

"I haven't talked with them yet." Sy looked over at the clock. "Christ, it's getting late; I better call. But I doubt that they'll have anything about Town Meeting Day. There's not much of a state angle."

"What's Willis's hot story?"

"He thinks he can get the governor to say that he's going to split with Johnson on the war. Willis got a good tip today. He's going to call him after it's too late for the *Patriot*'s early deadline."

Greenberg worked the cigar butt over to the other side of his mouth. "Yeah, that's a good story. He does pretty good work, doesn't he?" His voice was flat and his face blank, but Sy suddenly felt a new tension in the conversation. He carefully kept his own expression neutral. "He's had a couple of good shots. But then, he's got a lot of experience. Eight newspapers, in fact."

"Yeah," Greenberg said, again standing up. "That's what he said. And a degree from Columbia too."

Sy frowned in puzzlement. "Columbia?"

"Yeah, isn't that where he went to school? Columbia?"

"Oh yeah," Sy said, "that's right. Columbia." He remembered the job application. Willis had written that he attended—he carefully didn't say had a degree from—Columbia State College, which he later told Sy was a two-year teacher training school in North Carolina. Greenberg, probably with some encouragement from Willis, had assumed it was Columbia University and that he had graduated. Maybe he figured he had an MA in journalism. Sy smiled, but Greenberg had already turned his back and was going through the door of the office. "Hey, Matt. When are the kids coming in to take the calls?"

"About seven." He stopped and turned back to look at Sy. "I've got five of them coming in this year. Is that okay?"

"Sure. Tell Alice. And by the way, the sandwiches will be here about eleven. And this year they're for the composing room too. There should be plenty."

Greenberg took a couple of shuffling steps toward his own desk before Sy called him back. "One more minute, Matt. Close the door for a minute."

When he was sitting down again, Sy said, "Is something going on out there? In the newsroom?"

Greenberg shrugged. "What kind of something? There's always something going on out there; it's a zoo."

"No, I mean something new. I just got a feeling a couple of times lately that I was missing something, or maybe there was some kind of tension that I didn't know about." He looked closely at Greenberg. "You haven't heard any grumbling or anything out of the ordinary?"

Greenberg shook his head thoughtfully. "No. Nothing. There's the usual grousing. You know, sometimes it's louder than other times and the extra hours on town meeting always gives them an excuse. And there's been some complaining, or sniping, about Willis. But that's to be expected. You know—reverse carpetbagger, big-shot reporter from the *Atlanta Constitution*. That kind of thing. But it doesn't seem to bother him and it won't last long."

He stopped but Sy didn't answer, so Greenberg went on. "Is that what you mean? The chatter about Willis? Or is it something else?"

"I don't care what they say about Willis. He's a big boy; he can deal with the office politics." Sy decided Greenberg didn't know anything, hadn't noticed anything unusual, but he tried one more time. "It's just that a couple of times I noticed the newsroom was empty when it shouldn't have been normally, and that a couple of times I've seen groups of reporters standing around talking quietly and they shut up when I walked by. I thought maybe the same thing had happened to you."

Greenberg shook his head again. "Naw, I haven't noticed anything like that. I'll keep an eye open, but I don't think so." They were both silent for a minute, then Greenberg stood up. "I've got to get this thing moving. Relax, Sy, the surgeon general says paranoia is bad for your health."

The Oasis was empty and even the bartender had disappeared by the time Willis and Sy finished dissecting the paper. Willis had finished first and silently withdrew with his glass into the back of the booth, away from the beam of the wall lamp. Sy seemed fully absorbed in the paper, his drink hardly touched on the table in front of him. His paper was opened full-width to the double truck; he must be reading every goddam town meeting story. Willis was mildly curious since most of the stories except his own had seemed pretty boring, but he didn't mind because he didn't feel much like talking anyway. In fact, he didn't feel like doing anything in the world other than exactly what he was doing: sipping bourbon in a semi-dark corner, peacefully unwinding after one of the best days he had ever had of reporting and writing. He was as content as a man can get and still be awake—no itches, no twitches, no tingles, no regrets, and no worries. Well, maybe one: the bar was going to close in a few minutes.

He watched surreptitiously as Sy plowed through the back pages of the newspaper and finally folded it back to its original form and dropped it onto the empty space beside him on the vinyl seat. Sy took a long drink of his scotch and finally said with startling gusto, "Goddam, kid, goddam. We did a goddam good job with this one. Congratulations."

Seymour lifted his glass and raised it in Willis's direction before draining it off. "Where's Jake?" he said, turning toward the bar. He got up, reached for Willis's empty glass, and walked to the bar. Willis closed his eyes and slumped against the seat, but in a very short time Sy was back. "Better hurry if we want another. Jake said he's shutting it down right at two, even if we're the only ones here."

You could have ordered two this time, Willis thought, but he didn't say anything, just nodded his thanks to Sy and picked up the full glass.

"Willis," Sy said, "I meant it. You did good work today. Your town meeting story made me remember why I used to love to cover those things. Hell, I think next year I will cover one."

Willis covered his pleased embarrassment with a long drink but Sy wasn't finished. "What really makes me happy, though, is what you've done for the others, especially the young guys. You've started to show them what I always hoped Greenberg would be able to do—a sense of how newspapering can be when it's done right. I see it in the way they listen to you and read your stories, but more importantly I see it in their copy. They're really trying now, really working, and it shows in these stories." He lifted the newspaper from the seat and waved it in a little circle. "This is damn good coverage. Anybody who reads this newspaper carefully will know what town meeting is all about. I just wanted to thank you."

Seymour paused but Willis didn't know what to say, so he didn't say anything. "And I'm not even talking about your main story, the piece on the governor. That's a hell of a story and a solid beat that'll be picked up on the national wires tomorrow."

"Thanks," Willis said. "Thanks a lot. I've got to tell you, I can't remember when it felt so good to be newspapering."

He took another long swallow before leaning forward toward Sy. "It's me who ought to be thanking you. I never told you, but that first night, that night you gave me the job, I was ready to get back on the bus and leave."

Sy didn't answer other than to lift his eyebrows slightly. "I mean, I came back to the paper to tell you I wasn't going to take the job, but you changed my mind. And I'm damned glad of it. I haven't had such a good job since the *Observer*."

There was an awkward silence, and in the stillness they could hear the hum of a fluorescent light somewhere near the bar. They had arrived at a place neither had expected to find, and both were speechless in the dawning of that discovery. With a man and woman, the next stop on this unexpected journey would have been foreordained, but for these two the path stretching ahead was as unmarked and mysterious as the one that brought them here. Maybe, though, this was the end of the trip, a rest stop of such peace and comfort that there would be no need to go further. Maybe they could go on just like this, reporting, writing, editing, talking, drinking, putting out newspapers day after day until there were no more days, making newspapers and stacking them up in tall piles that never fell over and filled acres of space, like monuments in a beautiful cemetery.

Whiskey words, Willis thought as he stood up and reached for the other's glass, but Sy waved his hand away since his scotch was hardly touched. Willis took his own glass over to the bar where Jake was tidying up for closing. "Don't bother with new ice," he said as he put down his money. "The added advantage of drinking fast."

Willis heard the door open but he didn't turn around until he heard Connie's voice behind him. "Hey, Willis," she said, "it's nice of you to keep Jake company."

He turned, smiling, and saw that Connie wasn't by herself. A tall guy wearing a dark overcoat was standing just behind her. "You alone?" she said without waiting for an answer. "This is Vince Carmoli. Vince, this is Bud Willis, our new ace reporter."

As they shook hands, Willis pointed toward the corner booth. "Come on back," he said, "Sy's over there."

Connie looked truly pleased as she smiled and waved toward the booth. "Okay. We've got time for a quick one, right, Jake?"

He was already reaching for glasses. "Beer or what?"

"A beer for me," Vince said. "A Budweiser." Connie raised two fingers and Jake popped the caps on two long-necked bar bottles.

When they had settled into the booth and introduced Vince to Sy, Connie said, "He's a prodigal son. Or maybe favorite son would be a better cliché because you really haven't been very prodigal, have you? Vince grew up here and left for a while but now he's back."

Sy shook his hand. "You're not Pietro's son, are you?"

"That's the other side of the family," Vince said, "the respectable side. My side is the logger-woodchuck branch over in Addison County. Uncle Pietro even changed his name. He put an *e* at the end instead of *i* to make sure nobody mixed us up."

They laughed and Connie added, "Yeah, the extra *e* adds a lot of sophistication and it looks great on the store window."

Willis slid back into his corner, feeling very tired now and a little drunk, content to let Sy carry the conversation. He was too tired or too satisfied or too something to be any more than a little jealous.

"Vince went to school with my ex-husband," Connie was telling Sy, "at the University of Chicago. Then they went to law school together at Virginia."

"Doesn't sound to me like the track of a woodchuck," Sy said. "Those are pretty fine schools for a Vermont logger."

Vince took a short pull on his beer before answering. "One good teacher," he said. "That's all it takes, right? At least, for me it was. I went to a little school that had three classes and three teachers for kindergarten through grade eight. Three classes in each room. And for me there were only two teachers because Mrs. Spindler, my teacher for third through fifth, moved with the class so she also taught us sixth through eighth.

"That was before they consolidated all the little schools, at least in rural Addison County. By the time Mrs. Spindler was through with me, I was packaged, stamped, and ready to ship off to college. High school seemed like just a formality. I remember taking her my report card all those years, every marking period after I left her school, and she'd grill me about every mark. Just getting a good grade wasn't enough. She wanted to know what I had learned."

The others were just listening, drawn into the story by Vince's earnest manner of telling and his casual dismissal of his own part, as though he was without self.

"I don't remember ever even thinking about whether I would go to college, even though God knows no one else in my family ever had. She said I was going to college, probably sometime in fourth or fifth grade, and that was that. My parents just accepted the verdict like I did. I'm still not entirely sure how she managed the scholarship and the work-study deal."

Connie said, "Didn't you graduate from Chicago in three years?"

"Yeah," he said, "with two years of summer school. After Mrs. Spindler, college was a breeze."

"You're practicing law?" Sy asked.

"No, Connie left out that part. I never finished law school."

"Right," Connie said, "he quit halfway through his third year to go south with the Freedom Riders."

"Well," Vince said, "that makes it sound a little more noble that it really was. In the first place, I was only two months into the third year. And I wasn't doing all that well in law school. A lot of it just didn't seem to make much sense to me. The truth is, I really didn't like the law and the idea of practicing made me feel sick. So when a friend asked me to go south with her, I just took off. Even then I expected to go back to law school in a year or so. Of course, being a lousy lawyer, I overlooked the draft. I was in the South exactly six months before they called me up."

Connie broke in again. "Four years, right? Four years of typing army reports. I still remember some of the letters you wrote to Ben. Where were you? Kansas?"

"Yeah, for a good part of the time. Actually, I was moved around quite a bit. But Kansas was probably the worst. That's when I missed Vermont the most, I guess."

Vince finished his beer, set the empty bottle down, and looked at Connie, but before they could get up, Sy said, "How'd you get out of Vietnam?"

Vince relaxed back in his booth and said quietly, "I just told them I wouldn't go."

Sy laughed, but Connie said. "No, Sy, that's really what he did. He was in intelligence, right, Vince? It's called intelligence?"

He nodded.

"Anyway," Connie went on, "he told them they could put him in the stockade, but he wasn't going to Vietnam."

She leaned toward Sy and tilted her head ever so slightly to what Willis called the charm position, creating the look that says, "I really care what you think about this, because only you and I really understand what's going on here."

"You'd love this story, Sy, if Vince would tell the whole thing." Except, Willis noticed, she didn't give him a chance to tell it, hurrying full speed into the story. "The army didn't know how to deal with this renegade captain in the intelligence branch who refused orders to go to war. They could handle guys who ran away or punched their superiors or even those who tried to fake some disability. But they just freaked when he sat down and said he'd go to jail first."

She glanced quickly over at Willis. "Wouldn't that have made a great story for some Kansas newspaper? And you better believe the army knew it too."

For the first time, she turned to Vince. "They shipped you off to Korea, right? About as safe from the press as they could get you, short of prison."

"Well," Vince said, "you make it sound more dramatic than it actually was. Basically, I just used the tactics they taught the Freedom Riders down at the Highlander School. You know, passive resistance. Or sit-down stubbornness, as some of the civil rights people said."

Connie said quickly, "Anyway, it worked, and he finished out his hitch without going to jail and without going to Vietnam."

She looked at him with obvious pride, but it was not clear to Willis what else was in the look. He was quite aware, though, that she did not touch him, not even so much as the hand-on-the-sleeve gesture that was practically a Connie trademark.

She looked back to Sy. "I didn't mean to get into all that when we came over here. What I really wanted to say was that the paper today is great. Absolutely wonderful. It makes me proud to work for you, and I wanted you to know that."

Sy's normal glibness was stymied by this unlooked-for graciousness, and his tongue stumbled. Connie laughed gently at the unintelligible reply and said as she stood up, "Don't let me confuse you, Sy. We'll still disagree plenty and I intend to tell you about that too."

She turned away, evidently sure that Vince would follow, as he did. Two steps toward the door she turned and waved to Willis, who just nodded numbly.

"All right, guys," Jake called out, "I'd be on overtime now if I wasn't working for myself. How about bringing those glasses over on your way out."

CHAPTER FOUR
Thursday, April 4, 1968

Willis paced fretfully around the nearly empty newsroom. He checked the wire but didn't really read any stories; it was all crap anyway. He paused briefly to peer out the window, just long enough to see a car full of kids cut the corner too close and splash filthy gutter runoff water on an old lady trying to cross the street. Pissants. He flopped down at one desk, then jumped up and moved to another, then leaped up again and hurried over to the Photofax machine humming away in the corner. He took off the reel and unscrolled the pictures, stopping to look only at the Vietnam shots, and when he finished there was a mound of the flimsy paper piled up at his feet. He carefully began to reroll the paper, but it was slow work winding the slimmed-down spool and he quickly grew impatient. His hands weren't very steady and soon the paper was rolling unevenly, creasing the photos and growing into what clearly would become a giant snarl. Willis grabbed a pair of shears from the table next to the Photofax and snipped the paper that was still seeping relentlessly out of the machine. He put on a new empty spindle and tossed the half-rolled spool on the overloaded table. He looked around to see if anyone had seen him, but the newsroom was empty except for Merle and he was hidden behind the *New York Review of Books*.

Willis walked away from the mess of wrinkled wirephotos and went to the water fountain for a drink. He looked at the wall clock, checked his own wristwatch, then lit a Winston and took another halting turn around the newsroom, stopping again at the fountain. He passed a wastebasket and flipped his cigarette ash into it. A wad of Photofax paper burst into flames, sending a terrible chemical odor into the room. Willis slammed his foot into the wastebasket, putting out the fire but getting his shoe jammed. "Goddam it," he sputtered, hobbling around the room trying to knock the basket off by scraping it against desk legs. When he looked up, Connie was standing in the doorway laughing.

Shit. Connie had hardly spoken to him all week, hadn't even acknowledged his presence except a few times when she noisily got up and left the newsroom because he had come in. If he said something to her, she just sneered or glared or made some snide comment to someone else who happened to be standing nearby. It all started the night LBJ announced he wouldn't run again for president.

The next night Willis had asked what she thought of Johnson now and she turned away without answering, but on her way out of the newsroom she said to Hank, "Wouldn't it be great if every Texan—hell, every Southerner north of the Mason-Dixon Line—just went home?"

That was four days ago. Willis had known she was pissed because he'd refused to go to her meeting, but he had no idea how long she would hold the grudge. He hadn't wanted to go to the stupid meeting. He didn't even want to know what they were doing, although he really did know, of course; how could he avoid it? He might have gone just to keep the peace if Sy hadn't asked him to stay late and help with the LBJ story. Over the past month they had begun monitoring the late television news together, and with big stories they would write their own unbylined story based on the wire coverage from the *Times* and the AP plus the CBS News report. Just the night before, they had written their own lead on the bylined story about a breakthrough in relations between Washington and Hanoi. Willis knew some people in the newsroom were complaining about this collaboration, and he himself had an unspoken worry that he and Sy might be having a little too much fun, putting a touch too much drama in some of these stories. But it was hugely satisfying to watch these news events on television, crib from the source reporting by the *Times* and AP writers, and then concoct your own adjective-rich accounts. Imagine a wire service writing, as Sy had, that Johnson "tugged gently on his enormous earlobe" before announcing "the biggest surprise in American history since Pearl Harbor." Hell, it was more fun than sports writing. As for complaints from their own newsroom, Willis dismissed them as professional jealousy. After all, the whole newsroom had some sort of weird crush on Seymour.

Connie's anger was more troubling, and not just because Willis had the hots for her. He had pretty well given up on that hope anyway since the night with that Vince guy. He should have learned a long time ago to keep romance and his work separate. He should have learned it with Sheila, God knows, or in any one of several situations since then. This time, though, he meant to turn aside before anything even began, and he had already met a great-looking woman who tended bar up at the ski area. But even without romance, Connie could make life uncomfortable in the newsroom, and he saw big trouble ahead if she kept calling these meetings to talk about unions.

Now, caught here with his foot stuck in a wastebasket and her sneering at him like some goddess of righteousness, he suddenly was furiously angry and was about to swear at her when she cut him off, calling loudly across the newsroom, "Hey, Merle, you better look up and watch this." Merle put down his paper, carefully marking the page with a piece of copy paper. "Watch what?"

Connie walked toward Merle's desk but she did not lower her voice. "Watch what? Why, watch how a smooth ol' Southern pro moves around a newsroom. They say old Willis there was nominated once for a Pulitzer, and now I can see why. Can't you? He's quick on his feet."

Willis kicked the leg of the desk one more time, hard, then sat down in the nearest chair without looking directly at Connie. He bent over and pulled the basket off his foot, straightened up, and swiveled around to say something to her, but the phone rang on the city editor's desk where he was sitting. At the second ring he picked it up and said crossly, "City desk.

"Where? How many? Goddam. How many people? How many students? What do you mean you don't know? Look at them. How many are out there?"

Willis spun around quickly to see if Connie and Merle were watching him, and they were. He grinned. "Well, what's happening now," he said into the phone, mild mockery replacing the irritation in his voice. "Yes, right now. Oh. Well, I'll see what we can do. What's your name again? Okay, just don't do anything rash, not until we get there."

He turned to Connie and said, "There you go, Ace. There's your scoop, all ready and waiting for you."

She didn't answer, just looked blankly at Willis as though he had spoken in a language she didn't understand. But Merle couldn't resist. "What's happening at the college? Are you going over there?"

Willis moved over to his own desk and sat down before he answered, "They're rioting. Why don't you hustle over there and cover it?"

Merle had jumped up so abruptly when he heard "riot" that the *Review* fell out of his hands, scattering pages over the floor, and for an instant he couldn't decide in his excitement whether to answer Willis or pick up the paper. He started to speak, then stopped and dropped to one knee. Willis laughed. Connie shook her head angrily, making her blonde hair bounce on her shoulders. "Leave it on the goddam floor, Merle." She shoved her head forward, her jaw jutting toward Willis. "What's going on, Willis? What do you mean 'riot'?

And why should Merle get over there? Why don't you go? He's not even on duty yet."

Willis leaned back and put his feet up on the desk. "You hear that, Merle? Connie says you can't cover the riot because you haven't punched in."

Merle looked back and forth at the two of them. "Are they really rioting? What's the issue? The war?"

"She didn't say what the issue is, but it's probably the war. Or the draft. Or yippies. Or maybe it's just spring and the college kids are bored. The girl I talked to sure sounded like she wouldn't mind a little action."

"Listen, asshole," Connie said, "it's the college kids, including girls like the one you talked to, who're going to stop this stupid war. Or maybe you good ol' boy Pulitzer Prize nominees don't think they ought to stop the war? Maybe you're just like Johnson and just want another coonskin to nail up on your wall."

Willis leaned back and raised his feet to rest on the desk. He smiled broadly. "Good ol' boy, huh? That sounds like rank prejudice to me. What've you got against rednecks?" Damn, she's worse than Sheila about not letting anything pass. And just as blind in her convictions about what's right and what's wrong. She's sure these protesting kids are true believers, soldiers in the cause of truth and justice. She doesn't know and won't ever know because she won't accept it, even when everybody else knows it, that what they're protecting is their own hides. Wait until they get rid of the draft. Wait until this war is nothing but American have-nots volunteering to fight Vietnamese have-nots, just black kids fighting Asian kids; that's when the college campuses will forget the war. It'll be a simple lesson: no draft, no protest. But she won't believe it because she already knows what's right.

Connie glared at him in silence until he dropped the smirk, then she said, "Is there a story or not? What are they doing?"

The weak spring sun slicing through the window caught Connie's face, and Willis, still leaning back, thought, Christ, she has brown eyes, or at least they're not blue like I thought they were. But he said in a bored tone, "Who knows? After all, isn't this the first warm day in five months? The girl I talked to just said they were going to have a riot. Said a couple hundred kids were on the quad. I asked her when it started and she said it would start as soon as we get over there with a camera." He sniggered. "Sounds like a toy riot to me."

Willis swung his legs off the desk and swiveled around so his back was turned toward Connie and Merle, dismissing them and the campus riot. Connie glared at the back of his head until Merle said, "Well, I'm going over there. They're probably protesting the war. Maybe they'll take over a building."

He hurried toward the door, but two steps shy it swung open and the publisher's son walked in, brushing past without noticing Merle, who veered off course and, in the process, tripped over a pile of yellowing newspapers stacked up beside a desk.

Fletcher pushed the front lock of hair away from his eyes in a boyish gesture that he had, in fact, used habitually since boyhood. He extended his right hand at arm's length. Willis languidly raised his own hand to belt height and thrust it forward just enough to be polite.

"Glad to see you again," Fletcher said. He emphasized the point by showing a wide expanse of perfect teeth. His eyes gripped as tightly as his hand. "Nice work on town meeting." He yanked his gaze away abruptly and fixed it on Connie, who had taken Merle's seat and was watching them with unmasked hostility from across the room. "Well," Fletcher said, "we don't usually see Connie in the newsroom this early. I hope I'm not interrupting anything?"

"It's your paper," she said without smiling. "I'm just hanging around, and I don't have any idea what he's doing." Willis smiled when he saw that Fletcher was staring at her crossed legs. Never even heard her. He turned his chair around so he was facing Fletcher, whose fixed smile still beamed in Connie's direction but was aimed approximately at her knees. Finally, he looked back at Willis and said, "I heard a lot of talk about your New Hampshire story on McCarthy and Johnson too. People liked it."

"Thanks."

"And damn good timing too. Your story was the first thing I thought of last week when Johnson said he wasn't running again. Those are the kind of stories we get a payback on. We have too many stories that nobody reads because who's going to read the same stuff they can watch on TV? I know I'm not going to. A lot of those stories are—what's the word?—oh yeah, irrelevant."

They heard a chair smack into a desk and looked up to see Connie headed out toward the composing room door, walking quickly in short, choppy steps that clacked out disgust but that also made her short blue skirt bounce and jerk partway up her thighs.

Fletcher turned back to Willis and smiled, his eyebrows raised to what's-that-all-about position. "Prickly," he said.

*
**

Sy slammed through the door, his head darting around to see who was in the newsroom, just as Connie came back from the composing room carrying a Coke. Sy's scarf was draped loosely around his neck and he yanked it off with his right hand. He ignored Willis and Fletcher, shouting past them, "Hey, Connie, you've got to cover a press conference this afternoon."

"I can't." She sat down at her own desk and looked up at Sy but did not say anything more.

"Why not?" He looked at her out of the tops of his eyes.

"In the first place, I have to go somewhere else. In the second place, I don't start work until four."

Sy looked around the newsroom again and was about to say something when Connie raised her arm and pointed at Willis. "Why don't you send the hotshot over there?"

Sy looked over at Willis and Fletcher, who had stopped talking and were both watching them. "What are you working on, Willis?"

"Who's having a press conference?" Willis answered.

"There's a religious commune of some kind up in Moretown. They're complaining about harassment and they've called a press conference for this afternoon."

"Moretown? Christ, that's thirty miles away, isn't it? Is it worth it?"

"Yes, it's worth it," Sy said with some irritation. "Take the news car. And you better hurry if you've never been up that way."

"Wait a minute," Fletcher said. "Maybe it's not worth it. Won't the AP cover a press conference?"

Sy ignored him. "Get a map from Alice's desk," he said to Willis. "It'll take you about forty-five minutes to get there."

Willis nodded, but said, "How about Harry? Why can't he go?"

"Who?"

"Harry? No, I mean Hank—you know, the kid. Harry, Hank, Henry, whatever his name is." Connie snickered from the background.

"Wait a minute," Fletcher said again, moving slightly closer to Sy. "Are we going to cover every group that wants to whine about something? Whoever goes up there to Moretown is going to end up on overtime, right?"

Sy had started turning toward Connie, but he whirled around toward Fletcher, his face reddening. "We're going to cover every goddam group that I say we're going to cover. And I say we're going to cover the goddam press conference."

He turned to face Willis directly, the blood now pulsating in the tips of his fingers, in his toes, and most obviously in his pointed ears, which glowed like warning lights when his blood pressure soared. "And you're going to cover it, Willis. So get moving. Now."

Sy wheeled around to aim his hawkish glare at Connie. "And if you're not working, what in the hell are you doing in here? From now on, Connie, if you're in the newsroom, I'll assume you're working. Or rather, you assume that you're working because if I tell you to go cover a story and you don't do it, you can assume that you're fired."

Her jaw dropped open and she started to say something, but before any words came out Sy had turned away.

Several other people had drifted into the newsroom and Sy looked at them clustered toward the far end of the room. "That goes for all the rest of you too," he shouted. "If you are in this room, in this building, then you are working; you are on duty. So work."

No one laughed.

He turned back to Fletcher and Willis. They stood close together, tense and awkwardly off-balance, with their eyes flicking from Sy to Connie. She appeared frozen in place. Sy sent his angry look circling the silent room one more time, ending up back at Fletcher and Willis. Still, no one else moved.

"The car's in the parking lot, Willis." He said it flatly. "Call me from up there if there's a story. Go. Now. Right now." He turned away.

Everyone in the newsroom had seen Sy boil over into emotional anarchy, most often during confrontations with aggressive critics who dared to challenge a reporter or the paper's coverage, but this time was different. Much later, Ron and several others would remember the scene in painful detail, each of them describing their own surprise at the mean-spirited, humorless tone of Sy's attack. He acted, they said, like an angry bully. "Rabid," was Simmons's adjective.

It was a turning point for several of the people in that room, although they didn't really catch on at the time. Or maybe they did know it even then, but just didn't know they knew it. Maybe it's always like that; things happen, a cause suddenly causes, and everyone around knows immediately what the effect is going to be, but they have to pretend to themselves that they don't because if they know the future, they can't live with the present. From birth onward, the most certain forecast of all is the one outcome we spend our lives denying.

Later on, Sy himself called the episode that day in the newsroom strange and admitted his own behavior had been unusual even though he maintained up to the end that his surging fury was fully justified. Never mind that he acted in anticipation, not in reaction. Never mind that no one else could see the justice, or the lack of justice, that propelled him. For most of his life, he had stood alone whenever no one would stand with him, which was often, and he was not only content with his own stubbornness but proud of it and willing—more than willing, *eager*—to deal with the consequences of it. He knew, even if no one else did, that Connie's querulous readiness to fight needed to be checked. He knew that Fletcher's earnest longing for recognition was dangerous. He knew, with the surety of knowledge that comes from the inside out, that everything had changed even though nothing looked any different, or rather, that everything was on the brink of a change that would leave no one untouched. He knew all that, even though neither he nor anyone else could see or hear the avatar descending on them. Later he would take solace in the fact that when the god-beast was coming, he did not pretend not to know—that he dared to rage when others would have let fear and caution keep them silent. He did not, he would say, lack conviction.

After ordering Willis out of the tense newsroom, Sy turned and walked slowly toward his office, calling over his shoulder, "Fletcher, I'd like to talk to you." By the time Sy reached his desk and turned around to peer through the glass wall, Willis had disappeared, Connie was talking to a group of reporters, and Fletcher was approaching the open door of the office. He walked in, closed the door, and stood in front of Sy's desk.

"Well," he said, "you managed to piss on everybody out there, including me. Do you think that's a smart way to manage the newsroom?"

"I think it's my way to run a newsroom, Fletcher. It may not be the way you want to run the advertising department, but it's the way I want to run this department. And that means it is the way I'm going to run this newsroom as long as I'm the managing editor. Now then, your father said to talk to you about something — something about meetings?"

That was not precisely what Manny had told Sy, but it was close enough to defend if he had to.

Fletcher shifted his weight and looked away from Sy, but the office was so small there wasn't much to look at except the blank television set. He moved over and sat in the chair next to Sy's desk. It was the first time in a month that he had been in Sy's office. He had stayed away since Town Meeting Day, but being back in that chair brought back the memory of the tongue-lashing over Kittridge and the tax bill.

"Yeah," he said, "I thought it might be a good idea if your people and my people had regular meetings so they got to know each other. You know, so the news department and the advertising department could at least appreciate each other's problems."

Sy stared at him wordlessly, puzzled because it was not the answer he had expected. Either Manny had gotten it wrong, which was entirely possible, or Fletcher was playing mind games at a level Sy had thought far beyond his ability. He thought back an hour to the gut-churning conversation in Manny's office. The first thing Manny had said was that he had been told — passive tense, and he had flatly refused to say who told him — that newsroom people were meeting with pressroom union people. He wouldn't say which newsroom people. They had argued as bitterly as they had ever argued over anything about whether Manny had a right to withhold such information. In the end, Manny said he didn't care whether he had a right or not, it was his information and he was keeping it for himself. And evidently that's all he knew. Someone had reported that someone in the newsroom was talking to someone in the pressroom about unions.

Then Manny had said that Fletcher wanted to talk with Sy about "the meetings." And then, the last thing he had said was that Sy was not to mention the report about unions to anyone. "And I mean anyone," Manny said. "I don't want you to tell anyone what I've told you, and I don't want you to do anything about it." Manny rarely repeated himself, so Sy was surprised by the double admonition and he was even more unsettled when Manny slowly raised his gaze to dead center of Sy's eyes from its normal resting place on his collarbone and said for a third time, "Don't do or say anything about this to anyone."

He taxed his memory to replay every small detail of the conversation and he was certain of the sequence. First, Manny talked about the union. Then he mentioned Fletcher and meetings. Then he issued the uncharacteristic warning. The connection was inescapable, but then what was this nonsense Fletcher was saying?

A trap. A goddam trap.

Fletcher shifted in his chair. "I'm just talking about having joint staff meetings. The biggest headache my ad salesmen have is listening to complaints from their clients about what you put in the paper. I just thought it would help, like, you know, make things easier for everybody if my guys and your guys got together to talk sometimes."

Sy silently raised his gaze to a spot on the wall two feet over Fletcher's head. Fletcher hurried on. "Christ, I mean, what's wrong with that? It would give the salesmen a chance to pass on complaints and at the same time they would get to understand why your reporters write the stuff they do. Besides, don't forget this is a local paper and my people are out there every day talking to local folks. They talk to people in this town who know what's going on—real stuff, not just politics and government." He was talking faster and faster, worked into an embarrassed panic by Sy's silence and by the memory of their last conflict.

He hurried on blindly. "That reminds me—did we have the story about Chick Clark's daughter? Winning the trip to Florida?"

Sy's eyes flicked down to Fletcher's face, then rolled again toward the ceiling. He swiveled his chair about a quarter turn but still didn't speak. Fletcher said, "I was just thinking about meeting maybe once a month. Or so. I mean, Christ, they work in the same building every day. It's not as though your people would get contaminated or something."

Sy leaped out of his chair, pushing it hard against the back wall of the office. He opened his mouth then closed it again without a word, shoved his hands in his trousers pockets, and took two wide strides around the end of the desk. He stopped a foot from Fletcher's chair, too close for him to stand up but not quite touching him either.

"Fletcher," he said, staring nearly straight down at the upturned face, "we are never going to have what you call joint staff meetings." He raised his voice a notch. "As far as the newsroom is concerned, we're never going to have staff meetings—period. If you want to meet with what you call your people, why, go right ahead. You can spend the whole goddam day meeting if you want to, but not with my newsroom."

He leaned a menacing inch closer. "Forget it. No, more than that. Don't just forget about meetings; keep your salesmen and your clerks and your everything else away from the reporters at this newspaper. Your salesmen are just like the salesmen for every other outfit in this town. They don't have any more influence or any more access or any more anything else than any other smiley, smelly, spineless, supine salesman—or, for that matter, any other businessman or cop or politician or anyone else."

He loved the spontaneous alliteration.

"Are you getting me?" He jabbed a finger toward Fletcher. "News? Those sniveling, nickel-chasing chiselers wouldn't know a news story from a jingle. They may know how to tell an advertiser what he wants to hear, how to schmooze him out of his money. But don't ever think that reporters are going to listen to them about what stories to cover. In fact, if I haven't told you this before, I'm telling you now: If you or your salesmen think you have a news story, come to me with it. Do not—do not ever—go tell it to a reporter. If it's a story, I'll decide whether to give it to a reporter."

He stopped talking, but he did not move right away. Fletcher, gripping the arms of his chair, was white around the eyes, but he wasn't looking up at Sy. He slid his chair slightly backwards, just enough so he could stand up without bumping into Sy, but before he could rise, Sy took a half step and reclosed the gap. They froze in a silence that crushed down on them like a vacuum for a half minute before Sy suddenly spun around and walked back around the desk to his own chair. Fletcher was still gripping the arms of his chair and he did not start to rise until Sy was lowering himself into the seat on the opposite side of the desk. Neither of them spoke until, as Fletcher opened the door, Sy called out to his back, "Don't close it."

Sy watched him walk stiffly through the newsroom, his head up but not looking left or right. He'd been pretty hard on the kid. But screw it. Either he was too dense to feel pain or he was trying to trick Sy into talking about the union stuff. Either way, he deserved to have his ears pinned back.

Sy looked at the clock on the wall opposite Alice's desk: 3:05. All the other desks were empty. He stood up and began to scan the *Times*

wire, but after a few minutes he let the yellow telex paper drop back into a folded pile behind the machine. He left his office and strolled over to Alice's desk. "I'll be back in an hour or so," he said. She grunted.

After a minute, he walked on out of the newsroom and down the hall through the business office. A few people were working there, but the office did not seem as full or as busy as usual. He went on out the front doors and hesitated on the sidewalk before turning left. The gutters were running slushy streams, and he felt a sudden gust of wind sweep around the corner from the southwest. A thawing wind, just like Frost's, a wind to "scatter poems on the floor; turn the poet out of door."

He walked ahead of the wind for a block to a parking lot often used by the reporters. Several of their cars were already there. In the back of the lot a couple of young guys with long ponytails were huddled against the wall of a brick building, passing a joint back and forth. A large peace symbol had been painted on one end of the wall, and on the other end, in different paint, OFF THE PIGS was carefully lettered. The two boys, each wearing the scraggly beard of fledgling vanity, watched Sy but didn't try to hide their joint. He walked on, turning at the next corner and then, at the end of that block, turning right onto Third Street. Two more blocks and he was standing in front of the union hall, an old, soiled-to-black brick structure that at one time had been a school but in the 1950s had been abandoned by the city and bought by a group of labor unions. The first floor had been split up into several offices that now were used by various local unions. The second floor was a large, open meeting hall, also used by the unions, and the third floor was the meeting place for AA, or at least the AA congregation that could climb that many stairs.

Once, Sy had spent a lot of time inside the union hall while covering a long strike by the local carpenters union against the state's biggest construction company. He had written stories every day for weeks, including a long wrap-up piece that explained how the union had been destroyed, even though technically the strike continued, when the construction company managed to hire enough scab carpenters to fill all of its needs. Both sides hated his stories. The contractors complained endlessly because he refused to quit calling their employees scabs. The union men had bitterly denounced him as a traitor and his story as a lie. They had sworn the fight was not over and had demanded a retraction, but the publisher had stood firmly behind Sy and had even written an editorial reinforcing—

and lamenting—the judgment that the carpenters local was dead. Within days after the story, the pickets had disappeared from the construction company headquarters. Now, ten years later, carpenters here earned about half the wage they made in some states.

Sy stood outside the union hall, with one foot on the first step, looking up at the battered, heavy wooden door. Air conditioners hung awkwardly out of the first-floor windows, like epidermal tumors, but on the second floor white curtains fluttered through the open bottom sashes to the outside. It was the warmest day of the year so far, and even at three fifteen the sun was high enough to feel fine on Sy's head. There was no midafternoon traffic and the street was quiet, but he couldn't hear any voices coming from the open windows. He was listening so hard he didn't hear the police cruiser glide to a stop behind him at the opposite curb. Chief Jeff Bushey leaned out of the driver's side window and shouted, "Hey, Sy, thinking about getting an honest job?"

He turned away from the steps and crossed the street. "Chief, what would a man like you, who spends every day up to his elbows in dishonesty, know about honest work?"

Bushey's eyes squinted and the smile wrinkles froze as he studied Sy's face. Suddenly he pushed up the brim of his hat and renewed the smile. "Careful there, Scribe; somebody who hadn't known you as long as I have might not understand that you just like to play with words. Like the man said, words can be about as dangerous as a loaded gun." He stared silently at Sy long enough to make sure he had gotten the message.

Bushey was one of the few men Sy considered to be predictably dangerous. Lots of people were probably capable of violence through a sort of spontaneous combustion, he assumed, but not many were built with a capacity for cold, calculated, premeditated violence. He once did a quick and dirty analytical piece on recent first-degree murder cases and found that most killers who figured it out beforehand either used safe-distance techniques, like poison or time bombs, or else they hired a professional assassin.

Ten years as police chief without a major incident had done nothing to dispel the feeling Sy had about Bushey. He had written the stories about his hiring. A twenty-year marine, Bushey had seen action in World War II and in Korea and then some sort of duty involving military brigs. Sy had never found out exactly what was involved other than that Bushey evidently was on the right side of the prison bars. Sy had always suspected there was something odd about his discharge, although he never could find any evidence or any negative reports. All he really knew was that Bushey had retired at age forty with only the rank of buck sergeant and that he had been hired as police chief largely on the strength of a glowing recommendation from a ranking Marine Corps officer who was a native son of the city and maintained hometown contacts.

They talked for a while about city hall politics, then Bushey checked his watch, started up the cruiser, and drove slowly down Third Street.

Sy had been in front of the union hall for fifteen minutes and he had not heard any meeting sounds and had not seen anyone come or go. Of course, the meeting could be in one of the first-floor rooms. Maybe there was no meeting at all and the newsroom was empty because all the reporters were out working or were just taking advantage of the weather and were coming in late.

He moved again to the steps and leaned on the handrail. It would be easy enough to take a quick look inside and Sy had no qualms about spying, but Manny's stern warning stopped him. There couldn't be any harm in just walking down the street, but going inside the union hall would be hard to explain.

Still no sign of activity. Maybe Manny had gotten the whole thing wrong? Maybe he had misunderstood, or maybe the mysterious informant had made a mistake? Why would they want to start a union, after all? Suddenly Sy was disgusted with himself; that was the sort of softheaded wishful thinking he hated in other people — "debauchery of the public mind." For Sy, few things were more important than to know himself as a man, like Sandburg's Lincoln, who struggled amid illusions, fated to answer for himself.

Even if Manny were capable of making such a mistake, which he might be, Sy knew he could count on his own recent uneasiness and unformed suspicions. Something was sure as hell going on with the newsroom, and he would not delude himself.

He glanced once more at the union hall door, then walked away, thinking that at least he was still ahead of Fletcher who, he decided, didn't know a thing about the union problem. Sy wondered if Willis knew anything and decided that he must know but that did not necessarily make him part of it.

He headed in the general direction of the paper but detoured a couple of blocks so he could stop by the coffee shop. It was a little late for the afternoon crowd, so Sam was alone and had already poured a cup before he could tell him not to bother. He sat on a stool sipping the coffee, while Sam, who had left Prague in 1948 just ahead of the Communists, raved about Dubček. He always prodded Sy about news from Prague. After listening quietly for a few minutes, Sy looked around the empty lunchroom and said casually, "Seen Connie or any of the others this afternoon?" Sam said no and reached for the pot of coffee, but Sy shook his head and stood up to leave. He reached in his pocket for money, but Sam waved him off.

When Sy walked back into the newsroom, five reporters were at their desks, including Connie, who looked up at him and smiled.

Willis was glad he didn't have to argue with Sy about whether to write a story. Seymour always expected a story and he would stew a bit when Alice gave him the message about the press conference being a bust, but what could he do about it since Willis was on the road and couldn't be reached. He'd get back to the paper late, assuming he could find a roadhouse or even a diner to kill some time in, and by then Seymour and Greenberg would have planned the paper without counting on a story from him. Later he could tell Sy that he was sure he could get a story out of the commune but not from the press conference. In fact, he was already beginning to see a story, some sort of feature about this back-to-the-land, antiauthoritarian, anti-Vietnam, hippie-culture cult living in self-selected isolation from the world.

Willis slowed down again as Men Working signs warned him that the narrow paved road was about to turn back into a wide gravel road. You could guess how much political muscle a place had by how much of the interstate system had been finished. In Texas and most of the other coastal states it was pretty well finished; up here, they seemed to think four-lane roads were a sign of government waste. In most places, the forests crowded right up to the shoulders of the highways, and the skinny shoulders themselves didn't offer a driver much comfort. As far as he had been able to see they had built a lot of short stretches of superhighway, but very little interstate actually connected one point with another and only in one spot, in the far southeastern corner of the state, did the interstate actually connect with another state. His car churned up a thick cloud of dust behind him as he crept along, but his was the only vehicle traveling that afternoon so at least he didn't have to eat someone else's dirty wake. After about a mile, the gravel ended abruptly as the road made a sharp right-hand corner before turning into a narrow blacktopped bridge.

The river below looked, by God, like *Field & Stream.* Snowmelt had turned the stretch below and above the bridge into whitewater for as far as he could see. Half full, the rapacious river had swallowed all but the largest of the boulders, and waves slapping against these car-sized rocks sent spray over their tops.

Narrowed here at the bridge, the stream spread out as it roared downstream, threatening to tear out the fragile banks and their lightly rooted young hardwoods whose tiny, pale green leaves hung out over both shores. Upstream, a long-abandoned concrete and granite dam formed a six-foot waterfall that glistened in the afternoon sun, a shimmery curtain stretched between sheer bluffs. Willis stopped his car halfway across the bridge and slid over to the passenger's side, studying the downstream scene as if it were a landscape in a museum. The darker pools on the backside of the larger boulders must be where the exotic trout lived, waiting hungrily for a photographer to show up so they could leap at hand-tied flies cast by Ivy League professors. Fish with names that rolled off your tongue like mysterious places—steelhead, rainbows, brookies, and browns. Those were the kind of fish that glided through the dreams of boys like Willis had been, towheaded boys who spent their summer days snagging dull, blunt crappie and bream out of deep opaque creeks with steep red banks, boys who dangled worms into thick gray water that slid along slowly and silently and whose only exciting tenants were cottonmouths.

As Willis stared at the rippling water, a picture suddenly appeared in his mind, almost intact: himself, a boy, lying on the wooden porch floor, idly turning the slick pages of a magazine, thinking of a movie star whose name now was long gone but whose shape, fossilized in his mind, came back with full force. He flips the page, a green Studebaker appears on the left-hand side, and on the right is a picture of this spot, this very spot, only the focal point of the photograph is a man in hip boots, knees bent, vested body leaning back with his bamboo fly rod arched nearly double while in the foreground, fifty feet upstream, a spangled trout dances on its tail— a picture of a life so perfect that for an instant it even displaced the sweatered fantasy of the previous page.

It must have been here, by God, it must have been the same spot; it must have been shot from this same bridge, the afternoon sun sparkling off the same crumbling dam, only later, maybe May, when the water was lower and less violent.

He looked around, suddenly sure that someone was watching him. But the bridge was still empty. No cars in sight up or down the road. Far downriver the woods gave way to a plowed field on both sides of the river, and across the field he could see silos and a barn but no other sign of life was visible in any direction. Willis slid quickly back under the steering wheel and started the car.

He drove slowly along the river valley road, a mile or more before he passed another car. The highway twisted with the river, rolling up and down low hills and circling around the higher rises. In the distance, in the few spots that were flat enough and bare enough to see any distance, round-top mountains formed a solid white fence for the valley. Everywhere shoots had broken through, turning the patches of snow into mere accessories for the green cover, and the occasional dark, stooped, old bare apple trees were only reference points for the groups of slender poplars and birches whose early leaves caught the soft fading light.

The Bible got it all wrong, Willis thought. They gave valleys a bad name, all that talk about the shadow of death. This looks more like the valley of life, a place to live in, not walk through. There was a great quote in one of the Vermont history books Sy had persuaded him to read, something that Ethan Allen said about gods of the mountains not being like gods of the valleys, but he couldn't remember exactly what it was.

Then he remembered Seymour's rage in the newsroom and a shadow fell across his rising mood. He had seemed crazed, ranting at Connie and looking like he might actually attack Fletcher. It was as though the harnessed energy that made it exciting to work for him had suddenly broken free, out of control, like a stiff breeze turning into a hurricane.

Of course, Willis thought, he really has gone sort of crazy. He must have learned about the union. That's why he was ranting, and he thinks I'm part of it. That's why he sent me out here. Oh shit.

Then his mind went back to the stupid press conference, which also had jangled his nerves. Willis's eyes flicked involuntarily to the rearview mirror. Basically, it was a hippie commune like hundreds of others, full of kids with long hair and silly dreams, but it also seemed very different from the other free-love, cheap-dope, no-mind hippie havens he had seen. This one felt like it had a purpose, maybe even an organized vision. Perhaps it seemed different because there were so many children; he guessed there were about two dozen adults and nearly that many small children. But the real difference, he realized, was that the leader, the guy who called himself Thunderclap, was more than just foolish, he was downright spooky.

Willis and a kid from the local weekly paper had been the only reporters. While they waited to see if anyone else would show up, Willis wandered around the farm, trailed by a girl in a sack-like dress that hung nearly to her sandals and a boy wearing heavy boots and blue overalls over a stained white shirt that he kept buttoned tightly around his neck and wrists. When he spoke to them, their eyes struggled to focus, then sweet grins appeared on their faces and they would nod or shake their heads. He guessed they were both about 20, one dark and the other fair. Their young faces were full of grace. They were beautiful and genderless, as interchangeable and sexless as shiny depolarized magnets.

Their lack of power, unselfconscious vulnerability, made Willis seethe with irritation; at the same time, he was ashamed of his own self-concealing posture of authority. He embarrassed himself further by blurting, "Do you like being so isolated way out here in the woods?"

She smiled first, then he, and they looked at each other before turning their untroubled eyes back to Willis with a shrugging gesture that he took to mean the question had no meaning but that it was okay if he wanted to ask it.

Willis stared at them for a minute, then brushed past the still smiling pair and started off with a wide stride down one of the paths leading from the yard toward the woods. Just before the edge of the grass he looked over his shoulder and, sure enough, they were trailing along, single file, behind him. "Did somebody tell you to follow me?"

The boy, in the lead, stopped and looked blankly at Willis, his hands hanging motionless at his side. "Well? Did they?" The boy stared briefly, then he said, "Yes." That was all he said. Willis couldn't see the girl behind him, other than the long skirt flaring out on either side of the legs of his overalls. "Why are you following me?"

"Because he told us to."

"Who?"

"The Chief."

"Why?"

"I don't know."

Willis looked uncertainly into the boy's smooth face, but finding not even mockery, a sudden rage propelled him back along the path until he was an arm's length away. Not so much as a flicker crossed the boy's face. They stared into each other's eyes until Willis dropped his gaze, spun around, and walked off again down the path into the woods. He did not look back again but he knew they were there.

The path wound around in a circle, past a hodgepodge of rough-board shacks built in odd shapes and making use of assorted discards, such as automobile windshields and metal signs. Things Go Better, one roof proclaimed. He did not see anyone inside or near any of the shacks but they all had at least one dog tied to a stake in front. The hardwood trees, mostly maples and birch, had been cut back only enough to squeeze in the huts and the tiny packed-dirt clearings in front, now mostly mud, where the dogs paced or lay glumly watching the humans' footpath. The clearings and paths were clear of snow, but in the woods dried-out, granular white patches covered most of the ground except for bare spots radiating from the sap-warmed bottoms of the tree trunks.

At the end of the circle he was back in the front yard of the farmhouse, where people sat or sprawled on the porch and small children and babies played or slept in the matted long-dead grass. He thought no one had noticed him until he spotted a young girl near the porch who seemed transfixed by the sight of him. The beret gave her away immediately, but even then it took a few seconds for his mind to come into register with his memory. Time played one of its funny tricks and for an instant he had vivid recall of the girl and the bus, but it seemed to have happened in a different place in another, far-distant year. Could that trip have been only three months ago?

He must have tripped because he nearly fell, and then he heard a loud voice boom, "Careful of the babes. If you tramp on the least, you're tramping on the rest of us too."

It was a threat. It sounded to Willis at the time like a threat, without humor or playfulness, not conversation but intimidation. The voice came from the porch of the house where the sun glinted off the metal-rimmed eyeglasses of a man standing at the top of the steps. His bearded face was tilted downward and he raised a heavy arm to wave as Willis regained his balance. He looked huge, with a dark beard so long and so thick that Willis couldn't tell whether the fatigue shirt was buttoned at the neck or not. Unlike all the others, he had rolled up his sleeves. The man's hair curled out in all directions around his head, and there was enough left over to make a ponytail.

Willis looked around to see if he was motioning to the boy and girl, but they had disappeared. He made his way toward the porch, stepping carefully around the small forms sprawled unconscious on the ground or sitting quietly in small groups, murmuring and laughing. Not one of the children looked up at him or moved to avoid being stepped on. They're no more afraid than rattlesnakes, he thought—hell, less afraid; rattlesnakes warn you off.

Willis tried to concentrate on the dark man watching him from the shadowed porch, but he was distracted by the children and started to think of his own son, who would have been the age of one of the big kids here but in Willis's memory remained a toddler.

The news conference was a farce. Besides not having any news, the guy wouldn't answer any questions, wouldn't give his real name, and complained because there were no television cameras. He ranted about persecution by the police but wouldn't give any real examples, spoke for a while in rhymed couplets that did not make any sense, and raved about the war and a conspiracy between Wall Street and Israel to open up a new supply of oil from Southeast Asia. He seemed to think of himself as part preacher, part political leader, part philosopher, and part clown. It was like listening to Castro on speed.

Willis felt humiliated, sitting there with the rookie weekly reporter listening to the diatribe. After listening for more than a half hour without making a single note, he finally stood up and waved a hand angrily at Thunderclap.

"Listen, buddy, I came all the way up here because you said you had some news. So cut the bull and say what you have to say or I'm leaving. If you can prove any of this crap, you better do it soon."

No sound came from the crowd, not even a baby's cry, but they all turned carefully to look at the bearded leader. For a moment he just looked down at Willis, then he said slowly and deliberately, "It's all right, children, it's okay. Let him go. The press is part of the establishment, and like the rest of them these agents of greed and corruption are doomed. But not now. Not here. Let him go."

As he drove along the valley, crossing and recrossing the swollen river, Willis thought about how he would describe the commune scene for Sy. He'd make him laugh, imitating Thunderclap's paranoia, his booming prophet's voice spewing out snatches of scripture tangled up with Hallmark greeting card sentimentality and Jack Kerouac gibberish. And the whole diatribe spiced up at the end with a paean to LSD that Willis guessed was plagiarized from Timothy Leary. That's how he would describe it to Sy, he decided, and just then his eye was pulled back to the rearview mirror.

Far back, a car was coming around a wide curve where the road followed tight up against the river, hemmed in between the water and a wall of granite that in some places they had cut back to make enough space for two narrow lanes. Willis took his foot off the gas pedal, but the trailing car did not get any closer, and he speeded up, but it didn't drop further behind either. The dark car was just far enough behind so he could not tell how many people were inside. The two cars rolled along in near isolation, as though attached by an invisible cord, without overtaking any other traffic. Only once did a car pass going in the opposite direction. Willis remembered the feeling back at the bridge that he was being watched.

Willis accelerated suddenly as his car hit the midpoint of a wide left-hand turn and the other car disappeared, but as he went into the switchback curve to the right, he looked over and saw it cruising along silently into the turn, a long black burden that he was doomed to drag along like a bad memory. The road grew increasingly curvy and several times he lost sight of the car, but each time it reappeared. At some point Willis realized he was watching the road behind more than the one in front. Once he glanced down at the speedometer and saw the red needle splitting seventy, and he braked so hard the car began to fishtail before he got control of the wheel and himself. Ahead he saw an unpaved parking area notched out of the woods and, without considering why, he braked quickly and swung his car off the road. At the back of the turnout, a galvanized pipe protruding from the embankment poured a heavy stream of water into a shallow stone-lined pit. No one was using the communal spring.

Willis opened the door and had swung his left foot out when he saw the black car turn onto the gravel. Its tires flung stones noisily into the wheel wells. It was a Cadillac Sedan DeVille, with eerie, gray-tinted windows. He sat without moving, frozen like a rabbit caught in a headlight, his door half open and both feet resting on the ground. As the Cadillac approached, the passenger-side window descended slowly, revealing first a large head of steel-gray curls, then a round, jowly face, and finally a ham-sized forearm, lifted up then dropped into place over the chrome and shiny black paint. "We figured you was having car trouble," she said. "Fred said, 'The way he's speeding up and then slowing down, I bet he's either overheating or his carburetor is acting up.'"

She peered into his face, waiting alertly for confirmation or whatever else her greeting would fetch back. When Willis didn't reply right away, she went on. "He can't do much since his heart attack, but he says if you need water there's a pail in the trunk. It's another five miles before the store."

Willis held on to the top of the car door as he stood up, afraid his weakened knees would buckle without support. A wave of relief rushed through his body and spilled out in a huge smile. "Ma'am," he said too loudly, "my radiator and my carburetor are both all right, but I sure am proud to see you anyhow." He eased his car door closed and walked the three steps to the side of the Cadillac. He bent down so he could see across her more-than-ample chest to the driver's side. "It sure is friendly of you folks to stop like this."

Fred didn't look exactly friendly. A massive left forearm was draped over the steering wheel and he was half turned toward his wife's window. A spotless, thin-striped hat, like railroad engineers wear, was pulled halfway down his forehead, but the bill was not long enough to shadow either his giant nose or a lower jaw that protruded like an outcropping of rock over his bib overalls. His mouth was sealed in a line that ran parallel to the cap bill above it. He looked as powerful as a bull. If a heart that big stopped thumping, everyone nearby would notice the silence.

"I see you're driving Vermont plates," she said. It was a flat statement but somehow there was a question buried in it too, and underneath the question was yet another statement. In six words, she had said, "You're not one of us, but you're pretending to be. And who are you, and what are you doing here?" And she did it without being rude or even overtly curious. Willis waited but she didn't go on. "Yes, well, I'm a reporter," he said, "a newspaper reporter."

"That right?" she said. "A reporter. For the local paper?"

"Yes."

"We don't read that paper."

Willis felt as though he had done something wrong.

He glanced quickly past her gray-curl helmet to see if he could catch Fred's eye and maybe get a little fraternal encouragement, a nod or a wink. God knows Fred must have felt the sting of her unspoken indictments often enough. He saw only a massive face that reflected roughly the warm sympathy of a tombstone.

"Well, it's pretty far away from here," Willis said softly, looking skyward, away from both of them.

"It ain't that," she said. "We used to read it."

Oh Christ, here it comes. But it didn't. She just sat, her eyes narrowed, her mouth clamped, and her attention focused like a guard dog on Willis, a mute force irresistibly compelling him to ask:

"Why did you stop reading the paper?"

"We live in Florida most of the year since we sold the farm," she said. "We're just here summers, at the camp."

"Oh," he said. "I see."

"But that ain't why we quit the paper," she said, again chopping off the conversation in a way that forced him to fill the void.

"Why did you quit?"

Fred made his first contribution, driven out of his silence by sheer pride. "She was a correspondent."

"A what?"

"Town correspondent. She wrote the news from Granby. Filled a whole column every week."

Willis grinned a comrade's salute toward her, but she said only, "Fifteen years."

He looked blank but she and Fred just sat silently, waiting for a response. They looked as though they might wait a long time.

"Why did you stop corresponding?" asked Willis, clearly no match for their endurance.

"They quit having local news," she said. Willis frowned, shaking his head slightly in sympathetic disbelief at "their" foolishness.

"That ain't why we quit reading it, though," she said. "We quit because it's not right for the paper to support the hippies and them others when our boys are over there in Viet Nam fighting for the country."

"Aidin' and bettin' on the enemy," Fred said with satisfied finality.

She had not turned her gaze away from Willis since the car rolled to a stop and she still didn't look in Fred's direction, but she bobbed her head back toward him as she informed Willis, "He was three years in the Pacific, so he knows what he's talking about. Wounded twice."

Fred corrected her, "One was just a graze."

"Well," she said sharply, "you got two Purple Hearts."

Willis stared at the hero with what he hoped was proper respect.

"Two," she said, holding up the appropriate number of fingers.

That seemed to be all there was to say. After waiting just long enough for Willis to challenge the facts, if he dared, she said, "Well, I guess if you needed any help you'd have said so by now, so we'll go on along." Willis nodded, and the smoke-tinted window began its slow automated ascent, but just in time he said, "Wait, tell me your name so I can tell people at the paper that I met you."

"Ginny," she said. "Ginny Palmer."

"They'll all remember her," Fred called out as he dropped the Cadillac into drive.

Willis found a place to stop for a beer and a hamburger, but it surely was not a roadhouse. Called Jenkins Family Restaurant, it was located where a roadhouse ought to be, at a remote crossroads a few miles from the nearest town, but this place looked more like a farmhouse than one of the low-cut, windowless, cinder block honky-tonks he realized he had begun to miss. Roadhouses in the rural South were as common, as recognizable, and as comfortable as short-steepled churches; you could usually find at least one of each, sometimes squatting cheek-by-jowl, between every town or village. Up here, Willis had gradually come to understand, the villages were a little closer together, about a day's walking distance, but between settlements the only gathering places were barns and barnyards.

Jenkins Family Restaurant turned out to be, in fact, a remodeled farmhouse with an expanded dining room filled up by six square, four-place wooden tables, two of which were fully occupied. The other tables were absolutely bare, and Willis took one by a window, as far from the other diners as he could get. As it turned out, the Jenkinses did serve alcohol, or at least beer, although there was no sign advertising this accommodation, and Mrs. Jenkins, or whoever was rattling around inside the kitchen, produced a fine fat burger with a bonus of homemade french fries.

Overall, he had to admit as he drove the final ten miles to town, the restaurant had been perfect for what he wanted—to kill a little time, mull over the commune, and relax with a brew. He pulled into the newspaper parking lot a little after eight just as the radio began playing "Ode to Billie Joe," which he secretly loved. Willis sat listening to Bobbie Gentry, feeling mildly homesick, or not sick, really, so much as warmly nostalgic for some of the places and people he had left. Sheila was at the head of the list, or at least the memory of Sheila when they had first married and both worked for the *Montgomery Advertiser*. Then he thought of how blisteringly scornful she would be about this song and Bobbie Gentry and the whole sappy notion of Billie Joe McAllister. Christ, Sheila's sarcasm could peel paint off the walls.

The song stopped mid-chorus, leaving empty air after "jumped off the Tallahatchie . . ." and for a moment the radio was silent. Then a somber voice said, "This is a news bulletin. The Associated Press has just confirmed that Martin Luther King has died. He died at 8:05 Eastern time, some two hours after being shot at the Lorraine Motel in Memphis."

Willis leaped out of the news car and ran up the back stairs to the newsroom, bursting in on a scene that was even more chaotic than usual. People were swarmed over the AP wire machine, a smaller group hovered at the Photofax, and a stream of empty plastic cartridges fired off from the composing room slammed noisily into the wooden box that served as final terminal for the pneumatic copy-delivery system. In Sy's office, he and Greenberg were leaning over the *New York Times* wire. Willis could see the television flickering over their heads. Ron, Merle, and Hank were all at their typewriters, each one locked onto his own keyboard with furrowed-brow concentration. Willis looked for Connie and spotted her at the center of the group reading wire copy as it clattered out of the AP machine. She was holding up the ribbon of paper as it fed out of the machine so those at the back of the group could read the story. Even the guys from the sports desk were gathered around, trying to see either the copy or the photos. Telephones were ringing on at least three of the abandoned desks and Rocky was standing in the doorway between his kingdom and the newsroom, scowling menacingly at the general disorder.

As he started toward Sy's office, Willis noticed Alice slouched down in her chair reading the *Saturday Evening Post*, oblivious to the turmoil. The telephone on her desk jangled loudly at her elbow but still she didn't look up until she had carefully marked her place in the magazine, set it down neatly on the right side of her bare desk, and glanced at the clock. Finally, on the third ring she got the receiver to her ear and said, "Newsroom." The one word was distinct but as neutral as distilled water—no inflection, no greeting, and no interest. She listened silently for a moment, then looked up at Willis and extended the phone toward him. "It's for you," she said, already reaching over with the other hand for her magazine.

"Switch it to my desk," he said. He was not expecting a call and realized he was a little irritated, probably because he wanted to get to Sy and find out what was going on.

"Hello, Bud?" He didn't recognize the voice, but everyone up here called him Willis so he immediately assumed it was someone from the past. "Bud? This is Fletcher. I wondered if you had a minute to talk if I came down to the newsroom?"

"You mean right now?" He was stalling but also interested despite himself.

"Well, yeah. If that's all right. I could be there in about twenty minutes."

"Sure. I'll be here. What's it about?"

Fletcher paused, cleared his throat, and then said, "I'd rather talk to you in my office. Don't worry, it's nothing urgent. Just something about a news story. It's just that I'd rather no one else knew about it." When Willis didn't answer right away, he said, "If you know what I mean."

"Sure," Willis said. "Okay. Come find me in the newsroom when you get here."

Seymour was motioning to him from the glass office and Willis walked quickly over there. Greenberg didn't look up, but Sy said, "No commune story, eh? Just as well tonight. We've got our hands full and I want you to help."

Willis nodded, pleased and eager. "I want a couple of things," Sy said. "First, can you use some of your old sources or buddies to get some background, some lively stuff, for the King story? You know, some anecdotes, I-was-there quotes. Didn't you cover some of his marches?"

"Yeah," Willis said. "A couple. I'll call some people. I interviewed him once, for about five minutes. He was sitting in the back seat of a car, waiting for a driver or something. Maybe I could work in something about that."

"Good," Sy said. "Get the wire stories from Lindsay. He's got his hands full too, but Greenberg and I are both helping him. This is a hell of a story. Johnson has cancelled his trip to Hawaii."

Willis nodded and started to turn away, but Sy stopped him.

"That's not all. Merle is working on a story about the college protest this afternoon. Not much happened but a lot of people were there and we need a good story. I may ask you to help him with that."

"Sure," Willis said, "but how about Ron or Hank? They're both pretty good writers and they probably could smooth out some of Merle's syntax, at least."

"They're both writing good stories of their own. Ron covered a meeting of the McCarthy people and got some stuff that no one else has. They closed the meeting, but he found someone who would talk."

Willis felt one small stab of jealousy. "How about Hank?"

Seymour was shaking his head. "No, we can't hold his story either. I want you to do it."

Willis was beginning to feel hemmed in, in a way he couldn't quite understand. "How about Connie," he said. "Why can't she help Merle?"

Seymour stiffened. "Goddam it, Willis, because I told you to do it, that's why. Merle will be writing for a while and that'll give you a chance to make your calls. Then you can rewrite his story or help him rewrite it. We've got plenty of time. It's not quite nine."

He turned back toward Greenberg, dismissing Willis, and said, "Tell me, Matt, how come people around here work so hard to get out of working? It used to be that reporters wanted to write stories; now they just want to pass them off to somebody else."

Willis left in a huff and arrived back at his desk in a black mood. He didn't even see her coming but suddenly Connie was at his elbow, shoving aside a stack of newspapers so she could sit on the corner of his desk. "Anything out of the commune?"

"Of course not," Willis said. "I knew goddam well there wouldn't be."

He looked up and added, "It was a great drive, though. You ought to go up there sometime."

"I'd like to," she said. "Maybe we'll go together. I'm sort of interested in the commune too."

Willis's mind tilted. Too? What did *too* mean? The commune and him? He looked into her face for a clue but found only warm eyes and a slightly smiling mouth. She said, "Looks like a busy night here. But if you can make it, we're having another meeting at eleven. I'm hoping everyone who's interested will come. This is an important meeting."

She hesitated, but he didn't. "Yeah, sure. I'll try." It sounded weak so he went on. "I ought to get through with my stuff by then. Sy asked me to dig up some color on King."

She frowned and it took him a moment to realize why. "Christ," he said, "you know what I mean. I wasn't trying to make a joke."

She laughed but then said seriously, "Yeah, it must be hard when people are always watching for you to make a racist mistake. You were right today to call me on the redneck crack. It's all prejudice, isn't it? White on black, black on white, white on white . . ."

He nodded and right then he liked her so much he would have signed a union card or anything else she handed him. But she just smiled again and left, saying, "The meeting's at the same place. Come late if you can't get there by eleven."

It had already been a long day, but Willis no longer felt tired. He grabbed his address book out of the top drawer and began copying down telephone numbers. First, he'd call Clancy in Atlanta. He'd covered King since his early days at Ebenezer Baptist in Atlanta. Willis himself had first run into King even earlier, when he was a twenty-one-year-old rookie reporter and King a young preacher with the church in Montgomery. He never had seriously covered King or the civil rights movement, though, because at the beginning he was just a rookie cop-chaser, and by the time his career and the movement both took off he was doing mostly political stories. In North Carolina and occasionally in other places, politics took him into civil rights, but it never was really his beat.

He knew most of the South's good civil rights reporters, though, including a guy at the *Memphis Press-Scimitar*, and it only took a few minutes to have a list of eight that he could get some help from. He began working the phone, but at the same time he was watching his own newsroom—or rather, he was keeping an eye on Sy's office because as usual that was the center ring.

Willis was still smarting from the crack about not working. There was no doubt that Seymour could be a heavyweight asshole, but he was just as skillful as newsroom conductor. A steady stream of people filed into and out of his office, and when he was alone the telephone was glued to his ear. He had had the phone company put in an especially long cord so he could pace around the office, check the *Times* wire, and even walk partway out into the newsroom with the speaker cradled on his shoulder and the box dangling at the end of his arm. He also had plug-in earphones that he used to take dictation from a reporter when no one else was around or he didn't want to wait for the copy. Willis knew that Sy took some pride in being the fastest typist in the newsroom, which really was not so remarkable since most of the reporters typed with two fingers or, at the most, two fingers and a thumb for the space bar.

Willis watched as Greenberg and Pembrooke, one of the copy editors, nearly collided as each one hurried toward Seymour's door with their heads down, reading copy. He waved them both into the glass office, quickly read Pembrooke's paper, nodded, spoke a couple of words, and was intent on Greenberg's piece before the copy editor even made it back out the door. Seymour and Greenberg exchanged a few words, and by that time one of the proofreaders was waiting at the door. Sy motioned her in and Greenberg left, shouting as he cleared the doorway to Hank across the newsroom.

Willis lost track of the newsroom activity for a while as he talked with friends in Texas and North Carolina. He got the name of a *Chattanooga Times* reporter, but he couldn't get through to him. Finally, he reached the Memphis guy and that call gave him his story, including some stuff that he knew the wire services wouldn't have.

When he looked up to check on the newsroom again he saw Rocky standing in Sy's doorway and, although he couldn't hear them, he could tell they were both angry. Sy had stood up at his desk, his head thrust forward, and Rocky was tapping rapidly on the doorjamb with his pica rule. When Sy picked up the phone, Rocky turned and stalked bowlegged through the newsroom, red-faced and muttering.

Willis suddenly remembered Mark Twain's story about a newspaper editor in Tennessee. An old editor friend had shown the story to Willis years ago and he had reread it so many times he knew some of the lines by heart. Twain's slander-loving, fire-breathing, gun-toting Tennessee editor "scowling fearfully" and butchering reporters' copy "till its mother wouldn't have known it."

Willis snorted a laugh under his breath, wondering if Sy knew the story. "What's so funny?" It was Fletcher, standing at his elbow. He had forgotten all about him.

Shit, Willis thought, looking wildly over at Seymour's office, for one crazy second envisioning Sy pulling out a pistol and shooting Fletcher the way Twain's Tennessee editor dealt with his enemies. What he really was worried about, of course, was that Seymour would see him talking with Fletcher and storm out of his office yelling at both of them.

"Hi, Fletcher," he said quickly. "I'll be with you in a minute. I'll meet you down in your office."

The advertising director's office was just off the front entrance hall. When he walked in, Fletcher was slouched heavily in his desk chair. Sitting down across from him, Willis noticed a double row of framed pictures on the wall behind Fletcher's head but he didn't realize at first that they were reprints of *Saturday Evening Post* covers.

"What do you think about Martin Luther King?" Fletcher asked, his face revealing nothing.

"What would you expect me to think?"

"Oh, well I just meant you probably were as shocked as everybody else and, uh, I just wondered if you had any guesses or opinions about who, uh, who might have done it."

Willis lit a cigarette and didn't answer, so Fletcher ventured on. "I've never been down South. Except to New Orleans and Florida, of course. But it always seemed different to me, uh, I don't know, just somehow the people seemed different. I don't mean . . . that is, I just mean different, not worse or better or anything, just . . ."

Willis finally spoke. "No, Fletcher, they're not so very different. In lots of ways, in fact, they're just like people up here. Just like you, in fact."

Fletcher sat up straighter. "Yeah, well, I guess so. But that's not why I wanted to talk to you." He paused, then said, "I understand you went up to that commune today. I mean, I was in the newsroom when Sy sent you to the press conference."

"I know you were, Fletcher. I was there too, remember? What about it?"

Fletcher looked uncomfortable. He had taken off his tie and added a red crewneck sweater, but he pulled at his collar anyway, as though he was loosening a tie. He stood up, shook down his trouser legs to straighten the crease, then sat back down. "Listen, Bud, we've got a problem, or at least some of the businessmen think we may have a problem. You can help us out."

He stopped talking long enough to look earnestly into Willis's face. Whatever he saw evidently encouraged him to go on. "We're picking up some pretty scary rumors about that commune."

"Drugs?" Willis asked.

"Well, yes, drugs, among other things," Fletcher said. "But not just drugs in the commune. We're hearing about local kids going up there to buy marijuana and sometimes bringing it back here. But that's not all either."

He stopped talking and leaned forward slightly. "Some people are starting to believe they're hiding draft dodgers and stirring up unrest among youngsters from around here." He paused. He's letting that shocker sink in, Willis thought, but it's not going very far.

"But the worst is the child abuse. We're hearing horror stories about beating of children and weird religious stuff."

Willis was interested for the first time. "Has anyone seen this stuff? This child beating? What sort of religious stuff?"

Fletcher leaned back in his chair. "I don't know if they've actually got witnesses. But I do know that the hippies are not sending their kids to the public schools. And there's pretty strong evidence that they're not reporting things like births and deaths that happen in the commune."

Willis said, "That's a hell of a good story. Have you told Sy?"

Fletcher shifted uneasily and held up his hand, palm forward. "Not so fast. I just heard about all this tonight. I was at a meeting with some local leaders. Some state people were there too. But it's way too early to do anything or write anything. This is all off the record, of course. I mean, really off the record. I don't want you to tell Sy even."

Willis stiffened in his chair but he didn't say anything. He shifted his eyes away from Fletcher and they came to rest on the famous Norman Rockwell picture of a soldier returning home from war. In 1945, it was sentimental tripe; in 1968, it was a sick joke.

"Well?" Fletcher said. "Do you see what I mean?"

"So far, there's nothing not to tell," Willis said after a minute. "All you've told me is a bunch of rumors from someone, I don't even know who."

Fletcher nodded, sealing the deal, but then he must have had second thoughts because he said, "I mean it about not telling Sy. I don't want him to know."

His voice carried a tone that sounded like intended menace, but Willis saw in his face more terror than threat. He realized suddenly that Fletcher was scared of Sy, and Willis tucked away that revelation to think about later. When the owner is afraid of the editor, strange things can happen at a newspaper.

"So what do you want from me?" he asked Fletcher.

"Well, when they were talking at the meeting, I knew you were there but I didn't mention it. I didn't know whether you were writing a story tonight or what happened. So I just thought I'd let you know what I had heard."

"There wasn't any story," Willis said warily. "Just some fool with long hair who wanted an audience."

Fletcher nodded quickly to assure Willis that he agreed with his assessment. "Well, if you're planning to go back, or if you think there's any reason to look into that situation further, I'd be interested to hear what you find out. I mean, it might be worth taking the time on some slow day to go back up there to look around. Even if you still didn't get a story. If you did go, I could let these local folks know what your impressions were, I mean, just how the place struck you, even if there wasn't enough of what you would call solid information to write a story."

He smiled broadly. "You've been around enough so I'm sure you could get a good idea about drugs and stuff like that . . ." His voice trailed off but it didn't matter because he wasn't saying anything anyway, just trying to make some kind of deal. Willis couldn't quite grasp what the deal was supposed to be, but the whole conversation made him squirm as though someone had suddenly pulled out a handful of dirty pictures and offered them to him.

Then he remembered the hulking Thunderclap and the strange silent passivity of the kids he had seen at the commune. And he remembered his own sense of foreboding, the heavy paranoia that settled over him while he was there.

There might be a hell of a good news story up there. Whatever was going on between Sy and Fletcher wasn't his business anyway, was it? He said to Fletcher, "Well, yeah, I guess maybe I ought to find a chance to get back up there. That is, if you don't mind investing in a dry hole, because if I take a day and don't write a story, that's what you'll be doing."

It was Fletcher's turn to squirm. His hand jumped to his mouth and he began gnawing gently on the first joint of his thumb. Willis leaned back in his chair and raised his eyes to the Rockwells. "I mean, I've heard you say we need to be careful about spending money and I know you're worried about advertising competition; are you sure you want me to make this fishing trip? Because let's be clear, that's what it will be. Pure old trolling, as simple as that."

He looked squarely at Fletcher, who was still chewing, a frown twisting his normally smooth forehead. "It might even be on overtime," Willis said. "Seymour's keeping us pretty busy with routine stuff, so I might have to go up there on a day off."

How far could he be pushed?

Fletcher took a final bite of knuckle, then leaned forward with his forearms resting on the edge of his desk. "Look," he said, "let me level with you. There are some pretty highly placed people interested in this commune. Some very high people. They're counting on me to help them. But this is just between you and me. My father doesn't know about it and Seymour doesn't know anything about it.

"Besides, it looks to me like some of the stuff Seymour has you guys doing is pretty dumb anyway. Isn't it? I mean, this could turn into a really big story, and whatever time you spend would be worth more than some routine Council story or some so-called investigative story about how awful business is. Anyway, Bud, I think we understand each other."

He stood up and started for the door of his office. "I'm just going to poke my head back into the newsroom for a minute."

Willis shrugged and they walked down the hall without talking. Seymour and Connie were sitting on the edges of desks that faced each other across a narrow aisle. Seven or eight people, mostly young reporters, were standing and sitting around them. It looked peaceful, even cozy, like an impromptu college seminar sprung up in the midst of bustling action all around them, until Willis got close enough to see the hunched-up tension that made a lie of the casual posturing by Connie and Sy. If they had been cats, their tails would have been lashing, the pads of their paws spread wide.

Seymour's eyes swept past Willis and Fletcher and moved on around the circle, pausing briefly at each reporter. "Connie," he said softly, his gaze still wandering over her head to the crowd, "I don't know what you've got to do at eleven that's so goddam important, but I do know what this newsroom has to do. We've got to wrestle together a newspaper that tells one of the biggest stories of the year—hell, one of the biggest stories of our time."

She started to answer but Seymour cut her off. "That's not all. We've also got to make a reasonable shape out of Merle's story about the college protest. Wait a minute. There's more. We've also got a handful of local and state stories that have to be finished and put in the paper, and we've got to do all this better than anybody else is going to do it."

He looked around the room again. "And the people right here, these people that you're interrupting right now, are the ones who are going to make this newspaper."

Again she began to speak, but he went on. "One more minute, Connie, then I'm through. We're going to do all the things I said— all of us together, right here in this newsroom—in time to make a reasonable deadline so we can get a newspaper on the streets.

"That's our deadline, and it's our only deadline. I don't know what's driving your deadline and I don't care. But our deadline is to get this paper on the street. And if that means people who normally get off work at eleven stay later, then so be it. If they have to stay until twelve or one or two, then that's what they're going to do."

Finally, he stopped and stood up as though to leave, then he said as an afterthought, "Our job is making the paper. Reading it is the readers' job. And it gets thrown away all by itself."

Several people giggled. Connie broke in hurriedly, "Listen, Sy, we don't need a sermon on what newspapering is all about. We know all that. What we need is decent pay and reasonable working hours. We know how to make a newspaper; what we want is to put out a paper and still have a life. It may be okay with you to work all the time, to spend your whole life in here, but I don't think it has to be that way. I like newspapering too, but I also have other things I want to do."

She slid off the desk and was standing directly in front of Seymour, her lips parted to gulp a deep breath. Opening his eyes wide, arching his eyebrows in comic exaggeration, Sy said, "Oh yeah? And what might that be?" Several men laughed as a red glow spread across Connie's face.

"Wait a minute, Sy, I think Connie is talking about something serious." They all turned to look at Willis as he stepped forward.

Sy yanked his head around and said loudly, "Well, if it isn't Jeb Stuart, come to save the lady. Step right on in here, Willis. Let's hear what you think. I assume this means you've finished your own story, right?"

Connie raised her arm as if to push Willis away. "I don't need your protection," she said flatly. He shrugged and stepped back. "But you're goddam right I'm serious, and Seymour's going to find out just how serious I can be."

Sy looked at her, then turned his back and walked toward his office, spreading apart the ring of reporters. When he had gone a few feet and everyone was watching him, he turned around and said with rising anger, "Connie, I don't think you give a damn about newspapering. I think what you care about is power. And that's all. You want power. You're not interested in newspapering or in people. You're an imposter. What you're serious about is you. You just want to run this newsroom, don't you?"

Connie looked stunned, as though she had stepped on a scorpion, poisoned by an unseen stinger. She sat down abruptly on the edge of the desk and they all watched in amazement as tears filled her eyes.

"Lay off, Seymour. That's not fair and you know it. Leave her alone." It was Fletcher. Standing in the back and unnoticed by anyone, his voice drifted over their heads. "She has a right to complain and to be heard."

Those standing between Fletcher and Seymour moved apart, opening a space so they could see each other across the room. "You don't know what you're talking about, Fletcher," Seymour said in an even, cold voice. "You don't even know what this is all about. Go count your ad lineage."

If Fletcher heard him, he didn't show any sign. He looked over at Connie, then he turned toward Seymour and said, "You've got a warped view of the world. You might think that journalism is the only honorable profession and that journalists are the only honest people, but nobody else believes that. There are other things. Connie's right."

Seymour shouted, "Goddam it, Fletcher, stay out of this. You don't know a goddam thing about it."

Greenberg called from his own desk, "Hey, Sy, it's ten thirty. We've got to get this thing moving."

Seymour glowered once more at Fletcher, then at Connie, and moved with long strides back to his own office. The group of reporters quietly went to their desks and Connie picked up her purse and jacket from her desk and left the newsroom.

Willis went back to his telephone calls and when he looked up a few minutes later Fletcher was gone, Sy was talking with Greenberg again, and the newsroom noise was back to the normal high-pitched whine of a hive on a hot summer day.

He talked to enough people and remembered enough from his own reporting to write a pretty fair sidebar to the King story. Seymour ran it on Page One, underneath the photo of the Lorraine Motel balcony but above the fold. As he looked at the paper later Willis thought, that AP picture's going to make that motel balcony the most famous balcony since Romeo and Juliet, and there's my byline right below it. Sy also added an editor's note that described Willis as an investigative reporter who had covered the civil rights movement extensively for several of the South's most prestigious newspapers.

Willis also did some heavy rewriting on Merle's story, so between both assignments he was still working well past the normal deadline. It was nearly two when Sy finally gave the last copy to Rocky, who by that time was a two-legged bomb whose fuse was nearly gone. Willis, Seymour, Greenberg, and Lindsay, the wire editor, were the only ones left in the newsroom by the time the old press groaned into motion.

The others had drifted out of the newsroom one or two at a time ever since Connie left, but Willis didn't keep track so he had no idea how many actually went to the meeting. The bars were long since closed, so he went back with Sy for a drink at his apartment, which some reporters had recently begun calling "the grain store."

Greenberg and Lindsay both said they needed to get home, but each of them did accept a cigar from Sy before leaving.

CHAPTER FIVE
Thursday, May 16, 1968

Sy sat alone at a small table in The Cafe, drinking coffee but ignoring, or trying to ignore, the plate of toast he had ordered for some reason he would have been unable to explain. He knew he didn't want it and wouldn't eat it even as he told the girl to bring it, and now that it was actually there, neatly halved and giving off hot-buttered bread smells, he was mildly disgusted at the prospect. At nine thirty in the morning, the very idea of eating was slightly repulsive.

Coffee didn't count, of course, and he took another deep gulp. Time for one more. He caught the girl's eye, an easy trick since only two other tables were in use, and she started over with the pot. A new girl. Plain. The Cafe had a couple of longtime waitresses but generally there seemed to be a rapid turnover. Good economic times, he supposed, made it difficult to keep low-wage help.

Johnson had been saying you didn't have to choose between guns and butter; you could have 'em both. And so far he seemed to be right. The signs of prosperity were everywhere, and Vermont was having its biggest boom of the century. The war, Sy thought, the goddam war. He knew he was getting obsessed with it, much too preoccupied. He couldn't remember any story that had so absorbed his attention, seeped into his own life, with such power. When he wasn't thinking about it, he was reading about it or watching it on television. He was embarrassed by how devoted he had become to the Walter Cronkite news, the same news report he had once considered insignificant. One thing about the war: it sure as hell had brought television news to a sudden maturity he had not believed possible.

The damned war. It seemed to be on his mind all the time, even now when he knew he should be concentrating on why Manny had telephoned him. It was only the third time in twenty years that he had called Sy at his place. As always, Manny had been cryptic and mysterious, probably not intentionally uninformative but, nevertheless, absolutely unhelpful. The phone had waked him up, of course, so maybe some of the mystery came from his own grogginess.

"Sy?" Manny had asked. Who the hell had he expected to answer the phone at eight thirty in the morning? "Sy? Can you come into the office this morning? About ten, if you can. Yes, I mean, come at ten. I want to talk to you."

That had been all. The entire conversation, except for a grunt or two from Sy.

Manny had put in the "I want to talk to you" without providing the slightest hint of his mood or purpose. Probably about the union rumors, Sy thought. But why the urgency? Manny was nothing if not considerate. This was a publisher who delivered his own editorial copy to the composing room so no one would have to make a special trip to his office to pick it up. He knew Sy's late-night habits and he would not have called so early without being aware that Sy would know it was important.

For the past hour he had been trying to focus his attention on Manny because he hated to be caught off guard, but his mind kept careening off to the goddam war. The first thing he thought of after he hung up was the anti-war protest scheduled for the afternoon. Then he remembered the stories about the Paris peace talks and then the stories about the mass demonstrations the French students were calling a revolution.

He wondered if the French "revolution" would spread to the rest of Europe. It sounded as though this kid, the one they called "Danny the Red," might be the sort of symbolic leader who could transport his cause, or at least his energy. Hell, they had already recruited organized labor and it sounded as though they could shut down the French economy whenever they wanted. The French kids were rioting to take back their university from the encroaching police, a cause that you'd think would put the laboring class on government's side. The American kids were rioting to take back their lives from the State, a threat faced by everyone — at least, every draft-age man. And yet, oddly, the working stiffs in America were lining up with the cops while the French workers were manning the barricades.

Could Manny have called because he wanted to talk about the protests? No, certainly not, although he and Sy had already had one long talk about the French riots. Manny had spent some considerable amount of time in Paris in the '20s, and he once told Sy that twenty years later he had become physically sick and went to bed when the Germans took Paris. He still, even now, had a nostalgic attitude toward France. In an editorial, he had condemned the rioting Sorbonne students as "spoiled brats who have never felt a wound."

Sy was still thinking about the war and its dominating influence when he got to Manny's office. He was a few minutes early but he barged in without thinking of knocking or even pausing in the open doorway. So when he looked toward Manny's chair, he was stunned to see someone else sitting behind the desk. The guy was sitting there with the telephone to his ear, turned halfway toward the window behind the desk and speaking in low tones into the receiver.

They've sold out, Sy's brain screamed into his ear. This guy is the new owner. He was about forty, fit looking, with a face that you'd call Irish except that it had no broken blood vessels, not even in the nose. His neatly combed brown hair trailed a half inch over his collar. The collar was white, but when he swiveled the chair around, Sy was startled to see that the rest of the shirt, all of it except the collar and cuffs, was blue. It looked like a 1910 shirt with the stiff collar and cuffs attached separately, and for a moment Sy couldn't take his eyes off of them. A narrow red silk tie closed the rounded collar, whose two sides were connected by a thin gold pin that lifted the precise knot of the necktie into prominence.

A dandy, he thought. A dandy with a brogue. But then he took a real look at the rest of the guy and the ludicrous image evaporated. He wore the faintly pinstriped blue suit with the easy elegance of Joe DiMaggio, and his face turned out to be more interesting and less ethnic than he had thought.

"Ted McNally," he said, sticking out his hand. "You're Sy?" Not a hint of explanation as to why he was sitting at Manny's desk and no sign of embarrassment—no smile, no foot shuffling, and no gaze shifting.

This is a formidable person, Sy thought as he shook hands. "Yeah, I'm Seymour. Where's Manny?"

"Mr. Monrose? Well, Manny's—right here."

Manny walked into the office reading the *Patriot Press* and he looked up in surprise when he saw Sy. He glanced at his wristwatch, then said, "Hello, Sy. Thanks for coming in. I know it's pretty early for you, but Ted has to catch a plane at half past twelve."

Manny kept only two chairs in his office other than his own desk chair because he said any conversation with more than three people was a meeting and ought to be held like a meeting, preferably with a table between the parties. But then, Manny also refused to attend meetings. He sat down behind the desk and McNally took the chair next to the desk, leaving the one back against the wall for Sy. He pulled it over to the other end of the desk so he and McNally were both facing Manny and had to turn slightly sideways to look at each other.

"I've hired Ted to help us with the union problem," Manny said. "He's a lawyer and an industrial psychologist and he's done a lot of work with newspaper unions."

Sy interrupted, "Well, we don't have a union yet. It's only rumors so far."

"You're a little behind, Sy. They're already passing around union cards." McNally's tenor was a soloist's voice and it pulled the others' heads in his direction. "In fact, we believe they've got enough signatures already, or soon will have enough, to bring in the NLRB for a vote."

This news hit Sy like a sucker punch and it left him speechless. How could this thing have gotten that far without him knowing it? How in the hell could this slick lawyer from New York know more about his own newsroom than he did? Look at him sitting there so smug and sure of himself. What else did he know? What the hell was Manny up to, bringing this guy into all this, into our newspaper?

Sy looked at Manny but still he didn't say anything. He didn't know what to say. Was Fletcher part of this? Did he know about this McNally guy? About the union cards?

Manny blinked but he didn't say anything either. McNally seemed to be the only one with free use of his tongue. "I'm sure you know, Sy, that this changes all the rules. Or rather, this brings a whole new set of rules into play."

The voice was compelling in its dips and rises, and the words were charged by their simple directness. "We now have two goals—and only two. One is to come out of this with us, not the union, in control of the paper. The other is to avoid running afoul of the NLRB in the process."

He paused, but still neither of the others spoke.

"Okay. It is critically important for us to understand the National Labor Relations Board piece. The board is neutral, of course—a referee, judge, neutral arbiter. That's by the book. The reality is that the NLRB is a woven set of trip wires laid out in our path that we have to walk over but not set off."

He stopped, shifting his look from Manny to Sy and back, one hand resting on the arm of the chair and the other on the desk. The fingers on the desk hand began to tap quietly but rapidly.

"Are you sure about the union cards?" Sy finally asked, but even as he spoke he knew McNally would be more likely to leave home with a hole in his sock than he would to speak without being sure of his facts.

He didn't even answer the question, other than to nod dismissively and turn his head to Manny.

"We don't know the actual numbers," Manny said, "but we're pretty sure most of the newsroom has signed up, part of the advertising department, several of the clerks, and most of the men in the mail room."

"I thought the mail room was already unionized." Sy said. "Aren't they with the pressroom?"

"No." It was McNally, and Sy again felt himself tipped off-balance by his own lack of information. "No," McNally said again. "They never joined, but apparently they're ready now. The union wants to make this a 100 percent shop."

How the hell did he know that? Sy felt his anger rising and it soared when he realized he was almost afraid to say anything. He blurted, "Have you talked to the union?" He said it calmly, but again he felt instantly that it was a dumb question.

"Of course not," McNally said with a quick frown. "But I know the organizer they're using here and I've had some research done on him and on the national union leadership. They're going to be tough."

A dozen questions flooded into Sy's head but he hesitated, waiting for his racing mind to slow down. Finally, chiefly to use up some time, he asked, "Who's the organizer?"

McNally said, "He's a guy named Carmoli. Vince Carmoli. I think they're using him because he was originally from around here, but he's also very good, according to what I've been able to find out."

It was the third major shock for Sy and he felt his hands go cold and the blood drain out of his face. Anger turned to fury, obliterating the cold confusion that had kept him under control up to this point. A picture of Connie flashed in his head, and he leaped up from his chair, his face contorted by bunched muscles. Goddam her. I should have known. He glared at McNally and then at Manny, raging inside but unable to say anything. Manny, who should have expected an outburst, looked horrified, as though Sy had just spat on the floor. But McNally, for the first time, smiled up at him and said, "Relax, Seymour. Sit down."

He looked toward Manny and said, "Don't worry, he'll be all right. It's always a shock when you first hear these things. It's like a palace coup or something. Sy'll do fine when he understands what's going on."

"Goddam it," Sy roared. "Goddam you, don't condescend to me. I already know what's going on and I don't like it. And I'm going to do something about it." He felt like kicking the desk, and his hands balled into fists. He was glaring at McNally, who just smiled placidly without moving, but Manny jumped to his feet, his face suddenly blazing into fiery life, like taillights when you slam on the brakes.

"Sy," he shouted, "that's enough. Sit down."

After a moment, Sy did sit down, stiffly perching on the edge of his chair.

"Listen, Sy," Manny said, "Ted is on our side. No, more than that. Ted is going to tell us how to deal with this. And we're going to do what he says. Understand?"

Sy's face glowed nearly as red as Manny's, but before he could answer, McNally interrupted.

"Don't worry, Manny, there's no harm in Sy blowing off with us." He turned to look squarely at Seymour. "Explosions like that don't threaten or intimidate us." He paused, but when Sy didn't answer he continued. "But that's exactly the sort of thing that will set off the NLRB alarms. And it's exactly what you better not do with the union people, Sy."

Better not? Better not or what? The raging voice was inside Sy's head and it did not escape. McNally wasn't through. "They'll kill us if you do something that the NLRB says is intimidation or threatening. Let me be absolutely blunt: We might as well quit right now unless you can control your temper—or at least your outbursts."

Sy opened his mouth to speak, but McNally motioned him quiet. "I'm not trying to piss you off, Seymour. But you need to know that if what I'm saying is irritating, you haven't heard anything yet. They'll do their damnedest to make you mad, make you do something they can nail us for. It's not you they'll be after, it's the paper, and they'll go a long way to create an unfair labor practice."

Sy was boxed in, snared by the expert trap. He just didn't know as much as this guy. He had found out only after letting himself be led into a corner that he wasn't going to be allowed to punch his way out. He knew all about the expert trap; he'd seen it a hundred times and seen dozens of victims writhing in it. But he hadn't seen this one, the one that he ought to have known was coming, the one of all that he should have avoided. He looked over at Manny, but he had turned away and Sy couldn't even catch his eye.

McNally spoke again. "Okay, Sy, let's talk about what you can and cannot do. I don't mean just you; I mean everyone who is considered part of management."

Part of management? It was a hateful concept. Management? This is a newspaper, not a goddam factory.

"Management is anyone who is not eligible to join the union," McNally said, now dropping into what must have been a well-rehearsed instructor's spiel. "If you're in that category, it's best not to talk at all about the union. I mean, if someone tries to start a conversation about it, just say you can't, or won't, talk about it."

He paused for questions but there weren't any. "Okay then. That's clear? Okay. So, Sy, you in particular are enjoined from this kind of talk. As boss of the newsroom, you just cannot talk with anyone about the organizing. You can't ask how it's going, you can't answer if someone asks you how it's going, and, most importantly you can't suggest that you don't like what's going on."

"I'm a newspaper editor, not a goddam actor." Sy managed to say it relatively calmly. "What am I supposed to do? Sign a union card? Pretend I don't know what the bastards are doing behind my back?"

McNally lighted a cigarette and offered the pack around, but neither of the other two accepted. He sat back in his chair and said, "Well, now, that's a good point. Let's talk about what we can do." He exhaled a cloud of smoke, carefully directing it away from the other two. "We need a strategy and we all need to understand what it is. Now, first, what's our objective?"

He waited for an answer, puffing slowly with obvious enjoyment. Finally, when Sy and Manny refused to play pupil, McNally said, "Okay, this is really pretty simple, but it may not sound so at first. Your first instinct will be to try to beat the union vote, or even keep it from coming to a vote if they don't get enough cards signed." Sy was puzzled, and when he looked at Manny he saw that he was too, but neither said anything.

McNally continued. "It's almost certainly a hopeless task. Remember, signing the union card is really easy. There's no consequence and they'll all know it doesn't mean anything. So they'll sign, and you couldn't stop them if you tried; you'd just build sympathy for the union.

"We'll probably lose the organizing vote too. The fact that they've already sent Carmoli in here means they're pretty sure of getting enough votes."

He looked purposefully at Manny. "Besides, from what little I know about your pay scale, I'd say they can make a darn good case for needing a union." Manny's eyes widened, his color darkened, and he said, "Wait a minute. We pay what we can and I call it a fair wage, so don't—"

McNally grinned. "See what I mean about getting riled up? It's pretty hard not to, isn't it, Manny? But I'll say the same thing to you that I said to Sy: Stay cool. Do not get angry."

He took a final draw and neatly snuffed the half-smoked cigarette in Manny's pipe-filled ashtray. "So if we can't beat the vote, what is our strategy? Well, first we eliminate as many key people as we can from eligibility. I'll tell you in a minute how we do that, but first you need to know why. Our goal is to keep enough people ineligible so we can put out a newspaper if necessary without the union. It'll be hard, but what we want is to bring enough people into management—I'm talking about NLRB definitions now—so that if a strike ever should happen, they can't shut down the newspaper.

"Remember, the only real power a union ever has is being able to stop the revenue stream. They probably can't do that if we can keep on putting out a paper. And it's best, of course, if we can do that without hiring replacement workers, scabs. Everyone expects management employees to cross a picket line."

By now Sy was completely calm and paying close attention to what McNally said, and questions began to stack up in his head. "That seems totally transparent," he said. "Won't they oppose padding of so-called management, and why wouldn't that be an unfair labor practice?"

"I can't promise that they won't oppose it," McNally said. "I'm counting on past experience and on what I call the candy-first factor." He paused for effect. "I'm assuming there will be some people who obviously have reservations about the union. Some who, for whatever reason, the union expects to lose. They'll try to exclude those people themselves before the vote. And we may mount some feeble effort to block their exclusion. But we'll lose. You see? The union will want its candy—first the signatures, then the vote to organize—so they will want to exclude anyone they think will vote against them. If we put people on the management list, they'll be afraid they would vote against the union, so they won't oppose excluding them."

Sy nodded, beginning to roll over names in his head. Manny asked, "What about the NLRB? Won't they see through this?"

McNally agreed. "Sure, they'll see if they look. But they won't even look if the union doesn't protest." He looked from one to the other and a conspiratorial smile crossed his face. "Of course, if they could ever prove that this was a strategy, a plan to beat the union in the end game, then we'd be in trouble. But they never could because this strategy will never be discussed again. Right? Never, not with anyone.

"And, of course, this conversation is privileged. It's absolutely protected by the attorney-client relationship privilege. That's what makes a law degree so useful."

Sy suddenly remembered his first trip to a whorehouse. He was a freshman in college, and one Saturday night he and three other guys were drinking beer and one of them had suggested it. He couldn't remember any of their names, but he knew exactly how he had felt during the fifteen-mile trip. They never actually found the whorehouse, but Sy remembered the drive—him sitting in the back seat feeling excited, worried, undecided, eager, and more than a little disgusted, all at the same time. That's just how he felt now, listening to McNally. Except that the disgust was even more dominant, rising in his throat as he watched the sheen of self-satisfaction spread over McNally's handsome face.

McNally looked at his watch. "I have to drive to Burlington and I better leave if I'm going to get that plane. Any questions we need to deal with right now? I'll be back soon."

"Yes," Sy said. "I want to get these people excluded as soon as I can. What do I need to do?" He felt like he was asking permission to go to the bathroom.

McNally sighed, glanced at Manny, and said tiredly, "Sy, let me repeat a couple of points: First, this is not an 'I' deal. This is a 'we' operation. You don't do anything, not anything, on your own. Second, if we get too impatient, we'll screw this whole plan. I want you and Manny to make a list of people, and probably you ought to include people from advertising, the front office, and the mail room. Make a list of possible exclusions and send it to me. But don't write out any titles or any reasons for the exclusions. Just the names. Then we'll go over it next time I come up."

He paused, but Sy didn't know what else to say and evidently Manny didn't either.

"Don't look so glum," McNally said as he stood up. "We're going to beat this thing. I know it's all new to you but trust me, I've done it before. We'll win if we don't make any mistakes."

He smiled, shook hands with each of them, and left quickly in a wide-stride, square-shouldered exit that left a big hole in the room.

They sat without speaking for half a minute until finally Manny said softly, "He's done work for the *New York Times* and Gannett—"

Sy didn't have enough energy to return more than a muffled snort. He stood up, shaking his head, and left the office.

The newsroom was empty, as still and quiet as a warehouse. The air seemed stale, used up, and Sy opened one of the big windows to let in street noise and smell. He stood still in the center of the big room for a moment, then moved slowly to his glass office. He hunched over the *Times* wire but didn't really read any stories and then dropped down into his desk chair. But he couldn't think of anything to do. He sat for a while with his hands folded on his desk, and when he finally looked up at the wall clock it said eleven thirty.

Leaving the newspaper, Sy walked into a beautiful, warm spring day. He didn't actually make any decision about where to go but he walked straight to Vic's, and within ten minutes he was sitting at the tiny round table with a mug of espresso in front of him. A handful of cigars was piled next to the cup and he popped one into his mouth.

Vic finished waiting on a magazine buyer and sat down with his own mug. Vic was not a great conversationalist, but it wasn't that he didn't have plenty of experience he could have talked about. In his sixty-odd years he had done more occupations and lived in more places than anyone Sy knew. But he had once said that it bored him to talk about the past because he had already lived it. It had taken Sy many years to ferret out the basic facts of Vic's life, not because he was particularly secretive, just too disinterested to volunteer information. If reticence was a drawback to conversation, though, Vic had two other qualities that made him a good companion. He never asked questions, even though he listened carefully without interrupting, except to deal with a customer. And he loved cigars and strong coffee. He was ready to smoke and sip anytime he was invited.

"They say the town's going to be full of war protesters this afternoon," Sy said. "Does that mean you'll get a lot of business?"

Vic shook his head. "Political protesters don't seem to buy many newspapers or magazines." Sy had no idea whether intentional irony was buried in the comment.

They smoked in silence, the cloud forming over their heads growing bigger by the second. Sy said, "You were a boxer, right? And didn't you turn pro for a while?"

Vic nodded. "For a while."

"I think you told me once that you were only knocked out in one fight. You said it was some palooka you'd never heard of and that you were on a winning streak and never even considered losing to him. Right?"

Vic nodded again.

"I remember you said the guy decked you with a left uppercut you didn't see coming and never even knew he could throw. Right?

Vic nodded.

"Well," Sy said, raising his cup, "now I know exactly how you felt."

Vic took a swallow of coffee too, then he said, "It was my last fight. I quit."

Ernie was deeply absorbed in *As the World Turns*, so Willis watched quietly from the other side of the front desk until a deodorant commercial came on. The clerk stretched as though waking from a nap. "How's it turning today?" Willis asked. "Is Erika staying with Keith or going off with Lance?"

"Ah, shit. It's all horseshit," Ernie said. "She shacks up with a different guy every week." He hoisted himself out of his seat with some effort and ran a tiny, puffy hand through his greasy hair. "I'm just waiting 'til it's my turn."

Willis laughed as the rumpled clerk rummaged through a pile of mail on the desk, found nothing for Willis, and shrugged. "Not your day either, I guess." He started back to the television set but turned around again when Willis said, "I may be leaving. I'm thinking about renting an apartment—or maybe even a house out at the lake."

"We'll try to get along without you," Ernie said. Then he added in a tone that, with some stretching, might have been considered friendly, "This'd be a good time to be at the lake, but most of them places ain't winterized."

"Well, I don't really know yet. I'm just starting to look around. I'm beginning to think I may stay around here."

Ernie's thin upper lip curved in a sneer that revealed a blackened tooth. "I guess there's worser places to be. But I don't know where they are." He turned back to the small television set just as the screen flipped and Erika's mournful face replaced the wet, smiling, freckled face of the odor-free Dial model. Ernie reached over and turned up the volume, ending the longest conversation they had had since Willis moved into the Uptown.

Willis walked across the van-sized lobby to stab out his cigarette in the overflowing chrome ashtray standing beside the only chair. He tried to knock off the ash gently, but the pile spilled over onto the linoleum floor. He glanced quickly toward Ernie but saw only the back of his head, so he left the butts on the floor.

He knew that five months was too long to live in a hotel, even when it was as cheap as a rooming house, but he didn't know why. In fact, now that he was thinking about leaving, all he could think about were reasons not to move. Hell, you didn't even have to make up your own bed.

He stepped out into bright, early afternoon sunshine and felt a sharp stab in his chest when the clear, hard air invaded his lungs, air that was an intrusive presence, as real as rain. The outdoors was filled with a light as bright as Texas but lacking the Gulf Coast's glare.

He looked east toward the nearest mountains. He had watched the color change from white to red-tinted brown and now they looked like a solid, light-green curtain rising from the edge of town.

This was a funny place. It was the outdoors that mattered. It was the weather and the landscape—what you saw and felt and walked through—that made you feel good or bad. Never mind what the assholes like Ernie did; the people were just background for the real world of the senses. What mattered was the temperature and the clearness of the air, whether the sun was out or the wind was blowing. You could wake up with a headache in your sour-smelling, cell-sized, junk heap of a room and ten minutes later feel like a happy kid just because you were standing outside on a perfect day.

Willis looked again toward the mountain, suddenly puzzled as he thought of Sy, who never seemed to be aware of the outdoors. Did he notice how the air felt? He turned and headed downtown along the nearly empty sidewalk, but long before he got to the coffee shop he realized that his mind had switched outward and he was watching for something, or rather, that he was alert in a way he had not been when he started walking. He slowed his pace, and by the time he realized what had caught his attention he had stopped altogether, peering up at the top of the Penney's building on the opposite side of the street. Two men were looking over the edge of the roof, their heads turned away from him. One of them waved in a wide arc toward the other end of the street. Willis watched as they talked and motioned, evidently signaling to someone he could not see. He realized that the arm-waving figure silhouetted above was Chief Bushey. Shit. The protest. Today was the day.

Willis hurried along, wondering who Sy had assigned to write the story. Now, looking around, he spotted several suited men on the sidewalks, looking in store windows and strolling along with newspapers under their arms. He laughed. They're so goddam dumb. At one thirty on a weekday afternoon, how many businessmen were you likely to see ambling along the street, window-shopping, and even if they did, they wouldn't be carrying the morning newspaper under their arms.

He was walking at almost a racing pace by the time he reached the corner, and just as he turned he swung his head around for a last look at Bushey on the roof. He rounded the corner and smashed blindly into something bulky that gave slightly then stiffened. Before Willis had recovered enough to figure out what he had hit, he was shoved against the brick building, his arms pinned to his sides by powerful hands. When his eyes focused, he was looking across six inches of space into the bearded enraged face of the commune leader.

"God, I'm sorry I ran into you," Willis said. "Are you all right?"

The anger seeped out of Thunderclap's face as he began to recognize Willis, but he continued to stare intently at his captive and, with no apparent effort, he kept his arms pinned down.

"Are you with us or them?" The question came softly out of a mouth Willis couldn't see, buried deep in the black bush that hid all except his dark eyes.

"Who's them?"

"The pigs," Thunderclap said, finally letting go of Willis's arms. "Johnson, Nixon, and the swine who are rooting the Garden of Eden into a cesspool of corruption."

"How about Humphrey," Willis said. "Him too?"

The commune leader ignored the question, instead asking again, "Are you with us?"

"I'm a reporter," Willis said. "I'm not with anybody."

Thunderclap turned without saying another word and headed across the street, where Willis saw for the first time a small mass of hippies waiting on the sidewalk, as colorful and as still as a pile of autumn leaves. The group seemed to be mostly women and small children and they did not move until Thunderclap stepped into the group, scattering people in all directions until they reformed into lines and he led them down the street. A half block behind them,

Willis saw a man wearing a brown suit step out of the entrance to a furniture store and head in the same direction.

More cops than crooks on the street today. He hurried past the empty coffee shop without even seriously considering whether to stop and was nearly running again by the time he reached the newspaper building.

Ron and Merle were the only ones in the newsroom and they looked up and smiled as he came in, but Willis just waved and went straight back to Seymour's office. The door was open and he walked in as Sy hung up the telephone.

"The town's crawling with cops and feds," Willis said. "They're setting up like it was the O.K. Corral."

"I know," Sy said. "That was Kevin on the phone from the statehouse and he said a busload of state cops is loaded and waiting if they're needed. And when I talked to Bushey a while ago, he seemed awful jumpy. I don't know exactly what's going on, but he must think it's a big deal. Last time we had a protest, he just called in a couple of off-duty firemen and put them in cops' uniforms."

Willis was curious. "You're pretty friendly with Bushey, aren't you?"

"We're not friends," Sy said, "but we've helped each other out a time or two. He got the job because the paper ran some stories that got the old chief fired."

The vision of Bushey's dark form on top of the building flashed back into Willis's mind, then his biceps flinched as he remembered Thunderclap's iron grip on his arms. He decided not to mention either incident to Sy.

Ron appeared in the doorway but did not quite enter the tiny office. He glanced at Willis, then spoke to Sy. "Who's covering the protest? Merle says the college has shut down and the kids are pouring into downtown." The kid was nervous; his left eyelid fluttered out of control.

Sy sprang up from his chair. "Where's Greenberg?" He peered through the glass wall into the newsroom. "Is he out there yet?"

"Not yet," Ron said. "He'll probably be here in about half an hour."

"Okay," Sy said. He was pacing around the office, which meant three steps in one direction then about-face. "Willis, listen. I want you to organize this thing. Goddam it, it feels like this is getting away from us. I've got to go see the publisher. We can't wait for Greenberg. So, Bud, you figure out who and what you need and then get out in the street. One of these days one of these protests is going to turn into a massacre."

He brushed past Ron and started out of the office but stopped just outside the door. "Make sure you get plenty of pictures. Get what's his name up on top of Penney's with his camera."

Sy was gone, hustling past Merle, who tried to hide by bending far over and pretending to poke through the junk in the lowest drawer of his desk. Sy turned around and came back, stopping just inside the newsroom to shout to Willis, "Take Merle with you. And Connie."

A couple of other reporters drifted into the newsroom and Ron hurried out of Sy's office to talk to them. But Willis stayed. He was excited and a little rattled by his own excitement. He turned his back to the newsroom and began scrolling through the *Times* wire copy clattering out of the TTX. It seemed as though every other story had something to do with the war, even the pieces on the election campaign.

As he read, his excitement began to curdle into self-mocking irony. Vietnam was the biggest story since World War II and he was stuck here in this backwater, organizing coverage of a rinky-dink protest march by drugged-out hippies and bored college kids.

A byline caught his eye as the yellow paper rolled through his hands. By Robert C. Smith. A Saigon dateline. Willis remembered Bob Smith from the *Montgomery Advertiser*, a dopey kid from Texas or Arkansas who kept trying to muscle in on his bus-boycott story. He looked again at the *Times* byline, then let the roll of paper drop back onto the floor without reading the story.

He looked up into the blank glassy-faced television set staring down from its shelf. "No one reads anymore anyway," Willis muttered. And most newspapers are just trying to copy the television crap. Pretty soon, newspapers will be all pictures, charts, and briefs. Fuck it, he thought, but then he looked out through the glass wall and saw that everyone in the newsroom was watching him, waiting for him to do something.

As he walked out of Sy's office, several reporters moved toward him, but before they spoke he said, "Where's Peterson?" Ron nodded toward the darkroom and Willis said, "Get him out here."

He said loudly to the whole room, "Ron, Connie, Merle, and I are going to cover this protest. And we're taking Peterson, so if anybody else needs any photos, you'll have to take them yourselves. Where is Connie, anyhow?"

He looked up at the large wall clock just as the minute hand lurched the final notch onto the twelve, and he heard the newsroom door slap back against the wall. Connie strode in, taking off her sweater as she walked toward her desk.

"Hey, Connie," Willis called, "you want to cover the protest march?"

She looked up sharply. "You making the assignments now? Where's Greenberg?"

Willis smiled slightly, keeping his eyes on hers. The hum of voices in the room had stopped and he waited for a count of ten before saying, "If you don't want it, I'll get somebody else."

She opened her mouth to say something but changed her mind and, still watching him, nodded her head. He ignored the nod. "Ron and Merle and I are going out there. Do you want it or not?"

She didn't answer but she lowered her eyes, picked up a notebook, and started putting her coat back on. Willis wouldn't let it go. "Well, are you coming?"

"Yes," she said finally without looking at him. She started toward the door, but Willis said, "Wait a minute. Come on into Sy's office for a minute and let's figure out how we're going to do this."

Ron came back with the photographer hurrying along behind him, two cameras around his neck and one in his hands. They all crowded into the tiny office, Merle in the rear.

Everyone looked up as the chosen five hurried through the newsroom, snatching up jackets and stacks of copy paper as they passed their own desks, and sailing on out the door without slowing to speak to any of the other reporters. They cruised past Alice's desk so fast the wind in their wake rustled papers on her desk. She sighed loudly. Willis slammed through the double-door entryway onto the street and the others followed, forming up three abreast behind him as he stepped out at a fast walk toward the park.

Willis heard Peterson muttering as he stumbled along, trying to keep up while loading film into one camera and adjusting the straps of the two other cases so they wouldn't bang into each other and his chest. Willis quickened the pace a little, calling over his shoulder, "Connie, you and Merle work the crowd for color or whatever you can find. Ron, stay on Main Street, talk to merchants, hard hats, any veterans you see. Try to get the love-it-or-leave-it story. I'll take

Peterson up on top of Penney's and just move around with the main story. Okay?"

It felt fine to be in charge.

He caught a sideways glimpse of himself in the plate-glass window of Nate's Men's Store and broke stride long enough to turn his head toward the image. He felt a small grin forming, but then he saw Connie's reflected face peering over his shoulder. The flash of her smirk turned his pleasure of the moment into a mouthful of ashes.

She called out, "Aye, aye, sir," and the others snickered. Willis's hand darted to his fly to check the zipper. Anger coiled up inside his stomach. He turned the corner onto Main Street and felt a cold breeze blowing from the east. He suddenly remembered the flask he had foolishly left in his room. He'd thought of it then decided against bringing it. The other day, Sy had noticed the flask in his jacket pocket.

Willis started across the street without looking to see what the others were doing, but he knew the photographer was still following because he heard his leather gear squeaking behind him. He hurried on toward Penney's, halfway down the block. He looked up and saw that Chief Bushey and the other guy were still peering over the edge of the roof.

"What's the goddam rush," Peterson shouted. "They're still milling around in the goddam park." He was out of breath. Willis slowed so he could catch up. Peterson was younger than Willis but he was seriously overweight. Out of shape too. He'd never make it on a big-time story, like a civil rights march. Willis remembered Montgomery and Greensboro and his spirits brightened again. He'd won a prize in Montgomery. "Come on, Peterson, you may be missing the best shot of your whole worthless life. Let's get up on that roof."

The four flights of stairs left Peterson huffing, his jacket dangerously close to sliding off one rounded shoulder and his cameras hanging at odd places around his torso. Bushey turned around to look as they came through the door onto the roof. Willis waved a greeting. "Hello, Chief. We'd like to take some shots of the march from up here. We won't get in your way."

"You're goddam right you won't," Bushey said. "Who told you that you could come up here? Never mind." He turned back toward the street. "Take your pictures. I may want some of them later."

Peterson started to protest but Willis motioned him to be quiet. He waved the photographer toward the corner of the roof from which he could see both Main Street and partway around the corner into

Charles Street. Bushey and the other man were standing about eight feet apart and Willis walked over to stand between them. Neither man spoke, but both turned to watch him. He felt the tar from the roof pull at the soles of his shoes. The chief was in uniform and the other guy might as well have been: brown polyester suit, cordovan wing-tip shoes, stiff white shirt, skinny green tie, narrow-brim felt hat, a bulge under his jacket at the waistline when he leaned over the parapet, and, in case anyone had missed all the other insignia, a trench coat folded over his left arm. All three watched the activity two blocks away on the Green for a few minutes, then Brown Suit turned away and left the roof without saying anything to anyone.

Willis said, "How come the Bureau's here?" Bushey didn't answer. "Did you call them in?" Again no response. Finally, turning to look at Willis, he pushed up the visor of his chief's hat. "The Bureau, huh?" His lip twisted. Willis's eyes flicked away, and in that blink Bushey's ironic smile turned into a true grin that, combined with the now-revealed broad forehead, changed his face from dour to cheerful. The ex-marine—drill instructor, combat captain, intimidator of men—became the happy recruiter. "How do you like it up here in Yankeeland? You finding enough excitement in our quiet little New England town? You didn't expect to find Peyton Place or something like that, I hope."

"Well," Willis said, "I sure as hell didn't expect to find the FBI hanging around the tops of buildings. Those boys don't usually turn out for every podunk protest . . ." He let the comment trail off and waited, but after considering it for a moment Bushey evidently decided to ignore it. Instead, he offered up another mystery. Pointing toward the still-growing crowd in the park, he said, "Sometimes a thing can be more than it looks to be. Nobody would worry much about most of those people. Mostly women without enough to do, spoiled college kids, and paper-pushing men"—he glanced at Willis, "No offense," then went on—"do-good guys who feel guilty and want everybody else to too." He turned away from the park to look directly at Willis. "That's harmless enough, just a little naive. But their little games can create situations that aren't so harmless." Again he pointed toward the crowd. "There's probably enough drug-dealing going on down there to fill up every cell in the county. And that's only the so-called victimless crimes. I'm not even talking about the serious stuff."

The door leading onto the roof burst open, spilling out a small flock of blue-uniformed cops who couldn't all fit through the opening at the same time but who tried anyhow. There were four of them, and they rushed toward Bushey and started speaking before they noticed Willis or, at any rate, before they recognized him. The youngest looking, a soft-faced kid wearing a brand-new uniform, blurted out, "It looks like every hippie in the state is out there. That big creepy monster from Moretown has got his whole bunch with him."

A tall, thin man with sergeant's stripes on his sleeve stepped in front of the rookie and stood with his heels together, arms at his sides, as though he was prepared to make a report. He didn't speak but his prominent Adam's apple bobbed up and down in anticipation. Bushey, leaning against the parapet, squinted at him. "Well, Lester? What is it?"

"You were right, Chief. The whole park smells like marijuana. Should we . . ." He broke off and clamped his mouth shut when he noticed Willis, who had made the mistake of turning around so he could pretend to be watching the crowd and not listening.

"Don't do anything," Bushey said firmly. "Nothing. Just watch them."

He swept his right hand, fingers outstretched, in an arc that included all four of the cops. "Nothing. You all got that?" They nodded, shifting their feet restlessly. "What I want you to do is watch. I want you to take names. I want to know the name of everyone that smokes a joint; I want to know who's carrying what; I want the name of everyone that farts. But I don't want you to do anything. You see what I mean?"

The young cop spoke up again. "I think I saw some of 'em carrying flags in paper bags. What if they burn them? Can we bust them before they actually light the flags?"

Bushey looked away from the kid and rolled his eyes skyward, then jutted his head forward slightly. "Sergeant Lester, is something wrong with this rookie's hearing? Has he got a problem that you didn't tell me about?" He took half a step toward the young cop.

"Your name's Tommy, right?"

"Tom, sir. Tom Briggs."

"Okay, Tommy, I'm going to tell you again. You will do nothing until I tell you what to do. Nothing. You will watch and take names. Observe. Do you have the radio we gave you? I see that you do. That's good. If I want you to do anything, someone will come on your radio and tell you to do it. Got that? Okay. Okay, Tommy. Now, what will you do if someone burns a flag?"

Briggs swallowed hard. "Nothing. I mean . . ." he began to stutter.

"Goddam it, boy, you got the right answer. Nothing. And that better be what you mean, and all you mean, because if you do anything else, I'm going to stomp all over your ass."

The four cops all swung their eyes toward Willis, and Bushey said, "Don't worry about him. Bud's not interested in us; he's got a story about war protesters to write. He's interested in what they've got to say about peace and justice and American corruption. Right, Bud?"

Willis didn't answer. He had, in fact, become absorbed in watching the protesters shifting aimlessly around the park. There didn't appear to be any obvious leaders. The large octagonal gazebo where the town band sat for Sunday night summer concerts was full of people, but they were always coming and going. One minute the bandstand would be full of middle-aged, middle-class people, and the next it would be full of hippies, then a crowd of college kids would take over. The rest of the Green was full of people roaming around, evidently waiting for something but, at least at the beginning, showing no signs of tension or impatience.

As he watched, Willis realized that nearly all of the new arrivals were students. They gathered in small groups scattered around the Green, anywhere from three to a dozen in each group. Most of them wore black armbands. He tried to count the crowd, but it was like trying to count sheep in a grazing flock and soon he gave up the effort. Whatever number he used in the story would be disputed anyway; it always was. One side wanted a high number and the other side wanted a low number. Official estimates were no help since all of the officials — cops, city politicians, rally organizers — were partisans. In Selma, the locals had said Martin Luther King led a few hundred marchers; organizers said there were 7,000; most news reports said 4,000. Willis couldn't remember what number he had used in Selma, but he knew that he was just guessing like all the rest of them.

Suddenly, looking out over the shifting crowd, he realized there were no black faces. None. Willis pulled out his folded-up copy paper and wrote:

— No blacks marching. Why not?

— Mostly black kids dying in the war. Where are the black students?

As he moved to stuff the paper back in his pocket, his elbow shoved into the stomach of the young cop, who had sidled tight up against his back to try to read what he was writing. "Hey, Tommy," Willis said, "don't you know it's against the law to read a reporter's notes?"

The flustered cop looked quickly toward the chief, but Bushey had moved away. "Bullshit," he said. "There's no law like that . . . is there?"

"Sure. It's in the First Amendment. Don't they teach you that at the police academy?"

Young Briggs scowled and walked away, suddenly very interested in looking at the crowd in the park. Willis wished someone had been around to appreciate the way he baited the kid, and when he looked around he saw that one of the other cops had indeed been listening. Willis didn't know him, but he knew about him. He was just a little older than Briggs, a recent hire named Molinaroli. Unlike Briggs, he wasn't a local kid. Bushey had hired him right out of the MPs. He'd done back-to-back tours in Vietnam, and rumor had it that Bushey figured on moving him up fast through the ranks.

Willis inclined his head slightly toward the fleeing Briggs and smiled at Molinaroli, who not only didn't smile back but looked as though his idea of humor might be to toss Willis off the building. Willis started to stick out his hand to introduce himself, but the cop, with one final glare, turned on his heel and headed for the door. "Come on, Briggs," he called. "Let's go look at the other assholes."

The asshole comment stung for an instant, before Willis thought of how Sy would get a kick out of this story. He always liked goading the cops. Or anyone else in authority, for that matter. He turned back toward the Green, wondering if Sy would come out to see the march.

The small park was jammed full now. The energy of the crowd was more like a rising and sinking of the whole than individuals moving from place to place. He ran his eyes across the Green slowly until his sweep was stopped by a commotion around the flagpole near the bandstand. Someone wearing a field jacket with a large peace sign on the back was trying to climb the pole. He was high enough off the ground so that the half dozen hands reaching up only came to his ankles. At first, Willis wasn't sure whether they were boosting him or pulling him down, but then the jacket suddenly plunged and the grasping hands moved to pin the climber's arms.

Willis glanced toward Bushey, who was standing at the northern corner of the roof, facing the park and speaking into his walkie-talkie. Hunched over the edge of the building, the afternoon sun turning him into a silhouette, Bushey for an instant became Lon Chaney's Quasimodo peering out from the bell tower. Willis made a note on his copy paper, but he knew even as he wrote it that the image would never see print.

He turned back to scanning the Green, remembering that he had not seen Connie and the others in a long time. He couldn't find them in the crowd, but he did locate two television crews and he spotted a *Boston Globe* car parked on the far side of the Green. Again he had a sinking sense that he had missed something about this story, that it was getting away from him before he even knew what he was looking for.

He noticed that only a handful of people were in the gazebo and they appeared to be standing more or less in a line behind one man, who was in the bandleader's spot but facing the crowd. He should have been down there, not up on a roof a block away where he couldn't hear anything, couldn't even tell whether the guy in the bandstand was talking to the crowd.

"I'm going down there," Peterson said, nearly sending Willis over the edge of the roof because he had been concentrating so hard he hadn't heard the photographer walk up behind him. "They're about to start walking and I want some close-up shots."

"Jesus Christ," Willis said. "Are you still here? You ought to be down on the street."

"That's what I said. You staying up here?"

Willis shook his head, but he said. "Yeah. Yeah, don't worry about me. Just get down there and shoot the leaders. And watch out for anti-protesters too. And cops."

He watched Peterson leave and felt even more alone and worried. He walked over to Bushey's corner. "Well, Chief, I'm going down on the street. This is starting to seem like some sort of big deal. What's going on?"

Bushey turned his head, then pivoted his whole body around and looked closely at Willis before answering. "I can't tell you. At least, not now. Maybe nothing special's going on. After it's all over, come see me and maybe I'll give you something—be able to give you something."

Willis started to press him, but one look at the stony face convinced him that was the wrong move. "Thanks," he said, hurrying off the roof. He hustled down the four flights and caught up with Peterson, who had stopped right in the middle of the store's doorway to adjust his paraphernalia. He muttered under his breath as Willis pushed past him without speaking.

Outside, the sidewalk traffic seemed normal for early afternoon, but there was a slow-motion feeling because two blocks of Main Street had been blocked off to cars and was completely empty. The parking meters stood guard over blank spaces and the streetlights showed red on all four sides. The big clock in front of the bank said 2:44. Willis stopped, lit a cigarette, and ran his eyes up and down both sides of the broad street. He spotted several men who looked somehow out of place, even if he couldn't say exactly why. Only a couple of them looked like FBI types and they could just as easily have been insurance salesmen. Most of the people on the sidewalks seemed to be women, and he realized he had never considered that they might use women for this sort of spying. Why not?

He looked back at the clock—still 2:44. What the hell? Just then a group of young guys, all wearing work clothes and boots and carrying or wearing hard hats, turned the corner by the drugstore and strolled toward Willis. There were about ten of them, laughing and pushing each other. They stopped halfway down the block and moved out to the curb, still talking and horsing around but not advancing. Across the street, a little closer to the park, Willis saw another group of young men, and he now noticed that several of them wore Kane's Tire Company baseball caps.

Arthur Kane was the outspoken and outlandish leader of the city council group that had tried to stop the peace march. The council had bickered about the permit request for weeks, with Kane warning it would lead to every pestilence known to modern man. Every pot-drugged hippie, every bare-chested woman, every draft-dodging punk, and every Red-ruined newsman in America would descend on town, he warned.

The paper had gleefully jumped into the battle over the permit, with Sy aiming most of his guns directly at Kane, although at the outset more than half of the other city councilors also wanted to stop the protest. Kane was an easy target, but he was a worthy opponent for two reasons: He was rich, having turned a single gas station into a statewide string of tire stores, and he was credible as a politician, despite his sometimes idiotic rhetoric, because he looked and spoke like Gregory Peck. Kane was a native Vermonter, but somewhere along the way he had shed the accent and added a white Stetson hat, creating what was, for Vermont, an exotic touch. By his mid-sixties, he also had permanently cleaned the grease out of his fingernails and had picked up a closetful of tailored suits.

At one meeting, Kane had denounced the march as a strategy "concocted by friends of the enemy, to divide the community." Sy had convinced Willis to move the quote to the lead of the story, and in a column he had written, "Cowboy Kane is beginning to sound like

Birmingham's Bull Connor, who thought the idea of civil rights for black people was just some crazy dream of 'outside agitators.' If Kane wins this permit battle, can fire hoses and German shepherds be far behind?"

Willis remembered the overheated coverage of the permit debate as he watched the group of Kane workers milling around on the opposition curb. He had told Sy he thought the Bull Connor reference was a little embarrassing, although he didn't press it because his birthright made his own sympathies suspect when it came to civil rights. Besides, he had to admit that something had turned around enough council votes to get the permit approved. The vote had been six to five.

The whole issue had given the peace march far more attention than it otherwise would have gotten. Even the *Globe* had written about it in the New England section. That's why they're here today, Willis thought as he began walking again toward the park. He approached the group of playful young workers and guessed they were from the construction job going on at the foundry. They quit talking and gave him a narrow-eyed once-over as he passed, not belligerent exactly but ready to be, like hometown boys standing around the concession stand at halftime. The ones he noticed had New England faces, all points and angles, with guarded but inquisitive eyes. It was clear they were not going to step into his path, but neither were they giving up any space.

It amused him to think about Sy's belief that the people up here who resented the anti-war stuff were like the Southern bigots. Comparing this bunch to the rednecked, fierce-eyed, rotten-toothed crowds in Greensboro was like comparing porcupines and copperheads. The only similarity was that you didn't want to kick either one.

In North Carolina, the mountain-bred independence had gone bad, poisoned by poverty and preachers into a mixture of suspicion and petty meanness that lay just out of sight, ready to spring to life at the first hint of threat. The mountain ridges at some point had become walls, stranding their people and separating them not into idiosyncratic freemen but into captive clans, distinct as a population but clones of one another so that when the mob surrounded the young blacks at the Greensboro lunch counter, the hate was as defined yet as indivisible as the flames of a forest fire.

Here, the chosen isolation of hilltop farming had made men as hard, stubborn, and singular as the field stones they had dragged and piled into countless miles of fence rows. These people grew confident by triumphing over hostile elements, they gained calmness from the beasts they worked with, and they learned from an inhospitable land the value of providing for yourself. Here, self-worth was measured by self-sufficiency, and the same standard was applied generously to your neighbor, who had his own stone walls to build and who deserved, just by being there, the right to be left alone so he could do it. Consequently, the ones who had remained in these mountains were those who respected themselves and each other. Whoever recruited this gang of young laborers had gotten only what he bargained for, an observant troop, and was bound for disappointment if he had meant to buy any head bashing or if he had figured he could ignite some deep-pooled innate fury. Alerted to Willis's approach down the sidewalk, the genes of these native sons had edged them further apart, not closer together, each asserting his own ground to defend. Don't Tread on Me is the motto on the state flag here, and this crowd, in their green or blue trousers and steel-toed boots, was bound to their own heritage as surely as the sheeted Klansmen of Montgomery. There was plenty of suspicion and submerged racism in this tribe, but there would be no lynchings here.

At the Green, Willis worked his way slowly through the crowd, headed vaguely toward the bandstand but at the same time on the lookout for Connie and the others. Anti-war signs, symbols, and stick-mounted placards were sprinkled thickly. You could divide the factions by slogan. He tugged out the folded-up pad of newsprint, grumbling because one sheet of the wad stayed behind in his jacket pocket. Christ, other papers had gone to regulation stenographer's notebooks even as far back as when he worked for the lousy *El Paso Journal*, that bastion of progressive journalism that still routinely referred to local Mexicans not as citizens or residents or even as people, but only as "others."

Willis scribbled down as many slogans as he could see. Out Now seemed to be the message of choice for the middle-aged and blue-hair contingent; Hell No, We Won't Go belonged to the college kids; and the hippies seemed content with the peace sign stamped, sewn, painted, engraved, and tattooed on clothes, signs, satchels, and bodies. Two strange-looking creatures with wild, snarled bundles of hair atop white-painted clown faces carried a banner that read Hey, Hey LBJ, How Many Kids Did You Kill Today. They staggered through the crowd, lurching and jostling along in gaudy, baggy shirts and striped trousers that flared out wildly at the bottom, entirely covering their feet and dragging across the grass like upside-down sacks.

In the park it seemed like an entirely different show than the one he and Bushey had watched from the roof. Here it felt like a carnival: people laughing and moving out of the way of the weird pair happily yoked together by the LBJ taunt; two-foot-high children clutching parents' hands, with their solemn, awestruck faces tilted up as high as stubby necks would allow; the twanging of multiple guitars, sometimes competing for off-key awfulness; hairy-legged boys in boots or sandals and short trousers — near men, really — tossing around a saucer-shaped thing called a Frisbee. And everywhere the sweet smell of marijuana burning.

Willis roved through the crowd looking for the ubiquitous narcs, the despised gestapo that haunted this generation of students but was so alien to his own experience that Willis had never learned to spot them in a crowd, even when he knew they were there. Still some distance from the bandstand, he spied a suspicious-looking man wearing a jacket and tie, leaning against the gazebo writing something, a camera hung around his neck. But when he got closer, he recognized the notetaker as a *Patriot Press* reporter and he veered off in another direction.

He was still scanning for narcs when he realized he was being eased along toward the street, carried on a slow tide that was consolidating the people into rough-edged ranks and would deposit them on Main Street. Willis struggled across the current of the human stream and found himself alone on the sidewalk of Church Street. He ran to the corner, turned onto Main, and saw Ron standing right at the head of the line of marchers like some damned drum major, except that he was facing the wrong way and was scribbling furiously. Directly in front of him, evidently part of the interview, were four men: the rabbi who had been an early local leader in condemning the war; two guys Willis did not know, who both wore stiff round collars that were gleamingly visible in front but hidden in back under curling locks of beautifully brushed silver hair; and the Unitarian minister he had once interviewed for a stupid story about teenage pregnancy.

Willis stopped and stared. Norman Rockwell himself couldn't have set it up any better, for Christ's sake. *Four Preachers and a Scribe.* Brilliant cloudless sky. Giant spreading maple tree half framed behind the subjects. Ancient red-brick bank building on the opposite corner in the background. Jesus, it was a perfect scene. Onward Jewish and Christian soldiers. Only, it was a lie. Willis knew it was a lie, knew some key piece was missing from this picture. The image troubled him in the same way the whole anti-war movement troubled him. Somewhere, buried under the layers of peace-and-justice wrapping, lay a dangerous, unacknowledged self-interest—a driving, corrupt force that had managed to harness and ride a sad population's artless yearning for absolute truth.

Ron stopped writing, folded up his copy paper, and stepped aside so the sanctified foursome could start their procession. Willis called to him and Ron walked briskly toward the corner where he was standing. "I think I've got a pretty good story," he said. "This is a truly ecumenical protest. Just about every church in town is represented here, except the Catholics." He looked to Willis for some sort of confirmation, but he didn't get it. "Don't you think the lead ought to be the church angle? The unity of the protest movement?"

Willis waited a long pause before asking, "Who organized this crowd?"

"What do you mean? I guess the ministers organized it. They're leading the march."

"Did you ask them?"

"No, but I didn't . . . I mean, they acted as though they . . . What makes you think the churches didn't organize it?"

Willis swept his arm over the crowd, which had become much quieter, almost to the point of school-assembly orderliness. "Do these look like church folks to you? You think they read about this in the Sunday bulletin?"

Ron turned to get a full view of the crowd just as the cavorting pair with the LBJ banner pushed their way through to the front, lining up right behind the preachers. "This looks like a political crowd to me," Willis said with a patronizing smile. "I'd check it out if I were you."

Ron looked pained but, Christ, it wouldn't hurt the cocky Ivy League kid to hit a bump or two. He was already pretty good and getting better with every story. But he wasn't a pro yet. Willis started to walk away but stopped again to say, "I'll see you back at the paper. Why don't you stay with the marchers. I'll get up in front. Have you seen Peterson?"

Ron shook his head, still looking a little hurt, before walking back toward the head of the march. Willis moved quickly, headed back to Penney's. He'd decided to try to keep an overview perspective on this story, a descriptive piece. Sy liked color. Besides, he still hadn't seen

Connie or Merle and he hoped he could spot them from the top of the building if he didn't run into them before he got there.

He remembered that he hadn't seen Thunderclap or his commune group in the park, but before he could give it much thought he spotted the FBI guy just starting up the front steps of the post office. Willis hurried and caught up with him at the front door. "Hi, I'm with the *Times*. I saw you on the roof with Chief Bushey."

"Yeah, I saw you too," he said, sticking out his right hand. "I'm Special Agent Mike Isham. What can I do for you?"

"Well," Willis said, secretly a little unnerved by the directness, "I was just wondering what the FBI is doing here."

The agent smiled and jerked his thumb toward the glass door behind them. "I work here. This is the federal building, you know."

"I mean, not here . . . at Penney's," Willis stammered. "I mean, you know, what were you doing up on the roof?"

"Talking to Chief Bushey," Isham said flatly. "We're in the same line of work, you know."

"What about the protest?" Willis asked.

"Well, that's Chief Bushey's jurisdiction. I mostly do paperwork, and, if you'll excuse me, I have a desk full of it waiting for me upstairs." He turned and disappeared through the big glass doors into the marble lobby. Willis noticed that he went straight to the stairway without even looking at the elevator.

Willis looked back and saw that the marchers were just beginning to leave the park, formed up in a haphazard wedge with the four horsemen of the apocalypse making the front rank. He dashed into the Penney's building and ran up the stairs, breaking out onto the roof just in time to see two giant army helicopters bank off to the west, presumably headed for the Plattsburgh air base. Willis was disappointed to see that Bushey was not on the roof; he'd know what the choppers were doing over here. The kid cop, Briggs, was the only one on the roof, hanging well back from the edge so he could see the street but not be easily seen from below.

He whirled around when he heard the door open and began to say something, but Willis held up his hand. "Hold it, Tommy, the chief said it's okay. I won't give away your position." Briggs clamped his mouth shut and Willis walked past him to the very edge and peered over, pulling out his copy paper and putting it on the flat top of the brick parapet. The clergymen and the clowns with the banner still led the procession, which widened out behind them to fill up the broad street. Stretched out gutter to gutter with the ranks in close order, the crowd didn't seem as large as it had in the park. Willis even wondered briefly whether some people had dropped out. The sidewalks on both sides of the street were now quite full, with people standing three or four deep turned toward the marchers. They stood very still, even most of the children, but it was hard to tell why because there wasn't much in the way of entertainment—a few hand-scrawled banners, a dozen or so convention-style placards with unoriginal messages, and a couple of the guitarists, the ones who could pick and walk at the same time.

He watched as Ron skipped along at the edge of the march, spurting out once to talk briefly with the leaders, then dropping back to speak with individual protesters, walking with one for a few paces, then dropping back to pick up another. While Willis watched, he talked with five or six marchers that way.

Peterson also was at the front of the pack, dashing ahead, setting up and snapping a shot, then running again. He looked like a man suffering a dire form of punishment or perhaps caught in some terrible contest in which he had to keep repeating the same tortuous play over and over. Maybe he should have stuck with the darkroom job, his own little kingdom where no one dared disturb him and he could move as slowly as he wanted.

Willis searched the crowd for Connie and Merle but he could not see either of them. Finally, when about half the procession had passed Penney's, he saw Merle at the very tail end bouncing along, trying to write on his pad without dropping entirely out of the pack. He was with a hippie contingent, of course, and when he looked closely Willis recognized some of the people from the Moretown commune. Then he saw Thunderclap, all but indistinguishable among his flock, and suddenly Willis understood that the commune leader was not really noticeably tall or conspicuous in any way—at least, not from four stories up.

When the parade leaders reached the barricade at the end of the blocked-off portion of Main Street, they stopped and waited for the others. When the crowd had packed in tightly, one of the silver-haired preachers climbed up to stand on a yellow sawhorse. Willis could not hear him, but he could see that very quickly he hit the pulpit gear, an overdrive delivery that had his arms rising and falling, hands spreading out then closing in. At one point his balled-up fists revolved in a circle around each other, like planets in orbit. He spoke to the attentive crowd for about five minutes, then climbed down. Willis waited, assuming the crowd would begin to break up. But then another man, unknown to Willis and inconspicuous in the crowd, stepped up and climbed onto the vacant sawhorse. He wore the campus uniform—a crewneck sweater over a blue shirt, khaki trousers, and sneakers—and he spoke with much less physical prowess, standing spread-legged on the narrow board with his arms at his sides and looking slightly unbalanced. He spoke for a couple of minutes before a spotty cheer came from the crowd. He spoke again, and another cheer rose up. Then he jumped off the sawhorse and the crowd began to mill around in place, but soon the tight weave began to loosen and then unravel as people straggled out onto the sidewalks and some turned around to walk back down the street toward the park.

The spectacle simply fell apart, disappeared into routine. While Willis watched, the city crews took down the sawhorse barricades, and within minutes, even before everyone had reached the park, automobiles were turning onto Main Street and the parking spaces were filling up.

The whole thing had taken maybe twenty minutes and had no more import than one blink of one eye. Yet he would spend his entire day, one full cycle of his life, absorbed in this meaningless nonevent, thinking about it, analyzing it, describing it in tiny detail, and finally turning what would have been a harmless tick of the clock into a lie, a story freighted with the potential reverberations that go with all yarns. He would take the short interval during which traffic was stopped so a throng of people could walk in the street and turn it into a front-page report, "news" that then could itself be remade, possibly into "history." Or maybe, even before that, this story would become the parent of other "events": city council action, police action, church action, political action—all progeny of his report on this meaningless march and all destined themselves to become "news" and eventually "history." Because if he didn't write the story, or rather, if nobody wrote it, the blink would be all there was, as transitory as a song heard once on the radio and then forgotten.

Briggs was still on the roof when Willis started down, but at the second-floor landing he heard the tortured creaking of ancient wood as the heavy-footed young cop crashed down three steps at a time. When he passed Willis, one beefy hand held the walkie-talkie tightly to his ear and the other clutched the wooden handrail, which he used to vault along to the next landing. When Willis got to the street, there was no sign of Briggs.

Willis dawdled along the sidewalk, headed roughly toward the paper but moving more and more slowly as he tried to work out his lead on the story. The problem was that he didn't have one. He could cover a weak lead with some lacy embroidery at the top describing the crowd, but Sy would know the difference. Besides, maybe the kid had followed his advice and managed to dig up something, or maybe Connie had stumbled onto something and that's why she wasn't in the crowd. Shit. What if the *Globe* or the *Free Patriot* or, God forbid, the fools from the TV station had found a story? He thought fleetingly of the helicopters but dismissed the idea as a long shot, not even worth chasing down. They probably had nothing to do with the protest.

He turned the corner onto Charles Street and saw a small crowd gathered halfway down the block. He also saw that his entire team, including Peterson, was in the crowd. When he got near, Merle rushed up to him. "They've arrested one of the commune people, a kid they say stole a wallet during the march. I don't think he did it."

Willis looked at Merle's worried face and didn't answer. He pushed his way through the outer ring and saw three cops surrounding a figure in overalls standing against the building, his face inches away from the bricks. His hands were cuffed behind him, dirty-nailed fingers curled limply, and a cop stood on each side, one holding tightly to each arm above the elbow. Sergeant Lester stood a step away, facing the half dozen hippies clustered quietly on the sidewalk. He clutched a brown wallet in his left hand while his right hand rested lightly on his belt, just above his holster. Willis looked closely at Molinaroli and then at Briggs, who must have run all the way from Penney's because his face was covered with sweat. He decided they were tense to the point of being dangerous. He edged around to the side to get a look at their captive and was caught off guard by his first discovery of the day. The thief was the smooth-faced, yellow-haired boy in overalls who had shadowed him around the commune, holding hands with the pretty girl. Willis looked quickly around to see if the girl was in the crowd, but if so, he didn't recognize her. When he looked back, the boy had twisted his head around and stared directly at him with soft, calm eyes in which Willis could read no emotion. Christ, he was just as spaced out as he had been at the commune.

"Face the wall," Molinaroli said sharply, tightening his grip on the boy's arm. Sharp-eyed bastard; he must have noticed the look. "Hey, you," he said to Willis. "You know this guy?"

Willis said, "What'd he do?"

"We're asking the questions," Sergeant Lester said, stepping close to Willis. "He said, do you know who this guy is?"

"No," Willis said, "I don't know who he is."

The cop was still holding the wallet and Willis got a good look at it. The brown leather was faded and worn smooth, with broken stitches, and it was surprisingly thin. It reminded him of an old billfold he had as a child, a discard from some relative.

"Whose wallet?"

Sergeant Lester started to answer but Molinaroli interrupted. "That's police business," he said. "We're conducting an investigation here. If you don't have any information, move on." He looked around at the others. "The rest of you move on too." Several more passersby had stopped to gawk, so a couple of dozen people were now jammed on the sidewalk. Nobody moved. "I said to move on," Molinaroli said, his normally high voice rising to shrillness.

"Bull," said a woman's voice from the outside ring of spectators. "Bull. This is a public sidewalk." It was Connie. "If this is a crime scene, what's the crime? If it's not, then we've got a right to be here and we're damn well going to stay."

A couple of people had turned sideways to look back at her, opening a line of sight between Connie and Molinaroli. He looked wrathful but his wits were mired in his anger, so his voice couldn't get any traction and the sounds that came out were not intelligible.

"Peterson, get a shot of this," she commanded, shoving people aside so he could step forward.

Young Briggs was so agitated he was hopping in place. He lurched forward to block Peterson, but he didn't want to let go of the arm, so his movement jerked the captive backward. The movement startled Molinaroli, who yanked back on the other imprisoned arm, sending the boy reeling into the wall.

"Watch it," Connie shouted, and then Merle chimed in from the other side of the crowd, "Yeah, watch it." The cops evidently felt surrounded and they looked wild-eyed for a moment.

Willis laughed loudly and Briggs screamed, "Arrest that bastard, Lester. Cuff the son-of-a-bitch." Spit sprayed out of his mouth with the final word and sweat streamed down his face.

Willis turned away to keep from laughing again and saw three men hurrying toward the crowd. Thunderclap was in front, massive arms pumping and great bearded head lowered, followed closely by one of the ministers and the other guy who spoke at the rally. Whoa, Willis thought, it looks like Jesus charging into the money changers.

The hippie leader didn't seem to slow down or make any sound, but somehow he was through the crowd and standing a foot away from Sergeant Lester before anyone on the inside of the circle knew he was coming. "This boy has not committed any crime," he said loudly but evenly. "Let him go. Now."

"Who the fuck are you?" demanded Molinaroli.

Thunderclap continued to look only at Lester. "Are you in charge here, Sergeant?" Lester blinked. "If so, let this boy go. I'm told you believe he stole a wallet. Well, I was with him when he found that wallet. And so were a dozen other people. We all saw him find it on the ground. And we also all heard him say he was going to try to find out who it belonged to."

The crowd parted behind Sergeant Lester, and Chief Bushey stepped into the center. Willis had not seen him and didn't know how long he had been there. "Who are you?" Bushey said to Thunderclap.

"I'm called Thunderclap," he said without evident embarrassment or irony.

"I don't care what you're called," Bushey said. "What's your name?"

"My name is Johnson," he said after a long pause. "H. H. Johnson. Do you know what's going on here, Chief Bushey?"

Bushey looked hard at the hippie leader but didn't answer and finally turned to Sergeant Lester. "How do you know he stole the wallet?" he asked in a calm voice.

"Jesus, Chief, we saw him with it in his hand." It was Molinaroli. "He was walking along the street carrying the goddam thing in his hand. He must have been looking for a trash barrel to throw it in because it was empty—at least, the money was gone."

Thunderclap spoke up. "There was not any money. It was empty when he found it."

"Shut up," Bushey said. "You and all the rest of you keep your mouths shut until I tell you to speak." He looked first at the leader then included all the others in the sweep of his eyes and hand. It was as though he had banished not only speech but all noise; no feet shuffled, no throats were cleared, there was not even any traffic sound, just dead stillness and quiet.

"All right," Bushey said finally. "Now we'll find out what's going on here. You, Molinaroli, tell me what happened."

The cop moved forward quickly but did not loosen his grip, so the boy was jerked forward roughly. "Let him go," Bushey said sternly, heading off a protest that Thunderclap had stepped forward to make.

Molinaroli began to report. "We were standing over by that streetlight, Briggs and me, when this bunch of hip . . . this crowd of people turned the corner up there and started towards us. When they saw us, they sort of slowed down or got nervous like, and this kid here moved way over to the inside, sort of hidden among the rest. But I saw him holding something in his hand, then sliding it down against his side like he was trying to hide it. So when they got closer, I stepped into the middle of them to get a good look and I saw that it was a wallet, this wallet here that the sergeant has."

He reached for the wallet, but Bushey pushed away his arm and stuck out his own hand for Lester to give him the wallet. Merle suddenly said from behind Bushey, "Wait, Chief. I was with them, or rather, right behind them, and I—"

"Shut up," Bushey said, whirling around to look at Merle. "I told you all to keep quiet and that's what I meant. So just shut up."

He looked again at the crowd gathered in a semicircle around the cops and the kid. "I think we can settle this right here, but if need be, I'll take the whole bunch of you to the station." He looked at Molinaroli. "Go on."

"Well, that's about all there is to it. I mean, we heard on the radio that a wallet had been stolen, and next thing we knew here comes this hippie kid walking along with one in his hand. So we grabbed him."

Bushey sighed. "So you grabbed him. You just grabbed him." He looked over at the handcuffed boy. "You and Briggs there. Patrolman Briggs, did you read him his rights?"

"Huh? Well . . . rights?"

"You know, Miranda rights. You know the Miranda case, don't you, Patrolman Molinaroli?"

"Uh, yes sir. In 1966, the Supreme Court—"

"I know when it was, Patrolman. It's Briggs and you who need the refresher course. Were you in on this, Sergeant Lester?"

"I came up later, Chief. He was already in handcuffs and—"

"Okay. Never mind. How much money was in the wallet?"

"The owner said he had $86 in it," said Sergeant Lester. "That's what he said when he reported it was stolen."

Bushey opened it wide and turned it upside down. "Let's see, there's nothing, absolutely nothing, in this wallet now. Is this how you found it, Patrolman Briggs? Totally empty?"

"Yes sir. Empty."

"Chief?" It was Lester, speaking in a very small, very wary voice. "Chief? There was one thing in the wallet. Just one—"

"Well, what was it? And where is it?" Bushey held out his hand. Lester reached into the breast pocket on his shirt and fished out a folded, faded picture and handed it over to Bushey. He looked at it, turned it over, and held it up. "What is it?"

"It's a picture," Lester said. "A picture of a girl."

"I can see that, Sergeant. What about it?" Bushey looked puzzled. "Christ," he said, "it's not even a photograph. It's cut out of a magazine, isn't it? Why did you take it out of the wallet?"

"Well, Chief, the wallet belongs to Charlie Parker, you know." Lester's gaze became a little shifty. "And that picture, well, it's about the only thing Charlie really cares about. Anyway, I figured the wallet might be tied up a long time as evidence, so I figured I'd just take the picture and give it to back to Charlie."

Bushey stared with disbelief at Lester, then turned his cocked head toward the other two cops. Willis giggled but muffled it and was looking in another direction by the time the chief had swung around to glare at him.

Bushey looked again at the picture. "This is Charlie Parker's wallet?"

"That's right," Lester said. "Old Charlie has been carrying that picture around in it for ten years." He grew thoughtful, as though the question of time was the key to an important issue. "At least ten years. He shows it to everybody. Says it's his girlfriend."

Willis barely contained another laugh. He'd only been in town a few months and even he knew about Charlie Parker and his famous picture. Charlie was the town drunk, or one of them. He made regular rounds of all the bars every day, showing his picture and bumming drinks.

Willis sobered up when he looked at Bushey's face. He looked like a man on the verge of exploding. But he said quietly, speaking very slowly in a steady voice, "Charlie Parker says someone stole his wallet? And that he had $86 in it? And that's why you arrested . . . I mean, why you stopped this boy? Have I got it right?"

Sergeant Lester nodded without looking at Bushey, and Briggs said, "Yes sir. He had the wallet in his hand."

Bushey passed his hand over his face wearily. "Did you search him? To see if he had the money?"

"Not yet," replied Molinaroli. "We were about to when—"

Thunderclap spoke up loudly. "Wait a minute. You can't search him. You don't have a warrant." He looked around at Willis, then at Connie. "You're witnessing this." Then he turned back to Bushey. "If you search this boy, I'm going to get a lawyer. I'm telling you, we saw him find this wallet. It was lying on the ground in the park. He stepped on it and picked it up to find out who it belonged to."

The commune leader and Bushey were less than an arm's length from each other, stiff-legged and tense as pit bulls, their eyes locked. Looking at Thunderclap's face, Willis remembered the look of furious wild-man malevolence he had thrown at him that day at the commune. Suddenly the hippie stepped back a half pace and recited, still looking at Bushey but without anger, "The men gained an advantage over us, and came out against us in the field; but we drove them back to the entrance of the gate."

A frown of uncertainty crossed Bushey's face, then he shook his head from side to side in an elaborate gesture of ridicule and said, "Jesus H. Christ." Turning to Molinaroli, he said tiredly, "Turn him loose." Briggs began, "But, Chief—"

Bushey cut him off. "Let him go. Take off the goddam handcuffs and let him go." Again Briggs's mouth opened, but Bushey shouted, "Take off the goddam handcuffs. What part of that order—order—don't you understand, Patrolman Briggs? Let him go."

Briggs unlocked the handcuffs and the boy rubbed his wrists. He still looked blank, as uninvolved in this episode or in the world as he had looked when Willis first saw him at the commune with the girl. He looked at Willis and smiled shyly in recognition.

Thunderclap stalked off in the direction of Main Street, and Bushey wheeled around to march off in the opposite direction. He stopped and called out to the commune leader's back, "Johnson, is it? I'm going to check on that. You can count on it."

The crowd broke up quickly and the newspeople set off together toward the paper, jabbering among themselves. "Merle, you get to write this part. It'll make a great sidebar," Connie said. "You were with the commune people all the time, weren't you?"

"Yeah," Merle said. "Nearly all the time. But I didn't see him pick up the wallet."

Connie spoke directly to Willis. "That's okay with you, isn't it? For Merle to write the sidebar on the cops and the hippies?"

Willis shrugged. "Sure," he said, "sure. What are you writing? I didn't see you all afternoon."

Connie, still walking briskly, said, "I think I've got a pretty good angle for a reaction piece." She stopped and touched his arm to make him stop too, and the others all stood for a minute on the sidewalk. "Ron and I swapped assignments," she said, looking directly at Willis. "I know you said for him to get a reaction story, but I ran into some people who wanted to talk—hard-hat types—and he said he'd just as soon do a color piece anyway. So we switched. Okay?"

What could he say? Willis shrugged again, but he knew she was screwing him over. Connie started walking again and talking. "Actually, it sounds like Ron may have a hard-news angle. He found out that the McCarthy organization was behind the whole protest. They organized everything, right, Ron?"

Ron kept walking and didn't look at Willis or Connie. He was slightly in front of the others and called back over his shoulder, "Yeah, they were behind it, all right. But more than that, they did it secretly. They got it to look like the churches set up the march, got the permits and everything, then when the McCarthy guy spoke at the end, the applause and all looked spontaneous. Did you see all those college kids? The Clean Gene brigade? They bussed them in from all over."

Good move, Willis, he said to himself. Give the damn kid the knife he uses to cut off your own balls. He's got the news, she's got the reaction, and Merle takes the sidebar. Leaves the old pro with diddly shit. Connie said to him, "Sounds like the lead, huh? The political angle? Unless you've got something better."

Willis didn't answer. They walked on in silence until they were a half block from the paper, when he suddenly said, "I forgot something. I'll be back in a while," and turned around and hurried back the way they had come.

Downtown was back to normal, as though the protest had never happened. The late-afternoon crowds were the same people who filled the sidewalks on any given day, locals who had regained the territory as effortlessly as the sea takes back its space from a passing ship. Kids meandered along on their way home from school, reluctant to give up their freedom when there was still three hours of daylight left; first-shift workers hurried or dawdled, depending on what was waiting for them at home; and a few furrow-browed desk jockeys scuttled past guiltily, although at five fifteen most of this species were still in their cubicles. Willis strode past the now-peaceful arrest scene like a man with a purpose, giving no sign that he secretly feared he was on a fool's mission inspired solely by his desperate need to escape Connie's triumphant return to the newsroom.

The white-brick police station occupied a first-floor corner space in city hall, fronting on Main Street as much so the citizenry could keep an eye on the peacekeepers as the other way around. Willis peered in as he passed. Flimsy curtains fluttered in the open, screenless window and what struck Willis was the general hominess of the place—more like a rather shabby, egalitarian men's club than a seat of retribution. A long wooden counter cut the room in two, but it was more a division of convenience than a class divide. The walls were thick with certificates and framed photographs of uniformed men. On the near side of the counter, most of the floor space was bare except for a few beat-up wooden chairs. Several mostly bare desks stood behind the protection of the counter on the other side. Only one was occupied. Willis could see the bare head of Sergeant Callahan resting in his cupped hand, his elbow planted firmly on the desk in front of him. Since he was alone, he probably was asleep. But Willis also knew he never would be able to catch him dozing because Callahan had a renowned ability to hear footsteps even before the person actually opened the door into the station. The old wooden floors of city hall always creaked with weariness underfoot, but the boards directly in front of the police station door complained particularly loudly.

Callahan was already lumbering to his feet by the time Willis turned the doorknob. By the time he had closed the door and walked the few steps to the counter, he was looking into the impatient face of an overworked policeman who clearly didn't have time for nonsense like answering reporters' questions. Willis briefly considered, then rejected, a comment about the odd fact that the soft cushion in Callahan's desk chair was still rising to its full fluffiness.

"Is the chief here?" Willis asked.

"He's busy."

"Can I see him?"

"He's busy."

"Go ask him if I can talk to him for a minute, will you?"

"You don't hear too good, do you? I told you, he's busy."

"Yeah, I heard you, Sergeant, but what you don't know is that the chief told me to come see him. So how about going in there and tell him I'm out here."

Callahan frowned but he didn't move right away. He took a pencil from behind his ear and began tapping on the counter. "He didn't say anything to me about talking to the press."

Willis was getting annoyed by the stubborn old fool, but he also knew the whole idea of talking to Bushey was a waste of time. Maybe he ought to give up, go on back to the paper, and just write a color piece about the protest. He could do that quickly and get out of the newsroom early. Then he remembered Connie's self-satisfied smile.

"Goddam it, Sergeant, if the chief wants something put in the newspaper and you block it, you'll end up with your ass caught in a crack. I don't know what he wants, but you can be goddam sure that if I leave here now, whatever it is won't get done, and you can also be sure that I'm going to tell him you blocked it."

Callahan was so mad he couldn't speak, but his fury was overwhelmed by his fear of offending authority. He snapped the pencil in two, turned on his heel, and walked over to the chief's closed door. He knocked, but not too loudly, and entered without waiting for an answer.

Willis smiled. He knew Sy would like the bit about the pencil.

Callahan came back out and gave him an icy look. He didn't say anything but he left the chief's door open and waved his hand in that direction. Willis had won, but he was glad the old guy was harmless. Most places he had worked, you were taking a real risk if you tried to bully cops, even the low-ranking ones. In Georgia once, someone had cut the throat of Sheila's cocker spaniel and left it bleeding to death on their doorstep. Willis had always been sure the killer was a local police corporal he had embarrassed in a story.

Bushey sat behind a perfectly blank desk, his glossy shoes crossed on the edge of the highly polished gray metal top. The desktop was huge and it was made even larger by a narrower but still expansive arm that extended off one end and also was unoccupied, except for the chief's ornate visored cap. The desk was so big it made Bushey's feet and cap look small, even though they both were far above average. The outsized desk was even more conspicuous than it would have been in most offices because of the remarkable plainness of this room. After using this office for a dozen years, Bushey had left no mark on it. No pictures on the wall, no curtains on the window, no rug on the floor, no sign, in fact, that anyone lived here. Willis remembered that Sy had once called the chief's office "a Spartan's lair."

Bushey was looking directly at him as Willis crossed the doorway and stepped into the office. "What do you want," he said. There was no question mark in his voice and his tone was menacing, but his face was empty of any feeling and, except for his mouth moving to speak the four words, his body was absolutely still.

Willis hesitated briefly, waiting for an invitation to sit down, but he didn't get one. "I just wanted to ask you a couple of questions about the protest," he said lamely. "Thanks for seeing me."

Bushey didn't speak or move, his gaze unwavering. Willis looked away, then back to the chief. "Actually, I just remembered what you said earlier. About checking with you later. You know, about why the FBI was here and why this war protest was different . . ."

No response. Hell, he'd known this was a waste of time but at least it got him away from the newsroom. What the hell, push on. He sat down in the chair in front of Bushey's desk. "I spoke to the FBI guy. He said you were working together?"

Bushey sneered. "He said that, huh? Working together, he said. What else did he say?" He was still as motionless as a frog on a lily pad and his eyes never left Willis's face.

"Well, he said you and he were in the same line of work and . . ."

Bushey sneered again and started to interrupt but changed his mind. "Go on."

"He said you were a pretty good cop."

Bushey twitched in his chair, yanking his feet off the desk. "That condescending sonofabitch," he said. "He knows as much about being a cop as I know about menstrual cramps. He's an accountant, a paper-clip counter with a badge." He leaned forward in his chair and motioned toward the door. "That worn-out Irishman sleeping at the desk out there is more of a cop than your FBI guy."

Willis was beginning to feel better for the first time since Connie took his story away from him. He might get something yet. He reached toward his shirt pocket for his pen, but one glance at Bushey told him that was a mistake and he dropped his hand back into his lap, covering the folded-up copy paper.

"You're Bud Willis, right?" Willis began a nod but Bushey didn't wait for an answer. "I know a lot about you. Montgomery, Charlotte, Atlanta, El Paso, Atlanta again . . . right? Maybe a few other stops. Covered a lot of civil rights stuff, a lot of political stuff, right? Won some awards, right?" He was talking fast and not waiting for any response.

"Been here about six months, right? Kind of a down-the-ladder move for you, isn't it? Never mind. That doesn't mean anything to me." He stood up suddenly and walked to the window, turning his back to Willis. "Divorced, right? One kid. They're still in Georgia." He turned around and moved over to stand behind his own chair, both hands resting on its back.

Willis had long since lost the spark of excitement ignited by Bushey's bitterness toward the FBI. Now he was off-balance, confused, and a little frightened. What else did this guy know and how did he know it? And why did he always seem to veer back and forth between friendliness and bullying? He changed manner so often and so abruptly that Willis could never get a good grip on how to deal with him.

"So," Bushey said in a new tone, "the word is you're a good reporter, a professional." He paused. "I like dealing with professionals even when I don't much like the profession. But now I'm puzzled. I can't figure out why, if you're a pro, you never asked about the helicopters? How many times have you seen those big choppers around here?" He sat down in his chair, leaned back, and again propped his feet on the desk, careful to keep the heels on the edge so he wouldn't mar the shine on the desk or the shoes. He smirked. "How'd you win all those prizes without knowing how to ask the right questions?"

Willis squirmed in his seat but at the same time he felt the excitement surge back and his fingers crept toward his shirt pocket. "I saw them," he said. "They left at 3:20, headed west toward Plattsburgh. What were they doing over here?"

Bushey looked at him for half a minute, then finally said, "There's your story. But I don't know if I can trust you. You seemed more interested in some hard-luck story about a hippie kid finding a wallet or police brutality or whatever it was you thought was going on out there on the street." He paused but continued before Willis could answer.

"I wasn't surprised by the others, but I was surprised that you were going to miss the real story here."

Willis took a deep breath. "The real story is why the helicopters were here? Who called them in?"

Bushey said, "I'm going to take a chance here. I'm going to give you this story. But if you fuck me over on this, you'll regret it. My name better not ever, not ever, be associated with this story. Understood?" Willis nodded. "I mean it," Bushey said. "I don't like these trench coat snobs but I have to work with them, and their politicians can make a lot of misery for people like me.

"Okay," Bushey said, "you can write this down on that paper you're hiding in your lap, but don't put my name on it or on any other piece of paper."

Willis yanked out his pen and put the paper on the bare desk so he could write faster.

"One more thing," Bushey said. "This is a good story. Real news. I expect this to get more attention than some rinky-dink dumb-cop story. Right? We understand each other, right?"

"Sure," Willis said without hesitation. "Sure." He looked at Bushey's face and was not comforted by what he saw. How the hell could he be certain how Sy would handle these stories? "Sure," he repeated with a grin. "We understand each other and this sure as hell is a better news story than the lost-wallet story."

Bushey was silent for a full minute, never taking his eyes off Willis's face. Then he began to talk.

*
**

The newsroom was humming at its early evening pace and no one noticed when Willis walked in. As he passed Connie's desk, though, she looked up and the wonderful wide smile broke out, lighting up her whole face with those beautiful teeth that delighted whatever corner of humanity she happened to turn them toward on those rare times when she switched on the high beam. "Hey, Willis," she called, "thanks for being so great about the protest assignments. I think we've really got the stories worked out perfectly, with every angle covered just right." She waited, still smiling. For an instant he felt his triumph go sour, but not for long. "Thanks, Connie. I may have picked up another piece that'll make it even better." The smile began to crumble but he didn't see the demolition because he moved on quickly toward Sy's office.

It was empty, the door standing open, but the smell of cigar smoke was so heavy that Willis knew Sy had just left. His jacket was flung over the television set, so he hadn't left the building. Suddenly Willis was struck by the contrast between this office and Bushey's. Seymour's had no more personal items than the chief's—no photos, no plaques, no diplomas, no handmade ashtrays or decorations. But it did have a personality, an identity that told you a lot about the person who occupied the space. There might as well have been a sign saying This Person Has A Cluttered Mind, but it was just as obvious that the clutter, rather than being a burden, made the person comfortable. Mostly the clutter was paper, or paper products—books, magazines, scattered sheets of copy paper, and, most of all, piles of newspapers. In a glancing inventory, Willis spotted the flags of a least a half dozen different newspapers. He leaned on the doorframe and lit a cigarette. If someone else moved into this office, it would take him weeks, maybe years, to get rid of Sy's presence. Moving into Bushey's office would be like renting a hotel room.

"Sizing it up?"

Willis wheeled around in blind panic, so startled that he choked on his cigarette smoke. Seymour was a foot away, standing with a questioning half smile on his face.

"No," Willis finally managed to say. "No, I was just waiting for you, but I was a little afraid to go in for fear I'd get lost in this jungle."

Sy brushed past him and sat down at his desk. "What's up? Connie and Ron say they've got solid stories on the protest." He looked up at Willis, raising his eyebrows.

Willis stepped into the office and then turned around and closed the door, a signal that always snapped heads around in the newsroom. Sy didn't comment but he lowered his head into the top-of-the-eyeballs position that meant "This better be good."

"This wasn't a protest," Willis said. "Or, at least, it wasn't just a protest. It was a trap." He paused but Sy didn't say anything, although he was listening closely.

"You know the Winslow gang? The bunch that killed the New Jersey cop?"

"Sure," Sy said. "And I know they're supposed to have a Vermont connection. What about them?"

"Well, the cops, or rather, the FBI and maybe the Treasury guys too had information that Winslow and his gang were going to be here today. They were supposed to be in the march or deliver something to someone or, anyway, make an appearance here today during the protest. The town was crawling with federal agents. They had helicopters out at the state police barracks and they expected to make a really big bust."

Willis stopped but Sy still showed no sign of interrupting, so he went on, laying it out the way he had planned on the walk back from the police station. "The feds have been sneaking into town for the past four or five days, a few at a time so no one would notice. They brought the choppers in one at a time at night and kept them behind the garages at the state police barracks.

"They thought Winslow was going to meet some woman here, but I don't know exactly why. I'm not sure the cops—I mean, the feds—knew exactly why. You know, he and three others are wanted for robbing three banks in addition to killing the Jersey trooper. Jesus, apparently that was a bloody deal; they shot him in the face with a sawed-off 12-gauge when he stuck his head in their car.

"Anyway, they're really after these guys. It's a nationwide manhunt and it's been going on for two years. Vermont is one of the places they know Winslow has turned up. He's got some sort of connection to a commune, or maybe more than one.

"They say they're using the money from the banks to finance anti-war stuff, the Weathermen maybe, and maybe some of the violence on campuses. Christ, I had no idea this Winslow thing was such a big operation. I didn't realize it was tied into the anti-war movement, did you?"

"I knew the police said it was," Sy said. "But as far as I know, they haven't even proved that Winslow or anybody associated with him killed the trooper or robbed anything. All I've read is that he's the main suspect and they can't find him. Did you hear something else?"

Willis shook his head. He didn't know what to say. An image of Bushey's face sprang into his mind and, suddenly, protecting their deal was more important than keeping Sy's attention. Seymour said, "Go on. What happened to the trap?"

"Nothing," Willis said. "The feds figure Winslow got wind of it or maybe just changed his mind. They seemed pretty sure that at one time he was planning on being here.

"In fact, it seems just possible that the whole protest was set up to get him here. At least, some people think so. Some people think the feds really bungled the whole thing, that even if Winslow could have been pulled into such a trap, they blew any chance by turning it into such a massive operation. I mean, helicopters and fifty-five federal agents, plus the locals and state police. That seems like a pretty heavy assault to catch two or three guys, even if they did kill a cop."

Sy leaned back in his chair. "Fifty-five feds? It sounds as though you have a pretty good source, or at least plenty of details. What else do you know about the trap?"

"I've got half a notebook full of details," Willis said. "I know just about everything except why Winslow didn't show up." He stopped and leaned forward slightly toward Sy "But this has got to be a source story. I mean, I can't say where I got it." He wondered if Sy would press him. He knew he wouldn't block the story, but he might insist on Willis telling him who the source was. Most editors he'd worked for would have done that.

"Well," Sy said, "have you confirmed any of it? Can you confirm it?"

"Maybe," Willis said. "I'm sure that Isham, the local FBI guy, won't confirm anything. But I think the governor's guy, Cramer, will if he knows how much I already have — and if I protect him. I thought I'd call him after I told you about it. But even if he doesn't, what're you worried about? I've got this solid. I know it's right."

"What makes you think the governor's office was involved? He hasn't been too friendly with the federal government since March."

"They had to have been. You can't send that many federal agents into a state without consulting the governor. Hell, even J. Edgar wouldn't do that. Besides, you told me that a busload of troopers was loaded and ready to send down here."

"Okay," Sy said. "How about the locals? Bushey? Can he confirm anything?"

Willis shifted in his seat but he didn't shift his eyes. "Maybe," he said. "But don't count on it." The questioning made him edgy, but he was pretty sure Sy wouldn't stop the story. Seymour had been faulted plenty for being too reckless, but no one had ever accused him of being too timid about publishing a story, particularly a political story.

"Okay," Seymour said. "Call Greenberg and Connie and Ron in here, will you? I want you to tell them what you've got so we can plan these stories. Oh, and Merle too. Bring him in."

Willis stood up and started out but Sy called him back. "It's a good story," he said, "but something stinks about it. We're being used. Of course, when someone gives you a story like this, they're always using you. What troubles me is that I don't know how or why we're being used. I expect they're using us to get at Winslow, but I can't quite figure out how. Anyway, write your story but keep your eye out for what's behind it."

Willis turned again to leave, but Seymour stopped him again. "One more thing," he said. "Tell Bushey that I said we don't owe him a goddam thing. Nothing."

Willis opened his mouth to object, but Sy stopped him. "Just tell him, all right?" He turned his back to Willis, turned on the television set, and sat down to watch the beginning of the local news while Willis rounded up the others.

When they had all packed into the office there was hardly room for anyone to move. Seymour and Willis had the only two chairs that weren't piled full of papers, so the others stood jammed into each other. Sy continued to watch the news with the sound turned down very low until the first commercial, then he told Greenberg to switch it off and said, "They led with the protest and said they'll have some footage later, but it didn't seem like much of a story judging from the headline." He looked around at the others.

"I called you in here so Willis could tell you what he found out. It'll change the way we had planned to handle the stories. Go ahead, Willis."

He quickly told them the essential facts he had given Seymour, leaving out the source part and ending by saying he believed it was the largest contingent of federal agents ever assembled in Vermont.

"Well," Greenberg said, "that's a hell of a story. We'll have to lead with that and drop the other stories out of the same headline. I think we ought to banner it, don't you, Sy?"

"Wait a minute." It was Connie, and everyone turned to look at her standing just inside the door. "Not so fast here. What's the story anyway? What really happened about this federal agent deal? Nothing. They were here, or at least someone told Willis they were here, but none of us saw them and neither did anybody else. What's the big deal?" She paused, directing her look to Greenberg. "This sounds to me like a sidebar. The main story is still Ron's. The protest. That's the story here, not some phantom trap for someone who never even showed up."

She looked around but no one spoke up. "Besides," she said, "what do we really know here? Just that someone—we're not saying who, I gather—someone says these federal agents were in town. Big deal. Ron's lead is that the so-called peace rally was really a set-up for a politician who got the clergy to do his dirty work for him. That's obviously a better story. Bud, you said yourself that was a great story. Even my sidebar is better that this other might-have-been tale."

Connie looked to Ron and then to Merle for support, but Seymour cut in. "Connie," he said, "you surprise me. Don't you think you're being a little parochial? I thought you were the one who always complained that we paid too much attention to local angles. Remember the other night when you were arguing with Greenberg? 'There's a big world out there,' you said."

She started to protest, but Seymour waved her off and continued. "We've got to be careful not to let our personal — parochial, I mean — interests get in the way of news judgment. What Willis has got is a story about the federal government coming to town in a big way to trap one of the nation's ten most wanted criminals. A few hours ago this town had an army of armed men hanging off rooftops and lurking in shop doorways. For a while today, we were the focus for a covert law enforcement operation trying desperately to capture a dangerous gang. And you don't think that's a lead story?"

He looked around at the others. "Connie," he said with a small smile, "I'm afraid your perspective is slipping."

Willis wondered if she would swear at him, but it was quickly evident that she was speechless. Her face bunched up with a rage that made her helpless. Everyone was watching her but only Merle spoke. "Sy," he said, "wait a minute." His eyes blinked rapidly and his hands twitched as though they didn't know whether he wanted them to be down at his sides or raised in front of himself. "Wait a minute. I read a few weeks ago in *The Nation* that they really don't have any evidence on Winslow. They suggested the feds made up the whole thing. That they were covering up some sort of police scandal in New Jersey and they were just trying to pin something on anti-war activists. I mean, Jesus, maybe this is just part of the cover-up. Maybe they're just using us?"

"Well, you could be right, Merle," Sy said. "It's a bit far-fetched, but you could be right. But so what? It's still a good story and it's still the story that's going to lead the front page of this newspaper in the morning." He looked toward Ron and then at Connie. She had recovered and stood motionless but composed. "These are all good stories. All of you just write your own pieces. Greenberg will figure out how to play them and I'll make sure you have all the space you need."

He looked slowly at each of them in turn, impartial and imperious as a trial judge. "Go ahead," he said softly, and they filed out of his office.

As usual, Seymour personally made the final inspection of Page One before the composing room hustled it down to the pressroom. He reread every headline and caption, checked the date and volume number, and finally signaled the nervous apprentice that he could take it away. They were a half hour beyond the final deadline for getting the page to the pressroom and Rocky was glowering from his straight-backed throne, gently slapping the pica rule on the metal desk in time to some primitive rhythm inside his own head. The final page check was the right of the editor, as inalienable to Rocky as the rights of man. But he didn't have to like it.

Sy turned away and left the composing room without acknowledging Rocky, a ritual of aggression as clear as a dog peeing on a fence post, and Rocky's ritualistic reply was to snap off the bright overhead lights before Sy reached the doorway.

The newsroom was empty and Sy assumed everyone had hurried off to make last call, and he was surprised to notice some relief that he wouldn't have to have a drink with Willis or any of the others. At the same time, he also felt a twist of anger because they would certainly be plotting and scheming about the union. Sy was so tired the anger couldn't rise very high, though, and its ugly taste was quickly neutralized by his satisfaction over the paper. He wouldn't know for sure until he could get the whole thing printed and in his hands, but he had a feeling it would be the kind of newspaper you always intended to make but rarely did.

Sy checked the *Times* wire then flopped into his chair to wait for the press to rumble into life. He had waited here hundreds of nights, alone in the late-hour stillness, yet he never could be sure whether he heard or felt the press start. Sometimes the thrill of anticipation seemed to have been muted by the years, but not this night. He knew this paper was going to be just what he would have wanted it to be when he came to work that day if he could have known then what news he was going to have. It was going to look and read exactly as a newspaper should. Putting out a newspaper was like preparing a multicourse meal without knowing beforehand what you had in the larder, and most days the final result was stew, usually filling and often nutritious but rarely elegant and never perfect.

Sy felt one burp of resentment that everyone else in the newsroom would rush off to plot rather than waiting for this masterpiece, but it didn't last long. He had started the day too early and was just too exhausted. Then, suddenly, he was aware of the tremor in the floor and the low moan in his ears, and he moved quickly through the newsroom, checking the supply of paper in the wire machines and Photofax and turning off lights.

Eric and another filthy apprentice were grabbing great armfuls of first-run throwaways as they piled up on the conveyor. Nine-Fingers was bent over the stream of papers as they poured out of the folder, checking every tenth or twelfth paper until he found one in full register with even ink distribution and correct margins on every page. Sy waited on the other side of the conveyor until the foreman motioned that he had hit a run that passed his inspection, then he snatched two papers out of the line now coming off the press faster and faster. He thumbed hurriedly through the entire forty-eight pages, then left the building through the mailroom, passed the loading dock where the first bundles were beginning to pile up, and into the still May night.

He walked slowly back to his place, holding the warm papers under his left arm, free for the moment of thoughts about the union, Fletcher, or jerks like McNally. Instead, he brooded on newspapering until a nearly forgotten line popped into his head: "It is immoral not to tell." It might have been Camus; he wasn't sure. In any case, that sentiment would make telling downright godlike.

He opened the small door opening off Main Street into his building and paused for a second at the narrow stairway before turning to his right down a dingy, darkened hallway. They called it an elevator but it really was a freight lift installed in the old feedstore in 1918, the year he was born. Sy knew how tired he was because he almost never used the elevator. In the first place, it only ran from the basement to the second floor, which meant he had to hike up the last flight to his place anyway. Besides, the thing was so slow he could walk up faster, even if it was parked at the first floor when he pushed the button.

Two facing sides of the lift were barred steel gates that swung open fully to allow cargo loading from inside the building or from the alleyway outside, and the other two walls were heavy wooden planks chipped and gouged by God knows what sort of pre-tractor farm implements. Sy clanged open the gate and stepped into the lift, his heart speeding up a notch as it always did since the true reason he didn't use the thing was because he was afraid of it. A single lightbulb shone from the ceiling, but whatever comfort the light gave was taken away by its dimness, which did not inspire confidence in the reliability of the electricity that ran the lift. The only sign of mechanization came from a plaque containing three unmarked buttons that protruded slightly from one of the plank walls.

He knew that state law required regular inspections of elevators, even though he had never seen any certificate on this one, so Sy took it on faith that the thing was powerful enough to deliver a single man safely since it was installed to hoist and lower feed bags and heavy equipment. His mistrust, he realized, was aimed more at himself than the machine. During the torturously slow ascent, he often had a nerve-rattling urge to get out of the cage. Only an act of extreme self-control prevented him from flinging back the iron gate as it slid inch by inch past the brick wall of the shaft.

Safely inside his own place, Sy took off his windbreaker, dropped the two papers beside the big chair, and crossed to the kitchen to make a stiff drink. As he settled into the chair, finally ready to read his newspaper, he heard the large old clock in the other room strike three times. There were no other distractions.

CHAPTER SIX
Tuesday, June 4, 1968

Willis raced down the four flights two steps at a time, eager to get outside but unwilling to let the elevator's permanent stink of sour milk spoil the smell of June that had flooded through the open window into his room.

"Hey, Ernie," he shouted as he burst into the lobby, "figure up my bill. I'm moving out next Monday."

"Congratulations," Ernie said without turning away from the television. "It ain't hard to figure. Fifty bucks a week, $8 per night for a part week. Smart guy like you, you can probably even do it yourself. Plus 3 percent for the governor."

When the picture turned into an Avis commercial, he finally swiveled around and stood up to his full five-foot stature. "No charge for the bimbo."

Willis blushed despite his best effort, then compounded his discomfort by mumbling, "What bimbo?"

Ernie's leer spread into an even nastier sneer. "The one that came down from the fourth floor at seven the other morning," he said, inclining his small round head toward the elevator. "There's only you and George up there, and that blonde sure as shit didn't spend the night with him."

"You sure do know how to make your guests welcome, Ernie. Does the boss know what a good desk clerk you are?"

Ernie turned his head and looked like he would spit but evidently decided not to. "That bastard don't know nothing. He can't even remember my name. But it don't matter anyhow because who else would take this shitty job?" He added as an afterthought, "You want it?"

"No, thanks," Willis said. "I've got one. I am leaving here on Monday morning, though. I've rented a place on the lake."

"Like I said, congratulations," Ernie said as he turned away.

Willis was walking toward the door but he turned back. "Ernie, I'm also going to buy a car. I want something that runs okay but doesn't cost much. Where should I go?"

"Cheap but good, eh? Try the wishing well."

"Huh?"

"Christ, how should I know where to buy a fucking car? If I had a car, I wouldn't be stuck in this shithole."

Ernie had managed to damper Willis's rising good spirits, but they soared again a few steps away from the Uptown. The weather was perfect and the mountains were glorious in the sunshine. He didn't hurry, but as he passed the bank the clock clicked to eleven. Shit, he'd be late; Sy had said the meeting with the publisher was at eleven.

Willis had never met with the publisher. Five months on the job and he had only spoken to him as they passed in the hall or on the rare occasions when he ventured into the newsroom to see Sy. The old guy seemed okay enough, but how the hell could you tell? It seemed like Seymour was a shield, a sort of barrier that kept the publisher once removed from the people who worked for him.

This meeting was sort of mysterious too. Sy had just said the two of them would meet with Manny at eleven. He didn't give any reason. Willis had a vague notion that it might have something to do with a promotion. Sy had hinted at something like that a few days earlier, but he wouldn't say what he had in mind. The idea troubled Willis. He could use the money but not if it meant taking some kind of editing job. This beat, this floating reporter assignment, couldn't be better. He had the whole damn state and no limits on stories. In fact, he suspected that Seymour liked it when he strayed over into the turf of the statehouse bureau guys. It pissed them off, of course, but what the hell did he care as long as Sy didn't mind? Seymour more or less encouraged such encroachment, even ran some interference, and sometimes over a drink he laughed at the "creative tension" when Willis got a good state political story.

Willis, now walking briskly, decided the meeting more likely was about covering the national conventions. Why would the publisher, who barely even knew his name, meet with him about a promotion? He might be interested in the conventions, though. Sy had said they would cover both parties in August, and he had hinted that Willis could go to Chicago with the Democrats. Today was primary day in California and maybe the publisher wanted to talk politics. That was all he had ever talked about to Willis in their awkward chance encounters.

As he turned in at the paper's entrance, he suddenly thought with horror, Oh Christ, maybe he wants to talk about union stuff? The union was a problem Willis kept pushing ahead of himself without figuring out what he was going to do about it.

He hated the idea of joining. Hell, he hated the idea of joining anything. Besides, he had worked in union shops and it seemed to him what it really meant was that the competent people carried the lazy bastards who would rather bitch than work. At the Texas paper, the newspaper guild was run by clerks and fools who counted on the newsroom to get them good contracts but otherwise ignored the newspeople. Organizing was all right for the pressroom and the composing room, but in the white-collar jobs, the union just seemed to gum up the works at a newspaper.

But he couldn't say all that, of course. Christ, being anti-union was as bad as being racist. Besides, it certainly was true that nobody working in this newsroom made enough money. He didn't know about Seymour, but he knew that even Greenberg barely got by and then only with his wife working part-time. The pay for reporters was ridiculously low, but they all knew that if they quit, the paper could fill their jobs before they even got out the front door. Sy once told him he had fifteen job applications a week. He'd gone to a couple of union meetings, mostly to keep Connie off his back, and he had been impressed by Carmoli. This union seemed to be different from the boss-ridden locals he had always dealt with on stories or at other papers, and Vince was not so much an organizer as a real leader who believed in what he was doing and made others believe too.

The whole thing seemed like a waste of time and effort, though, when what Willis really wanted to do was find and write great stories. This state, this backwater of poor dairymen, small shopkeepers, and clean politics, somehow seemed to be a gold mine of good stories. He had a half dozen ideas in his notebook that he hadn't even had time to start on because other important stories kept cropping up. Willis couldn't explain it, but in this place he just seemed to have a Midas touch for news, real news, important stuff that was interesting now and would have an even bigger impact on the state later, sometimes years later. And when his story splashed on the front page today, by tomorrow it would be causing ripples throughout the state's power structure from the governor on down. Best of all, of course, was that these were the kind of stories Sy loved and he made them even more important by the way he played them in the paper and by his enthusiasm.

Willis turned the corner and stopped at the open door to the publisher's office. He raised his hand to knock on the doorjamb just as Sy raised his head, and their eyes met briefly before the other two noticed Willis. Shit, Willis thought, right now Sy looks about as enthusiastic as the hangee at a lynching.

"Come in," Manny said. "Come in, Willis. This is Ted McNally." Only then did he realize there weren't enough chairs in his office.

"Oh, I'm sorry, Willis. Would you mind dragging in another chair? There's one down the hallway."

Willis was glad for the brief escape. He didn't know what was going on in there, but suddenly all his defense systems were on alert. Sy had mentioned this McNally guy, some sort of lawyer and labor expert. Looks more like an Ivy League, Kennedy-type politician, Willis thought.

* *
*

Sy almost never had hangovers and he didn't think he had had that much to drink, but today he had all the symptoms. His head ached dully, his stomach churned, his mouth was sour, and his mind was staggering around aimlessly, searching for something to hold onto. Maybe he was getting sick. Or maybe he was allergic to McNally. It was a mildly amusing idea, but it wouldn't hold water because he felt this way before he got to the office, when he didn't even know McNally was in town.

He had been in town three times in less than three weeks, but Sy had found frequent contact didn't make him like McNally any better. He remembered with some bitterness how pleased everyone had been when competing airlines began early morning commuter runs between New York and Burlington. That's what they call progress, Sy thought. Now McNally and his tribe can get here by nine in the morning, sack the place by noon, and be back in Manhattan in time for a leisurely late lunch. Real progress: New York now can control not only the national news outlets but the provincial ones as well.

Mencken probably could do justice to the idea, but Sy couldn't, at least not now, not with his brain writhing in pain. He slumped back further in his chair and closed his eyes while Willis was shaking hands with McNally and getting settled into his borrowed chair.

Manny cleared his throat. "If you're still with us, Sy, why don't you tell Willis why we're here."

"Well," he said, sitting up straighter, "we're gathered here today to find a seat for Mr. Willis. That is, we're here to raise him to a new level. In short, to promote him." God, he thought, cut it out. This is not Willis's fault.

"Sorry for the lame joke, Willis. I guess I'm a little hungover." He remembered that Willis was not among the group still in the newsroom when the paper went to press last night and he wondered where he had been. Without looking at Manny or McNally, he went on. "We really are here to offer you a promotion. One that you clearly have earned, by the way."

Manny nodded and McNally fidgeted in his chair, glancing at his watch. "We want you to be state editor," Sy said.

Willis looked from Sy to the publisher, then to McNally. Finally, he said, "I'm not sure what that means. We don't have a state editor now, unless I've missed something. What's the job? Do you mean I wouldn't be writing anymore?"

"No," Sy said quickly. "In fact, you basically would keep on doing just what you do now, reporting and writing on statewide stories. The editor part is just . . . well, just—"

McNally broke in. "You would be the editor who supervised state stories. It's really quite simple. As state editor, you would be in charge of statewide coverage; in other words, you'd be in charge of the same stories you're doing now but with official duties over that coverage. See?"

Willis looked puzzled. "Would anyone else be covering statewide stories?"

"No," McNally said. "Just you. But if anybody else did, you would be the editor for those stories. Working with Sy, of course."

"What about the statehouse bureau?" Willis asked.

Sy broke in. "That's a separate operation. There's a bureau chief there and it's just capitol coverage, state government."

"Right," McNally said. "You and the bureau chief would be equal, only your title would be editor."

"I see," Willis said with a grin that might be called sly. "I think I'm getting it. What would this mean for the union?"

He had asked the question to Sy, but McNally leaned back in his chair and cleared his throat again, a cocky outfielder waving off his teammates and mutely signaling, "I've got this one." Looking closely at Willis, he said, "Well, this promotion would mean you were ineligible for the union. You would be considered part of management and thereby excluded from the vote next month."

He paused, but when Willis just nodded, McNally continued. "It also would mean a pay raise for you. I'll let Mr. Monrose tell you about that in a minute. First, though, I want to make it absolutely clear that this has nothing to do with the current effort to organize the nonunion departments of this newspaper. That is a separate, and a totally unrelated, undertaking. All we're doing here today is recognizing your work and offering you a new job that is commensurate with your abilities and your achievements."

He recrossed his legs and laced his hands together with his long fingers, ending the speech. "Manny?"

Sy knew there was a long list of normal, routine human activities that Manny hated and avoided whenever possible. One was any form of public speaking and another was any discussion of money. But he's trapped now, Sy thought. There's no escape, unless he bolts for the door.

"Yes, well," Manny began, "as for your salary . . . uh, Sy suggested . . . that is, we agreed that with your promotion, you should have a pay increase of . . . uh, uh . . . of, let's see, Sy, wasn't that 15 percent we talked about?"

"That's right," Sy said without any hesitation, although, in fact, Manny had balked at 15 percent and had said he would go up only 10 percent. Now, face-to-face with the victim of his niggardliness, pusillanimity won out over greed.

Sy felt better than he had all day, and for the first time he began to enjoy this real-life farce. McNally looked smugly confident, Manny was still cooling down to his normal pink, and Willis looked like he was about to burst out laughing, probably doing the arithmetic, which Sy had already done. It amounted to a raise of about $35 a week and would make Willis the highest paid reporter at the paper.

"Well," Willis said, "that sounds good to me. Great, in fact. I had just decided to buy a car and rent a place, so I can use the extra money. I've never been an editor but I suppose I can get used to it."

No one said anything, so he stood up to leave. "As for the union, I was going to vote against it anyway, but don't tell them." He grinned. "This will make it easier. I assume all editors and bureau chiefs will be excluded?"

"That's right," McNally said. "We won't tell anybody about this yet, and I hope you won't. We're preparing a list and, unless the union objects, everyone on the list will be excluded. If they do object, the NLRB will decide; but don't worry, I doubt it will be much of a problem for you."

Willis started for the door, then turned around and asked Sy, "When does this new deal began? I want to get a green eyeshade and sleeve garters."

Again, McNally jumped in to supply the answer. "We're going to give them our list next week. But your promotion doesn't have to wait. In fact, I think it ought to be effective immediately. Today."

He stood up and stuck out his hand, adding through a big smile, "So go ahead and buy your eyeshade. You'll look good as an editor."

***

When Willis had left, McNally quietly shut the door and straightened the creases in his suit jacket, adjusting the sleeves to expose a precise ribbon of starched cuff. "I don't think that could possibly have gone any better, do you?"

Sy thought, smugness, thy name is lawyer.

"Well," McNally began, "Fletch is driving me to the airport and I have to meet him in a couple of minutes."

Fletch? Oh brother.

"But while we're here, Sy, I just want to remind you how important it is for us not to give these union people any opening to bring in the NLRB investigators."

Sy looked at him blankly.

"We've heard," McNally said, motioning to show that he was including Manny and not just using the royal *we*, "that you had some sort of confrontation with Connie Bridges the other night."

"Goddam," Sy began, "now you've got spies in the newsroom to—"

McNally broke in, his voice calm and his mouth showing a fake smile, "See, Sy? That's just the sort of thing we're worried about. Making accusations like spying and swearing at people—that's the type of behavior that could cost us this whole ballgame."

Sy's head throbbed. "You mean I've got to let Connie Bridges or whoever else is with the union run the goddam newsroom? Just sit by quietly while they take over. Is that right?"

"Of course not. But you have got to stop being paranoid. Nobody is taking over your newsroom. The quickest way to make that happen is for you to bring in the NLRB. They'll take over and there won't be a thing you can do about it."

McNally looked to Manny, who was staring intently out the window.

"Listen, Sy," McNally said soothingly, "we know it's not easy to keep cool in these situations. It's important and we're counting on you."

The solicitous condescension was even more awful than the self-righteousness, but it also was smothering in a way that kept Sy from responding, like foam sprayed on a fire.

"Anyway," McNally said in a normal tone, "so far we're doing okay. Indeed, I think we've developed a good list of exclusions that the union probably won't challenge, so we're right on track."

He walked to the door. "I'll be back in a few days. Keep in touch, Manny. And I'll talk regularly with Fletch."

******

When he was gone, Manny and Sy sat in silence, not looking at each other. Two minutes or more went by before Manny looked up and said, "How do you think the California primary is going to turn out?"

He reached across his desk to retrieve the ashtray and, with a look in his face that Sy judged could come only from disgust, he carefully dumped the two cigarette butts into the wastebasket, then put two of his three pipes back into the ashtray. He fished a packet of imported tobacco out of his pocket and began to fill the favored pipe, taking obvious pleasure in the process. Smoking was a ritual for Manny and he made it look spiritual and sensuous at the same time. Sy relaxed in his chair. Watching Manny prepare his pipe and smoke it was like witnessing a ceremony, like observing a priest of eudaemonism.

When he smoked, it was as though he had suddenly gone away for a moment, temporarily entirely alone. First he decided which pipe to use. Then he chose between the three pouches of tobacco he always carried. When he had a pouch in hand, he peered into it and with finger and thumb stirred and picked through the tobacco, slowly adding a pinch at a time to the bowl of the pipe. Layered until it formed a tiny mound over the top, he then tamped it down with his index finger, turning the pile into a shallow hole. Finally, the stem clenched in his teeth, he fired it up with one of the kitchen matches that he always carried loose in his vest pocket or, in warm weather, in his shirt pocket and that he usually struck inelegantly with his thumbnail, unless some more satisfying striking post happened to be available. Curious, Sy thought, that he didn't carry some special striking object since the feel of the match, the sound of the scratch, and the sudden flare were obviously part of the ceremony.

At the end of the first full inhale-exhale cycle, Manny returned to the world, now partially screened by smoke. "I expect if Kennedy doesn't win tonight, he'll be all done."

"That's what they're saying," Sy nodded. "The Oregon primary wounded him much worse than the Kennedy people let on." He looked closely at Manny. "Are you going to support a candidate before the convention?"

Manny puffed thoughtfully. "I never do, as a usual rule, in primary fights. Except sometimes in state elections." He chuckled. "Especially when the foolish Republicans look like they're about to nominate some right-wing loser." He puffed. "But I've been thinking about coming out for Humphrey."

Sy threw up his hands. "Why in the world would you do that? It would be the same as endorsing Johnson. And that's the same as supporting this stupid war. Why not at least wait until after Humphrey is nominated. Then the choice will be him or Nixon, and God knows that'll be a tough one to call."

"Yeah, that's why I haven't done anything yet. I don't want to get locked into supporting Humphrey in November."

Sy was surprised. "You might really endorse Nixon?"

Manny seemed a little uncertain, then he looked at his wristwatch. Sy checked his too and was surprised to see that it was a quarter to twelve. Manny said, "Are you in a hurry? If you've got fifteen minutes, I'd like to talk this thing out a little; frankly, I just keep going around in circles in my own mind. Maybe talking will help me clear up my thinking."

Sy had one instant of confusion, suddenly unsure whether Manny was talking about the presidential campaign or the union campaign. Was this about Humphrey and Nixon, or Connie and McNally? Then he realized that of course it was the political situation. This was just like dozens of conversations he had had with Manny, covering countless hours in which they talked, argued, speculated, gossiped about politics, quoted from books and poems, and smoked.

He relaxed but decided against fishing out a cigar—too early, and his head still hurt.

Manny relit his pipe, a part of the ritual that he always repeated many times. "It's beginning to seem to me that this war has spread way beyond what it means in Vietnam and is poisoning nearly everything else too. I mean, this country is divided in a way I have never seen. There's no political middle anymore. Four years ago, Johnson tarred Goldwater as the extremist, but now it looks like everybody is an extremist. You've got to be on one side or the other—about everything."

Sy nodded. "Yeah, it's that way even in Vermont politics. Hell, even in local politics. At town meetings this year, every town fought out nearly every article on the ballot. Sometimes it was natives against the new people. Sometimes young against old. Sometimes it seemed to be rich versus poor. Whatever the division, they were at each other's throats on every issue.

"Remember what Lincoln said? 'Thought is forced from old channels into confusion. Confidence dies, and universal suspicion reigns.' That's what war does when the people are divided over it."

"You left out a line," Manny corrected. "'Deception breeds and thrives.'"

Sy suspected Manny might have mixed up the quotes, but he didn't challenge him because when it came to Sandburg, Manny was at least as sure-footed as he was. He felt on surer ground with politics—or with contemporary politics, anyway. "Well, goddam it, you wouldn't support Nixon as a way to end the division? He's made a career out of trying to divide the nation."

"I'm not sure," Manny said, "I've been thinking—"

Sy interrupted, "Come on, Manny. You were one of the first publishers in the country to condemn Joe McCarthy. Nixon is just a McCarthy with the sweats and without the populism. And what about the George Polk case? And Helen Gahagan Douglas? You blasted him for weeks on that."

Sy stood up and began to pace. "Manny, for God's sake, think of all the editorials you've written about the need to have honorable government. How could you support Nixon?"

"Well," Manny said quietly, "that's just the point I've been mulling over. Maybe there's no way to end this war with honor. If that's right, then maybe only a Nixon can preside over defeat with dishonor. The problem with Aiken's formula—declare victory and get out—is that to cut and run is dishonorable by definition. Maybe there comes a time when honor has to give way to something else."

Manny puffed. "The way I see it, Nixon is not an extremist so much as an opportunist. Have you listened to what he's saying about China? He sounds more like Bill Meyer than Joe McCarthy." His pipe had gone out again and he relit it. "I think the country is turning against Vietnam and that it will keep turning more and more. Nixon will see that—already has seen it, I expect—and he'll do what he has to do to stay with the country. Humphrey can't do that. He's sold his soul to Johnson to get the nomination, and that means he can't ever turn against this war.

"And I'm finding Kennedy pretty hard to stomach. He's a throat-cutting opportunist and I wouldn't trust him any further than I could throw him. You saw him when he was attorney general. You never knew where he'd come down on civil rights because he was scared to death of the Southern bigots. And J. Edgar Hoover."

Sy began to speak, but Manny held up his hand. "Hold on a minute. I'm trying to work this out as I go.

"George and Lola stopped in the other day." Puff. "He said he wasn't campaigning; just a visit." Wry grin and puff. "He also said he believes Nixon is the best hope for getting out."

Sy burst in. "So what? You know damn well that Aiken has never liked Humphrey. You're the one who told me about the time he wrote a letter telling him to shut up and not talk so much on the floor of the Senate. Besides, Nixon and Humphrey aren't the only choices, you know. What about Gene McCarthy?"

That idea didn't get more than a flicker of recognition as Manny waved it away with the match spent in his latest doomed effort to keep the pipe lighted. "He's rather interesting as an unusual politician, and that was a fine speech he made the other night in Oregon. I said so in an editorial. But how could you ever know what he'd do next? And try to imagine him as commander in chief. It would be like making Pierre the emperor of Russia. Even Tolstoy wouldn't have risked such a thing."

"Well then," Sy said, "give Bobby Kennedy another look. I know you think he's slippery, but God Almighty, would you really trust Tricky Dick any further?"

"It's not just a question of trust. Actually, I don't trust any of them, I guess. The truth is, I just don't like Bobby Kennedy. I know they say he's smarter than his brother and that he's already a better senator than Jack ever was. But I can't get over the way he disappointed all those supporters after leading them on for months; said he wouldn't run for fear of splitting the party, then turned around and jumped in after McCarthy's surprising showing in New Hampshire. All that noble serve-my-country stuff just makes you want to gag when it comes out of his mouth. And did you see him on television with the dog on the Oregon beach? What a sham."

Manny snorted out a self-mocking laugh. "So I guess in the end, politics really is all personal, isn't it? I don't like him, so I won't vote for him." He paused and his face began to glow. "No, by God, that's not all there is either. This country is in a crisis, and there's a right way to fix it and there's a wrong way."

Sy was surprised by the sudden shift. Manny had gone into a new mood.

"They're all opportunists in their own way. The Nixons and the Gene McCarthys and Bobby Kennedys. The George Wallaces and even the Nelson Rockefellers and the John Lindsays. But it damn well does matter which one we choose.

"The ones that worry me the most are those that would play to the forces of destruction. The ones who want to tear down everything in the name of moral righteousness."

Sy was getting lost. Was Manny talking about the right or the left? Before he could frame the question, Manny answered it, his face now bright red, his pipe discarded, and his hands waving.

"I'm talking about those who would lead the kids into the streets to protest just for protest's sake. Protest what? I don't know what they want now. Johnson's out and the others have all said they'd end the war if they get elected. What's to protest? Maybe they ought to protest Ho Chi Minh. He hasn't said anything about stopping the war." He was pleased with this thought and he leaned back with a thin smile.

"Why are they protesting?" Sy's voice was too loud, but he went on, even knowing he was off-key because Manny suddenly seemed to be identifying with Lyndon Johnson. "Some of them are out there because they don't want to be the last one killed before they call it off. Some of them protest because they don't think their country ought to be going around the world destroying villages, defoliating jungles, and dropping bombs on babies. And, of course, some of them are out there because they're mad or stupid or just bored. Some of them are so drugged-out they don't know where they are anyway, and some are there just because the others are there. But, Manny, you of all people ought to support their right to be there, to protest just because they want to protest."

Manny didn't exactly recoil, but he looked on with uncomfortable tolerance, as he usually did when Sy was under his own steam. "It's not like our wars, Manny. And these kids are not like us either. I don't really understand what's going on very well myself. But something important is happening. Something's changing that is going to make a real difference to this country. And it's those people out there on the streets who are changing it. Those weird kids. Those boys who don't think fighting is manly. Those girls who think bras and shoes are repressive. I think they're really going to make a difference."

Manny blinked, then blinked again before he said, "Well, I think what they're going to do is cause trouble. Trouble that somebody else will have to fix. Look what they did in Paris last month. The same thing could happen here. They're going to tear down things that people have worked very hard to build. They're attacking institutions and ideas that have made this country great. They have no respect for sacrifices others have made and no respect for property."

His pitch rose and his voice grew strident, prompting Sy to look closely at Manny. He saw a whiteness around his eyes and tiny gray creases in his face that had not been there earlier.

Manny slapped the top of his desk softly. "Well, maybe we ought to blame ourselves more than anybody else. Maybe we've encouraged them to be irresponsible and spoiled. Maybe we've made a mistake in supporting this rebelliousness." He jutted his round chin out slightly and said more slowly and evenly, "But we don't have to keep on making it. And I'm not going to go on with it."

Sy sat back in disoriented puzzlement. Not go on with what?

Manny picked up his pipe and took a hard drag, but there was nothing left to burn and only a dry sucking sound came out.

He looked at his watch again. "Well, Helen will be waiting. Let's talk about this again. If I do write an editorial, I'll probably wait until closer to the conventions."

He started to stand, then sat back down. "One more thing." He looked uncomfortable, like a shy kid about to volunteer in class. "I can see that you don't like McNally very much. And I must say, he's not exactly my type either." He looked out the window. "When he's around, I feel like my shoelaces are untied or like I've forgotten to do something I was supposed to do."

Manny turned again to face Sy. "But I believe Fletcher is right. We need McNally—or somebody like him. And Fletcher researched this. What he found was that McNally is the best in the business.

"I am absolutely determined to beat this union. They've been trying to get control of this paper for years, and now they're using these radicalized kids and this general atmosphere of distrust and dissension to try again."

Sy began to interrupt, but Manny said, "Wait. Just listen. Like him or not, we're going to do what McNally tells us to do. All of us."

He clamped the dead pipe in his teeth, stood up, and headed for the door. Sy didn't move until Manny took his suit jacket off the hook on the back of the door, put it on, and waited, with his hand on the doorknob.

Sy walked slowly back to the newsroom, confused and vaguely disturbed. He was more depressed than angry. What the hell had Manny really been talking about? Did he have some bizarre idea that Sy was supporting the union? What the hell had Fletcher told him?

Later, when he was called on to recount the conversation, Sy's memory mixed the politics and the war talk and the union talk all together. He couldn't remember exactly which of Manny's words had been directed at the protesters and which ones were aimed at the union organizers. When he was asked, he couldn't even say for sure whether he had felt the conversation had been a threat to himself. He knew that in some vague way the talk had been unsettling, but it was impossible to know what Manny had said that upset him. In fact, in trying to reconstruct the conversation, Sy began to suspect that the threat had come not from what Manny had said but from some more sinister place, from something he never spoke but transmitted through a silent medium.

The newsroom was empty, except for Alice, and very quiet. Neither of them spoke as he walked in. He saw his name on a message slip on the corner of her desk and stopped to pick it up. "I was going to take it to your office," she whined. "I haven't had a chance."

*
**

"What do you know about Sy's sex life?" Hank asked with too-careful casualness, glancing into the rearview mirror but not looking at Willis.

"I know everything I want to know," Willis said. "Nothing." He waited, but Hank still didn't look at him. "Why in the hell would anybody want to know more than that?"

Maybe Hank was just trying in his amateurish way to find out what was going on between him and Marlene? Willis knew there was strong interest in the newsroom in their affair, and partly for that reason he had been very secretive about it. Not that there was anything wrong with it. She wasn't married or anything, for Christ's sake. He remembered Ernie's nasty remark.

"You've got to admit it's a little strange," Hank said. "I mean, Seymour's pretty old but not that old, and nobody has ever heard of him dating, or even mention, a woman."

Willis leaned his back against the car door and stared intently at Hank. His springy black hair was pulled back tightly into a luxurious ponytail, leaving his rosy-cheeked, smooth-skinned face fully exposed. A short upper lip kept his mouth in a permanent chipmunk smile and sparkly dark eyes gave the finishing touch to unmarred boyishness. Soon the relentless stare made him uneasy and he took a quick look over at Willis before turning back to the road. Some color rose in his face. "Christ," he said, "it seems like a pretty normal question to me. I mean, is it so surprising that people wonder about his sex life?"

Willis was enjoying Hank's uneasiness although he really liked the kid, and besides, he had been remarkably generous in lending his car. Hell, he could even lay a legitimate claim to information about Marlene since he supplied the car that made it possible for Willis to pursue her at the ski-area bar. And here he was giving up part of his day off to take Willis around looking for a car to buy.

"Well, Ace," he said, "what makes you think I'd know any more than you do about Seymour's sex life? You've been here a lot longer than I have. What have you found out?"

"That's the whole point," Hank said, still a little peevish. "None of us knows a damn thing; he just seems to work all the time. But it seemed like you were spending some time with him. You know, drinking and stuff. I thought maybe you had picked up something, that's all."

"All I can tell you is that I've never seen him with a woman and I've never heard him mention one. No, wait a minute. I did hear something right after I got here. What was it . . ."

He thought in silence for a while, long enough for Hank to turn his head fully in his direction. "Oh yeah," he said finally, "but that came from Merle, not from Sy. Merle mentioned once that years ago Sy had been married or had a steady girlfriend, something like that. I can't even remember if Merle said it was here or before Sy came to this paper."

"Right," Hank said, "I've heard that too, but Merle was speaking about fourth-hand. I don't think he really knows anything either, not firsthand."

Willis thought it was time to change the subject, and since the best defense is a good offense, he said, "How about you? How's your sex life these days? Found any coeds?"

Hank blushed and didn't answer. They drove without speaking for a while. Hank had picked Willis up after his meeting with the publisher and they were headed for a used car lot he knew about on the outskirts of town. Willis had noticed it because of the huge banner that floated over the entryway: All Southern Cars. Nothing Finer.

His initial curiosity had faded when someone explained that "Southern" was a code meant to suggest "no rust" without actually claiming so and thereby risking a false advertisement charge. He had never been on the lot, so when they pulled in, he was surprised by how many cars there were. They were lined up in multiple ranks and he felt instantly lost and helpless. Willis had never had much interest in cars even as a boy and he had owned only a few. Generally, the newspapers had their own fleets, so as long as he was living in cities he avoided what he saw as the unnecessary burden of owning an automobile. It had been one of the never-resolved fights with Sheila, who said she felt trapped without a car.

"Do you know what you want?" Hank said.

"God no," Willis muttered. "This scares the shit out of me. Do you know anything about them? What to look for?"

A guy in a tan suit and a Dick Tracy hat leaned against the wall of a small building with an Office sign over the door. He didn't move when Hank stepped out and began looking around at the line of cars. But when Willis finally got out and moved around the front of Hank's car, the man straightened up and began to walk toward them.

"Morning, boys," he said, but he looked only at Willis. "I'm Felix, but everybody calls me Red." He reached up to sweep off his hat, exposing a bald dome encircled by a faded gray fringe. "I guess you can see why."

Willis noticed the American flag in one lapel and a VFW pin stuck in the other one. "Must be your politics, right?"

The patriot's eyes narrowed. "I don't have any politics. Don't trust any of 'em as far as I could throw 'em."

He motioned to Hank's dirty Volkswagen. "I hope you're not here to try to sell me that little bug 'cause we're not in the buying mood. But if you're looking for a good car, a good American car, you've come to the right place. Like you see, we're loaded. It's a good time to buy, all right."

Hank had started walking down the line of cars and Willis began to follow him. "Well," he said, "I'm thinking about buying a car. But I don't really know what I want. Just something fairly reliable. And cheap."

Red fell in step beside him. "How cheap?'

"I've got about $700."

"We probably could finance something for you. Where're you working?"

Willis didn't answer.

"Seven hundred as a down payment would put you in a pretty good car."

He pointed in the opposite direction from Hank. "How about a four-wheel drive? I've got a Jeep over there that's in good shape that I could let you have for $1,500."

Willis stopped and Red began walking in the direction he had pointed. "You been through a winter up here? If you have, you know how handy a Jeep would be. I remember my first winter. The year after the war. Christ, I spent half my time shoveling out my car."

Willis had followed him even though he had never even driven a four-wheel drive. They stopped at something that looked like a large gray box on wheels. He didn't even know they made a Jeep station wagon.

"This thing will go anywhere," Red said, swinging open the driver's door. "Of course, you pay for the four-wheel drive, but this one is a real deal. I only took it in a couple of days ago."

Willis climbed in. He felt a seat spring jab into his butt. "What year is it?"

"It's a '60," Red said, "but it's been babied. Look it over. I'll just go get the key."

Willis didn't know what to look over. He gripped the steering wheel and peered through the windshield. It felt sort of like a truck.

The passenger's door opened and Hank poked his head inside the Jeep. He looked at the roof and peered into the rear compartment, then he reached down and lifted up the rubber mat on the floorboard. Underneath was another rubber covering which Hank pried up at the upper right corner. When he peeled it back, they were looking down at a rusty floorboard that had a ragged hole the size of a softball.

Hank looked at Willis and shook his head. Red arrived back and held out a key, but Willis said, "I don't think I'm interested in a Jeep. What've you got for $700?"

Red stuffed the key into his pocket, gave Hank a scowling glance, and said, "Well, actually, I just remembered something that might be just what you're looking for. Come on."

He began walking fairly quickly back down the line of cars. When Willis caught up, he said, "This is a '58 Olds 98 that's got a lot of good life left in it. It's big and heavy and it'd give you some good, safe transportation."

They reached the red and white Oldsmobile while Hank was still poking around in the Jeep. "Come on," Red said, "tell your longhaired buddy we'll be back in a few minutes. I want to show you how this Olds performs."

He pulled another set of keys from his other front pocket and jumped into the driver's seat, motioning for Willis to get in the other side. The car was huge and Willis thought, Christ, I'd never be able to park this thing. They roared out of the parking lot, and the tiny drop-off as they entered the street sent the front end of the car bouncing like a pogo stick.

"Good springs," Red said, "and feel that power."

Willis felt the car surge as the automatic transmission shifted through its gears. "Does the radio work?"

"Sure," Red said, but he didn't move to turn it on.

Willis turned the left-hand knob but nothing happened. He looked a question at Red, who was too busy watching the road. After turning several knobs, Willis finally tried pulling out the left-hand knob, and the radio came to life feebly. He was able to pick up only static-broken stations at a half dozen places on the dial. "That's nothing," Red said. "Just the antenna needs tightening. You're going to like this car." He raised his right hand to the roof. "Look at this headroom. I like a car you can ride in without taking off your hat."

When they got back to the parking lot, Hank was sitting in a small black convertible parked right next to the little office. "Here's the car for you, Willis," he called. "A TR3. Triumph."

"That's a nice car, all right," Red said, "if you've got five grand."

Willis felt even more confused than when they started. He was on the verge of saying he'd take the Oldsmobile just to get out of the whole mess, when Hank walked over and said, "You know, Willis, I just remembered something. Why don't we go get some lunch and think it over. We could come back this afternoon."

Red scowled at him again and said, "Who's buying this car, anyhow—you or your bright-eyed buddy?"

Hank never changed his chipmunk grin but Willis got his message. "Well," he said, "I'll think about the Oldsmobile. Maybe we'll come back after lunch."

They climbed back into Hank's Volkswagen and Red walked off stiff-legged back to his office.

"I found his folder on the Oldsmobile," Hank said as they left the lot. "Guess where it came from?"

Willis shrugged.

"Rhode Island."

"Well," Willis said, "that's south of here isn't it?"

Hank said, "I just remembered someone told me about a guy who's supposed to be the best used car dealer in the state. It's about twenty miles, but this guy is supposed to be absolutely honest. It's a one-man show; he buys the cars at auction, does his own mechanic work, and sells them for fair prices. At least, that's what I heard."

"You sound like a shill for a used car salesman," Willis said. "Who told you about him?"

"Well, actually, I heard Vince talk about him. Vince Carmoli. He wasn't really telling me, I just overheard him talking. Apparently, this guy has been selling used cars for twenty years, but he never advertises and never gets any bigger, just what he can work on and sell by himself. The locals go to him Vince said."

Willis was beginning to feel a little panicky. He was starting to wonder if he ought to just forget the whole idea of buying a car. "Okay," he said, "let's check it out. But first let's get some lunch."

Mitch's was crowded as usual and they stopped just inside the door to look for a table. "Christ," Willis said, "every lawyer, banker, dentist, accountant, architect, and bureaucrat in town must be here. I didn't know there were this many suits in the whole goddam state."

"And ugly sports jackets," Hank said. "There's a table back in the back, behind the palm tree." They made their way toward the potted tree, but before they reached it, Willis heard his name being called. It was Bushey and he waved him over.

"Grab the table," Willis said to Hank. "I'll be right there."

"Hello, sport," Bushey said. "You're just the guy I wanted to see. I was going to call you."

Willis stopped, said hello, and stood awkwardly behind an empty chair. He didn't know the man sitting with the chief, but Bushey evidently assumed he did. Finally, the man stood up and stuck out his hand. "I'm Sten Quimby."

"Christ," Bushey said, "you don't know our state's attorney? What kind of super reporter are you?"

"I guess our paths just haven't crossed," Willis said, "but I know who you are. How's the campaign going?"

Quimby, already back in his seat, said, "Great. Couldn't be better." He lowered his head over the plate, leaving Willis staring down at his dark crew cut and the dandruff-sprinkled shoulders of his pale blue jacket.

Bushey said, "Willis, we want to talk to you. Come by my office this afternoon."

"Okay," he said, "what's it about?"

"I'll tell you then," Bushey said. "Sten and I will be in my office at three thirty. Don't be late." He turned back to his plate, and the prosecutor was already loading up his fork, so Willis said, "Okay," and made his way to the table where Hank sat watching him.

"What did the dynamic duo of law enforcement want?"

"I don't have any idea," Willis said. "Bushey just said he wanted to talk later."

"What do you think of Quimby, our drug-busting prosecutor?"

"I think he has bad manners."

"Yeah," Hank said, "and bad taste and bad politics and a bad reputation. But the guys at the statehouse bureau say he's running pretty strong in the race for AG."

"The law-and-order ticket's going to be hard to beat this year," Willis said. "At least, everywhere else it is. Most places that's just a race code, though. I don't see any law-and-order issue up here."

"I think it's more than race," Hank said. "Did you see how that guy at the car lot acted toward me? That was just because I have long hair. It's like the whole country is divided into two sides. Quimby, the Republicans, George Wallace—they're all on one side even if they don't like each other. They support the war and the cops. It's true that they're also racists, but they also hate young people and drugs and hippies and intellectuals and long hair."

Willis laughed. Hank's mouth was just too small to cover all of his teeth, so even when he was being thoughtful and somber his upper front teeth gleamed out of his boyish face.

"Who's on the other side?" Willis asked.

"Everybody else," Hank said. "Everybody who's not screaming for law and order."

"You mean everybody under thirty, right?"

"No. Just look at that protest last month. You said yourself that most of those people were middle-aged or older. And I went to school with some of the loudest law-and-order screamers. The Young Republicans want to bomb Hanoi into the Stone Age. Which is funny, when you think about it, because the Stone Age is where the Young Republicans themselves want to be.

"Hell, look at Quimby over there. He's not much over thirty himself, but he wants to lock up everybody who's not in uniform. Of course, he's just exploiting the political opportunity. God, I hope he doesn't win. Imagine him as attorney general?"

Willis was growing tired of the conversation. He asked, "How about Sy? Which side is he on?"

Hank took a bite of his hamburger and chewed thoughtfully before answering. "You never really know with Sy, do you? One day he'll quote somebody and sound like he's on one side, and the next day he'll use another quote to support the opposite side. You never really know, but I expect the truth is that mostly he just likes arguing. But you can't really tell with him, and lately he's been acting downright weird about everything."

"Yeah," Willis said, "I think it's the union. What do you think about that, by the way?"

Hank looked uncomfortable. "I don't really know." He took another bite. "I signed the card."

"Hell, everybody signed the cards. How're you going to vote?"

Hank looked so pained that Willis thought for a second he might cry. "Listen, Willis, can I talk to you in confidence? I've actually been wanting to talk to you for a long time. But it'll have to be private, okay?"

Willis nodded but he was thinking, shit, I don't want to get into this. Ought to have kept my mouth shut. "Okay," he said. "Private."

"Well," Hank said, "I'm going to vote for the union. But I'm leaving the paper in September. Actually, at the end of August. And I feel a little bad about helping to vote in the union and then bailing out. What do you think?"

"Where're you going?"

"I'm going to law school. George Washington."

Willis was startled. He had assumed Hank had another job because it had not occurred to him that anyone would quit newspapering. He was glad Hank was busy with his hamburger because he didn't want him to see how surprised he was. Finally, he said, "Law school? Why?"

"Actually," Hank said, "I've always planned to go to law school. I've been putting it off as long as I could to get the longest possible deferment from the draft. I've been just ahead of the draft for the past two years, since I got out of college, but now they're about to catch up with me so I'll get another deferment by going to law school."

Willis grinned. The sly little bastard. "How do you know the draft is catching up with you?"

Hank looked actually embarrassed this time, but he didn't duck the question. "My father has friends on our draft board. They told him my name's coming up soon."

He hurried on. "I mean, I really want a law degree. I like working for the paper and I may go back to a newspaper job after law school. But if I do, I'll be in a better position to go with a big paper.

"It seems to me that newspapers need a little more professionalism anyway, don't you think? I mean, the pay is terrible and that's because there are no standards. A lot of reporters don't even have college degrees."

Including me, Willis thought, but he said, "Have you told Sy you're leaving?"

"Well, no." He looked pained again. "I was going to and then this union thing came along. I don't want to let Connie and the others down. I mean, I want to stay at least long enough to vote."

He paused, rubbing a french fry into a little pool of ketchup. "Ron's leaving too. He's going to journalism graduate school. But he hasn't told either."

Willis grinned again. Another crusader for truth and justice—and draft deferment. "So Ron wants more professionalism too. Well, good luck to both of you aces. When's he leaving?"

"Same time. The end of August. He got into Columbia. Did you like it there?"

Willis finished his beer and signaled to the waitress for a check, ignoring the question. "We've got to hurry if we want to see that car dealer. We're going to be late for work as it is, and I need to be at Bushey's office at three thirty."

As they left Mitch's, Hank said, "Remember, what I told you was private. You can't tell Sy."

Willis nodded.

*
**

The second car lot was much smaller than the first, located more than a mile off Route 4 on a small road that wound up into the foothills. There was no sign, just a string of cars lined up on one side of a gas station that stood all alone on the bank of a racing stream. Hank stopped his VW behind the row of cars and they walked together up and down the line, but none of the two dozen vehicles had any prices or other information posted. Finally, when no one had showed up after five minutes, they wandered into the open bay of the gas station. A guy in coveralls was underneath the lift, changing the oil in a pickup truck.

He looked at them pleasantly and nodded, then turned back to the stream of black oil pouring into his giant can. When it had slowed to an occasional drop, he screwed the plug into the oil pan and rolled the can out from under the truck. He wiped his hands, which looked surprisingly clean, on a cloth pulled from his back pocket. "What can I do for you?"

"I'm thinking about buying a car," Willis said. "Are those yours?" He pointed toward the line.

"They are," said the mechanic. "For the time being." He waited for Willis to say more. Finally, Hank piped up. "He's looking for some pretty basic transportation, I think."

The man nodded. "How much were you thinking of spending?" There was no judgment behind the question, or even implied. It was a simple question with a simple answer and obviously a necessary one if they were going to continue the conversation.

"Seven hundred dollars," Willis said, then wondered why he had been so blunt. He glanced at Hank, who was watching closely but who also seemed unusually unguarded.

"Don't have much in that range," the man said, looking down the line of cars. "Most of these are twice that much or more. I can't make any money on cheaper cars."

He looked at Willis for a moment, fully at ease and ready to help if he could and still make a profit. "I go to auctions sometimes and they sometimes have cars in that range. If you want me to look."

Willis liked the guy, or rather, he had a sense that he could trust him. It wasn't so much that he looked at you when he spoke as that he seemed to be speaking totally without guile. Not innocent exactly, or naive, but just plain. That was it. This guy was just plain; what you saw standing before you was what he was and he was perfectly comfortable with it and it would be fine if you were too, but otherwise it didn't matter much one way or another.

"Well," Willis said, realizing that without meaning to he was letting his disappointment show, "I had hoped to get something today. I'm moving, and I'll need a car by Monday."

The man was quiet for a minute, thinking, then he said, "I guess the only thing I have for that much money is that Saab over there. The green one sitting off by itself."

Willis looked over at Hank, who didn't seem to have an opinion, or at least didn't give off any signals.

"What's a Saab?" Willis asked.

"It's a Swedish car. I don't know much about them," the man said. "Some girl from up on the mountain brought this one in. The brakes were gone and she said she just wanted to get rid of it. I told her I didn't really want it, but that I could give her $400. She took it."

The man was walking toward a dusty four-door, dark green car that did have a foreign look—a low-slung body with a hood that slanted downward. "I put in new brakes and I got sort of interested in the car, so I read up a bit. I think it's pretty well built. It's five years old."

He opened the driver's door, which was not locked. Willis went to the other side and Hank opened up a back door. "I didn't even look at the mileage when I bought it. But when I finally looked, the odometer said forty-four thousand miles. Couldn't swear to that, but the engine looks and sounds good enough to be true."

The key was in the ignition and he started the engine. It purred smoothly and quietly. "I've been driving it myself for the last couple of days."

"Hey," Hank said from the back seat. "This is real leather upholstery."

Willis sank into the passenger's bucket seat and reached over to turn on the radio. "Hey Jude" blared out of speakers in the front and back.

"How much do you want?" Willis said.

"Well, I'll tell you," the man said. "I suspect the car's worth quite a lot, but I don't think it'll bring much around here. Don't see many Saabs in Vermont. Guess I'd sell it to you for seven hundred."

Willis looked at Hank, who nodded.

"Okay. I'll buy it. I'll have to go back to the bank. Is it okay if I come back with the money this afternoon?"

"That'll be fine," the man said. "I'll inspect it and put a new sticker on it this afternoon." He turned off the engine and the three of them walked back toward the garage.

"My name's Willis," he said. "I'll be back before you close up."

"That'll be fine," the man said. He drew out his cloth and began wiping his hands again, smiling slightly at both of them before turning back to the open bay and the pickup. He stopped and turned back. "I nearly forgot," he said. "That car's got front-wheel drive. I should have told you. If you want to change your mind, that's okay."

Willis looked at Hank, who shrugged, and said, "They say front-wheel drive is good in snow. Is that right?" he said to the man.

"Well," he said, "I don't really know, but it makes some sense. Seems to handle real well on corners."

"Okay," Willis said, "I'll be back later."

As they drove back toward Route 4, Willis said, "I can't believe I just bought a car I never even heard of from a guy whose name

I don't even know. Worse than that, I bought a Swedish car with front-wheel drive when I've never even driven a foreign car. Do they drive different?"

Hank was bubbling with laughter. "I think you got a great deal," he said. "I'd trust that guy with anything, although I'm not sure why."

They puzzled all the way back to town over how you can tell who to trust and who not to.

Sy was at his desk in the glass office reading the *Globe* but secretly keeping track of when the reporters and editors showed up in the newsroom. They always straggled in, most of them between one and two, the time when the workday officially began for the city desk reporters. Some were always late, of course, and some always early. No one had ever kept track or even noticed. Sy had been getting to the newsroom early for the past few weeks, long before his normal time of four or five, and he knew they were all curious about his new schedule. He could see them glancing nervously his way, like antelope at a watering hole who know the old lion is nearby in the tall grass. He liked the image but he hated the feeling, the confusion of being unsure whether he was the victim or the prey, or rather, the awful sense that he was both at the same time. It was a new place for Sy, who until recently had thought he knew all the terrain of his life, knew where the traps were, and was never surprised by the peaks and valleys of daily life.

Willis and Hank came through the newsroom door together at two forty-five, laughing and speaking to those they passed. Sy was a little surprised because he hadn't realized they were particular buddies. He liked Hank okay, but he figured him for a union vote.

He thought about calling Willis into the office but changed his mind when he stopped to speak to Connie. When they laughed, Sy's body stiffened. His tooth began to ache. Willis moved on, stopping briefly at Merle's desk then on to Greenberg's, where he flopped down in a chair beside the desk and started talking. Greenberg had hurried in just a few minutes before Hank and Willis, late as usual, and he was still sorting out his desk, looking at telephone messages and checking over the day book. Sy watched them closely during their two-minute conversation but he was careful to be looking in a different direction when Willis left Greenberg's desk and walked over to his own.

Sy's surreptitious gaze roamed restlessly over the newsroom, pausing briefly wherever people were speaking to each other, as though he could will his eyes to function as ears and thus sort the rebels from the loyalists. This behind-the-glass survey of his domain, normally a source of comfort and even happiness, now released instead an emotional bile that churned his brain the way acid corroded his stomach. Sometimes, watching the newsroom coming alive to a fresh news cycle was like watching a sleepy, happy child slowly waking in his toy-filled crib. Sy often swiveled his chair around, propped his feet on the desk, and idly rested his eyes on the comings and goings of the newsroom while he made his routine telephone calls or skimmed his way through the daily stack of newspapers. Now he longed for that peace, the lazy, relaxed, but wide-awake feeling that something exciting lies ahead but not for a while, like a bass fisherman easing his boat into a still lake just before daybreak.

He noticed several people staring at him and he realized the *Globe* had dropped to the desk, fully exposing his spy mission. He felt the blood rush to his head, but he couldn't turn away, could not stop the relentless probing of his eyes. In near panic, he grabbed the telephone and pretended to make a call, all the while glaring through the glass, his head pivoting slowly back and forth across the room like a searchlight.

Greenberg lumbered up from his desk and started toward the office, but Sy spun around in his chair so his back was to the newsroom, the telephone still raised to his ear. This universally honored do-not-disturb signal was even more effective than a closed door and Sy knew it would stop Greenberg. He couldn't see him but he could picture the shrugging shoulders and mournful sigh as he turned back to his own desk. He pushed the dead telephone receiver hard against his left ear, as though the pressure could bring some order to his confused, stormy head. He had been waiting impatiently for Greenberg to get to the newsroom, but now he couldn't bear the prospect of a conversation.

Sy closed his eyes tightly and a blurred vision of the little table at Vic's popped up. He slammed down the phone and was halfway across the newsroom before Greenberg called out, but Sy just waved him off and hurried on out the door. On the street he slowed down and felt the rhythm of his breathing smooth out, but his mind continued to race pointlessly. By the time he got to Vic's, he was strolling, hands in his pockets and eyes calm, although his pulse still raced.

He turned around in Vic's doorway without going in. He wanted to be in the newsroom, not here. That's the only place he ever really wanted to be. Why should he let 'em drive him out? It was his. He made it. They—Connie and the others—were just playing games, power games, entertaining themselves at his expense. It was a rebellion, pure and simple. But not a revolt against tyranny, not a war against oppression. It was a crusade of Lilliputians, mean-spirited, mindless little people who didn't know that in plaguing him, they were tipping the balance in the real struggle. They didn't know that their own irrelevant bid for power inevitably gave strength to the Fletchers and McNallys of the world, reinforced the relentless grasping of the commercial interests that coveted newspapers as just one more potential profit center.

Sy's stomach growled loudly and suddenly he felt ravenously hungry, and he turned abruptly onto Center Street, away from the newspaper. His stomach growled again and he became aware of a dull pain in his gut. After his meeting with Manny and McNally, he had gone into the newsroom and had been unable to leave at lunchtime, bound to his desk in his glass spy's lair by some compelling, desperate need to know everything that happened in the newsroom. Before they arrived, he couldn't leave for fear of missing their entry. As people began to straggle in, he couldn't leave for fear of missing some secret meeting or signal. He sat, trapped like a spider who, having spun an intricate web, must wait motionless at the center of her masterpiece until some hapless fly entangles itself.

Now, finally free of the newsroom, he strode purposefully down Center Street, although he couldn't think of anywhere he wanted to go except back to the paper. He turned into The Cafe entrance but wheeled around immediately and kept walking. He passed every restaurant and bar with hardly a glance and just kept on walking faster and faster until he forgot about being hungry. His legs became pistons, pumping without thought or will and propelling him along the sidewalk with only the dimmest awareness of other people, several of whom nodded to him as he passed. He walked without a plan, turning corners randomly on impulse, barely conscious that he was leaving the downtown behind. At some point he realized he was in a residential area at the north end of town, but he kept walking until the tree-shaded sidewalk ended and he was on a bare, newly paved street leading into a new housing development that announced itself with two brick columns that stood on either side of the road, like stage-set guardhouses. A bronze plaque set in one column said North Star Estates.

Sy stopped, and for a moment he thought he was lost because he had never been up here. When he looked back, he saw the town below him, clustered generally but imprecisely around the Green. He hadn't realized how steeply he had climbed. Ahead, the housing development rose even higher, filling what used to be a large hay meadow with the "estates" that became ever larger as they neared the top of the rise.

Sweating slightly and unprotected from a bright sun that was not much past straight above despite the hour, Sy thought what a strange sight he must be—a middle-aged man, standing with no visible means of transportation and no apparent purpose, trying to get his bearings in this paved landscape that was inhospitable to pedestrians, intolerant of aimlessness, and hostile to wanderers. He turned around and searched until he located the top of the low newspaper building near the center of town and the Butler Block that included his place on the corner of Main Street. His head felt clear and his earlier sense of near panic had completely disappeared. He was only vaguely aware of his hungry stomach, and his lungs felt open and aired out. Without really deciding, he found himself walking peacefully back down the hill, like a seagull suddenly blown free from the disorienting tumult of a summer squall.

"For Christ's sake, I can't wait all day for him," Willis muttered to himself as he hurried out of the newsroom without speaking to anyone. The large clock over the door said 3:25. He had waited half an hour for Sy to come back and now he had to rush to get to Bushey's office on time. He had wanted to tell Sy where he was going, but for some reason he didn't fully understand, he didn't want Greenberg or the others to know he was meeting with Bushey and Quimby.

He was worried about the time so he didn't try to sneak into the station to catch Callahan asleep. "Hello, Sergeant." He paused to see if Callahan would challenge him but he didn't even look up from the logbook spread out on the counter, so Willis went on by and knocked at the closed door of the chief's office.

Bushey was behind his bare desk doing nothing, as far as Willis could see, and Quimby stood at the window, his back to the door and his hands stuffed into the front pockets of his dark blue polyester trousers, which were so long they bunched over his shoes and dragged the floor in back. He looks like a *MAD Magazine* ad spoofing Monkey Ward, Willis thought, but he said only, "Good afternoon, Chief."

"Careful, Willis," Bushey said, "things aren't always what they appear to be." Willis jumped. Christ, was he reading his mind?

"What do you mean?"

"Just that. Don't make assumptions about people. As of one hour ago, I'm no longer the chief of police."

Quimby turned around but he still didn't say anything, just nodded toward Willis, who was seriously puzzled now. "What do you mean? Are you quitting?"

"How do you know they didn't fire me?" Bushey asked. "See what I mean? You're jumping to conclusions." He stood up and walked around the end of his desk. "Relax, Willis. Don't look so nervous. I'm doing you a big favor here." He motioned to a small table with four chairs shoved under it. "Come on, Sten. Let's sit over here and tell Willis what's going on."

When they were all sitting, Bushey said, "I really am quitting as chief. I gave them two weeks' notice this afternoon. I'm going to work as an investigator for Sten, and after he's elected I'll be the senior investigator for the attorney general's office."

He pushed his chair back a few inches from the table. "And we're giving you this story exclusively. Just you. You can write it tonight as one of those 'this reporter has learned' scoops. 'Unimpeachable sources say' and 'city hall observers believe'—you know, that kind of bullshit. Then tomorrow we're going to hold a press conference."

"Well," Willis said finally, "I appreciate the break on this. It's a good story."

"You're damn right it's a good story," Quimby said. "It's bigger than you think too. This is going to wake people up. When a man like Chief Bushey goes to work for a candidate for statewide office, you people in the press have got to realize that crime and law-and-order are the big issue. The trouble is, most of the press is liberal too. That's why we can't stop these drugs and the other stuff that's ruining our country."

Willis looked at Bushey to see if what Quimby was saying made any more sense to him, but his face was blank, stiff as a mask, with no expression in his pale eyes.

"Are you going to work in his campaign?" he asked Bushey.

"I told you. I'm going to be an investigator in the state's attorney's office." He said it flatly. "I'm not a politician and I don't work for political campaigns."

Willis gestured toward Quimby. "He just said you would be going to work for a candidate for statewide office. What does that mean?"

"Ask him," Bushey said, his voice still flat.

"You know what I meant," Quimby said. "I meant that Chief Bushey knows how serious a problem we have with these lawless elements and that's why he's going to work for someone who is determined to do something about it. Me. Listen here, we're giving you this story because the chief says you'd understand what all this means and that you'd write it straight." His eyes narrowed and he cocked his head, pushing his face closer to Willis's. "Is that right?"

Willis looked at Bushey again. His scorn of Quimby was turning into anger, but he also was confused because he couldn't imagine why Bushey would work for a fool like this guy. Bushey just shrugged.

Turning to Quimby, Willis said, "I'll write it straight if you tell it straight, but so far you've told me two different versions of the same story. Which one is straight?"

"I told you it was a mistake to trust this guy," Quimby said to Bushey, but his snarl had turned to a simper. "You can't trust any of them."

Bushey was leaning back in his chair and Willis thought he was almost smiling. Finally, he leaned forward slightly and said, "Sten, this was just a little test. And you failed. If you don't learn to deal with the press better than this, you can't win this election."

Quimby opened his mouth to speak, letting out a soft nasal whine that Bushey cut off before it became a real word. "Just listen, for God's sake. I'm not scolding you, I'm just trying to help you with a problem that's obvious to everyone except you. So just listen."

He turned to Willis. "That's why I wanted us to talk with Willis. He's got enough sense not to let your obnoxiousness get in the way of his story." He nodded to Willis, but evidently he didn't expect or need any sign of agreement. "And he's enough of a pro to be thinking already beyond this one-day story. He's already wondering what I'm really going to do and what we're planning. Right?"

Willis nodded. He didn't say anything, but suddenly it was absolutely clear to him what was going on. This blockhead, Quimby, was working for Bushey, not the other way around. This was a Charlie McCarthy show and Quimby was the dummy.

"So," Bushey said, "let's get beyond the sparring and have a serious talk. Sten, you just listen for a while.

"Now, Willis, here's the deal. I'm pretty good at reading character and I've been studying yours for a few months. I believe we can have an arrangement that's fair to both of us. And to Sten. You interested?"

Willis had been propositioned by all kinds of people in all sorts of ways, but this was different. A distant memory from some book, maybe a Hemingway novel, flashed through his mind—some story in which triumph and fear, corruption and honor, secrecy and betrayal mixed together so that each element was disguised from the other and they were indistinguishable to the protagonist. He didn't know what kind of deal he was being offered here, but he knew it was not an ordinary source-to-reporter arrangement. This time the sense of excitement was flavored not only with caution about credibility but with a strong taste of danger, as though he was being asked not just to report an undercover story but to participate in one.

And of course he was interested. Whatever else you might say about Bushey, he was not a trifler and he was not a blowhard. "What I'm interested in," Willis said, "is the story. News."

"I told you so, Sten. This guy is a newshound. He couldn't turn down this story if he wanted to." Bushey was smiling broadly, a friendly smile that sealed the deal before it had even been described.

"What we're offering is this: Besides the exclusive on my resignation and employment by Sten, we're going to tip you off to a huge news story that's developing but may not break for a while. Maybe not for quite a while. But this is a hell of a story and it'll be yours alone."

Willis started to speak, but Bushey held up his hand. "Hold on a minute. Let me finish. That's what you get. The news. One story now and a bigger one later. And what do we get? Three things: First, you can't break this other story until we tell you to. I know that's a tough one for you, but it is absolutely necessary. You'll see why in a minute, but for now I'll just tell you that if you wrote it at the wrong time, lives could be lost. Second, you pursue this other story just like you would anyway. That is, after we give you the lead, you do just exactly what you would ordinarily do. Investigate like any other reporter would do. Last, and I know this is the toughest of all, I want you to agree to talk to Sten from time to time, ask questions, grill him, treat him the way reporters treat politicians. Only don't write anything. Let me be honest with you. Right now, he's a disaster when reporters corner him. He gets mad, he shouts, he lies, he threatens. You've seen all that. What I want is for you to help me train him."

*
**

"You were looking squarely at the future today," Sy said in a flat voice, looking directly across the table at Willis. "We don't often get to see how things are going to be, but today you did."

Willis glanced around nervously, but The Oasis was nearly empty and the few other drinkers were too far away to overhear, but he still didn't answer because he didn't know what to say.

"How do you like it?" Sy asked.

"What?"

"The future."

Willis picked up his glass and took a long swallow, drowning the panic that had started rising in his throat. What the hell was Seymour talking about? He couldn't possibly know about Bushey offering him a deal, but if not, what was he talking about?

"I don't know," he finally said, buying time. "It doesn't seem as clear to me as you seem to think it is. What do you think's going to happen?"

Seymour emptied his glass and held it up to signal Jake.

"Mr. McNally," Sy said, again looking at Willis. "He's the future. His tribe will take over the newspapers and they'll run them for the rest of our lives. At least that long."

Willis relaxed. "So what's new about that? The lawyers and the bankers already run our lives from the time we start shaving to the day we die. And then the morticians and the preachers take over. So what?"

Sy shook his head. "You don't get it. What you saw today was a surrender. The fall of Troy. Lee at Appomattox. Only, Manny didn't know it. He gave his newspaper to the Tribe of McNally and didn't even know it. What do you think of that?"

He turned away to look for Jake without waiting for an answer, and Willis didn't offer one.

Jake arrived and set the full tumbler on the table. "How're you doing tonight, Willis?"

"Okay, I guess, for a tired-out old reporter. It's been a long day."

"You better hurry up; it's not like you to let Sy get ahead of you. Even when he has a head start. You ready for another one?"

Willis hesitated, then said, "Not quite. We've got a little time, haven't we?"

"Yeah," Jake said, "time for one more, or maybe two at your normal pace. Call me."

He walked off and Sy took a long drink. "I'm telling you, everything's going to change."

"Say, Sy, how far ahead of me are you, anyway?"

"I'm way ahead." A sly grin gave his hawkish face a furtive look. "I can see the future because I've paid attention to the past. Manny thinks he's just fighting the union, but he's wrong. The goddam union is a problem, but he doesn't know what the real problem is."

He paused and Willis began to say something, but Sy cut him off and hurried on. "The real problem is that the union gives them an excuse. It's just a tool, an opportunity to take over the paper. They know he'll do anything to beat the goddam union, even if it means giving up control of the paper. And they know it."

"Who?" Willis looked closely at Sy, really listening for the first time. "Who's taking over?"

Sy didn't answer. He looked solemnly at Willis, drained his glass, and shouted, "Hey, Jake. Help us out here."

Jake brought over two full drinks and set them on the table. "This is it. It's already past two. On the tab?"

Sy nodded and picked up his glass. They drank in silence for a few minutes, then Willis said, "By the way, Sy, I'm thinking about going back up to the commune tomorrow. I got a tip today that could turn into a story."

Sy showed no interest and didn't bother to answer.

"Is that okay?" Willis asked. "I mean, it'll probably take most of the day and I won't have a story out of it for a while. Maybe quite a while."

Sy nodded but still didn't say anything.

"Somebody'll have to follow up on the Bushey story. He's going to hold a press conference, but there won't be any news out of it that I didn't have tonight."

Willis waited. He knew it would be a mistake to try to talk about the meeting with Bushey, but at the same time he half hoped Sy would ask him the right question. He was confused and wanted help understanding what he was feeling about it. But Sy still sat silently, looking down at the table and obviously paying little attention.

"I thought that was a pretty good shot tonight," Willis said, disappointment making him a little aggressive. "The story about

Bushey going to work for Quimby." Still no answer. "What did you think?"

"I think Bushey is a snake and Quimby is a nothing. No, maybe he's something — an insect."

Willis just shook his head and they finished their drinks in silence. As they got up to leave, Sy turned to him and, standing close, said, "Remember what I said. Mark this day, June 4. No, I guess it's already June 5, right? Anyway, on June 4, 1968, everything changed."

Willis murmured, "It already has." But Sy didn't notice.

The entranceway lamp was the only light visible through the glass doors of the newspaper. Willis could hear the low throb of the press even before they stepped inside. Sy led the way through the darkened business office, walking briskly without faltering or bumping into anything. Well, he's not that drunk, Willis thought as they hurried through the gloom. When they got to the empty newsroom, Sy said, "Check the AP wire. I'll see if CBS has any results."

When Willis got to the office, Seymour was slumped far down in his desk chair, staring dully at the TV screen. "The AP is sending advance columns," he reported. "The closest thing to news is a long, goofy Sunday filler about red squirrels."

Seymour sank further into his chair without replying. The television screen filled up with a milling crowd of laughing, jostling people packed into a long room. At first there was no sound, just the silent image of tense waiting. The camera panned desperately over the crowd, blindly searching for something more interesting than a mob of people waiting for someone to arrive.

"I guess this is better than reading about squirrels, at least," Willis said. He remembered countless times when he had been among the crowd impatiently waiting for some politician or beauty or crook or victim to stand among them. He and the other reporters always kept slightly aloof from the crowd. Only the lousy reporters, the dumb ones or those who themselves were on the make, were impressed or inspired by the celebrity. For reporters like Willis, the excitement of these moments came not from reflected glory but from anticipation of battle. For them, a person who stepped into that magical spot known as a "public event" became an adversary, a combatant in an ageless contest in which the newsmaker's goal was to trick the reporter and the reporter's goal was to expose the humbug.

Willis, remembering his talk with Hank, said, "I was talking today with a guy who said newspapering needs to be more professional. He said reporters need to be better educated. What do you think?"

Sy continued for a minute to stare at the flickering screen as though he hadn't heard, but finally he swiveled his chair around and said, "Of course they need to be better educated. But forget the professionalism. That's just another word for making more money. You been talking to the union people?"

Willis, startled, said angrily, "Goddam, Sy, you're obsessed. No, this has nothing to do with the goddam union. Christ, it was just an idle question. Forget it."

Seymour looked at him, then said, "Well, you tell whoever you were talking to what H. L. Mencken said about professionalism." He opened the top draw of his desk and rummaged among a mass of scraps of paper. "Here it is." He held a half sheet of paper almost at arm's length and read, "I well recall my horror when I heard, for the first time, of a journalist who had laid in a pair of what were then called bicycle pants and taken to golf: it was as if I had encountered a studhorse with his hair done up in frizzes, and pink bowknots peeking out of them."

Seymour tossed the paper back into the drawer. "That's part of what I was talking about earlier. What we're seeing right now is journalism tying up its hair in frizzes. One name for it is professionalism. And at this newspaper, the union is helping tie the goddam pink knots."

He turned back to the television set as an excited voice said, "Here he comes." Both men leaned forward slightly as a smiling Bobby Kennedy appeared in one corner of the screen, moving into view on a wave of bodies packed so tightly around him that it was hard to tell which head rode on which suit.

The sound of the shot was so incongruous that Willis heard the screams of the crowd before he understood what he had just seen. That's Rosey Grier. What's he doing to that guy? "Jesus H. Christ," Sy whispered. They were both on their feet, pulled out of their seats like baseball fans yanked upright by the crack of a bat. "Jesus H. Christ."

Kennedy was on the floor. They stared pop-eyed at the black-and-white bedlam, impotent witnesses to a horror they could mitigate only by murmuring to each other. They watched and told each other what they had just seen, commenting in monosyllabic exclamations, sometimes with sounds that did not even quite make it to the level of words.

"Okay," Sy said after a while. "We're going to get this in the paper. I'm going down to the pressroom. You keep up with this." Willis jumped. Keep up? He and Sy had used the television news a few times to supplement the wire service reports, inserting details and sometimes outright stealing the network's stories. But it took Willis a moment to realize that Seymour intended for him to write the story of the Kennedy shooting directly from the television images.

"Start writing as soon as you can," Sy said as he hurried off through the dark composing room. Willis, suddenly nauseated, began to follow but then caught himself. He heard the AP machine dinging hysterically, but he was pulled back to the noise coming from the television set. Maybe something had changed. What if he wasn't dead. Will we remake the paper if he's not dead?

On the screen, Ethel Kennedy's horror-stricken face peered angrily past her raised hand, into the camera beaming down from its towering position above the body she was trying to cradle. What a spectacular shot, Willis thought.

The chaos of sound had been brought to order, replaced by the CBS anchor's barely controlled outrage. The TV reporter in San Francisco was still babbling but the background noise from the hotel restaurant had been screened out. Willis picked up a notebook from a desk on the way back into the office and sat down in Sy's chair.

Sy was a little out of breath as he strode back into the office. He snatched the telephone and began dialing, then stretched out the cord so he could get closer to the television set. "Hello, Rocky? It's Seymour. I need somebody back down here to set some type. Yeah, right now. No, I've already stopped the pressrun. Only about 5,000. Yes, goddam it, right now. I don't give a shit about the overtime. No, goddam it, I have not called Lyman. Listen, you son of a bitch, if you don't get down here or send somebody else down here in fifteen minutes, I'll run the goddam Linotype myself. I don't care whether you call Lyman or not and I don't give a shit about your union rules. I'm making over this goddam paper and I'm going out there right now to turn on the goddam Linotype."

He slammed the telephone down and glared at Willis. "You better start writing," he said. His face was bright red from the top of the white t-shirt that showed under the loosened collar to the receding hairline. His eyes bulged slightly and his clamped jaw was undulating. "See what the AP is moving, but I am sure we'll have to write our own story."

Willis nodded without looking away from the television screen.

"I'm going down to make sure that bastard throws away the early papers. If the phone rings, don't answer it. It'll be either Rocky or Lyman and I don't give a shit what either one of them has to say."

Willis jumped up and hustled out to the AP machine. It was still screaming frantically and the ribbon of paper was streaming out in double-spaced spurts. He found dozens of one-sentence "Bulletins" and "Urgents," but taken altogether they didn't give nearly as much information as he had gotten from thirty seconds of television images. He read everything, learned nothing, and went back to the office.

Willis watched the television set for another ten minutes, then he turned around to the typewriter on a stand beside the desk and wrote:

SAN FRANCISCO — Bobby Kennedy, heir to a star-crossed political dynasty, was gunned down last night precisely at the moment of his greatest triumph. He was felled at 3:15 a.m. (EST) by two pistol shots fired at point-blank range.

He was rushed to Good Samaritan Hospital and there was some hope that he could survive the gunshot. A young man wrestled to the ground by Senator Kennedy's bodyguard and others was taken into custody.

But even if he lives, Kennedy clearly was grievously wounded and the best hope of this nation's anti-war movement collapsed with him in the chaotic hallway leading from the kitchen of the Ambassador Hotel in San Francisco.

It took five minutes, but by the time he finished the five-paragraph lead, Willis was in stride. He described the shooting scene as though he had been there. He threw in details that only an eyewitness would know. He described the stunned lost look on the face of Rosey Grier, the bodyguard, whose normal expression of menace was long known to every American football fan. He dredged up his own memories of Dallas on November 22, 1963, when President John Kennedy was killed and Willis was writing for the *El Paso Times*. He built the story sentence by sentence with the ease and smooth confidence of an ice-skater. He laced it with description and boldly summarized facts into conclusions in a breezy style more like a sports story than a dried-up news report.

Willis pounded out twenty inches of copy without checking his notes or going back to the AP machine. By the time he was through, the wire service had managed to cobble together a reasonably coherent story, except that the copy editors were so rattled by the institutional demands of timidity that at one point they said Kennedy was "allegedly shot." Willis snorted. "Check this, Sy. The AP must figure he might have had a heart attack."

Sy was editing Willis's copy a half page at a time. They both stopped working briefly and were listening to the TV anchor when they heard a growly voice say from behind them, "If you fucked up that Linotype, Sy, I'll have your ass." Rocky's face was covered with red splotches, as though the arteries had dumped out pools of blood under the skin. Sy looked around at him and smiled, driving more blood into the pools. Rocky yelled, "Lyman's on his way down here and he's pissed, asshole."

Sy smiled again. "Shove it, Rocky. Here's the first column of copy." He stood up and handed over the sheaf of papers. "By the time you finish setting it, we'll be done with the rest."

"How much are you making over?"

"Just the front page and the jump. I'll cut the new stuff into the original story. We won't wait for a picture."

Rocky walked off in a bowlegged strut, shaking his head. "Jason's coming in. I'll set the type until he gets here. It'll be half past four o-fucking-clock before we get out of here."

Willis was writing again and Sy was watching the TV guys fill airtime. "I've got another graf or two," Willis said, "and after that I'd just be drooling on paper. Do you have enough copy?"

"Plenty," Sy said, turning around to look over the typewriter at Willis. "We have plenty. Wrap it up anywhere you want. By the way, that's a pretty nice piece of work. By God, we'll be the only morning paper on the East Coast with this story. What a goddam year."

The next half hour was a blur. Seymour and Rocky shouted at each other as they put the hot type into the chase, Sy standing on one side of the table reading the lead lines upside down and backward and Rocky on the other side yelling at him to keep his hands off the type. Willis was assigned to read the ink-wet galley proofs paragraph by paragraph as the type came out of the Linotype and was slapped into a tray for proofing. The kids who tailed the press and otherwise served as dirty-faced lackeys to the pressroom foreman dashed into the composing room three different times to see when they would get the pages. Lyman came in and bustled around the composing room, ignored by everyone except when they needed to shove him out of the way.

At some point someone had made an urn of coffee, and Willis was drunk on caffeine-laced adrenaline when he left the office, besotted with a simple, uncut happiness that was like the joy that comes with the end of homesickness. The newspaper under his arm was still warm from the press. He laughed out loud when he tripped over the curb and careened off a parked car. "Read all about it," he roared at a passing milk truck, and when he passed a glass-fronted store he bowed to himself and held up the banner headline for his haggard reflection to read. He drifted down the street in the general direction of the hotel. At the Main Street intersection, he looked to the left into the darkness beyond the five-block strip of buildings. A pale thread of light showed partway up the sky as the sun climbed toward the top of the mountain range from the backside.

Willis slouched down on a sidewalk bench to watch. But he couldn't sit still, and he was up and walking again before enough light to read by had spilled over the ridgeline. No stores were open, not even Pop's Stand, although by the time he got there the news truck had dumped out the day's bundles on the curb. A sudden proprietary impulse took hold and he picked up the bundles and carefully moved them closer to the safety of the doorway, then looked around furtively to see if anyone could have seen him.

The streetlights went dark just as he reached the hotel. He paused at the entrance, tired but slightly depressed at the prospect of climbing the dingy stairs to his room. He stood on the sidewalk looking uncertainly up and down the empty street until he noticed a small green car parked at the curb and realized with a shock that it was his. He had forgotten about it, but now, seeing it there waiting for him, instead of feeling burdened by ownership as he often had in the past, he was lifted by a mild but distinct surge of satisfaction. A couple of blocks away a neon Schlitz sign came to life in the window of a bar and grill. He stepped off in that direction, whistling under his breath.

CHAPTER SEVEN
Saturday, July 6, 1968

The gear shifter, a short post with a big-knobbed grip, stuck out of the floor between the bucket seats, and Willis still felt a little off-balance riding along with his right hand so close to someone else's knee. He noticed it especially with Marlene, who liked to sit partially turned toward him. When he shifted into third, his knuckles grazed right past her leg. She didn't seem to notice, or at least she never said anything and didn't move her leg. It seemed sensible to keep his hand on the stick until he could shift into fourth, but they were just starting up the long hill leading out of town and every time she fidgeted, her bare calf glided past the back of his hand, gently stirring the hair on the back on his fingers. He didn't mind, exactly, but it was distracting. And he kept thinking about how Sheila would never have been so casually intimate, not even after five years of marriage and certainly not at the beginning.

They weren't very much alike. He couldn't imagine Sheila going with him to cover a story on her day off even though she loved being a reporter and newspapering in general. But Marlene jumped at the idea, even though she never even read a newspaper. She said she'd never seen a commune and had never been in that part of the state. He hadn't exactly meant to ask her, but he knew that the way he had told her about it sounded like he was inviting her. Actually, he had meant just to invite her to the party later at Greenberg's house.

He glanced sideways at her and she smiled. Marlene hadn't said very much since he picked her up but she didn't seem moody, just relaxed, quietly enjoying the day. He liked her smile. She wasn't as pretty as Sheila, but then, not many women were. And Marlene had something else—an odd, quiet sex appeal that not only snared Willis and the other barflies but also seemed to charm just about everybody else. She put out some mysterious signal, an appeal not of naivete or innocence, God knows, but something laden with a childish seeking, a vulnerability that created intrigue when combined with her sophisticated looks and bearing. The young guys at the paper turned into mush every time he brought her around. But maybe it wasn't sex at all but something else, because even Connie, Greenberg, and Mo, the ancient one-eyed proofreader, went out of their way to talk to her even though she clearly had no interest whatsoever in the newspaper.

Willis sneaked another glance, but she had turned to look out the window. She reached over into the back seat to crank down the rear window, then pivoted all the way around, leaning hard into him as she reached for the other rear window handle. As she turned back around, she brushed the side of his face with a quick, dry kiss.

"What a lovely day," she said, snuggling back down into her seat. "I can't wait to get into the woods at the commune. You don't think they'll mind me being with you?"

Willis shook his head, but she went on, "Because if they do, I'll just wander off by myself. I mean, when you're talking to people or whatever, don't worry about me. I just feel like walking in the woods."

As they topped the mountain, Willis finally shifted the car into high gear and they started down the steep back slope, flying now, with trees going by in a blur on both sides of the narrow highway. Hot sunshine poured through the windshield, and the wind thrashed around inside the car, making so much noise that conversation was not possible. Marlene's long, heavy hair flew in all directions and she made no effort to corral it.

Willis gripped the wheel with both hands but he felt entirely in control, sure of the little car's performance and comfortable with the highway's curves and dips. He'd been up here three times in the past month, often enough to recognize dozens of landmarks, but he was still surprised on each trip at the change in landscape. The stream had shrunk to a bubbling ribbon, a frolicking child of the madly roaring river he had first seen in April. Even in early June the water had moved with intimidating speed and force, but now, in mid-July, it seemed merely playful. The wooded sections where the valley narrowed looked impenetrably overgrown with brush, and the wider floodplain meadows were knee-high in grasses, weeds, and wildflowers. Some of the fields had been planted to corn, which was hardly taller than the grass, and a few had already been mowed for hay, leaving a yellowish stubble.

As they sailed past Jenkins Family Restaurant, Willis noticed that most of the cars in the half-full parking lot were from out of state. He shouted to Marlene, "Lunch? You hungry?" She shook her head and they drove on without speaking until he slowed for the turn into the unmarked and unpaved road leading to the commune.

"Are you sure I won't be in your way? I mean, I don't want to get in the way of your job." Her brow furrowed and she reached over to touch his arm.

"No. Quit worrying about it," he said without looking at her. He tried to hide the flash of annoyance, but he knew she had spotted it and that made him even more irritated. Why did she always need so much reassurance? The longer they were together, the more she needed. She was turned to look out the window but he could tell her feelings were hurt. Christ. What happened? Sometime in the past month everything flipped over. At first he was chasing her but she seemed out of reach and several times he almost gave up, figuring one of the other guys who were always hanging out at the bar had the inside track. Then she got friendlier and for a while it was just about perfect.

They had fun together, the sex was fine, they never fought, and, in general, being with Marlene made the rest of his life as satisfying as the newspaper part. It was the first time his job had not created friction with the woman in his life. For years it seemed he had to choose between newspapering and everything else, and he always felt a little guilty about working long days or odd hours. But Marlene worked at night too and she had not complained even once about him being late. Hell, she didn't even complain when he didn't show up at all. If he wasn't there when the bar closed, she just went on home and was always cheerful and happy when he called the next day.

So what went wrong? Why'd he often have this vague sense of being reproached?

She was still turned away, watching the woods as they bumped slowly down the rutted road by now so narrow that if they met another car, one of them would have to pull over and stop. He remembered how she had been funny and uncomplaining about the grubbiness of his room in the Uptown and how excited she was when he rented the lake house. He was suddenly sorry he had been irritated and he reached over to touch her hand, which lay limp in her lap like an exhausted little bird.

She smiled at him, a little sadly he thought, then turned back to the window. They passed the giant pine tree that Willis always took to be the marker for the entrance to the commune although no one had ever told him where the property boundaries were. How much land went with the commune? He ought to find out. At the tree, the road turned sharply to the left and a collapsed stone wall went off at right angles to the road, snaking through the heavy woods as far as you could see.

"There's a deer," Marlene said quietly.

Willis stopped with a jolt. "Where?"

"Right over there, next to the wall. See it? It's looking right at us."

He still couldn't see anything except trees and he leaned over her, closer to the window.

"Oh look," she whispered, excited for the first time. "She has twin fawns."

At that instant Willis saw a flash of white and a blur of brown as the doe plunged into the woods. He caught a glimpse of two smaller forms, both covered with white spots, then the woods were again perfectly still. The deer had been no more than fifty feet off the road but he never would have seen them if she hadn't spoken. Christ, they were like something in a dream, so that when you wake up you know something's happened but at the same time you don't quite believe it.

"How the hell did you spot them?"

"I saw her ear twitch," she said. "That's what you always have to look for—movement."

"You saw her ear?"

She smiled at him. "Weren't they wonderful? The fawns were lying down and they jumped up at exactly the same time. Do you think she gave them some kind of signal?"

"I don't know," he said, suddenly remembering how the baby sometimes would stop crying as soon as Sheila came into the room, even before she spoke or he could possibly have seen her.

They crept along for another quarter mile, driving at walking speed as the road rose gently. At the top the road turned and on one side the forest stopped, giving way to an overgrown apple orchard the size of a supermarket parking lot that sloped off sharply toward the south. The short, gnarled old trees were densely leafed, their heavy branches reaching wide, with some of them drooping nearly low enough to meet the unkempt, overgrown grass and briars.

The orchard, glistening green in the July sun, was beautiful and he stopped the car. A range of mountains, gray and indistinct at this distance, hemmed in the valley and lower hills and he knew at least one small town lay alongside the river, buried from sight now at the bottom of this green bowl. He could see separated stretches of road but no cars were moving, and it was as though no people were in this vast stretch of land laid out in front of them.

"Apple trees never die," Marlene said cheerfully.

"What do you mean? Some of these trees look half dead right now."

"The tops die but shoots come back from the roots. They're related to roses, you know."

He didn't know that and he didn't know whether to believe it. Sometimes Marlene's nature comments were downright weird, like something you might hear from the commune people. She seemed to know the names of all sorts of plants and what they could be used for and he didn't really have any reason not to believe her but, hell, she just didn't look or act like somebody who would know that stuff.

"How do you know all that stuff?"

She shrugged. She always shrugged and answered vaguely when he asked personal questions. "I just know it. I've always known it."

He knew she had grown up in Vermont but he'd been surprised when he found out she had never lived anywhere else. Somehow she just didn't seem as provincial as most of the local people he had met. She had the same direct what-you-see-is-what-you-get manner they had, but where they often seemed eager for talk or association, she was usually watchful and wary. At those times the heart-gripping vulnerability disappeared without a trace, leaving Willis with a vague sense of guilt.

"My mother grew up on a farm on the Connecticut River. Maybe she taught me," Marlene said in an obvious effort to be helpful, but she didn't seem very interested in the question.

"Look," she said with whispered urgency, thrusting her arm out the window to point. "She's back."

Partway down the orchard Willis saw a deer step timidly out of the woods into the grass. She stopped, head up, and a half minute later a spotted fawn stepped out to join its mother, followed in another few seconds by the second fawn.

Willis remembered that Marlene told him once she had lost a baby just a few weeks before her due date. She had just said it in passing, as though it had been a very long time ago, and she'd never mentioned it again. Now he wondered if seeing the fawns made her think of it. You sure couldn't tell; she sat perfectly still, watching the deer with a half smile on her face. He thought for the first time that it was odd she didn't have any children. She was nearly thirty and she'd been married to some asshole for a long time before she finally kicked him out. Funny that he'd never wondered about that before.

Willis let out the clutch and the car eased forward up the hill. Marlene watched out the window until they reached the top where the forest began again. Just inside the woods, near the edge of the orchard, sat the commune's first shack, a low, badly weathered little wooden building with a rusted tin roof and a row of windows high up on the wall, just under the exposed two-by-four rafters.

"Oh," Marlene said, "look at that old chicken coop. They must've moved it up here and turned it into a house. That's wonderful. It looks so cozy, and they can look out over the whole orchard."

Brightly colored curtains fluttered in all the small windows, but Willis still didn't think it looked particularly cozy. Some of the boards on the outside had been patched, the roofline sagged, and if the thing had ever had any paint, the evidence had been thoroughly destroyed. Christ, if you put this shack in among a bunch of Alabama sharecroppers' houses, it would ruin the neighborhood.

"Look at the curtains," Marlene said with a laugh. He looked closely but still it took a minute for him to realize they were made out of cut-up American flags. It was the sort of detail he ought to have in his story when he finally wrote it and he was embarrassed that he hadn't noticed the curtains on one of his earlier trips.

They eased past several shacks of various shapes, sizes, and construction, but they didn't see any people. Just dogs. Barks and howls echoed around the dense hardwood forest but none of the dogs ran up to the car. On past trips, some of the dogs had been free of their chains and they had swarmed around the car until someone called them off. When they came within sight of the main house, Willis still didn't see any sign of people, but as he stopped the car near the front steps, a short figure emerged from the open door and stood very still against the wall of the house.

Willis recognized her as soon as he was out of the car. The beret was jammed down nearly to her eyebrows and she seemed to have grown a lot taller, but there was no doubt about it being the weird kid from the bus. He had seen her a couple of times but she always disappeared before he could actually talk to her. Now she stood her ground, silent but clearly on duty.

"How're you doing?" he said. "Long time no see." Christ, he'd never said that in his life. What was it about this little girl?

She didn't answer but she moved across the porch to stand at the top step. She was wearing striped bib overalls over a sweatshirt and no shoes.

"Where is everybody?"

"They're not here," she said, looking directly at him. "Who's that?"

He looked around and was a little startled to see Marlene right behind him a couple of paces. He hadn't heard her get out of the car. She was smiling broadly at the girl.

"Oh," he said, "this is Marlene. My friend. Marlene." The girl nodded, or at least he thought she nodded but the motion was nearly imperceptible. "I can't remember your name . . ."

She still didn't help him out, just stared blankly down at them.

"What is your name?"

"Net."

"Oh yeah. Annette is it?"

"No."

"Paulette?"

"No."

He was starting to get irritated.

"Lynette?

No answer.

He was running out of names and patience. "Nanette?"

Silence.

"Christ. Fishnet? Bayonet?"

Marlene stepped in front of him and started up the steps. "Just Net," she said. "Her name is Net, that's all."

She reached out her hand. "I'm glad to meet you. Don't mind him, he's just grumpy."

To his amazement, the girl reached down and shook her hand. For a second he thought she was even going to smile, but she didn't.

"Where's everybody?" Willis said again. "And don't tell me they're not here. I can see that."

The girl said nothing.

"He just wants to talk to the grown-ups," Marlene said. "That's why we came up here. Can you tell us where they are? Or when they'll be back?"

The girl shifted her steady stare to Marlene and said, "They're down at the farm. Haying."

Willis was suspicious. He knew the commune didn't have any farmland. "Haying where?"

"Down at the Bradleys," she said. "They're helping them get the hay in."

"How come you're not down there?"

"I'm sick."

"Oh," Marlene said, "you shouldn't be here alone. What's wrong with you?"

"Flu. I've got a fever."

Willis felt himself shrink back but Marlene hurried up the final step and reached out a hand to touch the girl's forehead. "Yes," she said, "you do look flushed." After a moment she said, "But I don't think it's very high." She took her hand away. "You ought not to be out here, though. Go on back inside and go to bed. Is your mother down haying too?"

"No," the girl said, "she's gone to get some medicine."

"Okay," Marlene said, "we're leaving. You go on back to bed."

She turned around and quietly but firmly took Willis's arm to turn him back toward the car.

They drove slowly back down the narrow dirt road and as they came up to the pavement, she said, "Turn left."

"How do you know where the Bradley farm is?"

"I don't. But we came from that other way and I didn't see any haying going on, did you?"

She said it without irony or sarcasm, but he was annoyed again anyway. He hadn't even decided whether he would look for the Bradley farm. But he turned left onto the empty highway and they drove in silence for a mile or so.

"Maybe we should try that next right," Marlene said.

He couldn't see a sign or any other reason to think the farm was on that road, and he didn't want to take it because a tractor pulling a wagon had just turned into it and he knew they'd never be able to pass it on such a small road.

Before he could say anything, she said quietly, "I may be wrong, but they could be taking that wagon to pick up the hay."

They followed the tractor for a few minutes before the driver found a spot wide enough to pull over. He waved them around. Willis eased the Saab past and continued up the winding road. At least she didn't say they ought to ask if this was the right way; Sheila would have insisted. The car climbed a ridge, but the dense woods blocked their view in all directions. Five minutes later the forest ended and they were driving between two large fields, one of which had been mowed. In the other one, on the left, a small herd of tan cows grazed and rested.

The farmhouse stood at the end of the mowed field, an unimpressive, once-white structure that squatted as close to the road as it could get, cowering from the enormous unpainted barn that loomed over it from behind. Far behind the barn a tractor pulled a hay baler slowly along the rear edge of the mowed field, and ahead of it another tractor towed an odd-looking rake that gathered the cut grass and piled it into long rows. Between the barn and the baler a large, ancient truck was parked, its hood raised, with three or four men milling around it. Several other people sprawled out on the ground and a few others picked up bales of hay and piled them into bunches as they came spitting out of the baler.

The short driveway and most of the yard beside it were filled with cars and pickups. As they stopped the car and stepped out, they could hear the roaring of the engines and the rhythmic thudding of the baler. The solid door and all four windows on the front of the little house were shut, with shades drawn, presenting to the roadside as formidable a presence as such an unimposing structure could muster. They walked quietly around the side and dodged between the parked cars on their way to the hayfield.

Marlene stopped and turned toward a small porch on the side of the house. She smiled broadly, lifting her hand in a timid wave. Willis for the first time saw a huge, squat figure standing, feet wide apart, in a small open doorway. She filled up the whole space. Willis had already turned back toward Marlene before he remembered. My God, it's Ginny Palmer.

"I know her," he said softly to Marlene and walked over to the porch.

Ginny was drying her hands on a small towel. He was sure she remembered him, although she didn't speak until he did. "Hello. Remember me? Bud Willis. You and . . . uh, uh . . . your husband stopped to help me out a few months ago. Out on the highway."

"Fred," she said.

"Right. Fred. So how are you?"

She didn't answer and didn't even look at him. She had turned her fearless and fearsome gaze full on Marlene, who was still smiling prettily with no sign of discomfort. They looked at each other with some sort of mute understanding that Willis saw but could not fathom. They didn't seem to need or expect anything from him, but neither of them spoke so finally he said, "I'd like for you to meet Marlene. My friend Marlene."

Slowly Ginny finished drying her hands and with surprising grace shoved off from the doorway. She crossed the small porch in two rolling strides and reached down from the single step to offer her hand to Marlene.

"Glad to meet you. Come on up."

She led the way into the kitchen and stirred several pots on the gas stove before settling herself into a too-small chair at the head of a large oval table that would have filled up a normal kitchen.

"You still working at the newspaper?"

"Well, yes. Yeah, I'm still there."

"How about you? You work there too?"

Marlene laughed. "No. I don't think I'd be very good at it. I don't even like to read them."

Willis said hastily, in warning, "Ginny used to be a correspondent for the paper."

"I don't blame you," she said to Marlene, then turned her massive head to snap at Willis, "I don't read it either. I already told you that."

They sat in silence for a minute, then Marlene asked what she was cooking. Ginny began telling her in exact detail what and how much food she was working on, giving Willis a chance to look around. The kitchen seemed enormous, as big as the whole house looked from the outside, and he realized it was, in fact, half the downstairs. Divider walls had been taken out so the kitchen could be expanded to stretch the length of the house. It was clearly the command center for the farm, with doors opening toward the front of the house, toward the barn in the rear, and to the little side porch. The sink was full of dirty dishes and the drain rack beside the sink was piled high with clean ones. All the windows and all the doors in the kitchen were open. An idle wood-burning cooking range stood next to the busy gas stove. The winter stove was heaped with all sorts of junk, including a red-checked jacket and a toolbox. All of the counter space—hell, every inch of flat space of any kind—was also piled high.

Willis was puzzled. Ginny surely seemed at home and the place was set up just the way he would expect her to do it, but the way it looked just didn't seem right.

"We never found out 'til yesterday," she said. "You would have thought somebody would've told us."

Willis thought he must have missed something. She was looking at him and he nodded his head, but when she didn't go on he had to say, timidly, "Told you what?"

"About Sid."

Willis waited until he was sure she was not going to add anything. "What about Sid? Sid who?"

Her gray curls bobbed fiercely, shaking her jowls, and she blinked her eyes in surprise at his ignorance. "Sid Bradley. Who'd you think we was talking about?"

Willis squirmed and glanced at Marlene, but she was staring innocently out the open door. "What about Sid?" He took a wild gamble. "Is this his place?"

"Of course it's his," she said. "It's been his ever since we sold it to him five years ago. To him and Martha, that is."

"What happened to him?"

"I thought that's why you were out here. To write about it."

"No. Actually, we came over here looking for the people from that commune up on the other hill. Somebody said they were at the Bradley farm, haying."

Ginny looked toward Marlene, evidently wanting confirmation of this suspicious report, because when Marlene smiled and nodded, she turned back to Willis. "They're here all right. The whole field's full of them. Who'd you think all this food I'm cooking was for?"

She looked at Marlene again and said, "Fred eats a lot, but not that much." She and Marlene both guffawed.

Willis was beginning to feel a little irritated. "What did happen to Sid, then?"

"A tree fell on him." She let that news sink in. "Nearly killed him. He's in the hospital with a broke head, a smashed shoulder, and one leg mangled so they might have to cut it off."

"Oh, how horrible," Marlene said. "How did it happen? When?"

"Wednesday. I guess he mowed that field of hay in the forenoon, then after lunch he went up to the woodlot to cut some firewood. Cut a big dead sugar maple and a limb fell on him."

She looked at each of them in turn, timing her story. "They'll do that. He ought to have known better." She paused again for argument in case one should be available, but neither of them chose to participate more than a sad headshake. "Ought not to have been up there at all for the matter of it. He should have been tedding the hay and leaving the woodcutting for later. That's what Fred says."

She stopped again and rose to stir the pots.

Willis ventured, "Why was he cutting firewood?"

"He's got all turned around," Ginny said mysteriously. She sat down again. "After Martha died last winter, I guess Sid just couldn't handle it by himself. They say he did some awful funny things, got turned around so he was sleeping in the daytime and working at night. They say he'd milk at midnight, then again in the forenoon. Then he quit sleeping at all, they said. I mean, I guess he slept some—got to. But they say he'd be up all hours. Lights on in the barn all night, and when spring came he'd be spreading manure or working on fences all day, then in the barn all night."

She paused, but the story was rolling now and she didn't seem to need anything from her audience. "We came over to see him right after we got back in April and he seemed kind of strange. Mostly we thought he was just wore out, though. Fred told him he was working too hard, but Sid just acted like he didn't hear.

"Then later we heard he hadn't paid his grain bill, and somebody said he wasn't hardly shipping any milk. The milk truck'd come in and he wouldn't have more than half a load. That's about when he started selling firewood, I guess."

"So," Willis said, "you and Fred are over here helping with the hay?"

"Somebody's got to do it." She gave Marlene a sly look. "And there sure ain't anybody that knows this land better than Fred and me. We cut them fields twice a year for twenty years. Started right after the war. Working with horses then."

Willis stood up and looked out the open door. "Looks like Fred's getting some help. And here comes more—a tractor and wagon."

"That's Old Man Shatney," Ginny said. "Sid's old truck broke down and Fred called Shatney to bring his hay wagon."

Neither of them said anything, but she went on as though Willis had questioned Fred's wisdom. "Well, they got to get the hay in today. It's already been down too long and it's going to rain tonight."

"How'd you get the commune people to help?"

"They just showed up. Got here too early." She looked sternly at Willis. "But that's better than too late."

"Last time we talked," Willis said, "I got the idea you didn't much like hippies."

"I never said that. Don't tell me what I said. I said I didn't like folks tearing down this country. And I don't. And I told 'em that when they showed up here."

She pointed to the sink. "I was standing right there and he—that big one who's their leader—was standing right where you're standing now. Right in the doorway. And I told him exactly how it's going to be if they stay on this place while I'm here."

She looked smugly at Marlene, who smiled and nodded encouragement.

"I told him right to his big hairy face that I don't like draft dodgers and don't like marijuana, or whatever you call it. I don't like skinny dipping and . . ." She turned her sly grin toward Marlene again. "Course, I might know something about that 'cause it ain't just hippies that go skinny dipping. But I didn't tell him that."

Marlene laughed and Ginny went on, speaking again in the instructress voice she seemed to think Willis needed. "I said I didn't like homos and lisbons and that sort of goings-on, and I said I would not tolerate burning or mutating the American flag."

She turned again to Marlene. "Well, mister-man, by that time I was going pretty good and I could see he was getting a little antsy. But he didn't say nothing, not so much as a peep. So I figured he was getting my drift and I eased off. I said we'd be glad to have their help and that it was neighborly of them to come down to help Sid out. And he said Sid had been good to their commune thing up there, giving 'em raw milk and whatnot. And I said, 'Well, we're glad to have your help,' and I was going to fix up some supper and when the haying was done they'd be welcome to come on back to the house here and have some."

Ginny leaned her heavy forearms on the table, one atop the other. "That was about noon and I ain't seen any of 'em since. He, that big guy, said some of the women would help me with the supper but I told him I wouldn't need any help until it was cleaning-up time."

She gave Marlene another coconspirator's glance then tilted her head slightly to roll her eyes toward the ceiling. "Hippies ain't very clean, you know. Now, I say live and let live and I don't care what they do up on their side of the mountain, but we don't need any topless cooks down here." She maintained the stand-up comic's deadpan, waiting for their laughs. "And whatever they do up in the field, that's Fred's problem."

All three of them roared at the image of Fred and a field full of topless hippie women, and Willis leaped at the chance to get away. "Well," he said, "I've got to see that. We better get on up there."

Ginny said, "Ain't no need to hurry. When Fred came down to telephone Shatney, he said there hasn't been much for them to do since the truck quit and he had to do some work on the baler, so there's not that much hay to pick up yet."

Willis looked at Marlene and said, "I guess we'll go on up there anyway," but she stayed in her chair.

"No, I'm going to stay down here and see if I can help Ginny. It sounds like there's plenty of people in the field."

He looked quickly at Ginny but she was clearly pleased with the idea, nodding her massive gray head once and rewarding Marlene with a tight smile.

"Okay," Willis said, "but you better keep your shirt on."

He could still hear both women laughing as he stepped off the porch.

Willis started into the field without knowing what he would do when he found Thunderclap, but then, he had decided to come up here to the commune without really knowing what he was looking for. He had long since stopped charging the paper for the time he spent on this story. No one in the newsroom seemed to have much interest in it, including Seymour.

"What's the news hook?" Greenberg said when he tried to talk to him about the commune. "A bunch of hippies out in the woods smoking their brains out. No news there. Christ, Willis, you're just pissed because you're the wrong generation. You better leave those girls and their dope alone and stick with what you know—bars and barmaids."

Willis couldn't tell them about Bushey and Quimby. Besides, what was there to tell? Dark hints about some future raid that never seemed to happen. Meanwhile, Willis had spent so much time hanging around the commune that Thunderclap didn't even seem so crazy anymore.

The hayfield was now full of people, noise, and movement. The baler punched out compact bales about every ten feet, and the tractor with the wagon inched steadily around the perimeter, still far behind but slowly catching up to the baler. A half dozen men, nearly that many women, and a small swarm of children ran, walked, and sometimes tumbled along briskly in rough formation about the wagon, grabbing bales, carrying, or in some cases dragging, them to the creeping wagon. On top, a woman and a half-grown boy stacked the bales in a neat, solid block, working from the front of the sideless wagon toward the back. They had finished three tiers and were beginning a fourth about halfway up a slatted wall at the front of the wagon that was the only vertical support for the load.

No one was left at the idled truck and as he passed Willis noticed the remains of their earlier rest stop. Two roaches and two clips were carefully laid on the wide running board beside a small paper bag half filled with marijuana. It sat on the running board like a bag of candy, the top open as an invitation to anyone who came along. From the truck he could spot Thunderclap, and Willis stopped for a minute to watch. He moved in a steady jog, picking up a bale in each hand, slowing to a fast walk on the way back to the wagon, halting long enough for the stackers to get ready, then flinging the bales up one at a time and running back for more. All the time he seemed to be keeping up with what everyone else was doing, whether the stackers were getting behind, and especially where the children were. At one point Willis saw him sweep up a small child who was straggling behind and carry him at a jog until he caught up with a group of other kids.

Eventually, Thunderclap noticed Willis by the truck and waved to him, but he didn't show any sign of stopping so Willis walked forward on a diagonal course that would intercept the tractor and wagon. As Willis neared the moving entourage, Thunderclap tossed up his two bales and walked over to him. "Slow day for news, huh?"

"No news today," Willis said. "We don't have a Sunday paper, so that means nothing happens on Saturday. No news."

Thunderclap shook his head in obvious disgust. Sweat dripped from his brow into the overgrown beard, which was matted and speckled liberally with hay chaff.

"But no news is good news for me," Willis said, "because that means I can be out here, which looks like a lot more fun than pounding on a typewriter."

The hippie leader looked at him with frank appraisal, and Willis was pleased not to see any sign in his eyes of the suspiciousness that used to dominate their dealings. After thinking it over he said, "Well then, come on. Let's grab some bales."

"Go ahead," Willis said, "I'll catch up."

He walked back to the truck, where he sat down on the running board. He took off his button-down—collar shirt and after a moment's hesitation pulled his t-shirt over his head. He jogged across the field and caught up with Thunderclap standing at the back of the wagon, waiting to toss up his bales.

He looked at Willis's bare chest and shook his head. "That's a mistake, man."

Willis just smiled. He knew he didn't have to worry because he never got sunburned and he'd worked in places a lot hotter than this hayfield. They both jogged off to pick up bales.

In half an hour they'd finished loading the wagon, which, Willis realized, wasn't really a wagon but a wide, homemade trailer, and the tractor headed for the barn, going very slowly now because the load was high and the whole rig heaved and swayed like a boat in heavy seas. The stackers had climbed down to join the procession that meandered along in the wake of the machines, walking in ones and twos, mopping sweat and bits of hay from faces, necks, and arms.

Several of the commune people had nodded or said hello to him but no one had begun a conversation, and Willis walked along by himself, sweat running from every pore, most of it catching at his waistline where it soaked the tops of his protruding shorts and created a dark, two-inch wide ribbon in his Levi's. As he walked along and his skin began to dry, his arms began to itch, then to sting. Scraping away the hay chaff, which was caked so thickly it looked like tattered sleeves, he saw a whole new capillary system of tiny cuts covering both forearms, and pretty soon the mild stinging had spread to his stomach and sides, wherever the cut end of a bale had brushed against him.

"Can't wait to take a swim, can you?"

Thunderclap was suddenly at his side. He hadn't heard him walking up and his voice startled him. He saw his eyes flicker across his red-splotched chest. "Quick dip probably be 'specially welcome for you, huh?"

Willis noticed the hippie's own white shirt was fastened right up to his neck and the sleeves were buttoned at the wrists. He nodded, but he added, "Yeah, I guess so. If I have time, but I may not." He carefully kept himself from scratching or rubbing his cuts.

They walked along silently side by side for a few steps, Willis as usual a little uncomfortable with this large, strange man. He didn't know what to call him, so generally he just didn't use any name. How the hell could anyone say Thunderclap with a straight face? The commune people often called him Chief, but Willis couldn't bring himself to use that name either. He remembered the name he had given to Bushey the day of the protest, but Willis was pretty sure that was made up on the spur of the moment. In fact, Bushey had told him that wasn't his real name, although even the cops didn't seem to know his true identity.

Finally, mostly to break the silence, he said, "It looks like just about everyone at your, uh, commune is out here helping. I heard what happened to Sid Bradley. Too bad."

Thunderclap didn't reply for a couple of more steps, then he said, "You out here to write about Sid? Because if you're not, you ought to be."

Willis waited, but no more was offered, so he asked, "Why's that? You mean write about the accident?"

"No. Not about the accident; it wasn't an accident."

"What do you mean? A tree limb fell on him, didn't it?"

Thunderclap stopped. "That's the trouble with reporters. Even honest ones, which most of them are not. Even the honest ones don't ask the right questions."

He threw up both hands as though he were flinging away an armful of trash. "Of course a limb fell on him, but the question is not whether he had an accident but why he had it." He lowered his head and shook it violently, drops of sweat spraying out in all directions. "This is a man who has worked in the woods all his life. A capable, healthy, serious man. Now, why would such a man let a tree limb fall on him?"

He jutted his bullish head forward and shot a piercing look at Willis. "Did you even wonder about that? What drove him to such a weak place that he would let a tree fall on him?" He didn't even pretend to wait for an answer. "I'll tell you what it was. It was the banks and the lawyers and the hospitals. It was the government with its taxes and it was the capitalist system with its exploitation of all people who work with their hands. That's why Sid got hurt. That's why he's in the hospital and we're out here today picking up his hay. Because they drove him crazy. Because they didn't want him to keep this little farm. They drove him to a place where he was too weak to even do the things he had been doing ever since he was a boy—make hay and cut firewood."

Oh God, Willis thought, he's about to start spouting scripture. They were standing near the abandoned truck and he motioned toward it. "I want a smoke," he said and began walking in that direction. "Want one?"

Thunderclap didn't answer but he walked alongside. Willis picked his shirt off the running board and pulled the pack of Winstons out of the pocket, offering it to Thunderclap, who shook his head. After lighting the cigarette, he put the pack back in the pocket and started to put down the shirt, but Thunderclap said gently, with no sign of triumph or ridicule, "It might be a good idea to put that on." Willis shrugged, but he carried the shirt with him as they began walking again toward the barn and he slipped it on as they talked.

Thunderclap railed quietly but earnestly about greed, corruption, inequality, the war, and the common man. Willis listened and occasionally nodded or asked a simple leading question, but his attention wandered. He was still having trouble figuring out exactly what story he would write about the commune, but at the same time he knew Bushey was right when he kept saying there was a terrific story buried somewhere in this weird counterculture.

It depressed Willis to think of Bushey and his various admonitions, and it made him feel particularly alone—even a little uneasy—to remember their conversations. Bushey didn't know, of course, that he had become somewhat friendly with this bearded maniac, and Thunderclap didn't know that he was trying to get a story about the commune. No one, including Seymour and Marlene, had any idea that Willis routinely talked to the former police chief or that young Fletcher and his friends had their own interest in this situation. And as far as Willis had been able to discover, no one in the press or the government or even the various police agencies knew that Quimby was planning to use the commune somehow in his campaign for attorney general.

This story—or whatever else it turned out to be, because at this moment he couldn't imagine what he'd ever write—was on Willis's mind far too much. He'd never before felt so drawn to a story and at the same time entirely isolated from everyone involved in it. Sometimes, covering the civil rights movement he had worried that he was getting too close to one group or another, but he had never felt separated from his newspaper or other reporters and he had always been able to talk with Sheila or someone else about the stories he was working on. Both sides had accused him at various times of being a pawn for the other side, but he had never taken the charges seriously or questioned his own motives.

This commune story was different, and the more he worked on it, the more uncomfortable it made him. Everything was under the surface, and the parts that showed all turned into decoys. Quimby fed him rumors about child beating and neglect and even dark reports about burials that were never reported. But he never seemed to have any real evidence, or if he claimed to have it, he said it would be illegal to give it to Willis.

Bushey was more direct, but he too failed to show any proof. His chief charge was that the commune was somehow connected with a group of terrorists and that Thunderclap was actually a part of the Winslow gang, wanted nationwide for cop murder, bank robbery, drug dealing, white slavery, and God knows what else. Fletcher and his crowd of businessmen said the commune was a magnet for local kids who came there to buy drugs, alcohol, and weird sex and that it was a central station for an underground railroad that shuttled draft dodgers into Canada.

All of them hated the hippies for their open use of obscene language, for their disdain for normal work, and for their war protests. They all breathlessly quoted word-of-mouth stories and reports in obscure magazines warning about a coming invasion of Vermont by thousands of alienated people and convicted criminals eager to join this commune or one of countless others believed to be scattered in the rural mountains.

None of the various complaints fit very tidily with Willis's firsthand observations at the commune, except for the charges of widespread and flagrant violation of the drug laws. Pot was ever-present, and Willis never saw anyone try to hide or disguise its use. Neither, though, had he ever seen violent or abusive behavior toward children or anyone else. He had never seen a firearm or, for that matter, any of the hard drugs, like LSD, although he had caught enough oblique references in commune conversation to believe marijuana sometimes was just the appetizer drug.

They walked along in silence for a while, then suddenly Thunderclap stopped and flung out both arms in a wide sweep that covered most of the landscape. "These'll all be gone in a few years," he boomed.

Willis jumped, startled by the sudden prophecy. What the hell was he talking about? The mountains?

"They're just about gone already in the rest of the country. They are gone entirely from the Midwest and California. Swallowed up by greedy, gulping corporations that spit out farmers like grape seeds." He turned around to take in the field behind them. "They won't even bother to take over hill farms like this; they'll just starve Sid out and let the woods do the swallowing or the land developers with their goddam vacation chalets."

Willis did not usually listen very carefully to Thunderclap's raving, but now he was struck by a tone of forlorn sincerity. The words and delivery had the usual theatrical touch, but underneath was a personal sadness that caught his attention.

They toted, stacked, hauled, unloaded, and restacked hay all afternoon, working steadily but not frantically since the skies stayed clear until the final couple of loads, when clouds began to move in from the southeast. Fred baled with the determined, one-pace rhythm of a windup clock and, as far as Willis could tell, he never spoke a word to anyone, although, as the only one with farmer credentials, he was at least theoretically the field commander. Ginny will be proud of him, Willis thought. The tractor and attached baler cleared the field, moving in ever-tighter circles until finally the last windrow disappeared and, without ever changing speed, the noisy rig headed toward the barn.

The tall gambrel-roof barn was half full when they finished at four. Willis and several others made one more trip back to the disabled truck to gather up discarded clothes, empty beer and water bottles, and the bag of pot, which was not yet empty but considerably diminished. Willis had noticed, with some weary irritation, that by late afternoon some of the hippies were moving more aimlessly and accomplishing little work, particularly a young, big-eyed guy called Dennis who drifted around the field smiling, carrying a single bale that for a while he seemed to forget was dangling at the end of his arm.

*
**

When Willis got back to the house, Fred and Thunderclap were filling up the small side porch, one planted on each side of the door in kitchen chairs that they filled so thoroughly the bottoms of the legs were the only visible points of support. Between the two of them, Willis thought, that little porch is carrying well over a quarter ton, and he hoped the floor joints were in better shape than the deeply worn, weather-grooved banisters that fenced in two sides of the porch.

Between the two massive men a narrow strait led into the kitchen, but Willis decided not to risk the passage. He sat down on the top step, turned half toward the silent pair and half toward the still sunny little yard.

"Pretty good day's work," he ventured cheerfully, but a single short nod from Fred was the only reply. In sheer physicality—shape, mass, and posture—they were as identical as two stone monuments but at the same time as distinct as marble and granite. Sweat gleamed from both of their shadowed faces, their only uncovered parts, but Fred was crisp, clean, and smooth while Thunderclap was hairy, stained, and slouched. Remarkably, Willis thought, they appeared content, relaxed, and at ease with each other, like circus lions resting between acts.

Marlene came through the kitchen door carrying two Budweisers, and her smile became a gleeful little laugh when she saw Willis. "I'll get you one," she said, handing the bottles to the others.

Thunderclap nodded his thanks, took a long swallow, and set his bottle on the handrail. Fred looked at the beer as if it were a nearly forgotten old chum, then drank off half the bottle in one gulp. He tilted the bottle down from his mouth briefly, then upended it again, finally setting it down on his rail with barely one finger of beer left. He said nothing.

Marlene stepped neatly between them and smiled as she handed Willis's beer down to him, brushing his shoulder with her hand. "A bunch of the others went swimming," she said. "Are you going?"

Willis shook his head. "Me either," she said, "and neither is Ginny."

Fred snorted a chuckle. "She would if she wanted," he said with proud conviction. "She can swim like one of them things you see on television. Like a seal."

Willis pictured her gray water-sleeked hair and broad cunning face, half submerged, plowing steadily through the water.

Thunderclap spoke for the first time, although he made it sound like the continuation of a conversation. "Even if we get him enough hay and enough wood, he still won't make it through another winter."

They all looked at him, but no one replied.

"The creamery won't take his milk for another month, and the government inspector's going to quarantine him again next time he comes if the barn isn't clean enough."

"The bastards," Fred said in a low growl that made Willis wonder what he'd be like if he ever really got mad.

"How's he going to pay the mortgage?"

Fred shook his head and Willis copied him.

"They act like Sid's crazy, but it's the government and big business that's making him crazy," Thunderclap said.

"That's right," Fred said, "at least as far as farming goes. They got so many rules now you can't make a living. No matter how hard you work."

Marlene went back inside and they sipped their beer in silence for a while. Willis suddenly picked up a strong odor of marijuana and he saw that a couple of the commune boys were sitting in the shade of a car parked off to the side. They must have been there all along, hidden in the tall grass, maybe taking a nap. The smell of burning pot was powerful and distinct, and Willis looked over at Fred, but if he noticed he wasn't letting on.

Willis lighted one of his own cigarettes and held out the pack to the others. Fred shook his head. "One bad habit at a time," he said, raising his beer bottle. "I ain't smoked since my heart attack but you go ahead; 'cause I quit don't mean I'm going to try and tell everybody else what to do."

His eyes flickered to the right toward the pot smokers.

"You boys make pretty good farmhands," he said to Thunderclap. "Girls too, for the matter of it. If you'd been around five years ago, I might not have ever sold out."

Thunderclap asked, "Could you make a living on this place?"

"Sure," Fred said. "For a long time we did pretty good. Then everything started to change. First there was the bulk tanks. Then you couldn't have a wooden milking parlor; poured a lot of money right into the ground for concrete. Then the haulers for the creameries wouldn't go up certain roads."

He stopped, then started again as though he actually wanted to talk. "Of course, we didn't have a mortgage either. But then the government got into it with both feet and started fooling around with the price of milk. It got so you never knew what you were going to get. You'd get a fair-sized check one month and not hardly nothing the next."

He paused, gathering strength to continue what was for him a marathon of speech. "And all the time more rules. Can't do this, got to do that. It got so you had to be a crook just to keep farming. They made you into a crook 'cause you had to say one thing on one form and just the opposite on the next form."

He tossed off the last gulp of beer, and when the bottle came down his thin mouth twitched and his small eyes rolled wickedly. "Of course, we was still doing all right, me and her."

Willis laughed and Thunderclap nodded appreciatively.

"But then I had my heart attack and then it just didn't seem worth it. I was tired of fighting with the co-op and fighting with haulers and grain dealers and with government men out here every month thinking they knew better than I did about how to farm this place. So we quit. Sold out.

"Couldn't find no one to buy it at first. Finally, we sold to a real estate guy, and before you knew it he'd turned around and sold it to Sid and Martha. Funny thing. I've known Sid most of his life, but when we was looking to sell we didn't know he was looking to buy. Truth is, I was surprised they could afford it."

He shook his massive head and tugged on the short brim of his engineer's cap. "Then, by God, first thing Sid did was go out and buy that goddam fancy silo over there. I suppose somebody sold him that on time, but any fool could've told him he couldn't make the payments. Hell, he ought to've known himself."

Fred took off his cap and scratched his head. "Well, I'm just glad I got out when I did."

But Willis thought he didn't look very glad. His face had drooped and he looked as mournful as he had been content before he began his tale.

"Still," Fred said, "it don't seem right that Sid can work himself crazy and they still take away his farm."

They all looked up as a small red truck turned into the driveway. A wiry man wearing blue work trousers and a white shirt stepped out and walked briskly toward the porch. A patch over his breast pocket said "Tim." He carried a small book, rather like a newsboy's receipt book, in his left hand, and with his right he pulled off his baseball cap. A patch on the cap said "PSC" in large letters.

"Hello. Is Sid home?"

None of them answered.

"I'm from Public Service Company. I need to check the meter."

"He's not here," Thunderclap answered when it was clear that Fred and Willis were not stepping forward. "What's wrong with the meter?"

"Well, that's okay," the meter man said, "I'll just go down cellar. I know where it is."

"What's wrong with it?" Thunderclap asked again, suspicion putting an edge in his voice. "Electricity seems to be working all right."

The meter man covered his thinning hair with his cap and seemed to straighten up slightly. "Who're you?"

It wasn't clear who he was asking since he didn't seem to be looking at anyone in particular, and no one answered. He shuffled his feet a little, then finally said, "I'm going down cellar to check the meter. I've been here three times this week and nobody's been around and that's why I came back on a Saturday."

"Sid ain't here." It was the first time Fred had spoken since the meter man arrived, and he acted as though the earlier conversation simply hadn't happened. "It's his house and he ain't here."

Tim the meter man had put a foot tentatively onto the step, but when Fred spoke he hesitated, although he didn't back up. He's got some spunk, Willis thought as he noticed that while neither of them had yet stood up, Fred and Thunderclap had leaned closer together, further narrowing the passage to the door.

"Listen," Tim said in a tired but strong voice, "Sid's three months behind on his electric bill. I'm gonna check that meter and if it's working all right I'm gonna leave him a disconnect notice, and in two weeks we're coming back up here to pull the meter. Unless he pays the bill."

He still had one foot on the bottom step and now he finished stepping up. "The law says I've got a right to go into that cellar. Hell, I got a legal right to go in even if nobody's home. If I need to, I'll get the sheriff, but I've got to check that meter and that's what I'm going to do."

Now he was standing on the porch, but he waited a moment to see what they would do. Willis looked quickly at Fred and Thunderclap and was a little surprised to see that they both seemed apprehensive, intimidated either by Tim's boldness or by the authority of legal sanction. A ripple of doubt passed across both of their faces, and each one cut his eyes quickly to see what the other one was doing.

Tim took a step forward.

"No, you ain't." The voice came through the open kitchen door and it was followed immediately by the formidable body of Ginny Parker. "They already told you. Sid ain't here and you ain't coming in."

The meter man stopped, and it was immediately clear that he wasn't going any further although he did not yet turn around.

"You ought to be ashamed," she said. "And your company's shamed too. You call it a public service company but it's a public disgrace is what it is."

Sweat rolled down her face and she raised her hand to mop it off with a paper towel. "And don't tell me about the law. We all know who makes the laws. It ain't right and it ain't justice to cut off Sid's electricity."

Tim was still standing motionless, making no effort to reply.

"It ain't right," she repeated, "and somebody ought to do something about it."

Willis had been listening with a smile on his face, but suddenly he realized she was now glaring at him, not the meter man. Finally, he got it, and he spoke for the first time since the truck turned into the driveway.

"Tim," he said, "I'm a reporter for the newspaper." He stood up as the meter man turned around to look down at him from the porch. "I'm out here to do a human-interest story on how Sid got hurt and how his neighbors are all turning out to get his hay for him."

Tim blinked, for the first time showing confusion and uncertainty.

"I guess now I'll write about how the power company plans to shut off his electricity while Sid's still in the hospital."

Willis pulled a pen from his shirt pocket but he didn't have any paper, so he picked up his empty beer bottle and started to write on the label. "What's your last name, Tim?"

The meter reader stepped back off the porch to stand about two feet from Willis. "Wait a minute," he said, "you can't put that in the paper. I didn't know you were a reporter."

"I've got a legal right to write it," Willis said. "You can't stop me. Now, exactly when are you going to pull the meter?"

Tim began to walk away.

"Hey, Tim," Willis called. "Who should I ask for when I call the power company?"

The meter man hurried to his truck, tossed the receipt book through the open window, then climbed in and drove off without saying another word.

Willis watched him leave until he heard Ginny cackling. When he turned around, he saw that she had moved onto the porch and Marlene had squeezed in behind her to stand in the doorway. All four of them were looking at Willis, their smiling faces beaming silent applause at him. He started to step up on the porch, then thought better of it and sat back down on the step.

"Will you really write a story?" Marlene asked.

"Maybe," Willis said, pleased with himself but still a little surprised by his own role. "I'm not sure exactly what I'd write and it probably wouldn't do any good anyway. The disconnect rules are pretty fixed and I think the power companies have to follow them even if they get bad publicity from it."

"It ain't right," Ginny said again. "It wouldn't happen if the REA still owned the light company. Somebody ought to do something."

There was a long silence, and the coconspirators' triumph was fading fast when Fred finally spoke. "What if they read the meter and find out he don't owe nothing?" he asked.

They all looked puzzled, even Ginny.

"I know how to make the meter run backwards," Fred said solemnly.

Thunderclap jumped up from his chair. "Run backwards?"

"Yep," Fred said, "it's simple."

They all waited while he gathered his thoughts. "And I know how to make it run slower too, if you want to."

"How do you do it?" Thunderclap asked.

"You make it run backwards by just unplugging the meter and—it's just like a big lamp plug or something—just unplug it and plug it back in upside down."

He looked around at the other three for reaction. "And the dials run backwards, like the hands on a clock running the wrong way."

Thunderclap said, "We could run it backwards for a couple of weeks, then plug it back in the right way."

"That's right," Fred said, "and before we plug it back in, we'll take off the seal and sprinkle salt into the wheel mechanism. That'll make the dials run slower for a long time."

No one said anything for a couple of minutes, then Thunderclap said, "By God, let's do it."

Willis saw that for some reason they were all looking at him. Finally, he said, "On Monday I'll call the PSC public relations people. Maybe if I say I'm working on a story, they'll hold off on pulling the meter. That'll give it time to run backwards for a while, maybe even a few weeks."

No one said any more. Thunderclap and Fred went off together into the house as a pickup and two cars pulled to a stop and several young, wet hippies piled out, laughing and running toward the house. They stopped when they saw Ginny on the porch.

"Don't come in here wet," she said sternly. "And everybody better have all their clothes on."

Sy eased his huge old car up to the curb, shut off the engine, and sat quietly behind the wheel for nearly five minutes. He was parked half a block from Greenberg's house, and although the street was filled with empty cars he had a clear view of the sidewalk in front and the path leading up to the front porch. No one arrived during the time he waited, but then, he had known he was quite late. He thought again about just driving away, avoiding the party altogether, but even as he toyed with the idea he knew he couldn't do it. He had to go. It was the July 4 party, two days late, of course, since all newsroom parties had to be held on a Saturday.

It was eight thirty when he stepped off the sidewalk onto the front path—twilight, the time, Bacon said, when bats fly among birds and suspicions come out to mingle with thoughts. He could hear music and loud talk coming from the backyard and he walked quietly around the corner of the house. He paused for a moment, leaning against a drainspout. Most of the newsroom seemed to be there, laughing, talking, some throwing horseshoes, some cooking over a grill, and nearly everyone drinking. A keg of beer on a picnic table was the centerpiece.

"Hey, Sy, want a beer?"

Hank was walking toward him, and Sy hurriedly probed in his pocket for a cigar. He pulled one out, waved it toward the kid, and said, "Later."

Connie left a small group watching the horseshoe game and walked toward him. "Hi, Sy," she said brightly, "we've been looking for you."

Hank moved toward her with an exaggerated swagger, saying, "And here's looking at you, kid," but she ignored him.

Sy lighted his cigar and said through the smoke, "Hello, Connie. Looks like a good party. Where's Matt?"

"In the house. Tending to domestic affairs."

Sy lifted his eyebrows. "Anything wrong?"

Connie shrugged. "Not really, but you know Nancy. I don't think she's too crazy about having the newsroom invade her house, and Matt's been running around between the party and the family, making peace like some goddam diplomat."

What she said about Greenberg's wife was true; she didn't have much interest in the newspaper. But Sy hated Connie's bitchy, backbiting superiority and he was on the verge of calling her on it but he choked back the words. The union vote was to be held by the NLRB on Tuesday. Manny had been lecturing Sy nearly daily about avoiding confrontations and McNally had telephoned him three times, the bastard. He did allow himself a wordless sneer, however, and it was not wasted on Connie. Her face stiffened and she turned away from him, stepping quickly toward another group. Hank turned away too; another union vote for sure.

Sy stood at the corner smoking his cigar, not hiding exactly, but not eager to join the party. Saturday nights were a problem for him, or at least three out of four were troublesome because, without a newspaper to make, he didn't know what to do with himself. One Saturday a month, promptly at ten, he happily went off to Vic's house to play poker, and in fact he was going there this Saturday. Most weeks, though, Saturdays were a trial, a long evening spent either fending off invitations or staying at home to read, drink Scotch, and wrestle down a recurring impulse to haunt the empty, idle newsroom.

His eyes roved over the crowd. He knew most of them, of course, and he had seen many of the others from time to time on their occasional visits to the newsroom. Most of the reporters and editors and even Mo and the proofreaders were milling around the yard. Willis was one of the few he couldn't find.

He also took a close look for Vince. He expected the sly bastard to be working the party for votes. But he couldn't spot him. Christ, maybe he was with Willis?

"Sy. Hey, Sy."

The shout came from the back porch. Greenberg was standing on the top step, holding a large tray full of uncooked hamburgers and hotdogs. "Come on over and get a beer."

Sy nodded his head but still he didn't advance. Several people were looking in his direction and conversations suddenly stopped all around the party. Anger blazed into life as he glared toward Greenberg. Did he shout to warn them that he was here?

No escape. Now everyone was looking at him. The only noise came from the record player on the porch that poured *Porgy and Bess* out into the yard. Straight ahead a path was open to the barbecue pit, which glowed with hot coals, sending a light stream of smoke rising to the sky. Simmons hulked beside the pit, a hotdog jammed halfway into his mouth and his other hand holding a paper plate piled high with food.

Simmons, that fat goldbrick, was going to vote for the union just to make trouble. He thought of going over and tipping the plate out of his hand into the fire.

He stopped close to Simmons and carefully exhaled his cigar smoke away from him. "Hello, Lon. I see you're Johnny-on-the-spot as usual, so long as the spot is near the food."

Several people standing nearby laughed. Simmons often bragged that he got to car accidents before the cops and he once made the mistake of describing himself as Johnny-on-the-spot. In the newsroom, Sy called him Spot about half the time.

Sy waved a hand toward the meat sizzling on the grill. "This must be the scene of the crime. But I can see that you've got it covered."

More laughter, and Simmons's cheeks puffed out in anger but he didn't say anything. Everyone knew he was terrified of Seymour.

Greenberg set down his platter and said wistfully to Sy, "You playing cards tonight?"

He nodded. Greenberg loved poker, and he was the only one in the newsroom, other than Sy, who Vic had ever invited to play. But Nancy didn't like the late-night games and Matt had stopped playing.

"Matt, why don't we get up a game here?" It was Ron, who had walked up behind Sy. "There's got to be enough poker players in this crowd."

He turned toward the horseshoe players. "Connie, how about you; you up for a little poker? I know you like blackjack, at least."

"Sure," she said, "I'd probably play for a while." She looked toward Greenberg. "If it's okay with Nancy," she said.

Greenberg's permanently wrinkled brow knotted further. "Yeah," he said with worried enthusiasm. "Sure. Let's see if we can get up a game."

Sy felt Connie watching him. When he looked over, she smiled at him with a gloating victory nod that made his hand tremble and sent blood rushing into his face.

"Hey, Connie," Ron said, "how about Vince. Where's he?"

"Don't ask me," she said, turning her face away from Sy.

"How about Willis?" Ron asked, his eager voice rising. "He'll sure as hell play if he gets here. Is he coming, Matt?"

Vince and Willis? They must be together. Sy could feel his face darken with clamped-down fury. He turned and walked stiff-legged to the beer keg. Constructing insults in his head, he pulled the tap but then forgot it until he noticed a woman he had never seen before staring at him. The beer was running over his cup and pouring onto the ground. He wanted to kick her, but instead he ground the toe of his shoe into the earth where the spilled beer had pooled.

He took his cup to the outer fringe of the crowd, where he found Mo sitting alone, his back propped up against a giant maple. Mo had been excluded from the voting because the union claimed he had been a proofreader so long he had become management. Sy slumped down beside him and they began talking about movies. Sy had only read about most of them, but Mo had seen everything shown on the silver screen since Tom Mix and it was the one and only subject he really liked.

By nine forty-five some people had left and others had moved inside, but Willis still hadn't appeared. Sy stood up to go and said goodbye to Mo, who showed no sign of leaving as long as the beer held out.

It was fully dark now but the yard near the house was well lighted. He was a few feet from the porch when Willis and the blonde girl he had been hanging out with lately came out the back door. Their hair was wet and newly combed and they were both laughing. He waved to Sy, but several people clustered on the porch were talking to him. He seemed to have a small entourage.

"Where've you been, Willis?"

"Making hay," he said. People laughed. "It's a long story. I'll tell you later."

Sy beckoned to Greenberg, who followed him out into the shadows outside the circle of light. "What's up? You going to Vic's?"

Sy didn't reply until they were well away from the others, then he said, "Listen, Matt. They've got me boxed in. I can't make a move. So I want you to do something for me."

Greenberg's voice was cautious. "Sure, Sy. If I can. But there's not much any of us can do about the vote, you know. If that's what you're talking about."

He added tenuously, "They're going to win the vote. You know that."

"Goddam it, of course I know that." Sy's voice rose but he lowered it immediately to a near whisper. "It's not the vote I'm talking about. It's the people who aren't voting."

"Who? What're you saying?" Greenberg said in confusion. "I'm one of the ones not voting."

Sy's voice remained low, but now he was spitting his words. "Right now I'm talking just about Willis. Willis and Carmoli. What I want you to do is keep an eye on those two."

"Huh? Willis?"

"Shush. Just listen. I want you to let me know if Carmoli shows up here later. And if he and Willis talk. I think they've been meeting tonight."

"Azoy, Sy. What've you been smoking? What would make you think Willis is up to something?"

Sy's voice returned to nearly normal volume and pitch but it had a new smugness as he said, "If you don't want to be suspected, don't tie your shoelaces in a melon patch."

"Huh?"

"It's a proverb, Matt. You ought to know about proverbs."

Sy turned away. "Just keep an eye out." He walked toward the corner of the house, keeping in the shadow, and disappeared.

CHAPTER EIGHT
Wednesday, August 28, 1968

"What's the news?" Manny asked, looking up from his typewriter as Sy poked his head around the doorway. "Come on in. I'm glad you got here before the others."

Sy settled himself in his usual seat next to Manny's big wooden desk before he spoke. "Black, fearful, comfortless, and horrible."

Manny looked at him and blinked. For a moment he didn't speak, and Sy wondered if he knew the source. Finally, he said, "Wrong play." He picked up his pipe. "Or were you talking about the Democrats?"

"No," Sy said, "that was just a comment on the time of day. Why do we have to have these meetings in the middle of the night?"

Manny looked at his watch. "It's eight thirty in the morning," he said.

"For some of us that's the middle of the night."

"That's a sore subject," Manny said, waving two note-sized sheets he picked out of the pile of papers on his desk. "I've got nasty complaints about last night from the composing room and the pressroom. How late were you, anyway?"

Sy knew it was coming and that's why he brought up the time. He was relieved by Manny's tone, but he was also annoyed for being relieved. Why should he complain, anyway? Newspapers break deadlines to get big stories, for Christ's sake.

"We pushed them pretty hard," Sy conceded in deference to Manny's tone. "I expect we missed some of the late long-distance delivery connections."

"Delivery connections? The way these memos tell it, you made the paperboys late for school. And I haven't even heard from Andrew about how much overtime we had to pay. But I will."

He sat forward and picked up the front page of the paper. "But I've got to admit, this is a great shot of Mayor Daley. The cutline says they adjourned after one; is that right?"

"Chicago time," Sy said. "Two seventeen our time."

"You took this picture off the television set?"

Sy was a little startled. Manny had never mentioned the television set, which had been in Sy's office for five months now. For years Manny had refused to install such a "time waster" in the newsroom. When Sy bought one with his own money, Manny had simply refused to acknowledge its existence. But this photo was obviously a shot of an image on a television screen.

"Right," Sy said, "Peterson took it. I thought it came out fairly well."

Manny blinked. He looked well rested, as always, but his eyes, normally steady and focused, dodged around the room. He sighed.

"Listen, Sy, I'm glad we got the convention story. It makes me proud of the paper and it's the style of newspapering I've always liked. But you know that when we go to offset printing, you're going to have to quit breaking these deadlines willy-nilly."

Sy felt the good mood slip. "Willy-nilly? What's that supposed to mean? I held up the deadline to get a story that we ought to have in the paper. That's not willy-nilly."

He paused, struggling to get a grip on himself, but when Manny began to speak, Sy waved him off. "Wait a minute. Who's deciding when we go to press—the newsroom or the back shop? Is this a newspaper or a shopper?"

"Oh relax, Sy. When we get the new press, the deadline's going to move up an hour. That's all I'm saying. You've known that all along. And it's going to be a real deadline."

Sy suddenly felt exhausted, sapped of all the goodwill he had felt earlier when he woke up and recalled the night's work. It was a damned good paper and nothing had been able to stop it—not the union nonsense, not the deadline, and not all the other deadweight he had to carry around. Willis had delivered some good, solid stories, and between the *Times* wire, the AP, and his own writing from the television, they had as complete coverage of the convention as anyone could want. It was a good newspaper they put on the street, and if it was an hour or so late, so what? But Manny had taken away the earlier glow.

Sy shook his head slowly. "I don't get it. We're making all these great technology changes, making everything faster, but the news deadline is getting earlier. What're we doing all this for, anyway? Technology ought to make something better, not just cheaper to produce."

Manny just sat, his face showing limitless patience that only the old can summon. He didn't need to answer the question and he knew that Sy knew he didn't need to answer it because it really wasn't a question at all but a moan.

He looked away, fumbled with his pipes, then evidently decided not to smoke and instead abruptly pushed away the ashtray.

"The others'll be here soon," he said, "and I had hoped we could talk first. I'm writing an editorial and I'd like your view of this madness going on in Chicago."

"I think the Democrats are dead," Sy said. "They're committing suicide."

Manny nodded. "Anything to the Ted Kennedy rumors?"

"That's all over," Sy said. "The so-called draft movement got hot over the weekend, but it died yesterday. Cold dead, Willis says."

He felt himself relaxing, his mind easing into a comfortable zone. "No, this deal is done. Humphrey will be nominated tonight and then, as they say, the shit will hit the fan."

"That's what I figured," Manny said. "Too bad. I don't think Humphrey can beat Nixon and I don't think Nixon represents this country any more than Gus Hall does. And that guy Agnew scares the bejesus out of me."

"Right," Sy said, "that's the problem. Neither party represents the country but they've got a death grip on the process. Both of them nominate losers, and that makes it possible for a crazy like George Wallace to get some traction. I'll bet he gets 20 percent of the vote, and that means Humphrey couldn't win even if he wasn't welded to Johnson's Texas belt buckle."

Manny nodded. "Yeah, the poor bastard. I feel a little sorry for him out there with Daley running the convention and Johnson running everything else."

He paused, and a smile that Sy had come to recognize as unadulterated mirth spread across his pink face. "But don't think high-handed party tactics is anything new to the Democrats," he said. "In 1932, when it looked like the California delegation was going to bolt for Roosevelt, the police locked the convention hall and wouldn't let anyone out."

He laughed. "That was in Chicago too. And I remember that an AP photographer telephoned for an ambulance, and when they brought in a stretcher he put his plates under the blanket and sent out the only pictures that anybody got from that session."

Sy laughed.

"It looks as though Willis is doing a pretty fair job," Manny said. "He had three good stories last night. What made you decide to send him instead of one of the statehouse guys?"

Sy hesitated. "Well, Stevens went to Miami with the Republicans, you know." He stopped, but that obviously wasn't enough since Manny knew either of the other two statehouse reporters would have liked to cover the Democrats' national convention. "I just decided to give Willis a chance," Sy said lamely. "He's done a lot of good work for us this year."

He hoped Manny wouldn't push it. The truth was that Sy knew the other two had voted for the union. Since the vote, Willis had convinced him that he was not secretly supporting the union and that he would cross the picket line if they called a strike. But he couldn't tell Manny because McNally had ordered him repeatedly not to talk to anybody about the union and not to retaliate in any way against anyone who voted for the union. Bypassing the statehouse guys could be called retaliation.

The gap between him and Manny over how to deal with the union had widened over the summer. They both worked hard to avoid talking about it, but it had left Sy with few allies. He had been enormously relieved to find he could trust Willis.

Manny looked at his watch again, reached for a pipe, then snatched his hand away, and finally said with a bad actor's phony casualness, "What's the mood these days in the newsroom?"

Sy was instantly on guard. First they tell him not to talk to the reporters, then they want to know what's going on. Any answer could be a trap. He stalled.

"I went to a party at Greenberg's the other day," he said. "Most of the newsroom was there."

"Before or after the vote?" Manny asked.

"Just before. Well, it was about a month ago, actually."

A quiver ran across Manny's balloon-smooth forehead as he shot Sy a sharp look and said through slightly puckered lips, "A month ago? I mean what's the mood now, since the vote and the NLRB certification?"

Sy's caution broke. "How the hell should I know? You and your Irish gunslinger told me not to ask questions. Hell, not to talk to anybody. I just put out the newspaper; how would I know what's happening in the newsroom?"

Manny's face had returned to normal placidity. He blinked but didn't answer.

"I ought to be asking you," Sy said. "What's happened since the vote?"

"Nothing, I guess," Manny said. "McNally and Fletcher will tell us when they get here in a few minutes."

They sat silently for a minute, then Manny stood up and walked to the two windows on the west side of his office. He raised each of them as far open as it would go, letting in street sounds and a mild breeze. The old building didn't have central air-conditioning. Some of the individual offices, including Fletcher Junior's, had window units, but Manny had refused to have one. He said he wanted air the way it came from the factory, not reconditioned air.

"It's going to be hot," he said. "Even hotter in Chicago, I expect."

Sy didn't answer.

"What's the news from Prague?" Manny said.

"It looks like it's over, at least for now," Sy said. "The *Times* is reporting that Dubček is back in as of yesterday, at least as a figurehead. The fighting, anyway, seems to be over."

Manny was still standing in front of the windows. "So, the Prague Spring wilts in August." He turned around, shaking his head in wonder. "What next? What a year. Vietnam, Paris, Czechoslovakia, now Chicago . . ."

"You left out the assassinations and the burning of the cities," Sy said, "not to mention the crucifixion of Johnson and the resurrection of Nixon."

"Well," Manny said with resignation, "they'll be here in a minute and I guess we'll have to spend the rest of the day dealing with this union mess."

He shook his head and his pink face darkened slightly. "You'd think they'd see what they're doing. You'd think this year, this year of all times, they'd see how critical it is to have independent newspapers and they wouldn't be trying to tear them down."

His resolve finally surrendering to his self-sympathy, Manny lunged for the ashtray and grabbed a pipe without even going through the selection ritual.

"Dammit," he said, "you'd think the newspeople at least—at least they would see how important this work is. Why do they let themselves be led around by the malcontents and the professional rabble-rousers?"

Sy didn't even try to answer. He sat back as Manny filled and fired his pipe. He puffed out the first big cloud of smoke just as McNally, trailed by Fletcher, walked briskly into the office.

"Good morning," he boomed, creating a little wake of Old Spice— tainted air as he made a quick circuit around the office, grabbing up the other chair and setting it down firmly beside Manny's desk. "Fletcher," he said, "would you mind snagging a couple more chairs? I know your father doesn't approve of meetings, but we really do need to have a seat for everyone."

McNally strolled over to the open window and paused, looking out. "So, Sy, that's quite a show they're putting on in Chicago. I got a quick look at your paper on the way down from the airport just now. Pretty nice coverage. You had some stories I didn't even see in the *Times*."

He turned away from the window to face Sy. "But don't you think that headline was a little strong? 'Prague West.'" He flashed a patronizing smile. "I mean, really, it's just a political convention."

Without waiting for a reply, he made a decisive quarter turn to his left, dismissing Sy and giving the benefit of his presence solely to Manny. "I suppose we should be thankful that the market, at least, keeps these things in perspective, eh, Manny? Four days of screaming headlines and the Dow has hardly flickered. That tells us just how important and how, quote, historic, unquote, this nomination drama really is."

McNally waited for Manny to agree, but all he got was another cloud of tobacco smoke, so he went on solo, shifting now to a more solemn, philosophic tone.

"I really have a hard time understanding some of these people. We're enjoying one of the longest economic booms in history, the budget is balanced, the stock market is stable and rising. Maybe things are too good, too easy, so people like these protesters and dreamers like McCarthy can afford to joust at windmills."

Still finding no response, he returned to the window and slowly took off the jacket of his seersucker suit. He folded it carefully and tucked it neatly but without prissiness on the windowsill. "Maybe it's like this union business," he said, turning back to face Manny. "Just something we've got to work through — thoughtfully, carefully, and patiently. If we can do that, eventually they'll just go away and we and the country can get back to doing our business."

Sy was stunned, not so much by McNally's arrogance as by his own tongue tying caution. He should have shoved this nonsense back down his self-righteous throat about three sentences back, but he was still sitting meekly with his legs crossed. He had done some research and made some calls about McNally and found that he was a rising star headed for a partnership in one of the most prestigious Wall Street law firms, a high-priced outfit that handled all of a business's legal issues that were too sticky for local talent, from taxes to investments to labor. Sy couldn't remember the firm's name, but he recalled with some scorn that it was a string of six surnames strung together with nothing to separate them, as though they were too busy to take time for the commas, until the final one, Smith, which was set off by an ampersand.

He remembered the scorn and his lip curled, but still he didn't speak. He didn't say, "McNally, you arrogant little bastard, you're headed for a fall. You will trip on your own hubris." He should have said it, but he didn't. Instead, he sat with a sneer on his silent mouth and some unnamed but soul-strangling fear in his heart.

Fletcher came through the office door carrying one chair and dragging a second. McNally was just finishing the careful tending of his starched cuffs, which now were rolled two turns, exposing strong wrists covered with red-tinted golden hair.

"Say, Seymour," McNally called without looking up from his sleeves, "would you mind too much moving to one of those other chairs? I'd like yours so I can turn it and face Manny and the rest of you at the same time. Thanks."

Only the two seats Fletcher had just set up were available since Fletcher had taken for himself the one positioned at the other side of his father's desk. Sy stood up and moved, still without comment, to one of the new chairs. A seat in the gallery, he thought. As he was settling himself, Andrew walked into the office and took the other guest seat, first pulling it just slightly farther away from Sy's. Andrew was a clean-cut, mannerly, and dull accountant, recently promoted by Manny to the title of business manager. Sy was puzzled by the change and finally assumed it was connected to the union-busting strategy. He had never had much to do with Andrew, and when he did, the conversation was so boring he always found himself involuntarily staring at the accountant's mouth. Evidently, Andrew had been born with a harelip that had been wonderfully repaired, leaving no trace except that his broad upper lip was slightly but permanently smeared.

"Good morning, Andrew," McNally said cheerfully. "Thanks for coming. Great game by the Sox last night, and what about that Yaz, eh?" He threw Andrew a big grin.

Andrew never smiled, but now, flattered by the personal attention, he nodded vigorously, his scrubbed face turned up eagerly toward McNally. "I'll say. You know, that's only the third time Yaz has played first base," he said. "He's got a seven-game hitting streak going. And he's hit in fifteen of the last sixteen games."

"I managed to get tickets for the final game of the Series last year," McNally said. "Great seats, but what a heartbreaker."

He was still standing, but he turned around the chair vacated by Sy, pulled it a couple of feet away from Manny's desk, planted his gleaming black wingtip shoe on the seat, and propped his left hand on his raised knee.

"Okay," he said, "let's get started. We asked you here, Manny and I, for an informal planning meeting. As you know, the first negotiating session with the union is scheduled for tomorrow. Right now, we're planning to go ahead with that schedule unless something comes up at this meeting that makes us decide to seek a postponement. We've already delayed this session two times, and it would be better—from a strategic sense—if we don't cancel this one. But if you know some good reason why we shouldn't meet, let me know, because I'd rather risk a reprimand from the NLRB than fall into some surprise trap."

He looked around solemnly. "We'll be accused of stalling, anyway. It is, of course, better for us if this goes on long enough for everyone to get tired of it, and that's what's likely to happen so long as they can't pull off a successful strike. But we are not stalling. We are moving expeditiously but prudently, in good faith and in full compliance with the law. And that's what we should tell anyone who asks."

He paused, but no one spoke. "So no one knows anything that ought to make us nervous? No complaints that you know of about unfair practices?" He looked squarely at Sy, who stared back silently and managed with great effort not to acknowledge that the question had been addressed to him. If the bastard wanted to ask him something, he could do it directly.

"Okay," McNally said finally, "no one knows of any defections? No one who voted for the union has come forward to tell you that he had changed his mind? He or she, that is.

He looked at each one of them in turn and all shook their heads except Sy, who remained stone-faced.

"Well then," McNally said, removing his foot from the chair and checking the seat for dirt before sitting down, "if there's nothing we need to know, I guess we can move right into planning our tactics for tomorrow." He paused, glanced quickly at Manny, then turned to Sy.

"You can go if you want, Sy. We won't need you for this."

It was a sucker punch and he reeled numbly for a moment. Finally, he stammered, "What the hell do you mean? If you're planning strategy for the negotiating session, I need to know what it is."

"No, you don't," McNally said quickly. "You're not on the negotiating team."

Sy swung his head toward Manny, but he was filling his pipe.

"Goddam it," Sy said, "what do you mean I'm not on the team. Who is on it, then?"

"Well," McNally said slowly, "I am and Fletcher is and Andrew is. Each side has three negotiators, and we're our three."

Sy felt confusion shoving aside his anger. "What about Manny," he said, "it's his goddam paper."

McNally smiled tolerantly. "Look, Sy, you better leave the strategy to us. You never put the one with the ultimate authority on the negotiating team. Don't you get it? You always need to be able to say, 'We'll have to check it out with the boss.'"

Still confused and now embarrassed too by his own innocence, Sy said, "Okay, but what about me? Why can't I be on the team?"

McNally's tone hardened. "Look, we just decided it would be better if you weren't one of the negotiators. Manny and I talked about it. And Fletcher. Besides, we need Andrew because he's the only one who really knows the numbers and that's information we need at our fingertips during negotiations."

Sy looked around, but no one except McNally, his accuser, would look at him. Convicted and no appeal. An awful childhood injustice welled up in his memory. He had been accused of breaking something—God knows what—and before he could explain his innocence, he had been sent away to his room.

"All right then, that's probably for the best anyway, now that I think about it." It was his own voice, but he hadn't planned this speech; it just rolled out on its own. "This will leave me free to assign and edit stories about our labor situation."

Their heads snapped up and now all four sets of eyes were fixed on Sy.

"Yes, that's right," he said thoughtfully, warming now to the familiar role of telling people that he intended to expose them, "if I were on the negotiating team, then, obviously, I couldn't handle the stories. But now I'll be free to cover the union situation."

The other four were still frozen in horror, with McNally's eyes particularly wide with emotion.

Sy knew it was a bluff, but he had to play out the hand. "I've been worried," he continued, "about how we were going to handle the news coverage. I'd hate to leave it up to the *Patriot Press*, and the AP would be suspect because we're a member and they would be walking a fine line. But this could turn into a big story for Vermont, especially if they strike, and I'm glad to be able to handle it myself."

"Are you crazy?" McNally exploded, leaping red-faced out of his chair to loom over Sy. "News coverage? We're going to do our damnedest to avoid news stories and we're sure as hell not going to write them ourselves. What are you thinking of? This is not some game, you know."

He looked away from Sy to Manny. "The future of this newspaper may depend on how we handle this situation, and we can't afford to have Seymour or anyone else fooling around with this."

Sy looked coolly at McNally and smiled. His superiority was slipping, the smooth lawyer glibness submerging under his rising anger. He needed to keep twisting the needle. It was Manny, not McNally, who would call the shots, and he had to make him see that this hired gun was interested only in his paycheck. He didn't care whether he was working for a newspaper or a meatpacking company.

"Whoa, Mac, settle down," Sy said soothingly. No one ever called him Mac; he hated it. "You know, I've been covering labor-management wars for more than twenty years, and you're making the same mistake the companies always make."

He looked over at Manny, then stood up himself, a foot away from McNally and half a head taller. "In every story I've ever covered, the union is always ready—eager—to tell its story to the press, but management always has no comment. You know what that means? It means the public—the ones who buy the product and who speak to the politicians—hear only one side. They hear the union story but not the company story."

He spoke directly to Manny. "Is that what you want? Do you want the people of this state to side with the union?"

Manny's face was dark red and Sy could tell he was chewing the end of his pipe, but he didn't speak.

"Listen, Manny, the outcome of this union-organizing move is critically important to this state. You know that better than anyone. It may be the most important story going on right now in Vermont. We've got to cover it. That's more important that winning a fight, more important than making money."

McNally and Fletcher started to speak at the same time, but Manny shook his head and put out both hands to silence them. He didn't speak right away, slowly taking down his pipe and setting it carefully beside the others in the ashtray. When he raised his eyes and started to talk, it was obvious that he was going to deliver a speech.

"I have spent my entire life building this newspaper," he began. "During that time, I have had two primary goals: To make it stronger year by year, not bigger, necessarily, but stronger. And to use it for the benefit of the people who read it. These are the two principles that I try always to use when making difficult decisions. I use both. But they are ranked. Never equal. For I know that service comes only from strength."

He was speaking deliberately and calmly. He looked at each of them in turn, then looked back straight at Sy. "I resent your suggestion that I would use the paper dishonorably to make money. I never have and I'm not doing that now. It's an unfair accusation. And it won't work, Sy.

"I decided at the outset of this problem that I needed expert professional help. I told you that, and that's when I went to Mr. McNally. He has helped guide us through this trial, and I am more confident than ever that he is the person I want to rely on.

"We will continue to do exactly what he tells us to do. I will do that and so will you. But in all cases, the final authority for what we do is mine. And I will exercise it. So hear me: Not one word will be printed in this newspaper about this union situation that I don't approve beforehand. Not one story, Sy. And before I approve it, I will seek the guidance of Mr. McNally.

"I believe that's clear. And I hope my earlier instructions are also clear, but if they are not, say so right now. Otherwise, you can go."

Sy was still standing. He felt clearheaded and calm and suddenly freed from some burden. He couldn't stand the thought of looking at McNally or Fletcher, so he focused on Manny's dark blue eyes as he backed toward the door.

He opened it, and as he left said quietly, "Manny, you make the angels weep."

As he closed the door, he heard Fletcher snicker. "What's that supposed to mean?"

"*Measure for Measure*," Manny said.

"Huh?"

The newsroom was as empty as a tomb and Sy's steps echoed. Even the wire machines were still. He roamed around the cluttered room, stopping randomly to read things posted on the walls, mostly jokes, cartoons, newspaper clippings, and long scrolls of yellow teletype paper on which someone had written out fake news stories. Some of them were decades old. One of the fake reports began:

MONTPELIER — The Vermont Senate today voted to change its daily work schedule by adding an official three-hour nap time. "Most of them sleep most of the time anyhow," said the Senate President, "so we just made it legal."
The governor said he didn't think he'd notice much difference.

Sy remembered the night the story had clattered off the telex that connected the newsroom to the statehouse bureau. A young and still-gullible reporter had ripped it off the machine and run into Sy's office saying, "Jesus Christ, wait 'til you see this."

He remembered most of the incidents that prompted the various postings, which now filled almost all the wall space around the newsroom. The wall desecration was one more cause for complaint against the news staff, usually from the janitors but also from the ad salesmen and business office women, and Manny dutifully passed each of them on to Sy without comment other than one time when a new decoration showed up that looked like an abstract painting but on closer inspection turned out to be a large poster of a naked woman. Sy had quietly removed the offending poster and no one ever mentioned it. He suspected Simmons.

The composing room was as lifeless as the newsroom. The lead pots had not even been turned on. He walked over to Rocky's raised desk and thought about somehow fouling its gleaming bare surface but decided against it. Back in the newsroom he continued his slow prowl, dimly aware of being repelled by the idea of going into his own office.

He stopped by Willis's desk to read a carefully typed note on top of his typewriter. It was from Alice, who had insisted on having memo pads printed with her name on the top and whose only job pleasure seemed to be sprinkling them around whenever she had an excuse. This one said:

Chief Bushey Called. Said to call Him when you get back from Chicago. At States Attorneys Office.
Didn't give Number.
Alice, August 26, 1968

Two days ago, Sy thought. Wonder what he wants with Willis. But he was too tired to think about it. He looked at the wall clock: nine thirty. Sy decided to go to his place and go back to bed.

∗∗

Willis had slept only three hours but he was up early, still excited from the night and eager to get out of his stifling hotel room and onto the streets. He rushed into the shower and shaved blind while standing under the spray, all the time getting more antsy as he became wider awake. He hurried, still dripping, to his tiny room's single window but, of course, he couldn't see anything. The window looked out in the wrong direction, away from Michigan Avenue, and besides, the hotel was blocks from the convention headquarters in the Hilton and miles from the Stock Yard Amphitheatre. Wrong space, wrong place.

It was after nine by the time he had made the short walk to Michigan Avenue, and he was mildly surprised when he finally got there to find nothing at all unusual. Normal street traffic, routine morning pedestrian traffic. No cops. No protesters. Chicago might have big shoulders, but it was damned bland at nine on a Wednesday morning in August. The bloody confrontations of the past three nights had given way to peaceful commerce. The heartland, Willis thought with detached superiority, keeps its priorities straight; take their money with a smile during working hours and crack their heads after dark.

He walked at a leisurely pace south on Michigan, content that with a whole day to find his story he couldn't miss. His own delegation certainly would not yet be up to any mischief; probably still safely bedded down—he liked that image—back at the Pearson.

Marlene drifted unsummoned into his mind and he knew he ought to telephone her. He hadn't called since leaving home and he still didn't feel like it. Why should he? He'd known secretly for some time that it was over, and she probably knew it too. Well, he'd warned her from the outset that reporters don't get seriously involved.

The day was already hot, but a nice easterly breeze was blowing off the lake. When Willis decided to walk the two dozen blocks, he had felt a small bump of self-congratulation; it had been weeks since he had a serious morning hangover. He made it to the newsstand in about twenty minutes and began searching for the Vermont papers. This was the only newsstand he had found that carried all the out-of-town papers and it had been his first stop each morning. He found the competition, the *Patriot Press*, with no trouble, but for the second day in a row he couldn't find his own paper. "Goddam it," he swore aloud, still scanning the racks but already sure he wouldn't find it. "He missed the goddam connection again."

The guy behind the counter didn't bother to look up, further irritating Willis, so he kicked the bottom board of the stall, which got his attention.

"You got any other papers back there?"

"Sure, we keep the best ones out of sight so the out-of-town assholes can't find what they want and won't buy nothing. How 'bout you; you find anything you like?"

He was about fifty but he looked like he could get ugly, so Willis didn't fire back. He picked up a *Patriot Press* and a *Times* and handed over a dollar. The guy hesitated, fumbling in his drawer, but Willis kept his open palm out until he finally handed over all the change. Screw him.

He walked another block to a coffee shop tucked in next to Colonel McCormick's imposing Tribune Tower, grumbling to himself about not being able to find out what Seymour had done with his overnight stories. He'd filed three stories, good ones that nobody else had, and he wanted to see them in print. He also wanted Barbara to see his stories. Guilt surged up so abruptly he cast his eyes quickly around the shop.

He ordered a black coffee and said to the counterman, "All the excitement must be good for business?"

"Yeah, it's good business all right. But, man, it's awful what they're doing to the city."

"Who're you betting on," Willis ventured, "Humphrey?"

The counterman slid over the coffee and rang out the check. "What, are you joking? It's wired. Everybody knows that. Everybody but the crazies and the McCarthy kids. When Mayor Daley and LBJ say they're for Humphrey, then it's going to be Humphrey. You can take it to the bank."

He rang up the sale and tossed Willis a final gem: "Unless, of course, the whole thing's a big act and Johnson is going to fly in here today for this phony birthday party and allow himself to be drafted." He smirked at Willis. "I know a guy works at a bakery that just made a two-hundred-pound cake with LBJ written on top."

Willis took his coffee and newspapers to a table with a window next to the sidewalk. He began reading but he was still annoyed not to have his own paper.

Willis had called in his final story about midnight, but he'd dictated it to Merle on the city desk and he hadn't talked with Seymour. But he didn't need to; he knew he'd be standing up in his little glass-walled office, two feet from the TV set flickering from its perch on the filing cabinet. He'd be scribbling notes on folded-up copy paper cut from newsprint, writing left-handed, with his wrist twisted in a U, his long fingers reaching down from the top of the paper instead of up from the bottom. Willis pictured Seymour's head thrust forward in pugnacious concentration, a tiny tuft of dark hair visible under his nose where the curving beak and deep lip cleft had hidden it from the hurrying razor.

Willis suddenly smiled and slapped his hand on the table, sloshing coffee into the saucer. By God, Seymour had waited until the convention adjourned for the night, holding up the pressrun and missing all the delivery schedules. He'd waited to see the whole incredible spectacle. That meant he'd have the only newspaper on the East Coast with a story, maybe even a photo, of Daley exploding in fury.

Willis had been watching from the press box when Mayor Daley, after sitting most of the night scrunched down in smoldering sullenness, had suddenly, defiantly, taken control of the convention. Mouthing obscenities you could see plainly but not hear, like a giant frog spitting out toxic insects, the boss-mayor had commanded the presiding officer, who happened to be the Speaker of the U.S. House of Representatives, to shut it down. Daley slashed the convention into adjournment by slicing his finger across his fat throat like an enraged director calling down the curtain on some stage production gone awry.

Daley had been audacious, but he also had been smart enough to wait until most of the TV audience had given up and until it was too late for the daily newspapers to report. Daley had pulled the plug at 1:17 in the morning, Chicago time, far too late for any of the big Eastern papers. But, Willis smirked, he hadn't counted on Seymour. Daley could command his political party, but Seymour could command his printing press. It was a fair match.

Willis was still irritated but, by God, he had to hand it to Sy—a little crazy, but the kind of editor who makes people want to stay in this ball-busting business. Willis had worked for a lot of papers, nine in twelve years, but even though it was the smallest, this one might be the best yet.

He picked up the *Patriot Press* and read it with growing contempt. The coverage was at the same time hysterical and dull, confused and simple-minded. They didn't even have the rise and fall of the Teddy Kennedy boomlet. The coverage of the chaos outside the convention hall was skimpy and managed to be boring despite the bloody police clashes with war protesters.

He tossed aside the *Patriot Press*, signaled for more coffee, lit a smoke, and picked up the *Times*. They'd put this edition, probably the bulldog or maybe the second, on the streets of New York long before the convention session adjourned. But the *Times* coverage still seemed comprehensive, coherent, and, above all, useful. Willis read everything else before turning to Wicker's convention story. If Willis had a hero in this business, he reluctantly admitted it was Tom Wicker. He had a deep-seated suspicion of columnists, mostly lazy guys who used the editorialist's license to avoid the hard work of reporting. But Wicker, faithful to the reporter's bargain with the reader to deliver information but freed of normal newswriting boundaries, could turn the dreariest Washington process report into a lively story. He had a unique way, Willis thought with envy, of being involved without exactly taking sides.

When Willis looked up from his paper, a stream of young people was flowing past his window, walking purposefully south on Michigan Avenue. He drank off the tepid remains of his second cup, then hurried outside and nearly ran into Tom Wicker, who was stepping out of the Tribune building.

"Hey, Mr. Wicker," one of the young marchers shouted, "come on, we're going to the convention."

Willis stood quietly up against the building, unnoticed by marchers or Wicker. He saw a tired smile began on the somewhat jowly face of the hero, then watched it freeze into momentary paralysis when another marcher said loudly, "March, Mr. Wicker. Put up or shut up."

Wicker, his suit jacket slung across his hunched shoulder, stood watching the protest line recede down the street, his hand partly lifted in a friendly but uncertain gesture. When the last marchers were a half block away, he let his arm drop and walked in short, weary steps to his car parked at the curb and drove off past the young people toward the amphitheater.

The encounter further soured Willis's mood and he brooded over it on the bus ride back uptown. But he had forgotten Wicker by the time he got to the convention several hours later. First he had to cover a meeting of the Vermont caucus. He was not eager. What possible difference could the caucus make? Who cared? The whole damn convention was a charade and everyone knew it. All the posturing and arguing, all the rhetorical fireworks—none of it made a damn bit of difference. And certainly no one cared what happened to Vermont's twenty-two miserable votes. But he had to cover it since that was, after all, the justification for sending him to Chicago.

*
**

Back in Vermont, the assignment had seemed exciting, but now he was beginning to feel a little silly, like a grown-up caught playing a child's game.

The delegation was so small it could fit, with minor bulging at the seams, in a hotel suite assigned to the governor, who was the titular head of the state Democrats, although he was not officially a voting delegate. The suite was just beginning to fill up, and Willis slumped down on a miniature sofa at the back of the room, grateful to find an observation post detached and small enough to discourage potential seatmates. He'd spent much of the past four days with these people and had interviewed most of them at least once. For the most part it had been fishing in a dry hole and now he just couldn't work up the interest. Except, of course, now there was Barbara. He scanned the crowd for her, but she was one of the delegates who had not yet shown up.

Willis slouched on the sofa reading the *Tribune*, twisting hard to the right and leaning over the arm so he could catch the light coming through the window. He remembered reading somewhere that Chicago had once been known for "muscular journalism," but most of what he had seen in the *Tribune* was flabby blather.

The noise grew steadily louder as the room filled up and finally someone asked for quiet and started the caucus, but Willis didn't look up from his paper. He had just turned to the awful editorial page and was reading a paean to Boss Daley when she sat down.

For a moment he was frozen in place, afraid to look around. Her hip pressed tightly against his and her smell rolled over him, engulfing him in the sweet, exotic perfume of sex, past and future. He heard a gentle rustle as her flowing skirt folded casually over his leg, and her thigh, the one with the indented circle of smallpox vaccination, molded secretly to his. He stared with burning eyes at the paper clutched in both of his outstretched hands, seeing and thinking nothing, utterly reduced to skin-throbbing feeling. Finally, driven equally by public shame and reckless lust, he closed his paper, dropped it into his lap, and turned his head in her direction. Back straight, hands folded in her lap, she sat looking with deep concentration toward the front of the room where the national committeeman was making an impassioned plea for delegation solidarity.

A large opal on her right hand blazed with reflected light from the overhead chandelier, and although he couldn't see it from this angle Willis knew its even larger companion would be hanging around her neck on a slender gold chain. He wanted to lean forward so he could see the fire-spitting stone resting on her tanned chest, deep in the long V of the blue and white polka-dot dress. Without shifting her gaze, she lifted a bare arm, stirring a new wave of perfume, and lightly tucked back a stray strand of hair before letting her hand drop unobtrusively to rest on his hidden thigh.

Not until she casually slid the hand back to her own lap did Willis realize that the murmur of voices had stopped, and he looked up in panic to see most of the delegates twisted around in their fold-up chairs, watching him in obvious anticipation. His mind, racing now to recover from its momentary anesthetization, screamed unintelligible nonsense at him, something about an argument over whether he should leave, but he couldn't bring the numbed memory into focus and so he merely stared back blankly at the gaping crowd. Finally, the national committeeman—a decent, tweedy old gentleman from the northern part of the state—saved him, either because he suddenly understood Willis's predicament or because he wanted to move the show along.

"Well, I see. Indeed," he called out in a commanding, clipped bark, clearing his throat loudly, "obviously, Mr. Willis doesn't choose to intervene in our little family spat, and he's quite right to refuse. It is, after all, our decision whether he stays for the caucus or is excused."

Most of the turned heads had swiveled back to the front, to Willis's immense relief, and his rescuer continued, "Well now, we'll do this the democratic way, by free and open voting." He paused and peered mischievously over the top of his glasses. "Maybe we should film it for Mayor Daley's edification."

The room filled with laughter that seemed much louder than warranted. "Now," the committeeman resumed, twinkling and overly encouraged by his own wit, "the situation is this: Mr. Sprague—Delegate Sprague—has suggested that we conduct our business outside the, uh . . . the purview of the press. Which in this case means Mr. Willis, since the rest of the . . . uh, the, uh . . . the pack, if you'll excuse me again, Mr. Willis"—more laughter—"since the rest of the pack seems to think there are better ways to spend its time this afternoon than meeting with the Democratic delegation from Vermont."

A young woman, whose name Willis couldn't remember but who he believed was a McCarthy delegate from Brattleboro, stood up. "We have nothing to hide," she said, her voice rising as she spoke. "If we can't even keep our own work and actions public, we're no better than the Johnson/Humphrey/Daley gang. What this party and this convention need is more reporting, not less. Leave the press-gagging to the goon squads out on the convention floor."

Someone clapped, but she didn't wait, turning to look directly at Willis or maybe, he thought, color creeping into his face, at Barbara.

"Besides," the young woman said, "Willis has been with us for so long now that we don't have any secrets anyway." The delegates laughed, and when they stopped she added, as she resumed her seat, "and neither does he."

At the show of hands, no one voted to throw him out, not even Sprague, although Willis was hoping that he would. He didn't want these people to know his secrets and he wanted to know theirs only so he could write about them. He was not part of the group.

Christ, what if he just left? Too late. The governor took over the caucus and began applying pressure for the entire delegation to vote as a block and, of course, to vote for Gene McCarthy.

"I think all of you know I would never try to pressure anyone into voting a certain way," he began.

Willis, scribbling fast in his notebook, wrote, *But,* just as the governor said, "But I do think it's terribly important that someone send a message loud and clear to those who have taken control of this convention that Democrats will not be intimidated and will not be stampeded. And I don't know anyone better suited to send that message than the Vermont delegation."

Several people clapped, including Barbara, who then dropped her hand back onto her skirt where it lay covering Willis's leg. She obviously was wearing little or nothing under the billowy cotton dress.

"I have been appalled—I am appalled—at the rudeness, the belligerence, the downright fascist tactics we have all seen on this convention floor. I personally saw a television reporter slammed in the stomach with a police club, and I saw a delegate pledged to someone other than Mayor Daley's candidate dragged bodily off the floor."

Willis was paying attention now, or at least some of the blood coursing through his system was getting through to his brain. This was a sitting Democratic governor urging a rebellion against the leaders of his own party. He had been the first Democratic governor to split with LBJ over Vietnam and he had backed the insurgent candidacy of Kennedy and then McCarthy. But he had not ever spoken so emotionally and so publicly about revolt. And he was still just winding up.

"Outside the convention hall, we have seen even more disgraceful behavior. Last night in Chicago, the police rioted. That's a harsh indictment, but there's simply no other term for it. They rioted."

There was a murmur in the room, a low, indistinct noise. As the room fell silent again, he went on. "And today I can tell you that even the representatives chosen to conduct the business of this convention have felt the wrath of party bosses run amok. As you know, I was thrilled to be chosen a member of the platform committee. I thought at least we could express the will of the people through that document, no matter what happened about the nomination."

He paused to light one of his trademark cigarettes. No one in the room stirred.

"Well," the governor resumed, "I am sad to report today that I was wrong. We were cheated, lied to, and tricked at every turn. When we go on the floor later, you will be presented with a platform that represents not the people's will or the party's will or the delegates' will, but the will of Lyndon Baines Johnson."

He pulled on his cigarette and puffed a great cloud of smoke toward the ceiling. "We lost. We have lost."

Willis was behind as he filled page after page of his stenographer's notebook with huge, scrawling script that he hoped he would be able to read later. When he got to *We have lost*, he kept on writing, *Fourth party. By God, he's going to help start a fourth party.*

It was the news he had been waiting to find and now it had just landed in his lap—along with some other things, he thought with a quick glance to his left. But here it was. The governor was bolting the Democratic Party. It would be a great story back in Vermont and he would have it alone. He'd call Sy and tell him about it and then write it later.

". . . so," the governor was saying, "I'm going back for the official vote of the platform committee and I won't see you again until tonight. But let me leave you with one final thought. It's about loyalty.

"Now, loyalty is a fine, even a noble, thing. It's the glue that holds things together and you have to admire it wherever you encounter loyalty. But . . . but there are times when things that used to be valuable need to be taken apart. There are times when marriages fail. When a cherished job no longer satisfies. When a fan outgrows one team and shifts to another.

"When that happens, loyalty must be put aside. It needs to be overridden when more important, more noble values require that these old things be broken.

"We, this mighty nation, are right now engaged in a bloody war in Southeast Asia that we should end. We, the most powerful people on earth, are killing and burning and destroying a country and a weaker people that have done nothing to harm us. We are sending young Americans to die in a jungle for a cause that no one, no one—not Lyndon Johnson or Hubert Humphrey or anyone in this room—can explain.

"It's time to end this disaster. So I urge you, when it's time to vote, let blind loyalty be the final casualty of this dreadful war."

Two hours later Willis was in the press box high above the convention floor, looking out over the noisy, churning sea of delegates. Both press boxes were crowded as always, but compared to the floor of the amphitheater, the overhead boxes were clouds of tranquility. The convention bosses had issued only fifty-five floor passes for one thousand daily newspaper reporters covering the convention. They were supposed to share the passes but, of course, as with all else, the big dogs ate first and reporters for insignificant papers, like Willis, got the passes only during times when there was little or no floor action.

But Barbara had somehow gotten a bootleg delegate's pass for Willis and he had used it several times, to the envy of some other reporters. This was the first time since he took the Vermont job in January that he had been thrown in with the national press corps, and he hated his bush-league status. He had covered the civil rights crusades of the early sixties with some of the guys now on the national campaign trail for major newspapers, and it depressed him when they asked who he was working for now.

It made him feel better for them to see that he had what they coveted: at-will access to the floor. But if you wanted to know what was happening with the convention, the press box was a better place to be. Now, as they considered the party platform, from the box Willis could see it was less a debate than a controlled riot, like a lunchroom protest of prison inmates. They couldn't control the outcome, but that didn't make them like the menu any better.

Willis was directly above and in front of Mayor Daley's front-row seat, and he watched in fascinated revulsion as the bulldog face registered the glee of a triumphant tyrant.

The governor had been right; the Vietnam plank was a lousy joke, a phony statement drafted by Johnson's lackeys and, evidently, accepted by Humphrey. Of course, look what it got you if you dared to split with Johnson. Willis peered out of the box toward the Vermont delegation, which he could barely see. He laughed. That's what it got you. The convention floor was set up like a baseball diamond, with the podium as home plate (and Daley, of course, as pitcher). The Vermont delegates, thanks to the governor's early split with the president, had been relegated to deep right field, on the foul line and as far from the action as they could be put without falling out of the amphitheater.

He began to search for Barbara and at first he couldn't find her. Soon he was engrossed in just watching the delegation. Once, years earlier, he had been on a train sidelined near a stockyard. Searching for amusement, he had spotted in the distance a pen full of cattle and as he watched they seemed to go a little crazy. They milled around jerkily, turning first one way, then another, lowering their heads one minute and the next rising off the ground on their hind feet. He couldn't hear anything, but it was clear that something was driving the cattle nuts. Finally, he had decided the cows were being stung by hornets. He remembered that scene now as he watched the squirming, restless Vermont delegation, trapped in obvious torment at the back of the hall.

His eye, roving across the Vermont crowd, spotted a blue-and-white figure waving vigorously from the aisle. He knew instantly she was signaling to him, and he smiled in awe at her boldness. God, she was something. It made no difference to her that everyone would know she was leaving before the delegation even voted. If the television cameras happened to spot her, even the folks at home would know. It made no difference to her that anyone in the delegation who bothered to look could guess she was waving to Willis in the press box.

None of those things would stop her from doing what she wanted, any more than she was stopped from sleeping with Willis by the fact that she was married to a Republican insurance executive in Vermont who almost certainly would find occasion to talk with members of the Democrat delegation when they got home.

Willis saw her stop waving, turn, and leave by a rear door. Shit. He ought to stay for the vote, but it was absolutely predictable. He'd pick it up later. He still hadn't called Seymour, but it was still early, not yet even six in Vermont. He'd call later.

But he didn't, or at least he still hadn't called when he and Barbara walked hand in hand out the front door of the hotel just before sunset.

"Relax," she had said, lacing her fingers with his as the elevator door opened into the hotel lobby. "What're they going to do if they do see us? Democrats don't give out scarlet As."

He laughed, but it was a tinny, fake laugh because he didn't feel amused, and knowing he ought to have called the paper long before now made him even more edgy.

They crossed Michigan Avenue and strolled toward the lake and a parking lot where Barbara had left her rental car. The sky was darkening far out on the giant lake and the wind had picked up a little, sliding slightly to the northeast. They were headed for downtown where a big protest march was supposed to happen, but here, blocks from Grant Park and the Hilton, it was wonderfully peaceful. Barbara hummed quietly, swinging their clasped hands as they walked. She had changed into a dress the color of near-ripe grapes, fastened all the way up to a tunic-style collar, and, on top, an unbuttoned white sweater. The most visible opals were now the ones attached to her ears, although Willis knew the necklace was still around her neck.

"How old are you?" she asked abruptly as he stopped to light a cigarette. He laughed. "Thirty-three," he said. "Plenty old enough."

"That depends," she said. "Old enough for what?"

"Well, to smoke, at least. How old are you?"

"Old enough to have stopped." She walked on slowly.

He said tentatively, "Why'd you ask?"

"I just wondered. You look older than that, but you sometimes act younger."

He smoked silently, unsure where the conversation was headed.

"Have you ever been married?"

"Yeah. I was married, but it ended five years ago."

"Well then," she said, "you ought to know that marriages, like everything else, come and they go. So what's making you so jumpy? Mine has been over for nearly five years too, but we just haven't gotten around to doing anything about it."

They'd reached the car and she tossed him the keys. "I assume you have a license," she said.

He nodded and unlocked the passenger-side door for her. As she climbed in, she said, "October 29, 1929."

"Huh?"

"My birthday. Born lucky. That's me."

He drove slowly down Michigan Avenue, but they had to stop north of the river because police barricades closed off the bridge. As they began walking, the streetlights were popping on although the city was not yet really dark. They walked immediately into the crowd's fringe, still blocks away from the Hilton.

They merged into the crowd and began threading their way through, holding hands now to keep from getting separated. People all around them were chanting, "Peace Now. Peace Now." Not very far into the throng Willis picked up the faint, residual odor of tear gas but there was no sign yet of any police action. They kept moving slowly forward into the crowd, which grew thicker as they advanced. From inside the mob he couldn't get any sense of how many people were there.

Willis's stomach and mind were both fluttering with apprehension. How could he cover this story from here? He wasn't even sure he could get out of the crowd if he wanted to. He still hadn't called Seymour, and now God knows when he'd get a chance. He'd never before been uneasy about being trapped inside a story he was trying to cover, not even at the Selma march. The chanting was getting louder and closer, and when he looked around he saw that Barbara had taken it up. "Peace Now. Peace Now," she shouted.

The crowd was not moving; people all around were standing on tiptoes or jumping in place to try to see ahead of them. Willis, when he realized that he too was stalled, tightened his grip on Barbara's hand and pushed forward, making slow but steady progress despite some angry looks and words from those he shoved aside.

"Press," he called out over and over, a mantra that never made much sense in such circumstances but that seemed to work.

The tear-gas smell grew stronger, although it still didn't have the sting of a fresh blast. The chant changed: "Let's Go, Let's Go. What's Holding Us Up. Let's Go, What's Holding Us Up."

It was dark now, but Willis could see just ahead of them the Blackstone and the Hilton, windows blazing with lights high over Michigan Avenue.

"Stop the War. Stop the War." The new chant seemed to be amplified and he spotted loudspeakers attached to some of the lampposts. Willis saw that they were near the edge of the crowd, fairly close to a restaurant door on their right, and he leaned over to tell Barbara they were going to try to get inside. But the noise by now was deafening, even if she had not been yelling herself, and she just shook her head at him.

The screaming chant suddenly shifted: "Fuck you, LBJ. Fuck You, LBJ."

A shriek from thousands of human voices merged into an unintelligible roar, drowning out all other noises, and the crowd exploded, blown apart by a wedge of blue-helmeted riot police charging into the heart of the great mob.

Willis heard tear-gas canisters popping all around. He pulled Barbara, dragged her, against the wall of the nearest building. Screaming people lunged in all directions, flying like shrapnel away from the center where the police wedge had hit.

An elderly woman fell screaming in front of Willis, crying out as her knees scraped on the sidewalk, then rose and limped into the fleeing crowd.

Barbara had shrunk back hard against the building, one hand over her mouth and the other still holding on tightly to Willis's hand. A figure staggered backwards, crashing into her, then dropped to his knees rubbing his eyes hard with both fists. Tears poured in streams down his young beardless face, and, as Willis watched, a running policeman reached out as he passed and whacked the boy in the back with his truncheon, pitching him forward facedown. He was up and running blindly before Willis could reach him.

The night filled with screaming voices and the wooden thud of sticks hitting bone and flesh. Sobbing people—men, women, and children—dashed past with blood flowing from faces and heads.

Blue helmets were everywhere, and black boots slammed into bodies littering the sidewalk. Fallen victims were dragged by arms, feet, or one of each limb into patrol wagons brought up through the barricades to the intersection.

Within a couple of minutes, Willis was all but blinded by his own tears and the gas stung every exposed piece of skin. He heard a terrifying sound of glass breaking as one of the storefront windows shattered. He yanked Barbara forward and covered her head with his arm, ducking his own head as far as he could as glass rained down onto the sidewalk behind them.

Farther away he heard a new crowd cry: "Boo. Boo. Boo."

The crowd had been pushed back a hundred feet or so from the intersection, and Willis and Barbara left the relative sanctuary of the building and scuttled across Balbo Drive to the periphery where a double row of riot cops had established a new skirmish line.

Willis pulled his hand away from Barbara, reached a fresh notebook out of his pocket, and approached a panting cop in the first tier at the extreme left flank. A nightstick dangling from his hand swept up with spring-loaded speed and tore the notebook from Willis's hand before he could speak. He leaped backwards before the downstroke could crash into his skull. He scurried back into the crowd as the smiling cop squealed, "Write that, fuckhead." Willis, safely behind another body, looked for a badge number but the cop had taken off his shield.

The crying, screaming crowd, penned north and south between wooden barricades, had been compressed into an immovable human wall separated by three feet of pavement from the police, who growled insults and fidgeted in place like an aggressive offensive line waiting for the snap signal. Some protesters in the front row knelt and began singing "America the Beautiful," and for a few minutes the action seemed frozen into a still shot, then Willis watched in disbelief as a group of cops snatched up one of the yellow barricades and used it as a battering ram to charge into the crowd.

Unable to move out of the way, people in the path of the assault fell like cornstalks and were trampled.

A roar of mixed terror and fury rose from the trapped crowd as the blue helmets from the double line poured into the opening made by the battering ram, swinging their sticks and gloved fists, kicking, and spraying Mace directly into horror-struck faces.

As the police lines opened, people spilled through, and soon they were fleeing in all directions, most of them headed toward the park and the lakeshore but others dashing into hotels, restaurants, or any other accessible building.

But there were no havens. The cops, a fanged pack gone berserk, chased them screaming into lobbies and dining areas, clubbing heads and pulling down anyone they could catch.

Willis held his spot at the corner, instinctively sure that running away blindly would be their most dangerous option. He shoved Barbara behind him and backed up as tightly as they could get to the building. A fleeing body tripped on the curb in front of them and went down. A cop pounced, yanked up the girl's head by its hair, and sprayed Mace directly into her eyes before planting a stiff kick in her side and moving on in pursuit of other victims.

Before Willis knew what was happening, Barbara sprang out and began dragging the hysterical girl back toward their wall. "Come on," she yelled, "we've got to take her to the car."

They lifted the girl and began moving cautiously, sticking close to the buildings. Willis yanked them to a stop when he saw a cop running full speed in their direction, but he was pursuing a young long-legged guy who rushed along dragging a banner behind him.

The cop overtook him and stuck his wooden baton between the boy's churning legs, sending him crashing headfirst into the street. The cop slammed him across the shoulders with the stick, snatched his hands behind his back, and was taking out his handcuffs when suddenly he jumped off the boy and ran off. Willis saw that he was headed to the rescue of another cop who had fallen and was spread-eagled on the pavement about thirty feet away.

The boy was trying to scramble to his feet and Willis ran over to help him. He was sobbing, and when he turned his head Willis saw that his face was a bloody mess. He reached down to retrieve his banner, which turned out to be a North Vietnam flag, but Willis pulled him away, shouting, "Leave the goddam thing and get out of here."

By the time they made it to the car, the girl had stopped screaming and the boy was no longer sobbing, although he was still gasping for breath. Tears poured from the girl's red eyes and she still couldn't see. Barbara and Willis both gasped when they got a good look at the boy's mangled face.

"Get in," Barbara said, "we'll find a hospital."

"No," the boy said, "I don't want a hospital. I just need to clean up."

The girl was shaking her head. "Yeah, me too," she said. "I just want to wash my face and knees." They saw for the first time that blood was trailing down both of her legs from deep scrapes on her knees.

"Okay, let's go to the hotel," Barbara told Willis, and he nodded.

"Let us out and then park the car," she said when they got to the Pearson. "We'll go up to my room."

It took him ten minutes, and when he got to the room the wounded fledgling protesters looked much improved. Their names were Penny and Larry and it turned out that both were Chicago high school students but from different schools so they didn't know each other. Both remained adamant about not going to the emergency room, and when they had finished cleaning up their various injuries, Barbara and Willis agreed they didn't need stitches or other medical aid.

Penny's eyes were still puffed up and the parts that should be white were deep pink. "Visine and Band-Aids will fix you up," Willis said. "And all you need, young Patrick Henry, is iodine, Ben-Gay, and a little more sense. What the hell were you doing with that flag? It's like going in a bullring with a red cape but no sword."

Larry looked embarrassed, although it was hard to tell because his face was too swollen and cut up, but he didn't give ground. "Yeah, well, somebody's got to do something." He swept his hand from Willis to Barbara. "You guys haven't done much to stop the war except talk."

They must have looked hurt because he dropped his eyes and said softly, "My best friend joined the marines when he graduated last year. Now he's dead."

Penny began to cry again. Soon she and Larry were talking together in a running conversation that Willis found so elliptical he could hardly follow: Vietnam, draft dodging, honor rolls, SATs, LBJ, Nixon, Bob Dylan, their parents. The links were evidently perfectly clear and logical to them, but Willis soon lost the thread and began fretting about his own situation. It was nine—ten in Vermont.

Barbara called room service and ordered sandwiches and sodas for the kids, beer for Willis, and wine for herself, then she said she was going to take a shower. She pulled off her sweater and Willis noticed for the first time that one arm was heavily splattered with blood. She saw him looking and said, "No purple heart for me. That's Larry's donation to the peace movement, not mine."

When she left, Willis picked up the telephone and carried it as far away as he could, perched himself on the window ledge, and put in a collect call to the paper.

"Willis? Where in the hell are you?"

Seymour was already shouting without even saying hello.

"Where's your goddam story? Where's the caucus story? Where are you?"

He was still shouting, but when he paused for air, Willis could hear newsroom pandemonium and he pictured the scene in close detail but, oddly, he didn't feel any wish to be there.

"I'm at the hotel. The Pearson. I've been covering the march and—"

"Goddam it, what do you mean, 'covering the march'? I'm watching the goddam march on television right now and it's a bloodbath, not a march. Where the hell are you?"

Willis was beginning to get irritated. He thought about telling Sy to shut up, that maybe sometimes things happened that were more important than filing news stories. He suddenly remembered the young marchers telling Wicker to put up or shut up. Maybe he ought to tell Sy that it felt different to be involved with something rather than just observing it with passive judgment.

But he didn't say all that. "I told you," he said calmly. "I came back to the hotel to write the story."

Willis heard Penny and Larry giggling and he motioned for them to be quieter.

"Goddam it," Seymour said, more softly but still angry, "why didn't you call in earlier? I've been trying to get you for hours. Where are you?"

"I told you. But what difference does it make. Listen, I—"

"If you're in the goddam hotel, why didn't you answer your phone? I just called there about one minute ago."

"I'm in the hotel but at another phone. Listen, this place has gone crazy. The police rioted downtown and—"

Seymour burst in again. "I told you, I know all that. I'm watching it on television right now. It's still going on. What're you doing in the hotel? The convention is blowing up and the downtown streets are running blood. What the hell are you doing in the hotel?"

"I'm trying to get you a story, goddam it."

"Have you been to the convention? What's the delegation doing?"

"Yeah, I was out there for the platform vote. They voted unanimously for the minority plank on Vietnam but—"

"I know all that too. Look, you're covering the biggest political debacle of the century and it sounds like all you've got is wire service stuff. What do you think we sent you out there for? The platform vote?"

"Listen, Sy, I got a good story out of the caucus. The governor—"

"The caucus?" Seymour was shouting again. "That was five hours ago. I've talked to half the delegation since then and none of them have seen you in five hours. Where the hell have you been?"

A loud knock rattled the door and Willis turned away from the window just as Barbara walked out of the bathroom.

"Come in," she called.

"Room service," shouted a young Asian man as he rolled in a cart.

"Goddam it, Willis, what . . . who . . . are you shacking up out there?"

Seymour's voice had risen to a shriek. "Of course you are. And drunk too, right?"

"No, wait a minute, Sy. I—"

"Forget it, Willis." His voice was now subnormal, so low Willis could barely understand him. "Just forget it. I should have expected it, but I didn't. Forget it. But don't call anymore. I don't have time for it."

Willis started to answer then realized Seymour was gone, but he heard his voice, well away from the telephone, call out, "Greenberg! Tell everybody that if Willis calls collect, not to take the call."

Willis started to dial the city desk number, then he changed his mind. The protest kids were still sprawled on the bed, jabbering away to each other, but Barbara was watching him.

He smiled broadly. "There's some luck for you. They've got all the news they want for tonight." He picked up a beer from the cart and turned on the television set. "And I guess that makes me free. Let's see what's happening in the real world."

The Pennsylvania delegation was casting its ballots, but the convention already was bedlam because everyone knew that when the self-serving folderol was over, the votes were going to Humphrey and they would put him over the top.

When the Pennsylvania vote count was announced, the picture shifted immediately to the Hilton Hotel room to capture a foolishly beaming Humphrey lunging toward his own television set to kiss the black-and-white image of his wife, whose smiling face filled the screen. So while CBS filmed the candidate, another network, in its own attempt to film the first draft of history, had beamed in on the Happy Warrior's wife as she sat in the convention gallery.

A perfect ending, Willis thought, pleased to have an excuse for the bittersweet taste of righteous indignation that filled his mouth. Television instantly brings together a man and wife, a party and its insurgents, a nation and its leaders, all in one flash that washes out the thousands of conflicting images of the last week and even the last hour.

News before it happens.

It was just after midnight when Willis left the hotel. Penny and Larry had left earlier. It turned out she lived with her parents, both professors, not far from the Pearson. They were going to get her car and then she would drive Larry to his parents' house, an Episcopal rectory about five miles away. A match made in Hanoi, Willis called it, puzzling and annoying the teenagers.

He and Barbara watched the convention coverage for a while, but eventually she had made it sweetly but firmly clear that her fondest wish was to be alone.

Back in his own room, Willis found he couldn't sleep. He started to write, assuming that if he had an actual story to dictate he could convince Seymour to take it. But he quickly found he couldn't make the story work.

Or rather, he couldn't figure out what story he was writing. The caucus story about the fourth party? A pie-in-the-sky balloon that would crash to the ground in a week or might have already deflated — who cares.

A police riot story? Who would read it when they had already seen it in their own living rooms?

How about the story of a bread-and-circus performance staged by political knaves who would sacrifice their own children and subvert democracy to prove they were right? No one would believe it, at least not until it had been worked over three decades later by graybeard historians, like morticians fixing up a cold corpse.

In the end, Willis doodled at the typewriter for a while, then decided the time had come for him to shut up too. He put on his jacket and left. He had spotted a neighborhood bar a couple of blocks away and he figured it couldn't hurt to get lost, at least for a couple of hours.

CHAPTER NINE
Monday, September 9, 1968

The real estate guy had called it a cottage, but since he first laid eyes on it, Willis had never thought of his house as anything but The Box. "Let's go out to The Box," he'd say, and everyone would know what he meant.

Nearly square, its low roof peaked at not much more than twice a man's height and then pitched down so low that he had to duck to walk under the gutters. The shingled roof was plastered with lichen, and the unpainted half-lap siding, variegated by age, sun, moss, wind-driven rain, snow, and lake spray, gave The Box a grown-from-the-ground look—a giant mutated mushroom sprouted under a thick canopy of white pine that shut out the sun from all directions except the lake side.

He had come to like the place, fond in the same way commuters can grow attached to an interesting panhandler. You wouldn't want a permanent association, but after the wary suspicion of first acquaintance the relationship had settled into a comradely give-and-take. Lying in bed, wondering whether his bladder would hold out long enough for the new clock radio/coffee maker to finish perking, he realized he had become even more tightly connected to The Box since Labor Day weekend, when nearly everyone else had left the lake.

The change had been quite dramatic, even though it took him a few days to understand just how different it was. They had just disappeared, like the starlings that had nested all summer in the eaves, leaving vacant camps, abandoned docks and boathouses, and wakeless waters. Quiet had dropped on the lake, and the dust settled deeply on the rutted little road that wound along the shore. Some of the cottages had, like his, been turned into year-round houses, but so far Willis had not identified the ones that were still occupied. Even though Labor Day came early this year, he had seen few boats and hardly any cars in the past week. In the isolation he had begun to mutter inside his head to The Box, as though the two of them were sharing the time of solitude. Leaving the cottage one morning, he had said, "I don't know whether we still need to lock up or not; what do you think?" Later, driving to work, he couldn't say whether he had actually spoken aloud or merely thought the question.

His bladder buzzed him just as the coffee maker dinged, and Willis hustled out of bed and off to the bathroom. Over the toilet was a round window that the real estate agent had proudly claimed to be an authentic porthole salvaged from an ancient steamer up on Lake Champlain, and Willis was gazing blankly through it into the small backyard when a blue car turned off the road and stopped on the grass next to his Saab.

Marlene stepped out and immediately squatted down beside her car, hand outstretched toward the woods at the edge of the yard. Willis grabbed a pair of shorts off the hook on the back of the bathroom door and on his way through the kitchen he picked up a t-shirt. As he stepped through the screen door, a small calico cat that had been creeping toward Marlene suddenly bolted and leaped back into the woods.

Her head swung angrily toward him, but then she shrugged and stood up, smiling and wiping her hand on her blue jeans.

"She'll come back if she's really hungry," she said.

"What makes you think she's hungry?"

"Oh, the summer people always leave cats and dogs when they leave. They just abandon them. You find them hanging around all the lakes after Labor Day. Besides, didn't you see her? She's just a kitten and she's all skin and bones."

"Hell, if she's hungry, why doesn't she come over here and catch some mice? This place is crawling with them. They had a hell of a party in the walls last night."

Marlene smiled politely but she looked at him solemnly. "She's afraid," she said. "How does she know you're not like the people that left her?"

Willis shrugged. "Everybody makes mistakes. Maybe they just forgot her and didn't remember 'til they were back in Jersey or wherever."

"If you really want her," Marlene said, "I can coax her out. She'd probably make a very good mouser. They say tricolored cats are the best."

Willis didn't know what to say. He was getting a little irritated. It was always this way with Marlene, as though she was testing him or something.

"But I don't want to catch her unless you really want her. I mean, it wouldn't be fair."

"Hell," he said, more crossly than he intended, "you don't even really know if she is lost or feral or whatever. Maybe she's just prowling and lives somewhere with a perfectly nice family."

Marlene looked at him for a moment, then shrugged her shoulders and smiled weakly. "Okay," she said.

He turned back toward the house. "Come on in. Want some coffee?"

She followed him into the kitchen. Out of the corner of his eye he thought he caught her looking at the half-empty bourbon bottle on the counter. Damn, he had meant to put that away. But Christ, otherwise the kitchen was tidy and even clean by bachelor standards. No dirty dishes. He'd even washed the glass, which anybody should see meant he hadn't been drinking too much.

She sat down at the table but still didn't say anything.

"Coffee?"

She shook her head.

Willis took a long time filling his own mug and adding sugar and cream. Maybe this is a good time to tell her. He was sure, just from her vaguely sad demeanor, that she had known for a long time that it was over. Hell, it was over before he went to Chicago. Long before. Before Barbara. He'd been home nearly two weeks and he hadn't even seen Barbara during that time. And he had been with Marlene a few times, but still, it was over. Just one of those things. That's what he ought to say, but every time he began, she looked at him like a kid waiting to be scolded or hit or something.

He turned toward her and moved wearily toward the table. There, that's the look. She was watching him closely, her eyes wide and looking as though she might cry.

"I'm sorry," she said at last. "I don't want to hurt you."

He was startled. "What do you mean? I mean, don't worry. I mean, what do you mean?"

"I should have told you before," she said. "I know I should have. But I just wasn't sure."

He didn't know what to say.

"I really just decided for sure a couple of days ago."

"Decided what?" He felt a little panicked. Was she leaving him?

She folded her hands in front of her on the table and looked intently into Willis's eyes. "I'm moving into the commune."

"What? What are you talking about? You're going to be a hippie?" He tried to laugh sardonically but it came out more as a stuttering giggle.

Her mouth tightened. "I don't want to hurt you. Please don't be angry."

He stood up. "Look, you better think this over some more. I mean, not because of me necessarily." He looked down at her. "Although it does seem like you might have at least talked to me about it before this. But the important thing is that this would be a bad mistake. I mean, you can't just move into that commune. You don't know what it's really like."

"Actually," she said, "I've already moved up there. Yesterday."

Willis exploded. "With Thunderclap? You've moved in with Thunderclap?"

Marlene blushed all the way to her hairline. "It's not his commune," she said angrily. "There are more than fifty people out there. You're just like all the others; you've just got something against him."

"Goddam it," he shouted, "you don't know what you're doing. You're going to screw up everything."

She frowned in confusion, then stood up and walked briskly to the door. "I'd like to talk to you about this when you're not so mad. I hope you'll find me next time you come up to the commune."

Willis didn't follow her to the door right away. He sat back down at the table, mind racing and pulse throbbing. He sat long enough to grow calm, then took a long swallow of coffee. Shit. You just never know. Champ to chump before breakfast.

When he finally walked to the screen door, Marlene was just standing up, the calico cat snuggled between her elbow and chest. She got into her car, still carefully cradling the cat, and backed slowly onto the road.

The screened-in porch at the back of the cottage was a haven from the mosquitoes that sometimes swarmed into attacking armies, and Willis had spent a good part of the summer looking out over the pretty lake from that protected sanctuary. He could see all the way to the upper end of the lake where the brooding old hotel presided over the summer colony's activities, a matronly looking wooden structure now showing some shabbiness while at the same time making it obvious that it had known life on a grander scale. Earlier in the century the hotel had been the center of a rather ritzy spa—first a getaway for families of the robber barons and later a poorer but prouder enclave for New York intelligentsia. At least, that's the way Seymour had described it. Supposedly, Dorothy Parker, among others, had spent part of many summers at the lake.

Willis felt rather brooding himself, silently drinking his coffee on the shadowed porch where he was invisible from the lake, even if anybody had been out there to look in. Deep in his mind a tiny worry was beginning to scratch toward the surface; maybe it was a mistake to sign a lease on this place. In June it had reminded him of a little lake he had visited occasionally as a child, a spot he had once thought would be the best place in the world to live. He quickly found out just how different the two lakes actually were. The one of his memory was bathtub warm, crisscrossed with trotlines, and fringed with wide bands of weeds. This one was so cold, even on the hottest days, that a running jump was the only sane way in. It was the home port of small, elegant sailboats, not heavy, flat-bottomed, blunt-snouted johnboats, and it was the playground of lawyers and doctors, not subsistence fishermen. The fish here were trout and feisty smallmouth bass, not sluggardly catfish and fat largemouth.

In June he had dismissed the snide remarks about how a Southern boy would freeze to death out here in the winter. The cottage was insulated and it had heat. He tried to remember just how he had pictured lake life in winter, but he drew a blank. Probably he hadn't pictured it at all. But he did have a mildly disturbing idea that maybe Marlene had been part of whatever image he had on that June day when she had helped him move out here. He remembered thinking back then that anything would be better than the Uptown and that even absolute solitude would be an improvement over Ernie.

Now a picture did pop into his mind, but it was not cheering. He thought of Barbara and their walk along Lake Michigan. But he knew immediately and without doubt that Barbara was not going to spend a night, much less a winter, in this cottage.

By eleven he had finished the pot of coffee. The sun was high and the porch had become hot. Outside, he ambled without purpose toward the water. By the time he was on the short dock, he still had not seen any other sign of life on the lake, and, suddenly, instead of feeling forlorn he began to think how lucky he was, how brilliant to have seen what no one else could see, namely, that this was really the best possible time to be living on the lake. Here it was empty, a private retreat, but still as warm as summer, free of bugs, and offering its full charm to him alone. The air was clear in the sparkling way he had not noticed since June, and the sky was an endless blue. He jerked the t-shirt over his head, kicked off his sneakers, and dived off the dock, swimming strongly before he even surfaced.

He swam to the little platform anchored just shy of the boat channel and heaved himself up. The sun dried him quickly and he lay on his stomach lazily watching the shoreline. After a few minutes, the first sign of other life appeared in the form of a blue motion he glimpsed through the trees, headed down the road toward his cottage. She's coming back, he realized. Christ, now what?

He watched the slow progress of the blue flashes through the trees. She must have changed her mind. Something he said must have changed her mind. But what if she had misinterpreted? What if she said she wanted to stay with him after all? Christ. Maybe she was just bringing back the cat.

For several long minutes he didn't move; eyes closed, he hugged the raft like a turtle on a log. Finally, he stood up, jumped into the water, and swam steadily but without hurry toward the dock. As he climbed out of the lake, he heard the screen door slap shut behind her as she went onto the porch. He knew she was watching him put on his shirt and shoes. On the way up from the dock he strained to see through the black screening into the porch, but he couldn't see anything, not even a moving shadow. He grew increasingly annoyed, knowing she was up there watching his every step, but he couldn't even tell whether she was sitting or standing. Goddam it, you shouldn't have to be spied on from your own house.

As he opened the door he was still undecided whether to be friendly or testy, and the dilemma so distracted him that it took a full second for his mind to register what his amazed eyes were screaming at him. The delay made the impact of recognition more violent and he very nearly stumbled backwards down the steps.

"Jesus, Willis, that's no way to greet an old friend." Bushey sounded genuinely hurt, but his grin was malicious and he made no move to stand up from the porch glider where he sat, with his black loafers resting on the little glass-topped table. "You're either guilty as hell or scared to death. Who'd you drown out there? I hope it was just a cat."

Willis's mind was still muddled, and for a wild instant he thought that Bushey had grabbed Marlene or that maybe she and he were in some sort of conspiracy involving the commune. His eyes raced around the dark porch, searching for her. Finally, he remembered that Bushey too had a blue car. His heart slowed down and he felt the panic die, but he was still agitated. What the hell was he doing out here at The Box? He turned and carefully allowed the screen door to close slowly and softly. He still hadn't moved, and a small puddle was forming on the floor at his feet.

"You could give a guy a heart attack, sneaking up like that." He walked past Bushey into the kitchen and picked up his pack of cigarettes from the table, lighting one before returning to the porch. "Think of the headline: Ex-Cop Scares Reporter to Death. How would you explain that?"

Bushey laughed and lifted his feet off the little table.

"Christ," Willis said, "think what that would do to Quimby's election chances."

Bushey shook his head in mock disgust. "You news guys are all just alike. You all think you're a hell of a lot more important than you really are. What makes you think anybody would care if you had a heart attack?"

Bushey always managed to keep Willis just a little off-balance, never certain that he had really understood some comment or some gesture. Now, somehow, he had turned his own lame joke back on him and Willis didn't know where to go with it. He stood awkwardly, his shorts still dripping water, with the ash of his cigarette poised over his cupped hand.

He started toward the kitchen for an ashtray. Bushey spoke to his back. "How about some coffee? It's a long drive way out here."

He stopped and the ash dropped off onto the kitchen floor. "Okay," he said, irked but also glad to have a distraction. "It'll take a few minutes."

"You need a, uh, a friend out here," Bushey called. "To make coffee for you." Willis couldn't see him, but he knew he was smirking. "Whatever happened to your friend from up on the mountain? Marlene?"

Christ, did he see her leaving? How'd he know her name?

"She's still up there, I guess," Willis called.

Then he got nervous. Maybe he came out here following her or something? "In fact, she was just out here. For a quick visit."

Bushey called again. "How about your new friend? Barbara."

Willis nearly dropped the coffeepot. How the hell did he know about that?

"Her husband is a big supporter of my man Quimby, you know."

Willis still didn't respond. He puttered around the kitchen pretending to be busy. When he finally stepped back onto the porch, Bushey was leaning far back in the glider, swinging gently and smiling, his narrow-brimmed straw hat pushed far to the back of his head.

"Coffee be ready in a minute," Willis mumbled, lighting another Winston.

Bushey nodded, still smiling ironically. "I don't think he knows," he said.

"Who?"

"Her husband. At least, he hasn't said anything; but if he really doesn't know, then he's the only one who doesn't."

"Knows what?" Willis knew as he spoke that it was a pathetic comment, the guilty reply of an eighth grader withered into limpness by the infallible wisdom and absolute power of the accusing principal.

Bushey laughed, a loud snort of derision.

"Never mind," he said. "How was the convention, anyway? It looked like a hell of a show, at least on television." He paused, then added with a sharpness that Willis took to be double-edged, "That is, if you had time to pay attention."

This must be how a suspect feels, Willis thought. If you answer, it's probably a trap; if you don't, you're obviously guilty.

He hid behind a long pull on his cigarette, then went back into the kitchen and poured a cup of coffee. "Cream or sugar?"

"Black," Bushey said.

He brought in the coffee and, bereft of excuses, sat down gloomily in one of the tattered wicker chairs he and Ron had salvaged from the dump.

"Cheer up, Willis. You ought to be glad to see me, even if you don't know it yet."

Bushey lifted his cup and sipped with surprising delicacy. "We're going to win this election, you know. I know you don't think much of Quimby, and I have to agree that in another year he wouldn't be exactly a sure-bet candidate. But this year the Republicans are going to sweep everything and he'll ride in on the wave."

Relief surged through Willis's brain. Politics he could deal with, anywhere, anytime. He sat back in his chair. "First you've got to win the primary. What makes you so cocky about that?"

"That's what I came to see you about," Bushey said, reaching for a packet partially hidden next to him on the glider. "We've got a new poll that shows Quimby winning the primary by eight points."

He reached into the manila envelope and pulled out a sheaf of papers. "It was taken this weekend. You can't get much fresher than that."

He looked up expectantly, but Willis resisted the impulse to reach for the papers.

"It's a little late to do you much good, isn't it?"

"That depends on you," Bushey said with a forthrightness that startled Willis. "I came out here to give you the poll—the whole thing, since I know you'd never run selective results. I'm going to give you all the races: governor, light governor, attorney general. The whole nine yards."

He held the papers in his hand but didn't extend them toward Willis. "No strings," he said. "You do whatever you want with it."

Willis had no professional qualms about taking the poll. Some papers refused to carry poll results on the final two days before an election, but he had always thought it was a stupid policy. It was still news, for Christ's sake, if the poll was reliable and fresh. Once, in North Carolina, he had worked like hell to get a poll and finally succeeded, then had the story killed.

He waited, pretending to be considering. Neither of them spoke. Willis thought about going into the kitchen to get a smoke, but he didn't want to press his act. Bushey was capable of any sort of stunt, including taking the goddam poll to the *Patriot Press*. Still, the whole situation made him fretful. Why give the poll to him and not the *Patriot Press* in the first place? That was the Republican paper. His own paper had pounded Quimby for months. Seymour and the old man had agreed in this case that Quimby was a minor menace and ought to be stopped, so both the editorial page and the news pages had been relentless in attacking him.

Bushey said no strings, but there was no such thing when you were dealing with Bushey. He sat patiently holding the papers, with no hint of expression on his tough face.

Finally, Willis reached out his hand. "I can't promise what Seymour will do with this," he said. "He's funny sometimes."

Bushey laughed. "I'm not worried about old Sy," he said. "He'd cut his own brother's balls off for a good story."

He handed over the packet. "You might at least say thank you," he said.

Willis just nodded. He didn't even open the envelope, but he did tuck it carefully under the cushion of the chair next to his.

"By the way," Bushey said, "what's happening down at your paper, anyway? Is there going to be a strike?"

"Anybody's guess," Willis said. "But I doubt it."

Bushey eyed him closely. "I hear they're pretty determined, the union. I also hear the old man is really dug in. It sounds to me like it could get nasty sometime this fall."

Willis just shrugged but he was off-balance again. You never knew with Bushey whether he was giving or getting information, whether he was leading you somewhere—maybe somewhere you wouldn't want to go—or was just trying to find out how much you already knew about something.

"We're trying to stay on top of all situations like this," he said. "Anything that could affect the state, like a big strike, might end up on the attorney general's desk, you know."

Willis flinched. Christ, was he reading his mind? It wasn't like Bushey to explain why he was asking questions—or why he did anything, for that matter.

"Well, anyway," Bushey said, standing up from the glider, "situations like that can get ugly, and if it does, remember, we might be able to help out." He smiled. "Sometimes it takes something ugly to make you know who your real friends are."

Willis blinked, struggling for an answer, but he was saved by the telephone. He hurried into the kitchen to answer it, and Bushey waved goodbye and stepped toward the door. But Willis still hadn't heard the screen close when he said, "Hello," so he knew Bushey was listening.

"Willis? It's Connie. How are you?"

"Okay," he said, keeping his voice as neutral and unrevealing as possible. "How about you?"

"I'm glad I caught you," she said. "Ron and I were hoping you could have lunch with us. Today. It's his last day in town."

"Sure," he said, listening hard for sounds on the porch. "Where?"

"How about The Cafe? In about half an hour?"

"Yeah, I'll be there. Bye."

He hung up the phone and walked quickly onto the porch, but there was no sign of Bushey. He stood very still for a half minute before he heard the car door shut at the front of the house. By the time he had walked around to the driveway, the blue sedan was disappearing down the road.

*
**

Sy sat on his windowsill, fitfully reading *Richard III*, his eyes flitting between the pages and the sidewalks, which by now were nearly empty but earlier had been clogged with people hurrying to their jobs. He'd been there since before the rush hour even started, unable to sleep, his mind whirring, his pulse racing on caffeine, and his stomach churning from the too-early intrusion of coffee and nicotine. The stale air in his room was thick with cigar smoke that he didn't notice as he read the familiar lines. He loved the play even though he had come to it late, well into middle age, on the recommendation of Manny, who argued it was the best of all the histories.

But now his attention was pulled irresistibly from the play to Main Street, as though he expected to see something mysteriously important, and the words rolling endlessly in his mind were not Shakespeare's but McNally's. "If you interfere with the union, harass them in any way, we're going to suspend you," he had said yesterday. We? Suspend? Harass? The whole conversation, really a lecture, had dumbfounded Sy, closed him up so all he could do was look silently to Manny in a futile search for some sign that would explain what was happening.

McNally had read sternly from a letter announcing that the NLRB was going to conduct a formal inquiry into charges of unfair labor practices. He had read the bureaucratic language as though it had holy import and as though he had to interpret it for the others, even though the only information in the entire letter was the fact that an inquiry would be held—sometime. No explicit charges were made and no one was named as the accused.

When the letter used two long sentences to say only that no date had been set for a hearing, Sy had snorted and rolled his eyes until McNally rebuked him. "Seymour, this is serious. When are you going to grow up and begin to see that this is important?"

Sy had looked at Manny, who surely would appreciate the absurdity, but he was staring in the other direction, toward the window. Fletcher Junior was brushing imaginary crumbs off his shirtfront, and Andrew was nodding vigorously to second McNally's complaint.

That's when McNally had threatened him. "Our strategy is working just right," he had said. "I sense they're getting a little desperate. But that just means this is a crucial time for us. We can't afford to make a mistake. And, frankly, Sy, I'm worried that you might make that mistake—again."

He had paused, expansively and confidently giving Sy or Manny a chance to challenge him if they would, but no one spoke.

"So," McNally said with the finality of royalty, "if you can't keep yourself under control, we're going to have to keep you out of the newsroom. And you better take this seriously; you've had several warnings and this is your last one."

Sy had come to the meeting unsure what to expect but secretly hoping that Manny, at least, would be pleased with his handling of the union issue. He thought he had basically followed all the rules, even the silly ones. He had had no major run-ins with Connie, he had dutifully hired the two new reporters sent to him by McNally to replace Ron and Hank, and he had made hardly any effort to find out what was happening inside the union.

He was truly puzzled by the NLRB letter and believed the charges, whatever they were, must be directed at someone else. But sitting there under the imperious taunting of McNally, he had felt only helpless confusion. He couldn't reply. No guiding anger rose to help him, and no wit came to rescue his tied tongue. No one else in the room would meet his eye, but he knew they were all pitying his humiliation while at the same time delicately refusing to see or touch his flayed sensibilities.

After the meeting, the confusion and painful uncertainty had deepened hour by hour as Sy struggled through the routine of putting out the paper. At one point he saw Greenberg standing in the hall talking to McNally. He turned on the television news and sat in front of the flickering images for an hour, his door closed and his back to the newsroom.

Later, as he walked back into the newsroom after a supper break, Fletcher was standing at Willis's desk, bent over in close conversation. When he saw Sy, he stood up and walked off quickly, leaving through the composing room. Sy went over to Willis's desk, but when he got there he couldn't think of anything to say and simply turned away. He walked to the door of the composing room and stood for a moment, staring at Rocky sitting on his raised throne in deep discussion with Fletcher.

Back at his own desk, Sy had skimmed blindly through the wire stories and sat quietly, pretending to read copy. Finally, a little after eleven, he had left his office, waved to Greenberg, and made his way without speaking to anyone through the deadline-frantic newsroom. Outside, the night was cooler but still summer, and he walked slowly toward his place, the sweat drying under his shirt and his thoughts gradually coming into focus.

**

He was exhausted by the time he climbed the stairs and had felt immense relief to be inside his own living room, but then, suddenly, a stab of panic had hit him and without thinking he rushed back through the empty outer room to the elevator. He threw back the steel door, his heart beating wildly, but the grated lift was empty, the low-watt ceiling bulb dutifully offering its humble spray of light that did not quite reach the floor of the cage.

Sy had made himself a stiff drink of scotch and slumped into his easy chair. He picked up the newspaper on top of the stack beside the chair and began reading, but soon he crumpled it into a ball and flung it toward the corner. He had scribbled hastily and briefly in his journal, then dozed fretfully in the chair for a few hours, unable to wake up or to summon the will to go to bed.

At six the street sounds had roused him, and he felt better. He dumped some ashtrays and his half-full glass, picked up the wad of useless newspaper, took a long shower, and put on clean clothes. Afterwards, with coffee and a cigar, he had taken his perch on the windowsill and begun *Richard III*.

He spent the morning reading, smoking, monitoring the street, and replaying what had by now faded into only a single lost round in his continuing fight with McNally. He brooded on what McNally insisted on calling the "no-strike strategy," and suddenly it came to him: the so-called expert was destroying the newspaper. Despite McNally's tough talk, he was playing right into the hands of the union. Rather than forcing their hand, his delaying tactic was really giving Connie and Carmoli and the others time to build their strength, win public support, and trick Sy into making a mistake.

The more he thought about it, the more certain he became that McNally's campaign was going to be disastrous. The numbers were on his side and that's why Manny continued to support him. The union had made the mistake of leaving out of the bargaining unit enough people to put out the newspaper during a strike. That was the correct part of McNally's calculation. But he had ignored the psychology. He had overlooked the natural sympathy that the nonunion people would have for the strikers, and with his Wall Street mentality he had not considered the public's reaction.

All of them, except Sy, had assumed you could count on the union to act in good faith. They had not known that the agitators would keep stirring up things, making trouble wherever they could. Sy had seen them, had watched as they continually tried to undercut his efforts. He had seen Connie whispering with Alice and others not in the bargaining union. Even Willis. They had all known that Ron and Hank were leaving, but no one had told Sy.

He was pacing around his living room, excited now that he was able to untangle a line of thought. He kept remembering things, and each memory made the snarled knot smaller and lengthened the string of clear reasoning, like the time he saw Greenberg standing on the sidewalk outside the newspaper talking furtively with Connie and Merle. Why hadn't they gone inside to talk? He remembered back to the party and how they had all grown quiet when they realized Sy was there. Mo had been the only one who would talk to him.

Why couldn't Manny see that delay was an enemy? They ought to be forcing the issue, make the union strike and then break the strike. Sy had no doubt that they could win. The union was weak, a motley collection of small people banded together by petty ambitions like higher pay and shorter work hours. Sy and Manny could certainly turn back such a puny challenge, but he needed to convince Manny that McNally was wrong, that he was leading them into a trap. The problem was Fletcher. He and McNally were working together. That's why it was so hard for Manny to see the truth. He couldn't reject McNally's strategy without rejecting Fletcher. And by teaming up with McNally, Fletcher was able to turn his father against Sy. But what about McNally? What was he really up to?

Sy stopped pacing and stood concentrating on the question, looking down on Main Street. Why didn't McNally see that they ought to move now? A chill shot down his spine. Of course. It wasn't that McNally and Fletcher didn't know they were making a mistake; they didn't care. They weren't really interested in breaking the union at all. It was Sy and Manny they were trying to break. First, drive a wedge between them, get rid of Sy, and then wear down Manny until he agreed to sell the paper. Delay the strike but keep the pressure on and finally Manny would give up. Of course. McNally was probably working for some big chain that wanted the paper. He was the Trojan horse. And Fletcher was working with him.

Really agitated now, Sy felt as alert and as clearheaded as he had ever been. He shoved some cigars in the front pocket of his trousers and, twelve hours after leaving, headed back to the paper. The irony, he thought happily, is that McNally had been right; he couldn't afford to make any more mistakes. But the fatal mistake was McNally's; he had foolishly become so arrogantly sure of himself that he had inadvertently armed Sy. McNally was like Macbeth's falcon towering over the mousing owl.

A grin spread over Sy's face. Wait and see who gets hawked. Now, finally, he knew what he should do and who the real enemy was. All he needed was some information that would show Manny what McNally was doing. And information was something Sy knew how to get.

He felt acutely alert, focused on details he sometimes ignored. He checked his pockets for money, wallet, and keys, locked the door to his inside two rooms, checked to make sure the elevator was still parked at his floor, and locked the outside door opening into the stairwell. At the bottom of the narrow stairs, he locked the street door and stood in the entryway for a minute, glancing up and down the block. He walked along at a normal pace, feeling the annoyingly bright sunshine on his face.

A block ahead he saw a vaguely familiar figure moving away from him up Main Street. It could have been the union guy, Carmoli. Otherwise, he didn't spot anyone he recognized on the street. Nearing The Cafe, he realized he should be getting hungry and he slowed his pace, but food didn't have much appeal and he was reluctant to waste the time. At the entrance, he stopped, peering inside to see whether it was crowded. He jumped back when he saw Willis, Connie, and Ron sitting at a table midway toward the rear of the restaurant.

Sy spun his back toward the door, hunched his shoulders, and hurried on, resisting an impulse to shield his face with his hand. At first he was relieved, fairly sure they couldn't have seen him, but as he walked he grew increasingly angry. He hated feeling furtive. He was ducking around like some seedy lobbyist or corrupt politician. He stopped, poised to charge back into the restaurant to confront the conspirators. Then McNally's threat leaped into his mind, freezing his feet in place for a moment before he continued walking.

By the time he reached the newspaper, anger and shame had whipped each other into a boiling froth. He slammed back the front door and, head jutting forward, rushed into the newsroom. At first he didn't see anyone. Alice's desk was empty, and he checked the wall clock: 3:12. Then his eye caught a movement and he saw Merle in the back of the room, lounging in his desk chair and mostly hidden behind the *New York Review of Books.*

Sy was standing right beside his chair before Merle noticed him. He lowered the paper with a shy smile.

Sy demanded, "What're you doing?"

Merle shrugged.

"Goddam it, I said what are you doing? Are you working?"

"No," Merle said softly. "I'm just reading the paper."

"We don't pay you to read the *New York Review.*"

Merle shrugged again. "Of course not."

"Then what are you doing in here?"

Merle tried to roll his chair back but Sy stepped forward, closing the gap. He looked puzzled. "I'm just reading the paper," he said lamely. "I come in here nearly every day to read. I always have."

"Well, not anymore you don't," Sy said. "Things have changed . . ." He caught himself; be careful, they could say that was a reference to the union.

"Besides, I've always told all of you not to hang around the newsroom if you're not working. You know the policy."

"Policy?" Merle looked shocked. "I didn't know we had any policies."

Sy knew he was not being sarcastic, just being Merle. But he said, "Don't be a smart-ass. If you're not working and not putting this on your timesheet, get out."

Merle's eyes opened wider. He started to smile, as though he suddenly realized that Sy was joking.

"I mean it, Merle. Get out of here if you're not working. And if you are working, quit reading the goddam paper."

Merle stood up. "What time should I come back?"

"How the hell should I know," Sy sputtered. "What time are you supposed to come to work?"

Merle shrugged. "I just always come in when I feel like it. Sometimes in the morning, sometimes about noon."

"Well, goddam it, what time do you put on your timesheet?"

"Two o'clock."

"Always?"

"Sure."

"Well, then, goddam it, come in at two o'clock."

Merle hesitated, looking up at the wall clock, until Sy screamed, "Get out. Right now."

After Merle left, Sy took a quick tour around the newsroom, as empty as a graveyard now but still alive, like a baseball field in the hours just after a game when the lights are still on but the stands are vacant and the sounds seem to be echoing still. The only desks that stood out in the general disorder were the two recently abandoned by Ron and Hank. The side-by-side desks were identical and empty except for decrepit Underwoods half submerged in the center of the narrow wooden tops, stark symbols of betrayal that brought the dark blood rising back into Sy's face. He had once held high hopes for both of them—smart, educated, stable guys from the middle class who seemed to have chosen newspapering when any number of other careers would have been opened to them. Both going back to school, for Christ's sake—lawyers and academics, ghosts instead of men. Sy blamed the union. He remembered how grateful they had both seemed to be when he first hired them.

He stormed into his own office and went mechanically over to the *Times* wire, but he didn't read anything. He sat down, then popped up again and walked straight to Fletcher's office in the advertising department. The girl at the counter said Fletcher was out to lunch. Sy nodded, then poked his head into Andrew's cubbyhole. Empty.

He walked slowly and casually down the hall and ducked into Manny's office. He eased the door closed but not firmly enough to click the latch. It was the first time he had ever rifled the office during working hours. He made a quick search of the half-empty wastebasket. Nothing useful except an empty manila envelope from McNally's law firm. It was an outsized envelope and Sy held it in his hand for a minute, wondering.

The top of the desk was cluttered but it was a clutter of neat piles of papers, each stack obviously organized in some design that made sense to Manny, like a housewife's arrangement of china gewgaws in a whatnot. Sy rummaged through the piles, careful not to change the arrangement or mix up the papers in each stack. He skimmed several letters, although none had a connection to him or to the union. He found no inquiries about buying the paper, but he didn't expect to find those because Manny was so secretive about buy offers.

Sy didn't notice how hard he was sweating until a big drop plunked onto a pile of papers. He dabbed at the spot with his handkerchief. He stopped often to listen for footsteps but he continued with a methodical search of the desktop. He then opened the top drawer of the desk and probed perfunctorily through the other drawers, but he was getting more and more nervous. None of the drawers was locked.

After twenty minutes of searching he gave up and, with enormous relief, slipped back out the door into the hall. He stooped down and pretended to tie his shoe to give his heart time to stop racing. He mopped his sweaty face and leaned for a moment against the wall.

The search had been a long shot and he was not disappointed so much as relieved, both because he had not been caught and because now at least he was doing something. As always, if you had the nerve and just kept digging, eventually you'd get the information you wanted. It's what he always told his reporters.

Driving into town, Willis had begun to wish he hadn't agreed to meet Connie and Ron. He didn't want to talk about the union, he didn't want to hear their warmed-over views about the war and politics, and he didn't want to watch Ron squirming with delight every time Connie touched his arm or looked him in the eye. Christ, the kid never learned. The talk with Bushey had put Willis on edge. He wanted some time to study the poll and decide how to handle it, but he didn't want to tell Connie and Ron about it—not yet. And just before he left The Box, Barbara had telephoned, leaving him with one more reason to dread this lunch meeting.

They were already at The Cafe when he walked in, and he was surprised to see Vince at the table too. Ron and Vince both stood up when he arrived, and Connie smiled and waved to him. "Sorry, I've got to run," Vince said. "I have another lunch meeting. I just came by to say goodbye to Ron."

"Don't rush off on my account," Willis said. "I'm not in the union, but that doesn't mean I'm contaminated, you know."

Vince laughed and Connie said, "Not contaminated, exactly, but some people think you have a poison pen."

"What's that supposed to mean?" Willis said sharply.

"Relax, Willis," Ron said. "It was a joke."

"If you newspaper guys are not fighting with someone else, you knife each other," Vince said.

He smiled quickly to Connie and then turned to Ron. "Anyway, Ron, good luck with school. And thanks for your help. I hope to catch up with you again someday."

Ron nodded and he and Willis both sat down.

"See you later, Willis," Vince said as he walked off.

Willis took a quick look at Connie. She was fiddling with her napkin and looking down, a slight frown creasing her mildly sunburned forehead. Something's wrong, he thought.

No one seemed inclined to talk, and they had ordered and the food was on the table before they got past the weather and the goodbye banter.

"So, Ron," Willis said, "have you met your replacement? Yours and Hank's?"

Ron glanced quickly toward Connie before answering. "Yeah, I met 'em. That's all, though. They didn't seem very friendly."

"Just not your type, young friend. My guess is those guys haven't seen much college life. But that doesn't mean they aren't good reporters, you know."

"Come on, Willis. Those knuckleheads are scabs, pure and simple. You know that as well as we do." Connie said.

Bull's-eye. Willis sat back and grinned. He'd guessed that was what was bothering her.

"How do you know? I doubt Sy told you that."

"Quit playing games, Willis." Connie sounded more tired than angry or maybe just worried, but something had put the edge in her voice. "We all know that Sy didn't hire those creeps. We all saw his face the day he walked in the newsroom and they were waiting for him. I don't know who found them, but it sure as hell was not Sy. I suspect that high-paid, union-busting, lace-curtain Irish lawyer."

"Don't look at me," Willis said with a short laugh. "I sure as hell didn't hire 'em. I don't even know their names."

He tossed his head toward Ron. "Besides, if you want somebody to blame, blame him. He's the one who's walking out."

Ron looked frightened. "Wait a minute," he said, eyes darting from Willis to Connie, "Connie knew all along—"

Willis broke in. "Yeah, walking out of the union fight so he can go to school and bring more professionalism into journalism. Isn't that right, Ron?"

"No, that's not right, Willis. I mean, I am going back to school but—"

This time it was Connie who interrupted him. "Forget it, Ron. This asshole is just jabbing you. Hell, he's no better than a scab himself."

Willis laughed but he was stung. "That's bullshit, Connie. If you're really looking for someone to blame, start with yourself. You agreed to leave me off the union eligibility list and you left a lot of others off too. That's why you're in trouble now and you know it."

He took a long drink of water, but neither of them responded so he went on. "Christ, I'm not even supposed to be talking to you about this stuff and that's your doing too. So don't give me this scab bullshit."

"Forget it," she said. "We didn't ask you to lunch to fight. I'm just a little on edge. And I really do hate to see Ron and Hank leave."

"What's on your mind?" Willis asked.

She sighed. "It's just the whole situation. We're not getting anywhere. They're stonewalling and we can't find any leverage to move them. They're transparent but we can't prove they're stalling. And everybody is getting nervous. It's not just the newsroom. The others are even more edgy."

She put her elbows on the table and leaned her chin into her cupped hands, looking thoughtfully from Willis to Ron and then back to him. "Look," she said finally, "I'm really going out on a limb here, but I think I can trust you. And Ron is sure I can. So here goes."

Still she hesitated for a moment, looking closely at him. "We need some help."

He must have looked alarmed because she hurried on. "Don't worry. We're not asking you to join the union or anything like that. I just want your opinion—I know it'll only be a best guess—about some things. I mean, really, we just need some advice."

She paused, swallowed, and sighed. "Okay. Here's what we need to know. Remember, just your best guess. I mean, you've been around a lot of newspapers."

She stopped again and sat back in her chair. "If we called a walkout, could we shut down the paper? I mean, over the course of a week or so, maybe even three weeks. Could we wear them down and stop the presses?"

Willis relaxed. He liked being the authority, and it pleased him that after all her mocking of his experience, now she was asking his advice. What happened to her faith in the great expert, Vince?

He carefully controlled his expression—not the time to gloat.

"Well," he began in a thoughtful tone, "first I want to make sure both of you understand that I am absolutely neutral in this thing. I never have wanted anything to do with it, I have not taken sides, and I am not going to have anything to do with it. I'm just here to write news stories, and if the time comes when I can't do that, I will leave. So I'm a neutral observer and that's all, right?"

They both nodded.

"Also, this is just a guess, remember. But it is an educated one. I've been in a few labor situations, although nothing exactly like this.

"Anyway, my guess is that you can't shut down the paper. I have to believe they have lined up an emergency crew that can operate the press, and I'm sure Rocky can get the composing room work done. Hell, he'd probably do it all by himself if necessary. Anyway, that wouldn't shut them down. And the newsroom is no problem. As you know, a lot of us were left out of the union from the beginning, and as you see, newsroom scabs are a dime a dozen. A long strike would hurt their revenue, but I expect they've been salting away money for so long they could ride out a drought without much pain.

"So my guess is that you couldn't close the paper, and I know you couldn't do it in three weeks, probably not in three months."

Connie nodded, and for an instant Willis thought she might cry. But she didn't, and finally she said, "Thanks. That's what I was afraid of."

Willis couldn't resist. "What about Vince? He's the pro; what does he think?"

He was surprised by the hurt, or perhaps guilty, look that flickered across her face. "That's the other part of the problem," she said at last. "You've been fair with us so I'm going to trust you some more. But you must not tell anyone this."

She glanced around quickly to make sure no one was near their table. "Vince is leaving. The union wants him to take over a situation at a big plant down South that's headed for a strike. They really need him and he's pretty sure we're not ready for a strike here."

Connie looked over at Ron as though she wanted him to add something, but he was looking down at his plate, slowly running his fork through the leftover food.

"Whew," Willis said, "where does that leave you?"

"What do you mean?" Connie stalled.

"Come on," he said, "you know what I mean. What are you going to do when Vince leaves?"

"I haven't crossed that bridge," she said.

Willis looked from one of them to the other, his head scanning across the table twice, but neither would catch his eye. Christ, they're all going to leave—bail out of this mess and leave Merle and the others wondering what hit them.

He sat back in his chair, content for a minute to let Connie and Ron squirm in silence but also wanting some time to think. He signaled to the waitress for more coffee. It was too bad about the eager true believers, like Merle, but maybe when the dust settled they wouldn't be any worse off than when they started. Life would go on and maybe they had even learned something, grown up a little because of this run-in with the real world.

Over the past months he had spent some uncomfortable hours questioning his own choices. Sometimes he wondered about just standing on the sidelines taking notes. It was an old itch for him, but in the end something always happened like this; by and by, the heroes always tripped on their banners. And when they did, someone else always got bloodied. And someone else always had to pick up the injured.

When the rednecks charged the black revival meeting, where were the preachers? On their way to the next tent, counting their nickels and dimes all the way. When the cops cracked the kids' heads with sticks, where were the crusade leaders? Watching from air-conditioned hotel rooms on the twenty-third floor.

Willis looked with growing bemusement at Connie and Ron, sitting with long, mournful faces but already secretly a few steps removed from the coming debacle.

"So, Connie," he said finally, keeping his face carefully masked, "if it's already a lost cause, you might as well just move on to someplace you can do some good, right?"

She looked up sharply, ready to counter-attack but was stopped by Willis's apparent sincerity. When she didn't answer, Ron spoke up. "How about you, Willis? How long are you staying around here?"

"Me? I told you, all I care about is stories. I'll be here as long as good stories keep falling in my lap." He picked up the manila envelope from the table and waved it. "Like this one."

"What's that?"

"A poll. A brand-new poll on all the primary races, hot off the copying machine."

Ron whistled softly, but Connie stiffened.

"Where'd you get that?" she said. "It's too late to run it."

"The hell it is," Willis said. "Hell, it was only done this weekend. It's as close to accurate as you can get."

"Yeah," she said, "but you can't use it now. If it comes out in tomorrow's paper, it'll influence the voting."

Willis shrugged. "So what do you do? Stop writing news just because the news will influence the voting? Come on, Connie, polls—legitimate polls by independent outfits—polls are real news, just like issue positions are. More so. If X is ahead of Y the day before the election, then that's news."

"It's Quimby's poll, isn't it?"

She caught Willis by surprise.

"Who cares whose poll it is as long as it has all the races and you've got the complete poll. This is not a selective, partial poll, you know. This is the whole thing."

She was shaking her head vigorously, the blond hair waving from side to side. "God, I can't believe you'd carry water for that guy. He's a right-wing scumbag trying to cash in on the Nixon vote. That bastard never had an original thought in his whole life."

Ron broke in, bouncing slightly in his chair with excitement. "Christ, have you heard his latest ad? The slogan is No Insult Unanswered, No Crime Overlooked."

Willis laughed. "Whoa, Ace. I don't write about just the politicians I like. Hell, if I did, I wouldn't write anything. My job is news, remember? By the way, what happened to your vaunted professionalism? It's not very professional to take sides in an election, is it?"

"Come off it, Willis." Connie's eyes were flashing and her hand was chopping the air over her plate. "What's not professional is running a poll some sleazebag bootlegs to you the day before an election."

Willis smiled broadly at her. "Connie," he said cheerfully, "you better stick with helping Vince organize the starving workers. Leave the newspapering to us scumbags."

She shoved her chair back so hard it rattled the table. "You're . . . you're . . . Christ, what does Seymour say about your toadying for Quimby? Or Bushey, or whoever's pulling your strings?"

"Well," Willis said, still smiling, "the first thing he'd say is that you've got the wrong word; you better look up toadying. But I don't know what he'll say about the poll story; I haven't told him. But I assume he'll say, 'Good work, Willis.'"

She glared at him for a few seconds, then her shoulders slumped and she said, "Oh well, I don't need to worry about Seymour on that kind of stuff. He's a pig on things like the union, but you can count on him when it comes to news."

She slid her chair back to the table. "Anyway, that's your problem and his, not mine. And I really do appreciate your advice and your confidence." She looked solemnly into his eyes. "I truly don't know what I'm going to do yet. It's a real dilemma for me." Her eyes began to fill with tears that she quickly wiped away.

"We've got a meeting late this afternoon. The steering group. I'll tell them what you said. But don't worry, I won't use your name."

She stood up. "After that, maybe we can figure out what to do. And maybe I can decide what I'm going to do."

Willis nodded. "Are you working tonight?"

"Yeah," she said, "I'm taking my supper break for the meeting. How about later, after work, maybe we can find Hank and all have a drink together."

"That sounds good," Willis said. "I ought to be finished fairly early." He tossed a sly look at each of them. "I've only got one story to write."

She shook her head and reached for the check. "Come on, Ron, I'm paying. This is your farewell lunch, remember?"

"How about me?" Willis asked. "Are you paying for me?"

"You're on your own," she said, but she was smiling.

It was one thirty and the newsroom was still empty except for Alice, slumped at her desk, just sitting there, not even reading. Sy glanced up now and then to check the clock. He and Alice had not acknowledged each other since she drifted in and sighed her way around the newsroom, parceling out the day's newspapers that had been dumped on her desk, checking the paper supply in the wire machines, and turning the page on the giant calendar hanging on the bulletin board. She shuffled past Sy's office without so much as a glance inside.

The next time he looked up, Willis was standing in his office doorway, and Sy realized he had been hoping he would show up before the newsroom filled up.

"Hello, Willis, come on in."

Before he could answer, Sy stood up and said, "Better yet, let's take a walk. How about a cup of coffee?"

Willis nodded. "We can take a walk, but no coffee for me. I just finished lunch."

Sy looked closely at him and waited to see if he would say more, but he didn't.

"All right," he said, "let's just take a walk."

"Okay," Willis said, "but I can't be gone long. I have to . . . uh . . . run an errand. And I have a story I want to get to work on."

"What'll I tell people?" Alice asked Sy without looking up as they passed her desk.

"About what, Alice?"

"About you. If they want to know what time you'll be here, I don't know what to say. I never know anymore when you'll be in and when you won't."

Sy shook his head. "Just tell them I'll be back later. No—hell, don't tell them anything. Just say you don't know. What's wrong with that?"

She didn't answer.

Sy walked through the door, then turned back and stopped next to Alice's desk. "Tell them," he said, "what Thoreau said: 'To a philosopher all news, as it is called, is gossip, and they who edit and read it are old women over their tea.'"

Alice stared, slack-jawed.

"In other words," Sy said, "tell 'em that if they've come here about news, they've come to the wrong place."

Alice still looked blank, spit gathering at the corner of her mouth. Finally, as Sy turned to leave, she said, "Who's Throw?"

Willis was still laughing as they left the building. "The old man sure can pick winners for you," he said. "How long have you been putting up with Alice?"

"Long enough," Sy said, wondering how Willis knew that Manny had hired Alice.

"Speaking of such things," Willis said with careful casualness, "where'd you find the two new guys?"

"I guess they found me," Sy said. "Why?"

"Just wondering. You ought to know there's scuttlebutt that they were brought in by McNally as strikebreakers."

Sy felt his face darken and he turned away from Willis as though he was looking in the store windows as they passed. After a few steps, he said, "Sounds like you've been talking to Connie. When did you see her?"

He cut a quick sideways look toward Willis, but now it was Willis who was looking away.

"Not really," Willis said vaguely. "It's not Connie necessarily who's talking, just general newsroom gossip."

Sy asked again, "When did you last talk to her about the union and the paper?"

"I haven't seen Connie, except in the newsroom, in quite a while," Willis said, his head still turned toward the street traffic.

Anger swirled up so violently Sy almost broke his stride. He felt like kicking Willis, but he shoved down the impulse and just kept walking.

They covered half a block in silence before Willis said, "What'd you want to talk about?"

Suddenly Sy felt only deep sadness, the fury of surprise betrayal supplanted by common hopelessness. He walked a few more steps before replying, "I was looking for something, for some information, and I thought you might be able to help me."

Willis didn't answer.

"When you walked into the office," Sy said, "it seemed for a minute as though you might have come along just then because you knew what I was looking for, knew what I needed."

Willis shot him a quick, anxious look, but neither of them broke stride. "I'll help you if I can," he said cautiously, "but if it's union stuff you're talking about, you seem to be pretty much going your own way. I thought you were getting your advice from the lawyer, McNally."

"I met with McNally yesterday," Sy said, glancing at Willis and reassured to see that he obviously had not heard about that meeting. "He has his own game plan. And I have one too."

Willis showed less interest in this hinted mystery than Sy would have expected. He went on. "I need to know a couple of things. Most importantly, I need to know what the union's strategy is. And I need to know whether they think a strike will be effective."

When Willis didn't answer, Sy said, "I hoped you'd be with me on this. After all, you're not in the union; they left you out."

They were passing Vic's, and Sy thought about stopping but he didn't like the idea of facing Willis across a table so they kept walking. He didn't want to say any more but it was as though he couldn't stop himself. "I mean it, Willis, I really could use some help." He never begged anyone. "Will you help me?"

"I don't have any notion of what their strategy is," Willis said. "They don't confide in me and I don't ask. As for a strike, all I can tell you is that I'm going to keep working whether they strike or not. And as far as I know, all the others who are not in the union will keep working too."

Two city hall hangers-on were approaching on the sidewalk, and they stopped talking until they had nodded greetings and passed on. Then Willis said, "I think you already know that McNally gives me the creeps and all this whispering and posturing and game playing has made this job a lot less fun than it used to be. On the other hand, I'm happy not to be in the union and I wouldn't have joined even if they hadn't excluded me. I think this is an exceptionally fine little newspaper and I just hope they don't screw it up."

He slowed down enough to light a cigarette, and when Sy started to speak he waved him off. "Let me finish. I was going to say that in the meantime, I've got a notebook full of good stories that I want to write. I intend to go on writing them as long as you keep the presses running and are willing to print what I give you. And speaking of that, I'm working on a good story right now for tomorrow. You want me to tell you about that now?"

"Later," Sy said absently, unable to call up any interest in talking about a news story. "Tell me later."

They walked without speaking for a while, turning back toward the newspaper. They passed the bus station and Sy remembered the night Willis had walked into the paper looking for work. He recalled with a bitter irony how he had said he needed a job and he hoped Sy needed a good reporter. But it had turned out to be another one of those one-way deals; when he needed some reporting, some information, Willis wasn't there.

As they neared the parking lot used by the reporters, Willis said, "I've still got to run out to The Box to pick up something. I'll see you later in the newsroom."

Sy nodded without speaking as Willis walked off with awkward self-consciousness toward his Saab, ducking his head down and backward as though looking at his own track, like an uncertain performer walking into a crowd. He pulled out of the parking lot, turned left, and, as the car disappeared, it hit Sy with sledgehammer certainty: Willis was going to report to someone, probably Carmoli. But could it be McNally or Fletcher?

As he drove, Willis tried to concentrate on Barbara, to plan his speech and plot his performance. He knew she was going to tell him to get lost and he needed to figure out whether he would be outraged, sardonic, hurt, bitter, maybe just relieved, which is how he actually felt. She was a complication he didn't need in his life, a very nice diversion for a while, but for regular life she would be a luxury he didn't want to pay for. Still, it was important to close this little theatrical interlude in style, and ever since she telephoned he had been trying to focus on creating the right script.

But his mind wouldn't settle to the work. First there had been fretting over the Bushey meeting, and then lunch had distracted him. Now, headed toward the rendezvous spot, he was having trouble keeping his mind from wandering back to Seymour. In the first place, he had looked awful. Dark pouches sagged under his eyes and his shave was even more haphazard than usual. Mostly, though, it was the way he talked and the way his probing eyes roved continually without resting on anything.

Willis drove slowly, basically retracing his route into town from the lake. Barbara lived in a showplace spread up on top of a mountain, an old farm she and her husband had been building and rebuilding for ten years, providing the main source of employment for their one-store town. But she didn't want to meet there. She did want to be home by the time her son finished football practice, though, so they had arranged to meet at a tiny picnic area near the spot that her road intersected with the lake road. Convenient, Willis thought when she suggested it, but he had merely agreed without editorial comment.

Her white Jeep was already in the turnout when Willis drove in. She was sitting at the picnic table just inside the shade line provided by the large maples behind her and, as usual, she looked perfect. She smiled beautifully as he walked toward the table, and the scattered bits of dialogue he had tucked away flew out of his head.

He headed for the bench across from Barbara, but a wrinkle rippled across her face and he changed course, dropping down beside her with his back leaning on the picnic table. "I've missed you," she said.

He didn't answer except to cock an eyebrow skeptically.

"You can miss someone and still not want to see them," she said.

"I didn't know that," he said.

She looked closely at him, checking to see if he was mocking her, then shrugged and said, "Well, it's true." She laughed as though she were mildly embarrassed. "I search the paper every day to find your stories. And I read every one of them."

"Even the Republican stories?"

"Especially those. We have to know what the enemy is doing, you know."

Willis nearly asked if her Republican husband was the enemy, but he didn't.

"I wanted to see you," she said, "to tell you that we're going away."

"Going away?"

"Yes, we're moving."

Willis was startled, then he laughed softly. "Yeah," he said, "I know. You're moving into a commune, right?"

A puzzled frown settled on her face.

"And you're leaving right away, right?"

She shook her head slowly, "We're not leaving for a month. And I don't know what you mean about a commune."

"Never mind," he said.

She shook her head again, clearing away the nonsense. "Anyway, I just wanted to tell you before you heard it somewhere else. Carl, that's my—"

"I know who he is."

"Carl's been offered a big promotion. We'll be moving to Europe for a few years."

"No more protest politics, huh?"

She looked hurt, then angry. "This is a terrific opportunity for us. All of us. For Carl and the children. And me. You're not going to make me feel guilty about this."

"About what?"

"About any of it. About leaving or about you. In Chicago we never pretended it was anything more than it was, and you can't start pretending so now."

"Okay," he said, "you're right. And congratulations. I hope you have a great time in Europe."

They talked for a while about politics, then she looked at her watch.

"Before you go," he said, "what about the fourth-party movement? Is the governor still interested?"

She shook her head. "That's dead. Kaput. Stillborn, really."

She smiled at him. "There's your story. But don't quote me."

He nodded. He started to tell her about Quimby's poll but changed his mind.

"Hey," she said, "isn't that Seymour's weird car?"

He turned to look just as the huge black Citroën glided majestically past, headed toward the lake. It was Seymour's, all right, probably the only one in the state; an ancient, hulking luxury car he had brought from France years ago and that spent most of its dotage squatting like a deflated monster in the tiny parking space behind his apartment.

Seymour rarely used the car or left town at all, for that matter, and Willis wondered for a minute where he was going. Then he knew; he was going to The Box to check up on Willis.

Barbara stood up and stuck out her smooth, tanned hand. He took it and she pulled him in for a short hug, then she was gone and the Jeep kicked a bare track in the gravel parking area as it leaped onto the highway.

*
**

On his way back to town, Willis couldn't decide whether to confront Seymour about his spying mission. The newsroom was getting busy by the time he got there and he went right to work on his poll story. He decided to hold the fourth-party story for another day.

Two hours later Sy still hadn't appeared in the newsroom, and Willis decided he better tell Greenberg about the poll story so he could plan for it. Greenberg didn't raise the issue of whether to publish a poll so close to the election, so Willis didn't mention it. He had some good reaction quotes and they decided to give the story a big play on Page One as a sidebar to the main advance story about the primary election. Willis liked the play—another thumb in the eye of the hotshots in the statehouse bureau.

Greenberg said he hadn't heard from Seymour and that he had tried to call him, but he didn't answer his telephone. He shrugged, sighed, and said he guessed he'd put out the paper without Sy.

"How often does he do this?" Willis asked. "Just not show up when you're expecting him?"

Greenberg shook his head. "Never. I've been here for fifteen years and Sy has never missed work without calling in or telling me ahead of time."

They looked at each other, then each of them shrugged and turned away.

Willis went back to work on his story, making more calls and generally taking his time. It was the perfect story for such a day—simple, easy to report and write, and important. Still, he didn't really enjoy working on it. Something nagged at him, and he couldn't get Bushey's smirk out of his memory.

Halfway through the evening, Willis noticed Connie wasn't in the newsroom either and he remembered she had said she would be working. Funny.

He finished his story early and sat back, smoking and watching the newsroom. It seemed like he had been there forever—or long enough, anyway, to have grown proprietary. In fact, he was a little embarrassed to realize how attached he felt to this little newspaper, a sense of personal pride he had not known at his other jobs. Looking around, he began thinking how much the newsroom had changed since he first saw it, and impatient irritation crept into his peaceful contemplation. He watched the two new reporters sitting in Hank's and Ron's old desks but somehow isolated, set apart from the others. Interlopers, opportunists posing as reporters, even though he knew both of them had newspaper experience somewhere in the Midwest. The change was not just the new guys, though; it was far more basic, and he didn't like it.

Willis looked over at Seymour's unlighted office. God knows Sy had changed in these nine months, but he dismissed the idea that a single person, even someone like Sy, could take the life out of a good newsroom. And all the others were still there. Merle, banging away at his typewriter, sweat beading on his brow. Mo, green plastic shade low on his bald head, hunched over his desk, reading through a pile of copy with his one good eye. Simmons, reared back in his chair, talking expansively to the guy in the next desk and anyone else who would listen. Greenberg, up and down a dozen times an hour, his hand plowing through his graying hair, often with a burning cigarette squeezed between two of the furrowing fingers. All the others— reporters, editors, copyreaders—each straining at his own oar, lost in immediate personal ambition, but each one acutely aware of everything happening in the room and all of them at war with a common enemy, the clock on the wall.

He watched and smoked, growing more and more agitated, irked by the unidentified changes in the newsroom and angry at his own inability to figure it out. Fuck it. He stubbed out the Winston, gathered up the pages of his story, and hastily pasted them together.

"Here it is, Chief," he said, flopping the glue-stained story into Greenberg's overflowing basket. "I'm going out for a quick one but I'll be back to see if you need anything else."

He weaved his way through the humming newsroom without speaking to anyone. Christ, he thought as he left, a guy who loses two girlfriends in one day has a right to be a little surly. And to have a drink too, for that matter.

Willis had two Jake-sized bourbons at The Oasis but they didn't improve his mood. He didn't even feel like baiting Jake, so there was no conversation exchange. He just drank and brooded, slouched alone in the usual back booth, sullenly wishing for company but then hoping every time he heard the door open that it was not someone he knew.

He got back to the newsroom just before eleven. Seymour's office was still empty but Connie was at her desk. She waved to him as he walked past to Greenberg's desk.

"How's the story?" he asked.

"Fine," Greenberg said, sounding more than usually harried as he raised his eyes only briefly from the copy he was reading. "It's fine. It's already gone, probably out with the proofreaders now."

"No sign of Seymour?"

"No. Not yet."

When Willis turned away, Connie caught his eye and motioned with her head toward Seymour's office. They got there at the same time and went inside without turning on the light. She closed the door.

"I've got to talk to you," she said. "It's important."

"Okay. Shoot."

"Not here. I'm going to finish up the little thing I'm writing and then I'll meet you somewhere. How about Jake's?"

"This sounds interesting," Willis said. "I thought you were practically a married woman."

"Don't play games, Willis. This is serious. Will you meet me?"

"Sure. I'm through, so I'll go on to Jake's. I'll be there when you get there. Unless he runs out of bourbon."

Willis was still at the bar with his first drink, talking to Jake, when Connie walked in. She ordered a beer and they walked to a booth in the rear. She swung her purse off her shoulder, slammed it down in the middle of the table, and flopped down hard on the cushioned seat.

"Whew. You're not going to believe this," she said, taking a long gulp of beer.

Willis waited as she seemed to be gathering her thoughts. Finally, she began.

"You know I told you we had a steering committee meeting late this afternoon. Remember?"

He nodded.

"Well, we met at the union hall as usual. Just the committee. Five of us. Vince was running the meeting. We talked for an hour and a half, maybe a little longer."

She took another drink and leaned her forearms on the table, her head, its big eyes open wide, shoved forward toward Willis.

"We were talking strategy, you know, and it was not very organized. Everybody talking at once. Then, suddenly, Vince stood up and put his finger to his lips. He nodded his head toward the closet. You know, one of those old cloakrooms they used to have in schools when we were kids?

"Anyway, Vince motioned for us to keep talking and he tiptoed over to the closet. He yanked open the door and — you won't believe this — Sy was standing there."

She shook her head, still leaning far across the table and practically whispering now.

"Honest to God. He was just standing there, like something out of a movie. He looked awful. His face was gray and sweaty; it must have been hot as hell in there. His tie was loose, like always. But listen to this: He had peed his pants."

She leaned back and Willis thought for a second she was going to cry, but she didn't. "Willis, it was the saddest thing I've ever seen in my life. He just stood there with this huge dark circle on the front of his pants. He stood there blinking for a minute, then he walked slowly over to the door and left. I can't even describe to you how his shoulders were slumped."

"Holy shit." Willis slumped back in the booth. He felt like he had when they told him his dog had been run over. He wanted to know every detail, but he also wanted to run away so he wouldn't have to hear any more. He didn't want to ask any questions because it seemed like the story could only get worse.

He was glad Connie wasn't looking at him. Her head was bent so low over the table he could see only the top of it. Finally, Willis said, "Did anyone say anything to him?"

She shook her head but didn't look up.

"Did he look back or say anything? Not anything?"

Connie shook her head again.

He took a swallow of his drink. Suddenly anger swelled up and Willis snarled, "Did anybody laugh? Or snicker? Any of those guys with you?"

She raised her head and shook it again sadly. "Nobody said anything. Not a sound. It was awful. You could hear every one of his footsteps, and when he closed the door, it sounded like a gunshot."

Long strands of hair had fallen down both sides of her face and she pulled them back with both hands, sliding back on the seat at the same time. "No one said anything for a long time. Finally, someone got up and looked out the window and saw him walking down the street."

"What's the union going to do?"

She was instantly defensive. "They've got to do something."

"Yeah," Willis said. "I'll bet they do."

"Listen, Willis, why do you always have to sneer at everything? Vince feels as awful as I do. He told me he wishes to hell he hadn't opened that closet. That he had just pretended not to hear that noise and had just ended the meeting. But he can't do that now. And we can't just pretend it never happened, can we?"

She waited while Willis lighted a cigarette, but when he still didn't answer, she said, "So the union is going to file a complaint. We've got to. And the NLRB will hold a formal inquiry of some kind. It's really out of our hands you know."

Willis nodded and still didn't speak.

"That's one of the reasons I wanted to see you," she said. "This inquiry could get sticky. And I thought—Vince and I both thought—that it could get uncomfortable for you if you had to testify. I mean, not that you've done anything wrong, but if they questioned you too hard about what you knew and how you knew it, well, it seems like you probably know a lot about both sides since you aren't really taking sides . . ."

She paused, but he wasn't ready to say anything. He picked up her beer bottle but it was still half full, so he set it down again and carried his own empty glass to the bar. When he slid back into the booth, she said, "Anyway, I wanted you to know about all this. If Sy has a friend in the newsroom, it seems to be you. And I thought you ought to know. Also, I wanted you to know that the union is not going to ask you to be a witness or to testify or anything."

"Well, thanks. I guess." His mind was busily pulling apart her last little speech, wondering why she and Vince would be so worried about what he might say to the NLRB. He couldn't dredge up anything—no conversation, no information, no slips of the tongue—that they might be worried about. Still, there had to be something. Oh well, take your luck wherever you find it; he was glad if he could escape the whole NLRB mess.

They were both quiet for a while, sipping their drinks and watching each other with friendly interest. For Willis, the attraction was no less strong than it had been way back in January, but it was at the same time totally different now and he puzzled for a minute over the difference. What had changed, he decided, is that now there was no expectation, no anticipation. The attraction would never be any more than that; it was complete, without fruit and without promise.

"How's Marlene?"

The question startled him and he wondered, as he often had, whether she was reading his mind or if his face had just telegraphed his thoughts. He took a drink before answering.

"Marlene who?"

She laughed. "It's that bad, eh? I'm sorry. I liked her."

He shrugged. "Me too. Big loss."

Connie grinned and lifted an eyebrow. "Well, you don't look exactly suicidal."

"What's that supposed to mean?"

"Nothing," she said, "only rumor has it that you haven't been obsessive in your devotion lately."

Christ, did the whole goddam world know?

"Anyway," she said, motioning toward the door, "these guys will be glad to hear about your bad luck."

Hank and Ron were standing in the doorway and Merle came in behind them. When their eyes had adjusted to the darkness, they hurried over. Hank sat next to Connie, and Ron beside Willis, leaving Merle to drag up a chair at the end of the table.

Jake shouted from behind the bar, "Hey, don't harass the paying customers."

A worried frown crossed Hank's smooth face and Merle jumped up. "Relax," Willis said, "he's just reminding you." He dug some money out of his pocket and reached it over to Merle. "Get me one while you're at it."

When they all had their drinks, Ron turned to Willis. "Did Connie tell you about Sy?"

"Couldn't wait," he said, "all the dirty details."

A hurt look twisted her face but she didn't reply, and Willis nodded in turn to the other three. "And I suppose you guys couldn't wait to spread the word either. Did you write a story about it? Put it on the radio?"

No one said anything and they carefully didn't look at Willis. He took a long swallow, wiped his mouth with the miniature napkin, and said, "I remember way back—maybe two or three months ago— when all of you guys thought Sy was pretty great. A guru of journalism. Hell, Hank, you acted like he could walk on water."

They were all squirming in their seats now, and Willis could feel his own indignation growing, filling him up with its venom. "You all loved it when he bashed the bad guys, right? When he yelled at anyone who dared criticize the newsroom or any of your stories, right? Remember, Merle, remember when you fucked up that obit and the funeral home guy came screaming into the newsroom? Remember how Sy threw his ass out before he even got all the way to your desk?"

Willis finished off his drink in a long gulp. "It's different now, isn't it? Different when you're on the other side."

"Shut up, Willis," Connie said. "You're getting drunk. What'd you expect us to do? Pretend he wasn't spying on the union? Sy's problem is he think the rules don't apply to him. He thinks that he's right and that makes him immune from the normal rules. Well, he's wrong. And so are you. If you're so concerned about him, why don't you . . ."

She stopped, either because she couldn't think of what she wanted him to do or because Vince had walked up and was standing beside Merle at the end of the table. They all looked up at him as he stood watching Connie's tirade with tired, worried apprehension.

She began to speak again, then stopped, shook her head, and gave Hank a light shove. "Let me out," she said. "I've had enough of this."

She stood up, slung her purse over her shoulder, and turned to Willis. "You're a mean bastard."

She walked away, leaving Vince looking down on the others with a bewildered expression. He shrugged, offered a tight smile, and began to turn away.

"Hey, Vince," Willis said from back in his corner, "we've got to stop not meeting like this." Vince gave him a blank look. "If I were a sensitive guy, like some others," Willis said, glancing from Hank to Ron, "I might take offense."

Vince looked at Willis, then at each of the others in turn, smiled, and said only, "See you later," before he turned and followed Connie out of the bar.

"Cocky bastard," Willis muttered under his breath. He noticed the other three were looking uneasy, as though they too were thinking about leaving.

"Let me out," Willis said to Ron. "I may be a mean old bastard, but at least I'm not going to let you guys leave town without buying you a farewell drink."

Headed for the bar, he said over his shoulder, "I'm getting you one too, Merle. Looks like you and I may be the last guys standing when this mess is all over, so we better stick together."

When he left the bar with the three beers and his own glass, Willis was careful not to totter so they wouldn't think he was tight. He carried the three bottles in his left hand and concentrated on the level of the bourbon in his right. He made it without sloshing out a drop. He set down the drinks and said, "That right there is my parting advice to you boys, the wisdom of the ages: keep a steady hand on the glass."

They snickered but they were obviously still restless. Hank was slowly, methodically tearing his napkin into tiny same-size pieces. Ron tapped a striped swizzle stick on the table like a tiny drumstick, beating out a dull plastic-on-plastic rhythm, and Merle, still sitting at the end, was jiggling both feet at the same time, his knees bouncing at about 200 rpms.

Willis handed around the beers. "Okay, guys, let's forget the union and all that unpleasantness." He nodded toward Hank. "Let's drink to the practice of law and to the pursuit of justice," he said, lifting his glass and then turning it toward Ron, "and to professional journalism, whose goal, as we all know, is to comfort the afflicted and afflict the comfortable."

He took a long drink, set down his glass, and said, "Or have I got that backwards?"

The other three drank from their beers but still didn't say anything, casting surreptitious glances at each other.

"C'mon, guys," Willis said, "you're supposed to be celebrating, but you look more like you're mourning the death of an old aunt who left you out of her will." He looked around the bar. "Take a look at this place and be glad you're getting out. Hell, you could end up like Merle there. Or me."

"Right," Merle said with a weak laugh.

"Damn right," Willis said loudly. "You're getting out at exactly the right time too. That's always the secret to life: timing. Knowing when to get out. Take Seymour, for example. He ought to have gotten out a long time ago. Now look what's happened. His paper has gone to hell and he's driving it over the cliff. Or at least he looks like he's driving."

Willis gave the other three a close look to see if they had understood his sly perception about who was really running the paper. But none of them met his eye. Too dark to tell anyway, and besides, they obviously were too scared.

"Christ," he said, shifting to a safer target, "talk about timing. Just look at LBJ. All he's doing is picking up where Kennedy left off, but look who's the hero and who's the fool."

He took another drink and set down his nearly empty glass so hard an ice cube jumped over the side. "It's all in knowing when to get out. And you boys sure know, all right. I congratulate you." He paused. "Yessir, the ship is sinking and you're leaping for shore."

Both of their heads snapped up, and Willis hurried on. "Just joking. Just checking to see if you're awake. Now, let's finish this round and then I'll take you around to show you some guys about your age who don't have a good sense of timing."

He tossed off the last drops of bourbon as Ron said, "Not me. Thanks, but I'm pulling out early in the morning and I've got to get some sleep."

"Yeah," Hank said, standing up, "me too."

"No, no," Willis said, rattling the table as he stood up. "Wait a minute. It's still early. Come on, just one more drink." He saw that they were hesitating. "Yeah, c'mon, guys; I want to show you this other bar. Just down the street, but I bet you've never been there. Come on, one more beer and one more memory for you."

Willis headed for the door and stumbled slightly before he remembered to walk carefully. He didn't turn around to see if they were following. What could they do, just leave without saying goodbye?

On the sidewalk he waited until they were beside him, then he began walking before they could argue. He knew he was lurching a little but probably not enough for them to notice.

The other three were all still in tow as he shoved open the door of the no-name and he walked straight to the bar where the bartender was leaning on his elbow, watching television.

"Hey, Bob," Willis said, "getting rich tonight, huh?"

The bartender shrugged. "It's Monday; what'd you expect."

Two women sat at a table in the far corner, obviously not knowing or caring what night it was. The only other patrons were two guys at the far end of the bar. Willis had seen them before but they had never spoken.

"Beers for my buddies here," Willis said as the others joined him at the bar, "and a bourbon straight for me." He knew something was wrong with what he said, but he couldn't quite figure out what it was. "Make it a double," he said, "it's been a long day."

They took their drinks to a rickety table. Ron and Hank looked even more uncomfortable than they had been at Jake's.

"See those two guys?" Willis nodded toward the bar. "That's who I was talking about. Guys like them." He thought he was speaking softly, but he noticed one of the men at the bar had turned his head toward their table. They were both in their early twenties, strong, hard-looking guys with square heads and wide faces.

"Those guys," Willis said, "no sense of timing. They aren't headed for graduate school. Or if they are, it's a different kind. They're headed for Vietnam. Or else they've already been there. Anyway, you can be damned sure they're going wherever somebody else tells them to go. Poor bastards."

"Easy, Willis," Hank whispered, "keep your voice down."

The two guys had both turned around on their barstools and were looking directly toward their table.

Willis lifted his hand and gave them a casual wave. "Ah, shit," he said, "don't worry. They're too dumb to be dangerous."

He thought he had whispered, but Ron said, "Jesus Christ, Willis, shut up."

"They're probably loggers," Willis said, "or quarry workers. Check out their boots. Life expectancy is probably forty-five. That is, if they've already been to Vietnam."

One of the bar guys said loudly, "I like the one with the ponytail. He's cute. I'll take him."

"It's the drunk I want," the other one said. "And the fucking hippie with the beard."

Willis laughed loudly. The bartender moved quickly to the other side of the bar and came to their table. "Okay, out. Now. Get out now."

"Fuck you," Willis said, but Ron and Hank had each grabbed him by an arm and they lifted him out of his chair and were trying to drag him to the door. He broke one hand free, grabbed his glass, and tossed off the rest of his bourbon. "Okay, okay," Willis said, laughing again. "You guys are too nervous." He began walking toward the door, but as soon as he felt Ron's grip slacken, he wheeled around and stepped back to the table. He grabbed up a nearly full beer bottle and took it with him as he let them pull him outside.

On the sidewalk they walked quickly, half dragging Willis, Merle following, until they got around the corner out of sight of the bar.

"Goddam it, Willis," Hank said, "you could have gotten us killed. What the hell are we going to do with him?" he asked the others.

Willis straightened up and shook off their hands. "Chickenshits," he said. "Don't worry about me. Where's my car?"

He knew he was weaving as the four of them walked to the parking lot, but he wasn't worried; he had driven okay when he was a lot drunker. Now he just wanted to go home. He wished he had grabbed two beers off the table.

"Are we going to let him drive?" Merle said when they got to the Saab. "I could drive his car and you guys could follow me."

"Christ," Ron said, "it'd take an hour to get out to his place and back. Can you drive, Willis?"

"Fuck you," he said. "I can drive better dead-ass drunk than you can drive sober."

He climbed into his car and grinned at them through the window. Hank shrugged, and Ron said, "He's a grown-up." Willis looked in the mirror as he left the lot. They were still standing there.

He drove slowly down the empty street and was a block away when he noticed that he hadn't turned on the headlights. Be careful, he thought; that's the kind of thing a cop might stop you for.

Willis didn't pass any other moving vehicles as he maneuvered slowly through the downtown, making sure to stop dead at every intersection, even the ones with only blinking caution lights. He crept through the outskirts of town, his eyes flicking between the road and the rearview mirror. The windows were down and the cool night air was sobering him up. He reached for the beer clamped between his thighs but decided to wait until he was sure no one could see him tipping up the bottle. That's being smart. He smiled to himself and glanced quickly in the mirror to see the cunning smile. Smart thinking like that is what kept him out of trouble. Of course, you could be too smart. Like Seymour.

By the time he reached the highway he was tired of being cautious. He was driving fine, maybe even better than usual, more alert. He loved the way the Saab handled, responding to the slightest acceleration or tweak of the wheel. He finished off the beer and flung the empty out the window, throwing wide so it wouldn't break on the road.

The car was nearing seventy miles an hour when he hit the straight stretch, and without thinking so much as reacting, he jammed the pedal the rest of the way down. Everything felt just right, a perfect thrill, a moment of invincibility. The car raced through the night, headlights grabbing then losing the broken white line, over and over. Willis poked his head out the window briefly just to feel the thunderous air. The lights picked up the curve-warning sign and he lifted his foot, then pushed it down again immediately. He knew this curve like his own footprint. The wheel wobbled for an instant and his stomach flipped, but highway and stomach steadied again as the road straightened itself.

The speedometer was pegged but he couldn't quite read the number and couldn't remember how high it went. His eyes returned over and over to the mirror, but no lights appeared. About five miles from his turn, a car approached from the opposite direction and Willis suddenly realized he was astraddle the middle line. He yanked the wheel and the Saab rocked, but settled down again before the oncoming car had passed. It went by so fast he couldn't tell what kind of car, but for a panicky moment he thought he had seen a light mounted on the roof. Be calm. Turn off the lights? Duck into a turnoff? He had slowed the car, but then he mashed the accelerator again. He could make the five miles and get off on his own road before the cop had time to turn around and overtake him.

He was so busy watching for landmarks that he sailed past his turn. He jammed on the brakes and the car fishtailed for a hundred yards before he got it stopped. His heart was pounding. He threw it into reverse, turned off the lights, and started backing up as fast as he could and still keep it more or less under control. He was almost to the turnoff when headlights appeared far down the road. Fighting down an impulse to turn on his lights, he pushed the gas pedal down even further. He swung the wheel sharply and the car rocked into his road tail first, gravel slamming into the undercarriage of the low-slung Saab. He turned off the key and sat, panting slightly, his neck and back aching from being twisted around backwards.

The car glided past in a blur of light, passing with a low roar. He must have ducked down because after it passed he didn't know whether it had lights on top or how many people were in the car.

Willis sat for a full minute or more, long enough for relief to wash through him, leaving behind a dull lethargy. He thought long and hard about curling up on the seat and going to sleep, but as the sweat started to dry under his shirt, he felt cold. He struggled to develop a plan and felt a small shot of pride when he came up with one. He'd turn the car around, drive slowly to The Box, and go to bed.

By the time he reached the short turnoff in front of the cottage, he was exhausted, barely able to keep his eyes open. He shoved open the car door and left it open, groping his way inside, where he fell onto his bed.

CHAPTER TEN
Thursday, October 31, 1968

"Hello, Willis. You alone?"

Bushey was not exactly whispering, but his voice had a low urgency that demanded all of Willis's attention.

"Yep, all by myself."

"It's payoff time," Bushey said, and Willis could picture the look on his face, mocking himself at the same time he was being drill-instructor earnest. "If you've got appointments this afternoon or tonight, cancel them."

"Whatever you say, Chief, but you've got to remember that I do have a job."

"If you call it work," Bushey said. "But don't worry, this is part of your job. The biggest assignment you've had in quite a while." He paused. "Listen, Willis, I'm dead serious. I'm giving you a great story, the one I've been promising you. But you can't tell anybody. I mean nobody."

"The commune?"

"Quit guessing," Bushey said. "I want you to meet me at three."

"Come on now," Willis said, already impatient beyond reason to know the story and irritated by the whining tone he heard in his own voice. "I need more than that. I do have a boss and they expect me to show up at work."

Bushey laughed, dismissing the weak argument. "A boss? Who would that be?" He snorted again. "I don't have time for this shit, Willis. Meet me at the turnout of Route 138, where the spring is. And be there at three. Not too early. At three."

"Okay."

"And, Willis, by the way, say hello to your boss. If you ever see him." Bushey hung up.

The bastard. He knew all about Seymour, of course, and probably he knew what had happened to the newsroom. Willis hung up the phone and went to the back door to look out over the lake, rippling gently like a pale-blue jewel reflecting a sky so wonderfully bright and clear it seemed like a gift. But it was a lie, a promise he knew to be false even before he heard the kerosene heater moan into action back in the kitchen. When he first got out of bed, the ground had been covered by a heavy frost that only now was melting. Christ, it had snowed four days ago and stayed on the ground for several hours.

Willis lazily tidied up the kitchen, showered and shaved, and headed for the paper shortly after noon. His Saab was a little slow in starting and he remembered that he hadn't checked the antifreeze. He was pretty sure it was okay, but so many people had warned him that he was nervous about it. He wondered if too little antifreeze could make a car hard to start in cold weather.

Driving to town he noticed that the trees were suddenly bare, leafless hulks whose famed foliage not long ago had turned the state into a mecca for aged tourists. Christ, you'd think the geezers would want to go where things were coming to life, not dying. The roadsides now were paved with dull, shriveled leaves, pressed flat by the heavy frost. By spring they would be mashed all the way back into the ground. The sky was still mostly clear and a weak blue, but the puny sun didn't give off enough warmth to drive with the window open.

Willis stopped at his bank before going to the paper, parking in the gravel lot in the rear and going in the back door. Fiddling with his wallet and digging out his paycheck, he didn't raise his head until he was in front of the teller's window and he jumped when he found himself face-to-face with Frankenstein.

A muffled, girlish laugh came out of the mask. "Trick or treat," she said.

"Christ," Willis said, "I forgot."

All the tellers were wearing costumes. The monster-faced girl demanded that he accept a treat and he felt more than a little foolish walking out of the bank clutching a giant, witch-shaped lollipop, but no one seemed to notice. He stopped at the door and watched the other customers long enough to see that no one was surprised by the costumes or the childish decorations hanging all over the lobby.

At the regular parking lot near the office, the entry was blocked off by sawhorses and the space was entirely filled with floats in various stages of construction. He drove another block farther from the paper and parked in a metered space, muttering under his breath as he fished two dimes out of his pocket. They'd been running Halloween stories in the paper for a week, but Willis hadn't read them or paid any attention other than to grumble that without Seymour the news judgment was going to hell. He'd never lived in a town where anyone other than kids went crazy over Halloween. Christ, whoever heard of a parade on Halloween? When he was growing up, all they ever had were football parades and every fourth fall an extravagant motorcade staged by the joint forces of preachers and bootleggers, weeping babies and sobbing women riding on flatbed trucks with banners reading Rout Demon Rum, and Keep Christ In The County.

"Hey, Merle, what is all this Halloween crap?" he yelled as he walked into the newsroom.

Merle looked up from his paper. "It's a tradition, All Hallows' Even," he said, as though that would explain something.

"Goddam it, I know what Halloween is. What I want to know is why everybody's running around like it meant something. I mean, they're making a bigger deal than the Fourth of July. They didn't even have a parade for the Fourth, did they?"

Merle blinked.

Willis walked to his own desk, shaking his head. "Christ, it figures, I guess. You'd expect people in a weird place like this to think witches and monsters were a barrel of fun."

He sat down, thumbed through a small stack of messages, and picked up the *Times*. Most of the front-page stories were politics and war. Or, he noticed with a bitter sneer, a combination. The three-column lead story announced a breakthrough in the efforts to get peace talks started. He read four paragraphs before throwing down the paper. "Jesus Christ," he snarled, "a week before the goddam election Johnson announces a breakthrough. And do you know what it is? The North Vietnamese have agreed to a seating arrangement at the Paris talks. Jesus God Almighty, how dumb does he think we are?"

He snorted out an ugly laugh, but when he looked around, no one was paying any attention. Four or five people were in the newsroom, but if anybody heard him, they didn't give any sign of it. Even Merle was buried again behind his own newspaper. Irritated and a little embarrassed, Willis picked up the *Times* again. He read the political stories but not the war stories. He was weary of reading daily accounts of battles and body counts, dreary stories about places whose names he couldn't remember. Willis wouldn't admit it to anyone, but he preferred television coverage of the war stories.

The newsroom was filling up slowly as reporters drifted in one or two at a time. They walked quietly into the newsroom without talking, plopped down at their own desks, and began rummaging through drawers or reading newspapers. No banter, no shouting, no arguing. Christ, it was like the waiting room at a dentist's office. He looked at each of them, one at a time, then laughed out loud. "This is the crowd that ought to be wearing masks," he said loudly but to no one in particular.

Connie strode wearily through the door exactly at two and went to work immediately, sorting through her desk. She hadn't officially resigned but it was an open secret in the newsroom that she would be quitting after the election. Her public posture in recent weeks had been sad but stoic acceptance of the inevitable, a grieving victim of defeat at the hands of a vicious opponent. Sometimes she mustered the energy for a brave display of determined fortitude, gamely predicting a union victory even if the great day came too late for her to participate in the joyful liberation. Mostly, though, Connie just smiled weakly, sighed a lot, and showed by voice and gesture how very tired she was.

That was the public Connie, Willis thought with an ironic grin as he leaned back in his desk chair and studied her across the room. There was another Connie, though, one he had caught glimpses of when she was off guard—smiling as she read a letter that he presumed was from Vince, her face relaxing into composure as she pecked away at her typewriter, a sudden liveliness in her stride as she left the office, swung her purse over her shoulder, and stepped out briskly down the sidewalk. Little signs, but perfectly clear signs, he thought, the signs of someone happily planning her future.

Willis lit a cigarette and strolled slowly over, shoving aside a stack of books Connie had pulled out of the drawers and piled on the corner of her desk. He slid one buttock onto the cleared space and, half sitting, said, "Any breakthroughs?"

Connie looked up and with a very tired motion smoothed back some loose strands of hair, a corner of her mouth twitching slightly and her eyes showing hurt, suspicion, and, of all things, betrayal. "Who wants to know?"

Willis laughed. "Whoa," he said, holding up his hands in mock defense, "I guess not."

She didn't answer but continued to look straight into his face. Suddenly her eyes filled up with tears, and still she didn't turn away, not even when they spilled out and dripped into her lap.

"Hey, what'd . . . I mean, I'm sorry . . . What? Connie, I . . . what'd I . . ." Willis stammered and tried to collect his thoughts. He couldn't look at her directly. He swiveled his head around to see if anyone was watching. When he looked back, her eyes were clear, the tears stopped as quickly and as inexplicably as they had started. She was just staring at him calmly, her hands now folded and resting in her lap.

Finally, she spoke in an even, flat voice. "What did you want, Willis?"

"Nothing, really," he said softly. "Really, I just meant to say hello. I mean, you seemed to be worried or something and I just meant to ask if everything was all right."

She just nodded and waited for him to go on.

"I've got to go out on a story," he said finally. "I was hoping to catch Greenberg before I left. Or Seymour, if he shows up. I don't suppose you know when they're coming in."

She shook her head.

"Well, if I have to leave before they get here, will you give them a message? Tell them I'm working on what might be a good story and it may break for tonight. But it may not. So tell them I'll call when I get a chance."

He hoped she would ask about the story, but she didn't, merely nodded her head again.

"So," he said, "what's happening about Sy? Is he still suspended, or what?"

"How the hell should I know?"

"Well," he said, "I thought the union . . . I mean, you guys brought a complaint, didn't you, and I just wondered what was happening about it."

She sat silently for a long moment before saying, "All I know is that they're taking Sy's deposition this afternoon. The NLRB has scheduled a hearing and our lawyers are deposing him and some other people today."

Willis was startled. "Who else . . . I mean, I hope—"

"Don't worry," she said, "you're not on the list. I told you before not to worry. You'd be better off, Willis, if you learned to trust people sometimes."

He nodded and stood up. She was already bent over, reaching for something in the bottom drawer, and he walked back to his own desk.

Willis killed some more time reading the paper, hoping Sy would come in before he had to leave. No one seemed to understand Sy's situation since his suspension for spying on the union. Sometimes he showed up at his office, but he didn't seem to have anything to do with the newsroom. He'd just sit in there, watching the television news or reading. Only Greenberg ever went into the office, and he never stayed very long. And some days Sy never showed up at all.

Finally, leaving just enough time to meet Bushey at three, Willis snatched up a couple of notebooks and left the newsroom without speaking to anyone. He was glad to be out of there. The place was beginning to give him the creeps.

He went through the front door of the paper at a fast walk, head down, and almost ran over Seymour.

"Hey," he said, "just the man I wanted to see."

"Why?"

"Well," Willis said, "you're my editor. At least, I thought you were. And I'm going out on a story. It may be a pretty good one."

He looked at Sy for the first time and was surprised. He was wearing a suit and necktie. His red scarf was hung loosely around his neck and he was wearing, for the first time Willis could remember, large and very dark sunglasses. The real shock, though, was his face. He had shaved carefully, even the renegade patch in the cleft of his lip that was shielded by his beak, but he looked like hell, like an old man. His face was gray and blotchy and, when he took off the glasses, his eyelids drooped and the skin under his eyes was loose and wrinkled.

Sy's eyes brightened briefly, then he looked away. "You better tell Matt about it."

"I can't wait any longer," Willis said. "I've got to go." He wanted to blurt out the whole story, to ask Sy how to handle Bushey and what to do if they busted the commune. He wanted to ask for help, but looking at Seymour, he just shrugged.

"Just tell Greenberg that I'll probably be calling in a story later."

"I will if I see him," Seymour said. He moved toward the door, then turned back and said, "I'm going to meet with the lawyers, and when I saw you I half thought you were coming out to help me drive a better bargain."

It was a typically mysterious comment, almost as though he was quoting something, and Willis didn't know what to say. They looked at each other in silence. Finally, Willis said lamely, "Well, hang in there. And remember: Fuck 'em if they can't take a joke."

He and Sy turned away at the same time, and Willis checked his watch. He'd have to hurry to get there on time.

Manny turned away from his Royal and leaned back in his chair as Sy came through the door. "Sit down," he said. "So is this thing with the Vietnamese going to help Humphrey?"

"What thing?" Sy felt awkward, as he usually did when he wore a suit, sure that Manny would notice he had tried to dress carefully. He sat down quickly in the chair at the corner of the desk and pulled off his scarf.

"The peace talks," Manny said, looking closely at Sy.

Peace talks? Sy forced himself to stare back at Manny with a direct, blank gaze, pretending he didn't know this talk was a code, a word trap probably worked out earlier with that goddam McNally. Over the past two months he'd seen less and less of the publisher. He hadn't seen him at all during the so-called suspension, and after Sy came back to work, when they did talk the conversation was strained at best and often downright uncomfortable. Well, he could play the dodge 'em game as well as Manny, or better. If they wanted peace terms, let them say so out front.

"Who wants peace?" he asked in a level voice.

A furrow rippled quickly across Manny's brow. "I'm talking about Johnson," he said, "the thing he announced about making progress on seating arrangements at Paris."

"Oh yeah." Sy shook his head. Hell, it was all right with him if Manny wanted to keep this charade going. "Too little, too late," he said, pausing a moment in case Manny wanted to drop the code and talk directly about their own negotiations. Finally, he went on. "Nixon's going to win even with Wallace in the race." He paused again, then he couldn't resist adding, "You've got to remember, Manny, the tough guys always win. The really tough guys." Pause. "Like Nixon, I mean."

"Johnson's tough too," Manny said. He looked over at his typewriter. "That's just what I'm writing right now." He gave Sy a shy, uncertain glance. "I'm saying this might even be a real American political tragedy." He paused, waiting for an explosion or some derisive comment, but Sy just sat passively, waiting, keeping himself in check until he could see which way Manny was trying to lead him now. Sy knew the talk about tragedy was obviously a reference to his own situation.

Manny started again. "I mean, whatever you think of Johnson, he's been a huge and successful figure. He's won everything he ever set out to get, defying overwhelming odds. And he had every reason to think he could keep on winning, and he would have too if he had just been able to admit that he was wrong. All he had to do—back a couple of years ago when Mansfield and Aiken got back from that Vietnam trip and told him he couldn't win the war—all he had to do was admit he had been wrong. If he'd just said that, some people would have attacked him, but the majority would have forgiven him and he'd be a shoo-in to keep his job this year."

Sy sat back and grinned. So that's it. He wants me to apologize, to say I was wrong. Suddenly he felt like laughing, like clapping his hands. Now he had the missing piece, like when you get stuck with a sentence and then out of nowhere the perfect word or phrase pops into your mind. Now he had it. Manny just wanted to humiliate him, set him down a notch because he had been so far ahead of Manny and his hired guns. They'd tried to keep him down all along, but he had outwitted all of them; he'd defied their edicts, rejected their appeasement strategy. And now, in the end, he was the one who was busting the union. Not that fop McNally, and God knows not Manny or Fletcher Junior. But, of course, they couldn't just accept that. They had suspended him, but they must have known he'd keep right on working on his own to stop the union. And succeeded too. The organizer had gone—Vince, the phony ringer brought to turn the newsroom against Sy. And now Connie was leaving and everyone knew the union was collapsing. So now Manny had to rub his nose in it. Just admit to being wrong, eh?

He was still smiling at Manny, who was pretending to be puzzled, sitting across the desk with a quizzical look on his face.

"So," Sy said finally, utterly unable to keep the triumph out of his voice, "I take it you agree with Aristotle?"

Manny frowned and shook his head slightly in puzzlement.

"Oh, come on, Manny. You know what Aristotle said about 'withdrawing our wrath from the man who admits that he is justly punished.'"

Manny shook his head again. "Who said anything about punishment? I was talking about Johnson not being able to get himself out of Vietnam. What're you talking about?"

Sy just grinned at him, a sly, mocking smile.

"Well," Manny began again, reaching across his desk for a pipe, "whatever it is, that's not what we're here to talk about today." He looked at his watch. "Your deposition is at four, right?"

Sy nodded. "Right. I can't wait."

Manny shot him a quick glance, then went back to the pipe-packing ritual. When he had it going well and a small, thick cloud of blue smoke hung over his head, he said, "We've got some things I want to talk about before you go over there. I've asked McNally to join us and he'll brief you a little before the deposition. He'll be there with you, of course."

Bring him on, Sy said to himself, I can handle both of you, but he said nothing to Manny. Why help him out? He felt some inner satisfaction as he noticed how the old man had suddenly begun to droop with age. You could see it in the tired slump of his shoulders and in the dullness of his eyes.

"I, uh . . . We need to talk before he gets here," Manny said, then quickly retreated into a long, noisy pull on his pipe. Sy still didn't respond.

"Things seem to be going pretty well with the union situation," Manny mumbled without taking the stem out of his mouth. "Of course, nothing's really changed, and McNally would sputter if he heard me say that. But it's the truth and I know that you know it anyway. Right?"

"If you say so."

"Listen, Sy, forget the past. It's over. It's time we moved on."
Sy answered only with a sneer and a lifted eyebrow.

"I mean it, Sy. Why can't you just forget it? We both know that I did what I had to do. When they caught you in that foolish closet, I had to do something or the NLRB would have killed us. And you know it."

Sy still didn't answer.

"Damn it," Manny sputtered, "forget it, move on. Remember what your man Francis Bacon said: Those who dwell on the past are trifling with themselves."

Sy sprang from his chair. "Forget it? I don't forget anything, Manny." He strode over to the window and looked down on the street. "Including what one of your own favorites said about the past."

He turned to face Manny and grinned, a man laying down an ace. "Remember your Whitman, Manny: 'For what is the present, after all, but a growth out of the past?'"

Manny blinked. Stymied. Sy started to add on a *Tempest* quote but checked himself. Beware of overkill. He felt great. The time off had been good for him; he couldn't remember when his mind had been so sharp or quick. He watched Manny blinking, outdueled.

"Well," Sy said, moving back to his chair, "I thought you said you wanted to talk about something." He sat down and pulled out a cigar and slowly peeled off the wrapper.

Manny waited, savoring his pipe smoke, then he blew it out with a long sigh. "Okay. Well, here's what I've decided. I'm going to make some changes." He set down his pipe and looked directly into Sy's eyes.

"I am taking you out of the newsroom."

Sy felt his own breath rush out of him and, for an instant, he was paralyzed, unable to draw in more air as panic stabbed at him. Everything stopped, then his lungs refilled and his mind began to spin wildly. He heard Manny's voice but at first he couldn't catch the words, just sounds, until his hearing focused. ". . . assistant to the publisher. That is, assistant to me."

Manny smiled, a stupid, phony cocktail-party grin. "I'm not getting any younger, you know. Helen says I need all the help I can get these days."

Sy was picking up all the words now but his mind was still reeling with confusion. What did he mean "out of the newsroom"? What did Helen have to do with this?

Manny was still talking and puffing furiously on his pipe after each four or five words. "You'd write some of the editorials; and don't worry, there'll be plenty for you to do."

Sy still couldn't speak. His mind now was as spongy as it had been sharp a few minutes ago. From way back somewhere a voice was telling him, "Sure. Of course. This is part of the plot. They've cooked this into the whole rotten stew."

But Manny's voice, the one he had been listening to for twenty years, also was coming at him and it also was compelling, the same reasonable sound and the same reasoned structure that had always guided their conversations, and not only their conversations but their joint decisions, devising the very actions that had been his own life's work.

"So, Sy, I didn't have an easy time coming to this. But it is final. I know now that it's the right course." Smoke rolled out of his mouth and he peered through it, with his eyes locked on Sy's.

Suddenly, the panic lifted, the confusion cleared, and Sy quit struggling, letting the words roll unedited off of his freed tongue.

"McNally," he said, spitting the word. "You've sold out to that goddam McNally. He put you up to this. This is his scheme and he got to Fletcher and together they put you up to this."

"Shut up, Sy. That's enough." Manny was speaking as loudly as he ever did, the pipe flung aside and his face now all but drained of color, leaving only pink blotches. "McNally had nothing to do with this. And neither did Fletcher."

Sy's mind whirled blindly, grasping for an idea to hold onto. Willis. Maybe Willis had known about this, maybe that's why he had acted so strangely. He would confront him, ask him. Where had he said he was going?

At that moment the door to the office swung open and McNally came in, walking quickly and already talking as he carefully stripped off his kidskin gloves.

"Hello, Manny. Hey, Seymour, big day, eh? Hope I'm not late." He was beginning to shake off his overcoat when Manny spoke.

"Mr. McNally," Manny said sternly, raising his arm to look at his watch, "you're early. Too early. Kindly wait for us outside, if you will please. Maybe in Fletcher's office. I'll come down and get both of you in a few minutes."

The lawyer blushed but he didn't appear to consider protesting as he turned sharply on his heel and left as briskly as he had come in, leaving behind an awkward vacuum and a faint scent of manly perfume. Sy leaned back in his chair and watched Manny intently, wondering how he would explain this curious intrusion and his obvious lie about McNally not knowing, but at the same time feeling a mild tug of admiration for the old man; never too distracted to keep the hired hands in their place, even the expensive ones.

Manny glared at the closed door but he didn't apologize or comment on McNally's blunder. "Well," he said finally, "that's really all I had to say. I wanted you to know what I've decided before your deposition."

He was looking keenly into Sy's eyes, his own face fully returned to its normal becalmed smoothness. Sy remained speechless.

Manny sighed and picked up his pipe, but he didn't try to light it. He put it down on the desk and fumbled aimlessly with several sheets of paper. One caught his attention and he shoved it into the top drawer of his desk. Finally, he looked up and said, "Okay, Sy. Here's what I'm doing. I'm going to retire."

"What the hell does that mean? Retire?"

Manny blinked twice.

"You mean quit? Leave the paper? Christ, you're going to sell the paper?"

"No," Manny said wearily, "I'm not selling anything. I'm going to retire. I don't know exactly when, but Helen wants—we want—to travel. I haven't been back to Europe since before the war. I want to see it again."

Helen again.

"Besides, I'm tired. I'm seventy-two years old and I'm tired."

He waited again, and Sy tried to answer but he couldn't. He wanted to say something, but he couldn't figure out what it would be. *What about me?* That was the only thought he could frame, but he managed, barely, to keep from blurting it out.

Finally, Manny set down his pipe and stood up. "Well," he said, "I'm going to get McNally and Fletcher. I'll be right back." He stood up, then sat down again abruptly. "One more thing: I'm not going to tell anybody until we've settled this union thing. No one. And I'd appreciate it if you'd honor that. I told you because I thought you had a right to know. But I really don't want anyone else to know that I'm retiring. All right?"

He left, and Sy, his numb mind abruptly charged with multiple ideas, bolted upright and leaped around the desk, yanking open the drawer where Manny had stuffed the piece of paper. He knew with full certainty that paper would tell him what was really going on. He yanked out the top paper and read quickly. It was a memo from Andrew, three garbled sentences but the message was clear. The note reported that when they closed the books on 1968, Manny could expect a cash take-home bonus for himself of about $80,000.

It was more than four times his own salary for the whole year. Sy stuffed the paper back into the drawer and made it to his chair in plenty of time before Manny and the other two walked into the office.

*
**

Willis dawdled on his way out of town. He stopped for gas and chatted with Gus while he paid the bill. "Whole damn town's full of floats," he grumbled. "Took me ten minutes just to get this far."

"I'm not complaining," Gus said. "Not with gasoline at fifty cents. Every one of those floats is on a truck and every one of them needs gas and most of them stop here. More treat than trick, as far as I'm concerned."

Five miles from downtown he was totally alone, not another car on the highway, but he was still poking along. The sky had turned dull, a gray overcast as uniform in color and detail as a dingy sheet. Christ, what a place. Blue sky at noon, gloom before dusk. Noticing the time, he stepped down on the pedal but very soon he had eased up again, giving way to the sullen dread that had captured him.

He hadn't spoken to Marlene in nearly two months. She had called once and left a message at the office, but he hadn't tried to call back. How can you call somebody at a goddam commune? One day he had gotten in his car and started up there but turned around and went back to The Oasis instead.

Passing Jenkins Family Restaurant, he braked hard and swung into the gravel parking lot. Maybe he could grab a quick beer and tell Bushey he had a flat tire or something. But he knew even before reaching a full stop that he couldn't get away with it, and he turned the Saab back onto the highway.

There was still no traffic, and now fully resigned he began to make up some time. When he reached the spring turnout, his watch said 3:05. Bushey's blue sedan was parked far back on the gravel, nose facing outward. Near the front of the lot a large yellow school bus waited, entirely empty as far as Willis could tell. He drove slowly forward and stopped beside the blue car, which also appeared to be empty.

Stepping out of his car, Willis remembered how frightened he had been back in April when Ginny and Fred had followed him into this place. He wasn't exactly afraid now but he dreaded this encounter. He looked around but still couldn't see Bushey or anyone else. The blue car was idling quietly, the driver's door open, and the bus also was running, pumping dark smoke out of its exhaust pipe. Where the hell were they? He stood leaning on the front fender of Bushey's car, warily watching the highway and the entrance to the turnaround for a full minute or more. Suddenly, with no warning, the car horn blasted him upright and he swung around in panic, crouching, his legs ready to flee. Bushey stood beside the open door, reaching in, with his hand still pressing the horn.

"Jesus Christ," Willis shouted. "Where the hell were you?"

"Get in," Bushey said. "It's me that ought to be swearing. You're late."

Willis's pulse was still pounding as he climbed into the car. His heart raced again when he reached under his butt to move a lumpy object and brought out a holstered pistol. Bushey glanced over and laughed. He reached for the gun. "Give me that before you hurt yourself."

Bushey palmed the holster and with one swift motion whisked it across his own lap and deposited the gun somewhere near the floor in front of the seat. Must be a hidden pouch, Willis thought, and suddenly he remembered something Seymour had told him months ago. For years Bushey had suffered from terrible, crazy-making headaches that sometimes were so bad he thought of killing himself. He always kept a gun nearby, Sy had said, to be ready for the final headache, the one he couldn't stand. Maybe, Sy had suggested, he would have used the suicide solution long ago except for his crippled wife, who depended entirely on Bushey.

The car moved quietly across the parking lot, and neither of them spoke until they were pulling onto the highway. Bushey slid sunglasses over his nose as they turned west and gained speed. Must be habit or playacting, Willis smirked to himself. There was no sun visible, and even on a bright day sunlight would just bounce off those flat, shiny black eyes.

"What's the bus doing here?"

"We may need it," Bushey said. "There're a lot of kids at the commune, you know."

"So it is the commune, then?"

"Come on, Willis. Don't play games with me. If I wanted to play word games, I'd buy a fucking crossword puzzle. Okay?"

Willis didn't answer.

"Okay?" Bushey said again. "No fucking games, okay?"

Willis nodded. He didn't quite trust himself to speak.

"I promised you I'd give you this story and that's what I'm doing," Bushey said. "I said it'd be yours alone, and that's why you're here. I keep my promises."

Bushey was driving fast and he had been concentrating on the road, but now he turned his head full around to look directly at Willis. "This is up to you," he said. "If you don't want to be in on this, just let me know; I'll take you back to your car."

Willis didn't answer right away, but Bushey didn't turn his eyes back toward the road until he finally said, "Okay. I mean, sure I want to be here and I want this story." Bushey pivoted his head back to the left and Willis found enough courage to say softly, "Unless you drive off the road and kill us first."

A half mile ahead of them a car heading in their direction suddenly turned left across their lane and onto a dirt road. Something about the car caught Willis's attention and his eyes followed it. When they got to the turnoff the car was out of sight, but he recognized the road as the winding one leading to Sid's farm. Then he remembered hearing a month or so ago that Sid had died. He recalled the tiny obit they'd run, a three-paragraph summary of a man's entire life that didn't even say what killed him.

Willis wondered what had happened to the farm and he was about to ask Bushey if he knew, but before he had a chance Bushey began speaking, and he forgot all about Sid.

"Okay," he said, "listen up. I'm going to tell you what's going on here. But don't take any notes. There're lots of moving parts to this operation and lots of things are likely to change before we're done. I'm just going to tell you what we know and what we don't know and what the plan is. I can't tell you how it's going to turn out, but don't worry, we'll be able to figure out what to write later on."

We'll figure out what to write? Willis felt like screaming, "Stop the car. Let me out." But he didn't. He didn't say anything, and after a quick glance in his direction, Bushey said, "We've got warrants to search the commune—all the buildings and the land. Take apart the whole damn thing if we want. We're looking for evidence of drugs and child abuse. We know all that's been going on up there."

"How do you know?"

"We know," Bushey said, looking around again at Willis. "We know enough to get a judge to sign the warrant and that's all we have to know. And that's all you have to know too."

They drove in silence for a mile, Willis tongue-tied by confusion and getting more and more angry at his own timidity. He was intimidated and he couldn't deny it. We'll figure out what to write? The hell we will, he said, but only to himself.

And then Bushey blurted out another surprise that tripped Willis and sent his mind sprawling again into murky confusion.

"My real target is that creep who calls himself Thunderclap," Bushey said. "And this time I think I'm going to get him." He paused but kept his eyes on the road. "Once and for all."

Willis's reeling mind suddenly filled with the memory of the holstered pistol. Once and for all? Jesus.

Bushey laughed. "Don't panic," he said. "It's all legal enough, even for Boy Scouts like you and your buddy Seymour. You remember last spring when the FBI came to town? Well, we believe—hell, I know— that your buddy Thunderclap is really Winslow, the guy they were looking for then. He's the army deserter and bank robber who killed that cop in New Jersey. The FBI fucked up that deal, but now I know that he's the same guy and he's been hiding out up here ever since."

He glanced at Willis and grinned, satisfied by the utter shock that had spread across his face. "I've suspected this asshole since May when we had that run-in. Something about him didn't add up. But it took a while to put the pieces together. But I've got him now."

"Are you sure?" Willis said weakly. "I mean, how do you know for sure? And how do you know he's still at the commune? I mean, I haven't seen him or heard anything about him in quite a while."

Bushey smirked. "Don't worry, I know. Just take it that I have my source. You know all about good sources, don't you, Willis?"

Bushey drove along in silence for a while, his jaw muscles working slowly. "And you, young Mr. Willis, are privileged to be the first to know all this. With the sole exception of Quimby." He glanced over and smiled. "I needed him. We've got to do this the right way, right?"

Willis had recovered somewhat and managed to keep his voice even as he said, "You know, Chief, one thing that has always puzzled me is how you can put up with Quimby. I mean, he just seems like exactly the sort of spineless pol that you'd hate."

He waited for an explosion but it didn't come. After a half minute, Bushey said in a voice that had abandoned its bullying tone, "Well, that sounds like a serious question and one that you've actually thought out. At least, that's the way I'm going to take it. So I'll tell you why I put up with Quimby. Only, as always, you got to know that this is strictly between us and I'd deny under oath that we ever had this conversation.

"So you want to know what's up with Quimby?" He paused, thinking out the answer, then finally said, "Here's the best way I can explain it. This is a quotation, pretty much a direct quote from my all-time favorite movie. Edward G. Robinson said it in *Key Largo*: 'Let me tell you about politicians,' he said. He actually said, 'Florida politicians,' but I take it for all of them. Anyway, he said, 'Let me tell you about politicians. I make them out of whole cloth, just like a tailor makes a suit. I get their name in the newspaper. I get them some publicity and get them on the ballot. Then after the election we count the votes. And if they don't turn out right, we recount them. And recount them again. Until they do.'

"That's why I put up with Quimby. I made him out of whole cloth. Only, we won't have to recount the ballots." He turned to look directly at Willis. "But we would if we had to."

Willis watched the road and they drove on in silence. After maybe a mile, Bushey turned to him again and said with a grin, "Any more questions?"

Finally, he managed to say without much spirit, "I thought you said the warrant was for child abuse. Is it a federal warrant?"

"Don't be simple, Willis. Or pretend to be. If we went for a federal warrant, the wedge-ass FBI would be all over us, checking this and checking that until half the world would know what was going on. Christ, they'd blow it like they did the last time. We don't want that now, do we?"

The car was so quiet Willis heard the sound of Bushey's hands sliding drily over the steering wheel as he repositioned them. "Christ, Quimby's got to be good for something. He got the warrant last night without anybody knowing and we put together this whole operation today without interference from anybody. We'll have the bastard in jail and probably have a confession before anybody knows what's up."

He looked over at Willis, grinned again, and punched him gently on the shoulder. "When we're done, I'll call up that asshole down at the FBI and give him his case in a nice, tidy bundle. You'll have your national scoop. And the story will break just in time for the election, so Quimby will get his ticket into the attorney general's office."

He paused, staring straight ahead, and Willis could see the lowering sun reflected off his sunglasses. "And," Bushey said in a slightly lower voice, "I'll have the satisfaction of nailing Winslow and pissing on the almighty FBI all at the same time."

He laughed. "Neat package, huh?"

Ahead Willis saw the turnoff to the commune, the small road completely blocked by cruisers and unmarked police cars.

Sy flashed through the newsroom without speaking to anyone, brushing so close to Alice's desk that one of her notepads spilled onto the floor. He snatched shut the door to his office and dropped into his chair, only then looking out at the gaping faces staring back at him. Why in the world did he ever make an office with glass walls? He swiveled his chair around, his back to the newsroom, and grabbed up a newspaper, but he didn't read even the headlines.

The meeting had been awful, Manny ganging up with McNally and Fletcher to instruct him as though he were a surly child. "Now remember, Sy, this deposition is the real thing, the best chance they'll have to make you hang yourself. And you've already made the noose for them with that stupid stunt at the union hall. So be careful, okay?"

Sy had started to fling back an insult, but McNally had already turned his back and walked to the window and Manny butted in. "Just listen to him, Sy. Just listen. We're all just trying to get through this mess. So just be quiet for a minute and listen."

McNally turned back to face him. "I'm not going to be able to help you much. It's not like in court. I pretty much have to stay out of it even if they get rough with you, except in certain very defined areas. So you're going to be mostly on your own."

He paused and nodded in silent satisfaction when Sy didn't respond. "But we also have some tools. To begin with, don't volunteer anything. I mean nothing. Answer their questions with as little information as you can give. Yes or no or I don't know. Those are the best answers. 'Yes' or 'no,' and the best is, 'I don't know.' Right?

"Remember, we don't need to make our case here. This is their deposition. They're fishing, but they won't catch anything unless you bite. They'll insinuate and ask insulting things. They'll act as though they know a lot more than they do know. And they'll try to get you to admit something. They'll try to make you mad. So for God's sake, try to control your temper."

Blood surged into Sy's face and he started to push himself out of his chair, but Manny and McNally both shouted at him, "Sit down."

"And be quiet," Manny added.

"And don't act offended," McNally said. "You've done enough damage already. We were doing fine, just fine, until you pulled your bonehead stunt. Now we're working out of a hole and God knows where we'll end up. And it's your fault, Sy. Yours and no one else's. Not mine, not Fletcher's, and not Manny's. Yours. So try to redeem yourself."

Sy glanced toward Fletcher, who was staring out the window, a small smile on his face.

Remembering that gloating smirk and replaying the scolding in his mind replenished Sy's anger, and he spun around in his chair to glare at the newsroom gawkers, who all quickly looked away and became very busy at their own desks. He looked at the wall clock and decided he had just enough time to have a coffee with Vic before going to the lawyer's office.

Sy stomped through the newsroom without speaking to anyone and pushed open the front door, nearly slamming it into a young woman and a child who had been standing outside peering in. He stepped around them before the woman said, "Mr. Seymour? I'm Marlene. We met a couple of times when I was with Bud Willis."

Seymour liked the quiet, pretty girl Willis had been hanging around with, and he turned back to say hello. "This is my friend," she said, putting her hand on the shoulder of the girl who stood at her side staring intently and without self-consciousness into Sy's face, a small child wearing a pulled-down beret and some sort of dark cape.

"Oh yeah," Sy said. "Glad to see you. Looking for Willis?"

"Well, yes," the woman said. "We didn't want to bother him at work, but we hoped he'd be coming out or something."

"Sorry," Sy said, "but I believe he's out covering a story."

They didn't reply or move, just continued to stare at him.

"Away," he said, "I mean he's away, out of the building. Working."

The woman nodded slightly but still didn't move.

"Can I help you?" Sy said, an edge of irritation creeping into his voice. "Is something wrong?"

"We don't know," she said, but nothing more.

Sy's frustration grew stronger. "Well, do you need help?"

The woman leaned backward slightly, away from him. "No," she said finally, "I don't think you can help."

But they still didn't move, and Sy finally shrugged and turned away. "Well then, I need to be going. Nice to see you." He hurried off and turned the corner toward Vic's, but when he got there some new pimply-faced kid was minding the store, and he gulped down a quick mug of coffee, bought some cigars, and headed off to the lawyer's office.

The deposition—the inquisition, in Sy's view—was to be in the office of the law firm that had represented Manny and the newspaper for many years. It was one of the state's most prominent firms, linked for generations with governors and corporations as well as with hotshot litigators and lobbyists. Manny was a close friend of a senior partner, and Sy had been embarrassed for years that his newspaper was so tightly entwined with this powerful outfit. One of his first major battles with Manny had erupted when they wrote a front-page story describing how the firm had represented multiple interests involved in a complicated civil case. Manny had complained bitterly that the story was unfair, unnecessary, and contrived chiefly from innuendo and insinuation. The firm had done nothing illegal and the paper had no right to single it out, he argued. Sy defended the story and angrily accused the partner, Manny's friend, of trying to use his influence to block a legitimate news story. In the end, they had resolved the bitter contest as they had many others: the story stood, without correction or softening, and Manny wrote a strongly worded editorial defending the law firm and, in Sy's view, undermining his own paper's news story.

The fight was many years old, but the memory was fresh as Sy walked into the granite-faced office building, a landmark in its own right since, with five stories, it was the tallest structure in the city except for the Universalist Church spire. He pushed the button for the elevator, and when its door slid open one of the best-known and most successful legislative lobbyists stepped out, a squat but fit man who also had been a frequent target for Sy's journalistic arrows.

"Hello, Sy," he said in a too friendly voice, shoving forward his right hand. "Glad to see you."

Sy smiled back and shook his hand. "I'll bet," he said.

"Have a nice day," the lawyer said as he turned away, and Sy stepped into the elevator.

Bushey's car was second in the procession, right behind Quimby's as they moved slowly up the road toward the commune. When they reached the cleared space in front of the old house, the lead car pulled over far to the left and stopped. A uniformed trooper jumped out of the front seat, carrying a camera. He stepped quickly to the side and aimed toward the back door, shooting Quimby as the prosecutor bounced out and strode purposefully toward the porch.

"Jesus Christ," Bushey mumbled as he parked beside the lead car.

"Damn," Willis said, "you've created a monster, all right. But a photo would help the story. Can you get a roll of film for me?"

Bushey just looked at him and shook his head in mock disgust. "I always said you guys are just like the politicians; you have no shame."

The cleared area was swarming with cops, who quickly surrounded the house. Quimby strode onto the porch and raised his hand to knock, glancing over to make sure the photographer was in place. He rapped loudly, waited a few seconds, then pounded again on the doorjamb.

No one answered the repeated knocks, and Quimby, with two cops on his heels, opened the door and stepped inside the small, ramshackle house. A few minutes later they and two more cops, who evidently had gone in the back door, came back onto the porch, and Quimby looked over at Bushey and shook his head.

"Goddam," Bushey swore. "Okay, send them out to the shacks and pick up everybody—I mean everybody—and bring 'em out to the clearing."

He turned to a young trooper standing nearby and said, "Mark, go get the dogs, just in case. But keep 'em quiet."

Cops working in pairs were heading off down the various paths leading out of the clearing, and Willis started off toward the one he had taken on his first visit. He heard Bushey say, "You better wait here with me, Willis," and he checked his step, but then walked on without answering or looking back.

Soon after he entered the woods he met a trooper coming toward him, and he stepped off the path to let him by. Sandwiched between him and his partner were the boy and girl who had followed Willis on his first visit. They looked at him as they passed but no one spoke.

Willis made the full circle through the commune, and when he got back to the clearing he saw a couple of dozen people, about half of them children, standing or sitting on the grass, more or less surrounded by cops. The scene was entirely peaceful, no weapon in sight and no loud voices except for the tethered commune dogs barking away in the woods. The two police tracking dogs were milling around nervously on their leashes, but they showed no interest in the barking of their undisciplined brethren.

Bushey was just coming out of the house carrying a shirt and a pair of leather boots. "Bring them over here," he shouted to the dog handler. Willis walked toward Bushey, who was talking quietly with Quimby. He and the dogs reached them at the same time.

"Give 'em these things," Bushey said to the handler, "then try to pick up his trail. The bastard must have run off through the woods."

He turned to a trooper wearing sergeant's stripes. "How many others are missing, do you know?"

"No idea," said the sergeant. "You ask these jerks a simple question and you might as well not bother. They ain't saying nothing."

"Well," Bushey said, "how many do you have here?" He waved toward the small crowd.

"Thirteen grown-ups and eleven kids," the sergeant said, "counting anybody over about sixteen or eighteen as a grown-up."

He shook his head in dismay. "Not a single one of them is carrying a wallet or any sort of identification. Ask them a question and they just smile or look blank."

Bushey said, "Have you checked the kids for marks or bruises?"

"Not yet. Do you want us to?"

Quimby spoke up for the first time. "Wait a minute. We better get them over to the town hall first. I mean, we ought to have the social workers and all that so we can tell the judge how careful we've been." He looked nervously at Bushey. "I mean, we don't want to screw this up and have it come out wrong."

Bushey thought for minute, scowling. "Okay," he said finally, "and we need to separate the kids from the others. Load up the bus with the kids, and take the hippies in the cruisers. When we get there, put the hippies in the basement and guard them, and put the kids upstairs in the big room. The judge is going to be set up in the smaller room just off the big one."

Willis noticed for the first time that the school bus had been brought into the clearing. He was looking around for Marlene. He also was thinking about Thunderclap. How'd he manage to get away? Man, this was going to be a good story.

He began moving into the small knot of commune people, hoping they'd talk to him. A cop stepped in front of him and held up his hand. "Hold it," he said. "You can't talk to them."

"Why not?" Willis asked. "Are they under arrest? In custody?"

The trooper looked toward Bushey, who walked over and said, "Listen, Willis, this is my party. And if you don't like the rules, you can leave."

"How?"

"That's your problem, Ace."

Bushey turned away again but the cop stayed in place, blocking Willis. He shrugged and walked off, circling the crowd of commune people from outside the police perimeter. It didn't take long to see that Marlene wasn't with them. Did she run off with Thunderclap?

Cops went in and out of the house, toting out a few plastic garbage bags filled with God knows what. Finally, they seemed to have finished and began milling around in the yard, so Willis walked casually into the house to look around while they loaded up the bus and the cruisers. The inside was a bigger mess than the outside—five or six rooms with dirty floors, torn wallpaper, and big gaps of broken plaster. He couldn't tell whether people actually lived there or just used the space as a sort of common room. A couple of mattresses were on the floor, but no sign of sheets or blankets. He didn't find anything very interesting. He couldn't tell whether the clothing scattered around was really clothes or just rags tossed aside. The kitchen had some pots and utensils, but no real evidence of cooking.

The shelves were empty except for a few glasses and a few plates and bowls and one giant box of Cheerios.

*
**

The secretary led Sy back to what she called the conference room and, apparently, he was the last one expected because she closed the door behind him. The young lawyer who was officially Sy's counsel, since McNally didn't have a Vermont license, introduced him to two men sitting at a long highly polished table, two grim-faced lawyers representing the union. "And, of course, you know Mr. McNally," he said, waving toward the chair where the dandy sat just away from the table, right behind the seat designated for Seymour. The lawyer didn't bother to introduce the stenographer, sitting on a folding chair at her own little portable desk just to the right of the large chair at the head of the table.

The union lawyer, settled into the presiding seat, explained the deposition process, the rules and obligations, the threats and admonitions, and, when Sy didn't have any questions, he hurried into the oath.

". . . so help you God?" and Sy said, "I do," but what he was thinking was, "So, help me, God."

He couldn't see McNally without turning around in his seat, but he could feel his presence behind him. The first half dozen questions were perfunctory, just-the-facts kind of stuff for the record, tossed out by the younger, obviously bored union lawyer. Sy answered in a name-and-serial-number manner. Then the older guy, the beefy one with the too-tight collar, took over, pulling his chair close up against the table and leaning toward Seymour.

"Now, Mr. Seymour, we want to know about the day you spied on the union negotiating team." He paused, lifting his eyebrows as if inviting comment. But Sy bit his tongue. "I'm talking, of course, about the time you hid in the closet at the union meeting hall and listened to our negotiators plan their strategy."

Sy still didn't answer and he didn't drop his eyes from the lawyer's.

"You do know what I'm talking about, don't you, Mr. Seymour?"

"No."

"No? No, what?"

"No, I don't know."

"What?"

"Nothing."

The lawyer shoved back from the table and rolled his eyes. Then he began again. "Okay, let's start over. Why were you spying on the union negotiating team?"

"I wasn't."

"You weren't? What were you doing then?"

"Nothing."

"Nothing? You call it nothing to be hiding in a closet, spying on a union negotiating team that was planning its strategy?"

"Yes."

"Yes? Yes, what?"

"Whatever."

The lawyer's eyes were bugged out and he ran his hand furiously through his thinning hair. "Listen, Mr. Seymour, we're not playing games here. You're under oath. And I'm getting a little tired of this bull—" He turned to the stenographer. "Strike that."

"What?" Sy said.

The lawyer turned back toward Sy. "What was that, Mr. Seymour?"

"What?"

"What did you say?"

"I said what."

"What what?"

"Strike what?" Sy answered.

The lawyer turned to his partner who, for the first time, looked alert and interested in what was going on. The older one said, "Jerry, I'm not connecting here. You take over and see if you can get us back on track."

"Okay. Okay, Mr. Seymour, now let's go back a little. We're talking about September the ninth. A Monday, I believe, late on the afternoon of September 9. Do you remember that day?"

"Yes."

"And where were you that day?"

"Here."

"Where?"

"Here."

"In this office?"

"No."

"Where?"

"In town. Right here in this town."

"Okay. Where in this town?"

"At my office."

"At the newspaper?"

"Yes."

"And did you leave the newspaper?"

"When?"

"When? Well, when I said. In the afternoon."

"What afternoon?"

The older lawyer broke in, standing up with eyes bulging. "Listen, McNally, I'm getting sick of this. You better—"

McNally was on his own feet. "Seymour," he said sharply, "come on with me." To the others he said, "Excuse us. We'll be right back."

He led the way down the hall to a small room with a four-person table and walls lined floor to ceiling with books. He shut the door and pointed Sy into one of the chairs but didn't sit down himself.

"Okay, Seymour, now listen carefully. I can't make you stop playing games. But you ought to know that you're in a hole here and you're digging yourself in deeper all the time. This is not some sort of exercise to amuse you, and it's not some sort of conspiracy. We're dealing with a serious situation here and it's time you got with the program."

The airless little room was hot and McNally had begun to sweat, tiny crystal beads forming at his hairline. He waited for Sy to say something, but he didn't. Finally, McNally shrugged, turned his back, and said, "Okay, it's your funeral." He reached for the doorknob, then turned back. "I'm here as your legal representative and, just for the record, this is a warning from your lawyer. If you keep on being uncooperative, I'll have to resign—that is, stop representing you. Whatever it is you think you're doing, you're goddam well not going to bring me down with you."

He stopped but Sy still didn't reply, leaning back in his chair so he could look up into McNally's eyes. "Christ, Sy, what do you think you're doing, anyway?"

At last Sy smiled and said simply, "I don't know."

McNally's face glowed rage and he snatched open the door and stormed down the hall without looking back to see whether Seymour was following. But he did, and when they got back to the conference room, he resumed his seat and waited with calm patience, his own face as composed as a shadowed pool.

The older union lawyer stood up and said, "Remember, Mr. Seymour, you're still under oath." He asked the stenographer to read back the last question and answer, rubbed his hand thoughtfully over his mouth and chin, and said, "Now, on the afternoon of September 9, the union negotiating team was holding a meeting in the union hall. They were discussing strategy for the ongoing negotiations with the newspaper that employs Mr. Seymour as its managing editor. After about a half hour of talk, during which several important—strategically important—decisions were made, the head of the negotiating team, Mr. Vince Carmoli, thought he heard a noise coming from a coat closet that opened onto the room where they were meeting."

He turned to the stenographer. "Am I going too fast? Okay, thanks. Good." He stroked his heavy chin again. "When Mr. Carmoli opened the closet door, he was amazed to find that Mr. Seymour was standing inside the closet. He had, of course, heard the entire strategy session."

Standing directly behind his own chair, he had been speaking to no one in particular, gazing over the heads of the others at the table, but now he turned to address Sy directly. "Mr. Seymour, have I got all that about right?"

"No."

"Well, what part have I got wrong?"

"I don't know."

The beefy lawyer looked as though he might reach over and grab Seymour, but instead he turned his back, walked to the end of the room, then turned around again and said, "Okay, I'm going to try one more time. Then, if this keeps up, I'm going to call a halt to this deposition and we'll take this transcript to the National Labor Relations Board and let them deal with it. I know you understand what I'm saying Mr. McNally, and I hope your client does. Do you, Mr. Seymour?'

"Yes."

"Okay. Mr. Seymour, we believe that on the afternoon of September the ninth, at about four thirty p.m., at the Union Hall on School Street, that you, in the name of your employer, committed an unfair labor practice. More precisely, we believe that you spied on a private strategy session of our union, which at the time was in contract negotiations with your employer. Furthermore, we believe that you were acting on behalf of, and perhaps on the instructions of, your employer or his agent."

McNally cleared his throat and everyone turned toward him, but evidently he decided against interrupting and the union lawyer nodded his approval.

"Thank you. I won't take much more time but I want to make this record clear and complete. Our union charges that Mr. Seymour, acting alone but possibly with the knowledge of his employer, sneaked into the union hall, hid himself in the closet, and spied on our negotiators in direct and obvious violation of federal labor laws.

"Now, Mr. Seymour, do you understand what we are charging?"

"Yes."

"Do you agree with the situation as I have described it?'

"No."

"Do you agree that you were found hiding in the closet of the union hall?"

"No."

"Do you mean you deny that you were in that closet?"

"Yes."

"Mr. Seymour. We have six witnesses. They were six feet away from you. Christ, they even saw that you had . . . Strike that."

The stenographer said, "The whole statement?"

"No. No, just the last part—the part beginning with 'Christ,' to the end."

The lawyer shook his head as if to clear it. "Mr. Seymour, one more time: Were you in the union hall on the afternoon of September 9?"

"No."

The lawyer slumped into his chair. "Okay, that's it. I'm ending this deposition and we'll see you in front of the NLRB."

Willis decided not to wait for Bushey because he didn't want to miss any of the court action. Besides, he figured Bushey was staying around the commune more out of frustration and anger than any real hope of catching Thunderclap. The dog handler had made one complete circle around the periphery of the commune and his bloodhounds had picked up no trace of Thunderclap. But when they got back to the house and the handler reported to Bushey, he swore and sent them back out for another try.

"The sonofabitch has got to be out there," Bushey muttered to no one in particular. "He couldn't have got away. Unless someone tipped him off."

He turned to glare at Willis, but he just shrugged and said, "Come on, Chief. You know goddam well I didn't tip him off. I didn't even know until you picked me up. Remember?"

So when the bus was loaded with the kids and all the adults were packed into the cruisers, Willis walked over to Quimby and asked if he could ride with him to the town hall. The prosecutor shot a quick look toward Bushey, then said, "Okay. Sure. Get in."

Quimby rode up front with the plainclothes driver and Willis was alone in the back seat. Willis wasn't sure where the town hall was located. The town was split by the mountain range and it didn't have a real village. "How far is it?" he asked. "I don't remember seeing it out on Route 16. Where is the center of this town, anyway?"

Quimby swiveled around in his seat as the unmarked cruiser followed the procession out of the commune. "Only a couple of miles," he said, "but you'd never find it if you didn't know. It's on a dirt road, way the hell away from anything. It's one of those little town centers that has only a grade school, a little store, and the town hall. They really only use the hall for town meetings. Usually, nobody's there."

"So why are you taking them there? I mean, how come the judge is going to be there? Can you hold court anywhere you want?"

Quimby flashed a smile reeking with self-satisfaction. "You can if you know how to do it." He added, "Don't worry, this is all legal and airtight. We set it all up just right, and the best part is that only those who needed to know knew what we were doing."

"Why didn't you take them into town?" Willis said.

"Too far. We didn't want to drag these kids around for hours." Quimby offered his shit-eating grin again. "Besides, Scoop, if we'd done that, you wouldn't have had your scoop." He looked over to see if the driver had gotten his joke. "And if we'd gone all the way back to the courthouse, we'd have had reporters, lawyers, and other busybodies swarming all over the place."

It took about a half hour for the caravan to make the short trip. Finally, as they rounded a bend in the road and started down a gentle grade, Willis saw the hall, a two-story white clapboard building with a belfry tower topped by a weathervane, a structure as straight out of rural New England's history as grazing livestock and stone walls. Directly across the road was the hall's twin, minus the belfry tower, identified by a single word painted over the double front door: School.

Next to the school was a small store, clearly built to be a house, with a gas pump in front and a covered porch running the full length on the road side. All three buildings stood within fifty feet of the road and all three had their own parking lot on the side.

The bus was pulling into the schoolyard, and the cruisers were turning the opposite direction into the town hall lot. Several cars were already parked in each lot, but the store's parking area was empty.

Quimby motioned the driver toward the town hall and when they stopped he hopped out and headed quickly inside without speaking to anyone. Willis watched for a few minutes as the troopers unloaded the hippies from the cruisers, again trying to spot Marlene, then he followed Quimby into the town hall.

The prosecutor had disappeared, and Willis found himself alone in a large high-ceiling room that hadn't changed since it was built sometime midway through the nineteenth century. Age-browned wainscoting fenced in the room to waist height and a row of tall multipaned windows lined the east and west walls, but the north and south walls were unrelieved blank plaster except for the entryway at the south end, where he was standing. At the far end, a wall-to-wall platform raised a strip of floor about a foot higher than the rest of the hardwood flooring, and on the platform was a long folding table, totally bare except for a small raised block upon which rested a heavy-looking gavel. A single chair was shoved up to the table, directly in front of the gavel, and flanking the chair were American and Vermont flags.

Otherwise, the hall was empty of furnishings or signs of habitation, with the lone exception of an ornate iron and chrome woodstove positioned so that the warmest areas would be those nearest the platform. Christ, Willis thought, you'd freeze to death at March town meeting unless you sat on the platform or packed the whole room with bodies. He couldn't tell whether a fire was burning but the room was not uncomfortable now, although the sun was lowering and weakening in the west. When it was gone, the building would creak with cold.

As his eyes made a second pass around the room, he saw that a small door did, in fact, break up the far wall behind the platform. The same dull white as the upper walls; he had missed it at first. He walked over and opened it, finding a dimly lit stairway, and looking out the nearest window he realized the ground sloped off sharply below so that the bottom floor of the town hall was half basement and half above ground, with the building backed up tight on an alder swamp. Willis snorted. Of course, he thought, they built it on ground so steep, so unlevel, it couldn't be used for farming. No need to waste good level ground for public buildings when everybody knew there wasn't enough to go around as it was.

He thumped down the stairs, feet banging on the bare treads. At the bottom, another door opened into a much smaller room, also bare. It filled only about half the space of the hall above and he could see three doors spaced out across one end, evidently leading into even smaller rooms. Two state troopers were standing together near one of the doors and they looked toward Willis, but they didn't say anything and neither did he. One of them slipped quietly into the little room. On Willis's left, an outside door suddenly opened and another cop walked in, followed by a line of the commune people walking single file but not handcuffed or restrained in any other way that he could see.

After all thirteen were inside, several more cops filed in, fanning out around the perimeter of the room like watchful sheepdogs. No sign of Bushey, though. Willis spotted the boy who had been charged in the wallet theft and he moved toward him, inconspicuously he hoped, until the cop came back out of the small room and headed straight for him. "You better wait upstairs," he said when he was standing beside Willis, pointing toward the stairway door.

"Why?" Willis said.

"Because Mr. Quimby said so," the cop said, his unsmiling eyes peering from under the stiff brim of his drill instructor's hat.

Willis shrugged and stomped back up the stairs. He was still alone in the large hall, but after a couple of minutes the stairway door was flung open and a line of cops carrying folding chairs began to pour in. They were busy for about five minutes, up and down the stairs, each carrying two chairs at a time. When they had a couple dozen assembled more or less in rows before the platform, they carried up two folding card tables and two chairs for each table. They arranged them left and right, directly in front of the long table.

It's like some amateur play, Willis thought. The bit actors are the stagehands, changing scenes for the courtroom act. First to enter was the court reporter, bringing her own fold-up desk and dictation machine. In a few minutes the commune hippies were led into the room and seated in the front row, directly behind the small table. They were followed by Quimby and a trooper, and behind them came a young blond man Willis didn't know, wearing a suit and carrying a briefcase. He sat at the table on the left and immediately began dragging out lawbooks and legal pads, carefully arranging them on the card table. The young man and Quimby didn't acknowledge each other's presence, although Willis was sure they had been together in one of those small rooms downstairs.

Willis had dragged one of the chairs out of the back row and positioned it toward the front and far over to one side so he could see all the key spots in the room. His unauthorized repositioning of the chair drew a glare from a sergeant, but no one interfered. He had just stood up to speak to the blond lawyer when the stairway door opened again to let in a shriveled-up old man wearing dark blue trousers and a light blue shirt decorated with a deputy sheriff's badge and a "Bailiff" tag. He shuffled to the front and shouted out the usual "All rise" spiel, then shuffled back to hold open the door.

The old bailiff had called out the judge's name but Willis wasn't listening, so he was very surprised when Judge Wayne Talbot strode briskly into the room, calling out, "Be seated," before he even reached the makeshift bench. Willis knew the judge mostly by reputation, although he had once covered a trial over which he presided. Talbot was on the lowest rung of the trial-court ladder, but he was one of the best-known judges in the state. His fame rested as much on his courtroom behavior and his pre-judge career as on his legal rulings. With premature gray hair, the posture of an athlete, and the face of an actor, he looked more like a politician, which, in fact, he had been before being named to the bench.

He called the court to order, then said, "I'm going to depart a bit from normal procedures because, as we can all see, this is not a normal session of this court. It is, in fact, extraordinary in more ways than one but beginning with the fact that we are here, in this building, in this town."

He looked around the room, then continued with a small shake of his head. "And I don't need to remind you that in addition to everything else, this happens to be Halloween." Some of the hippies giggled and Willis laughed out loud, although none of the cops or lawyers cracked a smile, even when the judge added, "Which somehow seems appropriate."

Willis wondered how he had come to get this case. He was pretty sure Quimby and Bushey would not have chosen Talbot if they had any say in the matter. He was a Republican, of course, but during his time in the state senate, his had been one of the few liberal voices that carried any authority. He had championed, with little success, tax reform, election reform, welfare reform, and damn near every other kind of reform, including drug-law reform. During two active terms, he had made headlines and floor speeches on scores of issues, and his persistent theme had been "We need to bring Vermont into the twentieth century." As a result, the traditional wing of the party, the Mossbacks, to use Sy's term, actively disliked Talbot. Still in early middle age, he was a formidable threat to the conservative agenda. That's why they were relieved and, like everyone else, quite surprised when he was appointed to and accepted the judgeship.

But it was his style on and off the bench that had elevated Talbot's reputation to statewide recognition. The media loved him because he was glib, outspoken, quick-witted, and, as a legislator, always available for comment. As a judge he was more circumspect but only marginally more cautious. He was still relatively loose with his comments and his speech was casual, often barbed, and sometimes colorful.

"Mr. Quimby, we're going to start with you, as the prosecutor in this case." He spoke directly to the stenographer. "Mr. Quimby is the State's attorney and he will be presenting the case under consideration." Putting on his glasses, he held up an official information sheet and read, "The case is *State of Vermont versus . . . Randall Winslow et al.*"

He threw a quizzical glance at Quimby, then shrugged slightly and said, again to the stenographer, "Representing the defendants is Mr. Michael Jones. He is a public defender assigned by the State." Jones didn't look up from his note taking, and when the stenographer pushed up her glasses and signaled she was ready, the judge said, "If you will, please, Mr. Quimby, tell the court why we're here and what you want us to do."

With that, Judge Talbot sat back in his chair, pushed it gently away from the table, and fixed his gaze on Quimby, who was rising to his feet but casting his eyes around the room, evidently in search of someone.

"Well, Your Honor," he began, still looking toward the stairway door, "we're here under a warrant issued last night by Judge Newell, who is the presiding judge right now in this district and—"

Talbot interrupted "No, Mr. Quimby. Judge Newell is the district court judge assigned to this district for this term. But I am, as I would have thought you could tell, the presiding judge, at least for this proceeding. And I am not Judge Newell."

Quimby squirmed. "Of course, Your Honor. What I meant was—"

"Okay, Mr. Quimby, we know what you meant. Proceed. Tell us why we're here."

The prosecutor fiddled with his papers. "Well, Your Honor, this is an arraignment under an information signed by Judge Newell that I mentioned earlier—an arraignment on charges of child abuse, child neglect, truancy, failure to report certain health matters as required by law, and . . . uh, and a charge of being a fugitive from justice."

He paused as though expecting the judge to interrupt, but he didn't. Quimby looked quickly at the other table, but Mr. Jones was busy writing on his pad, showing no sign of speaking.

"We're asking, Your Honor, in light of the unusual circumstances as you pointed out, we, the State is asking that the defendants' right to withhold a plea for twenty-four hours be waived. And we're asking that the court deny bail in this case because of the very serious risk of flight posed in this, uh, unusual situation."

Now Jones was on his feet, but the judge motioned for him to sit back down. "Hold your fire for a minute, Mr. Jones. You'll get your chance." Talbot swiveled his raised finger to direct it at the other table. "First, Mr. Quimby, first you need to tell us who the State is charging with these crimes. The information said only 'Randall Winslow et al.,' and I, frankly, don't have any idea who 'et al.' is."

Quimby started to answer, but Talbot cut him off. "For that matter," he said, "I don't know who Mr. Winslow is. Is he here?"

"No, Your Honor. That is, I mean, he's not here yet. They . . . uh, the police and . . . uh . . . my investigator are still out looking in the woods for him. We thought—"

"Wait a minute," the judge said. "Are you saying that we're here to arraign someone who hasn't been arrested? You have a warrant but no suspect in custody. Is that right?"

"No. I mean, we have the others. They're here." He turned and nodded toward the front row, where the commune people sat quietly and attentively.

"Who are they?"

"Well, they're the ones with Winslow. The ones in the information that Judge Newell—"

"You mean they're 'et al.'? These," he pointed his finger at each of the hippies, counting down the line, "these thirteen people are the ones accused of child abuse and the other charges in the warrant?"

"Well, yeah, I mean, there may be more, but these are the ones we arrested at the commune."

The judge's voice carried a new edge when he said, "Mr. Quimby, do these defendants have names? They're right here in front of us, but are you telling the court that they're all being held under John Doe warrants?"

"We, uh, we don't know their names."

"Why not?"

"Well, they won't tell us. I mean—"

"So what you're telling this court is that you got a warrant alleging some quite serious crimes but you don't know the identity of the suspects, except one, and you don't know where he is. Is that right?"

"Well, uh, well, yes, but—"

"And this matter was so serious, so urgent, that you had to get the warrant on an expedited basis—in fact, in the middle of the night—and arrange for this extraordinary arraignment in the middle of nowhere. Wait. Let me back up for a minute."

The judge had been leaning forward across the table, his hands folded in front of him. He pushed away from the table and leaned back, tilting his chair onto its hind legs, and just stared at Quimby for a half minute. Finally, he said in a low, deliberate voice, "Mr. Quimby, I would like for you to explain to the court how and where you arrested these people. What were the circumstances of this arrest?"

Quimby looked startled, but then Willis was surprised to see him stiffen his spine and slowly fasten the middle button of his suit jacket, which he normally wore loose. "With the court's permission," he said formally, "it's not the State that's on trial here. We're not here to be cross-examined. Indeed, we're not here to examine at all. We're here for a formal arraignment and we had hoped for setting of bail conditions."

Still tipped back in his chair, the judge said, "You're right, Mr. Quimby, the State is not on trial. But you're asking the indulgence of this court in very unusual circumstances, as you've made very clear, so please indulge me. I'm confused about some things and I assume others may be too, particularly Mr. Jones and his clients, whom I have not yet allowed to speak. So if you will, help us move this proceeding along toward a just and proper conclusion. I'm sure that's the outcome we all want here. Right? Right."

He dropped his chair back onto the floor with a loud thump. "So, Mr. Quimby, once again I would like to ask a few questions. As much as anything else, we need these answers to create a record for this case. Which I'm beginning to think may have more import than I had realized at first."

He addressed Jones. "Mr. Jones, I will seek your indulgence too for a moment. But, again, let me assure you that you will get your opportunity."

The judge ran both hands through his springy hair, leaned forward, and said to Quimby, "I'm going to summarize this situation as I see it. Stop me when I go astray." He turned to the court reporter and said, "If I start going too fast, just let me know." She nodded and the judge continued.

"Okay. The State has accused these people and perhaps some others who have not been identified—or, for that matter, found—with mistreating children, whom we also have not seen. Am I to understand that these children and these defendants all live together?"

"Yes, Your Honor. They live in a, uh, in a commune."

"And this commune is located in this town?"

"Yes, just over the ridge, about five miles from here."

"And you arrested these thirteen defendants at that commune? Today?"

"Right, just about an hour ago, hour and a half, I guess. We raided the commune and—"

"You raided it? What does that mean?"

"Well, I and my staff and about two dozen policemen—state troopers and Sheriff's Department officers—moved into the commune, rounded up the suspects, and brought them here."

"Was there any resistance?"

"No. We had a warrant and—"

"Did anyone try to run away?"

"Well, no. At least we didn't see anybody. I mean, except Winslow, the fugitive suspect. He must have fled because—"

"Did you see him?"

"No, Your Honor, but—"

"Did anyone see him run away?"

"No."

"What is this man, Winslow, a fugitive from?"

"There's a federal warrant. He's wanted by the FBI. A fugitive from justice warrant."

"For this man Winslow?"

"Yes, Your Honor."

"And this man you believe was at the commune?"

"Yes."

"But you didn't see him?"

"Uh, no, Your Honor."

Quimby was shifting his weight from one foot to the other, shuffling his papers, and alternating his gaze from the judge to the table in front of him as he answered the questions. Willis was writing furiously, trying to get every exchange, but he felt the tension mounting in the room.

"So," Talbot said, "you have good reason to believe, I assume, that this man Winslow was at the commune?"

"Yes. I mean, we have evidence that the leader of the commune is the same as Winslow."

"The leader? What do you mean, the leader?"

"He's the head guy. He runs the commune. They call him . . . uh, uh . . . I mean, he's the same as Winslow."

"What name does he use at the commune?"

"Well, they call him Thunderclap. I believe."

"Thunderclap?"

"Yes, that's what they call him." He waved toward the row of hippies, then looked down and rustled through his papers. "He calls himself Johnson. H. H. Johnson. At least, that's the name he gave Chief Bushey, my investigator."

"He says his name is Johnson?"

"Yes."

The judge leaned forward and said, eyebrows raised, "As in President Johnson? And his initials are H. H., as in Hubert Humphrey?"

Quimby's face glowed red as he looked down at his papers and murmured, "Well, yeah, I guess so."

"So," said the now smiling judge, "when did he tell Chief Bushey his name was H. H. Johnson?"

"A few months ago."

"Was he under arrest then?"

"No."

"Why not?"

"Well, we didn't know then that he was Winslow."

"But now you do. And you have evidence of that?"

"Yes, Your Honor. And we have the warrant—"

"I know you have a warrant, Mr. Quimby. What I'm trying to do is figure out how you got it."

The judge sat back, rubbed his chin, and wrote something quickly on his yellow pad.

"So you have enough evidence to get a middle-of-the-night warrant. And I suppose you have evidence of the child abuse and other charges?"

"Yes, Your Honor." Quimby shuffled his papers but didn't offer any more information.

"By the way," Talbot said, casting his eyes around the hall, "where are these children? And how many of them are there? Were they all abused and mistreated?"

"Your Honor, they're across the street in the school. I believe there are eleven. And, uh, we believe they've all—"

"Wait a minute. What do you mean they're across the street? Did you pick them up during this raid?"

"Yes, Your Honor, we—"

"You took them out of their homes? You physically removed them from their homes?"

"Well, yes, Your Honor. I mean, we had to get them where we could examine them. And talk to them. We—"

"What do you mean examine them? Who examined them?"

"Social workers. And nurses. They're over at the school right now, examining them."

"Examining them for what?"

"Well, to see if they're all right. I mean, to see if they've been abused. And we needed to question them about—"

"Wait a minute. I thought you had evidence of child abuse."

"Yes. I mean, we know they've been mistreated and . . . I mean, we know that they've all been truant from school and we think many, maybe all, have been abused in various ways."

"What ways?"

"Well, punished, I mean, punished by being switched and paddled."

"Paddled?"

"Yes, Your Honor."

"They've been spanked with a paddle or something like that?"

"Well, yes, Your Honor. I mean, they've been beaten."

"And you have evidence of that?"

"Yes."

"But you don't know how many have been beaten? How about who beat them? Do you know which of these defendants beat them? And when, and why?"

"We know some of that, Your Honor. I mean we have general information about—"

"General information? You're alleging crimes here, Mr. Quimby. Specific crimes." He paused, then said slowly, "I think I'd like to see the evidence of these crimes that you used to get the arrest warrants. Could you produce that evidence for the court, Mr. Quimby?"

"Your Honor, we presented the evidence to Judge Newell. Last night. He was satisfied, Your Honor, and—"

"I've already pointed out once, Mr. Quimby, that I am not Judge Newell. So I would like to see this evidence so we can go forward with this proceeding."

"Your Honor, can I approach the bench?"

Talbot scowled, then nodded and motioned for Jones to come forward too. The three men leaned toward each other over the table and whispered for a minute or two. Willis listened hard for any raised voice, but other than the fact that no one was even close to smiling, he got no hint of what they were saying. Finally, the judge stood up, announced a short recess, and walked briskly toward the stairway door, the other two lawyers trailing close in the wake of his black robe.

Willis was dying for a smoke, but he also wanted to try to talk with some of the hippies. He decided to smoke first and hurried out the front door to stand on the broad wooden steps. A couple of deputies came out too, lighting up their own cigarettes as they cleared the door. They glanced at him but didn't pause and walked stiffly down the stairs to the parking lot. Some more cops joined them, apparently having left the hall by the lower doors, and pretty soon Willis could see them laughing and chattering away, a cloud of tobacco smoke forming over their little group.

He smoked his cigarette down, tossed away the butt, and peeked in the front door. He wanted to go across the street and take a look at the kids inside the school, but he was afraid of missing the judge's reentry. He paced around just outside the building, undecided. There was no sign of activity outside the school and he saw no one enter or leave the store. Then he spotted a pay telephone on the store's porch and headed for it at a near run. He dropped in a dime, got the operator, and made a collect call to the newsroom.

"Alice? It's Willis. Is Sy there? How about Greenberg? Christ. No, just tell them I'm working on a really good story. Yeah, a great story. Tell them it's about the commune and Quimby. That's all, just that. Tell 'em I'll call when I can but that I definitely will have the story for tonight. Okay."

He hung up, lit another cigarette, and hurried back to the town hall just in time to see Jones walk out of the stairway door and drop into his chair. Quimby came out next, and Willis was startled when Bushey emerged right behind him. Willis nodded to him, raising his eyebrows in a question. Bushey shook his head, just once, but made no other acknowledgement and took a chair on the other side of the room behind the commune people, who evidently had not moved during the half-hour recess. Pretty soon all the cops had filed back into the room. They waited for five or ten minutes, the room full of low voices murmuring. Finally, the bailiff shuffled through the door, squeaked out his usual command, and Judge Talbot hurried into the room and took his seat, looking out over the small crowd.

"The court is back in session," he said to the stenographer, "note the time, please." The judge sat for a minute, either thinking out his remarks or simply building dramatic effect, Willis didn't know which. Then he began, looking down occasionally at the yellow pad in front of him.

"This case on the surface is a relatively straightforward matter in which the State has brought a criminal charge under the laws governing protection of children from domestic abuse. It has some rather unusual twists and turns, including an apparently unrelated and serious charge having nothing to do with children. But by and large, the issues before the court today appear to be quite clear.

"The State, believing in its cause, has moved with its full might and authority to correct a wrong and right an injustice. It has employed the forces at its command to protect citizens otherwise powerless to protect themselves.

"We live in a confusing and difficult age. The certainties of an earlier time are crumbling one by one and the verities of the past are being transformed one by one into ambiguous paradoxes. And so, when right and wrong are presented to us in black and white clarity, we are tempted to leap to conclusions. When we see, or think we see, what needs to be done, we grow impatient with process and we are eager to get on with it.

"Over the past decade, our nation has seen many examples, and right now we are involved in a war that arose out of the same sense of righting a wrong, a war brought on by a demand for action, a war that in the end may become the lasting metaphor for this period of our history.

"Today, in this quiet backwater of Vermont, we're being asked by the State to right a wrong—as perceived by the lawful authority that represents us. But here's the problem: In doing its duty, the State intends to take away the rights of those it believes to be in the wrong. Unable or unwilling to satisfy the demands of the legal process, the State has short-circuited that process and in doing so has deprived the defendants of their rights.

"These rights are the most precious possessions of U.S. citizens, more sacred even than life itself, as we have proven in countless struggles over the past two centuries. Indeed, the monumental wisdom of the founding fathers was that they enshrined not only the rights of victims but the rights of the accused and refused to sacrifice one for the other."

He paused, and Willis, having given up on trying to get it all down verbatim, waited with his pen hovering over his pad and his eyes fixed on the judge. When the muffled clicks of the court reporter's machine stopped, there was no sound in the room. Looking directly at Quimby, Talbot continued.

"The State had no right to seize these thirteen people, no right to invade and search their property, and certainly no right to kidnap and incarcerate their children.

"The Constitution of the United States is perfectly clear on these points, and the Constitution of the State of Vermont reinforces and strengthens that clarity. The evidence, so-called, presented to this court falls woefully short of meeting the requirements for such actions by the State. And therefore, this court dismisses the warrant and quashes the information on which it is based.

"Furthermore, the court orders the State, as represented by State's Attorney Quimby, to deliver their children to these former defendants immediately and to transport them all safely back to their homes. Further, all property seized at their homes will be returned, except for any contraband that is clearly outlawed which will be kept in a safe place until further disposition by a Vermont court of jurisdiction.

"The other warrant before us, for the arrest of one Randall Winslow, also known as H. H. Johnson, on a charge of being a fugitive from justice, will stand. For now."

He looked around the room, which was as quiet and still as an empty church. Then the judge turned to the public defender and said, "Mr. Jones, I want to apologize to you. I promised you would get a chance to speak, but you didn't. Do you have anything you want say?"

Jones rose halfway out of his chair and mumbled, "No, Your Honor."

"Court adjourned," Talbot said, and left the room.

When the door shut behind him, everyone began moving at once, cops descending on Quimby and Bushey, hippies standing up and hugging each other, the court reporter folding up her apparatus, and

Willis trying to get to the prosecutor. When he did, Quimby just waved him off and a cop stepped between them.

He caught up with Jones at the front door, but other than a giant grin and a few inconsequential mumblings, he got nothing of value for the story. Next he tried to speak to some of the commune people, but again the cops kept him away. Finally, Willis decided he had all he needed for the story anyway and he began trying to figure out the quickest way to get back to his car. He remembered the court reporter and headed out the door in hopes of catching a ride with her.

Hurrying down the steps, he looked up just in time to see the door of the school open and a string of waist-high people pouring through, led by two women and followed by four more, two of whom were carrying babies. The whole crowd hurried across the street, brushed past Willis, and clambered up the stairs into the town hall.

Willis reached the parking lot just in time to see the stenographer pulling out. He waved but she didn't see him. The downstairs door of the town hall opened and Judge Talbot hurried through, his briefcase in one hand and his wadded up robe tucked under his other arm. He walked, head down, into the parking lot, and Willis hurried over.

"Judge Talbot? I'm Bud Willis."

"Yeah, I know," Talbot said without slowing down. "I saw you in there. But I have nothing else to say."

"Oh," Willis said. "Okay. But I have one more thing to ask you." Talbot looked at him warily. "Would you give me a ride to my car? It's right on your way down, on Route 16." The judge looked annoyed.

"I'm sort of stranded," Willis added.

"Yeah. Well, why not. Come on."

They walked across the lot and Talbot motioned to a black MG parked at the very end. He tossed his briefcase and robe behind the driver's seat and Willis folded himself into the passenger's side.

Seymour strolled into the newsroom just before seven, a huge, just-lit cigar in his hand. He passed Alice without speaking and she carefully kept her head down, eyes buried in *Reader's Digest.* The newsroom was half full, but none of the others looked up either, so he was nearly at his office before Connie gasped, then broke into a loud laugh. Sy turned to look directly at her, peering through the eyeholes of the Joker's mask. Last year he had worn a Batman suit on Halloween and climbed into the newsroom through a window, contributing to the long list of newsroom legends he had created. When Connie laughed, the others looked up, and Sy took a long pull on his cigar, blowing smoke out the grotesque turned-up mouth hole of the mask.

"Laugh on," he called in a voice muffled ominously by the rubber mask.

Inside his office he flipped on the television just in time for the final stupid Halloween joke with which Hubell signed off the local news segment. He read the pile of notes on his desk, including two from Alice saying the publisher wanted Sy to call. On the second one, she had written URGENT. He tossed the whole pile into the wastebasket and spun his back to the newsroom just as Walter Cronkite filled the screen. The phone rang twice, including a burst of six or eight shrill jangles, but he ignored it. He was taking the final pulls on his cigar when Willis hurried into his office just as Cronkite intoned, ". . . the way it is, Thursday, October 31, 1968. Good night."

"Hey, Sy," Willis said excitedly, "listen, I've got a great story . . ." He paused, waiting for Seymour to turn around, and when he did, a tiny squeal popped out of Willis's mouth.

"Christ," he said, "you scared the shit out of me."

"What's the matter, Willis, can't take a joke?"

"You'd of been sorry if I'd died before you got this story."

Sy pulled off the mask and Willis noticed again how carefully he had shaved and how old he looked, but he quickly forgot everything except how he was going to write the story. Over the years, he had found that talking it out beforehand, if you had someone sharp to ask good questions, helped shape the story.

Sy didn't seem very interested at first, preoccupied with stuff like how Willis had known about the raid and how he happened to be riding with Bushey. "What'd you have to promise him?" was his first question.

But very soon he was captured. Mostly he let Willis spill it out, moving chronologically from the time he and Bushey had arrived at the commune.

"Wait a minute," Sy said, remembering the young woman and the girl. "What time did you get there?"

"Just before four."

Sy nodded. "I nearly forgot. That friend of yours, the girl that used to be the bartender, showed up here just about that time. I'd forgotten, but didn't you tell me she had moved into that commune?"

"Yeah," Willis said. "But she wasn't there today."

"No. I just told you she was here at four. She had a girl with her and they were acting sort of strangely. Looking for you, but they wouldn't tell me why."

Willis frowned. Must have been the kid with the beret. He had forgotten to look for her at the commune but he would have noticed if she'd been with the others at the town hall.

"Go on," Sy said, intrigued despite himself.

Willis summarized some of the car-ride conversation, but he edited out the parts Bushey had said he would deny. On the drive back to the paper, he had thought hard about whether to write what Bushey had told him about Winslow. He knew that was supposed to be part of the background-only stuff. But some of it — a lot of it — had come out in open court, so he decided he'd write it all.

"Now listen, Sy. This is what all this is really about. This whole raid, all the child-abuse crap, was a setup, a trap to grab the guy who murdered that New Jersey state cop. Remember last May? When they were here looking for him? Well, Bushey found out that he was the same guy as the big bearded freak that was the chief at the commune. Remember?"

"Sure," Sy said, "and don't I remember that you got to be sort of friends with that guy?"

"Naw, we never were friends. Not really. I used to go up there occasionally, just snooping around, because I knew Bushey was onto something. That's all."

He fumbled with his cigarettes, finally getting one out of the pack and lit, then he looked up again and went on. "Anyway, he wasn't at the commune. Flown the coop. Bushey sent out bloodhounds, but they didn't get a whiff." He paused. "Great story, huh?"

"Yeah," Sy said, "go on. What happened?"

Willis described the roundup of the hippies, the caravan to the town hall, the makeshift courtroom, and the weird scene with cops milling around. "What do you know about Judge Talbot?" he asked.

"He's supposed to be a pretty good judge," Sy said, "and I don't have any reason to doubt it. I used to think he was one of the few public officials who understood what Emerson meant when he talked about integrity."

Willis couldn't quite remember who Emerson was and a crease rippled across his brow, so Sy thought he was trying to remember the quotation.

"'A little integrity is better than any career.' Not bad, huh? When's the last time you met a politician — or anyone else, for that matter — who thought integrity was more important than his career?"

Oh no, Willis thought, he's off again. But Sy smiled his sneer-tainted grin and said, "Of course, in this case I found out later that Talbot had a little help in switching careers."

"What do you mean? What kind of help?"

"Well, when he was a senator, he had a lot of trouble keeping his trousers zipped. And when his wife sued for divorce, she was about to spill a big pile of dirty laundry over his political career. That's when he took the judgeship appointment."

"Jesus, Sy, you're a dangerous guy. Have you got dirt on everybody?"

"Only the Joker knows," he said, holding the mask over his face, then setting it down and saying, "Anyway, what about Talbot?"

"He was the judge," Willis said. "He showed up to preside over the arraignment. Shocked the shit out of Quimby. He seemed to expect that somebody else, maybe the judge who issued the warrants, was going to be there. How do they get judges for special sessions like this one, anyway?"

Fully hooked now with this last element of official intrigue, Sy said, "Wait a minute. Go find Greenberg and bring him in here."

When Willis returned, followed by Greenberg, Sy said, "The court administrator assigns judges. He works directly under the Supreme Court, and when someone needs a special assignment, that's where it comes from."

They gave Greenberg the basics of the story, and when they were through he said, "Great story. Too bad we don't have any pictures. I don't suppose you had a camera?"

Willis shook his head, remembering for the first time the trooper with the camera. He didn't tell Sy and Greenberg.

"Oh well," Greenberg said, "we can use file shots of Quimby and Talbot. Maybe we have some shots of the hippies from the protest last spring. Didn't Peterson shoot about a zillion rolls of that thing?"

He left, and Sy and Willis began to plan the stories. They decided Willis would write three pieces: a main overview of the raid and the arraignment, a sidebar on the hippie commune, and a short sidebar on the judge's ruling and the unusual setting.

Willis stood up and headed for his typewriter, but Sy called him back. "Here's another idea," he said. "I'll write a political piece laying out the implications for Quimby's campaign with some background on him, Bushey, and Talbot. I know enough to put this thing into perspective from that angle, I think."

Willis was surprised. He expected Sy to add to his copy, maybe even some pretty heavy rewriting since he usually did when he was interested in the story. But he didn't often write under his own byline.

"Good idea," Willis said. "What do you think this will do to Quimby—help or hurt him?"

"It'll kill the bastard when I'm done with him," Sy said with more malice than humor. "How about writing the piece on Talbot's ruling first. It might help me if you have some good quotes."

"Okay," Willis said. "I've got plenty."

Everyone in the newsroom watched as he left Sy's office but he hardly noticed, riding a wave of excitement bordering on euphoria. It was like the early months when he and Sy had pounded out those late-night stories, like the Bobby Kennedy and Martin Luther King assassinations, working with some sort of unspoken conspiracy of purpose and mutual respect that made teamwork out of what normally is the most isolated human effort: thinking and writing. He hurried to his desk, dismissing a fleeting impulse to go out for a quick drink before starting on his stories.

Sy watched Willis as he rolled a sheet of copy paper into his typewriter and propped up a long yellow legal pad on the left side of his desk. The deposition, the notes to call Manny, even the goddam union had all moved to the back recesses of his mind. This was a story, something worth doing. He and Willis together could do something with this. "The shrill Trumpet sounds, to Horse: Away! My Soul's in Arms, and eager for the Fray." That's right. All he had needed was a friendly hand to brush away the spiders. And, like King Richard, he would not be awed by Fate.

He unburied his own typewriter, tossing off a pile of newspapers that had accumulated on top of it for the past month. He grabbed a legislative directory for 1965 out of the bookcase and opened to the senate section with the biography of Talbot.

A half hour later Willis came in with his two-page sidebar on the court session. Skimming it, Sy was amazed at the length of direct quotes, sentence after sentence of verbatim transcript from Talbot's ruling.

"Christ, Willis, do you take shorthand?"

"Nope."

"And you're sure about all these long quotes? I mean, we can't afford to have the judge or anybody else challenge the accuracy of this story."

Willis, bursting with satisfaction, said, "Trust me, Sy. These quotes will stand up to any test, including the official transcript when it gets done." He was glad he hadn't told Sy about the ride with Judge Talbot. "I've got 'em all. You want some more? Hell, I could tell you some things he thought about saying but didn't. If you want them —"

"No," Sy said, puzzled and still a little uneasy, "we'll go with these. Good work."

Someone shouted from the newsroom, "Hey, Willis, telephone."

"Send it in here," Sy yelled, motioning to Willis, who reached for the phone just as it rang.

"Listen, Ace, you took off in such a hurry that you forgot the pictures." Bushey was speaking softly, and Willis was glad because he didn't want Sy to hear his voice.

"Oh yeah. Yeah, thanks. I did forget. You still willing to let me have them?"

"When I make a promise, I deliver. The dispatcher at C Barracks has an envelope with your name on it and a roll of film inside. You can pick it up there."

"Great," Willis said, trying to sound casual. "I appreciate it."

"I told you," Bushey said, "I keep my word. And I expect you to too."

"Well, uh, sure. I mean, of course. What —"

"You know what I'm talking about, Ace." Bushey's voice was rising and Willis looked quickly at Sy to see if he had heard. He stood up and took a step away from the desk, turning his back to Sy.

"Well, I'm not sure," Willis said into the phone. "I mean, the *Key Largo* stuff isn't part of the story, and —"

"Goddam it, Willis, you know what I'm talking about. The sonofabitch got away, and that means you can't write that part. Understand? I told you I'd tell you when you could use that. And now I'm telling you that you can't. Got it?"

"Wait a minute," Willis said softly, unable to keep the pleading tone out of his voice. "I don't see how I can . . . I mean, he, uh, that guy . . . he was part of the —"

"Willis," Bushey said, his voice angry and rising, "leave it out. I'm not fucking with you. Leave it out."

Willis was trying desperately to figure out what to say, sure now that Sy must have overheard and would recognize Bushey's voice, when suddenly the telephone was yanked out of his hand.

"Bushey? This is Seymour." He was yelling into the receiver. "No, you listen. I'm the one who decides what goes in this newspaper. Not you. You have nothing to do with it. Do you hear? Nothing. And if you've got anything to say about what's in it, talk to me. Not to Willis and not anybody else. Nobody else."

Sy was breathing a little heavily, his mouth pressed up against the phone. "And don't you ever threaten one of my reporters. Not ever. You're nothing but a tinhorn cop with a chip on his shoulder. And if you ever threaten anybody from this newspaper, I'll get that tin badge taken away." He paused. "Do you understand?"

But Bushey had gone and Willis could hear the dial tone as Sy held the receiver away from his face.

He slowly walked back to his desk chair, carefully hung up the phone, and said softly with just the trace of a smile, "You don't think I was too rough on him, do you?"

Willis just shook his head. Sy had already sat back down and was picking up Willis's story, so he turned and left the glass office. Several people in the newsroom were watching, wide-eyed. Willis walked over to Merle's desk and said, "How about doing me a favor. I've got a lot to write. If you have time, would you hustle out to the state police barracks and pick up an envelope for me? It's waiting and it's got my name on it."

"Sure," Merle said, already standing up. "What is it?"

"A roll of film. Oh, and tell whoever's in the darkroom that it's coming and it's for tonight. Thanks."

The next three hours flew by at the speed time hits only very rarely, the supersonic passing when one speck of a lifetime is forever marked out as a special event. The newsroom's normal swirl and racket seemed to be more or less routine in all respects but it was just background noise tonight and it hardly registered with Willis, although at the same time he was fully aware of being the center of that tiny universe. He wrote and smoked and talked and thought, joked, and paced, all the time piling up pages of rough, triple-spaced copy.

Merle came back with the roll of film and Willis passed it on to Greenberg without ever saying where it came from. A half hour later Greenberg was holding the negatives up to the light. "Hot damn," he said, "these are terrific." He clipped the edge of two frames, then called Willis over. "Can you identify these cops or the hippies they're holding?"

Willis, always uncomfortable when he tried to read negatives, was relieved to see that one of the clipped shots included a cop he knew, and he was gripping the arm of the hippie kid who had been accused of stealing the wallet.

"Yeah," he said, "I know these two and the other one is just a crowd shot in the front yard of the commune. We don't need names for that one."

"Okay," Greenberg said, "we'll use both of them." He yelled to Sy, writing away in his office, "This spread is going to take up half the front page. Okay?"

Sy nodded without looking up from his typewriter, absorbed in his own writing but at the same time tuned into the newsroom in a way he had not been for months.

"Willis," Greenberg said, "whose credit line goes on the photos?"

"Nobody," Willis said, "just use them without a credit."

Greenberg shrugged and muttered as he walked away, "Modesty doesn't become you, Willis."

Willis was still writing at midnight, well after most of the reporters had disappeared and the harried editors were scurrying. It was the time when the production end of the process had begun to challenge the editorial side for dominance, a tug-of-war between those who wanted only to produce something called a newspaper as quickly as possible and those who wanted to create history. The clattering noise and the blue smoke from the typesetters flooded at ceiling height out of the composing room, and Rocky's ink-stained grunts shuffled between the two workplaces. Conversation, mostly shouted, had taken on the cacophony of communication between closely related species, like blue jays yammering at crows.

Sy had finished his story, instructing Greenberg to give it a rare double byline, with Willis's name listed first. He worked steadily on his and Willis's copy but otherwise he ignored the newsroom, holed up in his office, refusing to answer his telephone, and speaking only to Willis and Greenberg. He kept an eye on the door and at one point he told Willis that he was half expecting to see Fletcher or the business manager, perhaps even Manny himself, although such a visit would be without precedent. Sy didn't explain why, and he and Willis watched the news at eleven and congratulated each other when they saw no report on the commune raid.

Willis pulled the final sheet of copy out of his Underwood before twelve thirty, well before the final deadline, and pasted the last story together. He held it up as high as he could reach and it still dragged the floor, a dirty white ribbon of glued pages cut from cast-off newsprint. He dropped it on Greenberg's desk, then slumped into his chair, lighting up a new Winston and lazily looking around the newsroom, satisfaction filling every crevice of his being. He knew this night's writing had been among his finest ever, a mixture of great reporting and skilled recording, delivering to anyone who cared to read it not only the information but the tone and atmosphere of this long day's story. No twinge of self-doubt, no envy of war correspondents clouded this satisfaction. This was one of those moments when he had found what he was looking for and there was nothing to soil the feeling, not even a fear that they were becoming less and less frequent.

Sitting quietly, waiting for Greenberg to finish reading his last piece, Willis thought of Paul Newman; or rather, he thought of Fast Eddie, the pool shark in a great movie called *The Hustler*. He remembered Fast Eddie, the cocky, tough hustler, lying on the grass with his head in the lap of the beautiful but crippled Piper Laurie. He was telling her how it was when he was really on, when he was shooting pool and couldn't miss, when everything he did was perfect and he didn't even have to try. That's the way it was tonight. He couldn't miss. The words, sentences, and paragraphs just flowed out on their own until all the balls were gone and the game was over.

"Jesus, Willis, that's a terrific story," Greenberg yelled across the room. "Great work."

He picked up the story and headed into Seymour's office, but Sy met him at the door. "Don't bother," he said, "I've already read most of it. It's yours." He looked toward the composing room where Rocky was standing in the doorway glowering at anybody who would dare look back at him. "Yours and Rocky's. Good luck."

"Hey," Greenberg said, "aren't you staying around, Sy? Azoy, I may need some help. This is a hell of a night—"

"Must be if you're talking Yiddish. Always a bad sign. But I'm not staying. 'We have done that which was our duty to do.'"

"Huh?"

"Luke 17:10. You ought to know that. Oh, I forgot. You guys stop before those chapters, don't you?"

Sy stepped back into his office, picked up his mask and his jacket, wrapped his scarf around his neck, and walked out, saying, "Besides, Willis and I have some drinking to do."

He motioned to Willis and they started out of the newsroom just as the urgent bell began ringing on the AP wire. Greenberg headed off hurriedly, calling over his shoulder, "Hold on, I'll see what that is."

Sy halted briefly, then walked on toward the door. "Your problem," he called out. "If you need help, call Manny. Or McNally."

CHAPTER ELEVEN
Tuesday, November 5, 1968

The newsroom was as lonely as a warehouse, a still and stale home for cigarette butts and half-empty coffee cups. It stank of clotted glue, newsprint, and dried sweat. Willis stood in the doorway, repulsed but unable to think of anywhere else to go. The wall clock said eight forty-five, an ungodly hour when he should have been in bed, except that The Box was so cold he hadn't been able to sleep. At least it was warm here and he was thankful that he didn't have to speak to anyone.

He prowled around the newsroom but found nothing of interest on any of the desks or the bulletin board. He paused at Connie's bare desk, surrounded like an uninhabited island by all the others piled high with papers and trash. This was her last week.

The AP wire was halfheartedly spitting out copy that no one would ever read except bored editors of afternoon papers and barely literate rip-and-read radio disc jockeys. He skimmed through several yards of the neatly folded ribbon of paper, mostly election advances, perfunctory boilerplate as stuffy and uninspiring as the air in the newsroom. The election was going to be close; Nixon still slightly ahead in the polls but Humphrey was closing fast. Blah, blah, blah.

Willis sat down in Greenberg's chair, smoked a Winston, and thought about Seymour. It had been five days since the accident—accident?—and he was still in the hospital. He had been up once to visit, but what was the sense when he was still unconscious? He thought about telephoning to see if there had been any change. Christ, the hospital was probably one place you could call this early. He checked the list of telephone numbers taped to Greenberg's desk, dialed, and after two transfers finally got someone in intensive care. No change.

He made his way to Sy's office and began reading the *New York Times* wire. More throwaway advances and a few columns. He heard a noise and looked up to see Manny standing uncertainly beside Alice's desk. He looked even more uncomfortable than he usually did outside his own office, gazing around the newsroom as though he were lost and needed to ask directions. For a while he didn't spot Willis in the darkened office and he seemed about ready to turn around and leave. Willis felt like a lousy spy. Christ, it was the old man's paper, after all; he had a right to hang around the newsroom if he wanted.

Willis stepped into the doorway of Sy's office and said, "Good morning."

Manny smiled broadly. "Hello, Willis. Hello. Glad to see you." He walked toward the office. "I was just wondering if anyone had heard anything about Sy. This morning, I mean."

"Yeah, I just called the hospital. They said no change. He's still unconscious."

Manny had stepped into the office and looked around hesitantly until Willis motioned toward Sy's desk chair. He sat down with a grateful nod and Willis unloaded a stack of newspapers off the other chair and sat down himself.

"I haven't seen you, I mean, had a chance to talk to you since . . . since it happened," Manny said. "I mean, since the accident. I haven't even told you what a terrific job you did on the commune story."

"Thanks, your note meant a lot to me. Thanks."

Everyone knew Manny's preferred method of communicating with people who worked for him was through terse, typewritten notes that often were as incomprehensible as they were short but were usually meant to be complimentary. He left the criticism of reporters and news stories up to Seymour, who got his own share of the Manny notes, although by his own account those were not generally complimentary. He once showed Willis a manila envelope crammed with notes from Manny.

"Yes, it was a good piece of work," Manny said. "I hear the AP ran your stories and they got good play all over the country."

"Yeah," Willis said, "I've had calls from guys I used to work with that I haven't heard from in years. I guess they got pretty wide distribution."

"So," Manny said, "what's the next move?"

Willis's heart jumped, startled for a second by fear that Manny was asking about his own plans, but he quickly realized he meant the commune situation. "Well, there's really nowhere for them to go. They're looking for Johnson, uh, Winslow, or whatever his real name is, but otherwise Judge Talbot pretty well shot down their case."

"How about Quimby? What'll all this do to him?"

"Well, I expect his political career is over, at least for now. If they could have found Thunderclap, uh, Johnson, or whatever his name is and proved he was a terrorist, Quimby might have pulled it off. But it's too late now. He'll lose today because he took such a tremendous amount of flak over that stupid raid."

Manny nodded. "Your stories were pretty rough on him. And he deserved it."

"Yeah," Willis said. "Every news report in the state picked up that line Sy put in our story about 'state-sponsored child abuse.' No pol could survive that sort of hammering five days before the election."

Manny fumbled for his pipe, searching each one of his pockets before a ripple passed over his brow and he finally had to accept that he had not brought it.

"Yes, well," he said finally, "anyway, you did a fine job."

Willis nodded, expecting him to stand up, but he didn't. Manny sat, uncomfortable again, glancing down at the desk and then around the room before he looked again at Willis and said, "I, uh, I don't mean to pry, but I, uh, I would appreciate it if you could tell me about that night. After you and Sy left the paper, I mean. If you wouldn't mind too much. It's just that I keep thinking about him lying there for God knows how long and I can't get it out of my mind."

Willis didn't answer right away. He had told the story so many times it had become damn near a recitation. He had told the cops—three different times—he had told Vic and Greenberg, Connie, just about everybody else in the newsroom. He didn't mind telling Manny, but he didn't want it to sound rehearsed or disinterested.

"Sure," he said, "but there's really not much to tell. I mean, we left the newsroom about twelve thirty. Sy and I. We'd finished up the stories and Matt had read them all. We'd been working all night on those commune stories, so I guess Sy figured he wouldn't be much help to Matt with the rest of the paper. We thought he was pretty well finished anyway.

"We thought we'd go have a drink and come back, after the presses started, to get a paper." He looked at Manny, who nodded.

Willis, for some reason he couldn't grasp, felt compelled to say, "We did that a lot, you know. I mean, we'd go out for a quick drink after the composing room was finished when we were just waiting for the press to start."

Manny nodded again.

"Anyway, Sy and I went over to Jake's for a drink. I guess we had more than one. I mean, both of us were pretty well wiped out. Tired, I mean. It'd been a long day."

He looked sharply at Manny for any sign of disapproval, but his face was as smooth and bland as ever.

"So when the bar closed—at two, I guess—we headed back to the paper." He paused again, decided what the hell, and went on. "The cops asked me how much we drank. And I truthfully don't know. They asked me if Sy was drunk, and I don't know that either. I'm sure I was a little tight, at least. I mean, it had been a long day and we were belting the drinks down. Scotch. I remember thinking that Sy seemed a little weird and I remember thinking he might be a little drunk. But nothing really set off any alarm bells. Not for me."

He stopped to see if Manny would say anything, but he didn't

"Anyway, when we got back the press had just started. We grabbed a couple of papers and we were both surprised. We knew Matt had intended to banner the commune spread across the top of Page One. But we looked at the paper and saw the top-right story was the halting of the bombing in North Vietnam.

"I mean, that was the right thing to do and all—it was a hell of a big story, of course—but we just hadn't known that LBJ had stopped the bombing. It must have come in after we left. The AP bell rang just as we were leaving the newsroom. But we didn't wait to see what it was.

"So Matt made over the whole front page, shifted the commune photo and stories to the left side, and led with the Vietnam story. I mean, that was the right call, of course, but it surprised us. Christ, Matt must have been busier than a . . .

"Anyway, we went up to the newsroom and flipped through the paper. Everybody else was gone. Sy was quiet, just reading. Matt had had to move his political piece to the inside, but Sy didn't say anything about it. After a while Sy asked me if I wanted to come back to his place for another drink. I was dead tired and I had to drive back to the lake, so I said no, I was going home. After a while I was about to fall asleep, so I got up, said good night, and left.

"That was the last time I saw him."

Manny shook his head slowly but still didn't say anything. He rummaged through his pockets again even though he must have known he wouldn't find the pipe.

Finally, Willis said, "The cops quizzed me pretty hard at first. I guess they found out that some of us sometimes went back to Sy's place after the paper came out. But then I guess they found a cab driver who had seen Sy walking along by himself just outside his building, so they let up on me."

Manny nodded. "Yes, that's what they told me. You know, I never was in Sy's apartment. All those years and I never went there."

"Is that right? Funny. You never saw that goddam elevator, then?"

"No, I never did, although I think I had heard about it. Sometime way back."

"It was a death trap," Willis said. "Basically an open shaft with a shaky cage held up by rusty cables. I rode in it once but I never would again."

Manny looked closely at Willis. "What do you think happened?"

Willis shook his head. "God knows. I mean, I guess he just fell in. Stepped right into the shaft and fell down two floors."

"Headfirst?"

"Well," Willis said, a little wary because he didn't know where Manny was going, "what else? Maybe Sy just stepped in without looking, then flipped over as he fell."

Manny nodded again, but said, "They say he grabbed the cable, or they figured he did because his hands were cut up where he apparently gripped the cable. And it looked as though he held on pretty tightly for a while because the cable cut and bruised his chest too. Tore his shirt off."

Willis grimaced. "Christ, it must have been awful. He must have slid partway down the cable and then turned loose."

"Vic told me it was the worst thing he had ever seen," Manny said. "He found him, you know, on the Saturday two days later. Must have been awful for him too."

Willis's mind wheeled back to the day after the commune raid. He had slept late and hadn't gotten to the office until midafternoon. He spent most of Friday on the telephone, working on follow-up stories. The story had rocked the state, and everybody from the governor on down wanted to comment. He had kept watching for Sy, but he wasn't really surprised when he didn't show up. Then somebody dropped the *Patriot Press* on his desk and Willis found out why Sy hadn't come in. They had a short but prominently displayed story saying that the publisher had suddenly taken Sy out of the newsroom—"demoted," they called it—and reporting on the unfair labor charges filed by the union.

Christ, Willis thought, the ultimate blow—beaten on your own obit. No wonder he didn't come to work. Willis had tried to figure out who leaked the story to the *Patriot Press*. He had thought about dropping by Sy's place that Friday night, but he knew they would start drinking again and he was already feeling half sick from the hangover. Instead, he went home, had a couple of drinks alone, and went to bed early.

Manny was speaking again. "You know, if Vic hadn't gone by his place Saturday morning, God knows when someone would have found him."

"Yeah," Willis said, "Vic told me he'd gone by to make sure Sy was going to play poker that night."

There was a long, uneasy silence, so Willis said, "What have you heard from the doctors? I mean, do they think Sy will be okay?"

Manny shook his head, averting his eyes. "I don't know," he said softly. "I've talked to both of the doctors and they say there's no way to tell. They don't know how much damage there was to his brain, or even what sort of damage. They said he might just wake up one day."

"Christ," Willis whispered, "how long could he stay asleep like that? Is it a coma?"

"That's right. One doctor said it could last for years. But the other one said that isn't likely, although it's possible."

Manny paused, as though he was deciding whether to go on, then he said, "They talked about one case when a woman stayed in a coma for ten years. Brain-dead. Then she died."

Willis didn't say anything because he couldn't imagine what to say. Finally, Manny stood up, saying, "Well, if you hear anything, I'd appreciate it if you stopped by my office." He took a step, then stopped. "You know, it'd be all right if you just stopped by from time to time anyway. I mean, I'm usually there and if there's news or something, you could stop by . . ."

Manny sat back down in Sy's chair as though he had just remembered something. "By the way," he said, "how do you think the election's going to come out? Nixon?"

Willis sat back in his chair too. He suddenly felt guilty about not voting himself. He hadn't even registered and didn't know for sure which town he should vote in if he had registered. Manny was looking at him in a way that made Willis squirm, as though he was supposed to know something or do something. What had he asked? Oh yeah, the election. Nixon.

"Right," he said at last. "Nixon'll win, but the gap is narrowing. Too bad Humphrey doesn't have a few more weeks."

Manny nodded, waiting for more, but Willis just blinked and looked away, utterly unable to think of anything more astute to say. Finally, he said, still not looking directly at Manny, "By the way, what's happening with the union? Any change?"

Manny's face darkened. "Well, they tell me that it's winding down. In fact, McNally says that they may not even pursue the unfair labor charge. With Sy out . . . uh, not able to testify, you know, anyway, they may have to drop that case or just not push it. At least, that's what McNally thinks."

Now it was Manny's turn to run out of words, and he turned away. After an awkward moment he stood up and started out of the office. "Well, if you hear anything, let me know."

Willis nodded, greatly relieved even though he felt as though he had just failed some sort of test.

⁂

As soon as Manny left the newsroom, Willis hurried over to his own desk. He had heard his telephone ringing twice while they were talking and he'd been sitting there only a couple of minutes when it rang again. He grabbed it before the first ring had finished.

"Hello?"

"Willis? Is this Willis?"

"Yeah. Who's this?"

"It's me. Ginny. Ginny Parker."

Willis was immediately wary. He knew that at best he was in for a scolding, and maybe Ginny was bringing real trouble.

"Hello, Ginny. How've you been?"

"How do you think I've been? With all that's going on, what would you expect?"

"What's going on?"

"You'd know if you ever got out here."

"Yeah, well, I've been meaning to. But I've been pretty busy."

He could hear her breathing, but she didn't answer for a half minute. "Everybody's busy," she said at last. "I noticed you didn't make it to Sid's funeral."

"No, no, I didn't. Couldn't. I mean, I think I was away that day."

"Where?"

"Oh, just out of town on a story." He scrambled to change the subject. "What's happened to his place?"

"Nothing's happened to it."

"Is somebody living there?"

"Of course there is. Where'd you think I was calling from?"

"You mean you're there right now?"

"What else would I mean? Why'd you think I was calling?"

"Well, I really didn't know. I mean—"

"Well, that's where I am. Me and Fred have moved back in. Looks like it's ours again."

"Oh, I see. Congratulations. I mean, that just seems right somehow."

"Okay. But that's not why I'm calling. I called because you better get out here. Right away."

"You mean right now?"

"What else would I mean? Yes, right now."

"Why?"

"Never mind why. I can't tell you. But it's business. I mean, this is a news story."

"What's so urgent about it?"

"I told you, I can't tell you over the telephone. But I know a news story when I see one. I used to be a correspondent, you know. And you better get on out here."

"Listen, Ginny, I've got a lot of stuff to do here today. Couldn't this wait for a slower day? I mean, this is Election Day, you know. I've got a lot to write."

"You think I don't know that it's Election Day? And I know you're busy. But I'm telling you, you've got to get out here. Right now. This is a big story. All I can tell you about it is that it's something you've been writing about. So come on out here. We'll be waiting."

"Okay, Ginny."

"Goodbye."

And she was gone.

Willis chewed a fingernail, lit a cigarette, and paced around the newsroom. He couldn't think of anything he'd written that Ginny could be talking about except the commune stories. But except for the political fallout, nothing had really happened in the past few days. Bushey was pissed off and wouldn't return his phone calls, and Quimby either didn't know anything or wasn't talking.

Willis had been planning to drive out to the commune to see what was happening there, but not today. He assumed the cops were keeping an eye on the place in case Thunderclap showed up, but there'd been no news about him either. Apparently, he'd just disappeared into thin air, or rather, into the heavy woods. Hell, he almost certainly was in Canada by now even if he walked the whole way through the woods. He might have hopped on the Long Trail and hiked along the mountaintops right to the border.

He checked the newsroom clock. Still only a little after ten. He could drive out to Sid's farm and get back long before the polls closed.

The sun was bright and the sky clear as he drove along beside the river, glad now to be out of the oppressive office and moving along through a fall day that offered to the unwary no warning that winter was coming. The trees were mostly bare, except for the brown-leafed oaks, but the air was too warm and the sky too blue to be hiding any threat. He drove mostly with his window down, watching the water push its way around and over the boulders. He felt better and better as he drove, and by the time he reached the turnoff he was convinced that Ginny had called about some trifling story, maybe connected to Sid's death or maybe something had happened about the power company. Or maybe the commune people had been to see her or something. Anyway, he figured he would hear her out, get back to the paper by early afternoon, and deal with whatever story she had some other day.

He turned into Sid's driveway and nearly plowed into Bushey's blue sedan. Parked next to it was Marlene's little blue car, tight up against Fred's giant Cadillac. Holy shit. Bushey and Marlene? His impulse to back out passed as quickly as the flicker of curtain at the kitchen window. No escape.

Ginny was standing in the doorway by the time he was out of his car. "Hurry up," she said, stepping back into the kitchen, "and close the door."

Inside, Fred, Marlene, and the kid with the beret were sitting at the kitchen table. The table was bare—no food, no dishes, not even a coffee cup. It was clear to Willis that they had been just sitting there, waiting for him.

"What's going on?" he said. "Hello, Marlene." He nodded to the child. "Haven't seen you in a long time." She stared, unblinking and silent.

Willis's mind was chattering incomprehensibly and he fought to appear calm. The whole scene didn't make any sense. Marlene smiled at him and he thought, God, she's prettier than I remembered, but then she spoke, sending more confusion into his brain.

"Oh, Bud," she said, "I was so sorry to hear about Sy. Is he going to be all right?"

"How'd you know about that?"

"You know, word gets around."

Ginny was putting a kettle on the stove and she called out over her shoulder, "What'd you think, that you could keep it a secret?"

"No, of course not, just—"

"Well, you ought to know by now that just keeping something out of the newspaper won't keep it secret."

Marlene spoke again, putting her hand on the child's arm. "We, Anne and I, saw Sy on Halloween. We went by the office looking for you and he tried to help us."

"Yeah," Willis said, "he told me about that. But he didn't say what you wanted."

Marlene looked down at the table, glanced quickly at the girl, and said, "We didn't know what to do. Her mother had left the commune and wasn't coming back, and we were hoping you'd help us get Net to her grandmother's house."

"What happened? I mean, did her mother come back?"

"No. She's still gone. And Ralph too. Her boyfriend. They left a note saying they weren't coming back."

Willis looked closely at the girl but she just stared back, her face showing nothing. He remembered how she had reacted when the Greyhound nearly ran into the Volkswagen. He turned to Marlene, "You called her Anne. I thought her name was Net."

"It turns out," Marlene said, stroking the girl's arm again, "that it really was Annette all along."

Willis shrugged. "How about the grandmother?"

"Well, that didn't work out," Marlene said softly.

Willis looked around, confused, then he remembered Bushey's car outside and he tried to fit that into the puzzle. Maybe he was here to help the girl somehow? His brain clicked. "When did her mother and the boyfriend leave?"

"The night before the raid."

"Are they who tipped off the cops?"

Marlene frowned at him, cut her eyes toward the girl, then leaned back so Annette couldn't see her and nodded once.

"Ginny and Fred took her in," Marlene said quickly, then smiled again, "and me too, I guess. We've been here ever since Halloween."

Then Willis saw it all. The mother had tipped off Bushey— probably some reward—then somehow Marlene found out and she warned Thunderclap, who cleared out before the raid. But how'd he get away without a trace?

Fred had not said a word, and Willis looked over at him, awed that such a massive presence could be forgotten. Suddenly he remembered the car that had turned off on Sid's road just ahead of him and Bushey as they drove toward the commune the day of the raid.

"Hello, Fred," he said, "glad to see you."

Fred nodded, his face solemn but entirely noncommittal.

"Never mind who took in who," Ginny called out, pouring water over instant coffee in a large mug. "That ain't why I called you out here."

She set the mug down in front of Willis. "I figure you could use a coffee. I expect you're not used to being up so early."

His head jerked up in surprise, but she had turned back to the stove. "Thanks," he managed.

"I called you because of what's going on out there," she said, tossing her head toward the door. "Out in the woods."

Willis frowned, completely lost now, but she didn't seem to intend to say any more.

"What's going on out where?"

"He's trying to track him. And that might be a big mistake. I didn't know who to call, then I thought of you."

"Who's tracking who?"

"The police chief. Bushey. Didn't you see his car out there?"

"Yeah, I saw it. Who's he tracking?"

"Randy."

"Who? What do you mean?"

"Just what I said. Bushey is trying to track Randy through the woods. And I'm afraid he might do it."

Randy? Then it all connected. "Jesus," Willis said. "You mean Thunderclap's been staying here too?" He looked sharply at Marlene, who blushed and turned away.

"I told you," Ginny bellowed, "never mind who took in who. All you need to know is that he left here about two hours before daylight this morning, and three hours later Bushey showed up and said he knew he was staying out here and where was he?"

Willis sat down in the empty chair at the table. "Wait a minute. I'm confused. Thunderclap, or whatever his name is, left here this morning? Walking through the woods?"

"That's right. He's headed for Canada. He's been waiting these five days until the search cooled off. But he wanted to get up there before the weather turns bad."

Willis said, "And Bushey just happened to show up here? This morning? Has he been out here before?"

"No. Just this once. We figure he got a tip."

"Who from? Who knew Thunderclap was out here?"

Ginny's face darkened into a scowl and her jowls shook in rage. "His name is Randy. Randy Winslow. And I wish I knew who told. Don't we, Fred? If we knew, we'd know what to do, wouldn't we, Fred?"

"I believe so," Fred said.

Ginny went on, "We guessed somebody must have seen him, maybe somebody who drove up to bring something, or maybe that meter reader. Remember him? Anyhow, somebody must have seen him out here and told Bushey."

"Jesus," Willis said. "Is Bushey by himself?"

"Far as I know," Ginny said. "We didn't see anybody else."

"Is Thunderclap—Winslow—armed?"

Ginny looked at Fred, who said, "Don't know. But I'd bet he is."

Willis looked at Marlene, who shrugged, then nodded. "Probably. I know he has a gun."

"You can't blame him for that," Fred said, his huge jaw jutting forward. "They been trying to kill him for years. You ought to hear some of the stuff they've tried to do."

"Christ," Willis said, "he's a bank robber and a cop killer, isn't he?"

"That's all baloney," Fred said, "They just made up all that stuff because he didn't like the government. He told me all about it. They just want to get him because he's not scared to speak up and he won't do what they tell him to do. That's all there is to it."

They were all looking at Willis. He raised the coffee mug to his mouth and held it there, hiding his face more than really drinking because it was still too hot to swallow a big gulp. Christ, what could he do? He ought to just leave and call the state police, but how could he? What would Sy do?

"Well," Ginny said finally, "what're you waiting for? Finish your coffee and then go on. Fred, you better take your deer rifle." They all turned toward her, and she added, nodding vigorously so the gray curls bobbed up and down for emphasis, "Just in case."

"Wait a minute," Willis said, trying to keep panic out of his voice, "what are you talking about?"

Ginny looked hard at him, squinting through her glasses. "Talking about going out there to find them. That's what. You and Fred got to go see what's happened to Bushey."

Fred stood up and walked three steps to a door opening into the mudroom. He reached in and pulled out a rifle, dragging it by the sling, and opened the door to a wall cupboard whose top shelf was filled with boxes of bullets.

Willis cleared his throat, knowing he had to speak but without a clue as to what he could say. Ginny took the opening away from him, speaking now more gently. "We waited for you 'cause we figured that two would be better than one. Whatever Fred finds out there, he might ought to have somebody with him. Like a witness. And we figured you'd be the best one for that. I mean, you know 'em and you're a reporter and all."

"I think maybe we ought to call the state police," Willis said at last.

"Why? So they could find out about how he's been staying out here with us? Besides, what would you tell 'em? That Bushey—a cop himself, or used to be—came out here and went up in the woods?"

Marlene spoke now. "You know, Bud, Chief Bushey is still the law. I mean, as the investigator for the state's attorney. And all we know is that he came out here and went off into the woods looking for somebody. Why would we call the state police to tell them that, since he is an officer himself?"

Willis looked around at all of them—Ginny still standing up, leaning on the sink, Marlene and the girl looking like two scared children, and Fred stuffing bullets into the pocket of his red and black plaid jacket.

"What're you planning to do?" he asked Fred as he swung the rifle over his shoulder.

"Going to track Bushey. See which way he went and follow his trail for a while." He looked over at Ginny, but for once she didn't prompt him.

"I expect we'll meet him coming back. He had too big a head start and Bushey's bound to figure that out. That is, if he's any good at tracking; and if he's not, then he'll probably just get lost and come back anyway. Unless we go find him first."

The whole crazy situation still didn't make any sense to Willis, but he began to think what would happen if he did call the state police and they came out and Bushey just wandered out of the woods. Christ, he'd be pissed at Willis all over again. After all, he could have called in the state police himself if he'd wanted them.

They were all staring at him again. "All right," he said, gulping down the rest of the coffee, "let's go poke around for a while. But I'm not spending all day out there."

Ginny reached into the refrigerator and pulled out a grocery sack. "I made you some sandwiches," she said. "And there's some boiled eggs and some cake in there. And a jar of milk."

She reached the sack toward Willis, who took it because he couldn't think of anything else to do with it. He glanced once more at Marlene, who was looking away now, and then followed Fred out onto the porch. They walked briskly across the yard through the barnyard to the woods, where a well-worn trail led upwards toward the top of the small mountain that loomed over the farm.

Fred walked along at a steady but unhurried pace, not evidently looking for tracks or other signs until the worn path had petered out and the brush thickened and the land had begun to rise more steeply. To Willis, trudging along behind Fred, there seemed to be several possible trails, but they had underbrush too low for a man to walk past without ducking.

They had been walking for about twenty minutes when Fred stopped suddenly. "Bushey lost the trail here," he said. "Took the wrong game path."

"How do you know?"

"I can see. Clear as anything."

Willis waited, hoping for a moment that Fred would decide they had come far enough and turn around. But soon he started off again, turning slightly to the left but still climbing. After another hundred yards he stopped again. "He found it again," he said. "He's on the track again. I guess he's pretty good at it."

They walked on, now climbing more steeply. Willis was glad to see that Fred was even more out of breath than he was. He could hear him taking in and letting out air and he had slowed down. After another hundred yards or so Fred stopped and had to take in several chestfuls of air before he could speak. They were standing in a dense forest of hardwoods, mostly maples that Willis could recognize but also a fair number of smooth-barked gray trees nearly as big as the maples. The understory was much more open than it had been lower down, with fewer very small saplings. It was not a very interesting woods—a steep sidehill rising higher than he could see, with little variety in topography or vegetation.

When he could see that Fred was breathing a little more easily, Willis said, "Are we still on the trail?"

"Yes. I still got both tracks."

"Show me," Willis said.

"What?"

"The tracks."

Fred looked at him sharply, then apparently decided it was real interest, not a challenge.

Kneeling down, he said, "Look right here," and touched a slight depression where Willis could see now that the leaves had been flattened, leaving a slightly discolored indentation. "That's Bushey." He swung his heavy torso to the right and reached his arm across a yard of leaf carpet, jabbing his forefinger into a small patch of bare dirt. "And here's the other one." Looking closely now, Willis could see that the leaves had been scuffed away and the moist soil was imprinted with the crosshatch of a tread mark ending with a rounded scar left by the toe of Thunderclap's boot.

"How'd you learn to track? Deer hunting?"

"Army taught me," Fred said.

He stood up, brushed off the knees of his green work trousers, and looked ahead at the still-rising hillside.

"How high is this mountain?"

"Twenty-three hundred."

"What's on top?"

"Rocks. And some trees."

"What's on the other side?"

"Another one."

"How far?"

"Three-four miles."

"Where do you think he's headed?"

"Canada."

"Oh yeah. How far?"

"Sixty miles."

Fred leaned his rifle on a tree and pulled off his jacket. Willis was still wearing his sweater and had started to sweat a little, so he pulled it over his head and tied it around his waist. It reminded him of when he used to walk home from grade school.

"How long do you think we should follow them?"

Fred turned for the first time to look at him. He was still a little short of breath. "We'll go on to the top," he said, clearly avoiding the question and irritating Willis. Fred stuck the hunting jacket through the sling in a practiced way and started walking again.

The farther they went and higher they climbed, the more irritated Willis became. Why the hell was he taking orders from Fred, for Christ's sake? He was really breathing hard now and falling a little behind even though he could hear Fred grunting with every breath and he could see his shoulders heaving. After a while Willis spotted some giant boulders far ahead—too far ahead, in his opinion. He slowed, then stopped, but Fred didn't notice or if he did, he didn't care; he just kept shuffling along. He was forty yards or more in front when Willis began walking again and his lead increased gradually. Soon he could see a much smaller Fred plodding through the leaves, dodging and moving diagonally at times but clearly headed for the top.

Willis's head was down and he was really dogging it when he heard a bellow up ahead. "Hold it," Fred shouted. "Wait there."

Willis looked ahead and saw Fred, or part of him, the top half. He apparently was squatting or kneeling. Willis could see the top of the mountain, a rock-sprinkled bald spot beyond which the sky was unshielded and as blue as a swimming pool.

He sat down and waited, breathing in deep gulps. He had been carrying the lunch sack the entire way and he was glad to set it down. He was happy to be resting; then it hit him. Fred had found something and didn't want him to see it. He jumped up and tried to hurry up the hill, but he still couldn't get enough air and the land was so steep he was leaning forward. He grabbed saplings and pulled himself along wherever he could, but now he was basically restricted to one route, a narrow passage through the boulders and trees that obviously was used by all the creatures who made their way over the top of this mountain. It rose steadily but not in a straight line, twisting around large rocks and trees and dodging places where the ground fell away. He hurried as much as he could, but it took him a few minutes to catch up with Fred, who was still squatting down but swiveled around to look at Willis when he heard him huffing up the trail.

"He's dead," Fred called out.

Now Willis could see a form partly blocked by Fred, an oddly angled lump that didn't look exactly like a body but wasn't exactly the shape of a stump either.

Willis stopped, completely out of breath now, his chest heaving so he couldn't speak even though inside his head he was screaming, Who's dead?

Finally, he managed to rasp it out in a hoarse whisper, "Who's dead?"

"Bushey."

"Jesus," Willis said, or thought he said because he wasn't sure whether any sound actually came out.

He inched his way up alongside Fred. Bushey was slumped forward, evidently on his knees, with his top half folded over but not outstretched, his head hanging down at a ghastly cockeyed angle. Willis's eyes quickly riveted on the holstered pistol on Bushey's belt, exposed, with the white windbreaker hitched up over the handle. It looked like the same holster he had sat on in Bushey's car.

"Don't look at his face," Fred muttered in what was intended to be a warning but had the effect of an irresistible summons. Willis moved forward a step and peered around the slumped body, then yanked himself sideways, gagging. He would have thrown up if there had been anything in his stomach to come up. The top half of Bushey's face was gone, a pulpy mass of blood, flesh, and exploded bone.

When he finished retching he tried to look again, but his eyes made it only as far as the patch of ground in front of the body, a sodden mat of leaves splattered for four feet with blood and gore. His gaze dodged away, looking for a safer focus, but came to rest on the back of Bushey's head where a small hole was now horribly obvious, attached by a thin red line of dried blood to a clot that had formed where the collar made a dam.

Willis fled, leaping sideways to a large maple tree where he sagged down to sit with his head between his knees. He looked up when he heard Fred stand and walk slowly forward, stopping several feet ahead of the body where he squatted down and began pulling something out of the leaves. He gently raised up a thin wire that seemed to run along an inch or so above the ground. Willis watched, spellbound, as Fred exposed several feet of the wire, then stopped and slowly picked up a small lump that had been buried under the leaves.

"What's that?"

Fred mumbled, almost a whisper, "Trip wire."

"What? What is it?"

"Nothing," Fred said quite forcefully. "It's nothing." He turned to look at Willis.

"You better go back and call the police. I'll stay here with the body."

Willis just stared, desperate now to follow Fred's orders but at the same time sure that he shouldn't.

"Go on," Fred said impatiently, "we got to get 'em up here and we can't leave the body without nobody here."

Willis finally nodded, stood up, and left without saying anything more. Within a few steps he broke into a near run until he tripped and barely saved himself from sprawling. He half ran, half stumbled down the mountain, covering the entire distance in less than half the time they had taken to climb up.

When he got back to the farm, Marlene's car was gone, and he burst into the kitchen where Ginny was sitting at the table, working a crossword puzzle.

"Call the police. Bushey's dead."

Ginny dropped her pencil and pivoted the bowling ball head, her jowls swinging. She looked closely at Willis, then jumped up, moving much faster than he would have imagined possible. He heard her in the next room dialing, then talking in a low voice. Then her voice rose. "I told you, I don't know how. They just said he's dead. Yes. Yes, out here at our farm. Up in the woods. No, I don't know how far, just somewhere up on the mountain."

Willis went out on the porch to wait. He thought about calling the paper, but who would he tell? Alice? Greenberg wouldn't be in yet. And what would he tell him, anyway? A murder? Cop killing? He sat on the top step, as shaken as he could remember being in his life. He felt like just driving away, and he almost did when he thought of having to talk to Ginny while they waited. He started to stand up, but then he heard the screen slam and he sat back down.

"How'd he do it?" she said.

"Who?"

"Who? Bushey. How'd he do it?"

"No," Willis said, almost shouted. "No. You got it wrong. I said Bushey's dead."

"I know that. I heard you. That's what I said, how'd he do it?"

Willis's mind was so muddled he couldn't sort out any answer. He just looked up at her, looming over him with her log-sized arms folded in front of her stomach like a foundation built to support the structure of her massive bosom.

"It ain't my hearing that's wrong," she said, "it's yours. Did he shoot himself?"

"No," he said, "I mean, no, why would he—"

"Well," she said with ferocious irritation, "everybody knew that's why he carried that pistol everywhere he went. Didn't you even know that much?"

For one irrational instant Willis thought she might just kick him in the back, and he sprang forward off the step, turning around to face her. He tried to remember what he'd told her when he burst into the kitchen. Did he say anything about shooting? How'd she know he was shot?

"He didn't shoot himself," he said finally. "He was shot in the back of the head."

Now it was her turn to stare wordlessly, but she recovered speech quickly. "That don't prove nothing," she said, slowly lifting her right hand and twisting her arm so that her outstretched index finger was pressed to the back of her head in exactly the spot where the bullet had hit Bushey. She held the pose, looking hard at Willis to make sure he was getting the point. But his mind veered off as he marveled at the tininess of her hand stuck there to the blubbery arm without benefit of a wrist.

Then he remembered the pistol grip sticking out of the holster at the small of Bushey's back, and in the next picture that assailed his mind Fred was bending down, carefully tugging at the wire. Too many mysteries.

Ginny slowly lowered her arm but she didn't take her eyes off of him. He looked away, his gaze homing in on his Saab parked right behind Bushey's car. Then another puzzle.

"Where's Marlene?"

"Gone," she said.

"Where?"

"How do I know? She ain't my problem."

"Where's the kid?"

"Gone."

Ginny lowered herself onto the wooden chair beside the kitchen door and Willis kept his seat on the step, half turned away from her. Neither of them spoke for several minutes. From far down the valley he heard the first siren, a low moan.

"That'll be the rescue squad," she said.

He said to himself, Too late, but he didn't say anything to Ginny.

"Deputy'll be next," she declared. "Then the troopers, but they'll be later."

"How do you know?" Willis asked but not ever really doubting that she was right.

"There's not enough of 'em. They got too many roads to cover these days and not enough troopers."

The first siren, closer now, was joined by another. The ambulance and the deputy sheriff reached the farm at the same time, the police car wheeling into the little driveway just in front of the awkward high-bodied truck that rocked gently from side to side as it came to rest. The deputy and the two rescue squad men leaped out while their sirens were still echoing.

"Hello, Joe," Ginny called out. "I figured you'd get here first. But there's no need to hurry. They say he's dead."

The deputy nodded to her and looked sharply at Willis. "Who says?" he asked.

"This is Willis," she said. "He went up there with Fred. Fred stayed with the body and Willis came down and I called it in."

"You sure it's Bushey?"

Willis nodded. "It's him."

"You know him?"

"Yeah. Yeah, I know him. I work for the newspaper. A reporter."

The deputy looked doubtful, even more suspicious than he had been at first.

"What're you doing out here?"

"Ginny called me," Willis said.

"That's right," she said.

Joe looked puzzled, glancing from one to the other, but he didn't ask any more questions. The two rescue squad guys were standing at the back of their truck waiting for orders, dressed identically and, in fact, looking so much alike they could be brothers.

"Bring the stretcher," Joe called. "You," he said to Willis, "come on and show us where they are. How far is it?"

"Maybe a mile," he said, "near the top of the mountain."

The deputy hesitated for a moment, then said to Ginny, "When the troopers get here, tell them how to get up there." Then he had an idea. "Wait a minute," he said, although no one was moving anyway. He walked over to this car and pulled out a pair of walkie-talkies.

"Give 'em one of these," he said, "and I'll take the other one. Then we can guide 'em up the hill." He looked pleased with himself. "Let's go," he said, motioning for Willis to lead the way.

Nobody spoke as they puffed their way up the mountainside, Willis in the lead and glancing back from time to time to make sure they were still there. The sun was higher now and Willis was sweating hard. He was pleased when the rescue guys began to drop behind and he heard them muttering to themselves. Joe kept pace with Willis but he didn't push him for more speed. All of them were huffing loudly by the time they pulled themselves up beside Fred, who was still standing next to the kneeling form of Bushey, as though he hadn't moved since Willis left.

"Hello, Joe," he called. The deputy, gasping in air and wiping his forehead on his shirtsleeve, just nodded. "I guess he finally did it," Fred said.

Willis's head snapped up and he looked quickly at the deputy, but Joe didn't register surprise, curiosity, or anything else as he continued to mop his red face.

The rescue team had dropped the stretcher, and both of them were holding onto small trees, bending over as they sucked in deep breaths. Finally, one of them stepped around Fred and bent down over the body. He peered around to the front then jerked back slightly and whispered, "Jesus Christ. He's dead, all right."

Fred stepped around the stooping deputy, walked around the body, and bent over to reach for something. Willis saw that Bushey's white windbreaker was still hoisted over the holster at the small of his back, then he gasped when he realized the pistol was gone. He looked around quickly, but evidently no one had heard him.

"Here's the pistol," Fred said, still bending over and pointing to a spot about a foot ahead of Bushey's outstretched hand.

"Don't touch nothing," Joe said forcefully. "Not nothing." He hurried over to Fred and looked down. "We better wait for the troopers," he said, but his tone had shifted to uncertainty.

"It don't seem right," Fred said. "Seems like we ought to carry him down and not just leave him here like this."

Joe frowned and wiped his forehead again.

"They could be hours away," Fred said. "It don't seem right. It's not respectful."

Joe looked over at the rescue guys, then glanced at the stretcher. He bent low over the pistol, lying with its blue barrel half buried under leaves as though it had fallen nose first. He straightened and asked Fred, "You didn't touch nothing, did you?"

"Course not."

Fred snatched something in the air just above Bushey's slumping head. "Goddam flies has found him," he said.

No one spoke for a moment and the forest was as still and silent as a bank vault.

"Christ, it's sort of creepy," one of the rescue guys said, walking off a few steps and sitting down at the base of a tree.

Joe scuffed his feet in the leaves, then walked slowly in a circle around the body, looking down at the ground. "Fred," he said, "you know about hunting and stuff—you see any signs of tracks? I mean, besides his and ours?"

"No. I ain't seen nothing."

Joe frowned again, then thought of something else to do. He looked at the sky, then turned to the south where thin clouds were moving slowly at a very high altitude. "Think it'll rain?"

Fred looked up, scanning the mostly blue expanse. "Could," he said.

Joe thought of something else. "Say," he called to the rescue guys, "how long you figure he's been here?"

"Christ, I don't know," one of them said. The other one stepped over and picked up one of Bushey's hands. "Cold," he said. "Getting stiff."

Willis knew he ought to say something, needed to say something. But he couldn't think of what it would be. Would he tell this deputy sheriff about Thunderclap? He looked over at Fred, whose massive face offered no more hints than the sky.

"Maybe we ought to carry him down," Joe said. He checked his walkie-talkie to make sure it was turned on. "They could be a long time, and we can't just leave him here if it rains."

Willis was walking around the little group, moving past the bloodstained area toward the spot where Fred had pulled up the wire. He moved slowly and cautiously, glancing over to see if Fred would offer any kind of signal. He didn't, turning his back on Willis as though he was looking down the hill for any sign of the troopers.

Willis stopped at the spot where he thought the wire had been, but he wasn't sure. His eyes searched the ground but he couldn't find any spot that looked different from any other. "Hey, Fred," he called, "come up here a minute, will you?'

Fred turned around and said loudly, "Joe said not to move around."

"Yeah," the deputy called out, "and I meant it." He motioned for Willis to move. "Get back down here and don't mess up anything."

Joe pulled a handkerchief out of his pocket and used it to pick up the pistol. Then he realized he didn't have anywhere to put it and turned to the rescue squad men. "You got anything to put this in?"

One of them pulled a plastic bag out of a small pouch attached to his belt, and the deputy dropped the gun into it.

"Go ahead," he said, "put him on the stretcher. I guess I've got the scene secured. Let's get him down there. We'll wait for the troopers at the farm."

Fred picked up his rifle, which apparently Joe hadn't noticed propped against the tree, and slung it over his shoulder. "Here," Joe said, "you better let me carry that."

"You sure?" Fred asked. "It's kinda heavy."

"It ain't loaded, is it?"

Fred unslung it and pulled back the bolt, showing an empty chamber.

"Okay," Joe said, and Fred swung it back over his shoulder.

The five men, two of them carrying the corpse, waded off through the fallen leaves, obliterating whatever trail might have been discernible before their parade. Other than grunts and occasional bickering between the rescue guys about how fast they were going, the trip down was made in silence. They stopped three times for the stretcher-bearers to swap ends. Willis was still carrying the lunch, which Joe had examined carefully. As he poked through the sack, he had checked his watch to see if it was lunchtime but evidently decided that protocol wouldn't permit a picnic break. Willis carried the full sack back down the mountain because he couldn't think of anything else to do with it. His stomach was growling, but thinking about the food made him feel sick.

Back at the farm they loaded the stretcher into the rescue truck and had just slammed shut the back doors when the first green and yellow state police car rolled into the yard. A young trooper stepped confidently out of the car, carefully positioning his Smokey Bear hat squarely on his buzz-cut head.

Joe hurried over to greet him. "I secured the site," he said, "and we brought him on down. Might rain." He threw his head back and scanned the sky for evidence.

The young cop still hadn't spoken, checking out each of the five men in turn, his own smooth face giving away nothing. The rescue squad guys were both mopping sweat off their faces, one of them sitting on the running board of the truck. "We better get him to the hospital," the other one said to no one in particular.

The young cop spoke for the first time. "Is it really Chief Bushey?"

The others, by now so used to the idea that they had absorbed it into one of the world's facts that no sane person would question, just stared at him. "Well," the trooper asked, "is it?"

"Sure. Why, sure," Joe said finally. "I told you. We brought him down. He's in the truck if you want to see him."

Most of him, Willis thought, although he didn't say anything.

They heard the screen door slam and all of them turned toward the porch where Ginny was standing with her arms folded.

Just then they heard the siren screaming very close by, and no one spoke for the half minute before the second cruiser wheeled into the yard. Quimby leaped out of the back seat while the whine was still floating in the air. Yeah, Willis thought with a secret smile, he turned on the siren to announce his arrival.

Two troopers stepped out and followed Quimby as he advanced at a near run toward the rescue truck. "What happened?" he said a little breathlessly.

"He's dead," Joe said, squaring his shoulders and stepping forward. "Killed himself, it looks like."

Quimby frowned at him. "You sure?"

"I'm sure he's dead. He's in the truck. On a stretcher."

"What do you mean? Where'd you find him?"

"Up on the mountain," Joe said, looking a little nervous. "I secured the site."

Quimby frowned again, then looked around the group, his eyes stopping at the young trooper, who shrugged and said, "I just got here."

"Might rain," Joe said, looking to Fred for confirmation.

Quimby frowned at him again, then turned back to the trooper. "It's Bushey?"

"They say so," he said.

"Nobody's looked?" Quimby asked, then hurried over to the truck and tried to yank open the back doors.

"They're locked," the driver said, fumbling with a ring of keys. He opened the door and Quimby climbed into the ambulance but backed out so quickly he smacked his head on the doorway.

"Christ," he muttered, rubbing the back of his head, his face a sickly white.

Willis heard or felt a footstep, he wasn't sure which, and turned his head to the side. Ginny was standing just behind him. He noticed the three troopers had quietly positioned themselves, like sheepdogs guarding the perimeter of an edgy flock.

Quimby pulled out a handkerchief and wiped it across his mouth. He's really rattled, Willis thought, doesn't know what to do.

Quimby said to Joe, his voice a little too loud and a little too high, "Who told you to move him? How'd you find him?"

Joe just stared, his mouth gaping slightly. "I secured the site," he said finally, then his worried look eased a little as he remembered his other precautions. "Here's his pistol." He pulled the bag out of his pocket. "I was careful about prints."

Quimby took the plastic bag, holding it with two fingers. "How many rounds in it?" Joe frowned, then answered, "I don't know."

"Did you check to see if it had been fired?"

"No. Didn't touch it."

"Did anybody else touch it?"

"No."

Quimby looked around the circle, as though asking the others for confirmation, but no one spoke. He turned to the rescue squad guys. "Okay, take him to the hospital."

"He's dead," one of them said.

"Goddam it, I know he's dead. I want an autopsy. Take him to the hospital."

They nodded, climbed in the truck, and backed out of the yard. The others watched until, a hundred yards down the road, the siren began to wail.

Quimby shook his head and spoke for the first time directly to Willis. "What're you doing here?"

"Ginny called me," he said.

"When?"

He looked at his watch. "About nine thirty."

Quimby turned to Ginny. "How come you waited until twelve thirty to call the rescue squad?"

"That's when they got back," she said simply.

"Who? Got back from where?"

"Him," she said, nodding at Willis. "Him and Fred went up on the mountain to find him, and he came back about twelve thirty."

Quimby scowled.

"Fred stayed up there with him," Ginny said by way of clearing up the mystery.

Quimby frowned again, turning back to Willis. "You," he said, "tell me what happened."

Willis walked toward the porch, buying time. He sat on the top step and when Quimby had walked over, he said, "Here's what I know. Ginny called me at the paper and said to come out here. I've known her and Fred a long time, wrote a couple of stories about the farm and Sid and all that. Anyway, she called and I drove out here."

He paused, but no one else said anything. "When I got here, they told me Chief Bushey had been out here and had gone up the mountain, looking for a fugitive. They said they were worried and that Fred and I should go up there to try to find him."

Quimby shook his head as though clearing his mind. "Find Bushey?"

"Yeah."

"Why?"

"Well, they said he'd been gone a long time and they thought somebody ought to go find him."

"Why didn't they call the police?"

"He was the police."

Quimby opened his mouth but then closed it without saying anything, shaking his head again.

"Go on."

"Well, Fred and I went up the mountain, tracking Bushey. Fred tracked him, I tagged along. Anyway, we followed his trail and just before we got to the top we found him. Dead. Shot in the head."

Willis waited but no one said anything. There was absolute silence, as though "shot in the head" had been a command for all sound to stop. Finally, he said, "So Fred stayed with the body and I came back here and called—or rather, told Ginny to call—the rescue squad."

He paused again, and Quimby finally said, "Go on."

"That's all," Willis said. "You know all the rest. When Joe and those other guys got here, we all went back up there and brought him down."

Quimby looked around again at each of them, then turned to Fred. "Anything else?" he asked. "Anything to add to that?"

"Nope," Fred said, "I guess that's about it."

Quimby looked at the three state troopers, but they didn't offer any comments. He frowned again, then said, "Okay. We're going back up there."

He motioned to Fred. "Lead the way."

"He ain't had anything to eat," Ginny said. "Hadn't had time."

Quimby glanced at the sky. He muttered, "It'll be dark by four."

But Ginny wasn't listening. She walked past Willis into the kitchen and brought back the sack that had already made one round trip to the mountain.

"I made these for them before, but they didn't get a chance to eat," she said, handing the paper sack to Fred. "But you got time now."

Fred pulled out a sandwich wrapped in wax paper. Quimby looked annoyed but he didn't say anything. Willis spoke up, "I've already been up there twice. And I've got to get back to the paper."

He paused briefly, then started walking toward his car, glancing over at the troopers.

"Wait a minute," Quimby said. "I may want to talk to you again."

"I'll be at the paper," Willis said. "This is Election Day, you know." He knew it was risky to taunt Quimby, but it just spilled out.

Quimby looked angry but he couldn't seem to find any reason to make Willis go back up the mountain. Or maybe he still had political ambitions after all. "Well," he said finally, "don't go anywhere. I mean, stay where I can find you."

Willis nodded, took one more look at Fred, who was calmly chewing, then headed for the Saab.

"Hold it," Quimby said, "don't write anything about this yet. I'll put out a press release when we get back."

Willis didn't even bother to turn around, just waved his hand, climbed into his car, and left.

*
**

Quimby did put out a press release and a state trooper delivered it to the newspaper, but it was well after eight when he got there and Willis had already written his story, although he hadn't yet given it to Greenberg. The chaos of Election Day had a firm grip on the newsroom, which, to the young, discipline-steeped trooper, must have looked like a pen full of madmen. Willis watched him stop just inside the doorway, standing stiff with alertness, scanning the noisy room in search of someone he knew. The newsroom was full, with about half the population sitting at the buried desks and the other half roving randomly around in apparent pursuit of someone or something, most of the walkers trailing long tails of pasted-together sheets of paper. Tobacco smoke merged at the ceiling with the denser, darker clouds that rolled in from the composing room, diluting the effectiveness of the banks of fluorescent lights. After a minute, the trooper spotted Simmons, lounging as usual behind the mountain of paper on his desk with a telephone held more or less permanently to his ear. He put down the phone long enough to speak briefly to the young cop, then pointed toward Willis.

He walked over and stuck out his hand, holding a single sheet of paper. "The state's attorney sent this to you," he said, as Willis stood up beside his desk.

"Thanks. Anything new since this afternoon?"

The trooper didn't even bother to answer, simply nodding toward the press release.

"Did you get one of these to the *Patriot Press*?"

"I didn't," the cop said.

"Yeah, but Quimby called them, right?"

"He did whatever the procedure calls for," the trooper said smugly.

Willis gave him the hint of a sneer, then sat down and began reading the press release. The cop left, threading his way stiff-backed around the desks and moving bodies like a waiter weaving through a crowded barroom, careful not to let anything slosh onto him.

The press release gave the barest outline of Bushey's death, saying only that his body had been found on the mountainside, he evidently had died from a gunshot, an autopsy would be conducted, and an investigation was underway by Quimby and the state police. Fred and Ginny were not mentioned and there was no explanation of why Bushey was on the mountain.

"Hot damn," Willis muttered aloud, although no one was listening, "perfect."

He telephoned the number on the press release, the state's attorney's office, but he knew no one would answer; then he called the state police dispatcher, who told him nothing and didn't know how to reach Quimby. Finally, he called Quimby's house, but again there was no answer.

Bases covered, Willis read over his story one more time, pasted in a paragraph quoting the press release, and carried it over to Greenberg, who was hunched over his desk reading copy. "I think we'll have this pretty much alone," Willis said. "The *Patriot Press* and the wire services won't have much more than the press release, which doesn't say diddly-shit."

Greenberg looked up, blinking, obviously trying to refocus his mind. Willis had told him only the bare facts of the Bushey story, leaving out the call from Ginny and the part about how he and Fred had found the body. Now he stood beside the desk, smoking and waiting for Greenberg to skim the two-page story.

"Wow," Greenberg said, "good job. Where'd you get all this stuff? Sounds like you were there."

Willis shrugged. "I was. I mean, I was there when the body was found."

Greenberg's head snapped up. "You were there?"

"Yeah, Ginny Parker called me and said Bushey had gone up on the mountain looking for a fugitive. So I went out there, and Fred Parker and I hiked up there and found him."

Greenberg frowned. "How about the suicide stuff? Where'd you get that?"

"Read it again," Willis said with more confidence than he really felt. "All it says is that everybody who knew Bushey knew he had talked about suicide for years because of his headaches. That's all the story says."

Greenberg reread part of the story, then said, "Okay. We'll give it a shot. Probably below the fold since we've got all this election stuff. Tell 'em to dig out a headshot of Bushey."

Willis started to turn away but Greenberg said, "I could really use some help on the election, if you've got any time. Are you writing anything else?"

"Well, I don't really have another story. I've been out there all day. I could write about Quimby. I assume he lost, right?"

"Yeah, he lost. But the statehouse guys are doing the state elections. If you don't have any local stories, how about helping me with the wires and maybe with some rewriting of the state stories?"

"Sure," Willis said, "kind of tough without Sy, huh?"

"Yeah. Real tough."

"Any news on him today?"

"Nope. Still the same."

"Okay," Willis said. "I'll go read the *Times* copy, although it's way too early for anything solid yet."

"Thanks," Greenberg said.

Willis started toward Sy's office, a darkened, glassed-in hole at the edge of the newsroom that everyone had come to avoid like bad luck and yet remained the central focus for all of them every night as they put out the paper. As he threaded his way through the chaotic newsroom, he remembered his first gauntlet walk toward Sy's office and he was struck by a strange similarity. Many of the faces turned resolutely down toward their own typewriters had changed, but like that earlier time nearly a year ago no one wanted to take any notice of his passage even though now he at least knew each of their names and knew a lot more about some of them. This time even Connie kept her eyes down, pretending to be unaware of him and uninterested in his destination. He remembered how last January he had privately mocked them as shy egomaniacs, but now he realized that old unattributed newsroom witticism wasn't really on the mark. These people, these slightly unkempt scribblers, were not megalomaniacs, they were merely legalized voyeurs, self-proclaimed Peeping Toms licensed to watch from dark shadows the comings and goings of their fellow humans and then report their foibles back to the tribe.

By the time he reached the office, Willis's mood had soured into something approaching anger and he wanted a drink. He wheeled around without flipping on the light switch and stalked back to Greenberg's desk, saying loudly, "I didn't get any supper. I'm going over to The Oasis for a sandwich."

Greenberg threw a habit-inspired glance at the clock, then nodded his head, and Willis hurried out of the newsroom. The barroom was nearly empty, so he managed to catch Jake's eye and he raised a hand with three fingers extended. It was a signal they had worked out some months ago, meaning to bring three drinks spaced ten minutes apart. It was the only understanding they had managed to reach that could be considered communication, but it worked just fine for both of them. Jake was as different from the newsroom crowd as you could get and still be of the same species. He would never think of spying on anyone because he simply didn't care enough to watch them. He wasn't even very interested in himself.

"Hey, Jake," Willis said as he set down the third drink, "you want to hear a real scoop?"

"Sure," he said, drying his hands but ignoring the little pool he had spilled on the table, "tell me who's going to win the Harvard-Yale game."

"Huh?" Willis's mind reeled. He remembered vaguely that for some reason there was a lot of interest in this year's New England football classic, but he couldn't remember why or even whether the game had already been played. He said lamely, "How would I know?"

"Seymour would know," Jake said.

"Well, I couldn't tell you that," Willis said, "but I can tell you what happened today."

"So?"

"So Bushey's dead."

"So?"

"Shot."

"So? Big news. He's been talking about doing that for ten years."

Jake turned abruptly, walked behind the bar, and slammed through the swinging door out of sight.

Willis's rising mood sank again, deflated once more by Jake's unmasked scorn, and he sank back deep into the leather booth. But he had found out something. The suicide story, unless Quimby came up with something, was going to wash.

Christ, he thought, it's a funny world. He brooded for a while on his own predicament, but by the time he finished the bourbon he felt better and he knew he had to leave if he was going to get back in time to help Greenberg.

He had just stepped into Sy's office and turned on the television set when Fletcher sailed into the newsroom. Oh God, Willis thought, then relaxed when he headed straight for Greenberg's desk without even glancing at the office.

He watched as the hurrying Fletcher opened up with whatever was on his mind while he was still several feet away from Greenberg's hunched-over form. Willis couldn't hear a word, but he saw heads snap up all over the newsroom. Fletcher leaned over Greenberg, then straightened up, motioned toward the door, and stalked off, followed by a weary and clearly disgusted Greenberg, who trailed along slowly, both hands roving through his curly gray hair.

Willis felt sure Fletcher had heard about Bushey, but it was odd that he hadn't even looked around for him since he must have known Willis was doing the story. Then he thought maybe something's happened to Sy?

CBS was carrying election news and he watched, turned so he could also see the door of the newsroom. Greenberg was gone less than ten minutes, and when he came back Willis tried without any success to read his face. He slumped back down at his desk, reading copy even before he was fully seated, so Willis knew that Fletcher's mission had not been to report on Sy.

He peeled off a yard or so of the yellow paper piled up at the foot of the *Times* TTX machine and began reading election stories, still half listening to the TV drone. As reporters finished up their assignments, they began drifting into Sy's office to watch the television coverage. By midnight, four or five had jammed themselves into the tiny office, so Greenberg had to shove them aside to squeeze himself in, holding up a page ripped from the statehouse wire.

"Clean sweep for Republicans in the state races," he called out, "except for Quimby. He lost big-time."

A loud cheer broke out and someone slapped Willis on the shoulder, shouting, "Good work, Willis. Your commune story killed the bastard."

The others cheered again, then all at once they fell silent, like gossiping geese floating on a pond that suddenly sense a stalking hunter, only for this crowd, Willis knew it was the shadow of Seymour that fell over them. And over him too.

Greenberg left and the others began to straggle silently out of the office. When Willis looked up again, only Connie was still there, leaning on the glass wall and staring blankly at the TV. When she noticed Willis watching her, they both started to speak, but then each of them just shrugged, and after a minute Connie left too.

Willis read the wire stories and kept up with the CBS coverage, taking notes and occasionally conferring with Greenberg. The vote tally kept changing so it was like watching a horse race that never ended, round and round the track, neck and neck. He read some of the statehouse bureau stories and added some paragraphs to the one on the attorney general election. The normal deadline came and went, still without any clear indication of how the presidential election was turning out.

By one thirty the newsroom's work was wrapped up except for the main election story, the one Willis was going to write. Over the course of the evening his assignment had evolved quietly without him or Greenberg ever saying who was doing what. They just both knew that he would write the main story using whatever wire service reports and television election coverage they had.

Rocky had long since taken up his usual duty post just inside the newsroom, leaning on the door connecting to his own kingdom. From time to time he set sail like a tugboat leaving dock, churning in a straight line to Greenberg's desk where Willis could see him shaking his head and pumping his beefy arm up and down but evidently having no impact on Greenberg, who just waved him off without even looking up from his desk.

Willis grew fretful as the clock moved toward two a.m. but finally he became resigned to missing last call. At two fifteen Greenberg came back into Sy's office and said they couldn't wait any longer.

"Better wrap it up," he said, "unless it looks like there could be some clear signal in the next few minutes."

Willis checked the wires, listened for a minute to Cronkite filling airtime, then gathered up his notes, the *Times* stories, and the latest AP vote results and went back to his own desk. Sitting hunched over his Underwood, head down and fingers flying, he wrote:

WASHINGTON — Wednesday dawned with this country no more sure of who its next President would be than it was when this amazing political year opened.

In fact, the voters were not even sure whether they or the House of Representatives would pick the man who is to move into the White House Jan. 20.

The only certain fact at the end of a long night of ballot counting was that George Wallace was not elected. But the bantamweight former Alabama governor had succeeded in turning the nation's election process into turmoil.

Not even the usually cocky television networks would predict whether Hubert Humphrey or Richard Nixon would win the country. The lead shifted with each passing hour and the Electoral College vote was no more certain by 2:00 a.m.

At that hour, Humphrey held a narrow popular-vote margin, but Nixon held onto a small—but not decisive—lead in the Electoral College.

He handed the five-paragraph lede to the hovering Greenberg, lit a Winston, rolled another sheet of copy paper into his typewriter, and over the next thirty minutes pounded out a four-page, thirty-column-inch story and fed it a page at a time to Greenberg, who read it quickly, corrected typos, and passed it to a snarling Rocky for delivery to the typesetters. Willis knew it was a good story, a good writing job that he wouldn't have been able to pull off before this past year working under Seymour.

By the time Willis had finished writing, everyone had left except for Greenberg, who had shifted his battle station to the composing room. Willis wandered alone back into Seymour's office and flopped down in the desk chair, staring at the television but not listening. After a while he realized the telephone was ringing, and he shoved a pile of papers onto the floor looking for it. When he found the receiver, he grabbed it up and shouted irritably into the mouthpiece, "Hello? You still there?"

"Who's this?" demanded a brash voice that Willis recognized as the too-energetic kid from the statehouse bureau. "Is that you, Willis?"

"No," he said, "it's Gandhi."

"Huh?"

"Who the hell did you expect, Bob; yes, it's Willis. What do you want?"

The kid hesitated and Willis smiled. Good thing to keep these cocky young bastards off-balance.

"I, uh, I was looking for Greenberg."

"He's in the composing room. It's election night, you know."

"Yeah, yeah, I know. That's why I'm calling. Matt asked me to get a *Patriot Press* and let him know what they had. But they were late. The press just started and I grabbed one of the first ones out the door."

"Well, what do they have?"

"Just the usual election stories, no surprises there. No winner in the presidential race. Pretty routine, I'd say."

"Okay," Willis said. "Anything else?"

"Well, yeah. A couple of things. They've got this strange little story on Bushey. You know, the former police chief. He's dead. Did we have that one?"

"Right," Willis said, "we've got it. What does their story say?"

"Not much. Just that he was found dead of a gunshot wound and they're investigating. That's all."

"Okay," Willis said, "we kicked their ass on that one. What else?"

"Well, they've also got a story—on Page One—saying the union-organizing effort is over. Defeated."

"You mean at our paper?"

"Yes. They say the union has given up. Did you know that?"

"Christ," Willis said, "the bastards. They leaked that story just to get even."

"Well, is it true?"

"I don't know," Willis said, wary now because he remembered that Bob was part of the bargaining unit. "I haven't heard anything."

"Well, that's not all," Bob said. "In the same story, they say Seymour was fired just before his . . . uh . . . his accident. Is that true?"

"No," Willis said, "I talked to the publisher this morning and he didn't say anything like that. They must have got it wrong."

Willis figured the union had leaked that part of the story too, just to make trouble and to take a poke at Sy. Dirty bastards.

"Anything else?"

"No," Bob said. "That's enough. I'm going home."

"See you," Willis said, "and thanks. I'll tell Matt you called."

"Okay. By the way, how is Seymour? Any change?"

"No."

Willis hung up the phone and stood up. He was exhausted—too tired to move and too strung out to sit still. He checked the clock. The press wouldn't start for another fifteen minutes or so. He'd wait. Matt would be finished in the composing room soon. Sy's one inviolate rule was no drinking in the office, but Willis decided to break it. He fetched the flask from his jacket and ducked into the men's room. Two long gulps finished it off.

He had just gotten back to the newsroom when Connie walked in, looking even more forlorn than when she left. But the whiskey had kicked in for Willis and he called out cheerfully, "Hey, couldn't stay away, huh? Stick around; papers will be up pretty soon."

Connie followed him into Sy's office and slumped into the spare chair. "God, Willis, I don't know how you do it." She paused, cocked her head, and added, "Or why."

"Why's the easy part," he said. "I love it. I'd kill for a day like this." He had blurted it out without thinking, but the words brought back the image of Bushey kneeling in the leaves and he looked quickly at Connie, but her expression hadn't changed.

"Well," she said, "I've got to hand it to you. You're a damn good journalist. You seem to be always in the right place at the right time."

For some reason her compliment irritated him, maybe because it didn't seem like a compliment even though it sounded like one. "You've got two things wrong," he said. "In the first place, I'm a reporter, not a 'journalist,' whatever that is. And in the second place, I don't just happen on my stories. I work my ass off and I do whatever it takes to get them. That's the difference. You're more worried about whether something's right or wrong or whether somebody is acting the way they ought to act. I don't care about that stuff. I just want the story. That's why I'm in the right place. And I make it be the right time."

Her head was pulled back now and her eyes were open wide. "Whoa," she said when he had finished. "I was trying to give you a compliment, to say something nice. Nice just doesn't work with you, does it, Willis?"

He felt deflated, as though the air had been squeezed out of him, and he dropped into the desk chair. "Sorry," he said finally. "I'm sorry. It's been a long day and I guess I just sort of lost it."

She said nothing, but she didn't look as though she was accepting the apology.

"And there's something else," he said. "Bob just called. He said the *Patriot Press* has a story saying the union has given up and also saying that Seymour has been fired. I guess it just got to me for a minute."

First Connie looked startled, then the blood rose into her face and she said with fierce anger, "And you thought I leaked that to them. Right?"

"I don't know," Willis muttered, "I just—"

"Just what? Well, for the record, Mr. Ace Reporter, for the record, I didn't leak anything, and I resent the hell out of the fact that you would think I did."

She jumped to her feet and turned to leave, but just then Greenberg walked into the office. "Lovers' quarrel?"

Connie and Willis both blushed, and he said, "Christ, Greenberg, what a charmer you are. You were probably the kind of kid that pulled the wings off of butterflies."

"No butterflies around here," Greenberg said. He looked closely at both of them in turn, then asked, "Can you non-butterflies keep a secret?"

Connie nodded, but Willis said, "Of course not. If we could, how the hell would you fill up your paper?"

"Okay then," Greenberg said, "this is not a secret; it's an order to keep quiet."

He walked over to the half-buried filing cabinet, pulled open the bottom draw, and reached far inside, rustling papers. His hand emerged holding a bottle of Johnny Walker. "This is Sy's secret," he said, "and I bet even you didn't know about it, did you, Willis?"

"Hell no," Willis said, "what about his ironclad rule?"

"Sy's rules never applied to Sy," Greenberg said.

"Yeah," Connie said. "That's one of the things that was wrong around here."

They both shot her a nasty look, and Willis said, "Come on, Connie, ease up. He's not a threat anymore."

She burst into tears and Greenberg had to grab her arm to keep her from leaving. "Come on, Connie," he said, "it's been a long day and Willis doesn't do well when he doesn't get his bottle on time. Come on, sit down, and let's all have a drink while we wait for the paper. God knows I need one."

He led her to the chair and looked around for something to sit on himself. Finding nothing, he reached out his arm and swept a huge pile of papers off the desk onto the floor and sat where they had been, opening the scotch at the same time.

"Housecleaning," he mumbled.

Willis said, "You're in a fine mood, Matt."

"With good reason," he said, "we just put out a damn fine newspaper, among other things."

"Well," Connie said, brightening up a little, "it's not such a great day for me. This is my last day at the paper, you know."

The others nodded and Greenberg passed her the bottle. She took a short drink, wrinkled her nose, and said, "Probably if I liked this stuff better, it'd make me a better reporter."

"Nothing wrong with your reporting," Willis said, "it's just that you're more interested in other things."

"I'm sure that was meant to be snide," she said, "but I'm going to take it as a compliment, or at least as understanding. Because you're right; I am more interested in other things."

"Like union organizing?"

"Yes, that too. And I guess that's why I feel so depressed." She looked at Willis. "I don't know how the *Patriot Press* got the story, but they got it right. The union is pulling out, giving up, beaten."

"That's official?" Greenberg asked.

"Well, it's official but not officially announced yet. They probably won't ever actually announce it, but the national has told them to pull the plug and all the staff people have already left here."

"With Merle and others holding the bag," Willis said.

"He's no worse off than he was," she said. "Where's the harm?"

No one spoke because they were surrounded by the answer to her question and no one wanted to say the name.

Finally, Greenberg reached to take the bottle from Willis and said with a forced lightness, "So, Connie, we need to drink to your last day. Let's see, we better have two drinks—one for you and one for the union, since you're both leaving."

He took two short pulls on the bottle, reached it toward her, then pulled it back. "No," he said, a hint of coyness creeping into his voice, "three. We've got three final days. Counting mine."

He raised the bottle again.

"What do you mean?"

"What I said. This is my last day too."

"You're quitting?"

"Fired," Greenberg said. "Fired."

"When?'

"Tonight."

"Tell us."

"You saw Fletcher come in tonight?" They nodded. "Well, he came in to tell me not to run your story on Bushey. Or rather, he told me not to run the suicide part. Said Quimby had called and told him about it and that we were not allowed to mention that or some of the other details you had. He ordered me to run just the press release."

"What did you tell him?"

"I told him we were going to use your story. All of it."

"What'd he say?"

"Said I was fired."

"And?"

"I said only his father or Sy could fire me, since they were the ones I worked for. I said I'd leave when one of them came down here and told me to leave."

Connie and Willis both started to laugh.

"Yeah," Greenberg said, "I figured the odds that the old man would come down here tonight were about the same as that Sy would."

"So he left?"

"Yep. Not very happy, I'd say."

Willis was jumping up and down, trying to reach over the desk to slap him on the back. "Goddam, Matt, goddam. That's terrific."

"Yeah," he said, "until tomorrow. Or rather, until I get home and have to tell Nancy."

"Oh, Matt," Connie said, "what'll you do?'

"Well, I don't really know. Probably try to get a teaching job or maybe PR, God forbid. All I really know is that we're not leaving here. I decided a long time ago that while I like newspapering, it's not the most important thing in the world. Not to me."

They sat silently for a while, Willis and Greenberg passing the bottle and Connie shaking her head no. Finally, they heard, or felt, the rumble of the press, and Greenberg stood up. "Well," he said, "I'm going down to get a paper and then go on home."

"Me too," Connie said.

The three of them walked silently down the stairs, picked up a handful of papers from the pile laid out for them, and said good night. Only Willis went back upstairs to the newsroom, where he settled into Sy's chair to read and finish off the scotch.

CHAPTER TWELVE
Tuesday, December 24, 1968

Can silence—absolute, pure absence of sound—wake you up? The question was filling his mind when Willis's eyes popped open. He didn't know where it came from, it was just there, as though someone had spoken it directly into his brain, injected it somehow so the question filled up all the space of consciousness. But it didn't stay long, because his bladder also was full and even more demanding of attention than the stupid question. He threw back the covers and the cold punched into him before he even made it to his feet, long before he could grab the new bathrobe and get it wrapped around his naked body. It was the first bathrobe he had owned since his mother quit buying them for him but, by God, he was glad to have this one. Hurrying out of the bathroom to stand by the kerosene stove, the silence question resurfaced in his mind and he stopped dead still in the middle of the room, listening. But the silence was gone, if it had, in fact, ever been there, and he heard noises—several sounds, dominated by the whispering hiss of the heater, but underneath that the sounds of wind, of creaking wood, and the rustle of papers. Rustling papers?

Willis, truly awake now, shot glances around the room, looking for the source. At first he couldn't exactly track the noise, partly because nearly every flat space in the room had some sort of paper on it. Finally, his eye, helped by his ears, spotted a movement from the potato chip bag on the floor in the corner. As he reached to pick it up, a mouse darted out, swerving just in time not to collide with his foot.

He threw a halfhearted kick toward the fleeing mouse, but it was a hopeless gesture made up half from sudden fear and half from self-disgust. Weeks ago he had noticed mouse shit in one of the kitchen drawers and tracks through a pile of sugar he had spilled days earlier on the counter. If it hadn't been futile, in fact, he wouldn't have kicked at all because he was barefoot. He hurried over to the bed and searched around under it for his slippers but he couldn't find them. Slippers were another domestic luxury he had once left behind until Connie gave him this pair of sheepskin moccasins as a parting gift that she said eased her guilt about leaving the paper. Now, she had said with a hint of the seductive smile that once set Willis's pulse to pounding, she wouldn't have to worry about him during the long winter.

His eyes roved again around the messy room, looking for the lost slippers, and finally he saw the toe of one sticking out from under the sofa. He also saw the telephone, upside down on the floor, tethered by the springy cord to the receiver, which also was under the sofa. He was puzzled for a moment about the telephone and was about to blame the mouse until he suddenly remembered Sheila's call. He got mad all over again. In the first place, she had forgotten that his time was two hours later than hers, and in the second place it wasn't fair to surprise him that way, putting Timmy on the line without any warning. It was so late at night he couldn't think of anything to say except a lame, "Merry Christmas, Trooper." Besides, by that time he was confused because Sheila had been hammering him for five minutes about whether he had sent Timmy a present and she had practically accused him of lying when he said it was on the way. How the hell did she know how long it would take to get to El Paso? She also accused him of being drunk, which also was not right. And if he was, why the hell had she put Timmy on the line?

Anyway, that was why the phone was under the sofa, and he retrieved it but there was no dial tone and the damn thing seemed to be dead. One more thing he had to get fixed. His days had become an endless series of chores, boring routines highlighted only by niggling annoyances calculated to trip him up. He hadn't written a decent story in a month. Daylight had become so stingy that with his work schedule, if he slept a reasonable number of hours, he missed most of it. The Box was always dark and cold and he had begun to hate coming home, hated the long after-midnight drive, and hated the fifty-yard-long driveway that was always muddy, icy, or buried in snow. He seemed to be the only one still living on the lake, judging from the lack of car traffic on the road that wound around it, even though at least the town was still plowing that road. Christ, what would he do if they quit?

Willis hurried into the kitchen to make coffee—the goddam clock radio had quit working—but hesitated with the kettle under the tap, terrified that the water would be frozen again. He tried to look out the window to see what had happened overnight, but the panes were iced over so it was like trying to see from the inside of one of those glass-doored freezers in the grocery store. He yanked at the faucet handle, and when he heard the water rising to the spigot relief surged through him with a force far greater than called for by the tiny triumph. The pipes had frozen twice already since Thanksgiving. But at least the landlord had paid for those disasters. The Saab also had let him down twice, and both times he had to call a tow truck for a total cost of nearly half a week's pay.

The hot shower helped, but then he had to face that awful time in the freezing bedroom between dropping the bathrobe and getting the outside layers of clothes in place. He hurried so fast that he grabbed the wrong socks, the dirty pair he had foolishly dropped on the chair where he also had left his pile of clean laundry, and he'd pulled them over his cold feet before he noticed how stiff they were. Fuck it; what's one more day?

The coffee also helped, even the lousy instant Maxwell House, mostly because it was strong and hot, and he drank it hovering as close as he could get to the hissing kerosene stove. He was hungry but a quick open-and-shut survey of the refrigerator closed that option. A picture of the overheated diner halfway to town swam into his head, and his spirits lifted for the first time.

Two minutes later he was opening the front door, bundled up as much as he knew how to dress for frozen hell. Snow, piled a foot deep, tumbled slowly over the threshold into the living room. The Saab, parked as close to the door as he could get it, was an overgrown white lump, and the long driveway stretched ahead, an unbroken white hallway roofed with sagging branches of the spruce trees that lined both sides. The whole world was still, the only sound or motion coming from the dollops of wet snow dropping randomly from the overburdened limbs. It was as quiet as a graveyard. "Merry Fucking Christmas," Willis muttered as he fought the door closed over the buried sill and shuffled through the new snow. He probed with his gloved hand for the door handle and yanked open the driver's side door. Snow cascaded from the roof and both sides of the door, spilling onto the seat and floorboard. Willis reached behind the seat and pulled out the ice scraper, but it clearly just wasn't up to the task. He put it back and, shaking his head, replaced it with the snow shovel that he had learned to his sorrow had to be kept handy.

After clearing the car, he debated, but only for an instant, whether to shovel out the long drive. He was already wet up to his elbows. Hell, they'd told him the best thing about Saabs was the front-wheel drive. "It'll go anywhere," somebody had said. If it would start, of course. But it did, reluctantly, and Willis managed to get it turned around, headed in the right direction. Fast or slow? He couldn't remember what they had said, so he made the mistake of trying in between. The Saab did fine at first, gliding through the soft snow as sure-footed as a mule. But twenty yards out something happened, some buried rut or ice patch or maybe just some slight unevenness in the hidden path, and the car swerved a little, just enough to make the tires spin. The steering wheel yanked to the left and the Saab halted, engine racing, tires screaming, and Willis yelling—first, encouragement to the little car and then a string of obscenities.

An hour later he stood at the end of the driveway, soaked from the inside with sweat and from the outside with melting snow. The town plow had passed halfway through his ordeal, tire chains clanging and huge curved blade stripping the snow off the dirt road into four-foot-tall piles on the side. Willis had heard the roaring beast coming and for a moment his hopes soared, but the driver just waved cheerily from the giant rig and sailed on past. A one-minute detour by the monster truck could have swept the driveway bare, but instead the plow had added to the burden, turning a foot of fluffy snow at the end of the drive into a hard-packed, imprisoning snowbank.

Willis was wrung-out. He trudged back to the Saab, sank into its damp seat, and drove slowly but easily out of the driveway, relieved to be free but still a long way from happy. The parking lot at the diner—that's what they called it, even though it wasn't a dining car at all but a very old caboose that some enterprising Vermonter had salvaged many years ago and retrofitted—was nearly empty, too late for the breakfast rush and too early for lunch, and he parked next to the door. Grease-soaked exhaust streaming out of a pipe on the side wall smelled wonderful, soothing his growling stomach and offering his mind its first updraft of the day, a rare whiff of eager anticipation. Inside it was as warm as he had imagined, and he picked up two newspapers stacked by the cash register on his way to a back booth. He began to read and didn't even look up when the waitress set down a steaming mug of coffee, eating tools wrapped in a paper napkin, and a menu. She started to leave, then turned back, saying, "Say, didn't I see you on television a while back?"

Willis looked up into her broad, unsmiling, aging face. "Maybe," he said. "I've been on a couple of times but not for a while."

"Yeah," she said, "you were on that show they have on Sunday mornings, that news program where you ask politicians about stuff. Right?"

"Right," he said, flattered despite himself and wondering if she was going to say any more. When she didn't, and instead started to turn away, he blurted, "What'd you think?"

"I don't know," she said, "I didn't watch all of it. But I never forget a face."

Right, Willis thought, I've been in here a dozen times in the past six months and she never noticed, but one glimpse on the boob tube and she never forgets. He checked out the menu and quickly decided on the most expensive breakfast, the one promising the most food, about two pounds' worth, he guessed. The waitress was leaning tiredly on the counter, and when he looked up she heaved herself upright and began the heavy-footed trek, but he headed her off with a shout. "Number ten. And more coffee, please."

He flipped through the *Patriot Press*, as always looking first for anything about Bushey or the commune or anything related to it. He still half expected Quimby to reopen that mess, and he knew that if he did, the first thing he'd do would be leak it to the *Patriot Press*.

But not today at least, he thought as he put aside the hated opposition paper and picked up his own. Another day without a Willis byline on Page One. Well, hell, it was Christmas Eve. No news, the whole damn paper filled with features and recipes. A second-day story with a fairly big headline about the *Pueblo*. Stirring up the warmongers, he mumbled to himself, but at the same time he felt some sort of weird patriotic impulse. After all, how could the United States let some podunk country like North Korea just seize its ship, torture the crew, and hold them as prisoners for a whole year? Christ, he remembered the *Pueblo* had been the top story about the time he got here nearly a year ago. Funny. The world had hardly changed, despite a full year of bloody wars, murders, riots, and every other type of turmoil and, now that he thought about it, neither had he, despite a daily diet of great stories and what seemed at the time to be a steady stream of life-changing events. He couldn't remember what he had done last Christmas Eve. He probably had spent some part of that day sitting in a greasy spoon restaurant repairing a hangover. Funny.

Forty minutes later Willis left the diner, warm, mostly dry, and stuffed, a toothpick dancing in his mouth. Bushey and Quimby were on his mind again because as he paid the check the waitress had said, "You know, now I remember who you are. When you were on TV, they said you'd written the stories about that commune and Chief Bushey and all that."

He nodded, hoping not to encourage any more conversation.

"Did they ever figure out what happened to him? Or what became of that hippie from the commune?" she asked.

"Suicide, they said," Willis mumbled.

"Ha. I don't believe that one either," she shot back. "There's more to it than they're letting out."

He pocketed the change, nodded, and left, glad now for some reason that he had left a particularly good tip. It wasn't exactly that he felt guilty or even really uneasy about the Bushey story. He had sorted it out pretty well and decided he'd done the right thing. He had not told any lies, and he could have been wrong about the pistol being in the holster. Hell, it was a hell of a day and he could easily have been mistaken. Shit, the ballistics test said the bullet they had found buried in the ground came out of Bushey's gun, and that pretty much meant there was nothing else to say. And anyway, what was the likelihood that Fred would have done such a thing, covered up everything for Thunderclap? He just wouldn't have, that's all, even if he could have figured it out so carefully, which he couldn't. Besides, what the hell? Even at the worst, one bad guy ambushes another bad guy who's trying to kill the first guy in the first place. That's just the way things work, that's all. His own part was actually pretty straightforward—just doing his job, reporting what he knew, or at least reporting everything that he knew from any official sources. He hadn't written anything that would let anybody know he'd actually been there, but he hadn't withheld anything either. He had known a lot of reporters who held back information, usually to protect a source or to suck up to a source, and he always hated that way of operating. But he'd never done that and not this time either.

So he wasn't uneasy about the Bushey story and Quimby wasn't pushing it. He had answered all of his questions—in two different sessions, in fact—answered them without hesitation since there was no issue of revealing sources or protecting privileged information. It wasn't any sense of guilt, but the whole damn thing was on his mind too much, pretty much all the time. It was as though he had some secret, not exactly that he was hiding something about himself, but just that he knew things no one else knew. And yet, that sounded like he was hiding something, not writing some story that he ought to write. And that wasn't it, not at all. At first he had even felt some little tingle of power, a sense of moral superiority coming out of the way he had handled the whole affair. Not everybody could weave his way through such a thicket without stumbling into trouble. In his private contemplation, at one point he remembered something from *Huck Finn* that rang absolutely true in his case. *Huck Finn* was still Willis's favorite story, although he was a little shy about saying so and would never admit such a thing to Seymour. But he remembered how Huck had wrestled with his dilemma over helping Jim to escape and how he had worked it out so that his mind was easy. What if he had turned Jim in? How would you feel about *Huck Finn* then? It wasn't exactly like that in his own case, of course, but something like that, and at any rate he had by now fully made peace with himself. Just like Huck.

Still, he wished he could talk with Sy about the Bushey situation, just in general terms, to find out whether Sy thought Bushey would actually kill himself and whatever else he might say about him since they had known each other for a long time. He was thinking of Sy as he spit out the toothpick and headed across the parking lot toward the Saab. He decided to stop by the nursing home on his way to the paper. He hadn't been by in a couple of weeks and there was no hurry about getting to the paper since he'd be the only one there anyway. Christmas was the only day they didn't publish, which meant that Christmas Eve was the only night of the year when no one would be in the newsroom.

His car was hidden behind a giant red plow truck and, as he approached, the driver he had seen earlier walked around the rear end, headed for the diner. The bastard nodded his head and gave Willis a snaggletooth grin as they passed each other. The truck, engine idling noisily and pouring reeking blue diesel fumes into the air, was jammed in so close to the Saab that he had to squeeze himself through a door that would open only halfway. His black mood returned full force and Willis had a fleeting impulse to let the air out of the bastard's tires, but he didn't.

There were two nursing homes in town and the one Sy was in, The Maples, was considered the better of the two, although God knows why. The sprawling, low-slung building squatted in a flat field, brick-facade front facing the street, with two long, aluminum-sided wings stretching backward around a small courtyard now covered deeply in snow. Every fifteen feet or so along the wings, a single window marked out each resident's designated opening onto the world. Two black-barked, now leafless, sugar maples, just the height of the building, stood like scrawny sentinels at the entrance. Willis's depression deepened as he turned into the newly plowed driveway and drove under the roof protecting the wide front door. Maybe it was the roof that gave the place its reputation for class, since the inmates and their friends arriving at the other old folks' warehouse had to get out of their cars without benefit of The Maples' porte cochere. The protected area included two parking spaces, and Willis took one of them, ignoring the Handicapped sign.

The lobby, too small to deserve such a title, was empty, not only of people but of any hint that people might ever have done more than walk through. The strip of carpet was badly worn and now soaked with melted snow, and the plastic sofa against the wall was about as inviting as a cold bath. The windowless walls were decorated with photographs of The Maples itself, including a series of shots showing various stages of construction. No human image marred the display. A forlorn-looking plastic wreath hung on the door leading to the interior. Willis walked to the glass window opposite the entranceway and peered into a cubicle that also was empty, the swivel chair turned backwards as though the occupant had left in a hurry but Willis knew better since the tiny greeting office had been just as empty every time he had been to the nursing home. He was about to open the door into what he thought of as the Chamber of Horrors when he noticed the sign No Smoking: Oxygen In Use, and hastily reversed course. Outside again, he smoked a cigarette all the way to the filter before reentering the lobby. He didn't even bother to look into the glassed-in reception room, walking straight through the door into the bedlam of the nursing home.

The wide, brightly lit hallway was teeming with people, mostly women and all in motion. White and pink uniforms swirled in all directions, weaving continually to dodge oncoming carts, wheelchairs, and doddering patients shuffling along in various stages of undress. Willis made the mistake of pausing just inside the doorway, long enough for an ancient, shriveled, little man to appear in front of him, twirling unsteadily in tight circles, his toothless mouth agape and his unfastened bathrobe flaring out to reveal that it was his entire costume. One of the pink dresses emerged from the crowd and a dour-faced woman snagged the old man's arm, guiding him away down the hall.

Willis fought down the impulse to flee, fixed his eyes straight ahead down the corridor, and headed for Sy's room, far away near the end of one wing. Without looking left or right, he walked the gauntlet of old, discarded, but not-yet-dead human beings, some slouched in wheelchairs, some standing propped up in their walkers, some slumbering in chairs shoved off into little alcoves, and one ambitious old man crawling along on all fours toward the door. Groans, cackles, obscenities, and sobs assailed his ears but he walked on, carefully keeping his eyes from focusing anywhere except on the lighted Exit sign at the end of the corridor.

Seymour's room was mercifully empty and he shut the solid door behind him, silently thanking whatever architect designed the soundproofing that closed off the patients' rooms from the common areas. He stopped just inside the door, shoved a little off-balance by the sudden transformation from chaos to shocking stillness. He knew how complete his relief was when he realized that his chest was heaving and the deep breathing he heard was his own. He looked toward the bed but his eyes avoided the propped up form, instead locking onto the bottle that dripped a clear liquid through a transparent tube attached to Sy's outstretched arm.

Finally, he tiptoed over to the bed, as though its occupant were sleeping. Weak sunlight from the window fell over the still form. Willis was struck by how neatly Seymour's hair had been combed and he had been shaved far more carefully than he would have done himself most days. He protruded from the bedcovers only from his shoulders up, lying on his back, face aimed straight at the ceiling, and yet he didn't seem like a corpse, maybe because Willis could hear his soft, regular breathing. He jumped when he took a second look at Sy's face because his eyes were wide open, staring upward.

"Jesus," Willis whispered. After a minute he screwed up his courage and slowly passed his hand across the bed about a foot above the staring eyes. There was no movement, no change at all in the unseeing gaze. But after he had dropped his hand, the eyes blinked, reopening to the same blank stare.

Willis walked to the window and peered out over the bleak side yard where the snow lay like a tattered blanket, with tall weeds poking up in patches scattered around the field. He turned when the heard the door open as a young man strode briskly into the room, carrying a small flashlight in his hand.

"Hello, Mr. Willis," he said, sticking out his hand. "I'm George Thomas."

Seeing Willis's blank stare, he said, "Doctor Thomas. I'm Mr. Seymour's neurologist."

"Oh yeah," Willis said. "I didn't recognize you."

"That's probably because we haven't met," Thomas said, moving on toward the bed. "But I know you because I've seen you on television and I've seen your byline."

Willis didn't know what to say. He knew he had met one doctor, but he had remembered him as considerably older. How come he wasn't wearing a white coat or something? Not even a stethoscope.

"You might have met my colleague, Gene Slocum."

Willis nodded but the doctor wasn't looking at him, bending now over the still form in the bed. He raised the small light and directed the tiny beam into Sy's right eye.

"His eyes were open," Willis said foolishly, "when I came in."

The doctor didn't answer, shifting his ray of light to the other eye. After a minute he clicked off the light and turned back to Willis. "What a damn shame, huh?"

Again Willis didn't know what to say. He'd never encountered such a loose-acting doctor. But then, he'd never known a doctor as young as this one, or at least who looked so young. Christ, he looked a good many years younger than Willis. Maybe he was a resident or something? Finally, motioning toward the bed, he said, "Can he hear us?"

Dr. Thomas smiled. "No. No, I wish to hell he could, but he can't. But if you'd feel easier, we can step outside to talk. I hear you're a good friend of his."

In the hall, the doctor led the way to a closet-sized room with a small desk and two wooden chairs. He dropped into one and waved Willis to the other. "I follow your stories pretty carefully," he said, "especially the political stuff. You have a damn fine newspaper. Much better than I expected to find in such a small town."

"Thanks," Willis said. "It's mostly due to him. To Sy."

"That's what I hear. As I said, it's a shame."

"What're . . . uh, what're the chances for him? I mean, can he recover?"

"Hard to say. In fact, it's impossible. We've learned a hell of a lot about this sort of case over the past ten years, partly because of the damn war, but the truth is we've barely begun to understand what goes on in the brain."

Willis nodded. "How about the other injuries? He was pretty banged up in the fall."

"Yes, it was quite a fall," the doctor said, with what Willis thought might have been a hint of skepticism, perhaps even sarcasm, in his voice, "but except for his head, everything else has pretty well healed."

Willis felt himself floundering around for words. "Is he unconscious? I mean, obviously he is, but is it a coma? I didn't know his eyes were open. They weren't the last time I was here."

"No, probably not. His eyes opened about ten days ago. Just one morning when the nurses came in, they were open. Just like they are now."

The doctor sat back in his chair, looking thoughtful. "As for whether he's in a coma, we don't really know. I mean, what does it mean to be in a coma? Unconscious? Awake but unable to feel, see, think, respond to stimuli?" He ran a powerful-looking hand through his long, thick brown hair, looking intently at Willis but not, apparently, really expecting an answer to his inquisition. "My personal guess is that he's in some other state, some place that we can't even name yet. There's a condition known by the very unscientific term 'vegetative state,' but what does that mean?"

"Vegetative?" Willis said. "Jesus Christ."

"Exactly," the young doctor said. "Whatever else Seymour is or is not, he's not a vegetable."

"What does it mean?"

"Well, it means what you just saw back there," the doctor said, inclining his head in the direction of Sy's room. "It means someone who shows no sign of awareness but whose eyes open and close in a cycle of sleeping and waking. Sometimes their eyes will rove around, fix for a while on one spot, then move again or close. They'll groan, or maybe a hand or leg will jump. I've seen people who seemed to be pointing at something. But they're not."

"I've seen people in comas," Willis said, "but I didn't know their eyes could be open."

"As I said," Thomas said, his voice slightly clipped, "it's not technically a coma. In fact, people don't usually stay in a coma very long. After a while, usually no more than a few weeks, they either wake up, die, or move into this other condition, this vegetative state."

"So what happens then? I mean, how long can they stay that way?"

The doctor didn't answer right away, waiting until Willis turned his head toward him and they locked eyes. "Decades," he said at last. "Sometimes they stay just like that for many years, never any better and never any worse."

It was the doctor's tone as much as what he said that made Willis feel like screaming or running or pounding on the little desk. And the next comment, also delivered as an authoritative, just-the-facts declaration, did nothing to ease his panic. "Of course," the doctor said, "sometimes a patient will just wake up one day, regain consciousness, and return to more or less normal life." He paused again while Willis tried to digest that tidbit. "But that doesn't happen very often."

Jesus, Willis thought, decades? He had a vision of Sy lying in a semi-dark room for twenty years, maybe until the end of the century, then waking up like Rip Van Winkle. Willis would be in his fifties, maybe older, maybe an old geezer in a nursing home himself.

"Well," the doctor was saying, his voice now less somber and a boyish grin on his face, "let's hope for the best. Maybe he'll come out of it before the new year." He stood up, stuck out his hand, and said, "Nice to see you. If you have any questions, give me a call, although sometimes it's hard to catch me at the office. But I'll be out here from time to time checking on him, and you can leave a message for me."

"Wait, Dr. . . . uh, just one question." Willis blanked on the name. George? Thomas? "Uh, do you think he knows anything that's going on? I mean, how can you be sure that he can't hear? Maybe he can hear but just can't respond? Maybe he is just paralyzed or something?"

The doctor smiled, almost laughed, and said, "There's certainly a lot we still don't know about these sorts of injuries, but we're not altogether primitive. You can take my word for it, he doesn't know what's going on. Whatever's happening in his brain, it's not recording. Believe me."

They left the tiny office and the doctor strode off briskly down the hall. Willis, without considering what he was doing, walked slowly back to Seymour's room. He eased the door closed and stood still, looking around. Nothing had changed. If I come back in ten years, he thought, will it be just like this? "Time stood still," a deep voice intoned in his head, and a giggle squirmed out of his mouth. One drop of the clear liquid slid slowly down the plastic tube into the arm exposed on top of the bedcovers.

"Hey, Sy," he called out, "what's up? Had a good sleep?"

He went to the window, took a long look, and giggled again. The outside landscape hadn't changed either. "Yep," he said, turning toward the bed, "just like it was way back in 1968. You haven't missed a thing."

He looked down and gasped when the eyeballs suddenly swiveled to the right, aimed directly at him. "Christ," he said, "don't do that. Can you hear me? Sy, can you hear me?"

Willis moved quickly out of the line of sight, around to the foot of the bed. The eyes didn't change, still fixed on the spot where he had been standing. He looked around guiltily toward the door, then pulled out a cigarette and lit it. "Who's to know?" he mumbled through the smoke.

"Sy," he called out in a normal voice, "what're we going to do? What the hell are we going to do?"

He began pacing the room, around both sides of the bed, to the window, back to the door, and reverse. "I mean, we're in a hell of a mess." He smoked the Winston down to the filter, ground out the ash on the tile floor, picked up the flattened butt, and dropped it into an empty wastebasket near the bed, where it fell with a dull ring. "Don't tell 'em I did it," he said.

Willis walked back to the window and stood silently for a while until he felt wetness on both cheeks. It had been so long since he had cried that at first he didn't quite get it, but then a tear plunked down onto the window sill. "Yeah," he said, wiping his face on his sleeve, "a hell of a mess." He turned back toward the bed. "And it looks like you're not going to be much help getting us out of it." His voice choked, and for a horrifying moment he was afraid he was about to begin sobbing, but he took a couple of deep breaths and hurried out, casting one final glance at the still form before he quietly closed the door.

As he went back through the lobby he glanced at the glassed-in booth, but it was still empty. "I guess they're not selling tickets today," Willis said aloud, but no one was there to hear him. Now he felt desperate to get away, and he jumped into the Saab, turning the key before he was even settled into the cold seat. But nothing happened. Nothing. No sound, no click, nothing. He turned the key again, over and over, but the result was always the same. He climbed out wearily, raised the hood, and propped it open with the little metal stick. Then he stood back and looked into the engine compartment, but he might as well have been staring into space or into the brain of an opened-up head. It was a total mystery to him.

After a minute he gave the fender two vicious kicks just as the front door to the nursing home opened and a man came out, followed by a boy skipping along behind him. They were laughing, and Willis felt foolish, unsure whether they had seen him. The man stopped and called out, "Having car trouble?"

"I sure am," he said, "damn thing won't start."

The man walked over, followed by the kid who had turned shy and was hiding behind him. The guy was wearing an army field jacket and a black navy watch cap and the boy had on miniature versions of the same clothes, right down to the leather-top, rubber-soled boots. Longish red hair stuck out from under both caps, and both of them had jug-handle ears.

"You guys twins?" Willis asked.

The boy looked puzzled, but the guy laughed and said, "Never seen him before." He leaned over the fender and reached into the engine. "Battery terminals are pretty corroded," he said, "and loose," and then, "try it now."

Willis climbed in and turned the key again and he heard a series of muted clicks, but the motor didn't turn over.

"Okay," the guy said, "I think you need a jump. I've got cables in the truck."

He turned toward the main parking lot. "You stay here, Buddy. I'll get the truck and be right back."

Willis asked, "You want to get in?" but the boy shook his head, standing perfectly still and watching after his father. Willis couldn't keep his eyes off of him. He was so absorbed he hardly noticed the pickup approaching until it pulled in beside the Saab. A huge Christmas tree filled up the back end. Big Red climbed out, pulling jumper cables from behind the seat, and lifted the truck's hood. Little Red maneuvered as close as he could get to his father, then moved with him step by step, never more than a foot away from him.

They had the car started in a couple of minutes and Willis started to get out, but the man said, "Better keep it running. It'll need to charge up for a while. And you better get somebody to clean those terminals."

"I will," Willis said, "and thanks. What do I owe you?"

"Nothing," the guy said, "forget it."

"You're a lifesaver. Thanks."

The boy was smiling now, holding onto his father's sleeve. "Merry Christmas," he called, waving shyly.

They drove off and Willis followed them out of the parking lot, wondering about the Saab's reliability and still thinking about the little boy. He'd gone only a couple of blocks when he slapped the steering wheel and said, "Okay, I'll do it. By God, it's settled and I'll do it." He headed straight out Route 4 and a half hour later he turned onto the snow-covered gravel of the parking lot at the garage. He found the mechanic alone in the closed-in double bay, the heels of his boots sticking out from under a black car and country music playing softly from a radio on the workbench.

"I brought the Saab back," Willis said as the man rose from the car creeper he had been lying on.

"Got a problem with it?" he asked, wiping his hands on the red rag.

"Well," Willis said, "sometimes it won't start. A guy told me it may be just the battery. I don't know."

"Where is it?"

"Outside." He motioned beyond the closed door of the bay, but they couldn't see the Saab because the windows in the door were iced over. "I left it running."

The mechanic went over to the door of the empty bay and said, "Bring it in here."

Willis drove it in and the man signaled him to cut the engine. "Pop the hood," he called. After a two-minute examination he slammed down the hood and said, "Terminals need cleaning and it probably does need a battery. Punch-outs show it's four years old and you can't expect much more than that out of any of them."

He walked over to the driver's side and spoke through the open window. "By the way, when did you change the oil last?"

Willis couldn't remember, but he did have a foggy recollection of having it changed once, back in the summer. "Well," the mechanic said, "I checked it and it could use changing again. Not burning any, though. How's it worked out for you?"

"Great," Willis said, "just what I needed. But I don't need it anymore. How about buying it back?"

The mechanic didn't answer right away, other than to give his head a motion that could have been a negative but also could have just been surprise. Finally, he said, "I don't buy 'em except at auctions because I make my money in buying cheap and fixing them up. This one looks like it's still in pretty good shape—probably worth about what you paid for it, at least. But I couldn't make anything that way."

"Maybe I'd take less," Willis said.

"Well, I wouldn't want to beat you on it. But I wouldn't want to lose either. But here's an idea. You could leave it here and I'd try to sell it for you. Skiers'll be coming in soon. No guarantees, but if I got more than you paid, I'd keep the difference. If you end up getting less, then I'd just charge you a little for keeping it on the lot."

Willis thought it over, but not for long. "Okay," he said, "that sounds fair. Sometime after Christmas I'll bring it back out here and leave it." He stuck out his hand and the mechanic shook it, though not very enthusiastically, after wiping his own hands once more.

"How about a battery? Can you put one in now, just so I know it'll start in the morning? It'll need one anyway if I sell it, right?"

"Well, yes, you will. But I'll have to charge you for it. I mean, you'd have to pay for the battery now."

"Sure," Willis said, "go ahead. But I'll wait for the oil change until I leave it here with you."

It was only a little after four but already fully dark by the time he got back to town. He'd stopped off for a couple of quick drinks and felt better than he had when he left the nursing home, but the newspaper office was eerily quiet and dark, no lights showing anywhere and no sounds. In the newsroom, even the wire machines and the Photofax were silent, and it was the only time Willis had ever seen the water tap turned off in the darkroom, the developing trays turned upside down on the counter. The place was creepy, so still and empty it reminded him of some scary movie from his childhood, a mad scientist's laboratory or some important office suddenly vacated because all the people had been vaporized. He looked out of a newsroom window onto the street below, which was full of people hurrying along, most of them carrying bags or boxes. At the corner, the Salvation Army soldiers were on duty, ringing their bells and nodding their thanks.

Yep, joy to the world, Willis thought as he walked back out to the front desk where he had spotted a small mountain of mail piled on the counter. He shuffled through it and was surprised to find a half dozen envelopes addressed to him, all with the distinct shape of Christmas cards. He didn't usually get that much mail in a week.

The first one he opened was from the oil company that filled the tank at The Box. Then came one postmarked Winter Haven, Florida. Below the usual greetings tripe, which he didn't bother to read, was an entirely legible, carefully lettered message, and below that a signature, which he read first: "Ginny and Fred." Above it she had written with red ink, "We're thinking of you. Thanks and Happy

New Year's." He shoved the card quickly into his desk drawer for some reason that he couldn't trace.

Next in the pile was one of the boxy envelopes with no return address but a local postmark, and inside was not a card but a folded sheet of lined paper. He looked first at the signature: "Love, Marlene." She was writing to say goodbye since she was leaving town, probably for good (where to?). She had planned to see him to say goodbye in person but changed her mind. By the time he got the letter, she'd be gone. She couldn't (or wouldn't?) tell him any more and she was sorry things had sort of fallen apart between them. He shouldn't blame himself (why would he?). She hoped he'd be all right (what the hell did that mean?). Good luck.

He read the note again, but it still didn't make any sense. He hadn't seen Marlene since that day out at the farm when they found Bushey, except twice he had caught a glimpse of her on the street. But this note sounded like they'd just broken up or something. He read it a third time, searching for some hidden message. Then he tore up the paper into tiny bits and dropped them in the wastebasket. The next card was from his bank, and he tossed it without opening the envelope. The next one, postmarked Washington, was a card from Hank, with a long note congratulating him on the commune stories and raving about how great law school was.

At the bottom of the little pile was a card from the state's attorney's office, with a short nonreligious holiday message above Quimby's printed name and, at the bottom, five words scrawled in outsized script: *I'll be seeing you soon.* There was no signature.

Willis shoved that one into his drawer too, then pulled it out and reread it before putting it back with Ginny's card. He leaned back in his chair, thinking about the cards, when suddenly a shadow fell across the door, a half step ahead of Fletcher Monrose Sr., who stopped just inside and looked around the newsroom.

"Oh, hello, Willis, glad to see you," he called out so cheerfully that Willis actually believed him. "I saw a light on and couldn't imagine who would be in the newsroom. I wouldn't have expected anybody, except maybe Sy, to be here on Christmas Eve."

He looked a little embarrassed, maybe about mentioning Seymour, but he set down the shopping bag he was holding and walked across the newsroom toward Willis. "You know," he said with a shy smile, "the truth is that I came up here because when I saw the light, I had the crazy idea that he might be here. Crazy, huh? Guess I'm getting too old."

Willis smiled and found himself feeling a warm sympathy for the old man. "Not at all," he said. "You'd be surprised at how often I find myself walking around talking in my head to Sy. How crazy is that?"

Manny nodded and they both forced small laughs to cover the sudden awkward silence until Willis spoke. "But we're both safe from him now," he said, "because I know Sy is still at the nursing home. I just left there."

Manny laughed, a real laugh, although not very loud, then he said, "I would have thought you might go home for Christmas. Couldn't you talk Matt into giving you a few days off?"

"Well," Willis said, "I have to admit I didn't even try. I really don't know exactly where home is, other than the place I rent at the lake. I mean, my ex-wife and I don't have much to do with each other. She's married again, and that means I don't have much to do with my son either. And my only other relative, except for a bunch of cousins that I don't really know, is my older sister. And she lives in California, and we're not really very close anyway."

Manny nodded. "I guess Christmas can be kind of a lonely time." Then he showed the shy grin and said, "But as far as I'm concerned, it's mostly just a lot of bother." He motioned toward the shopping bag. "As you see, I'm not much of a present-giver. The essential last-minute shopper, I guess."

Willis nodded. "Yeah, well that's one nice thing about my situation. Nobody expects Christmas presents. Except my son, of course." He winced, remembering that he had forgotten, again, to buy anything. After Sheila's call, he had decided to buy Timmy some binoculars and get them shipped off so at least the postmark would be before Christmas Day. But he had forgotten and now it was too late.

Manny was still talking. "So, anyway, my preference would be to publish on Christmas Day. It's always seemed a little embarrassing just to shut down, as though somehow the world stopped on this special Christian holiday. I mean, we just pretend that the whole world is Christian."

He fumbled in his pocket and dragged out a pipe, showing no signs that he planned to leave soon. "You know what Swift said, don't you?"

Willis felt his own face freeze and Manny quickly said, "Jonathan Swift, you know. Anyway, he said, 'We have just enough religion to make us hate, but not enough to make us love one another.'"

Obviously embarrassed again, either by Willis's discomfort or by his own pedantry, he plunged on. "To be honest, though, I've never been able to justify putting out a Christmas Day newspaper. The cost is just as great as any other day, but there would be absolutely no advertising. Besides, it's a tradition, not publishing on Christmas. And who'd read the newspaper on Christmas Day anyway? That's the argument my wife always uses. And Fletcher Junior and Andrew always team to up point out how it would be just a waste of money."

He was searching through all his pockets, and when he finally came up with a tobacco pouch, he rammed the pipe into it as though an enemy were hiding inside. "I used to catch it from all sides," he said. "They'd say I was crazy to consider putting out a paper, and Sy would rant that I was being a money-grubbing merchant by not publishing."

Willis didn't know what to say. Finally, he offered lamely, "Well, yeah, Sy could be a hard case. He came down on me plenty of times."

"Oh," Manny said, "that reminds me. I nearly forgot. I've got something in my office that I . . . uh, that I've decided I want to give to you." He turned around, saying over his shoulder, "Come on back with me." He stopped so quickly Willis nearly walked into his back. "That is, if you've got time. I mean, it is Christmas Eve and you may have things you need to do . . ."

"No," Willis said, "I've got plenty of time."

"Me too," Manny said, walking briskly now and speaking over his shoulder. "I've been hoping to get a good chance to talk to you."

In his office, Manny hurried over to his swivel chair and settled in with a long sigh of relief, as though he had been longing to be there for a long time. "Sit down, sit down," he said to Willis. "You know, I wish I had a Christmas drink to offer you. Seems like this would be just the right occasion. But I don't. It's about the only absolutely inviolate rule we keep around here, no drinking in the newspaper. It's a good rule. Drinking has ruined a lot of good newsmen. But right now, I wish we could break it."

Willis gave a passing thought to offering to go out to his car for the flask, but he dismissed the idea and took the chair pulled up to the corner of the big desk. A tall stack of books that looked like black ledgers stood beside the desk, the pile reaching almost to the desktop, and one of the odd-shaped books was opened and lying upside down in front of Manny.

"That's what I wanted to talk to you about," Manny said, waving toward the stack of ledgers. "Those are Sy's journals."

Willis's head snapped up in disbelief. Christ, his journals? He knew Sy kept some sort of daily diary, but God Almighty, what's Monrose doing with them and did he read them?

The pipe stem was firmly clenched in place now and a stream of smoke spewed out of his mouth as Manny said, "Did you know about the journals and about the note?"

Willis shook his head.

"Well, you know when they found Sy—I mean, when the police got there and all—they didn't know what had happened. So they treated it like a possible crime, or suicide, and they searched the whole apartment."

Willis nodded.

"And they found the journals, this whole stack of them, and inside the cover of the one on top . . ." he paused and pointed to the one on his desk. "This one. Inside was a typewritten note saying that if anything happened to him, the journals should be delivered to me."

The old man stopped, fingered the book on the desk, and shook his head. "That's all it said. It was signed by Sy but it wasn't dated and it was written on newsprint—you know, what the newsroom uses for copy paper—and it was hard to tell how old it was."

"And the police just gave them to you?"

"Well, not right away. They didn't even tell me about them at first. Then about two weeks later, Mr. Quimby called me and asked me to come to his office. By that time it looked like Sy might not die, and I guess they just dropped the question of whether it might be a suicide because he said he was ruling it an accident and that I should take the journals."

He leaned back, puffing thoughtfully on his pipe, although Willis had a feeling that he also was watching him closely through the cloud of smoke. He didn't know what to say. Finally, Manny said, "It has seemed queer to me that they apparently never seriously considered anything except accident or suicide. I mean, how did they know there was no foul play? Sy, God knows, made plenty of enemies over the years."

"Yeah," Willis said, glad to have something to say at last, "including Quimby himself. There are a whole lot of people around here—in this town and in the state, for that matter—who weren't crazy about Sy."

"That's what I thought," Manny said. "So why do you suppose they didn't investigate for foul play?"

"All I know is that Quimby told me they were pretty sure he had been alone in the apartment and that there was no suicide note or any other reason to think it was anything except an accidental fall."

He lighted a cigarette and they sat silently for a moment until Manny said, "He made an entry that night in his journal."

"Have you read it?"

"It's here," Manny said, putting his hand on the book but not exactly answering the question.

"You can be sure Quimby and his crowd read it," Willis said.

Manny met his eyes briefly, looked down again, and said, "Yes, well, you ought to know that the very last entry was about you. Or rather, partially about you."

Willis felt his heart slam into his chest.

"That's what I wanted to talk to you about," Manny said. "Don't worry, it's nothing bad or worrisome, but I thought you ought to know that."

Finally, Willis managed to say, weakly, "What'd it say?"

"I don't know that I understood it all," Manny said. "I mean, it was a fairly long paragraph. Anyway, I thought you ought to see it."

Willis couldn't help staring at the opened ledger on the desk, but he managed to keep from reaching for it.

"In fact," Manny said, "this whole journal, the one for this year, has quite a few entries about you. I guess you and Sy spent a lot of time together?"

"Uh, well, yes. I mean, you know, I guess we did."

"Anyway, I gave it a lot of thought and I decided you ought to see the entries that were mostly about you."

Willis's first reaction was to be horrified, and he was on the verge of saying, "No. No. I don't want to." Then the panic eased and his mind was flooded with a mixture of curiosity and ego. What did Sy really think of him?

"Well," he said, "yes, I'd like to see them. I mean, if you think he wouldn't mind."

"I gave that a lot of thought too," Manny said. "I had the journals for a week before I even opened one. At first it just didn't seem right to be reading his private diaries. But I changed my mind. Why would he have written that note if he hadn't meant for me to see them? He could have left a note saying destroy these. Or he could have sent me a note separately saying not to read them, or whatever. I finally decided he had been moving that note into each new ledger, every year, always leaving it on top in the current one. So what else could he have meant than that I should get them and read them?"

Willis, again, couldn't think of anything to say. He was still staring at the upside-down ledger on the desk.

"And then," Manny said, "I decided that you ought to see the entries that are about you. So I'm going to make copies for you."

He picked up the book on his desk, glanced at the open page, and said, "It appears that he wrote in the journal every day and, as I said, over the past year a good many entries have included comments that I think you'd be particularly interested in." But Manny dropped the book onto his desk rather than handing it to Willis. He leaned back in his chair, closed his eyes, and took several extravagantly deep pulls on his pipe and held that posture for so long Willis began to think he had forgotten about him altogether. Finally, Manny opened his eyes, peering through the cloud of smoke floating between them, and said, "Sy had high hopes that you would stay with our paper for a long time. And I share those hopes."

Off guard, Willis didn't reply right away, and the old man hurried on. "I know Matt Greenberg feels the same way. And I just wondered if you have any plans? I mean, for the near-term future?"

"Well," Willis finally said, "actually, an old friend of mine has offered me a job. In Texas."

It was an exaggeration, not really a lie. Mike Dunn had telephoned from Houston after reading the commune series on the AP wire. He and Mike had worked together a couple of different times, and now he was managing editor in Houston. He hinted strongly, without ever exactly offering a job, that he'd like Willis to work in their statehouse bureau in Austin.

"I figured I might take it," Willis said. "It would mean I could be closer to my boy." He smiled. "And the weather would be a lot easier to live with."

Manny didn't return the smile; in fact, he looked as perplexed as his smooth, benign face could look. "I was afraid of something like that," he said. "I knew your stories on the commune would get a lot of attention. Several publishers I know sent me notes about the series."

Willis cleared his throat but couldn't think of anything to say, so he lit a cigarette.

"Well," Manny said, "I'd like to persuade you to stay. I appreciate your candor about the Texas job. There are some pretty good papers in Texas. But there may be some attractive opportunities here, you know."

Willis lifted his eyebrows. "I thought I already had the best job at the paper," he said.

Manny, obviously preoccupied with some thought of his own, didn't even answer. Then he said, "Look, Willis, I'm going to be absolutely candid with you. You've been open with me, and I'm going to tell you a couple of things that no one else knows. I trust you not to make me regret my own candor." He paused, puffed, then added, "I know from his journals and from what he told me that Sy trusted you completely."

Willis was a little embarrassed. "Thanks. I, uh, I promise you that of course I won't repeat anything you say."

Manny smiled shyly. "Actually, it's a relief for me to talk to someone about some of this." He glanced at his watch. "But I don't want to hold you up and make you late for something."

"No, no," Willis assured him, "I'm not going anywhere, but what about you?"

"I'm going to be late, but that's all right with me. I'd rather be here. Anyway, I thought you ought to know that we've decided to resume the search for a new managing editor. As you know, we sort of put that on hold after Sy's accident. But now we're opening it again. I, uh, I thought you might be interested in applying, I mean."

"Wow," Willis said, "I never even thought about it. I mean, I've never been any sort of editor."

"Of course," Manny said, "I couldn't promise you anything. I mean, it won't be my decision, not mine alone. I've turned over the recruiting to Mr. McNally. He's had a lot of experience with that sort of talent search."

"You mean he's going to hire the managing editor?"

"No, not hire. He's just conducting a nationwide recruiting effort." He blinked, a crease that might have been an interrupted frown rumpling his smooth brow for a second. "I've never done anything like that before, but maybe it's time we got a little more professional."

"It seems to me you've done all right. You and Sy. I mean, you've got a pretty good newsroom."

"And a union. Or, nearly a union. It was a near miss," Manny said. "Anyway, I think you'd be a pretty competitive candidate, if you wanted to apply."

"What about Greenberg?"

"Matt may apply too. But he may not either. He's told me in the past that he didn't want to be managing editor."

Willis decided to push his newfound position of confidante a little. What the hell did he have to lose? "By the way," he said, "what happened with Greenberg, anyway? I heard a rumor a couple of months ago that he'd been fired?"

The old man's face darkened, but he didn't get angry or dissemble his answer. "Yes, he was fired. Or at least, Fletcher tried to fire him. But I reversed it."

"You rehired him?"

"Not exactly. In the first place, Fletcher didn't have the authority to fire him. Matt was correct; only Sy or I could fire him. In the second place, he shouldn't have been fired. He did exactly the right thing in refusing to be told by Quimby what to print and not print. When Fletcher told me the next morning what he had done, I called Matt up immediately, woke him up, and told him I hoped he would come back and that I wanted him to be acting managing editor."

"Whew," Willis said, "that must have been tough."

"No, it was easy. I didn't have to think twice. The hard part was whether to make him acting editor. I mean, at that time we didn't know what was happening with Sy's condition. But the whole thing started me to thinking. And I decided it wasn't right to go on the way I was going."

"What do you mean?"

"I mean, it wasn't fair or right not to deal with the whole issue of what would happen to the paper after me. I don't know if Sy told you—I couldn't tell from the journals—but I had told him that I was retiring. I told him, in fact, on the day of the accident. Anyway, I had decided to retire and that Fletcher would become publisher."

"No," Willis said, "he never told me. I didn't know you were retiring."

"Yes, well, I am," Manny said, "but I've changed my mind about what to do with the paper." He sat back, relit his pipe, and again it was as though he had forgotten Willis was there. Finally, he looked at him again and said, "This part, this next thing I'm going to tell you, must remain absolutely secret. I mean, I hope you won't talk about any of this, and I know I can trust you. But this part no one knows. Not even my wife."

Willis nodded, as surprised as he would have been if Manny had told him he was really the Virgin Mary.

"I'm going to sell the paper."

"Sell it? To who?"

"Whom," Manny mumbled absently through the smoke.

"Huh?"

"I don't know yet," Manny said, "but probably one of the big papers. They're buying up a lot of small dailies these days. Even the *New York Times* is buying papers. It's a good market and I think I could get one of the best large papers interested. Maybe the *Globe*."

"I thought you hated chain papers. Sy always said you thought the chains, like Gannett, were ruining papers and killing competition."

"I do think that. I hate chain papers and I think they'll destroy the kind of newspapering I believe in. Inevitably, they will have to put making money ahead of newspapering."

"Yeah," Willis said, "I remember an editorial you wrote about that." He smiled. "I heard from one of their reporters that the *Patriot Press* bigwigs didn't appreciate that editorial."

Manny's face darkened again, then he smiled. "No, I guess they didn't. I got a quite snippy note from the publisher."

"Sy loved it," Willis said. "I remember him talking about it."

"Yes, well, be that as it may, I have decided to sell the paper. I still think chain ownership is wrong, but the tax laws have made it just about impossible for an individual to buy a daily newspaper, even one as small as this. The chains have too much advantage and can offer many times as much money as an individual could."

Willis tried to look sympathetic, but apparently his thoughts betrayed him because Manny looked at him sharply and said, "I know, I know. I could take less than top dollar, right? You're thinking, like Byron, that avarice is an old-gentlemanly vice. But damn it, I'm not going to give away this newspaper. It's worth a lot of money because we've made it worth a lot. All of us who have worked damned hard."

His face was still smooth but the pink had shaded to near purple, and Willis tried to speak but the old man cut him off. "Anyway, the price will be what the market says it is, and anything else would be irresponsible, just plain foolish."

Willis did not often flash back to his childhood—in fact, he rarely thought of it and remembered only a very few incidents—but now one of those long-buried images swam into his mind's eye. It was summer and he was in a car parked on a downtown street in front of the bank. His father yanked open the door, slid under the wheel, raised his fist, his sweating face as dark as Manny's, and slammed it into the dashboard. "The bastards," he said with great fury. "The rich get richer and the poor get poorer."

That's all he remembered and he looked away quickly, afraid Manny would read his mind, toward the corner of the desk where the ornate carved wooden clock ticked into the sudden silence.

"Yes," the old man said in a normal voice, "it's getting late and I need to go. But I wanted you to know my plans because it didn't seem right to urge you to stay at the paper without telling you. Not that selling it would necessarily change anything, you understand. I mean, I would only sell it to a respectable owner, of course, so there wouldn't be mass upheaval or anything like that."

Willis nodded, then asked, "What about Fletcher? What'll he do?" He meant for it to be a casual question, a vacuum filler, but Manny slumped back in his chair again and popped a new match with his thumbnail, sucking nosily on the pipe until it came back to life.

"Fletcher will be fine," he said. "It's time he and I both faced facts. This is not the right work for him. He's just not cut out for it. I guess I've known that for a long time, but I've always thought about it from my point of view and I should have been thinking about him. It really didn't hit me until the firing incident. When I heard what he had done to Matt, I suddenly knew that running this newspaper is just not the right thing for Fletcher."

He paused, then added, "Plato had it right. He said in *The Republic* that every man should do what he is best fitted to do. And nothing else, he said. Fletcher needs to learn what he is best fitted to do and now maybe he can."

Willis nodded because he didn't know what else to do, until Manny said, "Besides, he's going to be pretty busy for a while and I doubt he'll feel like spending sixteen hours a day down here at the newspaper."

"Doing what?'

"Well, this is another secret," Manny said, but he was smiling now. "Fletcher's getting married. That's where I'm supposed to be right now. Helen is giving a big dinner party and they're going to announce the engagement."

"Well, tell him I said congratulations," Willis said. "Is it Mary Alice?"

"Yes. Do you know her? Yes, of course you do. She works in city hall."

"Yeah, I know her. Tell Fletcher I said he's a lucky man. When's the wedding?"

"Soon," Manny said with a near-lewd grin.

Willis nodded, stood up, and was about to say goodbye, but Manny held up his hand to stop him. "There's one more thing I want to tell you," he said. "It's about Sy."

Willis took his seat again, thinking, Christ, I don't want to hear this.

"I just wanted you to know that you don't have to worry about his financial situation. I have set up a trust fund that'll pay his medical and nursing home bills as long as he needs it. And the paper had an insurance policy for him that will kick in, and a little money will accumulate every month until he can go back to work."

"Well," Willis said, "that is a relief. I mean, I wondered what would happen about the bills and all. I, uh, I think it's pretty fine of you to do that."

Manny waved off the remark, standing up himself now. "There's just one more thing." He was showing the shy grin again. "I'm also paying the rent for his apartment. I intend to keep it for him for as long as it seems reasonable to hold it."

"That's fine," Willis said again.

"Well, the reason I told you that is that an idea just occurred to me. The apartment is vacant now, of course, and I thought you might want to use it, for the winter at least. I know Sy wouldn't mind, and it would be a lot easier than trying to live out at the lake during the winter."

"Thanks. Thanks very much, that's mighty generous and I—"

Manny cut him off, now smiling broadly. "Consider it a bribe," he said, "to get you to stay here."

They left the paper together, Manny careful to be sure all the lights were off as they went.

CHAPTER THIRTEEN
Wednesday, January 1, 1969

The lobby was empty except for the desk clerk slumped in his chair behind the counter, his back to the elevator. Willis stepped out carrying his luggage, walked softly to the counter, and peered over, a little surprised to see that the quietly sleeping form was not Ernie but a bald, much older, and much larger man. The little bastard must have a day off, although he had been on duty when Willis checked in a little before midnight.

"Hey, Ernie," he'd called cheerfully as he pounded the desktop bell. "Happy New Year. Glad to see me back?'

"Thrilled," Ernie said, turning reluctantly away from the New Year's Eve coverage of Times Square. "You been here before?"

"Come on, Ernie, I lived here for nearly six months."

"Right, how could I forget? In that case, you know the rules and I don't have to tell you. Rate's still the same." He looked at Willis for the first time. "If you're alone."

Willis had put down the money and started to turn away.

"Plus tax," Ernie had said, shaking his head. "Guess you forgot that, huh?"

They'd done the signing-in ceremony in silence and Ernie was back with his best friend, the TV set, by the time Willis headed for his third-floor room. He'd just assumed Ernie would be there when he checked out and he'd get to say goodbye.

Now, at dawn, Willis stood at the counter for a minute, then decided not to wake Baldy. He set the room key down on the desk and turned to take a last look around. The lobby was no cleaner than it had been a year ago, small puddles of filthy melted snow slowly evaporating on the rubber mat in front of the counter, and it didn't smell any better either, not much better than a low-rent gym after a low-class boxing match.

Willis eased out the door, set down one of his suitcases, and paused at the entrance just long enough to turn up the collar of his overcoat. No warmer than last year either. Well, goodbye and good riddance, Uptown, and to you too, Ernie; you deserve each other. He stepped off briskly toward the bus station, whistling tunelessly and nearly silently, feeling a little smug to be in motion and not hungover so early on New Year's Day.

The streets and sidewalks were empty, the sun not yet a wintry glow at the top of downtown's tallest building. As he turned the corner, the clock in front of the bank showed six fifteen, and just as he got there, it obligingly clicked into temperature mode to tell him that 1969 was starting off at two degrees below zero. By the time he reached the bus station, he was congratulating himself on the decision to leave this icebound backwater, and even the surly kid at the ticket counter couldn't lower his spirits.

"Bus on time?"

"How the hell should I know."

"Supposed to leave at six thirty, right?"

"If you say so."

"What do you say?"

"I don't say nothing. I just sell the tickets."

"Okay. One-way to New York City. And keep up the good work."

The waiting room was empty, the tiny lunch counter shut up tightly. Willis again congratulated himself. Holidays were the best possible time to travel, with some minor drawbacks. He contemplated the puddle surrounding the coffee machine, wondering how deep the murky water might be, and finally stepped into it, fed in his quarter, and retrieved a cup of coffee that looked like—and probably would taste like—the bilgewater now covering the soles of his shoes. There was no sign of the bus by six thirty, but the front door of the station banged open and a young, uniformed soldier hurried in, a duffel bag slung over his shoulder and a civilian suitcase in his other hand. He hustled over to the counter, bought a ticket to somewhere, and settled down in one of the plastic seats as far away from Willis as he could get. More good luck for me, Willis thought; the poor bastard's already so homesick he can't stand the idea of talking to anybody.

The Greyhound nosed up to the curb at six forty-five, its arrival announced only by the fart-like expulsion from its air brakes. Three minutes later, as Willis was still trying to stuff his largest suitcase into the overhead rack, the bus jolted back to life, knocking him off-balance so he fell into the seat, which, thank Christ, was empty. Most of the others also were empty, although the entire back seat was filled with the snoring body of a large someone buried under a military overcoat.

He peered alertly through the outsized tinted window as the bus maneuvered through the deserted streets, more interested in the little city now than he had been during the time he considered himself part of it, although there was no hint of nostalgia in his contemplation, not even when he passed near enough to see the newspaper office. From the outside he thought the bus might appear rather sad as it rocked its way out of town, but inside it was warm, even cozy if you overlooked the odors, and as safe as the womb.

The town ended abruptly, giving way to open, snow-covered fields that showed no sign of the sprawl Willis had seen nearly everywhere else on the East Coast, and when they cleared the city limits the bus surged as the anonymous driver, totally obscured from sight in his high-backed seat, pushed down the pedal to make up his lost time. Soon they were roaring past the obscure signless car lot and Willis caught a glimpse of the green Saab still parked in front of the garage door where he had left it.

His plan so far had been flawless. Leave off the car, get a lift back to town, spend the night at the Uptown, and get away on the first bus out—no goodbye parties, no fuss, no arguments. The only real flaw was losing a month's rent. He stared contentedly at the fields, trees, and distant mountains flashing by, his mind as unfocused as the blurry landscape until suddenly he became aware of Tennessee Ernie Ford's voice inside his head groaning, "Another day older and deeper in debt." He'd been carrying "Sixteen Tons" around in his head just about as long as he had been newspaper hopping around the country, only this time he wasn't deeper in debt and he didn't owe his soul to the company store or anybody else. In fact, he had more cash in his pocket than he had amassed in a good many years, enough to stake himself until he found the next good berth. And he didn't put much stock in souls, as a general rule, although even as that thought slid past he felt the nagging pull of a dreaded duty.

Inside his smaller suitcase, carefully placed for easy access, was the manila envelope left for him by Manny. He had checked it out only enough to find that inside was a skinny three-ring binder containing the copied pages of Sy's journal. The old man had left the sealed envelope on Willis's desk several days earlier and they had not run into each other again, although Willis had left him a note saying he was leaving.

Willis had put off reading the journal, although he wasn't entirely certain why he dreaded it and in fact he also felt a strong interest in finding out exactly what Seymour actually thought of him. Still, the prospect of reading Sy's private diary was unnerving. Maybe he ought to just toss it? Who'd ever know?

He felt his good mood begin to fade and he slumped against the window, hoping he could call on a usually reliable escape, sleep. But with his eyes closed he began to feel the swaying of the big bus, and then the zinging of the tires penetrated loudly into his ears, the dry heat blowing up his trousers tickled the hair on his legs, and the chattering inside his head reached the pitch of bedlam. Maybe the merits of sobriety have been greatly exaggerated, he thought, remembering hangovers fondly as a tried-and-true pathway to sleep. After a while he gave up, reached into the small suitcase, and took out the manila envelope. The first entry, he noticed with a sudden surge of interest, was dated one day after he had arrived in town, just three days short of a whole year ago.

Thursday, January 4, 1968

It's late but even so I suspect I may ramble, mostly because I'm riding a mysterious wave of alert anticipation and it makes me feel like writing. The mood of staleness I wrote about last night has vanished, replaced by some nearly forgotten sense of eagerness. Likely the mystery is no more profound than a delayed reaction to the new year.

But whatever the cause, I'm glad to be out of the shadow. As my 50th year opens, I hope to keep my eyes away from the rearview mirror—or any other mirror, for that matter.

Deep winter has settled in with its usual trappings, but the familiar locked-down feel of January has become confused by a restlessness that I believe has migrated into Vermont, riding over the mountains on winds stirred by the turmoil churning the rest of the country. Even here we have been slapped awake by the war, the spreading race revolt, and the long-overdue agitation on the campuses. For my part, I welcome the upheaval, but God knows what it will mean for the newspaper. I believe we're ready but, curiously, I fear Manny will turn out to be the weak link.

My next quarrel with him will be over the new man, Willis. I hired him on the spur of the moment although I had told Manny that I wouldn't hire anyone until he and I had discussed it again. He'll say I broke my promise, and that's true, but it's also true that in the end he would have agreed to hiring a new reporter, and sometimes I get tired of this endless wrangling over money. And he'll get over his pique. If truth be known, I was inclined immediately to hire him because of his name since, just last night, I was reading Frost and was captured for the first time by "The

Self-Seeker." This Willis doesn't appear to be particularly like Frost's, but after spending several hours with him I am convinced he's the right person for this job and this paper is the right place for him. I suspect he'll turn out to be more like the Correspondent in Crane's story since I think that for Willis, life hasbeen a dangerous, choppy ride in an open boat and God knows whether he'll ever make it through the breakers to shore, but so far he hasn't lost heart. And I believe I can keep him rowing. The question, of course, is whether Willis is really the Correspondent or the Oiler.

There is no question, though, about his Southern accent, and I'll be interested to see how the wiseacres in the newsroom react to it. My guess is that the impulse to ridicule will be short-circuited by the hint of buried anger that sometimes seems to be just below the surface in Willis.

News was skimpy tonight but ominous nevertheless. The Administration is grumbling about Laos, Cambodia, and Thailand. The whole situation is confusing and scary. A red herring? A new war? LBJ seems capable of almost anything, blinded by hubris yet goaded by the terrible fear of inadequacy and failure. I anticipate a disastrous year in politics, a Republican resurgence in the nation and in Vermont. But, as always, a great year to be putting out a daily newspaper.

Jefferson once wrote that newspapers are vehicles that "serve to carry off noxious vapors and smoke." On a personal level, there's nothing like making a newspaper to carry off any noxious vapors that are troubling you. And the same is true of a daily journal. Log entries have an unambiguous beginning and end, a completeness otherwise unknown to our lives since we can't remember birth and can't ever know death. Today is unique, as different from yesterday as light is from dark. Tonight's scribe is a stranger to last night's, just as Wednesday's newspaper is only vaguely related to Tuesday's.

Pure white clean sheets
Warm only inside —
The war begins anew
-30-

Willis closed the notebook, stared out the window for a minute, then reopened it. The handwriting was as readable as type, really not writing at all but printing, with the blocky, uniform letters simply hooked together as though some second-grade prodigy wanted to fool a teacher into believing he had made the transition to cursive. Thinking back, he couldn't remember ever seeing Sy's handwriting. It felt like discovering a secret, like finding out someone you knew well was really much older or younger than you had thought. He read through the first journal entry again, and this time he could hear Sy's voice saying the words, all except the little verse at the end. What the hell was that all about?

He went back to reread the part about himself. The only writer he knew named Crane was the guy who wrote *The Red Badge of Courage*, and he remembered one night way back when Seymour had been talking about it. He'd said it was the only novel about the Civil War that rang true no matter whether you were from the North or the South. Willis felt the uneasiness creeping back, the self-doubt that had often been part of conversations with Sy, a vague wariness that he might be caught out as an imposter or, worse, a fool. In this case, he even knew the reason. *The Red Badge of Courage* had been assigned reading in an English course at Columbia State College, and he had only read a pony version but aced the essay test anyway with some fancy writing. Now he had absolutely no memory of a Correspondent or the Oiler. Maybe they were in some other book by Crane? What the hell is an oiler, anyway?

Thursday, February 29, 1968

This was our free day, the gift deposited in our accounts every four years by order of Pope Gregory, like a present left in trust by some long-forgotten ancestor, perhaps a mischievous great-great-great-great uncle with a twisted sense of humor. This year, those of us who live to the end will get 366 days. So far, 1968 hasn't done much to earn a bonus, and for the most part I could have been just as happy without this gift.

Another angry but petty argument with Manny led us nowhere and fixed nothing. He seems preoccupied with trivial, meaningless nonsense, like complaints from advertisers and silly letters to the editor from known cranks and fools. He's as jumpy as a flea, asking sharp-edged questions about people in the newsroom and moaning continually about ad revenue, overtime pay, and such things. He's so fretful it's making me nervous. The whole damn newsroom seems on edge.

With a couple of exceptions, we have the strongest staff I've ever put together, and Willis is rapidly becoming the linchpin, although from time to time I have wondered whether the curious restlessness in the newsroom began about the same time he arrived. The young reporters follow him around like acolytes, even the two Ivy Leaguers. I have high hopes for both of those boys and they could learn a lot from Willis. Ron especially needs some tempering, a little more self-awareness. Tonight he stormed into the office bubbling over about a story, flinging his overcoat on the floor and oblivious to the drop of water hanging from the end of his red nose.

As long as we keep a Willis in our newsroom, we needn't worry about Mencken's fear of the rising social position of journalists: "I well recall my horror when I heard, for the first time, of a journalist who had laid in a pair of what were then called bicycle pants and taken to golf: it was as if I had encountered a studhorse with his hair done up in frizzes, and pink bowknots peeking out of them."

Curiously, Willis seems to have a steadying influence on the staff, like a French farmer I once knew who worked with horses. They would grow calm, even docile, as soon as he walked into the barn, even though to me it looked as though he had completely ignored them. I'm not sure even Willis and I working together can keep the newsroom docile, though, and it's becoming increasingly clear that there's a conflict brewing with Connie. The byplay between them is more entertaining than troubling to watch and it will resolve itself quickly. My guess is that she could derail him if she wants, and I also suspect he's harboring some important secret. I doubt Willis would even acknowledge it, no more than I would acknowledge mine to anyone. "I could a tale unfold whose lightest word would harrow up thy soul."

Night and day
Roam over the frozen earth;
Fixed and free.
-30-

Willis again set aside the journal notebook, further puzzled by the three-line poems and even more intrigued by the mysterious reference to secrets. He turned again toward the window as the first hints of morning began to reveal the barren, snow-covered roadsides and far-distant mountains, barely visible as murky bumps on the horizon. Even now, escaping as fast as the Greyhound could go, it made him nervous to think that Sy suspected him of having "an important secret." He tried with no success to recall some event back in February that could have prompted suspicion, unable to remember exactly when the things that he could remember had taken place. The AWOL soldier? Maybe that was in February?

A billboard whizzed past the window, followed quickly by a smaller sign that turned into a Burma-Shave—like series of signs that Willis couldn't really read but that he knew were hawking a tourist trap and a motel. Then the motel itself, a ramshackle cluster of small cabins, flashed past, the Vacancy sign blinking forlornly into the creeping daylight.

Willis began to recall one of the early successes in his short Vermont career, the series of stories on billboards. One of the photo spreads used with the series had been of this rundown motel with its row of faded leaning signs and unappetizing cabins. The idea for the series had been Sy's and he had coaxed it along like a midwife, sometimes using quiet encouragement and sometimes mild admonishments but always standing by, ready to be a sounding board when Willis needed to talk about the stories. He remembered how the publisher had congratulated him on the stories and how he had taken the offensive on the editorial page when critics in the business community complained loudly that banning road signs would hurt the economy.

His feeling of gloom and uneasiness grew with the thoughts of Sy and Manny. He knew that stopping by the nursing home again wouldn't have made any difference, but at least he ought to have told the publisher in person that he was leaving. What kind of creep would just slip out of town before daylight without even saying goodbye? My kind of creep, Willis thought, but at least he could have the decency to read the journals. Sy clearly had put a lot of effort into them, and Manny had taken a lot of trouble to copy them and separate out the ones about Willis.

He read steadily for an hour or more before drifting off to sleep somewhere in northern Connecticut. He awoke with a start to find the bus empty, the interior lights on, and the door open, with strong daylight pouring through the opening. Outside his tinted window he saw a Stamford station sign and he jumped up to go look for a cup of coffee. But just as he got to the door, the bus driver charged up the steps, brushing Willis aside and yanking hard on the pneumatic door handle.

"Still just you and me, buddy," he said as he settled into the driver's seat.

"Shit, I wanted a cup of coffee."

"Too bad. You was sleeping so sound I didn't want to wake you up. Ought to be able to get one in White Plains."

Willis silently cursed the fat-assed driver, but the bus was already backing away from the docking station and he flopped down into his seat, glad now to have a target for his irritation. But now he was fully awake and unable to ignore the journal notebook.

Thursday, August 8, 1968

Too depressed tonight to write very much. Maybe I'll just try to list the obvious reasons for my black mood:

—The union has turned our newspaper into a nightmare, a twisted production operating for the wrong reasons with the wrong people all going in the wrong direction. I have to force myself to go into the newsroom every day.

—Manny refuses to talk about it and never tells me anything that's going on.

—Willis and even Greenberg seem to have betrayed me. Nearly every day I see one or the other, sometimes both, whispering to someone out in the hallway or on the street.

—Vietnam has turned into a lethal quagmire with no way out; the death toll soars.

—The rest of the world is headed toward some kind of precipice with the Soviets about to crack down on Prague and no one making any effort to stop them.

—And now, tonight, the Republicans nominated as president Richard Nixon, a half-crazy loser, and for vice president a totally corrupt small-time politician named Spiro Agnew.

It's all got me so confused, so muddled, that I sometimes feel dazed. When I came home tonight I found myself standing in front of the elevator outside my place. I don't know how long I'd been standing there and I couldn't remember whether I'd walked up the stairs or ridden up. "Half the time I don't know what's troubling me."

I can't go on. I'm going to bed.

It's now about 4 a.m. and I can't sleep. I woke suddenly from some weird dream that had Lloyd Bridges in it and my mind veered back to a TV show I used to watch a couple of years ago, a Saturday night series written by Rod Serling called The Loner. It

was about a former soldier turned loose at the end of the Civil War from a Confederate POW prison to wander around in a country that is clearly lost in schizophrenia. The series was a bust, yanked after a few weeks, but it was one of the few gems I've found floating in the other slop of television "entertainment."

I've been a loner all my life. God knows what would have happened to me if I hadn't found this newspaper and this place. I am still a loner, but until recently I've never felt alone or lonely. When did it start? Was it when Willis got here? When the union people sneaked in? The lawyer? Manny's creepy change of character?

Something is happening here, Mister Jones.

Tell us what comes next, Dylan?

Hide and go seek

The raven spies on a kill;

One wins and all lose.

-30-

Willis read on and on, becoming more puzzled with each new entry. Sometimes he recognized phrases or thoughts he had heard from Seymour, but mostly the journal entries just became more and more strange. It was clear that Sy had become obsessed with the union organizing and that he felt betrayed by everyone, including Manny and Willis. In certain entries the paranoia exploded into wild ranting, but in others a certain sly cunning seemed to be leading a reader somewhere, always ending up, though, with the incomprehensible verses.

He read steadily, only rarely peering out through the large tinted windows onto a bleak, increasingly urban landscape.

Thursday, October 31, 1968

The scariest day of the scariest year of my fear-haunted life.

Willis dropped the journal like a hot coal. He had been reading steadily for many miles, and at first didn't even notice the date. But the handwriting caught his attention, the words angling downward on the page and the script shaky and uneven, only remotely resembling the earlier entries. Then he noticed the date. Christ, Sy must have been really drunk that last night . . . or something.

The terror lifted briefly tonight, washed away by scotch whiskey and Willis with his terrific news story. But the brief flash only made the darkness more intolerable. "I am one, my liege, whom the vile blows and buffets of the world have so incensed that I am reckless what I do to spite the world."

I spoke those words to Willis tonight, but he had no earthly idea what I was talking about. I'm not even sure he's ever read Macbeth, much less remembered any lines. And yet, in calmer, more peaceful moments I can see clearly that if newspapers have any future, it will depend on finding and keeping people like Willis in the business. Whatever his other failings, no one ever will see his hair done up in frizzes.

Whatever happens, though, will be too late for me. I stumble and I can't go on, blinded as foretold 100 years ago by Emily Dickinson.

> *Tell all the truth but tell it slant –*
> *Success in Circuit lies*
> *Too bright for our infirm Delight*
> *The Truth's superb surprise*
> *As Lightning to the Children eased*
> *With explanation kind*
> *The Truth must dazzle gradually*
> *Or every man be blind—*
> *-30-*

Willis closed the journal notebook, more confused than ever about Sy and the accident and especially the final poem. Tell it slant? What the hell kind of advice was that for a newspaper man to quote? He rode on, his mind swerving, dodging, lost in confusion as the mile markers zinged past.

* *
*

Willis had been inside the Port Authority terminal before, but now he couldn't remember when or why and he had no idea where to find the telephones. He wandered around the massive terminal for ten minutes, and during that time he waved off four different panhandlers, each time feeling a stab of worry about his own future. Finally, he found the bank of pay phones. Alice answered on the fourth ring and for a second he thought she was going to refuse the collect call, but she didn't and he said hurriedly, "Listen, Alice, I really need to talk to the publisher. Can you switch me over to his office?"

"I thought you had left," Alice said with her usual accusing tone. "They said you were gone."

"Alice, listen, I'm in New York City and I've got to talk to Manny. Is he there today?"

"How would I know? I'm the only one in the newsroom. It's New Year's Day, you know."

"Goddam it, Alice, can you switch me to the publisher's office?"

"He might not be in his office."

"Goddam it, Alice, just—"

The line went silent, then he heard a click and Willis swore again, sure that she had cut him off. But then Manny's voice said, "Willis? Is that you? Where are you?"

Relieved, he said, "Yes, it's me. I'm in New York. Didn't you get my note?"

"Yes, I got it this morning. We just got back and this if the first day I've been in the office. I've been trying to call you but no one seemed to know where you were. Your note just said you were leaving, and even Matt didn't know how to reach you."

"Yeah, well, I'm sorry to have pulled out so abruptly. I tried to see you but they said you were away, so I just left the note."

"Right. Helen and I left right after Christmas for a few days in Florida."

A long silence followed, each waiting for the other to speak. Then a conversation began that Willis never meant to have, didn't expect, and that changed everything.

Manny: "Have you read Sy's journals?"

Willis: "Yeah. I read them on the bus. That's why I called. I wanted to ask you—"

Manny: "So you read the final one? On the night he . . . uh, uh, uh, fell?"

Willis: "Yes, that one too. And I was wondering . . . I mean, I have several questions, but I hoped you could tell me about those odd little verses at the end of each entry?"

Manny: "Verses? Oh, yes, of course. Those are a form of haiku."

Willis: "Hey, you?"

Manny: "No, no," giggle, "it's called haiku, an old Japanese form of poetry."

Willis: "They seem sort of mysterious, like a secret message or something."

Manny: "Well, that's common for the form. But it's true that when I read them I suspected Sy was playing some sort of word game. A puzzle or code or something. Some sort of secret message."

Willis: "A code? But who did he expect to read them?"

Manny: "Well, I haven't really studied them. But I know that during the war, Sy was a code expert, or at least he had some secret assignment that he never talked about. I believe he may have been working secretly with the French Resistance."

Willis: "Christ, he never mentioned anything like that to me."

Manny: "No, he never talked to me about it either, except a time or two something slipped out. I've always suspected that he saw some horrible things during the war. Maybe even participated in some terrible . . . uh, uh . . . events."

Willis: "Do you remember that one entry when he wrote about secrets? He said maybe I had some secret?"

Manny: "No, I guess I don't recall that one."

Willis: "He wrote . . . hold on, I'll find it and read it to you. Here it is: *I could a tale unfold whose lightest word would harrow up thy soul.*"

Manny: "Oh, that. It's something *Hamlet* said."

Willis: "*Hamlet*?"

Manny: "Yes. He knew nearly the whole play by heart, you know."

Willis: "Really? No, I didn't know that. And what about these codes? Do you think that's why he kept the journal? I mean, so he could write in code about the war?"

Manny: "Well, I doubt that it was that complicated. That journal went on for years, you know, not just the year when you were here. I expect he just liked keeping the daily record. The very first entry in the first journal is a quote from Francis Bacon. Hold on a minute, I'll get it . . . Here: *In sea voyages, where there is nothing to be seen but sky and sea, men should make diaries; but in land-travel, wherein so much is to be observed, for the most part they omit it.*"

Willis: "Yeah, I see what you mean. It's like he wanted a record or something."

Manny: "Well, yes, I suppose so. Anyway, you read all the ones I gave you? And so you know that shortly before his fall, I told him I was retiring? Leaving the paper?"

Willis: "Yes. I read that. That's why I called. I wanted to know what—"

Manny: "Well, that's why I wanted to talk to you. You probably wondered about what I said when we talked on Christmas Eve. I mean, about selling the paper and all that."

Willis: "Well, yes. I mean, I was thinking about that conversation when I decided to leave."

Manny: "Well, I've changed my mind."

Willis: "About selling the paper? About retiring?"

Manny: "Yes. I'm not going to retire and I'm not going to sell the paper. I thought about it a lot. In fact, that's all I did on this trip to Florida—think about it. And I'm staying here."

Willis: "Well, that's great. I mean, with you and Sy both gone, that just wouldn't be the same paper, and I—"

Manny: "So I'm staying, and I wouldn't want anyone . . . I mean, anyone at the paper . . . to think I will be leaving, and I wanted to ask you—"

Willis: "You needn't worry. I didn't tell anybody, and I wouldn't tell."

Manny: "No, that's not what I meant. What I want to ask you is whether you'll consider changing your mind too. About leaving, I mean."

Willis: "Well, I mean, I don't know . . . As I said in my note, it just seemed like the right time for me to move on."

Silence.

Willis: "Then I read what Sy had written. I mean, about the paper and about me and you, and I just really started missing being up there. And I felt crummy about the way I left. And, anyway, that's why I called you."

Manny: "Where are you, anyway? Where are you calling from?"

Willis: "From the bus station. In New York. New York City."

Manny: "Well, listen, Willis, what I wanted to talk to you about is to ask you to come back. I want you to come back and take Sy's job."

Willis: "Sy's job? What about Greenberg?"

Manny: "He doesn't want it. He likes being news editor."

Willis: "What if Sy—"

Manny: "Look, Willis, hear me out. We can't know, of course, whether Sy ever will recover. But even if he does, I'm afraid he'll never be able to run the newsroom again. That was clear even before his . . . accident . . . I had already told him that, before that night. If he comes back to work at the paper, it'll be as my assistant. So what I'm saying is that the job will be open no matter what happens with Sy."

Willis: "I don't know what to say. I've never even thought about running a newsroom. Do you think I could do it?"

Manny: "Yes, I'm sure of it. And so was Sy. You read what he wrote—"

Willis: "Move on. Here's a buck, move on."

Manny: "What? What'd you say?"

Willis: "Sorry, I wasn't talking to you. There was a guy here asking for money. You know, a bum."

Manny: "Anyway, what do you say? I think we could put out a hell of a good newspaper. Especially now that the union thing has gone away."

Willis: "I think so too. I just don't know if I'd be any good at being an editor. I—"

Manny: "Look, Willis, I've seen your work. Other than Sy, I don't know anybody more committed or more capable of doing the type of newspapering that I think needs to be done. Now, mind you, I can't make any promises about the long term. I mean, I'm 72 years old. I won't be here forever. But for as long as I am here, and that'll be as long as I can still bang out editorials on a typewriter—or whatever comes along to replace the typewriter, as some people are saying— as long as that, I can promise you that our paper will be independent and that our goal will be to put out as good a newspaper as we can make."

Willis: "This is a big surprise to me. I'm sure tempted, but I have a couple of questions. If you don't mind—"

Manny: "Go ahead. Anything."

Willis: "Well, what about Fletcher? I mean—"

Manny: "No, that's all right. Fletcher knows I've changed my mind about retiring. In fact, his situation has changed and that's one of the reasons I started rethinking my plan. He just got married, you know, and he and his wife are leaving at the end of the month for Europe. They both love it over there, and they're planning to live somewhere in Europe for a few years. Anyway, he'll be leaving the paper and who knows whether he'll ever want to come back to it. At any rate, he doesn't have much interest in the news end of the business even if he does come back."

Willis: "Well, that's nice. I mean, sounds as though he and Mary Alice are headed off into a pretty nice life."

Manny: "I hope so."

Willis: "One more question: What about Mr. McNally? I thought he was—"

Manny: "Well, Mr. McNally is no longer a factor. He and I . . . well, we . . . I mean, he and I had a rather serious disagreement. It's a long story, but the upshot is that he's no longer associated with us or our paper. Don't get me wrong; he did a fine job with the union and all. But in the end, we just had different ideas about the future and how a newspaper ought to operate. I had a long telephone conversation with him this morning and the upshot was that he's out of the picture and I've taken over the job of finding a replacement for Sy. Just me."

Willis: "Wow. You've been busy for a guy on vacation."

Manny: "The telephone, I think, is one of the modern inventions that can be truly called an improvement."

Willis: "Anyway, this is a lot to think about . . . I mean, I don't want to be coy, but it's just that I'm really surprised by all this."

Manny: "There's one more thing to put into your considerations. As I told you the last time we talked, I've committed to keeping up the rent on Sy's apartment. And if you agree to take this job, I'm sure he'd be pleased to have you move into the apartment. Otherwise, it'll just be empty until, well, until something changes with Sy, so you could move right in if you wanted, and I'd keep paying the rent, of course."

Willis: "Gosh, Manny, I really don't know what to say. I mean, if I took the job, I could take over the rent payments, unless Sy comes back, but—"

Manny: "Listen, don't worry about the rent. After all, if we worked it out this way, the paper could pay the rent and it would be a business expense. See?"

Willis: "Yeah, I guess so, but—"

Manny: "Well, we haven't even talked about salary and that sort of thing. So, listen, how about coming back up here and let's have a proper meeting and then you decide. Okay? Want to think about it?"

Willis: "No. I'll get the next bus out of here. I don't know the schedule, but I should get there sometime tomorrow."

Manny: "I'll leave the door to Sy's apartment unlocked. Just leave your stuff there when you get in and then come down to the paper. I'll be there until five thirty tomorrow afternoon."

Willis: "No, don't bother with the door. When I get there, I'll just go to the Uptown. Ernie will be glad to see me."

Manny: "Who?"

Willis: "Never mind. It's a joke and I'll tell you about it when I get there."

Manny: "Okay, see you tomorrow."

Willis: "Right."

Manny: "Just one more thing. Something to think about on your bus ride: 'The newspaper brought them together, and the newspaper is still necessary to keep them united.'"

Willis: "Huh?"

Manny: "He meant the American people, of course, but—"

Willis: "Who?"

Manny: Tocqueville. Anyway, think about it and I'll see you tomorrow. Goodbye."

Willis stood for a long time beside the telephone, then without really making a decision he walked to the ticket counter, found out the next bus back to Vermont would leave at six thirty p.m., and sat down on a filthy metal seat to wait. Tocqueville? Who the hell is that? He jumped up, glanced at the clock again, and headed for the street. He had plenty of time to find a bookstore and check it out. He might even find a place along the way to get a drink or two.

About the Author

Bill Porter was editor at two small newspapers when such an enterprise was still viable. Many of the reporters who were his colleagues and his adherents would go on to become some of the best known and most powerful people in their generation of American journalism.

Bill was a Southerner who recognized in his teens that the values of his home, still emerging from Jim Crow, were not his own. Despite six decades living among Yankees, he retained his accent, although, speaking with that accent, he often claimed otherwise. As a former colleague once wrote of Bill, *He talks like Demosthenes, with the stones still in his mouth.*

The stories that came from the act of reporting were as much a product of those newsrooms as the news itself. The reporter who gave blood to an injured source to get the interview. The memorization of a secret report to meet the source's prohibition on taking notes. The newsman stowing away among rescue workers going to an accident on the Cog Railway. The scribe who would pull the first copy off the press at a rival paper, reading any scoops to the rewrite desk of his own publication. The secret listening post which gave entry to the governor's office.

Bill often said that the best thing about working for a newspaper was that the mistakes and the triumphs only lasted a day. A writer distraught over an error would receive a three-word reminder of "just fish wrap" from Bill. Of course, the triumphs evaporated just as soon.

Of all the tales of upstart politicians humbled, of funny tragedies, of tricks and traps and lucky breaks, one was told the most. On June 5 of the most tumultuous year in modern American history, Bobby Kennedy was shot in California. Bill and the reporters and editors on the night desk held the pressrun, wrote off the television broadcast, and put out the only morning paper on the East Coast to carry the story.

Kate, Mae, Bill and Alphie